FAITHLESS

ELLE CHARLES

FAITHLESS

FAITHLESS

Copyright © Elle Charles 2018

Cover design by Rachelle Gould-Harris of Designs by Rachelle
www.designsbyrachelle.com

For all enquiries, please email: elle@ellecharles.com
www.ellecharles.com

ISBN: 978-1-69-783797-1

First publication: 2 July 2018
First Edition

Author Note

Faithless is long, slow burning romance read. It is the fourth instalment of the Fractured series and is a full-length novel.

Please note, this novel can be read as a standalone book, but throughout the story, there is cross-referencing to events within the last three novels. Although it isn't essential to have read the full Fractured series, it is advisable due to the story arc, the various character backgrounds and their relationships.

Contents

Prologue

THE FALLEN CANNOT be saved.

The ghostly words drift over the atmosphere as the cold chill of winter whistles through the trees, confirming the northerly snow shower forecast today is imminent.

I look over my shoulder at the small congregation of mourners filing out of the cemetery. They talk amongst themselves or pin their gazes on me. Some impart sympathetic smiles, while others glare with pure disdain, revealing their true thoughts. Holding their hateful stares, refusing to be the one to back down and give them further fuel for the fire, I stand and take it because today will be the last day that I have to.

Eventually, they part, exposing someone I never wanted to see again. My breath catches in my throat because I wasn't aware he was given permission to be here today. Flanked by two men in uniform, the chains around his limbs hinder his movement, but the clink of shackles is louder than it should be considering the distance separating us.

Overcome with grief, my hand instantly finds my temple. Gently grazing my finger over the fresh scar, running from the corner of my eye to my eyebrow, a distant wail of pain echoes inside my head, remembering how it came to be just a few short weeks ago. As my hand continues its descent, finally resting upon my neck, it invokes yet another unwanted memory.

Staring at the slow retreating form of the man I was once in love with, I finally see what everyone warned me of. I see the truth behind the lies, behind the façade he flawlessly crafted to fool everyone. But that mask started to slip long before even he realised. And let's face it, there is only so long someone can hide who they truly are.

"You fucking bitch!"

The scream rings in my ears as he strains against the chains and tries to make his way towards me. The guards quickly restrain him, but the damage has already been done as the remaining parishioners watch his show of lies and deceit.

"You fucking lied, you bitch! This is all your fault. I'm going to fucking kill you. You've ruined my life!"

"Move it. Now!" a guard orders, shoving him in the opposite direction with brute force.

I quickly shift behind a tall headstone and crouch down with my head in my hands, waiting for the silence to return.

"You're fucking dead, bitch! Dead!" His diatribe continues to penetrate the peaceful surroundings, loud and venomous, enough to raise the dead.

Wiping my tears in vain, he has caused yet another ripple in the calm. Because of his family's reputation, whoever witnessed his little tirade will automatically believe it.

I press my forehead to the headstone and listen, heartbroken, as the doors of the armoured van are slammed shut. I slump back against the stone, grateful he is gone, but I know this will not be the last time I shall face him. The next time shall be in a place where his fate will, hopefully, be sealed indefinitely.

"Hey," Lynsey, an old school friend greets softly, approaching my hiding place. As I stand, I come face to face with the same circle of friends I used to hang around with in high school. Needless to say, I haven't really spoken to them in a long time. For obvious reasons, we no longer have anything in common anymore.

"Hi," I whisper and give her the most convincing smile I can muster.

"I guess we were all wrong about him." Her eyes drift towards the security van now exiting the grounds.

I follow her gaze but don't respond. Mentally, I'm too preoccupied fighting back the urge to break down and tell everyone they were right, and I was wrong.

"I'm really sorry. Are you going to be okay?"

I shrug nonchalantly because that's one of the few questions that have been asked of me repeatedly these past four weeks. And I absolutely hate it.

Are you going to be okay?

Are you sure you'll be fine?

Okay.

Fine.

Two words I can no longer stomach to hear. There is nothing okay or fine about me, maybe there never will be again, but only time will tell if my theory is correct.

"Sure," I whisper, mortified that she has just seen first-hand a small level of the abuse I suffered. Still, there is nothing else I can say.

I could lie, I suppose, but anyone with a heart will see through it instantly.

"Thanks for coming, Lynsey." She bequeaths me a sad smile and pulls me into an unreciprocated hug.

"I'll see you around. You take care of yourself, okay?" I nod, unsure how I'm going to manage that.

She eventually lets me go, and the girls say their goodbyes. Watching them walk away, I shield my eyes from the sun penetrating the wintery clouds.

My sight shifts from my former friends to the imposing figure, standing at the arched stone entrance. His presence casts a dark shadow as the sun glimmers down, highlighting his attire. From one wolf in sheep's clothing to another, it's almost mocking that the men I once trusted implicitly have contributed to my unwarranted demise. But now I know better.

Studying him, he wears his usual expression of disappointment. It's nothing new, but I thought, on today of all days, compassion would burst through his staunch façade. Sadly, I was wrong in my romantic idea that wishful thinking would overrule.

"Norman?" My mother calls as she walks up behind him. She stops short, glancing with despair between our father/daughter impasse until he storms out of the cemetery. She lifts her finger in command to stay and dutifully chases after him.

I loiter on the spot as the bells ring from the spire, disturbing the stillness. The seconds pass uncomfortably, and I close my eyes in resignation, aware she may not return.

It isn't a secret in our closed-off, dysfunctional family that there is a possibility he won't allow it. Honestly, I should consider myself lucky he decided to put on the charade of being the grieving, caring father by presiding over today's service. How he's managed to pull the wool over the eyes of the village we live in is no small feat. If they only knew the truth of my existence for the last three years. If only they knew a lot of things, rather than listening to the lies and hearsay.

The bells chime again as I walk around the graveyard. They confirm thirty minutes have slipped by with still no sign of my mother returning. Why I thought she would, I have no idea.

I hold the flowers to my chest and stop and stare frantically at the spot I vacated just an hour ago. Sickness and fear claws at my insides as I watch the gravediggers fill in the now occupied hole, disrupting the last precious moments I have left in this place.

3

"Sorry, love, but you can't be here," one of the men says, slamming down the spade and rubbing his hands together to ward off the cold.

"O-oh." I baulk, succumbing to the pain because those seven little words have just shattered my world further.

Honestly, if I can't be here, where else can I go? I had a home, now it's gone. I had a family, and now, that too is gone. I had everything until it was ripped from me.

It's safe to say my New Year hasn't started the way I anticipated. And nothing will ever be the same again.

I clutch the carnations for dear life and hesitate because his statement has thrown me. My feet refuse to move because I *need* to be here. Holding his eyes, I want to beg him; to plead to let me stay just a little longer.

He reads my thoughts perfectly and yanks the shovel from the ground with fierce determination – a show of who has the upper hand here. The second man's eyes flit between his mate and me, then he takes a sip from the steaming thermos mug in his hand.

"Hang on," he says, pulling a crumpled sheet of paper from his pocket. "Are you family?" I nod furiously, hoping he will see my desperation. Kindness envelops his face, and the age lines soften around his eyes.

"Tony?" he calls to his colleague. "Let's give the girl some space."

He continues to speak, but it might as well be white noise filtering my eardrums. Maybe it's the cold, or maybe it's the strain of the day and the weeks preceding finally taking their toll. But truthfully, it's none of the above. I ceased to hear anything the moment crying stopped, paving the way for the beautiful, deathly sound of silence. My world ended a month ago, and I've been in limbo ever since.

"We'll be back in an hour, love. We can't give you any longer than that. I'm sorry." The man reaches out and squeezes my arm in comfort.

"Thank you," I offer, grateful for his compassion.

As I sit down on the freshly dug earth, the brass plaque glistens atop the coffin; a tiny ray of hope penetrating the bleak conditions.

I wipe my eyes and stare at the headstone. Softly tracing the gilding, memorising each letter, guilt flays me, and I mentally fight against the urge to throw myself in.

I've repeatedly been told that time is healing, that one day I will look back and not blame myself. Yet there is no one I can hold responsible or shift culpability to. This is my failure. I recognised the signs long ago, and I should have screamed my fears at anyone who would listen. I should have done so many things... So many things that shall now haunt me until the day I die.

All the moments of the last few years blight my broken soul. Thinking back to when our journey first started, I never thought this is how it would end. But it has, and now I'm left to pick up the pieces alone.

Except, have I been anything else for the last three years?

Laying down, I rest my head in my hands and speak things I know will never be heard. Confessions that will never be forgiven.

In my heart, I need to be absolved.

"I'm sorry," I whisper. "I'm sorry I didn't protect you. That I wasn't good enough. I tried, but it was too late. *I* was too late."

Footsteps approach and I lift my head, expecting to see the men returning. Instead, I see a sight that almost stops my already slow beating heart.

My mother.

"I thought you'd gone."

"No," she whispers.

"Did you see him?" I ask, wondering if she and my father witnessed the latest show of lies. "Did you hear what he said?"

"I did, sweetheart," she replies sincerely.

I sit up and wipe my nose on the sleeve of my plastered arm. My heart is breaking, obliterating. I want her to hold me and tell me everything is going to be okay. That I will make it through this and come out of the other side stronger, fighting with such determination, I won't even recognise myself. But they are just misguided fantasies to appease my soul. Nothing can erase what has been and gone - nor can it erase the blame I carry inside.

Tomorrow, next month, next year... It doesn't matter how long because I will always be that poor girl who couldn't save a life.

Mum smiles sadly, then picks up a carnation, kisses it, and drops it in. "They like to gossip, but they know he's lying, sweetheart," she says after a drawn-out pause and sits beside me.

"Do they?" I query. "This is all my fault."

"No, it isn't," she says firmly, tugging me onto her lap. I lean my head back against her shoulder, and my body shakes as I emit my anguish. Her soft hands stroke my cheeks and forehead, soothing me, trying to pacify the rage inside at this injustice.

"Do you think she hates me?" It's a stupid question, and one I know will never be answered.

"No, never."

"I feel so ashamed," I confess.

"Don't you ever say that. You did everything right. *Everything.*" She turns me abruptly, and her eyes latch onto the locket around my neck. "If anyone should be ashamed, it's me. I let this happen. I allowed him to leave you floundering when you needed us. I turned the other cheek because I was ordered to, because I was too frightened not to, and I'll never forgive myself for it."

To hear her speak such things is heartbreaking because I've never blamed her. Our family, the dynamics of it, has never been easy to manoeuvre. My father rules tyrannically; he doesn't know any different. He's a product of his own beliefs. It has made him hard and unwavering. Over the years, his firm faith has slipped into something that none of us no longer recognise. The man he was is gone, lost underneath his strong, disciplinarian authority.

When we were growing up, some days we couldn't even breathe without causing his temper to snap. And God knows I have been on the receiving end of it more often than I would like to admit.

"I love you, Mummy," I murmur, calling her the name I haven't since I was eleven and realised how uncool it was.

"I love you too, my special girl," she replies, also calling me the name she hasn't in years. She always used to say I was special because I wasn't expected. I was just…there.

Hiding.

"Come on, let's go home," she says, standing awkwardly.

I get to my feet and pick up the flowers. Removing one from the bunch, I drop the rest into the grave and lay the carnation on the headstone. Mum tugs me close and seizes my hand tight as the gravediggers make their way over to us.

"Thank you," I tell them.

"Take care of yourself, sweetheart," one of them says, giving me a tight nod.

Mum tucks me into her side as we move through the narrow winding paths. The bells begin to toll again, and my body instantly halts, rigid and stoic, while a thought comes to me.

"Where's Da-" The word lodges painfully in my throat.

"He's gone to the rectory. He won't be back until later."

"What about…"

"Also at the rectory. Come on, it'll just be us."

I gaze bleary-eyed out of the window while Mum drives slowly through the village streets. I memorise my childhood surroundings, possibly for the last time, as we pass the place I want to forget about entirely. It's the place I spent the last few years, mostly living in fear.

"Have you spoken to them recently?"

"No, they don't care about me. I was just a burden on their precious reputation. Everything they did was to save themselves from talk and ridicule, it was never to protect me. And they proved it, didn't they?" I mutter rhetorically, while the house of horrors blends into the scenery behind us.

I shut the car door and swallow hard, fearful to look upon the house that was once my home. Trudging up the path, taking in the Creeping Jenny snaking up the trellis, it feels like the world has stood still, and the time I spent away is just pure imagination.

My fingers drift over the front door, and I rim the letterbox, recalling the day I stood on this very step. Begging, crying. I was praying for a dream that would never come true.

"Honey?" Mum nudges me aside as she unlocks the door. I follow her inside, and the memory of my father's voice that fateful day permeates through the atmosphere. It infuses to the back of my mind, deep into the solitary place I banished it after the event. The sound of the lock draws me back to the here and now. Turning around, Mum strokes her finger down my face, her eyes full of mutual love that we have been cheated out of by another's will.

"Have you eaten today?"

"No, I couldn't keep anything down. The story of my life lately," I reply as she strides off to the kitchen. Following her dutifully, I stop outside the living room on impulse. The picture in my mind's eye taunts me because inside this room is where the nightmare partially began.

"Honey?" Mum calls again.

"Coming," I reply in a whisper and hurry after her.

An unwelcome sensation chills my blood as Mum quickly makes us a couple of sandwiches. Pulling out what used to be my usual chair, she puts a plate in front of me, and I pick up half of the sandwich and contemplate. I doubt I'll be able to keep it down, but I'm not helping myself by slowly starving to death.

Shoving it into my mouth, and my stomach churns instantly at the thought of trying to digest it. It's been so long since I've properly eaten

7

anything, I'll be amazed if I don't throw it up in the next thirty minutes.

"Where have you been living for the past month?" Mum asks as she rubs my hand. "I thought you were still with *them* until I saw her ladyship in the supermarket and she asked how you were. I lied, of course, but where have you been?"

"A hostel." I sigh. "I couldn't exactly go back there considering the charges, and after what Dad said to me, I thought it best for all of us if I stayed somewhere else until all of this was over. Now that it is, I have choices to make."

The mug in Mum's hand suspends dramatically in mid-air, then slams down on the table, sloshing tea over the top.

"You better not be saying what I think you are." Her anguish is ubiquitous, and I lift my eyes from the mess and inconspicuously shake my head.

She really expected me to stay. To walk these streets every day, pretending to be living, but I can't do that. There are too many memories here and too many heartaches. And far too many people who know my story, and those who spread lies because they don't.

"Mum, I can't stay. The looks, the whispers, even those brave enough to say stuff to my face. I can't... Please don't be mad at me," I plead.

"I'm not, sweetheart. I just wish I could change the things I've done for the last three years. I should have been stronger and stood up to your dad. You know, I never used to be so weak. Everything was fine for a long time. We were young, in love, but when he got appointed here, I was expected to be seen and not heard. It was an order from my successor that I took very seriously. It was easy when it was just the two of us, but when you girls came along that demand became harder and harder."

"Mum, please," I beg, desperate for her to stop because I'm aware of those hard demands.

"No. I'm woman enough to admit that I should have done better by you. I'm not blind. I understand why you sought solace away from this house."

"And look how that turned out for me." I drop my eyes to my hand and turn my ring repeatedly. "I've made such a mess of everything."

"No, darling. You haven't." Mum places her hand over mine, caressing it lovingly. And I smile; the first real smile I've managed since New Year's Eve.

I glance outside as the room dims a little, and the day begins to fall into a murky grey outside.

"Where will you go?" Her question is quiet, fearful, snagging my attention from the window.

"I don't know." I shrug and lie.

She nods singularly, absorbing my confession, until she stands, scraping back the chair on the floor. She leaves the room and returns a moment later clutching her purse.

"I realise I can't make you stay. You're a grown woman, and you've been through more than most have already." I bite my lip in discomfort as she purges her true thoughts. "Here," she says, and drops an envelope on the table.

I lift the flap and flick through the wad of notes inside. "I can't accept this."

"Yes, you can," she responds firmly, sliding her thumbs under my eyes. "It will help you get on your feet. Just promise you'll write and tell me where you are. You might be a grown woman, but you'll always be my baby."

I nod and curl my arms around her since she is unaware today will be the last time I shall see her. I will write, but I can never return. It breaks my heart because even when times were tough, she was always less than a couple of miles away. But when I wake tomorrow, I'll be in a different city, with no one to care or comfort me.

Mum's hold slackens, and she leads me out of the kitchen and up the stairs.

Inside my old bedroom, warm familiarity shrouds me, seeing the things I was forced to leave behind. I open the wardrobe door and brush my hand over the stuff still hanging inside. I remove a few items and put them on the bed. Glancing at my mum, she is holding one of my old school bags.

"Do you have anything left at the hostel?"

"No, just a few items the staff gave to me when I arrived. *They* still have all my stuff."

"Don't worry. I'll get everything back for you," she says sadly, tucking the clothes inside the bag. Sitting down on the bed and absorb the space for the final time. I pick up the picture from the bedside table of two little girls posing, with pigtails, missing teeth, and matching pink cardigans. The bed moves and Mum's body heat envelops my side as she manipulates me closer.

"How is she lately?"

"She's good. She tells me she's enjoying uni. I think she's lying," Mum says coyly, and I smile. Of course, she's lying. She's doing what *he* told her to, not what she wants to.

"Do you think she'll forgive me?"

"Absolutely. She thinks you walk on water. The only reason why I sent her away is because I knew she wouldn't let you leave. I'm sorry I didn't allow you to say goodbye."

"No," I whisper. "If the roles were reversed, I'd do the same. I'd fight kicking and screaming to make her stay."

"I'll talk to her; make her understand. Just promise me you'll write to her. Say what you need to and don't hold back. She deserves your honesty."

"Even if my honesty makes her hate him? Even if it rips this family apart?"

She nods. "There's been far too many lies in this family for far too long. In truth, this family has been in tatters for years."

I chew my lip and acquiesce, then hold out my hand. "Will you take me to the station?"

"Of course," Mum says, her palm tight in mine as I grab the bag. "Grudgingly, mind."

Walking down the stairs, I scrutinise everything. Memorising and reminiscing, I stop at the bottom and stroke my fingers over the picture taking pride of place on the windowsill. Picking it up, I'm surprised it is even allowed it to be exposed in his house.

"Take it," she urges. "I have another copy. I have some more you can take, too." She then gathers up a stack of framed pictures.

"Thank you," I whisper, taking them eagerly.

"He's always loved you in his own way. He just doesn't know how to express it."

How I want to refute her statement and scream out that they are lies, but I don't. Instead, I hold the frames to my chest and leave the house for the last time.

I clutch the seat belt, experiencing the newest wave of discomfort sweeping through the car.

The journey to the station has been fraught with my nerves and Mum's apprehension. When she agreed to transport me, I don't think she appreciated the enormity of my request. The tension peeling off her is palpable. As much as I want to tell her I'll be okay, we're both aware it may not pan out that way. I might have been mentally and emotionally alone for the last three years, but physically, I always had someone close – if I needed them.

"Are you sure you still want to do this?"

I nod, but I don't dare look at her. Regardless that I'm terrified, I need a fresh start. Even if I end up returning with my tail between my legs, begging for help. I need to find myself again.

I shut the car door and slide my hand into Mum's as we head into the station. Studying the departure and arrival boards, I slip off my rucksack and pull out a few notes from the envelope.

"Departure is in fifteen minutes." The clerk slides over my one-way ticket.

"Thank you."

I turn around, but I'm stopped short as my mother cries openly. It is only the third time I have seen her this way. The first was three years ago, then one month ago, and now today.

My own eyes water in reciprocation and I wrap my arms around her. "Please don't cry for me. I'll be fine."

"I love you. So, so much."

"I love you, too," I reply, tearful. "I'm going to be okay; I swear." Looking down at my hand, I remove the ring of inconvenience and press it into her palm. "Get rid of this for me."

She sighs, wipes her eyes, and shakes her head. "Removing it doesn't make it final and binding."

"I'm aware. Once I'm settled, I'll start proper proceedings."

"Let me know if you need money. I'll sort something out."

Shame consumes me as I walk onto the platform because it feels wrong to expect her to financially rectify my mistakes.

"That's me," I say, as the overhead announcement confirms boarding.

"London? Sweetheart, no, please don't go!" she pleads in desperation. I understand her worry, and I'd be lying if I said I wasn't feeling apprehensive.

"I promise I'll stay in touch," I reply, fighting to stay composed in her wilting presence. It's hard, but I'll save my tears for when I'm out of sight.

She bundles me into a final embrace and whispers in my ear. I know she loves me, but for years she has been caught between a rock and a hard place. It's a shame that the only time she can openly express her affection is here, in a moment when she knows she is losing me forever.

"I love you," I impart for the last time as I struggle to break free from her suffocating grip. I board the carriage, and turn back at the door, but am unable to handle it when she drops to her knees on the platform, heartbroken.

Easily locating my seat by the window, I roughly wipe my eyes and sit down while Mum gets back up on her shaky legs. The train begins to slowly depart, and I flatten my palm to the glass. Locking eyes with each other, it seems she has the same idea when she places her hand on the other side and runs alongside until the platform runs out.

Tears sting my eyes, while my hometown fades into the distance behind me for the final time. I slouch back and mentally separate myself from everything that has happened these last few years; starting with every impulsive, teenage decision I've ever made, and ending with the greatest. Catching sight of my reflection as another train passes, I know this isn't the end.

I smile as the conductor moves down the gangway, checking tickets. Sitting alone at the table for four, I discreetly study the couple opposite as they tease each other lovingly. They can't be much older than me, and it's depressing because, for a short time, I also dared to dream of love. I also used to believe in fairy tales and happy endings.

Now I don't believe in anything. And if there is one thing life has taught me, it's that I can no longer love or trust another human being.

I glide my finger over my temple, tracing the three-week-old scar, and finally concede my father was right.

The fallen cannot be saved.

And that is the hardest lesson this lost lamb of God has finally learnt.

Chapter 1

Twenty-one years later…

THE SHARP PAIN lingers as I stretch my neck, forcing me to remember the events which have brought me here. Events which have ignited memories I'd long locked away, never to be raised to the surface or thought of again.

Looking around the room, John's jacket is still hung over the chair – the same place it has been since I was admitted three days ago. And for the first time in three days, he isn't here.

I sit up and rub my tired eyes, but the fresh bandages on my wrists capture my attention. I hold up my hands, identifying the soreness overpowering my limbs, and I purse my lips, not wanting anyone to hear the pitiful cries pushing their way up my throat.

I roll my shoulders and arch my spine, as someone stops outside the door. The movement casts a shadow over the thin strip of light, and I wait with bated breath for someone to enter, but no one does.

Optimistic I'm going to be left alone, I pull back the sheet covering me. Flicking on the lamp, the room illuminates softly, and I study my legs, particularly my ankles. The abrasions circling them are undisguisable, and my heart sinks, recollecting in perfect detail my unprovoked assault of the last week.

Rubbing down my calves, documenting every bruise, the door finally opens. A woman I've never met before clears her throat and enters. Her shoes squeak across the floor, and the soft thump of a clipboard hits the mattress.

I quickly cover my legs and assess her properly. Realising *what* she is, I avert my gaze and grind my teeth, because now I can't play possum. That said, I don't feel up to playing poster girl for the broken or becoming the latest clinical study for the resident shrink, either.

"Hello, Mrs Dawson." Perching herself the edge of the bed, her empathetic expression is mocking in kind.

"Miss," I correct her pathetically.

She doesn't apologise but smiles her understanding. "I'm Doctor Althea Green. I'm a specialist in the-"

"I don't need a shrink," I cut her off in a whisper.

"Miss Dawson, I'm a psychological therapist, not a *shrink*," she replies, irritated.

"Same difference."

With an annoyed flick of her brow, she picks up the clipboard and begins to flip through the pages. "It says here that you've been suffering nightmares for the past two days. That you feel-"

"I know what it says!" I cry out in indignation. "I told you, I don't need a shrink."

Shame, embarrassment, and a hundred other emotions I dare not verbalise run rampant through me. But the most prevalent emotion is anger. Anger that someone saw fit to decide my fate, thus removing my control.

Again.

"I respect your opinion." She sighs. "No one knows you better than you know yourself, but I'd like to help." She stands up, pulls a notebook from her pocket, jots something down and rips off the page. "That's my direct number, should you change your mind. If I don't see you again, take care, Miss Dawson."

I train my eyes on the paper as she slips out of the room. Picking it up, I wonder if I can walk into her office and purge my dark soul. Shaking my head at the preposterous thought, I scrunch up the paper and lob it towards the bin.

Laying down, my eyes water involuntarily until a single knock plays upon the door, and it opens without invitation.

Doctor Stuart Andrews enters, clutching two disposable coffee cups. His all-seeing, assessing eyes, make me incredibly self-conscious, and I give him a vacant expression.

"How are you feeling?" Closing the door with his hip, he sets the cups down and drags the chair to the side of the bed. "Marie?"

"I'm fine," I lie.

"Really?" he counters sceptically.

"Where's John?" I ask, looking over the top of his blonde head, not wanting to get into a deep and meaningful with him. Yet we both know we will. And by asking unnecessary questions, all I am doing is biding my time and holding off the inevitable that will happen before he walks out of here.

"I don't know, but here are your release forms."

"Thank you," I whisper, laying them on my lap. "How's Kara? I kind of fell asleep on her this afternoon."

"She's already gone. Sloan was adamant she wasn't staying any longer than necessary. You know what he's like," he replies sarcastically.

I purse my lips and avert my eyes because that is one less premeditated subject to delay my truth.

"Marie, talk to me. Anything you say will be in confidence." The tension swirls between us because I don't know if I can trust him.

Touching the side of my face, I involuntarily run my finger over my temple. I wince and shift my hand over my eyes, but Stuart links his fingers in mine and lowers my arm.

"The bastard did a number on some old scar tissue. We stitched it as neatly as possible, but unfortunately, it will be more prominent when it heals." I open my mouth, but nothing comes out. "I noticed it a long time ago, Marie. Don't worry, you'll still be pretty," he says with a mollifying smile. "Want to talk about it?"

"No," I whisper and squeeze his hand in mine.

"Marie, you need to talk about it. All of it."

I shake my head, my nose and mouth twisting. "I can't."

"One day you must, or it will consume you."

I bark out a laugh. "It's already consumed me, Stuart. There's nothing left here to devour."

He leans over the bed, removes a pair of gloves from the box and slips them on. Unravelling the bandages on my wrists, he assesses my injuries closely. Relatively satisfied, he carefully lowers my hands, and his soft fingers examine my bruised eye socket and the surrounding split skin.

"What happened?" he probes gently again.

Salty tears well in my eyes, recollecting in painful, unspoken detail. "I always thought I was the strong one. That if Deacon ever turned up, I'd do what we all say we would and grab something and use it, but I didn't. I failed again."

"No, you didn't," he murmurs, drawing back his hands and removing the gloves.

I gaze up at the ceiling and press my skull against the metal bar running over the top of the bed.

"He was already waiting. I looked straight into his eyes. I didn't help myself, Stuart. I didn't fight. I didn't do anything. I just fucking stood there!"

"Marie, you..." he starts, but I shake my head vehemently.

15

"No," I reply with finality because I dare not tell him the rest. I haven't even told John, and it would be unfair to air my grief to anyone but him first. Regardless, I wasn't lying to Kara when she queried if he had done *that*.

Long, unsettling minutes pass, and seeing that this conversation is prematurely finished, Stuart stands.

"Look, every now and again, we all need someone. There's no shame in admitting you're not coping."

"I know, but I'm fine. Really."

He lets out a mirthless laugh. "Marie, you can fool everyone, but you can't fool me, or John. There's a great counselling team here. I once offered it to Kara, but unlike her, I'm hoping you'll give it a go. One session, that's all. She's called Doctor Green, you'll like her." I subtly shift my eyes to the floor where I lobbed her number half an hour ago.

Stuart sticks the post-it to the release form, then kisses my cheek. "It's not my place to say, but John's concerned that you won't be his Marie when you leave here. And I'll admit, I don't think he's mistaken." Satisfied he has aired his opinion, irrespective if it will be taken into consideration, he says goodbye and closes the door behind him.

I turn to the window as morning lightens the horizon. Fear snakes its way through my soul as I stare aimlessly.

Truthfully, I can lie as much as the next person. God knows I've made it an art form. But Stuart's right; they are both unmistaken in his last assumption because I'm not John's Marie anymore.

Three days ago, I was accepting of my life and the direction it was headed. But all that changed the moment I woke up tied to a chair, unable to breathe, having already had the living shit beaten out of me. The woman I was – the one I honed to perfection and the one John fell in love with – she's flown.

The impact of those few hours opened my eyes for the second time in my life. They verified that the vicious circle of life would always be turning and always be victorious. It would never stop. And I would never be destined for more than what I'd already been given - something that had been snatched away in the cruellest way imaginable.

Lost in bygone nightmares, I flinch when a flash of colour paints the sky, and I switch off the lamp and watch the storm clouds roll in. The first crack of thunder brings imminent darkness. To say I feel an affinity with it is an understatement - it appears to be the only place I seem to exist in perfect harmony.

Pressing my forehead against the glass, I'm cognizant that the proverbial sands of time have already started to shift again. And just like before, I will not be able to stop the grains from falling. It seems anytime I have a chance of happiness, the badness is just lingering beneath the surface, predicting the exact moment to strike and devour. For so many years because of this, I remained alone and loveless, existing but never living.

By existing, I went through the motions daily, putting on the façade of someone successful, well presented and put together, but inside I was nothing. I was hollow.

But living, however, was always for those who had something to live for. Someone special, something precious. I didn't have either of those things, and so I made do with the card that life had dealt me. The one I picked imprudently that turned out to be nothing but a life of pain and loneliness.

Then one day, when I had finally given up all hope, a glimmer of light appeared in the shape of an ex-army powerhouse. A man who is beautiful, inside and out. Caring, selfless, and completely astute, bearing an uncanny ability to read the minds and invade the hearts of those broken. I, being one of them. I knew the moment he turned up on my doorstep I'd never be able to say no.

Inhaling deeply, I know one day in the foreseeable future I shall have to make choices again. Choices that will swing the already precarious balance. And that balance is my undisclosed past.

Embattled by the memory, I rub my forehead, ineffectively unable to expel the shit that has lurked inside for over two decades.

Trudging to the holdall on the floor, I rummage inside and dig out the last of my clean clothes. Dropping them on the bed, I pick up the fresh towels and move into the small shower room. This is one of the only privileges I have. One that Stuart's position and influence have afforded me, and I'm thankful.

I lay the towels on the toilet lid and pick up my small wash bag from the cistern. Capturing sight of my reflection, my face is marred with dark purple bruising; yellow in some parts, almost black in others. A sickness lingers in the pit of my stomach, and I grip the basin for ballast, thinking back to the times I had once sported the same colourings.

I close my eyes as a painful howl rips through my conscience. Two decades worth of memories pulls to the forefront of my mind. They lead the onslaught of things I want to forget, things I'm too ashamed to confess and permanently free myself of. But unfortunately, forgetting is no longer an option - a senseless assault ensured that by making me the victim again.

Turning on the shower, I step inside. Rubbing the soap over my tender skin, the pain manifests, and my resolve crumbles.

The tears come thick and fast, and I'm grateful that no one can hear me, because I'm not a crier, not anymore. I was once. I used to cry every day. It was the only outlet I had for the repressed anger I'd accumulated for the life that had cheated me, beat me, broke me, and finally, took whatever was left. It was negligible because it left me with nothing.

Turning off the shower, I grab the towel and wrap it tightly. Faint footsteps resound from outside, and I open the door to see John in profile, studying his phone. I inch closer, and he lifts his head. He smiles, then rakes his eyes down the length of my body. Under his assessing gaze, I squirm, because this is the first time he has seen the full devastation.

For the last three days, aside from when I've had visitors, I have pretended to be asleep. It's selfish, but I don't want to tarnish his image of me. He thinks I'm strong and beautiful, that I can handle anything that is thrown at me, but he's wrong.

"Angel," he says gently, edging towards me.

Meeting him in the middle, my arms snake around his waist and I rest my head against his chest.

"Hi," I reply quietly, not knowing what to say. The words trapped inside will in time be verbalised. Not just those that have transpired to put us in this position, but those that initially put me in this position a lifetime ago.

In my heart, I know he's waiting for me to break, to snap spectacularly. And it won't be long before I do because no one can contain their pain for very long. Eventually, it beats even the strongest.

I pad towards the small pile of clothes and start to worry my lip. Staring at him diligently, I wonder how I'm going to ask him not to watch, or better yet, leave. But that's not an option; I already know he will refuse. I've struck lucky so far and managed to change without him being present. Unless he's looked when I have been asleep, he has no idea what lies beneath.

A light finger trails down my back, and I jolt in shock, fearing it.

"John…" My tone is guarded, and I clutch the towel tight. I'm not ready to let him see the rest of me. It's the same way that I'm not willing to talk about it because he will finally see the psychological damage, that, in my opinion, is far worse than the physical.

His face falls, and his pained expression is unambiguous since he can't hide his emotions. God knows he thinks he can, but he fails every time.

"You blame me," he says, and it is more of an observation than a question. But regardless, I respond with the only truth I have.

"No, I don't."

A resigned sigh flows over my shoulder. "No? Well, at least look at me and say it."

I fist my hands, rotate and glare at him. In this instant, considering what I've been through, I have every right to be reticent about being touched. I refuse to voice what he should already know.

Reading my thoughts correctly, he takes a step forward, and I step back because he is going to revoke my control. I make the decision quickly, rather than agonising over it, and I lower my head as the towel hits the floor.

Time ceases as we stand at a stalemate. Me, my eyes studying my toes; him, still motionless less than a foot away. I want to look at him. I want to see what he is thinking, but I know what my body currently looks like. I've heard it being discussed by the doctors. I've read it on my medical records, and I've seen it with my own eyes. And in time, my injuries will fade, but the memory will not.

Just when I'm ready to give up hope and snatch up the towel, his booted foot moves into my line of sight. His hands reach forward, and he glides them over my waist. Standing nude in front of him, aware he is studying every cut and bruise, memorising them, documenting them, is the most exposed I've ever felt.

"I feel ashamed, John. I can't bear for you to look at me like *this*," I admit.

"Shit, beautiful. Is that what you think?" He takes my hand and kisses it. "Don't shut me out, angel."

"I'm not," I plead pathetically.

He smiles sadly and shakes his head. "But you are. You have been since the day we met. I don't doubt what you feel for me, but I've learned to live with the fact you don't trust me. If you did, you would have told me about your life before Kara. You don't discuss anything; family, growing up, boyfriends. I know none of it. It's as though you didn't exist until she came along. I also don't dare raise it because I will be shut down. So instead, I've learnt to live with the titbits you'll freely give me, hoping one day you'll trust me enough to let me in completely."

I open my mouth, desperate for him to stop speaking words we both know are correct and just, but I'm rendered speechless by his tender display of affection, as his lips caress the back of my hand, all the way to my elbow. As he reaches under my backside, my legs automatically sweep around his waist. I link my fingers at his nape and rest my cheek on his shoulder while he kisses my forehead. His hand rubs up and down my back soothingly as he lays me on the bed. Looming over me, he kisses me, first hard and fast, then slow and reverent. Alternating between the two, I drown in the moment and sigh as his thumb circles my cheek.

"I love you," he murmurs. "There's nothing I wouldn't do for you. You know that, right?" I nod, my tongue sliding over my bottom lip, savouring him. "I'm sorry I wasn't there."

"It's not your fault."

"Yes, it is." He strokes my chest delicately. "I took a chance, it backfired. I never thought he would come after you. If I did, I would've ended the bastard myself."

"Darling, don't. I will never, ever blame you."

"I should've been there. I swore I'd always protect you. That I'd save you if you ever needed me to." His voice rises, revealing his guilt. His distress.

I press deeper into the mattress and take a breath. I want to tell him that he has saved me; every day for the last eighteen months, but I know he will want an explanation if I do. So rather than raise unnecessary questions I know he will pursue until he gets the answers he desires, I clench my hands tighter around him.

"Are you ready to go home?" he whispers over the top of my head, and my body shudders at the thought of stepping foot back in that house. "My home, angel. *Our home.* Not that place. Never again. As soon as you're up to it, we'll clear it out and put it on the market. Then it's gone. Erased."

I grip him closer while he presses kisses against my hair. Truthfully, nothing in this world can erase what has happened. And yet again I am back on the turning wheel, proving that life runs in cycles, and maybe this won't be the last time I nurse my wounds on a hard, hospital bed.

Still, I'm no longer disillusioned that this life won't show me further pain in the future. Bad luck comes in threes. I just have to hope that if it does happen, I will survive a third time and that the casualty of this war won't be the love of a good man who is yet to learn my truths.

Closing my eyes, I think back to the day he invaded my life, bringing his light, and hope for a future that had evaded me for so long.

Chapter 2

Eighteen months earlier…

OPENING THE BATHROOM door, the steam billows out the same moment I do. I grasp the towel at my front and groan when the phone starts to ring. As I dash down the stairs, the machine kicks in.

This is an answering machine. Please leave your message after the tone.

"Hi, Marie. It's me!"

"Oh, God, no," I murmur, rolling my eyes at the sound of Samantha Jones' exuberant tone. Whenever this girl calls me, the outcome is bleak. And calamitous.

I listen, unimpressed, waiting for her to speak the words that are going to cause me to have a nervous breakdown within the next five minutes. Narrowing my eyes at the machine, she waffles on pointlessly, until she finally says the words that might cause the ulcer I'm sure is growing in my stomach to burst.

"Just to let you know that something came up tonight, and I won't be able to work my shift."

My mouth falls open in horror, and I instantly see red. I can't believe she is doing this. I appreciate I gave the team extremely short notice, but she knows how important this night is. Not only is it in aid of charity, but it's also at the Emerson Hotel. And the last thing I need is for the selfish little bastard of an owner to be disgruntled. It is also safe to assume that if tonight is a spectacular fiasco, said little bastard will muddy my name from Land's End to John o'Groats.

I look up, praying to all that is holy that this night will not fail. It will not fall apart at the seams, and I will have an intact reputation come tomorrow morning.

"Anyway," Sam carries on. "I know how important it is, but there's no need to worry. I've already talked to Kara, and she's going to cover for me!"

My head jerks and I almost choke on my tongue upon hearing that declaration. Kara, my daughter for all intents and purposes, doesn't do waiting on the rich and ungrateful – her words, not mine. She's the names and numbers girl. She mans the office, takes the bookings, and keeps us on the straight and narrow.

"Well, that's all I wanted to say. Hope it goes well. Bye!"

"Sam? Sam!" I snatch up the handset, but she's already gone.

With the phone to my chest, I debate whether I should call Kara to clarify what the hell is going on but think better of it. I really don't want to know what's going on in Samantha's life. As a matter of fact, it's safer for all of us if we just avoid it altogether.

But, unfortunately, somethings just can't be swept under the rug. And if the newly hushed gossip already doing the rounds between the girls on my team is anything to go by, the downward spiral has already started to turn again. I only hope she doesn't drag my girl down into that probable pit of destruction with her - which seems to be her only destination in the foreseeable future.

I place the handset back on its base and turn back to the stairs, but a flash on the wall from outside snags my attention. Edging closer to the window beside the door, I push aside the blind and peer inquisitively at the grey Range Rover parked on the other side of the street.

Calm flows through me because this isn't the first time I've seen that car. Over the years, it has been a regular visitor. But visiting whom, I do not know.

I tilt my head in surprise when the window slides down, and a man wearing dark aviators and a flat cap stares straight at me. Shocked, I gasp and step back.

Shit! I'm well and truly caught. In nothing but a towel, no less.

Twitching the blind again, the man is still staring at my house. Fear clenches my heart because this is the day I've always feared. Grabbing the door handle, I'm relieved it's locked. As my paranoia kicks in, I hurry into the kitchen, again testing the handle.

My heart beats out of control as I anxiously creep back down the hallway to the front door. Playing peeping tom from inside my own home, I press my nose to the wood and squint through the spyhole. Glancing left to right, the car is gone. I step back with my hand over my mouth, wondering.

Opening the table drawer, I pull out my phone book and thumb through it until I find the number of a man I know will always help me. I lodge the book open and debate the right course of action since I possess no solid proof my life is in any kind of danger to necessitate his services again.

Except, as far as danger lurks, I've spent so many years forging a path forward, I wouldn't know what was waiting just behind me. My focus has always been to look straight ahead and never back.

Everything behind me is in the past. And whilst I'm not entirely committed to that theory, it's the best I've got.

Still spooked and apprehensive, I close the book and toss it into the drawer. With a final look outside, I head back upstairs.

I drop the hairdryer on the floor and style my hair into a small, low bun. Applying a little makeup, I slick my lashes with mascara and zip up my makeup bag.

I shift from foot to foot at the side of the bed, studying the choice of three black dresses from my collection of many. The decision should be easy, because regardless that they are three different styles, they are all, ultimately, LBD's.

Fed up of procrastinating, I randomly pick one out and grab a matching underwear set from the drawer, along with a pair of sheer, nude hold-ups. Perching myself on the edge of the mattress, I roll one nylon over my leg and then the other.

Resting my elbows on my knees, I stare around the room. As always, everything is faultless and perfectly placed. There is no excess baggage. I guess I could go as far as to say the only excess baggage in my home is me. On that melancholy thought, I remove the dress from its hanger and slide it on.

Standing in front of the mirror, the weariness in my eyes stares back at me. It's subtle and unassuming, but it's always there. I sigh because now is really not the time. Mentally stowing away the personal failure for later, I spray on a little perfume, pick up my heels and close the door behind me.

Reaching the rear entrance of the Emerson Hotel, tonight it's make or break. I'm not stupid to believe that the owner - who informed me in no uncertain terms that tonight better pass without hitch or event or there will be consequences - will be watching me like a hawk.

I grind my teeth, still furious of the demands that a man - one young enough to be my son - laid down on me. I appreciate age is irrelevant, but his behaviour was rude, uncouth and completely unjustified. Clearly, he forgot that he approached me for this little venture, at the eleventh hour, just to be awkward.

Notwithstanding his conduct, when his assistant called to inquire if I had the capacity to cover, I couldn't refuse. Not because of the amount of money I was coerced with, but because memories are a powerful thing, and this isn't the first time I have catered for this hotel.

The first time was some eight years ago, and it proved to be a defining moment in my life. It was the day that changed everything. Because that night, when my path crossed with that of a homeless, teenage girl, fate finally deemed me fit to be a mother.

My eyes drift over the steps as I remember the filthy teenager in misshaped, tatty clothes, eating a meal with such gusto it could've been her last.

I smile in recollection because good things happened out here that night. I gained a daughter, Kara gained a mother, and a little of the world's wrongs were righted.

I jab my finger into the intercom button and wait. Eventually, it opens and a young woman I only saw from afar at the initial meeting two days ago, greets me.

"Hi, I'm Laura. You should've come around to the front."

"It's nice to meet you, Laura. I'm Marie Dawson."

"I know who you are. Mr Foster has spoken *very* highly of you." She smiles, and I stare manically at the back of her head as I follow her down the staff corridor.

Mr Foster spoke highly of me? Highly unlikely!

Entering the staff room, I glance around at the walls in need of a fresh coat of paint, observing it is still the same as it was the last time.

"You can leave your stuff here. I believe most of your staff have already arrived," Laura says, handing me a company phone – God forbid I have any issues – and leaves me alone.

I sit down at one of the tables and pull out my mobile. I still have no call from Kara to confirm nor deny her attendance tonight, but I do have a text from my shift supervisor to say he's already here. Locking my things away, I smooth down my front and head out.

As I approach the ballroom, the noise emanating is loud and jovial. Pushing through the French doors, I delight in the vision before me. My staff, including my shift supervisor, are milling around the room. Some are straightening up the chairs and the centre displays, others are polishing the glasses and silverware, ensuring their reflections shine back at them.

I subconsciously rub my temple and sigh. Such ostentatious wealth will be displayed here tonight, but underneath the glitzy surface, there are always cracks.

I know because ostentatious wealth once controlled my life. Albeit, it was only for a short time, but still long enough to leave a lasting scar on my soul.

Six hours.

I'm counting it down.

Six hours until it's over. Six hours until I can take off these shoes. And six hours until I can, hopefully, go home.

Working the room, I take a fleeting glance at the attendees and then back to the man who hired me. Sloan Foster - complete with the obligatory, beautiful women vying for his attention - looks like he owns the world.

I nab a glass of champagne from one of my boys passing through the throng of guests and watch optimistically as Kara moves towards the table she begged me to relocate her from. Observing her and arsehole Foster, I realise the story she told me was incomplete. When she rehashed it, in between gulps of anxious breath, I thought it was all one-sided. But now, looking at him, seeing the way he is looking at her, the attraction is apparently mutual. Even from this distance, there is more in his stare than a playmate for the night. I might have spent many years alone, but even I can distinguish his intentions from his lustful gaze.

"Shit," I mutter. As much as I want Kara to live a normal life – whatever normal maybe – I fear the ramifications of this little tryst, should it blossom from the fake fantasy of this room into the harsh reality of the real world. The real world, of which, she has already experienced far too many of its harsh realities.

Removing my attention from Kara, my eyes drift around the room, ensuring the event is flowing without catastrophe. Although I doubt it would be noticed if it did since the owner seems far too content keeping his focus on something else I also consider my responsibility.

As I network around the room, singling out those who look like they hold an account at Coutts, I engage in conversation easily and leave when it's run its natural course. Retreating from the current small group of my choosing, discussing the state of the economy with depressing enthusiasm, I head off to the ladies.

Washing my hands, I bend towards the mirror, and the overhead lights emphasise the scar adorning my temple. Beginning just under my brow and ending at the corner of my eye, it's a visual memory of pain. After all these years, the puckered skin is barely noticeable, unless you are up close and personal.

I graze my finger over it in compulsion, and the distant sound of screaming is released from the dormant place I have kept it imprisoned.

The memory is broken by the clamour of women behind me. Beautiful and boisterous, they recap the evening with glee. More than once the owner's name is mentioned, and more than once I try to forget the unhealthy interest he is showing in my girl. I shake my hands over the sink and head back out.

Walking the perimeter of the ballroom, I slow my stride when a large, muscular man enters my peripheral vision in the sea of guests.

Dressed in a black tux, complete with bow tie, the material fits perfectly over his imposing arms and shoulders.

Seriously, tall, dark, and handsome has nothing on him.

I watch curiously, completely engrossed as he leads a young blonde onto the dance floor. My concentration is unbroken as he holds her securely and moves her in and out of turns. Partially concealed behind a group of animated, but still relatively sober men, I gaze, mesmerised, wondering if my ex *ever* looked at me like that.

A look of undeniable love. A look that speaks volumes.

I exorcise that demon from my head because *he* is the last man I want to be thinking about. My fingers inadvertently drift over the scar again, flooding my conscience with distant memories. They forego what came before, and again, start with how this scar came to be. A single, harrowing event that guaranteed I would never live a full, beautiful life.

With a final look at the man who, for the first time in years, has caught my attention, his movement slows. As if someone has whispered I am staring with morbid fascination, his head tilts, and he smiles. It's a smile of recognition, but I've never seen him before in my life.

Deep set, worldly eyes ensnare mine, and my body elicits a sharp, unexpected tingle from top to toe. Caught off guard, with my body emanating a hormonal hum I've not felt in years, I shuffle awkwardly but have nowhere to hide.

The woman at his side follows his line of sight, and enlightenment glosses her face. Stretching up on her toes, she grins enthusiastically and kisses his cheek before walking away.

Enthralled, unable to avert my gaze, he takes my stare as a challenge. With one hand fisted at his side, the other beckons me over, and I shake my head as sensibility begins to flood back in.

Poised and beautiful, the man is masculine in a way that sees him standing head and shoulders above all others. He carries the same confidence that once blindsided me. I was so swept up in it that I didn't see the falling façade until it was too late.

The sound of shattering glass breaks the connection, and I turn to the bar to see the remnants of a champagne bottle littered across the floor. Without a second thought, I rush over, but one of the waiters is already cleaning it up.

I glance back to the dance floor, but the man who captured my attention, and dare I say, my long-forgotten desire, has gone.

A sensation of imminent loss deepens, but it's a loss I don't ever want to experience again. It has meant I have lived alone, but regardless of how lonely I might be, I know I'm safe. I'm safe from harm, from pain, and ultimately, I'm safe from death.

I inconspicuously stretch up, fooling myself into believing I'm observing the room when, in fact, I'm searching for my mystery man, as Kara approaches.

"Hey, do you mind if I take five?" she asks.

"No, you go ahead," I reply. "Grab a drink on your way. Only a small one, though!" I lift my hand and show her my definition of small with my finger and thumb. She smiles, rolls her eyes, and requests a spritzer.

Inside the hot, busy kitchen, I walk around the industrial metal tables as the desserts are being laid out. Bending down, scrutinising them to ensure they are immaculate, the door swings open. The ambience is instantly vanquished from cheery to icy, as Sloan Foster strides in. His eyes scan the area repeatedly, evidently unable to find who he is looking for.

"Where is he?" he asks tersely, a slight American accent making an appearance.

"He's outside having a cig, boss," someone replies.

Not knowing where to put myself, I look up at *the boss,* and he smiles.

"This evening is an outstanding success," he says sincerely. "My mother would be proud. Thank you, Ms Dawson."

I'm at risk of choking on my own tongue. Never in a million years would I have ever thought he would be praising me. Clearly, he appreciates the time I have put in to get this event rolling on only two days' notice. Granted, his kitchen staff are working overtime because even I can't perform miracles, but the rest of the grandeur gracing the ballroom is all my hard work. And calling in numerous favours which I will eventually have to repay.

"Thank you, Mr Foster. I appreciate your approval."

He nods, but his concentration is elsewhere. Without further delay, he pushes through the door and leaves it swinging in his wake.

"Carl's going to get it when he finds him!"

"I wouldn't want to be in that little bastard's shoes!"

"Someone ought to go and clear out his locker!"

As the further musings of the kitchen staff are aired unapologetically, I discreetly snag a strawberry tart and spin around to hide my theft.

I push through the door with my shoulder, while a raised, aggravated voice drifts down the corridor. A young chef stomps towards me, and I flatten myself against the wall as he rants and curses, before kicking open the kitchen door.

Taking a bite out of the tart, I think Sloan has just found his missing staff member.

"Wow," I whisper, savouring the pastry. Rubbing my hands together to dispose of the crumbs, the sound of a familiar female seeps into my ears. Suspicion gets the better of me, and my feet lead me towards the back door.

I halt when I see Kara and Sloan near the steps. Witnessing their interaction, I mentally question if I should interrupt. Instead, I step back into the shadows and watch. Kara downs the glass of wine in her hand, and worry grips me when Sloan reaches out and tucks a strand of hair behind her ear. My mouth falls open the same moment her eyes close. It's a revelation, because, for the first time in years, I realise his touch doesn't adversely affect her. And for the first time in years, I'm jealous that she can give him something that she can't give me.

I train my eyes on the floor, listening to Sloan speak quietly, soothingly, until I turn away. Walking back down the corridor, my mind awash with emotion, I open a random door and slip inside. Standing amongst the crates and boxes, I remember, and remembering is never good for me.

In the days before I choose the path I'm currently dragging my heels over, once upon a time, my ex would say he loved me. But now, seeing the admiration and devotion in the look I have just witnessed, I remember the most painful thing of all – I was young and stupid – because while he loved to lead me astray, he never loved me at all. He never held me when I was doubtful. He never wiped the tears that I cried - most of them created under his heavy-handed anger. But most of all, he never cared enough to protect what should have mattered the most. All he cared about was himself. He cared about where his next night of drugs and debauchery away from our bed was coming from. He cared about everything, except what was waiting for him at home.

I inhale deeply as soft footsteps approach, and I crouch beside the shelving unit as Kara and Sloan pass by the open door.

Composing myself, praying that Kara is floating on cloud nine and doesn't notice, I step out. Malingering at the French doors, she looks conflicted. I tiptoe behind her, but she is so wrapped up in the moment of watching the man walk away, she doesn't see me.

"So, what did Mr Beautiful want?" I ask although I'm already aware of what he wants. She doesn't look at me and remains mute. "Hmm, hmm, thought so. When?"

"Tomorrow." Her reply is far too quiet, and I move in front of her. I shake my head at her unknown shortcomings. She has no idea who he is or what she has got herself into.

"You do know this was his event tonight?" Wrong thing to say, because she now looks ready to vomit. I'm not sure if I should say the next thing, considering it's something that she has first-hand experience of, but since I also know what it's like to suffer, I run my mouth anyway.

"The rumour mill says that his mother suffered from domestic abuse, so he devotes a lot of time to it, and some rather substantial donations apparently. He also owns... No, never mind. Come on, let's start cleaning up."

Holding the door open for her, she glides through, almost like she is walking on air – or floating on cloud nine. I don't blame her. I'd probably be the same if I had a good-looking man in my sights.

And speaking of which, the one who snagged my attention earlier is now blocking the ballroom entrance with a mixed-race man. From this distance, it is apparent they are ribbing each other. Again, instinctively, he turns right on cue. First, his eyes follow Kara, making her way through the room, and then they land on me. My breath hitches because tonight has proven something different to what I always believed.

I give him a small smile, and he returns it with a nod of recognition. The man next to him grins broadly at me, and I can't hold back my smile. Eventually, he turns, and with a final look over his shoulder, he's gone again.

I lean on the bar, mentally berating myself for an opportunity lost, because I know I shall never see him again. But if the handsome stranger has given me anything tonight, it's the realisation that I can't continue to live with regret, and that I still have a life worth living.

For the last twenty-one years, my life has been languishing in a graveyard with the dead, but I'm still very much alive. And tonight is the first time I have felt it.

Chapter 3

I COLLECT UP the random receipts and a single hair bobble as I wipe the duster over the sideboard; having forgotten how dishevelled the house gets when it isn't only me living here.

Picking up Kara's school picture, I carefully clean the glass and smile. My mind relapses, rewinding back to the moment I found that emaciated, broken child attempting to steal a meal for the night. Of everything I have done in my life, she is one of my better choices. A balm to the soul of a woman broken, defined by poor selection and foolish endeavour. She has often told me she can never repay me for saving her, but truthfully, she saved me. One fractured soul sent to ease another. She came along at the right time. She gave me a reason to believe again, to have faith that life is worth the heartache I had already endured.

She is my second chance.

I continue to flutter around the living room, straightening up and fluffing the cushions. Inhaling deeply, the smell of Victoria Sponge drifts in from the kitchen.

"Almost," I say rhetorically.

I close the living room door, ready to check on my rare sympathy baking when my eyes catch the thick envelope that was delivered to my office yesterday. I pick it up with a resigned sigh, wondering how many times I'll receive these until he gets bored of playing with a toy that doesn't want to play.

Flicking through the familiar pages, a knock reverberates throughout the hallway, and a figure darkens the frosted glass door. With narrow, curious eyes, I stuff the papers back into the envelope and toss it on the table. Another knock echoes impatiently, and I mutter, smoothing down my very casual dress of stretched, oversized top and faded leggings – the cleaning attire of choice.

"You're early. Have you forgotten your keys, honey?" I shout, not recall seeing them.

I await Kara's reply as I tug the droopy material over my shoulder, and run my hand over my perspired face, speculating what the hell has happened now. For her to be knocking on my door persistently again, can only mean one thing – trouble. The kind of trouble that comes in the shape of the very misguided Samantha Jones.

Again.

After bailing on the event weeks ago, I honestly thought she was determined to get better. That thought diminished the moment Kara knocked on my front door and dropped her bags on the floor.

Honestly, I often wonder why she stays and puts up with it. I also wonder how long it will be before she returns to the flat they share. Selfishly, I wish she would just move back here indefinitely. I know she's too old to still be living at home, but I wish I'd never let her move in with Sam. It's right up there with every other regret I need to repent for.

"Right, what the hell has she done now?" I open the door with my head down.

A silly, schoolgirl error.

My downcast eyes widen when I see boots – *large, black boots* – in front of me. Slowly lifting my head, I gulp back the saliva pooling in my throat, and my eyes roam in unexpected delight.

Overly washed, faded denim sits snugly over thick, muscular thighs, while a firm stomach, poorly hidden under a fitted, equally faded t-shirt flexes intermittently. I stare long and hard at the flawlessly formed, intensely broad chest and shoulders, honed to perfection. Involuntarily licking my lips, I finally look upon his face, and a fawning sigh escapes my throat.

Holy shit!

It's him.

My body lurches, but my fall is caught by my hand slamming against the door. It's not a reflexive reaction; it's the action of a desperate woman not wanting to show a man he has even a touch of power over her. My heart beats faster, harder, and I hide my anxiety by shuffling on the spot to straighten myself. Again, it's clumsy and poorly executed.

"Hello, beautiful. Remember me?"

As if I could forget!

These past few weeks, I have thought nonstop about the mystery man who roused my dormant desires in the middle of a crowded room. I wish I could say I left those wanton cravings the instant I left the building, but sadly not. For the first time in two decades, he has broken through. He has managed to get to the part of me that some have tried to over the years but never succeeded.

As I reflect, he arches a brow, defining a scar on his features – *his extremely attractive features*. Staring into his eyes, something glimmers, like he knows me, yet I don't know him.

"Erm... Hi," I greet nervously, looking behind him to see if any of my neighbours are out. As my shitty luck would have it, even the nosy old bat next door has far better things to do today. "What are you doing here? And how do you know where I live?" I ask, my mouth and throat dry from the very sexy, masculine man blocking my front door.

"I know a lot about you, Marie Dawson. Not only do I know where you live, evidently-" he waves his hand out. "I know where you work, the car you drive, the wine you drink, the ice cream you stash in the back of the freezer, and the chocolate bars you hide in the top cupboard for times you want to comfort eat. I know you, Marie Dawson."

My mouth opens and closes. How on earth do I respond to that? I don't know if I should be pleased that a man is taking an interest, or terrified that not only does he know where I live, but he knows things about me that someone I have only seen once from afar, shouldn't.

The tension swirls around us while he continues to study me. I squirm under his calculating gaze as a creeping sensation travels through me. Starting with a slow build up, I recognise these sensual feelings from when I was a teenager.

"I'm sorry, but can I help you?"

"Is that a trick question, beautiful?" He smirks and slaps a work-roughened hand on the architrave.

My brow quirks at his playfulness, but the trick is on me because I'm suddenly ravenous for something I have refused to give in to for years.

I purse my lips, trying to formulate a response. He continues to grin, but his stance relaxes somewhat. The door hinges squeak in my daze, and he takes a step inside. But I'm so mesmerised by his rugged, unconventional beauty, I don't realise until it's too late.

"Excuse me, but what do you think you're doing?" I ask flustered. Now over the threshold, he's so close, his knee brushes against my thigh.

"I'm coming inside since you weren't forthcoming in extending an invitation. I know you're not an exhibitionist, Marie, but you don't really want to have a meaningful conversation about our future on your doorstep, do you?"

His tone exudes confidence, and I feel my lungs constrict and the air being forced out. I lift my hand to my chest as he gazes down my body in approval. And again, I tug at the fabric, because unfortunately, the cleaning top of choice is that old and stretched.

"I don't want you coming inside, full stop!" My temper is rising. "And our future? Are you delusional?"

He lifts a brow. "I prefer optimistic, angel, but there's no denying the attraction. Yes, I think I'll be playing a big part in your future. Why fight fate?"

"Jesus Christ!" I exclaim, exasperated.

I have no idea what on earth he's talking about, or what I'm going to do. Logic tells me if he was here nefariously, he would have done whatever it is he wanted to already. But since he's standing here, his body parts intentionally grazing mine, discussing our non-existent future, I'm abundantly aware there is only one way to get rid of him.

"Oh, just come in, for crying out loud!" Standing aside, I wave my hand sharply towards the hallway for him to enter. He strides inside like he owns the place and instantly begins to scope out my home.

I shut the door hard behind me, and he spins around and rubs his chin thoughtfully. Closing the minute distance between us, he reaches out and strokes his fingertips over my collarbone. My eyes shut involuntarily, and I sway under his touch, breathing in his scent, feeling lightheaded and drowning in Eau de Man for the first time in over twenty years.

"Please, stop," I request pitifully, although my body is silently screaming at me to keep my stupid mouth shut.

"Open your eyes, Marie." His husky, seductive rumble encourages my lids to slowly lift, and his hand moves from my upper arm until he is massaging my nape.

"You need to stop doing that," I murmur, revelling in the sensation, wishing I could confess my true thoughts and ask him to never stop.

"Why?"

"Because." It comes out low and breathless.

His hands reluctantly retreat, and he glances at the hallway table. Fear churns in my stomach as he picks up the envelope. I rudely snatch it away and stuff it into the drawer. Slamming it shut, I perch my backside against it.

"Look, I have a hectic day ahead, and I'm working tonight. So, please, who are you and what do you want?" I throw my hands on my hips; I'm done being polite. Regardless that he makes me feel things I shouldn't, I don't have time for his fun and games.

Taken aback, he huffs and crosses his arms over his chest, accentuating his deliciously toned pectorals. "Fine. Kara's room?"

I cock my head slightly. *Kara's room?* "Why?"

He shrugs. "Because." He flippantly throws my dismissal back at me.

Accepting the reality that he isn't going to leave until I give him what he wants, I admit defeat. "Second door on the left." I point to the ceiling.

He wastes no time, and his boots pound up the stairs. With the elimination of his intoxicating presence, I race up after him and lose a tatty slipper in the process before kicking off the other.

"Sorry, but who the hell are you?" I demand, thoroughly pissed off, running into my bedroom – the second door on the left. Clearly, when answering his question, I was subconsciously thinking of the multitude of things he could be doing to me. If his neck massages are anything to go by, I can't imagine the rest of his talents will disappoint. And it's not every day a prime specimen of man shows up at my door, calls me beautiful and rouses my dormant parts from their eternal slumber.

I halt as he stands inside my bedroom, his hand drifting over the fresh linen. I swallow; it's been a long time, far too long. And seeing his eyes capture everything in my most private space, it's causing me to sweat profusely from panic and, dare I say, anticipation.

"Interesting," he murmurs, swaggering over to me. Cocky, confident, self-assured. He stops inches away from my body, and I can feel the heat roll off him like a hot summer's day. I breathe in unobtrusively, inhaling the pheromones he is unknowingly releasing. He takes another step, again purposely brushing his large frame against my smaller one as he moves onto the landing.

"Kara's room?" he asks again.

I point to the adjacent door, and we do the uncomfortable dance of trying to bypass each other. After the second unsuccessful attempt, he reaches under my arms and moves me aside.

I follow him into Kara's room and watch in a subdued, trance-like fashion, still affected by his handling of me, as he looks around appreciatively. It's almost like he is seeing something familiar or something that makes sense. He drags down a holdall from the top of the wardrobe and starts to pack up some of her clothes and toiletries.

"Look, you have five seconds to tell me who you are and why you're here. Otherwise, I'm calling the police."

"Orders." He blatantly ignores my question of his identity and picks up the boxes of contraceptive pills from the chest of drawers. "Good girl," he murmurs appreciatively and drops them inside the bag. Opening the top drawer, his expression turns uncomfortable. "Do you mind?" He looks at me and motions to the pile of bras and knickers. Well then, at least he has some manners not to touch a woman's underwear when not invited to. I'll give him points for that.

I halt with the scraps of material in my hands, and he bequeaths me a reverent stare that burrows deep into my heart and shatters open the gates I had tossed the key to many, many years ago.

"Who are you?"

"I work for Sloan Foster," he confirms, gauging my response.

Oh...

"He's my son."

...shit!

"He wants Kara's stuff taking over to his house."

"I beg your pardon?" I bark out a startled laugh, wondering what hit him on the head when this suggestion was *ordered* of him.

He moves quickly and presses me up against the small expanse of wall beside the wardrobe.

"Hmm," he murmurs and skims his nose up the side of my throat. This is far too close for comfort. And sanity. "Heavenly. I wonder..." His lips delicately flutter over my cheek, heading towards mine.

Shocked, turned on, and a little terrified, my mouth falls open with a gasp. I try to hide it by quickly shuffling out his hold and stuffing Kara's things into the bag faster than an opportunist thief on the rob.

I know I shouldn't be doing this. I'm also aware she's going to kill me when she finds out, but right now, I just want him out of my house. And if this is what it takes, then so be it. I want him far, far away from me, and these colossal feelings I haven't had a stirring of in years.

My mind runs away with me as I chuck socks and tights into the bag. The man is bizarre, yet very, very addictive. Stealing a quick glimpse, he's something, and that something is also definitely too young. Aside from some facial scarring and the barely visible age lines, he's got to be at least ten years younger than me.

"That'll do for now."

Lost in thought, I reach up and grab another bag, but I'm brought crashing back down to earth with the thud of his boots stomping out of the room.

I toss down the holdall and run after him. Reaching the front door, he is already throwing the bag inside the back of a Range Rover. He slams down the boot and marches back towards me. I press my body against the wood to let him in because it would be pointless to shut him out now. He's got what he came for.

I turn to close the door, but his car piques my attention. It is the same one that has been parked on the street from time to time. I shake my head and slap my hands on my hips, revealing my disapproval through the purse of my lips and the narrowing of my eyes.

Realising he has been caught, he rubs his chin and sighs. "Like I said, I know you, Marie Dawson. And I'd like to know you better."

He grins as he glances around the hallway again. It's omniscient and incredibly infuriating. With a cocked brow, he picks up my mobile from the table.

"Hey! I gave you permission to enter, not to manhandle my things!" I say, my hands flailing all over, trying to grasp my mobile.

"Would you?" he asks distracted, fiddling with my phone.

"Would I, what?" I hiss.

He jerks his head and the corners of his mouth curve. "Let me *manhandle* your *things?*"

My cheeks flush, and I could slap myself for walking straight into it. "Oh, don't flatter yourself, mister!" I reply curtly and reach for my phone again.

He holds up a flat palm in warning, while the incessant beeping continues to accompany the tension. With a victorious grin, he hands it back to me.

"There you go, beautiful. Maybe now you'll calm down-"

"I am calm!" I reply in the least calming tone I possess. His brows quirk, and he continues from where I cut him off.

"Agree to dinner, and then maybe let me *manhandle* your *things* after."

I was wrong; I'm not remotely attracted to this man. The longer I spend in his presence, I just want to stick him with a fork until he bleeds to death!

When I don't reply, he ups the ante of vulgarity.

"No? Would this work better if I let *you* manhandle *my* things? Just so we're on the same page, I'm more than willing. As a matter of fact, I can't wait."

"You *are* fucking delusional!"

"And you've got a dirty mouth, angel. But by fighting back, I know you're thinking about it. And trust me, I have plenty of uses for that wicked tongue of yours."

I'm speechless. Absolutely speechless.

No one has ever spoken to me like this before.

I swipe my forehead in agitation and slit my eyes at my mobile. He continues to smirk in satisfaction at my silence, then pulls out his own phone and taps the screen. I flinch the instant mine begins to vibrate in my palm.

"Hmm, just the reaction I was hoping for." Leaning into me, his hot breath drifts over my temple, awakening my senses further. "I wonder how you would flinch if *I* was to vibrate in your palm?"

"How dare you?" I gasp in disgust. My face is heating up a hundred degrees, but with his eyes penetrating profoundly and our lips almost touching, I feel myself falling.

"Very easily, and one day, I'll dare you." He straightens up and slaps my backside. *Hard.* My mouth drops open at an action that can be construed in two ways; an act of sexual deviance, or an act of reproof.

Still in shock, rubbing my mistreated rear, he laughs victoriously and strides towards his car with a confident, sexy swagger. Composing myself, still experiencing the sting of his hand exciting my latent desires, I follow him sheepishly.

"Just so you know, when I call the police to have you arrested for sexual assault, I'm going to need a name," I say calmly, praying it sounds confident and plausible.

He spins around in surprise; that beautiful, bastard grin of his is firmly in place, but God he wears it well. Too well, unfortunately. He makes haste towards me and firmly grips my waist. Nervous butterflies soar inside my belly the moment pushes me against the 4x4.

I moan low, feeling him hard and proud against my abdomen, while my legs beg traitorously to wrap around him and squeeze. A crazy passion engulfs me, igniting every nerve ending. I squeak out involuntarily when he presses harder, and my hip bones dig into him, while his muscles dig into me.

He breathes deeply, scenting me, and I press my hand against his shoulder, worried what my neighbours will think if they see me being manhandled by a very hot, strange man on my own property.

Chance would be a fine thing! I titter at the thought.

"Something funny?" he queries.

I shake my head, as I feel my cheeks flame further.

"You want a name, beautiful?"

"Yes," I reply, octaves higher. "And stop calling me that!"

He strokes the side of his jaw against mine and releases me. Slowly gliding his hands down the sides of my breasts, all the way to my hips, he stares with a certain something I'm not sure I am able to verbalise.

"May I?"

"May you, what?" I ask in a clipped tone.

"This," he says, cupping my cheeks. Then his lips touch mine, and it feels like my body is being brought back to life. My blood surges through my veins, while electricity sparks every cell, remembering what it feels like to join with another like this. His kiss is soft, seductive. Surprising. And I want to curl my toes at the sensation. Caressing his mouth against mine with such gentleness it's enough to take my breath away, I whimper.

"Goddamn, angel," he murmurs, shocked.

My heart thunders in my chest, and I close my eyes. My hands clutch his strong arms the moment his tongue glides over my closed seam, and I mewl, inadvertently authorising access again. Moving my lips in sync with his, he takes the opportunity to manipulate the advantage and slides his tongue over mine.

Inside my head, I know I should be pulling back, scratching, slapping, and screaming blue murder. But truthfully, I never want this moment to end.

His lips leave mine, only to be replaced by his finger, barely tracing my bottom lip. "Heavenly, just as I anticipated. Look at me, darling."

Opening my eyes, his are dark. Dangerous. His thumbs stroke my cheeks while his fingers cradle the back of my head. Suddenly unsteady, due to the pre-orgasmic tingle my body is experiencing, his other arm snakes around my waist to balance me.

"That was the first, but it won't be the last. I guarantee it."

"Hmm, presumptuous, aren't we?" The words leave my mouth without a second thought. Even after that kiss, I'm startled by own vindictiveness. He chuckles, and I hate to say it, but I do like his style of presumption.

"Absolutely. If I want something, I take it." Guiding me aside, he climbs into his car. "How about dinner tonight?"

I shake my head, failing to conceal the smile that is betraying me. "No, I told you, I'm working," I say, trying to fathom what the hell has just happened. And why my life is suddenly taking a very sharp turn in the same direction Kara's has recently.

"Can't, not won't." He winks, and my heart shudders.

Shit.

"You want a name, angel?" He slips on his sunglasses and starts the engine.

I nod, still disorientated from his amazing kiss. "Well, it would be logical since our tongues have already danced an intimate tango."

He sighs and reaches his hand out. Arranging my baggy top again, making me self-conscious, he delicately traces my collarbone. "That's not the only intimate tango we'll eventually be dancing together, darling."

"God, you're so crude."

"Maybe, but in time I'll have you begging for more. I'm Walker, by the way. John Walker. I'll be seeing you later, angel."

He turns to the windscreen and slowly pulls off from the kerb. Watching the car disappear at the end of the street, I stand there, lost, touching my lips like a teenager who has just had her first kiss.

I trudge back into the house and lock the door. The smell of imminent burning lingers over the atmosphere, but to hell with Victoria Sponge, because comfort food has nothing on a man who kisses you like he is starving for your touch when he doesn't even know you.

Clutching my mobile in both hands, I lodge my flailing body against the wood, trying to understand what has just transpired. Unable to comprehend it rationally, I head into the kitchen.

Removing the inedible cake from the oven, I drop the burnt offering onto the table. Yet, bizarrely, I'm not angry in the slightest. Instead, I sit and smile.

"Heavenly," I whisper, privately acknowledging the foreign sensations flooding back through me since the dam as finally been obliterated and razed to ruin.

And it's all thanks to a confident and very dominant, beautiful man.

"John Walker," I murmur rhetorically. His name sounds good rolling off my tongue, and I crudely wonder what else would be good on my tongue.

Touching my lips again, later can't come soon enough.

Chapter 4

STEPPING INTO THE ballroom, as always, it looks pristine. I smile with pride. It's events like these that make what I do worthwhile. The late nights, early mornings, and unsocial hours. All of it. Right now, it's worth it.

My eyes work the room, delighted by perfection, until they narrow, landing on something, or more precisely, *someone*. At the opposite side, chatting animatedly with a red-headed man is the insufferable, but shamelessly irresistible, John Walker.

"Shit," I mutter under my breath, realising his earlier comment about seeing me later was literal.

I sigh in approval as I gaze at him. Admiring his toned, tapered physique in yet another perfectly fitted suit, yes, I definitely approve of what I'm seeing. My tongue glides across my bottom lip as he laughs with his companion until our eyes meet. Straightening my spine, that unwanted, but welcome sensation drifts up my back, and I turn away, embarrassed he has caught me watching him.

But who am I kidding? Since I saw him at the last event, and more recently, this afternoon, when he manhandled me, fondled me *and* kissed me, he's all I can bloody think about.

I'd be lying if I said I didn't feel a snippet of pride that he finds me attractive. I'd also be lying if I said I wouldn't be interested in knowing where this might lead if given half a chance.

As I carry on assessing the room, my eyes land on Kara, cutting a radiant path through the crowd. My heart breaks watching her avoid people. It's soul destroying to see her close in on herself when put in situations she is uncomfortable with. I guess it's predictable, but I hope if anything good comes out of this *relationship* she has recently found herself in, it's that she will finally learn how to live.

Wondering if that's probable, my optimism disintegrates when a woman stands and, even from this distance, it's clear that she is letting my girl know her place on the social rank. As I approach them, I can already see the devastation take Kara over the edge. It's a broken look, something I have also gone through many times in the past. That feeling of being inferior, of not being good enough.

The moment I am in reach, I slip my arm through hers and feel the flinch. Moving us away from the table of bitchy women, I stop at the bar and pull out a stool.

"I should be really angry with you, but it's impossible when you look this amazing and happy! Well, happy until that vapid bitch opened her mouth, I guess." I pull out a napkin and hand it to her. Wiping away her tiny tears, John Walker approaches and strokes her face lovingly.

I stare, mesmerised, as he speaks to her. His words, the beautiful softness of them, they're a complete contrast to the man I met earlier today. Captured by the moment, I refocus to find him staring straight at me.

"Oh, Marie, this is Walker. Walker, Marie," Kara introduces us.

"Marie, it's a pleasure to see you again, angel," he says confidently, using that flaming name.

I glower, hands on my hips, hopeful my expression is one of unimpressed. His eyes narrow ever so slightly, and I move my head from side to side, fearful he will tell Kara that I allowed him to move her stuff out. I presume since she isn't raging like a bull in a china shop, she doesn't know.

Yet.

He brazenly rakes his eyes over me and smiles broadly. Every muscle clenches, but after this long of being alone, it feels nice to be appreciated. Wanted, even.

In the corner of my eye, I notice Kara's hand cover her mouth, hiding a giggle. I whip around with a glare and give her the 'mother means business' look.

"I wish I could say the same!" I spin around, feeling my face heat. "Two glasses of champagne, please," I request from the barman. I concentrate on my breathing, in and out, slow and even, until a sharp slap registers on my arse. *Again.* I gasp and whip my head around just in time to see the overly confident git get lost in the crowd.

"Marie?" Kara whispers.

I shake my head because even *I* dare not get into *that* conversation right now. Passing her a glass of fizz, I divert her attention by conveying all I know about her date tonight. I rattle off anything to dissuade her curiosity until she eventually asks the question I have been shamelessly avoiding.

"So, tell me how you know Walker?"

The mention of his name causes my grin to stretch from ear to ear, with absolutely no chance of hiding it.

"Stop changing the subject," I spout in true pot, kettle and black fashion. "And no, I had nothing to do with it!"

"Nothing to do with what?" she asks suspiciously.

Instead of answering since that would result in lying, I give her few more words of my motherly wisdom, then push her off the stool to go and dance with her man before someone else does.

Watching her walk away, my sight catches John's again, and he motions me over. I shake my head vehemently, but my feet demonstrate defiance and move. His triumphant smile widens the closer I get.

"Finally come to your senses, beautiful?" His enthusiasm is far from discouraged, but with men like him, it never is.

"Are you always an overly confident, arse assaulting bastard?" I fire back acerbically.

"Only where fine, fiery blondes are concerned."

I sigh in discomfort, entirely out of my depth. I have no idea how to flirt anymore. If I'm honest, I don't think I ever learned to begin with.

Taking in the room, I study the women present, the ones making eyes at Sloan Foster and the small motley crew of men he has been chatting to all night, including the one in front of me, and I realise something. I realised it when John stormed into my house this afternoon, but here, in this room of brazen wealth, with men that look like models and girls vying for their attention in the hope of snaring a wealthy husband, it's more than a passing thought.

"Do you not think I'm a little old for you?" The words leave my mouth innocently. I mean no harm or offence, but we both know it's a fact.

He scoffs. "No. I like an experienced woman."

Experienced? Yeah, right!

I laugh. "Mr Walker, I'm sure you'll find most of the women half my age in this room carry more experience than I ever will. If it is expertise you are desiring, you need to bother one of them."

He crooks his finger, and foolishly, I lean into him.

"Angel, the only thing I desire right now is to test out your expertise," he whispers, studying me reverently, waiting to see how I am going to react.

I close my eyes in discomfort. I'm no stranger to the opposite sex, but I'm most definitely a stranger to this type of crass talk.

"I guess this means I can't *manhandle* your *things* later?" He cocks a brow and rubs his chin thoughtfully.

I shake my head in anger because he's made me feel like a worthless whore. And I haven't felt this way in nearly two decades – not since I finally got rid of my despicable bastard of an ex.

"With all due respect, Mr Walker, no one has ever made me feel as uncomfortable as you have today. It may have escaped your notice, but I'm working, and you've exploited far too much of my time already. Goodbye." I turn curtly on my heel.

An acquiescent sigh resounds, and a small tug on my elbow impedes my escape.

"If I've upset you, I'm very sorry. That wasn't my intention. Look, let's start again. John Walker, thirty-six, former army officer, now private security. It's very nice to meet you."

Thirty-six? Well, I guess he isn't that young, after all.

I smile and yield. "Marie Dawson, forty, caterer. It's a pleasure to meet you." Taking his hand, warmth spreads through me, and I get that funny feeling from earlier. Not that I have managed to vanquish it between then and now, but whatever was left simmering is beginning to boil over.

"Would you like to dance, Miss Dawson?"

I cast my eyes over the floor, then smile and nod. It's been years since I've danced. "Yes, I'd love to, Mr Walker."

John leads me out onto the dance floor, and one hand grips mine while the other sits snug on my waist. It's firm and welcoming like it belongs there, and it makes me feel far more secure than I should, considering it has been a long time since a man has held me like this. It's also enlightening, and my body reacts willingly, stepping closer, needing to feel, needing to be fulfilled.

"Careful, beautiful. Otherwise one of us is going to find something we like very much." I burst out laughing. It's crude and lewd, and I can't get enough of him.

He twirls me away in time with the music and then reels me back in. His hands linger on my waist until they dip lower to the swell of my bum. Settled in his strong embrace, I allow myself to throw caution to the wind.

Just for one night, I want this.

I want him.

I slide my front to his and touch my head against his chest. Moving in perfect tandem, I feel myself letting go.

The current song finishes far too quickly, and John leads me off the dance floor towards the bar.

"What time do you finish?" he asks quietly.

"Late," I whisper. "Responsibility of owning a business – I'm always the last woman standing."

His brows quirk in reciprocation, mulling something over until he skims his finger down my face and closes in for a very chaste kiss.

"Still heavenly. And very, very beautiful," he says humbly.

He releases my hands and slowly walks away. As he becomes lost in the crowd, I grip the edge of the bar. Breathing heavily and swaying slightly, I wonder how long I can hold off what I know is inevitable.

And once the inevitable happens, I wonder how long I can hold off the other side of my life from becoming known and crashing all over the proverbial fan.

I slump onto a stool, my sanity on tenterhooks while my mental turmoil rises from the dead. I request a shot of brandy - purely for medicinal purposes - and down it in one, trying not to gag.

I slide the empty glass back over the bar, put on my professional face and push off the stool.

Standing tall, observing the night, pride fills me, but not entirely. Because deep inside, a part of me will always be hollow and frozen; defunct to any type of love that is bestowed upon me.

I know I don't deserve this man's attention, or whatever he may be willing to give me. But for the first time in twenty-one years, I'm willing to take that risk.

The staff door thuds shut behind me, and I sit on the step. I tap my foot impatiently, pissed off that the taxi I pre-booked isn't here already. I don't enjoy sitting alone in dark alleys at three o'clock in the morning.

Holding my bag to my chest, a Range Rover rolls to a stop in front of me. Looking left to right, my breath halts in my throat, until the window winds down. Relief fills me when John smiles from inside and opens the door.

"Hop in."

"No, I booked a taxi, but thank you," I reply.

"A taxi? No, get in."

"Mr Walker, thank y-"

"It wasn't a request, angel. Now get in."

Comprehending my choices are limited, I rise from the step. Climbing into the car, John takes my bag and lobs it into the back. My eyes cross in annoyance at his blatant disregard for my things until they meet his. But the protest I'm dying to scream out doesn't come, because his look is searing my soul in ways I cannot explain or pick apart.

"Thank you," I say, and his eyes widen. I don't know why he's so shocked; I can be hospitable. Granted, when stuck in a tight spot – the spot he apparently wants to shove me in – I can still be cordial.

Just.

I study him inconspicuously as he reverses the car back onto the street. He stares straight ahead, while the dark night and the lampposts pass by.

Pulling up outside my house, I stall in getting out. I don't know why, but something inside is hesitant. Looking back at him, he removes his hand from the wheel and reaches into the back for my bag. My fingers drift over his as he passes it to me, and an instant shiver takes hold. Noting my reaction, he grabs me.

"John, I..." I don't know what I want to say.

"Shush," he replies before his lips meet mine in a frenzy.

Quickly unbuckling my seat belt, he drags me over the gear stick and onto his knee. Stroking his hands down my sides, everything ignites furiously. From my mouth, which had forgotten what it felt like to be kissed until today, to my nipples, which are hardening beyond belief, and finally, my abdomen, squeezing heatedly in anticipation.

My arms move of their own volition and grab him hard. Falling further under his spell, I moan into him, powerless to stop my own hands from exploring his extraordinary taut muscles and the way they are flexing with each movement.

Long minutes pass under the shade of darkness. The sound of lips upon lips fills the space until a car horn blares, and I pull back nervously.

Placing my hand over my mouth, I stare into his eyes, sparkling with unknown promise. He strokes his finger down my face as he unbuckles his seat belt. Sliding out from under me, he carefully lifts me from the car. On solid ground, he cups my jaw and smiles. The stretch accentuates his ruggedly handsome features and the scar decorating his hairline.

He gently releases me and tucks me into his side, while the tingle already running riot through my body heightens. Retrieving my bag, he puts it over his shoulder, plants his arm firmly around my waist and walks me to my front door.

I take my bag from him, pull out my keys and open it. As I feel around the inside of the wall for the switch, his neck stretches and his brow creases like he is listening for something. Watching him for a few tense moments, he stares down and softly presses his lips to my forehead.

"Thank you for dancing with me tonight," he says, displaying a tender side I didn't think he possessed when he first turned up this afternoon.

He steps back, preparing to leave, but for some unknown reason, I don't want him to go. Yet I know I can't invite him in. Of all the choices I have made these last two decades, I must tread these unknown waters carefully, because if I don't, I know they may drown me. And possibly him, if whatever this is becomes something else. Something deeper, something I want but never allowed myself to dream was attainable.

"I..."

"No. You don't have to explain." He drags his thumb down my cheek. "I don't expect anything from you. I don't want you giving it away to me. Instead, I'll work hard for every breath and every moan. For every touch and every shudder. For every precious moment you see fit to give me, I'll earn each and every one."

I nod, disappointed, while internally everything is screaming at me to give it away. I want to let him in. Into my house, into my bed, into my lonely heart, and I can feel my resolve weakening with each mental muse.

John sighs, aware this moment is severely testing my judgement – and possibly his.

"Have dinner with me. Please," he asks gently.

Sucking on my bottom lip, I nod, not reluctantly, but because I want to. At the grand old age of forty, and after two decades of denying myself happiness, I deserve to be wined and dined. I deserve the chance to feel real affection at long last. I deserve whatever he is willing to give, until the day his giving becomes resentment.

"Yes, I'd love to."

He frames my face and kisses me gently, and that lovely, subdued bliss envelops every cell with each brush of his mouth upon mine. I close my eyes, savouring the moment, inhaling his aroma and the way it feels to be held in an embrace as close as this again.

"I'll call you, angel." Letting me go, he motions inside, and I cross the threshold. "Close the door and lock it," he says firmly.

I keep my eyes on him as I do as per his request. Leaning back against the wood, his heavy steps beat over the pavement until his car starts. When the engine drone has finally disappeared into the night, I switch off the light. Fishing out my phone, I dump my bag on the table and jog upstairs.

Twenty minutes later, I step out of the shower. I pause in the middle of my bedroom, having a sudden, sharp vision of him being stood here no less than twelve hours ago. Turning to the dresser, I drop the towel and touch my breast, still feeling the prominent spark from his caress. My hands drift down my front, pausing at my belly.

Consumed, the unfortunate spell is broken when my phone chirps. I pick it up and smile like a Cheshire cat when his name brightens the screen.

Sleep tight angel x

I put my mobile on charge, slip into my shorts and camisole, then flick off the lamp and climb into bed.

Studying the ceiling in the dark, his endearment burns brightly in my eyes.

Angel.

It's apt.

Although I'm confident my father wouldn't agree. And as I lay here, my body humming with unfulfilled pleasure, a part of me wishing he was here with me, touching me in ways I haven't desired in so long, I'm inclined to agree.

Because there is one thing my father was right about – I am no angel.

And John Walker might be the second reason why I fall from grace.

Chapter 5

Present day...

I PULL UP the collar of my coat to shield myself from the brisk wind. Leaning over the seat, I grab the flowers and engage the locks.

With the bouquet in one hand and the other turning my uncharacteristically quiet phone in my pocket, I walk the path I've walked so many times over the last year. Moving over the hardened maze of gravel – compacted through years of wear and tear – I smile as I pass other visitors.

"Hello," an elderly lady greets, while her husband tips his flat cap in salutation.

"Hello," I reply. I don't know them, and I'll probably never see them again. But in this place, we all share a morose common interest, one that joins us without realising - we have all left those we love to rest here for eternity.

With a parting smile, I walk towards the rear of the grounds, and my sight drifts over the neatly cut lawns and headstones. From the newly positioned marbles, gleaming brightly under a low winter sun, to the centuries-old weathered sandstones, some leaning precariously as the passage of time has altered the foundations upon which they were first erected.

I pass carefully between the graves, mindful of cutting corners and literally walking over the dead. Tugging my coat around my front, I stop and kneel. Examining the headstone, I reach forward and brush off the tiny clumps of mud dirtying the engraving.

"That's better, isn't it?" I murmur rhetorically. I know I'll never get an answer, and in an alternative universe – one where she's still alive and kicking, and one where I'm still livid and screaming – the answer I want probably wouldn't be the one I'd get.

I smile to myself, envisaging her finger flip of a response, and remove the dead flowers from the vase. Picking up the fresh bunch, I unravel the plastic from the stems, artfully arrange them and sit back.

"Aside from all the stupid shit you did, girly, I miss you. Kara misses you," I say quietly in the relatively busy grounds where, usually, you can hear a pin drop. Bringing my knees up, I rest my hands and chin atop of them. Closing my eyes, a streak of blonde hair flashes inside my head, accompanied by the small sound of giggling.

"I'll always miss you," I murmur, unsure as to whom I'm confessing that truth to. Although it's barely audible, it is a declaration I often make when no one else is around. In times when I don't have to disguise my sorrow or conceal the way life had beaten me before it had really begun.

With myself, I don't have to lie.

Contemplating my rumination, a shudder runs through me. I can't explain it, but it's always the same when I come here. It's a sensory explosion, drawing out my fear of someone watching me. Yet I know that is impossible. Apart from my guilty conscience, no one knows I come here.

They don't know from the day she was buried, I've been the one to replace the dying flowers fortnightly. They don't know I'm the one who cleans the headstone monthly. And they sure as hell don't know I sit here, speaking of things to purge my guilty soul, desperate to feel something close to the eventual emancipation of my concealed heartache. Moreover, the real reason why I do these things without seeking knowledge or glory is that here I can pretend. I can make believe the long-forgotten lies don't exist, and I can find forgiveness and restitution.

Here, I don't need to hide.

Here, I can seek atonement.

Except my quest for atonement has come some twenty-odd years too late.

My mind races through a million and one memories that have been catapulted to the surface, but the vibrating in my pocket recoups my focus. Plucking out my phone, aware it wouldn't stay silent for long, I purse my lips.

Nicki.

I glide my finger over my temple in contemplation, debating if I should answer. The choice is made when the vibration stops, and the screen fades to black. Minutes later it chirps, indicating a new voicemail. Again, I'm going to ignore that, too, because a call from her can only mean one thing right now: problems. And problems are the last thing I need today, not on top of everything else currently going on.

Rubbing my forehead, I adjust my position. "I'm sure you already know, but baby Foster entered the world yesterday. A boy, Oliver," I tell Samantha, starting a one-sided conversation, hoping she can hear me wherever she may be now. "He's a little early, but he's strong and healthy. You'd be in love with him if you saw him. He's inherited his father's dark looks, but his mother's beautiful innocence is there, too."

My heart constricts because yesterday was one of the best days of my life. Meeting baby boy was a revelation. It penetrated the chasm and roused deep-rooted fears that nothing else ever has. It was also one of the worst because it confirmed a silent truth, one I haven't been able to voice for fear of its ramifications. It proved I will never be able to achieve picture perfect. An amazing man promised me it all, but I'll never be able to promise the same.

"And Kara..." I divert my thoughts back to a place of harmony. "You'd be so proud of how she's turned her life around. I know you both had your differences towards the end, but she loved you very much, even after everything that happened."

I take a breath and glance down at my wrist in sad recollection. Regardless of my suffering that fateful day, my fate could have been far worse. The truth of my theory is resting six feet under me, and I'm not ignorant of the fact I might've shared her fate.

"I just wish I'd have done things differently when we first met. I'm sorry, Sam. I'm sorry I failed you when I didn't give you a chance."

I blink back the unshed tears languishing behind my eyes as the sound of the organ begins to play from the church. The opening chords are more than familiar, and the verse of a hymn I remember well kicks in.

I pick myself up from the damp, cold ground. Brushing off the fragments of grass and mud from my behind, I reach for the remainder of the flowers.

"I'll see you in a fortnight, darling." I bend down and press my lips to the top of the stone.

Separating the remaining lilies, I walk a well-memorised path around the surrounding headstones. I gift a flower here and there on the unadorned graves and turn with my last offering. Staring up at the statue – an angel in prayer – I touch the weathered stone. As always, I automatically seek out the other effigies dotted around, keeping a vigilant eye on the departed.

"Watch over her for me." I drop the lily onto the base. "And keep her out of trouble," I request, as a solo soprano voice drifts over the breeze.

Approaching the building, the voice draws me closer and closer in instantaneous compulsion, and the urge to walk inside is too strong to ignore.

I loiter in front of the old double doors and hesitate with my hand on the brass handle. Apart from the wedding and two funerals I attended two years ago, it had been a long time since I had set foot inside one of these places.

Too many memories, too many dreams – all of them frayed and tattered before I even reached eighteen.

"Excuse me." A voice seeps into my reverie, and I turn abruptly.

"Sorry," I say and move aside for the elderly gent to pass. He holds the door open while I stand frozen until he huffs and lets it go.

I whip out my hand before it shuts in my face, and the musty smell of wood, stone and aged fabric, assaults my senses. Shifting my eyes to the front, the collective voices raise higher and higher, reaching the crescendo before the climactic finish.

Morbid curiosity overcomes me, remembering the years, both the terrific and the tumultuous when I would be one of the small voices in the group. The years I was forced to abide by the values and beliefs imposed by this place.

But that was then, and then I was young and impressionable. And this now, and now I'm older and unreceptive.

The glimmer of the crucifix compels me as I slip into the end pew, and time drifts away. A part of me remembers this far too vividly, and inside, my conscience is screaming at me to run before I am coached back into believing in something that would never exist.

I slouch in the seat as the vicar addresses the sporadically seated congregation, but all I can see is a version of a man who was supposed to care for me, protect me. Yet he never did. Instead, he did the only thing he could to safeguard his image - he left me to fend for myself in a world that was judgemental and cruel.

Sighing softly, I pick up the hymn book. Thumbing through the worn pages, the choir starts to sing again. As I murmur the words, I gaze up at the vaulted ceiling, and the intricate architecture takes me back in time.

Closing my eyes, I remember the last time, in a life twenty-three years ago, that I sat in a pew and prayed in vain...

A hand squeezes mine tight; a small comfort to the void cracking further in my heart. Turning around, my eyes latch onto those of my mother, and her finger traces down my temple and jawline, conveying her compassion and sadness.

"Okay?" she whispers, and I nod pathetically. As she wraps her arm around my shoulder and draws me closer, I wonder if she knows I'm lying. I've been lying for so long, it's very much second nature.

I turn back to the front, seeing past the attendees, the pulpit, the altar, and look at the presiding vicar. His condescending gaze meets mine while his voice rings out, echoing off the walls, tormenting my fragile state.

Fidgeting in my seat, not knowing how much longer I can sit here, I stand abruptly. Frantic hands grab my hips, but I manage to shuffle them off.

Running between the pews, I slam the doors open and collapse on the ground in the doorway. Balled up and at risk of losing the little sanity I have left, I never knew this kind of pain could exist...

With my hand over my heart, I gasp and look around, thankful no one has noticed. Getting to my feet, my curiosity dead and gone, I shuffle out of the pew.

Outside, I inhale deeply, trying to calm down and equally batten down the memories since I refuse to allow this day to be marred any further than it already is. Striding towards the entrance, I click the car remote in my pocket as I cross the road.

I glance back at the building as I start the engine. I was right back then; I've never felt pain like it since. And the reason why I haven't is that I have never allowed anyone to get close enough to let it grow and manifest.

Until now.

"John," I whisper, shame emanating my tone. Dragging over my seat belt, I'm aware the next time I feel that kind of pain again, it will be from him.

"What are you doing?" I ask myself in the rear-view. It's a rhetorical question only I can answer. It also isn't a question of what I'm doing; it's a question of what I've already done. Regardless of my litany of reasons, whether real or romanticised, after all this time of intentionally avoiding the truth, I can honestly say I'm finally out of excuses.

I twist the key in the ignition, ready to drop the handbrake when ringing blares through the cabin.

"Hi, honey." I connect the call.

"Hi. Are you driving?" Nicki's bubbly tone is loud and clear.

"I will be in a minute, but you're on the Bluetooth." Dropping the handbrake, I check my mirrors and pull off from the kerb. "Problems?" I ask cautiously as I give way at the junction.

"No, but what time are you coming back?"

"I'm on my way now. Why?" I query suspiciously.

"Nothing, just some woman keeps calling from The Salvation Army. They're closing their offices in a couple of hours, and she's adamant she needs to speak to you."

"Okay, I'll call back when I get in. Anything else?"

"John called."

"Is he okay? Kara, Sloan? The baby?"

"They're all fine, but you just need to call him."

"Alright. I'll see you in twenty, thirty minutes," I reply. "So, tell Dev to get back to his own office, unless he wants to order stale cream buns and chase up overdue invoices!"

"I heard that!" Devlin's voice seeps down the line.

"Good. Go back to work! I'll see you soon, honey."

I brake gently as the line of vehicles stop. Pressing the menu button on the dashboard, I tap through the directory and dial.

"Walker."

"Hi, it's me," I greet lamely, because who else is it going to be when my name flashes up on his screen.

"Hi, angel. Can you ring me back? I'm driving."

"Sure, but Nicki said I had to call you. I'm worried."

"We're fine. Call us, say an hour?"

"Okay," I confirm, flicking on my indicator. "I love you."

"I love you, too," he says, much to the enjoyment of his unabashed boys in the background.

"Goodbye, Marie! We love you, too!" Parker shouts, followed by squelchy kissing noises.

"Shut it, sunshine! And turn that station back on!" is the last thing I hear as the line dies.

Activating the car locks, I stride towards the building. Fisting my security card, the door opens and Devlin – John's nephew – bounds out.

"Marie, looking lovely as always!" He grins, obviously thinking he can charm me into submission. Thankfully, I know his game. As much as he likes having a quiet lunch with his girlfriend, he likes it even better when there is food of the gourmet standard on the go. My daughter is right about one thing – the man is cheap.

"Thanks. Did you leave any of the samples?" I query, pondering how many of the freebies that arrived this morning are still in the fridge.

"A couple. I'll pay you!" he replies, striding towards his car.

"They were free!" I retort.

Leaning against the door, his hand flairs out. "In that case, they tasted even better! There's nothing like free to whet your appetite. I'll see you later, Auntie M!"

Auntie M! God, I feel so old when he calls me that.

"Hey, have you heard from Sloan?" I approach him as he pulls a black beanie over his chestnut hair, covering his half-inch black earplugs. He breathes into his cupped hands and rubs them together.

"No, I didn't want to push it after he kicked us out yesterday, but Tommy's spoken to him. Apparently, little lady is still exhausted, but she's happy not to be staying in hospital any longer than necessary. Understandable, really. He's a big boy for premature though, isn't he?" he says, a huge smile on his face, identical to that that everyone else has been wearing for the last twenty-four hours.

"Hmm, he's a healthy weight. Good thing she didn't go to term." I grin, satisfied when Dev's face contorts the same way every man's does when he is expected to talk babies, births, and everything in between. "Anyway, I'll see you later," I say, kissing his cheek. "Have a good evening."

"Yeah, me, myself and I will have a fabulous time! I don't suppose there's a chance I can steal Nic away early, is there?"

I shrug. "Maybe. Call and ask me later, I might be in a generous mood. Or I might be thoroughly pissed off, and my misery may want to keep hold of its company!" I grin and wink. "Bye, darling."

The sound of Dev's BMW rumbles idly as I enter the building and jog up the stairs. Reaching the office, I find Nicki at her desk looking guilty.

"Hi, honey. Don't worry, I've just seen Dev. Do you mind calling Martin to let him know we'll have the new selection going forward?"

"Sure. Sorry about Devlin," she says contritely, tucking her blonde hair behind her ears.

"It's fine. I don't mind him being here. He's free entertainment." I toss my bag and jacket onto the tub chair.

"True. So how did it go?"

"The usual. You know what accountants are like," I lie regarding my whereabouts this morning. I'm not an idiot; she knows I'm lying my arse off considering our accountant resides on the next floor down. Still, I trust her to keep my confidence, irrespective of what she thinks that confidence is.

Her lips purse and her eyes narrow as expected, but she doesn't say anything. "Want a cuppa?"

"I'd love a coffee. Thanks, honey." Picking up this morning's post from her desk, I flip through, but nothing of interest stands out.

"There are a few messages for you," she says, returning with my coffee. "Sophie called. Stuart has to cover sickness tonight, so she isn't coming. Jules rang, but she said to call her back when you're not so busy. There are a few more, but the general consensus is we're on our own tonight."

"Okay."

"Oh, there was also a voicemail from the estate agents – Veronica, someone or other." Turning around she starts to move out of the office.

"Nicki? The Sally Army?"

"Yeah?" She stops inside the doorway.

"Have you got the number?" I drop the post down and lift my mug.

"Yeah, let me just grab it," she says, scurrying out of the door.

"Did she say what she was calling for?" I blow the top of the mug before taking a sip.

"No, just that she needed to speak to you urgently," she replies and sticks the post-it on my desk. "Her name is Mary Johnson. You might still be able to catch her." The landline starts to ring again, and she turns. "I'll get that outside." My door closes with a thud and my hand trembles.

With a heavy heart, terrified of what this woman so urgently wants to speak to me about, I pick up my mobile. Dialling the number, it is answered on the third ring.

"Hi. Can I speak to Mary Johnson, please?"

"May I ask who's calling?"

"Marie Dawson. She left a message for me."

"Yes, of course. Hello, I'm Mary."

"Hi, how can I help you?"

"Miss Dawson, I work as part of a team who locate and trace missing people, relatives, mostly. It's one of the many things the organisation does to reunite families," she says, very matter of fact. It's almost as if she is reading from a textbook.

"That's great, but I don't know how I can help. Who is this missing person?" I query, raising my mug with a shaky hand because I know at least one.

"I'm sorry, Miss Dawson, but I can't give out that kind of information. Data protection."

My head jolts. I fully appreciate data protection laws, but I think she forgets that *she* called *me*.

"Okay, but how am I supposed to help if you can't supply the information to assist?"

"No, of course." She laughs singularly and pauses for a beat. "Miss Dawson, do you know a Magdalene Turner?"

My body sways, and tears pool in my ducts at hearing that name after all this time. My mobile falls from my ear, landing on the desk the same moment the mug slips from my hand, smashing down and spraying the picture of John and me in hot liquid. It's practically poetic. Or a sign of things to come.

"Hello? Miss Dawson? Hello?"

I pick up the phone and end the call. Wrapping my arms around myself, I turn to the window and stare at the skyline. Dark clouds roll in, darkening the day further. And as of five minutes ago, that darkness deepened to an impenetrable black.

Opening my mouth, I confirm the first of my unspoken truths.

"Yes, I know her."

Chapter 6

I REVERSE THE car into the driveway and cut the engine. Getting out, I retrieve the dry cleaning and the cheeky bottle of plonk from the boot.

"Good afternoon, Mavis," I call out to Mrs Thompson, one of the elderly neighbours that make up the street, as she tends to her beloved rose bushes. Yes, even in winter, she's pruning the stalks. Her head moves slowly – she does *everything* slowly – and she waves her secateurs at me.

"Oh, Marie! I've got something to ask you!" she says with such enthusiasm I know I can't escape into the house. Trust me, her conversation is colourful and plentiful – and I've listened to it many, many times over the last few years.

"Are you okay?" I query, dragging myself to the fence. Whenever she has something to ask, it is usually health related. It isn't unusual for either me or John to run her to the hospital or the doctor's surgery whenever she has an appointment. John says he does it because he likes to think that when he is old someone will do the same for him. I always tell him he's wishful thinking. Naturally, the sarcastic git counters, saying he'll never break a habit of a lifetime.

I, on the other hand, do it because I'm a pushover.

"I'm grand, dear!" Mavis waves the sharp pruning scissors in the air again, demonstrating her agility with worrying effect. "Are you and John finally going to stop living in sin?" she asks, nodding her head enthusiastically.

I chortle in surprise, almost choking on my tongue. "Sorry?"

"Are you getting married?"

Glancing down at my hand, realisation hits. "Oh, no. Maybe one day. Why?"

"Well, it's just that a car was parked outside your house for an awfully long time this morning."

"Oh." My tone is far too blasé but considering the average age of this street is seventy, anything out of the ordinary is fodder for entertainment. Although it doesn't explain the question of matrimonial bliss. "I wouldn't worry, probably just someone lost or a wrong address. Sorry, Mavis, but why would you think we're getting married?"

"I'm getting to that!" she mutters exasperatedly. "Anyway, the same car was here again this afternoon. You just missed it by about..." She closes her eyes, recollecting her thoughts. "...Twenty minutes."

I instantly look up and down the street, but the same cars are parked outside the same houses.

"Okay," I reply slowly, drawing my attention back to her.

"Anyway, a vicar got out!"

"A vicar?" Anxiety runs through me because I only know one vicar, and hell would freeze over before he came knocking on my door. "What did he look like?"

Her eyes widen. "No, it was a woman! She was about your height, and I think she was also blonde. I don't know, my sight isn't brilliant these days," she says, rolling her eyes.

"Very strange," I murmur, gazing up the street. I rotate back around, but Mavis has already returned to tending her garden, having said her piece.

"Happy New Year, Mavis," I call out, but she doesn't look back, just waves her hand. I shake my head, but I know this routine. When the gossip has subsided, and nothing exciting is happening, she just turns and walks away. Most would take her impertinent dismissal and lack of parting greeting to be an insult, but at ninety-two, the woman has earned the right to do whatever the hell she likes in my eyes.

Opening the front door, an eerie silence welcomes me. As per our discussion this morning, I already knew John wouldn't be home. Before kissing me goodbye, he promised he would be back to spend some time with me before I leave tonight. Like most company bosses, he makes his own hours. While he isn't afraid to roll out of bed at an unholy hour to get the job done, he flat out refuses to be sat at his desk, shuffling papers, and arguing the toss with clients past four o'clock.

Hanging the dry cleaning on the banister, I head into the kitchen and put the bottle of wine in the fridge. My eyes drift over the table to my daily delivery of post, and I quickly flick through before doubling back down the hallway and up the stairs.

In the bedroom, I strip off my suit and stand in front of the full-length mirror. Staring into my eyes, the haunted look I have carried for far too long ghosts my irises, but today it's hardly surprising. I step back and lament as my phone rings from where I tossed it on the duvet.

"Hi," I answer and sit on the edge of the bed.

"Hey, beautiful. You didn't call me," John replies, very matter of fact.

"I've just got in!"

"Now that statement speaks volumes. Dare I ask how much you spent, or shall we just re-mortgage the house, no questions asked?" he asks with a chuckle. *Sarcastic git.* He knows as much as I secretly like shopping, I also love a bargain.

"I haven't hit the sales, actually," I confirm grudgingly. "But if you must know, I have been to the cemetery." I wait for his response, but the awkward pause says it all.

"Angel, you should have said this morning. I'd have come with you," he replies sincerely.

I roll my eyes because everyone is always trying to redeem themselves for not helping Sam when it was apparent she needed it. Not that I'd have expected her to have accepted help if we did. But I'm just a hypocritic because the reason why I go is to redeem my own sins.

"I prefer to go alone. I took some flowers and told her about Oliver. Oh, and I also picked up the dry cleaning so you can take that off your list," I say, diverting his attention for obvious reasons. "Anyway, Mavis just collared me."

"When?" he groans, expecting the usual.

"Oh, she's fine, but she thought we were getting married."

He chortles heartily. "I should have gotten you a smaller ring."

I pull a face in agreement because, yes, his version of an eternity ring is rather ostentatious.

"No, there was a vicar here today. Twice, apparently. Do you know any?"

"Vicars? Darling, you know me and religion don't go hand in hand."

"I know, but what about your army mates? Any chance one might have seen the light?"

He snorts incredulously. "Nope. Same views as mine, but if this man-"

"Woman," I cut him off.

"Oh, even better! If she turns up again, tie her to a kitchen chair, feed her some of your bake off finest until I get home and then she can officiate." He laughs to himself, but I know it's no joke because he would. Without a doubt.

"Sure, and I'll tell the judge I thought confessional was a door to door service," I say flatly. "Anyway, what was the urgency in calling you?"

"What time are you expected in the seventh level of hell?"

"ASAP." I enunciate each letter. "Ideally, I should be there now, but Nicki said she'd start overseeing proceedings. And I'll have you know the kid is paying me a vulgar amount of money tonight. God knows I need it with the money pit back on the market."

His sigh resounds down the line, but I continue prattling on before he can comment. Heaven forbid, I have avoided talking about *that* series of unfortunate events for the last week.

"Am I still going to see you before I leave?" I query, hoping he will fulfil his promise of an hour or two of his undivided attention.

"That's why I'm calling. I've got a meeting."

"You're standing me up?" I ask with fake disgust.

"Angel." He placates tenderly. "Standing up is a very ambiguous statement when it comes to you. With you, I'm *always* standing up," he says coyly, emphasising his insinuation. "But this afternoon, I'm afraid I am standing you up."

"Huh," rolls off my tongue.

"I've got a friend dropping by who I haven't seen for a while. He says he's got a deal to discuss and he is adamant he can only meet today. He's picked the best frigging day for it. I'd prefer to spend a few hours rolling around with you since you're deserting me tonight."

"It's not desertion, its work!" I counter exasperated. "Besides, you don't take me to work."

"True, but it's still desertion, angel," he replies.

Catching my reflection in the mirror, I can't help but ascertain the relief etched across my face. "I promise I'll make it up to you."

"So will I. I'll call you at the stroke of midnight," he says.

"I'll be expecting you."

"You can guarantee it. Better yet, find a quiet room where you won't be disturbed, and I'll make it the best damn call of your life."

"Promises, promises," I mutter.

"I always deliver on my promises, starting with the very first one I ever made to you."

"I know," I whisper, remembering the words that left his mouth the first night we spent together. They are as clear as day. So clear, in fact, he could be repeating them right now.

"You remember."

"I'll never forget." I sigh content, lodging the phone between my cheek and shoulder as I reach around my back and unfasten my bra. It drops to the floor as I slide down my knickers and wrap a towel around myself.

"I'll let you go. I'll call at midnight. I love you."

"I love you, too. Bye." Hanging up, a restlessness overcomes me as I look around the empty bedroom. An empty nest. Some days that's how it feels. Now, as I approach forty-three, it's the one thing I long for more than anything else. It wasn't always this way, but the dull ache in my gut that I've never dared to identify grows. Shaking my head, I don't know why I do this to myself. Although unconfirmed, I'm not oblivious to the fact that that ship might have sailed already.

Entering the bathroom, I turn on the shower, and the steam begins to cloud the enclosure. I quickly wash my hair, then squeeze a dollop of body wash into my palm. Rubbing my hands down my legs, my fingers glide over the raised, scarred flesh at my ankles.

It's been nearly eighteen months since the night I was knocked out in my own home. Battered, broken, and bound to probable death, that night I feared I wouldn't make it out alive. Unfortunately, it also dug up memories from the grave that I never wanted to relive. For decades, I had fought hard to free myself of the burdens I carried, and eventually, I found a way to live without repentance. To live in the here and now and never look back. But that night made me realise I can't hide forever.

In the days that followed, several doctors told me the injuries I sustained were superficial, and my skin may not scar. They also said I was incredibly lucky.

They were wrong on both accounts. The marred flesh ringing my limbs confirms it. Still, I guess I am lucky. I was lucky two years ago, the same way I was twenty-three years ago.

Both days, I walked away with my life.

Both days, I know I wasn't meant to.

Turning off the shower, I slide on my robe. In front of the condensed mirror, my hazy reflection stares back at me.

"Lucky," I whisper, stroking my blemished temple.

Yes, I am.

But eventually, all luck runs out.

Chapter 7

THE BLUSTERY CHILL picks up around me as I sit on the stone steps at the rear of the Emerson Hotel.

Staring up at the stars, they gleam vividly, beautifying the night sky. A single tear rolls down my cheek as I wish and wonder and know it can never be.

The distinct whistle of fireworks shoots up, decorating the sky with colour and sound. They bleed bright against the darkness as the smell of sulphur permeates the atmosphere.

Curling my fingers around the flute of non-alcoholic wine, I down it in one. Taking a breath, I squeeze my eyes shut as the chaos finally begins.

"Ten! Nine!"

A new year is on the periphery. A day every year I wish I could hide away from. A day I pretend I'm fine while secretly reliving a past that will haunt me until my last breath.

"Five! Four!"

I put down the glass and rest my head in my hands. As always, I've finally learnt to feel nothing as the countdown reaches zero.

"Happy New Year!"

In the distance, Big Ben's bongs begin to chime, and the collective voices of those celebrating in the city grow louder and louder - a wave of sound to accompany the explosions overhead.

The big band playing the first chords of Auld Lang Syne seeps out from the ballroom. The cacophony of partially muted voices inside replaces the enthusiastic counting echoing in the deserted alleyway. From the completely sober to the completely paralytic, they resound in ear-splitting verse and chorus.

In time with the song, a distant memory plays on repeat inside my head, forcing me to reminisce on the event that materialised on this night all those years ago. And it's an event that has damaged me beyond belief.

I remember the fireworks and the way they painted the sky. I remember the look of excitement in the eyes reflecting back at me in the windowpane. Then sadly I remember the scream of my name, and the sound of doors slamming.

Ultimately, I remember the moment it all ceased to exist when the sound of silence consumed everything.

And it's been silently consuming it ever since.

A shiver careens through me, recalling the precise moment my young life was thrust further into the perpetual darkness that had been slowly devouring it.

The images linger threateningly – the bedroom, the landing, the banister, the stairs. Each one is so real, so vivid, it could be happening all over again right now. I remember everything, and that's what makes it the most painful memory in a mental vault filled to the brim with them. And regardless of how hard I try, even after all this time, I still can't beat the feeling of failure.

Lost in my own self-pity and loathing, my mobile vibrates softly on the step beside me. Lifting it to my ear, I shuffle inside and close the door with a loud, satisfying slam.

"Happy New Year, darling," I answer. Reactivating the security panel, I pad down the staff corridor and hang back at the French doors that open into the ballroom.

"Happy New Year, beautiful. Let me be the first to tell you this year that I love you," John says reverently. Each word is honest and amplified, causing a lovely trigger effect in my sad heart.

"And you," I reply, my attention piqued by the hotel patrons swaying in various lines, hands joined, singing boisterously.

"Are you missing something in that response?"

I laugh a little, pursing my lips. "No...but I love you too, Mr Walker. How's that for satisfactory?"

"Not good enough, but I'll let you make it up to me when you get home."

"How very generous of you!" My body flushes from the impending making up he has just orally guaranteed.

"Speaking of home-"

"No." Because I know exactly what he wants to speak of. "You Walker men! First, I had Dev begging to spring Nicki early, and now you. Between the two of you, the show would be running itself!"

"Angel, when there's free booze, free food, and no strings attached sex on offer, everything runs itself. Small mercies, beautiful. I don't ask for much."

"I know you don't, but I can't just leave Nicki. Besides, it's not like I'm fluttering around the ballroom demonstrating my ability to dance or scale the social ladder. At best, I'll be lucky if I get a glass of that expensive crap Sloan serves up!" I ramble, pointlessly justifying reasons he is already aware of.

"True." He laughs heartily.

"How was your meeting?" I query, wondering how his night has fared so far.

"Fine, but why the selfish sod wanted to meet tonight is beyond me."

"Are you still there?" I ask while my eyes scan the frivolity on the opposite side of the glass, witnessing the hell that awaits.

"No, I'm at home, planning ways to get you naked the moment you walk through the door. Any and all ideas are welcome. So far I have plonk and a long, hot shower. So secure a bottle of that expensive crap under your dress, and I'll retrieve it later." His coy tone induces my insides to melt. It's a sensation I have become accustomed to these last few years.

"Oh..." I gasp seductively, playing his game until the seduction morphs into shock as the door flies open and almost hits me. "Oh, shit!"

"Marie?" John shouts anxiously in my ear.

I slam my back against the wall as a middle-aged man with a middle-age spread fills the doorway. His anxious eyes search the corridor behind me, seeing past the liquor-induced fog that he's in the wrong place.

"I'm sorry, but..."

I place my hand over the mouthpiece and smile. "The toilets are in the foyer, sir," I answer his implicit query, pointing back the way he came. With an embarrassed smile on his alcohol reddened cheeks, he nods gratefully and slinks away.

"Angel?" John's distorted voice drifts from my mobile.

"I'm here. Just an encounter with a drunk. Darling, as much as I would love to talk dirty with you, I really must go," I tell him, needing to get back out there to Nicki and whatever calamities have occurred in the last thirty minutes I've been hiding.

His exasperated huff and subsequent sigh penetrate my eardrum. "I don't like it, but I understand. Look, I'll wait up for you, but one day, one of these nights *will* be mine."

I purse my lips and squeeze my eyes shut. In the two and a half, nearly three years we've been together, I've always promised at least one of these nights *would* be his. It's a falsehood I'm not ashamed to admit.

"One will. I promise." I lie again. "I'll see you in the morning."
"It *is* morning," he stresses.
"Now you're just being pedantic." But the correct word would be petulant. Or sulky.
"No, I'm just a simple man with simple needs who wants to make love to his wife until the sun rises," he says with a sigh.
A simple man with simple needs? Who's he trying to kid?
"I'll let you go. See you later, angel."
Whispering goodbye, I hang up and loiter at the door. A portly gent passes by on the other side, a hip flask crudely exposed in his trouser pocket, while each hand nurses a shot of liquor.

I sigh, taking in the scene. This night will always be a debauched affair, but watching the alcohol being consumed faster than my staff can fill it, saddens me. Yet once upon a time, I would have been doing the same thing right about now. Emptying one glass after another, struggling in vain to find an effective method to alleviate the pain. Still, finding a way to dig myself back out was harder than I could've ever imagined.

I swipe my hand over my forehead as a twinge of pain accompanies the sickness swelling in my belly. Touching my temple, I delicately trace the faded scar. Most of the time, it's barely noticeable, appearing to be more of a natural contour, but under these bright, stark conditions, and the fact a second, more prominent scar now runs alongside it, it's more than evident of its true nature. It is also the only physical reminder I possess from this night twenty-three years ago. The mental ones, however, are not singular. And I have far more than I would ever like to count or remember. But I do. Try as I might, time doesn't heal. It doesn't make things better and it sure as hell doesn't allow you to forget.

I tuck a stray strand of hair behind my ear, as I stop on the outskirts of the ballroom. It is still standing room only, not that I would expect anything less. This is the only night of the year where the party kicks up after midnight, rather than winds down.

Peering out from behind one of the pillars, I survey the grandeur. From the opulent crystal chandeliers, casting pearls of light across the ceiling, to the ornate, conical wall sconces. Ivory floor-length silk frames the bevelled sash windows, complemented by identical satin covering the tables. The crystal centrepieces - illuminated by soft flickering candles - sit proudly in the centre of each.

"Happy New Year," a gentleman says as he passes with his wife on his arm.

"And you, sir," I reply with a smile and continue to observe the festivities.

The music is still playing, the alcohol is still flowing, and the canapés are being served at every turn to line the stomachs of the sozzled and merry.

As I intentionally avoid a small group, congregated together like pack animals, discussing whatever the insanely wealthy talk about, I nab a glass of champagne and almost down it in one.

Looking at the glass, now half full – which seems to be an unfortunate reoccurrence in my life – I wonder how many I would need to pass out and wake up in the morning without recollection. It's wishful thinking because nothing can eradicate deep-seated memories blanketed by devastation. And trust me, for a quarter of a century, I've bleeding tried.

Filled with Dutch courage, I place the glass on a vacant table. Striding past one of the windows, I catch my reflection. My eyes work up the long, navy gown I had doubts my petite, vertically challenged figure could pull off successfully. From the long skirt to the fitted body and straight cut strapless bust, it is both elegant and simple.

I straighten my shoulders and rest my hands on my hips, daring to stare long and hard at the woman I've become. The truth is, after everything I've been through; the things I've seen, the things I've done, there is *nothing* I won't do to protect those I love. It's a lesson I learnt the hard way – *twice* - but I refuse to have that pain on my conscience for a third.

Heading towards the bar, a guffaw of laughter rises above the noise, including that of the big band, playing their regular offering of Sinatra. Sometimes, I want to ask if they know how to play anything else.

I perch myself on a stool and request a shot of tequila. Someone once told me you knew it was a big night the moment the bottle hit the table, but for me, I use it sporadically to numb the pain that has occupied the pit of my belly for a generation. It's the place it settled after it had already devoured my heart and soul.

I knock back the shot and hiss as it slides down my throat. Putting the glass down, I circle the rim with my finger. The barman returns with the bottle and shifts in a silent question of whether I want another. I shouldn't; I know this, but tonight, I allow him to assist in my impending, self-inflicted drunkenness. And I will allow myself this opportunity to try to forget.

"You might need this, too." He winks and places a bottle of water in front of me.

I down the second shot, causing my oesophagus to burn from the sheer strength of it. Chasing it down with a large mouthful of water, my sobriety is already battling inside for dominance.

Spinning around, I spot Nicki at the opposite side of the room, networking, conversing gracefully with an older gentleman. A grin tugs at my mouth, having witnessed her change from a slip of a girl who was frightened of her own shadow, to the beautiful woman now reaching into her leather portfolio, handing over the company business card with confidence.

Watching her face brighten always causes a bloom of hope inside my chest. She used to be so sullen and withdrawn – much like someone else I once took under my wing. In some respects, I guess you could say it's personal redemption to help those broken to eventually fly. Still, if only I could heal my own broken wings... I sigh; my psyche is delving far too deep today.

"Good evening," a Yorkshire drawl catches me off guard. Turning around, a tall, dark-haired man grins and drops his head a little.

"Evening. Are you having a good night?" I query, seeing that the rest of a jolly group nearby undoubtedly are. They will pay for it in the morning - if the litre bottles of vodka doing the rounds are any indication.

"I am now."

A small, nervous laugh emits my throat. "Good," I tell him, unsure how to respond. "That's good. Well, have a nice night," I tell him, embarrassed that I don't know how to flirt socially – not that he knows that, or that I have any reason to anyway - before turning on my heel.

"Happy New Year, Marie," Michael, one of my part-timers greets, rolling his eyes as a howl of drunken laughter seeps up beside us.

"And you, darling. Make sure you have a couple of these later," I say, pointing at the champagne as I swipe a glass of sparkling water.

"I will," he replies with a wink and blends into the finery.

Taking a sip, my head becoming a little clearer, I mingle around the room like a pro in the disorderly fray.

"Ah, Marie!" Ken Barker, my son-in-law's number two, calls from afar. With a forced smile, I pad over, inconspicuously smoothing down my dress as I go. Welcoming me into the little circle of guests surrounding him, priority number one I've learned from experience at these pretentious shindigs is that appearance is everything. If you don't have money and connections, wing it.

"Good evening, Ken," I greet. He kisses my cheek ever so politely as his smile falters.

"Happy New Year," he replies through gritted teeth, revealing his infuriation that he is being made to be the face of the company tonight and left to the money hungry wolves.

"Yes, but I can also think of better ways to be celebrating." I grin at him as he knocks back his champagne and grabs another. Polishing off the second glass quickly, his face lights up when a couple steps forward.

"Mr Lowe!" Ken says, sucking it up to the generously sized middle-aged man, and he shakes his hand firmly. The woman on the man's arm – who could pass for his granddaughter, not that I have room to talk about age differences - looks bored, and her eyes flit around the room in a way that reveals she isn't awed.

"Richard, let me introduce you to Marie Dawson. Caterer extraordinaire!" My head lulls to the side, and I gawp at him when shrugs and seizes the opportunity to escape.

Thanks for nothing, I think, as he literally runs away.

"Good evening, Mr Lowe. It's lovely to meet you," I say, recognising him as the owner of the very posh and exclusive Roseby Hotel. It's impressive, and I appreciate why the woman on his arm isn't impressed. She has probably attended what feels like a million of these events. I know how she feels.

Lifting my hand, his lips touch the back, and he drops it down while understanding streaks across his forehead. "So, you're the elusive Ms Dawson that he talks about so much."

"I'm sorry?" I frown in confusion.

"Foster," he replies quickly. "I can see why he refuses to give me your number." Richard tips his head back, sipping a glass of wine, but his eyes fixed on me. "Speaking of which, I don't recall seeing him."

"No, he and his wife welcomed their firstborn into the world yesterday. I'm sure you'll agree that takes precedence over this evening." I offer a polite smile, but he just nods impartially.

"Well, I've been told a lot about you over the years. I'd love for you to cater for my hotel sometime. Usually, I use my event organiser, but I think we could come to some arrangement."

"Oh, you have a beautiful establishment, Mr Lowe. Thank you, I'm very flattered." I smile, genuinely pleased by his direct proposal.

Due to his propensity for absolute perfection, it is well known in my circles that he has his own in-house coordinator. It is entirely unheard of for him to solicit outsiders, hence why I've had no prior dealings with him.

I take another sip of my water and debate whether it would be so wrong to cater for the enemy. There's a reason why Sloan has never offered up my name, and it must be more than being his competition. Still debating if this would cause cataclysmic ructions in the family, he speaks again.

"Maybe...dinner...one night this week and we can discuss it further?"

My mouth drops open, because while I am a little bit of a wallflower, I'm not a goddamn idiot, and that was more than a business proposition. My eyes narrow at his hopeful expression, but he knows precisely what he's doing. Looking at the woman on his arm, she is still impassive. And completely oblivious to his discreet flirting. That, or she has learned to look the other way.

"That's very generous, Mr Lowe, but-"

"Richard," he cuts me off, smirking salaciously, raking his hand over his thinning, grey hair.

"Richard... I'm sorry, but I don't think dinner is an appropriate setting for a possible business venture. However, I would love to discuss any proposal you may have in further detail at your office."

"Absolutely," he replies coyly. "Your reputation is impeccable, and your services have been recommended numerous times over the last few years."

My pride rises a notch, and I make a mental note to thank Sloan for putting my name out there - whether I wanted it to be out there or not.

"Excuse me," the nameless young woman requests, dropping her arm from his and glides through the room with supermodel quality you can't buy.

Suddenly, something in the atmosphere changes and Richard steps forward. His hand comes out, and I instantly step back. Shifting uneasily, my mounting discomfort is causing my irritation to escalate.

I look between him and the guests, wondering if I can gauge his thoughts.

And how quickly I can run away.

"Would you like to dance, Marie?" Richard asks, his arm already making a determined trajectory towards my waist.

Flustered, I spot Nicki at the other side of the room, talking to James, the reception manager. She waves, looking every bit as fed up as I now feel.

And now, she is also my means of escape.

"I'm sorry, Mr Lowe, but unfortunately, there's something urgent I need to attend to. Please excuse me," I spout out quickly, shying away from his wayward arm.

"Of course. I shall have my assistant contact you to arrange a meeting." He lifts my hand and kisses it, all the while his eyes never leave mine. "It's been a *pleasure* to finally meet you."

I fake a smile, as a creeping sensation snakes down my spine. The glint in his eyes, the way he accentuated *pleasure*, maybe this isn't such a good idea after all. Or perhaps I just need to ensure Nicki is present at every meeting I will ever have with this man.

Safety in numbers – it's never been more appropriate than right now.

"Thank you. Have a lovely evening." I drop my hand and turn abruptly. Marching away, I make a beeline for Nicki, hook her arm, and pull her into a small alcove.

"Marie?"

"Don't ask. But if someone calls to arrange a meeting at the Roseby, make sure it's at their offices, during the day, and not some swanky restaurant after dark."

"Okay," she says perceptively, looking over my shoulder, trying to pinpoint who has rattled my cage.

I hastily step behind the bar and pull out the staff rota. As I study it, trying to work out whether it is feasible - or fair - for me to run out of here at the speed of light, I catch Nicki's hopeful stare. I glance at my watch and rest my chin on the back of my hand, doing a quick mental headcount.

"Do you want to go home, honey?"

Her eyes widen, but she shakes her head. "Marie, I can't. There's still so much left to do here."

I smile and grab her hand. "I'll take care of it. Go home. Dev will be happy to see you."

She groans and moves her head from side to side in annoyance. "He asked you, didn't he?"

I simultaneously laugh and nod. "He did, and I'm obliging."

"Marie, I didn't ask him-"

"I know you didn't. Honestly, honey, I don't mind finishing up."

"Are you sure?"

"Nicole," I say sternly with a smile. "Go."

"Okay, thanks," she replies sincerely, with a mixed expression of vacancy and elation. Embracing me in a hug, she pulls back. "Happy New Year!" Unable to disguise the rapture in her tone, she bunches up the long skirt of her black dress and makes fast work of legging it towards the staff corridor.

"I see she has better things to do," James says, sneaking up behind me, and places a kiss on either cheek.

"That she does. Happy New Year, darling," I say, reciprocating his grin. "How's it been for you?"

He shrugs and rolls his eyes. "Not as good as it's going to be for you in ten minutes. You've been let out of prison early for good behaviour."

I furrow my brow, misunderstanding. "Sorry?"

"His highness just called. He said I had to run through what needed to be done and then you needed to go home."

I grit my teeth, infuriated. In hindsight, I should have seen this coming.

"No, James, I can't. I'm not an employee; I'm the owner. I can't just come and go as I please. This is my responsibility."

"Marie, don't do this to me. My orders are clear, and I get the impression my boss isn't the one making them."

"John," I mutter, shaking my head. "Look, if Sloan calls back, come and find me and I'll talk to him, but I'm not leaving." James opens his mouth, but I place my finger over it. "And that's the end of it."

He looks up to the ceiling, rolls his eyes and huffs. "You must really hate me!" I cock my head to the side at his dramatics. "Fine, but when Sloan sacks me for gross misconduct and failure to follow instructions, I'm coming to you for a job!"

"And I'd hire you in a heartbeat!" I laugh as he turns and strides towards the foyer.

As I twist back around, my eyes deceive me when they latch onto the shimmer of a red dress, adorning a woman on the far side of the room.

An instant frisson of sickness churns in my belly because it seems hindsight isn't the only bitch in town tonight; *it* and fate are playing second fiddle to a woman who embodies the word to perfection.

Touching my marred temple, I'm psychologically catapulted back into the past as the woman leads her husband to the dance floor. An image of them over two decades old, and two decades forgotten, slams itself into my mind.

Still studying them closely, hiding their shame and putting on a highly glossed charade, incenses me. Acting as if they haven't got a care in the world when something in theirs caused mine to stop turning, proves injustice still prevails in the rich and wealthy. And I, of all people, know first-hand how shit can be buried indefinitely when money is flaunted.

I turn quickly, thankful they haven't seen me. It's pure luck really, considering I've pretty much spent all evening hiding and leaving Nicki to run the show.

Moving to another seat - one obscured from the dance floor - my hand wobbles as I knock back another mouthful of water. I crane my neck, and my eyes drift over the now sparsely populated room since the drunken revellers have begun to call it a night.

Letting my hair down, literally, to hide, a throat clears.

"Hello again."

I rotate in annoyance and come face to face with the man who accosted me earlier. Bright-eyed, standing tall and proud, he is also probably one of the only sober people left in the room.

My eyes trail him from head to toe. It isn't the best time to be assessing whether to tout him for business, but I'm unable to halt the endeavour. From the expensive tux, covering his apparent well-kept physique, to his raven hair, delicately peppered with salty highlights, to his dark, undeniably handsome features.

As I continue to study him, I decide he can't be that much older than John. Honestly, it's hard to tell, and I'm shit with ages at the best of times.

Still, he isn't a patch on my man. In my eyes, no man ever will be.

"Hi," I greet with a forced smile.

I cast a subtle glance over my shoulder at the dancing queen, then observe him inquisitively. To my horror, he also turns – directly to where I was looking - before edging closer. Settling himself on a stool, he requests the most expensive champagne available – not the stuff that Sloan gives out freely at these ostentatious gatherings.

"I'm Marie-"

"No," he says abruptly, his eyes firm and unwavering on me. "No names. Let's just have a drink together, ring in the New Year and enjoy an intelligent, sober conversation."

"Okay," I reply, uncomfortably intrigued. "I've frequented many of these events, but I don't think I've ever seen you before," I comment, staring into his dark, mysterious eyes. "Are you an acquaintance of Mr Foster and his family?" I politely pump him for information.

"I've worked around the country for the last decade or so," is all he says, as he looks back at the dance floor. "Friends of yours?"

I let out a panicky laugh – one I wish I hadn't when the contours of his face harden for reasons unknown.

"No. I've never met them before." I lie because I'm good at that. I've been lying for so long, one day I won't know what's true and what isn't. One day, the falsities and facts will be divided, and so shall I.

With narrow eyes and an unconvinced nod, he holds out his hand. Placing mine atop of it, he kisses it, and I clench my fingers uneasily and pull back.

"Lovely to meet you, Miss Dawson. It's nice to be able to put a name to one of the most beautiful women in the room tonight."

"Thank you," I reply, still finding it difficult to accept compliments. More so, when I'm trying to remain incognito, and he is making it doubly hard with his forwardness, not to mention his nebulousness.

"Beautiful and bashful," he says playfully, and I squirm under his observation. He then pours two glasses of the overpriced fizz and pushes one towards me.

"Well, here's to an interesting, and hopefully, happy New Year," he says charmingly, although I identify his perceptive tone.

I hesitate because between him and Richard Lowe, I wish my decision to be selfish, raise my white flag and abandon this fledging ship had come sooner. I'm now half inclined to hunt down James and take him up on his offer.

Screw being the last woman standing. Right now, I just want to go home.

"So, are you here with anyone?" His question is quiet, but his eyes roam, wondering which of the drunken men still flailing all over the dance floor is my date this evening.

I recoil at his unambiguous enquiry for two reasons. One, because now I am entirely alone. And two, because he has just put the dampers on any intention I might've had of pressing him for business. Clearly, my type of business is probably not the type he has in mind.

Realising I've been quiet for too long, I start to stammer out a coherent response; one I am still unable to put into proper words and sentence.

"Hmm, I can see why he likes you." He knocks back his champagne and pours another. "That torch has burned for a long time. I'm not surprised it's still burning."

"I'm sorry, but do I know you?" I clamber off the stool, and my eyes dart between him and the door, uncomfortable at where this line of interrogation is heading.

"No, but I know you... *Marianne... Beresford.*"

I gasp as the name leaves his mouth. It's a name I haven't heard in over twenty years because Marianne Beresford is dead. My eyes widen, creasing my forehead, and I turn to run until he grabs my wrist, hindering my escape.

"And I'm not the only one," he adds in a thinly veiled, if not true, accusation. "Because they do, too." He twists his head to the doorway, and I follow his line of sight as the two ghosts of my past retreat from the ballroom.

"Let me go. Now!" I hiss, as hot air breathes over the tiny hairs on my neck.

"Secrets are a terrible thing, Marianne. Eventually, they all come back to the surface, regardless of how well you think you can hide them. Tell me, what will you do when the truth is out? How will you lie your way out of reality when you're finally forced to face it?"

I shudder when his fingertips ghost over my nape. Tears well in my eyes as the sensation deepens, channelling further into the place I remember the penultimate nightmare.

Time stands still, and I can't remove my eyes from the entrance, pondering when, *if*, they will return.

The man remains silent, and I spin around, ready to spit out my poorly concealed venom, but he is gone. I stretch up on my toes, just in time to see him walking out of the room.

I rub my hand over my throat, the fear intensifying. I deliberate if pure coincidence has occurred tonight, or if there is an ulterior motive. I know *they* haven't seen me because *she* would have no qualms about letting the entire room know. But him? The man of no name, bearing a fountain of knowledge he shouldn't be aware of, I must question wherein lies the connection.

Breathing deeply, I slap my hands on the bar. The overhead lights bounce off the diamonds in the ring John presented to me just seven days ago. An eternity ring; its significance needs no explanation.

A love for infinity, endlessly spanning time.

The second solitary tear of the night rolls down my cheek, reinforcing what I've feared since the day John Walker first rocked up into my life – I can't conceal the truth forever. I'm damn lucky I've managed it this long.

How? I have no idea.

With that thought in mind, I stride out of the ballroom. Locking the staff room door behind me, I slump down on the sofa.

I stare blindly at the floor because tonight, it seems, fate has started to weave its wicked web to bring about the end – my end. The one I've feared since the moment I stepped off a train with a bag full of meagre possessions, and a head full of broken dreams.

Balled up protectively, I know the day is coming when I will finally have to admit my failings from a lifetime ago.

Closing my eyes, I fear it won't be long.

I glance at the dashboard as I pass the notes to the driver. It's still dark outside, but four-thirty blinds me with its brightness. Climbing out of the car, my bag swings against my legs as I rush up the path.

The silence is welcoming as I lock the door and kick off my heels. Jogging up the stairs, a soft sheen of light seeps from under the bedroom door. Tentatively opening it, the bedside lamp casts light and shadow over a sleeping John. I approach on my tiptoes, and carefully remove the book from his hand. Kissing his forehead, I turn off the lamp and linger for a second before leaving the room.

In the kitchen, I dim the lights, pour a generous glass of wine, and set it down on the table. Retrieving my purse, I bypass the random receipts and business cards, until my fingers touch the worn paper at the back.

Laying it on the table, I close my eyes, fantasising of a time when I still had my Faith.

And I still dared to dream.

Chapter 8

THE SOUND OF a car alarm repeatedly blares outside, forcing me awake. Blinking rapidly, I lick my parched lips and groan. My stomach is delicate, and my head hurts; deserved retribution for downing a bottle of sympathy wine last night.

Rubbing the sleep from my eyes, I stretch and twist the clock around. I sigh; no one should have to be awake at this godforsaken hour. Switching off the alarm, a content, sleepy murmur seeps from beside me, and I look over my shoulder and grin.

Enthused and emboldened in my ropey, hungover state, I tentatively stroke my fingers along the smooth contours of his forearm. Moving up his bicep, I draw small circles over his shoulder, across his collarbone and then down his chest. I suck on my bottom lip, and gently drag my fingernail over his flat nipple, testing his limitations. As anticipated, his body jerks and his breathing quickens.

A devilish thought overcomes me, and I shuffle onto my knees. Encouraged, I hover over him and slowly descend. Lowering my mouth to his flesh, I bequeath him a soft kiss. My breathing comes out hot and heavy, and I smile in self-gratification when his arm spasms by his side, his body reacting in stunning, silent approval. Raking my eyes up his front, he is still asleep - or at least he's pretending to be, for all intents and purposes.

Absorbing the expanse of beautiful man laid out at my mercy, I circle my tongue around his nipple and sit up. Dragging my gaze lower, he is indeed responding as he kicks out his legs; the action adjusting the sheet barely covering his groin in the process. I groan subtly, turned on by the vision of his talented length, subconsciously hardening under my administration.

"Darling?" I whisper sweetly, balancing my weight on one hand. Curving my leg over his body, straddling his thick thighs, I smooth my palms down his stomach. I pause inches above his self-confessed favourite body part and bend down and intentionally drag my eager mouth over his hard tip. He groans unexpectedly, and his body jerks violently. Licking my lips, I fist my hand around him, wanting to torment and tease the same way he does me.

Consumed in my thoughts, undecided whether I should wake him with my hand or my mouth, a hand slap ripples across my behind.

"Hey!" I shriek as he pulls me forward and down, rocking his centre to mine.

"There are laws against taking advantage of a defenceless man," he says hoarsely, his eyes still closed.

"You're not defenceless!"

His lids flip up, and he grins. "No, but in five seconds you're going to be."

No sooner has the last word tumbled over his lips, he pushes me back, and rips my shorts and underwear down my legs. Throwing them over the side of the bed, he drags me back over him and holds firm at my ribcage. I tighten my knees on either side of his hips, while his fingers stimulate the underside of my breasts. Sliding my hands across his chest, soothing his abused nipple with my thumb, he smiles sleepily.

Here, chest to chest, nose to nose; there's no other place than inside his arms that I've ever felt secure. Wanted. Loved. Truthfully, John Walker is the most beautiful specimen of man I've ever seen. To me, he's perfect in every way possible. Strong, selfless, and entirely dependable. And for all those reasons and more, I fall deeper in love with him every second of every day.

"You love it, really," I whisper innocently. "Being taken advantage of is your favourite position."

"I won't deny it, beautiful; I do love it." He smiles gloriously, massaging my spine in long, languorous strokes. "I didn't hear you come in last night."

"This morning," I counter. "Besides, medieval England had knocked you out." My eyes skim over the door stop sized book on the bedside table. "I didn't want to wake you."

He rolls his eyes and grins. "It's a real page-turner, angel."

"Hmm, I'll take your word for it."

"The kid said he was going to sort out cover," he says accusingly.

I sigh. "He did, but I can't just leave my staff, regardless of how fantastic and efficient they are. You know it's not good practice. I let Nicki go early." I unnecessarily justify my actions.

"Lucky Dev." He lets out something crossed between a huff and a laugh. "Martyrdom will get you nowhere."

I shrug. "No, but it might gain me a good spot in heaven one day."

"Hmm, speaking of heavenly good spots..." He pivots his hips suggestively, and his hard length stimulates my soft core. His irises darken, and I roll my pelvis in a slow figure of eight, chasing more.

Trailing his hands from my back to my front, he stops and teases my pubic bone, and my eyes close voluntarily.

"That, right there, is a very good spot, Private Walker."

"It is indeed, and it's Lance Corporal Walker." His hands leave my body, and he flops them down above his head. "Now, feel free to take advantage. The longer, the better." He grins easily as the light of day approaches, highlighting his beautiful, rugged features.

"You just like to watch," I retort, my cheeks flushing at the insinuation.

"Damn right I do." He smiles roguishly. "That's a beautiful shade of pink you're wearing, angel, but if I wanted to watch, we wouldn't be in this position," he replies flippantly, in a tone that says I should know better. And I should, because he likes to be in control. He likes to be above me. He likes to do things that make me incoherent and mindless, and my being on top hinders it. But in this instant, he's letting me have control.

"You're very crude, Walker."

"I'm honest, Dawson."

He brings one arm forward from above his head, captures the back of the neck and pulls me down. Pressing his lips to mine, his mouth is soft, pliant, and very addictive. My tongue tangles with his, and I moan into him the moment he cups and kneads my backside hard and rhythmically. Swaying my body gently, the slide of his shaft against my core elicits a rapturous ache to develop in my tight breasts.

"Angel." The word resonates from his lips to mine while he pillages my mouth akin to a starving man. His hands sit softly on the base my neck, and I shudder the instant his thumbs begin to draw circles over my throat, while his fingers hold me in place at my nape.

"Darling…" I swallow hard. The sensation is parallel to cut glass sliding down my oesophagus.

His jaw grinds and his expression contorts, studying my reaction. This is too far outside of my comfort zone, and he knows it. But every now and again, he likes to test my progress. Progress, of which, for years, I haven't made any.

Truthfully, of all the ways anyone can touch me, this I cannot bear. It's abhorrent to even think about, let along experience again.

"Darling, please stop," I implore anxiously because he already knows a diluted version of the last night I saw my ex. The night the bastard held his hand around my throat and squeezed until my vision blurred and my body became disorientated from it. He doesn't know what came after, but that is a story for another day.

"Trust me." His request is barely audible, and I acquiesce because I do. "I'd *never* hurt you like he did, angel," he says softly, caressing the centre of my throat, much to my displeasure.

"I know, but it's there. It's always there, and I don't know if I can ever get past it," I confess, silently forgiving the moment he chose to bring the past into our bed.

He nods in comprehension, then bestows me with tender kisses, trailing them up the soft column of my neck, making me forget momentarily.

Adjusting me effortlessly, my thighs stiffen further astride his, and I cradle his head in my hands. Our mouths fuse together the same moment his fingers walk up my thigh and tease my folds. He rims my opening leisurely, then eases a digit inside. I gasp at the comfortable intrusion, and stretch my neck, giving his skilful mouth unfettered access. Groaning shamelessly, plunging up and down on his hand, he works lower, kissing and sucking as he goes.

His fingers continue to sink in and out, circling and stretching my wet heat, readying me for him. Adding a second, the pressure increases, until the heel of his hand is massaging my aching clit.

"Don't stop," I beg. "Don't stop."

The first spike engulfs my abdomen, and I tighten my arms around his neck and flatten my palms on his shoulder blades. Consciously seeking the fuel that will set me on fire, I undulate my hips in a deliberate, proprietary grind, calculated to make me come apart and shatter spectacularly.

"Oh, God!" I cry out, my body on fire. I ride his hand hard, pushing my core into his palm, constricting his fingers inside me. He withdraws his fingers with a tug and traces one delicately over his bottom lip. Sucking it into his mouth, his face is a picture of exquisite pleasure as he tastes me.

"I love it when you vibrate on my palm," he says knowingly, jerking up his pelvis.

"I know you do." His incredible steel length strokes the crease where my thigh meets my centre, and I reach down and caress his tip again. "But I'd prefer to vibrate on something else." I writhe harder, creating undeniable friction, using him to my advantage.

I stare with determination into his dark, sensual eyes. They glimmer with promise; promising me the world with unspoken truths and unspoken desires.

He reads my tacit thoughts correctly, then dislodges my hand and rips my satin camisole over my head. Cool air washes over me, from my shoulder blades to my backside, chilling my overheated limbs, cooling my overheated desires.

Palming one breast in his large hand, he rolls my nipple between his finger and thumb, beading it further. I shudder when his tongue rounds my stiff peak, and I rake my fingers over his head, holding him in place while he covers my areola. Taking it whole into his mouth, he nips and sucks ruthlessly.

"Darling, that's good." My body responds immediately, and I move my hips back and forth. Sliding his shaft along my folds, I manipulate him to where I want him, needing to feel him deeper, to fill me completely. His thumb nudges my engorged skin, all the while the hard contours of his length further stimulate my soft curves.

I toss my head back as he continues to suck with determination at my breast, and a surge of rapture finally consumes me. "Oh, God!" My body jerks and shakes under the wave, hitting hard and fast.

"Beautiful," he murmurs, sending incredible vibrations through me. "Playtime's over, baby."

He bites my nipple playfully, then suddenly, my body is flipped over, and he puts his full weight atop of me. Twisting my blonde strands between his fingers, his expression turns sombre, still relaxed and amiable, but something has definitely changed in the last few minutes.

Gripping the inside of my thighs, he parts my legs and licks from knee to apex, and I raise my hips. Dragging his thumb down hard against my opening, my abdomen furls and tightens, and I expand my legs brazenly.

My lower body arches, writhing as he curves his arms under my thighs, and brings them over his shoulders. Separating my folds, he guides his tongue to my centre, lapping at my swollen flesh before thrusting inside. My thighs cradle his head, and I rotate against him. Fucking me impeccably with his mouth, my body spasms as he plays me like a finely tuned instrument.

"Fuck, you're so ready," he says, the movement of his lips reverberating on my highly sensitive apex.

"Ah, God," I whimper, now used to the sounds I make when I'm wanton and willing. "That's so good, it hurts."

"How do you want it, angel?" His teeth tug intimately. "So turned on," he says on an exhale.

"Give it to me the Walker way," I reply, clenching the sheets.

"What do you want first? Hard fucking or slow loving?"

"Both," I request breathless, the same moment he adjusts my legs and starts to taste his way up my front. A few minutes feels like a few hours until he finally reaches my mouth.

He gently lifts my shoulders and places a few pillows underneath. Hovering over me, he lowers until our lips meet, and I can taste myself all over him.

He retreats methodically and smooths his hands over my breasts. Cradling each tender mound of sensitive flesh, he drags his fingertips around my areolas, pinching my nipples before he slides his hands under my backside.

"Watch," he whispers his demand.

I peer down, seeing his shaft poised at my entrance. Moving forward, penetrating a mere fraction, then withdrawing, he knows he's going to send me over the edge the longer he plays this game.

"Darling, please. I need-" The words I need to plead are forgotten as he finally slides himself inside. Everything clenches, and I lift up from the bed, mewling at the marvellous sight of his beautiful steel length slowly impaling me. Each amazing inch invades my tight walls, adding pressure as my body accommodates his fullness.

I bring my fingers to his cheek, and he turns his head, chasing my touch with his lips. Kissing each pad, he gazes down between us, savouring the sight of our union. Full to capacity, he presses harder, deepening the most intimate sensation one can have with another.

"Darling, move," I request softly, while the tingle of sweet ecstasy builds between my thighs. I whimper incoherently not sure if I can hold off not succumbing to the pulsing quickening in my core from the way he is searing me deep within.

"I will, but where do your hands go, angel?" His look of unadulterated love is unmistakable, and he strokes my face tenderly, encouraging me.

I manoeuvre one hand in between us, and slowly touch myself. When I initially did this with him, after our first night together, when it was apparent I needed more than penetration to climax, I was mortified. Now, I accept I have a man who will fulfil me regardless.

He will encourage and command me, take me high and low, and everywhere in between. He'll never leave me wanting. He'll give me everything, whether it is slow, tender loving, or fast, dirty fucking.

Further obeying, I place my other hand on my breast and squeeze and roll. With a light kiss on my lips, his eyes wide and pleased, he pulls back his hips, then plunges back in.

My body rejoices at the movement, and I curve one leg around his arse, as he influences my other knee out and down. Watching him slide in and out in long fluid strokes, is the most shameless, erotic thing I've ever witnessed. Each plunge hits hard, and the carnal sound of skin upon skin fills the room. I throw my arms out, my nails scratching the sheets, while my body prepares for the inevitable. I shift my leg from his behind, curl my toes and drag them up and down the back of his leg.

"Oh, God, that's good. I'm going to... I'm almost..." My abdomen shudders harder, and a second orgasm tears through me without shame. I rotate my hips and rub myself, deepening the coiling consuming my centre.

"That's it, baby, chase that high." His eyes remain fixed on my hand, pumping with fierce determination while I squeeze him inside me.

I continue to pant out; my back arched, my legs braced, seeking further fulfilment. Angling himself over me, he grabs my hands and drags them to the headboard. Holding them in place with one hand, he moves my leg and positions it on his shoulder. Shifting his weight onto his forearm above my head, he bears down, producing a sublime ache.

"Okay?" he asks softly, gyrating deeper. I nod on a moan, fully validating this is more than okay. I clench hard around him, and he grins. "Bad angel." His tone carries a playful authority, using his favourite intimacy moniker. But seriously, when he makes me feel this good, this often, he can call me whatever angel he wants to. "Want to come again?"

"Yes," I beg since my body is silently relishing another release, although my brain is adamant we can't take it. But with my body now in control, my hips lift and lower, and I tangle my fingers in his. As I continue to drive up and down with renewed vigour, gaining momentum, his eyes are dark and dangerous. I hold his gaze as he penetrates me beautifully, hard and fast, then gentle and slow, making me completely mindless. Tipping up my backside, his hard length thickens and pulsates deep within, and my body shifts back with each unforgiving plunge.

"John..." I whimper as he kisses me, concealing my plea. His tongue is rough and punishing, vanquishing all coherent thought as it dances furiously with mine and consumes me.

"Let go, angel." Slamming himself hard inside me, the slight pain is welcoming, and I meet him stroke for stroke. Riding each other to the point of exhaustion, he holds me down while a hot spurt of heat enflames my core and he groans.

"Fuck, baby!" Lowering my leg, his length pulses and his slick flesh rubs mine, and he finally roars out. His release starts the chain reaction for my body to fly high again.

I moan furiously as he drags me up, grabs my arse, and slams me hard and repeatedly into him, draining it out, prolonging the sensation.

"Fuck, I love you," he says, toying with the damp tendrils of hair that are stuck to my face.

"I know." I sigh out content.

With one last forceful surge, he exhales heavily. "I love fucking you, too. Ready and responsive; always wet, and very wanton. You're perfect for me."

I gasp and feign appalled, but I know it's true. So instead, I slap his arm playfully.

"You're a lewd, crude man, John Walker!" He pushes into me again, causing me to moan further in delight.

"And you, Marie Dawson," he grins and cradles my face, "are a bad, bad angel, but fuck if sinning isn't worth it with you!"

I curve my arms around his shoulders and kiss him. "Yes, I love you, too, John Walker." I rub my nose against his.

He chuckles. "You love little John more," he says sarcastically, powering up hard while referring to the name I wrongly bestowed upon his penis when we first started seeing each other. Fortunately for me, it was very wrong.

"He's okay, too, I guess," I reply flippantly as a little shudder peaks in my core again.

"Well, that's good, because he really loves little Marie. And she's not just okay, she's fucking phenomenal!" He laughs, placating my unforthcoming rebuttal as I shake my head.

"Seriously, I love the whole package. Always have; always will." His expression changes from playful to hopeful, and he begins to open his mouth again, but I place my finger over his lips.

"Not yet," I murmur as he sighs redundantly. Seeing his disappointment, I feel terrible. I know he wants more, and it's a more that he is more than vocal about these days.

One day, I know he will make me say yes. It won't be a forced yes, it will be a reluctant one. Not because I don't eventually want to, but because I don't know how to without consequences.

I gaze down at the eternity ring that is more fitting as an engagement ring. And a little voice inside my head tells me it probably is. I lift my head and watch him as he watches me.

The silence develops between us, the same way it always does when he implicates marriage, and I refuse to discuss it with him. I honestly wonder why he stays when he wants something I am outwardly unenthusiastic to enter into. It's a miracle he has managed to get *this* ring on my finger.

Realising nothing further can be said, he gently eases out of me and stands. With his length still standing to attention, and his hands on his hips, he smiles sadly.

"I love you, angel. You're a part of me here." He touches his heart. "You have been for a hell of a long time. Longer than you realise. One day, you will be Mrs Walker, and it's a day I will wait patiently for."

"Darling, please I-"

He shakes his head, cutting off my pleading. "Don't overthink it." He leans down and kisses me. "Go back to sleep. It's early, and I've got a meeting in a couple of hours."

"A meeting? Another one? It's New Year's Day!"

"Says the woman who rolled into bed three hours ago."

"Touché. Anything interesting?" I query delicately.

"No, just some information I need. It's nothing important." He averts his gaze, and my eyes narrow at his vagueness.

"Okay," I whisper.

"It won't take long. I'll probably be back before you're awake."

"Well, I'm awake now. *Very awake*," I emphasise. "So, provided you've got the time and energy, you're going to have to tire me out again before you go." I climb out of bed and sway my hips suggestively, sauntering across the room. "And I'm in desperate need of a long, *hot* shower." I close the door behind me as he groans.

I stand underneath the spray and slap my hands on the tiles. Resting my forehead against the wall, the cubicle door opens, and persistent hands snare my hips and turn me around. My body slides against his, and I walk my fingers up his chest. I press my finger to his bottom lip, and he takes it into his mouth, sucking lightly before nipping the tip.

"How do you want it?" he asks and jerks his head wilfully. I reach up on my toes, cover his mouth with mine and delve my tongue inside. Taking what I want, I suck and kiss his collarbone.

"Angel?"

Kissing an invisible line down his front, he tilts up my chin when I reach his stomach. My action needs no explanation and dark desire clouds his eyes. My knees touch the base, and I take him in hand, stroking reverently, rejoicing in the way he's already pulsating again. I align my eager mouth, peer up his body and watch his eyes flutter in anticipation. Smiling to myself, I take a breath and blow lightly.

"I want you on my tongue."

Massaging lotion down my calf, John walks in with steaming coffee and a lemon muffin. Handing me a mug, I sip it as the bed moves, and he lounges across the bottom in only his boxers, accentuating his strapping physique.

He pushes the small plate towards me and smirks in satisfied. "I thought you might be hungry for something else on your tongue."

I flush and smile shyly, but yes, I am hungry. Breaking off a small chunk, soft searching fingers trail up and down my ankle.

"Happy New Year, beautiful. How was your night?"

"It was okay," I confirm because I won't insult his intelligence when we both know it was crap. His brows pull together, and I shuffle. "Well, let's see. First, I met the elusive Richard Lowe. He offered me a meeting to discuss catering for him. That was...nice." Actually, it was the most unnerving work proposition I've ever had, but with powerful men it always is.

"Really?" he asks surprised, taking a mouthful of coffee.

"He was very forward with his request." I leave it at that because I don't want to fight about something that may not materialise.

"Well, that's fantastic. As long as catering is all he's expecting," he replies candidly, and I chortle, disgusted by his tone.

"That's incredibly unfair, even for you."

He huffs, puts down his mug and crawls towards. "Baby, the man is a dog. He's been cheating on his wife for years, and he has no qualms about where he sticks his dirty dick!"

My eyes slit, and I scowl at him as he palms my hips. "Well, thanks for the vote of confidence, but he won't be sticking *anything* anywhere near me!" I slap his hand.

"Angel," he says, catching my wrist firmly. "I can't blame a man for hitting on you. God knows if we'd met under different circumstances, I would be fighting off the competition. I just don't want you being put in a situation with him."

"The only situation I can see right now is the one you are imagining!" I tell him curtly.

"It *isn't* imagination. You're a beautiful, successful, and incredibly sexy woman. Any man would be blind not to see just how attractive a package you are."

And when he puts it like that, how can I fight?

I settle back down and furrow my brow. "Do you want me to say no?" I ask, without anger or duplicity. If he says yes, I will.

"No, of course not. This is a fantastic opportunity. I just want you to be careful and alert."

I nod, smoothing my hands over his front. "Don't worry, I think I'm at least twenty years too old for his tastes anyway."

His brow quirks. "What do you mean?"

"Nothing. Just an observation." Circling my finger around his nipple, I ghost my lips over it.

"So, what was second?" he asks with a groan.

I smile, somewhat confused, looking into his inquiring, obsidian eyes. "Hmm?"

"You referred to Lowe as the first."

"Well, after being propositioned for *catering*," I stress the word for my own sanity, causing him to smile. "I met a strange-" I stop myself, but I'm too late.

"A strange…?"

"Man. He was rather weird." I frown, still wondering who he was.

My thoughts are running away with me, but the couple from hell were present which means he quite possibly had some unholy alliance. It wouldn't surprise me. The underhand tactics they have resorted to in the past have proven they are unscrupulous when it comes to getting what they want. And the truth they will bury to protect their social standing. I just never thought I would ever see them down here. Although I guess I should have expected it one day considering the man's profession.

"What's his name?"

"I don't know, he refused to give it. He was tall, dark-haired, your age, maybe a little older. He seemed secretive," I say, shifting back in time to see his eyes narrow. Something I've become good at is reading him. This expression is annoyance, and something else.

"Probably just another drunk," he says with rare indifference, but his jaw tightens inconspicuously. "I should've been there with you. I'm sorry, angel."

"I think you've made up for it this morning. Go, you'll be late for your meeting." I touch my lips to his.

"He can wait. A few more minutes won't kill the bastard."

He twists us over effortlessly and strokes my hair, untangling the damp strands. I yawn; this morning's exerting activities now taking their toll. His hand moves down my front and stops on my stomach. I shift, uncomfortable in my own skin while he traces a small patch of indistinct, silver marks.

With his concentration fixed on my abdomen, I know what's coming. I've been dreading this conversation for the last couple of days. But if I'm being completely honest, I've dreaded it since the day Kara announced she was pregnant.

"You know, one day, I won't mind sharing you." I look up into his eyes, which reflect the honesty of his carefully worded request. "Provided you don't mind adding to your fat child marks."

I feel numb and disoriented as he kisses me and drifts his fingers over my stomach and hips.

"That'll be us one day," he says softly, wistfully. "Little girls, or boys, with cherubic features, blonde hair and blue eyes. Just like Mum."

My eyes shut in painful recollection; the picture in my mind's eye already perfectly formed.

My heart sinks as I bite my lip because it's getting harder and harder to dig myself out of the hole I'm burying myself in.

When we first started seeing each other, I didn't realise this would happen. That I would fall completely in love. That I would be willing to put my life into the hands of another and know, unequivocally, he would always cherish it. And above all else, he would lie, steal, and kill to protect it.

"Maybe one day. I love you," I whisper, breaking my own heart, because old habits die hard, and every time I say it, I feel like a fraud. My love for him may not be fraudulent, but who I am is. And eventually, the sad truths I'm concealing will shatter the world he loves.

"Good. I love you, too," he replies, as equally as quiet.

Unable to respond further, I nestle into his chest. With his broad arms caged around me, I start to drift off. His gentle fingers caress my face, lulling me into perfect bliss until he whispers the words that will eventually change everything.

"Will you ever let me in?"

Chapter 9

THE OLD GRANDFATHER clock chimes, carrying over the quiet atmosphere as I sit at the computer.

I rub my temples as a headache begins to take effect from the combination of a late night, an early morning, and the resulting lack of sleep.

I stretch my neck from side to side to work out the stiffness and grab my dirty mug. Trudging into the kitchen, I fill the kettle and flick it on to boil.

Ten minutes later, fresh tea in hand, I kick the office door shut. Moving towards the window, with the mug cradled to my chest, the dark clouds culminate, casting dark shadows and obscuring what was a bright winter's morning.

I sigh heavily as I gaze at nothing of significance on the horizon. If yesterday wasn't already depressing enough, I know there is a distinct possibility my mood may darken as today progresses - especially if I'm left alone to fester. And festering is what I've been doing for the last few hours, waiting for John to resurface.

Reaching for my mobile, I twist it on the spot. "I'm not that girl anymore," I whisper. That girl being the one who waited for her man to come home. Sitting on the steps, watching the clock tick by, waiting in vain. Everything I did back then was in vain, but I was still to learn that unvarnished truth.

But learn it I did.

The spreadsheet glows brightly from the monitor as I turn back to the desk. Pulling out the chair, I place down my mug and get comfy.

Forty-five minutes later, I slap my hands over my eyes. Daring to part my fingers, I glare at the screen. The numbers mock me because I can't make the bloody spreadsheet add up to save my life – not even with auto sum. I'd like to say this is the first time the calculations have misbehaved, but sadly, it isn't.

I shove the papers into a file, giving up on this ill endeavour. Right now, I have two choices. Tomorrow, I can either grovel to Patrick, the resident accountant in my building, or I can call him tomorrow and grovel. Neither is particularly appealing, but a late return will not be acceptable to Customs and Revenue. I'm also pretty confident Her Majesty will frown upon it, too.

While I weigh up the pros and cons of the envelope that screams possible tax penalty, the landline rings.

"Hello?" I answer.

"Hello, stranger!" The familiar twang fills my ear, and I smile, because the way she speaks, anyone would think we don't talk on a regular basis. Heaven knows she is the only way I achieve rational conversation these days.

"Happy New Year!" I impart for good measure. "What time is it there?" I ask, calculating it must be around six in the morning her time.

"Where?" she replies, confused. "Marie, my flight landed earlier this morning. Didn't John tell you?"

I shake my head in annoyance. "No, he didn't." The words come out a little bitchy, but I thought the days of us little women languishing in the dark were over.

"Typical. Well, I feel utterly exhausted, but I'm dying to see you."

"Where are you? At the hotel?"

"No, I'm at the house. My God, has John turned into Sloan recently?" she mutters, infuriated that I haven't a clue of what is going on today.

Listening to her babble on about delays, dispassionate flight attendants and turbulence, she eventually comes up for air.

"How long are you going to be?"

"I'll be there in an hour or two. I just need to finish something."

"Wait, are you working?" she asks critically. "Today?" Now she just sounds plain exasperated.

"Yes. Yes, I am! Some of us do have to work, you know."

"Pfft!" is her response. "Well, tell your man you want to stop working. He can afford it."

I snort in disbelief. "You tell him."

"Don't worry, I will. Look, just get your shapely backside over here, lady."

"I'm trying!" I grit out.

"Try harder!" She laughs and hangs up.

I put down the phone, save the spreadsheet and log off the computer. Double checking the windows and patio doors are secure, I throw my bag over my shoulder and lock the front door.

Almost an hour later, I climb out of the car and admire the reasonably clean paintwork of the Audi Q5 John presented to me after my attack. In the days after my assault, my Merc, which I eventually learned to love, disappeared from the driveway. And it has remained gone.

As I approach the security panel at the imposing gates, I glance towards the empty security cabin. Once upon a time, this tiny four by five hut had someone manning it day and night. These days, with no imminent threat to life, it now sits empty.

The whirr of electricity disrupts the quiet surroundings as I tap in the last number and the gates part. Climbing back into the car, I manoeuvre down the driveway towards the mansion.

Unlocking the front door, the sound of cooing and laughter greets me, and I drop the bags next to Jules' cases, which are all lined up in a uniformed row. Following the chatter, I stop in front of the mirror and check my appearance.

Gone is my short blonde bob, now, it is brushing my shoulder blades. Staring at my reflection, a glimmer of someone I used to know stares back at me.

"Well, it's about bloody time, lady! And, pray, what time do you call this?"

Twisted up in yesteryear, I swivel on the spot, unable to hide my grin at her sarcasm.

I feign innocence and glance at my wrist. "Excuse me, but *you* called *me*. And *I* call it being fashionably late. You should know, you're the one who taught me the value of making a grand entrance."

"'*Grand entrance*'," she mutters and waves her hand out. "Well, don't stand on invitation, come on in!" Lounging against the door frame, the woman towers over me by almost a foot.

"Why, thank you!"

This tit for tat camaraderie is something we've had going on for years. I will always remember the day this leggy blonde bombshell turned up on John's doorstep with three large suitcases, a Prada bag and a severe case of jetlag. In the days she spent with us leading up to the wedding between our children, we bonded. In all the years I spent alone, crafting an existence that kept me sane, I never imagined I would have a best friend again.

"Fashionably late!" Jules mutters, following behind me.

"Hello, darling. Happy New year," I greet Kara, who is sitting on the sofa, rocking her newborn. I give her a chaste kiss, and I'm grateful these days the uneasy flinch has lessened drastically.

"Hi. And you," she replies with a smile but looks over my shoulder, watching her mother-in-law ramble on behind us.

"The last time I was here you were *fashionably late* then, too. I can't say I blame you. I'd think twice if I had a six foot two Adonis, built like a brick shithouse, refusing to let me leave the bed! I guess can dream. I can dream a lot!"

I cover my face in mortification. "Children present."

"I think he's too young to understand," Kara says, stroking the flash of dark hair on her son's head.

"She meant you, darling!" Jules bursts out laughing.

Kara tuts for good grace. "Well, I think I'm finally ready for grown-up girl talk since I definitely know where babies come from. But I also know where I'm not wanted. Here you go Grandma, he needs changing." She leaves me holding the baby with a gobsmacked Jules and walks out of the room as I fling my bag on the sofa, and the changing mat hits the floor in front of me.

"Thanks." Dropping to my knees, I blow kisses at my grandson and lay him down. Unfastening his Babygro, I catch my counterpart in my peripheral vision.

"It's been a long time since I've done this. And you've never done it at all," Jules says, fresh nappy and wipes in hand. "Here, you need to-"

"I know what to do." I pull the side tabs and removing the offending nappy. "Who's a stinky, stinky boy?" I say playfully, cleaning him up, trying not to gag or projectile vomit.

Ten minutes, half a pack of wipes and a fresh nappy later, I fasten his Babygro and lift him to my chest. Gazing down at his innocent, shining eyes, his features already dark and brooding, my heart shudders. Familiarity envelops me, and I inadvertently catch Jules' serene expression.

"It's a good look on you. Have you..."

I give her what must be a death glare because her shoulders lift, and her head tilts, leaving the question hanging in the ether. *Interesting.* Even she dares not to raise this topic with me. Sometimes I wonder if she has spoken to John about it.

I hoist myself and baby boy off the floor, and inadvertently absorb that lovely smell all babies possess.

"Right then, where were we?" Jules starts. "Yes, *fashionably late.* Don't hold back, I want details. All of them, especially the good ones."

"You sound desperate."

"I am!"

With a betraying smile, I purse my lips and shake my head. She knows I don't kiss and tell. *Usually.* God knows over the last few years she has tried, and unfortunately, one poorly executed evening last year, basking in the summer sun, after far too many pitchers of Pimms on the deck, I spilt my guts over the man she had hired to be the protector of herself and her children. Regrettably, my drunken rambling, complete with hand gestures, was my comeuppance for being such a lightweight. And she's never let me live it down since.

"Nothing much to tell but said Adonis did leave me alone in bed this morning," I lie. "And considering *your* appearance is a week overdue, I guess you should be lucky *I* turned up at all." I bite back the amusement that is rounding my cheeks.

"It hasn't been for the lack of trying," she replies and strokes the back of Oliver's head. "God, I've missed you, lady." Her arms open, and I reciprocate the gesture and fall into her, baby and all.

The door opens, and Kara walks in and scrunches up her nose. I reluctantly pass back her son, and she tucks him into the Moses basket. Jules' arm curls around my shoulders and we stand as one and peer down at sleeping beauty.

"Three generations," she murmurs, pulling Kara close.

"He's amazing, honey. I'm so proud of you," I say, beaming at my girl, who is clearly madly in love with her early arrival.

"He's gorgeous. He looks just like Sloan did when he was born," Jules says proudly, and I curve my lips but am unable to assimilate. I never knew Kara as a baby, but by God, I wish she was mine in the real maternal sense.

"Speaking of Sloan, where is he?" I look around the room, finally noting his absence.

"Oh, he's gone to meet someone."

My brows lift, and my mouth drops. "He's left you with your premature, two-day-old son to meet a *client?*" I ask infuriated because *here* is where he should be, especially when his son was a month premature. I blow out my breath. Livid doesn't quite describe the way I'm feeling right now.

"Marie, I made him go. He hasn't slept since the birth, and he's making me more overwhelmed than anything else. He needs a break from worrying, and I need a break from overbearing!"

"Well, that's taken you long enough." My sarcasm is unmistakable, and I know I've hit a nerve when she narrows her eyes. "Who is he meeting?"

She hesitates, conflicted. "I'm not supposed to know, but I overheard him talking with John this morning. They're meeting Dominic Archer. Apparently, John was with him last night, too."

"Oh." I nod. "The ex-army mate. Do you know him?" I ask Jules, hoping it sounds casual.

"No, never met him," she replies nonchalantly. "But what I do know about him, is that he's brilliant. And by that, I mean there's nothing he can't find. ID's, intel, official records, even those sealed to the public."

"How?" I ask without thinking.

She shrugs and puffs out her cheeks. "No idea, but you can't run or hide when Dominic's involved. Trust me, the stuff he dug up on me, no one knew, but he did. Who do you think faked my death?" She waves her hand easily. "How do you think my son got all the info on you over the years?" She jolts her head towards Kara, who stands there looking vacant and speechless. "John calls in the favours, but Dominic's the brains behind it."

I glance down at my feet, mentally speculating if he knows all about me. And if John already has a file, hidden somewhere... I exhale because that's impossible. Adrian made it so.

"Want a drink?" Kara asks as she switches on the baby monitor. I want to say yes; preferably the most intoxicating liquor Sloan owns that will knock me out until the next century. "Marie?"

"Sure," I confirm as she leaves the room. Turning to Jules, I purse my lips and rub my forehead.

"Are you okay?" she queries.

"I don't know. Did I just overact?"

Her lips upturn softly. "Hmm, maybe a little. Sloan didn't want to go. He was very adamant, but she made him so she could have Oliver to herself for a while. It hasn't occurred to him how lucky he is yet. I appreciate the sacrifices he's made, but he needs to understand he can't always be here. He also needs to realise that a mother needs to bond with her child."

"And you're going to tell him as such, aren't you?" I query humorously and wait for her retort as she slides her arm into mine.

"Why, of course, that's what mothers are for," she replies as we follow Kara into the kitchen. "Whether he listens to me is another matter entirely. And if he kicks me out and cuts me off, I'm coming to live with you!"

Still laughing, I quickly wash and dry my hands then pull out a stool and reach for the mug Kara has put down.

"Sorry, honey. I didn't mean what I said about Sloan abandoning you both."

"It's okay; I like this abandonment." She smiles slyly. "He's coddled me for two days, and at times I feel like I can't breathe."

Jules takes a seat, leans on her elbows, and studies me keenly. All my senses prickle, because it's uncomfortable to be in her sights, not knowing what she is going to say or ask next.

"You look good. Happy. Content. A lot better than when I was last here that's for sure."

"Hmm," I murmur, schooling my response. "I am. Life is great. I guess being happy and in love helps."

"Speaking of love, how's John?"

"He's good," I answer with apprehension, nervous about where this is going. "Why do you ask?" The question comes out imperturbably, but inside I already feel the panic. Whenever anyone asks about us, it's always the same.

"It's nothing, but I just got the feeling he was...I don't know, distant when I spoke to him last week."

"Oh," I murmur innocently and take another sip of coffee.

The baby monitor comes to life and the three of us still until he settles back down.

"So, what have I missed? I asked John, but he told me since he didn't have the right appendage he wasn't privy!"

I chuckle, but Kara is faster to the punch than I am.

"Really? Those boys gossip worse than women in that ramshackle shed of theirs! Some of the stuff they discuss is positively obscene!"

Her reply is right on point, although John's response doesn't surprise me. The last time I asked his opinion on something, he advised me since he hadn't grown a pair of tits yet, what the hell did he know? And while he made such a vulgar statement, it didn't stop him from giving me his opinion on the dress in question when he stripped it off me. Not that I'm going to tell them *that*.

"Right you two, out with it!" Jules demands.

"Honestly, there isn't much to tell. Charlie and Jake, you probably know more than we do," I reply.

"Which is nothing! I'm only her mother, you know."

"Well, Soph and Stuart are still plodding along," Kara confirms.

"Have they set a date yet?" she asks, hopeful, which quickly turns into despair when Kara shakes her head.

"No. Soph just brushes it off, so now we've all stopped asking."

Jules baulks. "My God! She's the must unenthusiastic bride-to-be I've ever known! Poor Stuart," she mutters. "And the misfits? Dare I ask what those two are up to?"

"Same old; women, work and whining," I chime, nursing the mug between my hands.

"What about Jeremy? How's he been?" she asks sombrely. Her sadness is always apparent whenever she speaks about him. It's no secret Remy spent a lot of his childhood in her house. It's also no secret the demons he carries inside are slowly eating away at him. He hides it well, but these last few years have changed him – mentally and physically.

"He's partially closed off again," I tell her, noting Kara's immediate sadness.

Jules sighs. "I guess closed off is better than packing his bags and absconding in the middle of the night."

"True," I reply uncomfortably. "But who knows what goes on inside his head. So much lives in there he probably can't think straight half the time."

"What about the girl he was seeing? Pretty thing. Eve, wasn't it?"

"Oh, he's still seeing her," Kara says with a small smile. "I don't think it's as easy as he would like us to believe, but he deserves to be happy."

That he does, but I think it's definitely safe to assume it isn't smooth sailing. A conversation I had many moons ago with the girl in question snaps into my head... No, a rock and a hard place are infinitely easier.

"I've extended my offer of dinner repeatedly, but Evie never seems particularly taken. It's like she's frightened to get too close. Whenever I raise it with Remy, he's just his usual reserved self."

"Hmm, that's not surprising. I'll have a chat with him when I see him. Make sure he's not going to start going off the rails, doing his disappearing acts, or sticking needles in his veins again." She downs a mouthful of coffee and swings her head to me. "And you and John? What's happening there?" she queries, far too politely.

"What about us?"

"Don't play dumb with me, lady! God knows *I'm* never going to see any kind of action again, so I might as well live vicariously through you."

Kara titters, putting her hand over her mouth, while her cheeks turn crimson. "Children present," she mutters sarcastically.

"Cover your ears!" Jules exclaims, then points at me. "M, the mouth opens, and words come out. So out with it already! I'm desperate, remember?"

"We're good," I offer sheepishly, not to embarrass Kara any further. Or myself, for that matter.

"Good?" she repeats. "I think I need to intravenously feed you more wine, it's the only way you ever talk."

"And what does that tell you!"

"Okay, baby steps. How's the house sale going?"

I huff out, put my mug down and rub my temple. "John didn't say?" Jules eyes narrow. "The sale fell through last week, on Christmas Eve. They called at midday, just before they were closing, to say that the buyers had been for a final visit and decided against the purchase. Best laugh? The agent then had the cheek to ask when I would be settling the account since it has been on the market for longer than anticipated," I say verbatim, mimicking Veronica – the local friendly estate agent – with venom.

"Oh, I'm sorry."

I shake my head. "It is what it is. This is the second time; I don't know if I can cope with a third."

"You know what they say about threes." Jules stands and comes around to my side. Pulling out the adjacent stool, she sits and grabs my hand. "Did they give any indication as to why they withdrew?"

"No, although I have my suspicions. In the past, whenever a potential buyer got within twenty feet of the place, the nosy old bat next door would come out with tea and sympathy, expressing her horror that I was beaten and almost left for dead. Apparently, she regales it with glee and vivid detail. Each time more elaborate than the last according to the agent. Trust me, they are just as unhappy about it as I am."

"M, honey, it's just neighbourly gossip. We both know that talk is cheap!"

"Not when you're desperate to offload, it isn't!" I shriek. Seriously, this topic is enough to give me premature heart failure.

"I guess now's not the best time to tell you that I'm looking to move back permanently." She grimaces and backs away a fraction.

"No, that's great!" I grin, glad I will have my partner in crime on the same continent. "Do you want to buy my house?" I ask enthusiastically as an afterthought. Outwardly, I'm jesting; inwardly, I'm far from joking.

She smiles sadly, shaking her head for emphasis. "Like you'd ever come and visit me if I did. Seriously, if I thought you would, I'd say yes."

I roll my eyes, but she's right. "I appreciate the gesture. It's just obvious that it isn't the lack of potential buyers in the market hindering my sale, it's the street gossips. I've lost count of how many would-be purchasers have walked in and then walked straight back out because of it. Honestly, I'm starting to think I can't give it away. At this stage, I'm considering sticking a sign outside declaring all squatters welcome. God knows no one wants to buy it. Even a ball and chain would probably refuse to swing towards the bloody thing!"

"Well, let's hope this year brings good things," Jules says, raising her mug. I clink mine against hers, but sadly I don't share her good spirit.

The baby monitor slowly comes to life, and the sounding of Oliver fussing heightens. "He's ready for a feed. I won't be long," Kara says as she stands and leaves the room.

I glance around the kitchen, seeing the new additions of a steriliser, breast pump, and a collection of upturned bottles on the worktop. Turning back, I capture Jules' thoughtful expression.

"What?" I ask softly.

"You're great with him, you know. A natural mother. Are you really not tempted?" she asks with incredulity.

Natural mother? Tempted? I let out a dry laugh.

"No, I think my eggs are definitely past their use-by date." I squirm in my place, refusing to chat about this with her when I refuse to do so with John.

"Nonsense. Women are leaving it later and later now, and science is amazing these days."

"Jules," I murmur, but the woman just doesn't know when to stop.

"And John would be an excellent father - ask Sloan and Charlotte about his unorthodox parenting techniques." She grimaces in recollection. "Now there are a few stories that will give you nightmares!"

"Jules, please," I plead stubbornly, fed up this aggressive pursuit she seems to have taken on for no reason.

"Okay, fine," she concedes.

I purse my lips. Two words I used to despise so much, muttered in the same sentence, on a topic I've never dared to embrace. *Typical.*

"M, I'm sorry. I didn't mean to push," she apologises, quite contritely for once. A rare family trait I'm now used to.

"It's fine." In a bid to ignore the elephant in the room, I collect up the mugs and put them in the sink. Washing my hands, my phone sparks to life and shimmies over the island.

I slide my finger over the screen and pick it up. "Hi, darling."

"Hey, beautiful. So, I've just arrived home, ready for round three with the missus, but the missus isn't here." I chuckle at his simple, caveman tone.

"No. I've been very preoccupied with a beautiful young boy. Are you jealous?"

"Absolutely, but stay longer if you want to," he says, but fleeing is more than appealing right now.

"No, let me just say goodbye, and I'll see you soon." I end the call and join Jules back at the island. "I forgot to ask, but how long are you here for?"

"A few weeks, maybe a month. I'm undecided. How about brunch sometime this week?"

I nod and mentally run through what I have on this week. It isn't a lot, but it never is this soon after the Christmas period.

"Sure, as long as you promise not to make me house hunt with you," I say playfully as she links her arm in mine and we walk into the living room.

"Anything's possible. Would you really mind?"

"No, I like seeing how the other half live." I wink, retrieve my bag, and drop my mobile inside. "Do you fancy coming over for dinner one night?"

"Definitely," she says as we stroll down the hallway, then she grabs two cases and hauls them up the stairs.

The sound of content gurgling and sweet words of encouragement leak out from the nursery as I stop outside.

"I'll see you later, lady," Jules says as she hugs me and strides down the landing.

I push back the door and halt when I see Kara is breastfeeding. "Sorry, honey."

Her head jolts up, and she smiles. "No, come on in." She extracts her sleepy tot and covers up. Holding him lovingly, his front to hers, she massages his back, and he lets out a small burp.

"I just thought I'd let you know, I'm off. John's back, which means your beloved will be home soon."

"Okay. Do you want to hold him before you go?" she asks.

"No," I whisper, as she tucks him into the Moses basket. "I wouldn't dream of waking him up for a selfish hug." With a heavy heart, I touch the soft, sleepy head of my first grandchild. He stirs momentarily, pursing his tiny pink lips together. "Dream beautiful dreams, little prince."

I turn back to Kara and embrace her. "He's gorgeous, honey, and you made him. I was wrong, too."

"About?"

"When Sloan started to pursue you, I thought it would end badly, but I was wrong. I was wrong about everything."

Kara hooks her arm in mine and smiles, unsure what to say. "I'll walk you out."

At the bottom of the stairs, I slide into my jacket and rummage through my bag for my keys. "Jules and I are meeting for brunch one day this week, come if you and baby boy feel up to it," I offer, headed towards the door. "Failing that, I want to see you at mine for dinner on Sunday." She nods, knowing she isn't getting out of that regardless. With a kiss on my cheek, she loiters at the top of the stone steps as I climb into my car.

As I stop at the gates, they part with a slow creak, and I look up to the sky. A small ray of hope penetrates my heart as the gloomy clouds separate, and for the first time in twenty-three years, this day isn't as dark as I anticipated.

Chapter 10

I WRAP THE towel around my head and stand in front of the mirror. Wiping my arm over the glass, the condensation comes away with it. I sigh, critiquing my appearance, or more notably, any further lines to add to my forty-three years. It's pointless, of course, because they don't just appear overnight. Although us woman are convinced that they do.

I pick up my toothbrush, and my fingers graze over John's. Warmth spreads through me because I finally have everything I've ever wanted. I have a man who loves me, a house I call home, and a beautiful life. Once upon a time, it was an elusive dream - one that was out of my grasp for so long - but now I have it.

I smile, because all these things he has given me, unequivocally, not expecting anything in return. Occasionally, he's pushed for more, and I have quenched his thirst for knowledge, but not in any profound detail. It's a sad truth, but details are trivial, because no matter how many ways I can spin it, the outcome will never, ever change.

Sometimes, I think time wasn't on my side in this life. I often wonder if I am destined to fare better in the next.

The doorbell rings as I pull light cord, and a flurry of activity resounds from downstairs. I tilt my head over the bannister, just in time to see John enter the office, along with whoever is calling, before I close the bedroom door.

Perusing the wardrobe rails, I grin at the variety of polos, combats, and jeans, all ironed to perfection. If there is one thing I have learnt in the time that John and I have been living together, is that order is paramount.

And so is the ironing.

I push each of my almost identical black suits aside, needing to find the best one I own. Not to impress Richard Lowe - who John still has reservations about - but to make the best impression on his board.

As per my request, Nicki deflected his repeated dinner invites, after he personally called, and she went through his assistant instead. Needless to say, my suspicions were correct. And needless to say, I haven't informed John of that, either. No need for him to fly off the handle again with unfounded assumptions that will never materialise.

I flick through a second time until my fingers stop at the cream dress I wore for Kara's wedding. Pulling it out, my eyes drift to the window, wondering if the unpredictable weather of late will ensure it ends up soaked with an essence of dirt by the end of the day. I wouldn't be surprised, it's just my luck.

Sitting in front of the mirror, I begin to apply my face - the one I paint on for the world, to hide the one I'm ashamed of – when my phone starts to ring. Glancing at the clock, it's has just gone eight. And there is only one person who will be calling.

"Morning Simon," I answer playfully.

"Good morning, M. Is he still there?"

"Hmm. Do you need him?" I ask, repeating the exact same conversation we've had every morning since John moved me in without my knowledge the day before I was discharged from hospital eighteen months ago.

"No, just checking. Has Evans arrived yet?"

"I don't know," I reply, although he has just confirmed who is calling at such an early hour.

"Well, when you've finished having your way with J, tell him he's late. And to bring coffee, bacon butties, and some of those glazed doughnuts with the sprinkles on. Have a nice day!" He hangs up, and I rub my forehead in disbelief. These morning calls are getting stranger by the day.

Half an hour later, with my hair perfectly styled and my war paint in place, I grab my bag and jacket and close the door.

My foot clears the bottom rung, and I stop outside the office as John's laugh resonates. I dawdle in the small recess, watching him pace up and down in front of the window.

"Kid, why on earth are you asking me?" He pauses. "Have you not looked in that book I bought you?"

I put my hand over my mouth to suppress my laugh. Something else that has also been happening every day is Sloan calling. The number of times I have stood out here, listening to them on speakerphone discussing something to do with Oliver, but never reaching a resolution, is adorable.

"Sloan, put some of that gel on his gums and call Doc. Better still, call Sophie. You know the little man loves the crazy girl." He pauses again, then sighs. "I'm going now, but if you need anything, get your wife to call mine."

Hearing the phone drop on the desk, I tap on the door and push it back. "Morning."

"Angel," John greets gruffly. I stop at his knees and bend down for a kiss. My lips linger, and he breaths in content. "It's a good morning, indeed."

"Is he teething?" I ask the question but already know the answer.

"No, he's just being a pain in my arse again!"

I pierce him with a glare, but he's right – Sloan's a pain in everyone's arse.

"Doc had a look at him yesterday. He said it's a little early, but he's got a tooth just waiting to come through. Why the kid calls me, I don't know. I guess I could give baby boy some metal and wire to bite down on!"

"John!" I admonish, feeling his arms tighten around my waist, massaging rhythmically. "Simon called."

He snorts. "Today's request?"

"Coffee, bacon and doughnuts." I lick my lip, still tasting him. His eyes darken, and he wheels his chair closer.

"Stunning. Not seen you in this in a while." He grips my hips with a knowing smile. "What time's your meeting?"

"Half nine."

He nods, mulling something over. "You remember what we talked about last week?"

I roll my eyes and grind my teeth. "Of course, we've talked about it every week for the last seven," I reply, exasperated. "It's a meeting with the entire board, not a personal tour of his house ending in the bedroom, commenting on his sheets!"

Pissed off at my reply, he holds his hand up. "Don't. I'm just protecting what's precious and mine. He touches you, says anything untoward, or so much as looks at you in a way you find uncomfortable, I'll happily break his legs." And just when I thought this day couldn't get any worse, he raises the bar. "The man is a lying, cheating, dirty bastard, and he makes no qualms about it."

"You know, I've put off this meeting for weeks. So many, in fact, it makes me look unprofessional. And the reason why is because every time we have a conversation about it, we end up having a fight instead. I don't want to fight, John. I want your support and encouragement," I huff out, utterly dejected, prepared to admit defeat.

Realising he has thoroughly upset me, he tugs me close. "I love you. And I'll do anything to ensure you sleep easy at night. I'd fight for you; I'd kill for you. There's nothing I wouldn't do."

I rub my hand over his hair and acquiesce. "I know, but I spent a lot of years getting by on my own. It's not like I've never met a sleazy git who thought something other than food and drink was on the menu. I survived before you, and I'd survive witho-"

"*Don't* finish that sentence. It's *never* going to happen. While I remember, Jake went by the house yesterday." He reaches behind him and hands me the pile of post from the desk.

"Bills." I take a punt. "More bills," I say, flicking the brown envelopes. "And more bills!" I smile, recognising one from the bank and another from HMRC, which shouldn't put a smile on my face at all. As a matter of fact, I should be ripping it open and bracing myself for whatever it says.

John holds out his arm as I put the post down, and I plonk myself into his lap. Holding his gaze, I wait. Until waiting proves ridiculous, consuming precious time I don't have.

"Do you have anything to say to me?" I query delicately, as not to start a situation I have no interest in getting into a tizzy over.

He stares at me, his eyes wide and wondering. Wishing me good luck is going to kill him. Anyone would think the words were bloody fatal. Yet that isn't what I want to hear this morning. He's about to open his mouth when the work line rings.

"Sorry, angel, but I need to take this."

Convenient.

"Okay." I control the huff my throat is desperate to emit, slide off his lap and leave the room. These days I've stopped asking who calls. Namely, because he gets calls at all hours from all sorts of people.

Entering the kitchen, my annoyance is simmering just below boiling point. Lobbing my bag onto the worktop, Jake is sat at the table, a slice of toast at his mouth, his eyes on this morning's broadsheet.

"Morning, darling," I greet as I put the kettle on. "Does Charlie not feed you before you leave the house?"

He looks up with a vacant expression and runs his hand through his messy blonde hair. "Cooking isn't really her thing. She couldn't boil water if her life depended on it."

I cock my brow, and he gives me what he probably thinks is a charming grin. Stuffing another slice of toast into his mouth, his eyes subtly glance towards the office.

"So, I hear you might be getting into bed with the enemy by the end of today." He lifts the pint-size mug of tea to his grinning lips, and I wonder how much he heard since I was the one to bring sheets into the conversation.

"Possibly, but I wouldn't quite put it like that," I reply and drop two slices of bread into the toaster. I perch my backside against the unit as Jake flicks through the paper until the toaster pops up.

"Sloan and John weren't particularly chatty when I asked, but what's tricky dicky offering?" he asks as I join him at the table.

"Initially, it's only four events. Although I might just see if I can do a couple at first. Test the waters, so to speak."

"Sensible," he says, looking over his shoulder, down the hallway, to where John's voice is still resonating in muted tones. "Just be careful with him. Rumours are circulating that he's-"

"Stepping out on his wife?" I finish in response, covering my mouth and the masticated toast. "When I met him on New Year's Eve, he had a girl on his arm who was barely legal. Unsurprisingly, he wasn't even remotely ashamed. Look, I'm aware of *what* he is, and while I don't agree with it, it's money. Besides, if we all ran our businesses based on morals, we'd all be starving and homeless."

"Agreed," is all he says as the office door opens. "Just be alert."

I stare down at my plate with apprehension. Since every man in my life has warned me to be vigilant with him, I'm seriously considering walking into his office today and telling where he can shove his contracts. From an outsider perspective, you could say it's because I will be working for the competition, but of all the things my son-in-law is; overbearing, bossy, impossibly annoying and hard to please, he's never unfair. And he's never told me not to take the meeting, just to be *alert*.

"Angel?" John calls out.

"One minute." I dump my plate and mug in the dishwasher. "Oh, do you have anything to say to me, Jacob?" I query innocently.

Jake looks around with a nonplussed expression. "Good luck?" he says, taking a guess.

I huff out. "Yeah, thanks. I'll see you later."

"Sure," he replies with a crooked grin.

I can feel my eyes narrow, but I let it go. Something is going on here that I don't know about. I'm not stupid; these boys can't hold their own water. And considering in the past whenever something has happened, and I've been in the thick of it, I can read the signs easily.

Although, I shouldn't be surprised since today is the first day in forever that John hasn't woken me up with kisses. Either on my cheek, down my neck or across my shoulder. He's a living, breathing alarm clock of the best kind. And pondering the implications as to why makes me curious. Yet, just like everything else I need to deal with today, I don't have time to reflect on it.

Grabbing my jacket and bag, I move back into the office to find John standing at the window. From his perfectly fitted, faded jeans that mould over his hips and backside, to the snug t-shirt that stretches over his delectably muscled torso, defining every contour.

Walking towards him, he takes me into his arms and holds tight. "I forgot to say good luck," he says softly, pressing his lips to mine.

"Thanks," I whisper in disappointment. "I'm going to be late." Turning on my heel, I hurry towards the door, but strong arms snake around my waist, impeding my escape.

"Angel?"

"I'm sorry. It's nothing, really." But it is something. It's the fact that he can't be happy for me. It's also the fact that he doesn't trust me. He hasn't said it, but every time we've had a conversation about today, it has been unconsciously implied. And it infuriates me abundantly because he doesn't realise what exactly he means to me. My fault, of course, because whenever he asks I deliberately change the subject to something less embarrassing and more palatable.

"It's just nerves. You'll be amazing," he says, glancing at his desk as the phone starts to ring.

"The kids or the boys?"

"The boys," he replies.

"You better go. Simon already thinks I've got you tied to the bed. God knows what he thinks Jake's doing."

"Now that's a fascinating idea. I think I've got a length of rope somewhere in the garage," he says playfully. He slowly lifts my hands until my back is prone, and my bum is pressed hard against his groin. The atmosphere is thick with equal need until it is vanquished with the ringing of his mobile again.

"I'm going to beat that little sod when I get my hands on him!" He spins me around and cups my cheeks. "Call me with the verdict." Kissing me at length, he eventually lets me go.

Climbing into my car, I flip down the visor. "Good luck. And happy birthday," I congratulate myself since someone in my life ought to give a shit.

I drop my bag on the marble vanity, and gaze into my eyes, seeing the weariness behind their vibrancy. Smoothing my palms over the flyaway strands, I re-position my diamond studs and spritz on a little perfume.

"Marie Dawson. Lovely to meet you all." I smile brightly at my unimpressed reflection. "Hmm, I suppose that will do," I tell her. As expected, she doesn't respond.

In front of the full-length mirror, I hitch up my tights. Checking my dress hangs right, and my jacket isn't bunched, I deem it is as good as it's going to get.

With my bag over my shoulder and my portfolio under my arm, I exit the ladies. Ready to face the proverbial firing squad, I brace myself for the outcome before the show has even begun.

I step over the threshold of the immaculate presentation suite, and ten stoic faces meet mine as the massive oak door slams shut behind me.

"Good morning, gentlemen," I greet with a smile, and place down my portfolio.

"Good morning, Marie," Richard says brazenly from the head of the table, propping his elbow on the wood. I maintain my composure and move towards the laptop with my USB stick.

Well, here goes nothing.

The worst tricky dicky can say is yes, right?

Ninety minutes later, I lean over the conference table and collect up the presentation handouts.

"That was very well executed and precise. I'm impressed," Richard says from behind me as the last of my audience depart. "I like a woman who goes for what she wants."

I bristle, uncomfortable in his assumption of my *going for what I want.*

"Thank you, Mr Lowe. Excuse me."

He waves my way open nonchalantly, and I quickly do what I need to. Namely, needing to escape sooner rather than later.

"How about lunch?" he asks coolly, perching his large frame on the edge of the table. "We can celebrate your birthday."

I turn hesitantly, loathing the fact he has remembered when the man I share my bed with hasn't.

"Come on, Marie, just a friendly birthday lunch. I promise I'll behave myself." His hands lift in yield, but something tells me he isn't used to behaving himself very often.

"I'm sorry, Mr Lowe-"

"It's Richard, Marie. I'd prefer if you used my first name," he says, almost menacingly.

"Richard," I reply cautiously since I definitely don't want to be trying his name on for size. "I already have another meeting arranged after this, so, unfortunately, I'll have to decline." It's a barefaced lie, but necessary to ensure I can walk away without an unwanted lunch date I might not be able to refuse if he doesn't stop this passive-aggressive way of trying to get me alone.

"Well, that is unfortunate." He sighs in annoyance. "How about a belated lunch one day when you're free?"

I recoil, but thankfully, my response is unnecessary, when the door opens and a beautifully coiffured woman – a girl, really - enters. She glides across the floor and stops next to Richard, who nods some unknown order. From the corner of my eye, his lingering gaze goes after her as she clears away the dirty cups and saucers. I shift in discomfort, feeling very out of place and annoyed that some men just can't keep it in their trousers.

"Thank you for your time today, Richard."

"The pleasure is all mine, Marie," he says suggestively. "This is the first draft of the contract." His hand lingers on mine as he passes me the thick, bound document. "Have a read through and let me know if there is anything you would like clarifying. If everything is satisfactory, I'll have my assistant email the final draft. Then we will have a meeting to discuss *my needs*."

I smile grudgingly, spying the coffee jug on the table, wanting to douse it over his head and show him exactly what *my needs* entail. Sadly, I also like buying expensive dresses, indulging in eating, and having money in my pocket, so it's only inside my head I'm living that iniquitous fantasy.

Instead, I hold out my hand and grimace when his lips touch my skin. I make a mental note to scrub it with bleach until the first layer of my epidermis is making way for the second.

I drop my hand, bid him goodbye and move towards the door. My reprieve is short-lived as he follows me. Quickening my pace, I impatiently, discreetly, tap my foot as the lift refuses to arrive. Finally, one pings open and I step in. Pretending to fuss with my bag, Richard grins wickedly.

"Happy birthday, Marie," he says smugly.

"Thank you," I reply as the doors finally close. Breathing a sigh of relief, I practically collapse against one side. Never have I met such a lecherous, unscrupulous man in my life. And trust me, I've met a lot over the years.

Perusing the papers, I'll make damn sure everything in them is entirely satisfactory because there is no way on earth I want to be in his presence alone again.

Except if I do sign on for this gig, I know avoidance isn't possible.

And maybe yes isn't the worst thing he can say.

Chapter 11

I BREEZE OUT of the building with an added spring in my step, thankful for a relatively easy escape. Pulling out my phone, I dial whilst trying to avoid the bodies of the lunchtime exodus going about their business.

"Walker Security," John answers on the second ring.

"Hi, it's me."

"Hey, beautiful. How did it go?" he asks with calm suspicion.

"My presentation went very well, thank you. The board were happy."

"I'm sure they were. Was tricky dicky happy?"

"He seemed to be," I tell him, keeping the conversation on neutral ground, not wanting to start another argument over a deal that I'm still to sign on the line for.

He breathes in content, and I'm sure I can hear a smile in there somewhere. Ever since I confirmed the meeting to 'tout my wares' - which definitely carries a different meaning for Richard Lowe than it does for me - I've had the poor man acting as my audience.

Granted, Sloan wasn't impressed when I asked him what he thought of my sales pitch the many times he has been subjected to it in the past. Sticking me in a tight spot - which is virtually immovable when he glares at you - I caved and told him. He wasn't too happy to be *sharing me*. The sly git even went as far as to get my girl to try to convince me to cancel. But alas, we ladies stick together, and it takes more than him peddling his threats of withholding my grandson to make me submit.

But it was close, I'll admit.

"Well done, I knew you could do it. Although I'm not sure how the kid's gonna react. I guess he might have that aneurysm after all!" he chortles.

"Stop, you're making me feel guilty!"

"Good!" He continues to laugh heartily. "Come on over. I'll leave the boys in charge and take my favourite lady out for a celebratory glass of champagne."

It's very tempting, but that's an offer I must refuse. "There's nothing to celebrate yet. I haven't even read the contract properly. Besides, I have a desk full of stuff that I need to sort out, and I still need to arrange last minute cover for later this week. Unless you want to convince Simon and Tommy to don penguin suits again on Friday night. Surely it's better than their usual of downing free booze and picking up women."

He bursts out laughing. "You're wishful thinking again. After the last event that they agreed to waiter for you, I don't think it's an experience they will forget anytime soon."

"No, nor I," I mutter, the night coming back with vivid clarity.

So, it was only supposed to be a joke to make them uncomfortable. Unfortunately, that joke backfired when they agreed. *Enthusiastically*. Needless to say, they weren't supposed to offer themselves up with the starters, but they did. Their two-for-one deal was also never part of the agreement, but alas, that was also something else they flaunted with amusement between the mains and desserts to any woman who looked remotely interested - which happened to be quite a few of them, if memory serves correctly. That night I was caught between laughing and crying at their antics.

"Darling?" I murmur, ready to extend the olive branch.

"Yeah?"

"About this morning. I'm sorry."

He sighs. "No, I am. I overacted and made you feel less than you are. I'll admit I don't trust that bastard, but I *do* trust you."

"That means a lot to me, but so does your approval," I say, happy he has backed down. For now, at least. "If you want me to rescind, I will. I just don't want to fight."

"No, of course, I don't want you to. I'm proud of you, angel. I always will be."

"Thank you. I love you. I'll see you later."

"I love you, too," he says after a pause and hangs up.

I get into my car and belt up as my phone starts to ring. I groan, recognising the number, and grit my teeth in anticipation of what she is calling for now.

"Hello?"

"Hi, Marie. It's Veronica Harris."

"Oh, hi. I didn't expect to hear from you," I reply, hopeful she is calling me for something other than a query of when I will pay her bloody expensive invoice. I'm fed up with the calls from her friendly accounts department enquiring as to the progress of the sale. The sale, which I might add, is their forte, not mine. I accept putting the sign up in the front garden and walking people around the place, but it's their job to advertise and, with a bit of luck, sell the damn thing.

Taking a deep breath, I brace myself for another useless call, one that neither takes us a step forward nor a step back, it just leaves us all languishing in an indeterminate state.

As time has rolled by, my upbeat demeanour has waned significantly. Once upon a time, when there was government talk of green shoots on the housing horizon, and that the recession was over, I was hopeful. Well, those green shoots obviously don't apply to me, because I'm still paying a mortgage on a house that I haven't set foot inside of in years.

In the weeks that proceeded mine and Kara's brutal assaults, I could barely walk up the path without having a panic attack. The day I finally did manage to get inside, my heart broke, realising it was tainted and no longer my home. And every beautiful memory I had of raising my girl there was now going to be just that – a memory.

"Good news! Remember the couple we showed around last week?"

"Huh-uh," I acknowledge throatily.

"Well, they put in an offer this morning." Judging by her tone, it apparently isn't as good news as we both hope, and I wonder how much of a discount they are after this time.

"Market value?" I query.

Veronica inhales like she is preparing me for the worst. "It's ten grand under, and although I said you would probably still accept, I thought I'd check with you first."

I stare up at the Heavens, thanking whatever invisible God is up there for finally giving me my wish. It might be ten less, but this is the best news I've had in a long time.

In the last eighteen months of the house being on the market, I've had numerous offers and the last one which fell through spectacularly at the eleventh hour, after the buyers found out what had happened there. Damn the frigging internet - and the nosy effing neighbour! The house is a noose around my neck. An empty, unwanted money pit. But finally, I have a reason to be optimistic again.

"That's wonderful news."

"I know. They were hesitant at first, but they are first time buyers, and it was the most house for their money. Shall I call them and say you will accept?"

I smile, feeling the dead weight finally being lifted from my shoulders. "Yes, please do. Thank you, Veronica."

"Not a problem. If you let your solicitor know, I'll send across the particulars. It might take a few weeks for the buyers to get their mortgage documents through, so it gives you time to get things sorted. I'll speak to you soon!" She hangs up in delight. Delight that she is finally going to get her horrendous percentage for making a few phone calls and displaying a few pictures, not that she is helping me get rid of the financial ball and chain at long last.

I fire the ignition and hope blossoms my chest. Finally, the wheel is beginning to turn in the right direction again. First the events contract and now this. With any luck, it can only get better.

Can't it?

Unlocking the office door, it is dark and empty since Nicki is attending a tasting event this morning. I toss my belongings on the desk, boot up the computer, and head into the kitchen, mobile in hand, scrolling through the internet.

I reach for the milk the same moment my phone starts to ring. *Private Caller* decorates the screen, and I leave it to ring off, as I do with every other blocked or unrecognisable number. If it's that important, they can leave a message.

Five minutes later, I settle in at my desk, slide over the keyboard and forget everything for a while.

Biting the pen between my teeth, I smile, impressed that the spreadsheet has behaved itself for once, and I won't be calling Kara to sort it out. Or, when she refuses, paying another trip downstairs.

Lost in happy thoughts, a light tap plays on the door.

"Why are you knocking?" I call out playfully as Nicki enters. "Hey, how was it?"

"Really good, surprisingly," she confirms.

In the years that Nicki has been working for me, she has continued to impress, both in her work and her confidence. Just like Kara, it's taking time for her to come out of her shell, but it's happening.

"Excellent. Did they provide any price guides?"

She nods and pulls out the brochure and her mobile. "I also took some pictures, since we know everything in this book is shopped beyond belief." She slides into the opposite seat and leans over the desk, flicking through the picture gallery. "They also have an amazing entrée selection."

I quirk my brow, knowing she has definitely sampled those this morning. "Wow, these look nice," I murmur, astounded, that for once, what is in the books might actually represent what is on offer, and not just two slices of bread slapped together and cut into a triangle for effect.

"How did the meeting go?" she queries, turning off her mobile.

"We got it, but we really need to look at the contract in detail," I tell her because this is no longer a solo effort. Unlike Kara, Nicki takes an interest in all sides of the business.

"That's great. Scary, but great!" She gives me a coy look, cautious in voicing whatever is on the tip of her tongue. "How was flirty Lowe?"

Ever since New Year's Eve, that has become his moniker in our office. One day, I know there is a distinct chance that one of us will end up calling him it. Although I guess it's better than if we called him tricky dicky…

"Flirty! Uncomfortably so, but money is money. Guess what?"

Her eyes narrow in question and her head moves slowly from side to side.

"I've just accepted an offer on the house." It's still sinking in, and a part of me is trying not to get my hopes up just yet.

"Oh my God, that's fantastic!" she says in surprise. "Would you like a celebratory coffee?"

I nod at her offering. "Please, although a celebratory rum and coke would be better."

She grins and rolls her eyes. "Oh, the post just arrived." She places the small pile down on the desk then leaves.

I flick through the letters, seeing the usual. Junk, bills, and a suspiciously thick envelope. Sliding my finger under the seal, I pull out a document I haven't seen in years. Shock rocks my body, and I snatch up the envelope. With no sender's address, there is nothing to confirm where it has come from. I quickly close the door while flipping through the pages to the very back, seeing what I already knew was going to be there.

Nothing.

Nothing which I also rectified a long time ago.

The sound of Nicki returning causes my heart rate to accelerate. I shove the papers under a pile of overdue invoices, as the door opens, and she places down my coffee and a small fairy bun.

"Happy birthday, and congratulations on a successful pitch."

"Thanks, darling." I smile, trying to come across as being interested, but after what I have just seen, everything else can disintegrate into the ether.

"You okay?"

"Sure. It's been a trying morning."

"Alright." She nods. "I'll do a ring round, see if anyone has had dealings with this company. I'll let you know what the outcome is." The door closes quietly behind her, but the sound is still deafening.

I slide the decree out from under the pile and sigh. It's been over twenty years since I served these. Then one day, after giving up all hope and convincing myself he was never going to sign them, I discovered a five-year loophole that guaranteed I would be shot of him once and for all. But my luck isn't that good, and I know his gifts will keep on giving until they can give no more. I know I'm destined to carry on receiving these until the day I die because they are a reminder of what I took from him.

Years ago, when copies first started to filter through – albeit sporadically - I had no idea how he managed to locate me, let alone send them to me. These days, it's easier than ever with the internet being so readily accessible, but how he found me back then is hardly surprising. Educated, influential hands in deep pockets of the rich, legal kind will buy you anything you want - even the names and addresses of those who wish to remain anonymous. Nothing is sacred when money is involved. Dirty, clean and everything in between. Nothing is untouchable when it is wafted in front of the despicable or desperate.

"Fuck," I curse, digging out my old phone book, needing a number I haven't dialled in years.

Placing it on the desk, I dislodge the envelope, and a folded card catches my eye. Daring to look at it, my breathing falters, because of all the depraved shit he happily and willingly put me through, this is low, really fucking low. Even for him and his twisted, fucked up family.

"Son of a bitch!" I hiss, realising time is running out, and the life I had buried twenty years ago has finally been resurrected from the dead. And how long I can keep *it*, or *him*, from entering my present is a question I dare not address.

Picking up the phone, I dial and wait to be answered.

"Hello, I don't know if you can help me, but I need to speak to Adrian Taylor."

Chapter 12

I STARE AIMLESSLY at the clock as the hour hand hits six. Rubbing my tired eyes, I finally call it a night since Nicki left an hour ago.

Tidying up my things, I absentmindedly disturb the outstanding stack of work sitting precariously on the edge of the desk. My brow furrows as I pick up my old divorce petition – an unwanted birthday gift from my bastard ex.

"I'll never be free," I mutter and shove it inside my bag.

I activate the alarm and march down the stairs. The motion sensor lights turn on as I pass, confirming I'm the only person left in the building.

Outside, the theory of my loneliness is confirmed, since my car is the only one remaining, and suddenly I don't feel so secure. A couple of years ago when I was first looking to move premises, one of the things that stopped me was the security aspect. At the time, it was more for Kara's security than mine, although I've never been foolish enough to think I am completely safe. It was a defining factor in my choice, and I was lucky that the tenants of the floor I now lease were also looking to move.

I click the car remote and fling my bag on to the passenger seat as my phone stirs to life. Typical, not a bloody peep all day, now everyone will want to chat. Plucking it out, I swipe the screen to find a new message from my transatlantic counterpart. I leave the message unread, climb in and start her up.

Reversing out of my space, another car enters, and I huff out, fed up that every driver this side of London seems to think they can park up for a night on the town. It makes my blood boil when my reserved space is periodically occupied by shoppers who are too tight to pay for parking just around the corner.

I ride the biting point and watch in astonishment as the driver fails to put his vehicle between two white lines correctly – after five botched attempts - and parks up virtually horizontal. I shake my head, amazed that some certifiable idiot passed this clown fit to drive.

Heading into the busy rush hour exodus, the day is falling into night, and the streetlights illuminate in intervals. Slowing behind a packed double-decker, my eyes cast over my bag and my stomach somersaults as my thoughts run away with me. A car horn bleeds into my ears, killing my morose thoughts, and I lift my foot off the brake.

Finally arriving home, the house is in complete darkness. I grip the steering wheel as fear churns inside. The last time I pulled up to a house in total darkness, that darkness broke me, beat me, and pretty much left me for dead. After that day, I realised I still had a reason to fear the dark.

I unclip my seat belt and remove the personal attack alarm and self-defence spray from my bag. Clutching my fighting paraphernalia, they are John through and through, but I guess nothing declares undying love like legal weapons of the feminine variety.

I click the car remote and approach the house. The drone of an engine stops some distance away, and I turn to see a Maserati idling further up the street. Uncomfortable minutes pass, until the window winds down to reveal the driver. His dark hair is highlighted by a flickering lamppost, and even from this distance, there is something uncannily familiar about him, but I can't place where I might have seen him before.

I swallow as the car drives off at a perfunctory pace, leaving me with a head full of tumultuous fantasies that blur the lines of reality inside my mind.

Turning back to the door, I turn the key and push it hard, indenting the small expanse of wall behind it further.

A sliver of light bleeds from the dining room, and I edge towards it, spray in one hand, phone in the other. Prepared for the unthinkable, I tap nine nine nine and steady my finger above the screen. I might have been fooled once, but I'll be damn sure not to be fooled twice.

The silence devours as I edge closer. Crooking my elbow, I take a breath, slam my rigid arm down on the handle and kick the door open. I hold the spray in front of me as John spins around from the table, where he is lighting tea lights in the candelabra in the centre. Relief floods through me, but a sob emits my throat.

"Oh, shit!" John curses.

"What the hell are you doing?" I cry out.

He drops down the matches and rushes towards me. As he holds me tight and rubs my back in comfort, I never expected to be crying on my birthday again. Far too many times in the past I had spent it this way.

"I didn't mean to frighten you, angel." He pulls back and glides his thumbs over the apples of my cheeks, as the canister hits the floor and clatters. "Shush, don't cry."

"Your car isn't outside," I say between sobs. "I thought... I-I..." I press my head into his chest and listen to his heartbeat. Strong and steady, like the man housing it, protecting it. I lean back and gaze into his dark, penetrating eyes.

"No, angel. I wanted to surprise you, but I've fucked this up royally."

I dry my eyes and finally notice his attire. He is wearing a crisp, white shirt, with the collar open and the sleeves rolled up his forearms, and the black tailored trousers, shiny belt and shoes are definitely out of place on him. And as much as I love my army throwback, I love my rugged man in black, too.

My focus drifts over the table, enraptured by the flicker of flames, and the glimmer of the fine china I only bring out on special occasions. Seeing everything laid out meticulously, it hits me.

"You didn't forget," I whisper as he takes the alarm and places it on the table.

He moves his head from side to side with a smile. "No. You should know I'd never forget. Happy birthday, darling."

"You didn't have to do this."

"No, I did. I've made you feel like shit for weeks because I didn't like the idea that another man found you desirable. I just wanted to make it special. Now, I wish I'd booked a restaurant."

I tightly wrap my arms around him. "You're forgiven. Always," I whisper, scratching my nails over his five o'clock shadow while kissing his jaw. "Do I have time for a quick shower and a change of clothes before dinner?"

"Depends," he says, cocking his head with a mischievous grin. "Do you want dessert before or after the main course."

I can't control my grin as I grab his hand, lean over the table, and blow out the candles. "I think I'll have dessert first."

He influences me close and devours my mouth. With a moan, I reluctantly break free and drag him into the kitchen to turn off the oven and hob, and then out into the hallway.

"Excellent choice, angel," he says, but halts when he sees the front door still open.

"Sorry. I figured if someone was in the house, at least I'd have a fighting chance."

"Good girl," he whispers. It's not condescending, it is the fact he has continuously drilled safety into my head. For the first time in years, I've adhered his advice. I think he sometimes believed it was in vain, but it never was. I just prayed I would never have to use it.

"I left my bag in the car," I say, fishing the keys from my pocket and hurrying to the front door. My feet suddenly leave the ground, and he tosses me over his shoulder. I laugh unapologetically as he swats my backside for no apparent reason, instigating a lovely tingle.

Dangling over his shoulder, I click the remote as we reach the car, and he opens the door and grabs my bag. He strides us back into the house, punches in the alarm code, dumps my bag on the floor and carries me upstairs.

In the bedroom, he lowers me down and stands back. Slowly unbuttoning his shirt, I lick my lips in anticipation. I mirror his action, but he stops me.

"Hands to your side, angel. I want control."

I lower my hands submissively and dig my fingers into the duvet. His muscled torso flexes repeatedly, and I gaze up at him as he balls up his shirt and throws it on the floor. Unfastening his belt, he leaves the two ends hanging and flicks open his trousers button.

A flurry of tension courses through me, and I curl my toes, already feeling his unbridled heat pass over me.

I smile the moment he crawls onto the bed and nudges my legs apart. Sliding my calf over his muscular thigh, his dexterous hands ignite my flesh, moving up inch by inch. Grabbing my ankles, he drags me further down the bed and my dress bunches, before he shoves it further up my waist and cradles my hips. He balances one hand above my head, and I fall deeper when his lips meet mine. Our tongues slide together in long, firm strokes, but this kiss isn't polite or gentle, it's about loving and trusting someone so much that the idea of giving them absolute power is entirely liberating.

The carnal sound of desire echoes in the room until he eases me up. His hands snake across my shoulders, and the crisp chill drifts over me as he unzips my dress, instigating goosebumps to flair over my skin.

"Darling." I quiver as he tugs the fabric over my head, then throws it over the side of the bed.

He manipulates me back down, circles my foot in his hand, and lifts my leg. Lodging it against his shoulder, stroking slowly, he tilts his head and kisses the ball of my ankle.

His soft, yet possessive kisses continue as his hands descend my limb until he reaches the place I want to feel him the most. Between the flick of his thumb over my sensitive flesh and the soft suction of his lips on my inner thigh, my thoughts, my being, all begin to unravel.

"Close your eyes, beautiful." Breathing in, my back vaults wantonly, and I do as per his request.

My legs spasm the instant he pulls my knickers aside and runs his tongue the length of my core. I cry out, unable to contain the fire building, threatening to engulf me and eviscerate me in flames. I open my eyes and withdraw my hand from the side of the bed and reach down and smooth it over his head. His dark, piercing gaze meets mine from between my legs while he continues to work me with his tongue.

Rapture flutters in my belly and courses through my veins, because for all his hard edges, he has some pretty smooth lines, too. And when we're together, stripped down with nothing to hide, those lines are a no longer a mystery.

"Playtime, angel." He crawls back up my body and flips us over. He palms my hips while I straddle him, and his velvety steel length nudges my covered clit.

I stroke down his face to his neck, and he grunts content. Circling his Adam's apple, I move lower. Savouring his contours, my fingertips explore the divots of his military honed physique. I swirl my finger around his belly button, and his stomach contracts instantly. I grin with wicked intent and trace my fingers along the delicate hair trailing to his groin. Teasing his zip, I pull it down slowly, then push the waistband from his hips. Stretched out beneath me, he elevates his lower body to give me room to undress him. Frustration gets the better of me as I try to drag down his trousers, and he chuckles and rolls us over.

"Allow me," he offers hoarsely. Climbing off the bed, he drops his remaining clothing in a heap on the floor.

In nothing but his beautiful, naked, chiselled glory, he reaches over, hooks his fingers into my lacy shorts and whips them down my legs. Throwing them aside with a salacious grin, he cocks his head.

"Where do you want me?" he queries with faux innocence.

I shrug, fulfilling the promise he made years ago when he said I'd never have to give it up easily. And tonight, as much as I want to, I won't.

"In your hand?"

I shake my head.

"On your tongue?"

Again, my head moves from side to side, and my sultry gaze drifts down his hard, agile length and then to myself. *That's* where I want him.

"Good because that's definitely where I want to be tonight." He grins, accentuating his unconventional beauty.

He crawls back onto the bed, showing his restraint is a thing of wonder. Every movement is disciplined, precise and meticulous. He doesn't hurry or show any loss of control as he moves up my body painfully slow.

Parting my thighs, he positions himself comfortably in their broad, welcoming curve. His forearms rest on either side of my head, and he cages his body above mine. I breathe in, my senses alive, fully consumed by the spicy, scent of man infused with desire.

I blow out a long, low exhale, and watch his lips part. Tilting up my abdomen, again he makes no return gesture, and I wrap my hands around the back of his neck, while my thumbs drag down his bottom lip. He nips the pad delicately and quirks his brow.

"I've never loved anyone as much as I love you. As much as I will *always* love you." He smiles and tangles his fingers in my hair.

"I love you, too." I grip his shoulders and stretch up, desperate to taste him.

Fusing our lips together, my tongue glides against his, relishing his unique taste. I smooth my hands down his back and squeeze his tight arse before moving to his front. Teasing the fine hair on his abdomen, I stroke his hard shaft, tracing the vein on the underside delicately. He gasps in response, jerking in my hand, exposing his waning control. Spurred on to play harder, I fist my fingers around his silky, steel girth, and pump from root to tip, over and over. He groans through gritted teeth, and I glory in the sound, appreciating his carnal reaction as he convulses slightly.

"Is that good?" I ask innocently, exerting more pressure.

I grin when his eyes narrow and he growls deep in this throat. He throbs in my hand, inducing the wetness between my legs to grow more apparent, while the inevitable tingle takes effect. I smirk, not only enjoying his reaction but my own, too.

I squeeze him hard a final time and swipe a finger over the head, removing a bead of moisture. Touching my hand to my lips, I flick out my tongue and taste him.

"How do you want me, Lance Corporal Walker?"

He smiles broadly, beautifully, and dips his length to my aroused core, sliding it up and down between my folds, coating it in readiness.

"How do I want you?" he repeats in thoughtful consideration. "Bobbing up and down on my dick, riding it until you pass out."

"Can I vibrate on it?" I ask eagerly.

He drops lower and grinds into me. "It would be a crime not to. Now, guide me to heaven, angel."

I curve my spine and raise my hips as he shuffles closer. I pump his substantial length slowly and position him. His engorged head feels terrific, piercing my core. Digging my fingers into his shoulders, I hitch my heel to his arse as he enters me slowly. My legs widen impulsively, providing room for him to gain further traction until they fall to the side entirely as he fills me. I moan loud, unashamed, while he stretches me to the fullest.

"Is that good?" he asks innocently, but he knows it is.

"God, yes," I groan out, aware of everything happening in my body right now.

"Good, but I want you better. I want you mindless. I want you begging for it," he says, then he clutches my hips, retreats back, and plunges deep again.

A gasp catches in my throat, and my body quivers under the impact. Slamming in and out of me repeatedly, I undulate promiscuously, and my hands scratch at his back. I need to feel him closer. I need to feel him more than I currently am. But I know that isn't possible because no two human beings could ever be closer than this.

I clench my ankles around him when my body starts to tremble beneath him. He pumps hard and rhythmically, staring with intense need with every thrust. I'm torn, as much as I want to close my eyes and blindly feel my way through the journey of his body consuming and encompassing mine, I want to remain focused on him. I want to watch him fall apart under the beauty of our mutual high.

Rearing back, he takes me with him. His chest is slick, and my nipples glide against him, unable to gain purchase. He grasps under my bum and sits me comfortably astride his thighs.

With a faultless grip on my waist, he lifts me up and down, and my breasts bounce under the motion. He sucks a stiff, aching peak into his mouth, and I vocalise my gratification as he continues to suck and nibble until he finally releases it.

"Bobbing, beautiful," he says with a chuckle. "Fucking stunning."

My hands hold securely at his neck, and I brace my legs as I slide up and down on him, my sex completely slick and aroused. Bobbing, riding his dick, I give him what he wants. I swivel my hips, loving how he pulsates inside me. My body is on fire, and I pant out in time with him.

"Fuck, baby, that's amazing. Keep. On. Going."

"Darling...I...need...please..." I gyrate unforgivingly, internally rejoicing each time his thick tip touches incredibly deep inside me, stroking my cervix.

"Ride me harder, angel," he demands, and I oblige instantly, lifting up and slamming myself back down. "Fuck!" He swells, and molten heat rushes deep as he finally reaches fruition.

He roars out his release, tightening me in his embrace. I continue to move, whether he likes it or not until he drops his hand between us. The deep undulation in my core endures and amplifies as he rubs my clit in hard, repetitive circles. Licking my lips, I squeeze my eyes shut and gasp out the instant my orgasm crashes over me like a thousand waves drowning me in subliminal, potent bliss. My chest heaves and my core compresses around him, and I come on a loud, satisfied moan.

He kisses me deeply, and I cradle his head gently, unwilling to move. Pressing my cheek against his shoulder, I smile to myself as I count the accelerated beats of his heart.

Large, spread fingers massage my spine, and in his arms, I feel genuinely tiny. And truly protected.

"You bobbed, you rode, but are you ready to pass out?" he asks smugly.

I slowly lift my head and grin. "Yes, but now I'm just hungry," I tell him serenely, falling deeper in love with him, staring into his soulful eyes. Stoking a finger down my face, he lets it linger at my collarbone.

"Give me ten minutes, and I'll assuage that hunger." He jerks his pelvis into mine, and I roll my eyes and tut gently. "Although maybe I should feed you first. I don't want you falling asleep on the job."

"What? Like you did on New Year's Eve?" I smirk, interested to see how he will lie is way out of that.

"That's only happened once!"

"Ah! Convenient, selective memory loss," I mumble and reluctantly slide off him, both loving and loathing the sensation.

"I wasn't done sinning with you, angel."

"No, but I'm done with you. For now. If you promise to feed me, I promise to ride you until I pass out afterwards."

I fall back against the bed, thoroughly depleted. Rolling over, I attempt to tug the sheet around me, but he pulls it away. It's asinine, especially now, but I've never been comfortable being exposed, even in moments like this. My initial experiences of love and sex were misguided from my very first time. It was never warm or loving, it was a few minutes of all take and no give from a boy who got what he wanted and left me in a world of wondering what the big deal was.

Two and a half decades later, I finally understand all the enthusiasm.

"What's got you grinning?" he asks, as I trail my fingers up his chest.

"Nothing." It's the only sensible explanation I can give. I sure as hell can't tell him what I'm really ruminating on. "I'm just thinking how good it is between us."

With a cocked brow, he rolls us over and adjusts me to straddle his waist. His expression is serious, as he flattens his palm over my chest and rolls my nipples.

"So, what number am I?"

"Darling, please," I reply in discomfort. Just like nudity makes me uncomfortable, so does discussing my past experiences. All two of them - including him.

"Okay, maybe one day you'll tell me." I lay down atop of him and let his words fade. "Until then, happy birthday, angel." He reaches down to his discarded clothes and sits a jewellery box on his chest. I inadvertently purse my lips in worry and stare at him.

"Open it," he urges softly, and tentatively reach for the box. Flipping up the lid, I gasp at the pale blue gemstones, set in platinum.

"They're beautiful. Thank you." I clutch the box, stroking the stones repeatedly.

"Let's have a shower, then dinner." He glides his thumb over my bottom lip and steals a kiss.

"Sounds perfect."

He gently shifts me aside, stands and retrieves his trousers. Looking down the length of them, he pats the pocket. He hesitates as he sets them down, and I narrow my eyes in query.

"Ask me no questions, I'll tell you no lies," he says while he sweeps me up and strides into the bathroom.

Standing under the hot stream, the water cascades over my chest. His hands rub tenderly over my stomach, circling my abdomen, and he rests his chin on my shoulder.

"You know neither of us is getting any younger, angel."

"I know," I whisper, fearful.

Without further elaboration, he reaches for the body puff and commences to cleanse my front. I lean back against him, eyes closed to shut out his unambiguous, unfinished statement.

Twenty minutes later, I slip a pair of boy shorts over my legs and look across the room. John glances up instinctively as he ties the drawstrings of his charcoal pyjama bottoms.

"I'll go see what I can salvage for dinner," I say with a smile and head to the door.

"Wait," he says, moving towards me. Leading me back to the bed, a look of worry plagues his brow. "There's something I need to do. Something I should have done a long time ago." Picking up his trousers, he fumbles in the pocket and reveals another small box. Turning around, he tucks a few damp stray strands behind my ears.

He visibly swallows while he looks down at the box then lifts the lid. "Mrs Walker," he mutters curiously. "That has a nice ring to it, doesn't it?"

I cock my head to the side, knowing where this is going, and instantly despising the answer I've had prepared for a long time.

"So nice, in fact…" He inhales shakily and gets down on one knee. "That I want to make it permanent. This isn't the way I planned it, but I didn't want an audience in a restaurant, and I didn't want the kids getting wind of it just in case you refused."

"John…" I shake my head, not knowing what to say to deviate him from this path.

"Darling, I know you have issues. I've known it from the first stolen kiss, the first reluctant date, and the first incredible night we spent together. I get it; I do. You've admitted more than once that you spent your life alone by choice, but you haven't been alone for a long time. If you say no, I understand, but I don't want to wait any longer. So, Marie Dawson, will do me the honour of marrying me?"

He turns the box around, and my breath catches in my throat at the imposing diamond. Rising to his six feet plus height, he holds it between us. My heart beats rapidly, because the moment I have simultaneously longed for and feared, is finally here.

Right here. Right now.

Daring to touch the ring, I emit a nervous breath. I would love to be his Mrs Walker, but we've been the way we are for so long, and after the way my first marriage ended, I always thought I'd never be here again. The first time around, I never had a proposal. In fact, the wedding was arranged by my ex-mother-in-law, I just turned up. I was young and foolish; I didn't know any different.

"Angel," John's voice seeps into my reverie. "After nearly three years together, I need something more substantial than your fears of the past. I'm not your ex. I'd never hurt you like he did."

But little does he know, he will. It won't be intentional, it will be because his heartbreak leaves him no other choice.

"Talk to me."

Meeting his eyes, he opens my palm and puts his ring into it. It weighs heavy under the confessions I still need to make.

"There are a lot of things I don't speak of because it's too painful to reminisce about a past that I've finally left behind. One day I will tell you everything, but I never wanted to accept your ring and then have you hate me for it."

He cradles my head and rests his forehead against mine. "I'm not expecting to marry you next week, or even next year. I just want everyone to know that this beautiful woman is mine. But don't misunderstand, I don't want to be engaged for the sake of it. I want it to be because we *will* be getting married."

Tears slide down my cheeks, burning my skin. Closing my eyes, my soft whimper is undisguisable and heightened in the silence of the room. The litany of reasons I have for saying no bear no impact on his last disclosure. It is my own selfishness that is making me question my response.

"The best I can offer is one day," I whisper. John tilts my chin up, his eyes are wide and surprised. I curve my lips a little, but I have thoroughly ruined his proposal.

"Is that an inadvertent yes?"

I nod, but the word refuses to tumble over my lips. "One day," I whisper again.

He reels me into his chest and takes the ring from my hand. "Let's try this again, shall we?" This time, thankfully, he doesn't get down on one knee. "Marie Dawson, will you do me the honour of making me an honest man and becoming my wife, *one day?*"

I nod to hide my shame. "Yes, one day."

No sooner is the first word confirmed, the ring is already being slid over my finger. Staring into his shining eyes, I can't bring myself to feel happy for saying yes – or one day. He is the third best and right choice in my life, and I'd be foolish to let him go over something that may never see the light of day.

"I love you," I whisper sincerely because that is a truth I'll never be ashamed to confess. He lifts my hand to his mouth, kisses it, and draws me closer. His lips then claim mine, and I shriek when he unexpectedly throws me over his shoulder.

As he walks us down the stairs, he accidentally kicks my bag which he dumped on the bottom step, causing it to tumble and empty over the floor.

I shuffle down and scramble towards it, or namely, the old divorce papers that have slid out from the envelope. My breath quickens as John beats me to it and flicks through them.

"Angel?" His brow creases and his look of confusion is unmistakable.

"I was cleaning some of the cupboards in the office and found them under a stack of old tax returns. I must have put them there to shred and forgotten about them." I reach for them, but he moves his arm back.

"This is the reason why you're reluctant to say yes. You think that one day it'll be our names on a piece of paper, ending us, terminating what we once shared."

"No, I don't." I shake my head vehemently and stride into the kitchen. I head straight for the fridge and yank out a bottle of wine. Downing a large mouthful, the door creaks, and John leans against the architrave.

"Yes, you do. But you forget that just like you, I've been there. Trust me, what we have will go on and on. There will be no terminating us. No divorce, no separation, no needing space. It'll be you and me until the end. And I'll fight for it with every breath until my last."

My eyes close in provocation at his statement of infinity. "That's a beautiful theory, but sometimes all that glitters isn't gold."

"What do you mean?"

"I mean, I thought I had love once," I confess pitifully, watching the light reflect off the stone. "I was married and separated by the age of twenty, and finally divorced by twenty-five. I experienced more in a few short years of matrimony than what some do in a lifetime. When

I first met you, I didn't know where we would go, but as time ticked by, I realised what I had back then wasn't love. I learned to see no evil in the way he would treat me, and I learned to hear no evil in the way he would speak to me. And subsequently, I spoke no evil in relation to any of it. It was cruel and painful, and sadly that vision of love was mine. I had nothing else in my life, and he twisted and manipulated that to his advantage. It was all I knew for three, long painful years, until..." I sigh and close my eyes.

"Until?" John whispers.

"Until the day that stupid, misguided teenage *love*, turned into absolute, unadulterated hate. Those papers-" I tilt my head towards them, "I had to fight tooth and nail through the courts to get them finalised, because every time I sent them to him, he refused to accept what was already a foregone conclusion. I went through six years of hell to be free again. For a long time after, I separated myself from the world, and for a while, it was enough. It was enough that I had time to heal, to lick my wounds and start afresh. Everything I ever wanted was gone, and I accepted that. I accepted I was destined to live out my days alone until Kara entered my world. She made me realise that regardless of how bad life can be, no matter how diabolically you've been treated, you can still trust people, even love them. Then one evening, I saw someone across a crowded ballroom." I smile in recollection of the memory.

"And then two weeks later you knocked on my door. I was terrified to share my heart again, but with you, I dared to dream. I dared to dream of a future of what it would be like to be your wife. And *one day*," I say with a smile. "I will be your wife. And it will be the day I can walk down the aisle and know that you know everything. But until then, it will just be one day." I sniff back my tears and down the remaining wine.

The sound of the papers slapping down on the table resonates then strong arms cocoon me. I lean back as he presses a determined kiss to my skull.

"One day," he says gently and turns me around. "One day we're going to finish this conversation, and one day we will bury the past that haunts you for good. But until then, I'm good with you being my one-day Mrs Walker." He smiles, caressing my cheeks and gifts me a parting kiss. I study his back as he removes a couple of plates from the cabinet and sets them out.

"My past that haunts isn't pretty," I murmur, spreading the papers across the top. Tracing my finger over the name that haunts my past – and my present - I know the contents of these pages verbatim.

"I can imagine," he says on a turn.

I chortle singularly. "No, you can't. You could never, ever imagine."

He sighs and shakes his head. "Love and war both carry atrocities we don't want to speak of. Look," he says, serving up the reheated, spoiled dinner he lovingly created. "This is a conversation for another time." And just like that, he's drawn an invisible line in the sand.

I slide into a seat, pick up my fork and eat small mouthfuls of lamb and asparagus. Suddenly, my ravenous appetite has taken a back seat. I'm no longer hungry; I'm doubtful, and I just want to close my eyes and forget tonight ever happened.

Tipping the bottle of wine, he pours me another glass, and I observe him carefully, uncertain if he wants me paralytic to talk or to stay mute. I graze my teeth over my bottom lip, while guilt mentally slaps me. Placing down my fork, I study my engagement ring. How I would've loved to have said yes without equivocation.

"I really ruined it for you, didn't I?"

"No, you didn't." He laughs, covering his mouth with his hand. My head drops at his well-meant dishonesty, because I know I have. "Well, maybe a little, but my bruised ego will survive. It's large enough." He reaches over, and his fingers squeeze mine. "Just promise me something?" I raise my brows in consideration. "When one day finally arrives, please don't leave me standing at the altar like a sorry bastard."

I laugh. "Never. It doesn't matter how long it takes us to get there, you'll always be mine, which means you'll always be stuck with me." *Even if you no longer want me,* I think sombrely, but dare not offer it up for argument.

"Good," he replies, as his phone rings. "Leave it."

I perk up my brow. "You don't want to know?"

"No, it's probably a client. They can wait until morning."

Slipping off the stool and onto his waiting knee, I cage my arms around his neck. "Why don't we go back upstairs, and you can assuage my hunger. Maybe celebrate our new engagement while we're at it." My teeth tug his lip, and I feel him harden underneath me again.

The phone rings again, and he groans out, although who knows if it is disturbance or desire. Possibly both.

Securing his arm around me, he drags over his mobile. "I need to return this call, angel," he says, annoyed. "Why don't you go upstairs and warm the bed. I won't be long."

"Okay," I reply, kissing his jaw. "But don't be too long, or I'll start without you!" He groans desirously as I pick up my glass and the bottle and sashay to the door.

"Oh, before I forget."

"Yeah?" I look back, fun and flirty and wink at him.

He smiles, unable to hide it. "There was a message on the machine earlier."

"Oh?" I reply somewhat lacklustre, wondering why on earth that is relevant to me.

"A prospective client. She asked if you could call her back regarding a consultation for a reunion."

"A reunion?" I mutter, edging out of the door. "That's something I've never done before. Did she leave a name and number?"

"Hmm, a Magdalene Turner."

I halt in the hallway, while my whole world stands still and fails to rotate. Until recently, I haven't heard her name spoken in twenty-three years. But her memory is always more than a passing thought because I'm coupled with her right down to my DNA.

We are two sides of the same coin.

And she is also one-fifth of the shameful past I hide.

A presence lingers behind me, and I jerk when John moves my hair aside and kisses my neck.

"I've no idea how she got the house number, but I left the message on the machine, so you can call her back."

I clench the glass tight; dropping it would raise those questions I don't want to own or confess.

"Sorry, I must have given it to her by mistake," I murmur, continuing the deception. "I'll call her tomorrow, see what she wants."

"When you do, ask if she needs any security," he jests, slapping my arse before he strides back into the kitchen. I don't respond and walk up the stairs in a daze.

In the bedroom, I close the door and put the bottle on the dressing table. Pouring another glass, I debate whether or not to drink myself into oblivion and pass out through alcohol poisoning before John comes back up.

I catch sight of my reflection and slam my fist down on the dressing table. "You selfish, senseless, stupid bitch."

But truthfully, I've been deceiving myself for months, thinking the Salvation Army wouldn't communicate the outcome of the disastrous call from New Year's Eve.

Glancing down at my one-day, would-be engagement ring, I dared.

I dared to dream.

I dared to have it all.

I dare not dream to have it all any longer because dreams are fragile and unobtainable. And my dreams are nothing but beautiful nightmares of a life that broke my spirit. It broke me before I was even old enough to become cynical and jaded.

I twist the ring on my finger, and stare at my reflection, wondering if she hates me so much that she has chosen now to finally destroy me. But she's too late because there's nothing left to take.

"Why Maggie? Why now?"

Knocking back the full glass of wine, I climb into bed. Tugging the covers up to my chin, I close my eyes and pray for leniency.

And a dreamless sleep.

Chapter 13

"MAGGIE, GIVE ME that back!" I shout, racing through the park in the summer sun.

Maggie laughs maniacally while my cotton scarf flaps in the breeze behind her. She speeds off effortlessly, demonstrating the reason why she is always picked first in every sprinting event for school sports day.

I stop, out of breath, and drop my hands in defeat. Rubbing my hand over my face, I jog back to my mum. Flopping down on the bench beside her, she smiles and passes me a sandwich and a bottle of pop.

"I don't like her today," I grumble between mouthfuls of egg mayo.

"She'll give it back to you, honey," Mum says, brushing her hand over my clammy cheek. My mood perks up instantly when she digs out a Marathon bar and passes it to me.

"Thank you." I put down my sandwich, rip open the wrapper and take a bite. Turning around, Maggie is at the other end of the park, waving my scarf victoriously.

Show off.

Looking back at my mum, the gentle breeze blows her wavy hair, and she tucks it behind her ears. A strand comes loose and hangs down over her cheek, ending where the locket she always wears sits on her neck. I reach over and open it. Inside one half, is a picture of the three of us.

"My special girls," she says, squeezing my fingers.

I stare at her, knowing when I'm older, I want to look just like her. My mum is pretty. I know all girls say that about their mum's, but mine really is. She has the same blonde hair that Maggie and I have, and we share the same blue eyes and freckled nose. I hate my nose, but I love my eyes and hair.

Finishing the chocolate bar, I pick up my sandwich again. A light thudding on the grass snags my attention, as Maggie skips over with a triumphant smile on her face.

"Couldn't catch me, could you?" She sticks her tongue out and shakes her hips from side to side in a deranged dance.

"Shut your ugly face!" I snap back, pointing my half-eaten sandwich at her.

"Well, if I'm ugly, you are too!"

"Am not!"

"Are too!"

"Am not!"

"Are too!"

"*Magdalene! Marianne!*" Mum calls, stopping our sisterly cat fight instantly. In our house, the moment our full names are spoken, the line has been drawn - although Mum usually isn't the one raising her voice. I shift in discomfort, wondering if she will tell Dad and he will punish me later. Maggie might have pinched my scarf, but I'll still be the one to blame. I always am.

"Give your sister her scarf back, Magdalene," Mum orders as Maggie dallies and stares down at her feet, still clenching the material in her hands. "Now, Maggie."

"I didn't do anything!" Maggie whines.

"Don't make me tell your father."

Maggie's expression grows fearful, and she quickly hands it back to me.

"Do you have something to say?" Mum presses her.

"I'm sorry, Marianne," Maggie whispers shamefully.

I hold my scarf and stand. Passing it back to her, she smiles and hugs me. "I love you."

"I love you too, ugly!" She sticks out her tongue, swipes my bottle of pop and takes off with it, but this time I'm determined to get it back.

I chase after her, and eventually, we tumble onto the grass together, laughing. I stretch my arms out and stare up at the sky.

"Marianne?" I turn at Maggie's timid tone. "Will you tell Daddy what I did?"

I shake my head; I'd never tell him. "No, it'll be our secret. Promise."

"Do you think he'll be nice when he comes home from work?"

"I don't know," I whisper.

Her little finger curls in mine and we lay there, staring up at the sky, all misdemeanours now forgotten. The fluffy clouds float by overhead, and the sun blinds me, while I move my arms up and down at my sides.

"Come on, you two. We need to go to the supermarket," Mum says as her shadow edges closer.

"Can I have some midget gems?" Maggie asks.

"No, wine gums!" I counter.

"We'll see. Baby, what are you doing?" Mum asks.

I lift my head and grin but continue my rapid movements. "I'm being an angel."

She laughs and reaches both hands down to pull us up. "You need snow to make angels, but you'll both always be my angels."

We skip out of the park with Mum in between us, but she slows as a woman approaches. A boy, a few years old than me, is walking just behind her and stops when the woman does.

"Hello, Patricia. How are you?"

"I'm fine, Liz. My, my, aren't these two growing up?"

"Yes, far too quickly, in fact."

"Beautiful, too."

I look up at Mum, her smile is one of pride, and her hand squeezes mine. At her other side, I'm sure she is doing the same with Maggie, who is staring at the ground and fidgeting awkwardly.

"Yes, they are. Will we be seeing you at church on Sunday?" Mum asks the woman, who baulks.

"I don't know, Duncan is very busy with work at present. Well, it's nice to see you, but we must be going. Come on, Joseph," she snaps, then grabs the boy's arm and shoves him in front of her.

"So, what do you both want for dinner?" Mum asks.

"Spaghetti!" Maggie makes her request, but I don't respond. I'm too busy watching the woman shove the boy in front of her near to the pavilion.

"Marianne?"

"Sorry?" I murmur.

"Dinner?"

"Oh, spaghetti, please." I look back, but the woman and boy are nowhere to be seen. "Who was that lady?"

"Mrs Beresford, and her son, Joseph. You might see him when you start high school next term."

I nod and hold her hand tighter. "She didn't seem very nice," I mumble, but Mum just smiles as we cross the road to our car.

I gaze out of the window as Maggie sings along with the radio, her leg rocking.

My mind wanders, lost in daydreams until they are lost in the void, and the past darkness becomes the present day.

My eyes snap open, and my body slams up from the desk, forcing me to wake from the dream that has made an unexpected appearance inside my subconscious.

Covering my face with my hands, my breathing is hard and laboured, and the resulting perspiration dampens my skin. Acid rises in my throat, and I swallow it down, refusing to go back there again.

There, being the caustic place I never wanted to remember. A place that last saw the light of day a lifetime ago.

I glance out of the window as day breaks outside. The haunting silence consumes the quiet, disturbed only by the recurring tick of the clock. Studying it, a fact I've never been ignorant of is that time is fleeting.

And eternal.

I slouch back in the chair – where I found myself at three o'clock this morning because the past invaded my sleep – and remember the final time I saw my sister and mother. In a bleak cemetery, under a cold winter's sky, on a day that will be forever etched in my memory, is the last day we were all together.

Now fitful dreams are all I have to remember them by.

Pressing my hand against my chest, these days my dreams are clouded and sporadic, but last night – after hearing Maggie's message – they culminated in my subconscious and played on repeat. They interchanged flawlessly, from one long forgotten memory to another, but each one taunted me, damned me. Reminded me of yet another failure.

But the memory of chasing Maggie on that hot summer afternoon is nothing in comparison to the final memory of my mother, running after a train that would never stop. That hateful, unforgiving image of her on her knees in tears, is heart-breaking. For years, it was the only one that was prevalent and reoccurring. And after all this time, you think I would've accepted it, but I haven't.

It's been twenty-three years since my mother begged me not to leave on that cold, desolate day. Unaware to her as I sat on that train and watched her, she broke my heart. But whereas mine was broken, hers was probably obliterated, because the promises I made on that platform never materialised. Apart from the few letters I wrote - which aside from the initial ones, the rest were never answered - I have never seen or heard from her again. It's a painful and morbid thought, but maybe I never will. For all I know, she might have passed away already, but I've never been brave enough to set the wheels in motion to find out.

Wiping away the solitary tear, the pain I have carried every day since then stifles me, chokes me, and with each passing night, the dreams suffocate further.

But last night, unlike the dreams that came before, this one was different. Instead of breaking down inconsolable, she smiled and waved me goodbye. I know there is some deep, symbolic meaning in my inner psyche, but if only that were an accurate reflection of what happened. Because on that day, the train did disembark, and my journey did continue. It transported me to a city where - unknown to me in my young naivety - I would never know what it's like to live anything but a half-life of loneliness.

But in a city of millions, loneliness was the safest option. I didn't need it, of course, because twenty-four years is a long time. Or twelve - if I was incredibly unfortunate and uncharacteristic good behaviour prevailed. Still, to be lost in a sea of millions is akin to searching for a needle in a haystack. And just like that proverbial needle, I prayed I was never found.

Still, I was a foolish young woman who prayed in vain because I was found.

A creak from the landing floorboards resonates, and heavy feet jog down the stairs and stop outside the office. Quickly dropping my head down on the desk, the door opens.

"Angel," John murmurs, displeased.

He slides his hand down my face reverently before he carefully rolls the chair back. I mutter, for good lying measure, as he picks me up and places me down on the old sofa. The soft, supple leather supports me comfortably, and I know if he doesn't leave soon, I really will be at risk of falling asleep again.

He briefly touches his lips to mine, and I squint, spying his running shorts and vest, exposing far too much of his physique as he turns. The office door closes, and the incessant beeps of the alarm system puncture the quiet until he is gone.

I stand and stretch out the stiffness in my neck while staring at nothing of significance. Mentally brushing off every tumultuous thought of what may come to pass, I pace back to the desk and reach into my robe pocket. Arranging the delicate chain on the top, I open the two halves of the locket.

Special girls.

I caress my little finger over the smiling blonde in the middle and swallow hard. The lump in my throat is prevalent, remembering the triumvirate of laughing girls posing. The faint aroma of strawberry shampoo and delightful giggles fill the morgue-like atmosphere, recalling the day vividly. My lips curve and I close my eyes, evoking the memory of trying to exert control and failing miserably. Yet that was a failure I will never be ashamed of.

In the three years leading up to the day I stepped on that train and never looked back, I had a lot to be remorseful for. The choices I made, the life I choose, in the end, it was all in vain. I lost the respect of a father who, more often than not, was cold and loveless, but more than that, for a short time, I lost my mother.

Still, my biggest regret, one I can never reverse, is that I lost my trust in love, in life and in everyone who ever cared.

But ultimately, I lost something that was so precious to me, I thought I'd never survive.

I lost my Faith.

I press the two halves together and rub the front, removing some of the discolouration that has tarnished the gold over time. Unfastening the dainty clasp, I slip it around my neck.

Trapped, suffocating on memories, the front door opens, and slams shut, and John runs straight upstairs.

Removing the necklace, I drop it back into my pocket and glace up at the ceiling, listening to the familiar gait move around the bedroom. Exiting the office, I retrace his steps and push open the bedroom door.

I slip off my robe and tuck the necklace back into my jewellery box. Straightening up the bed, I pick up his discarded sweat-soaked clothes. Rolling my eyes, it amazes me that someone who has had tidiness drilled into them still has the ability to create chaos in the space of just a few minutes.

I clutch the garments in my hand and follow the sloshing sound onto the landing and push open the bathroom door. Tilting my head around the spine, the best sight in the world greets me. John Walker - naked, wet and totally oblivious to my presence.

I toss the dirty items into the linen basket and sit atop of it. Propping one leg on the lid, I rest my chin on my knee and watch him. Even through the steamy glass enclosure, the way he moves is mesmeric. From his densely defined deltoids to the muscles framing either side of his back, to the way his arse pulls taut and relaxes. Everything the man does is mesmerising.

He rakes his hands over his head, flexing his beautifully honed body. The water cascades down his back, over the double dimples at the base of his spine, highlighting the war wounds he has collected in battle. Yes, scars and all, my man is beautiful.

The glass door opens, and his curious look transforms into a broad, devilish grin, and he motions me to come hither. I slowly walk towards him, and he reaches out and slips the thin straps of the satin chemise off my shoulder. The delicate fabric falls to the floor with grace, and he slides his hand around the back of my neck and coerces me into the cubicle.

"Are you here to wash my back?"

I shrug. "Undecided. But if you're really good, I might let you vibrate in my hand."

The sound of the water falling is drowned out by his loud laugh, distinctly recollecting the first time he ever said such crude and innuendo-laced words to me, and of course, my resulting reaction as they hung ominously between us.

Leaning in, he tips up my chin and kisses my neck. Manipulating our positions, he quickly curves his hand around my side and presses it against my tailbone. My nipples brush and my breasts flatten against his wet chest. Smiling up at him, he lodges his thick thigh between mine, generating perfect stimulation at my apex, and snakes his hands down my spine. Palming one rear cheek, he lifts me quickly, and I cage my legs firmly around his hips, although I know he would never let me fall.

Moving me under the shower, he delicately soaks my hair, taking care not to get water in my eyes. Holding my head back by my nape, he grunts, then nips at my lips, until I open and allow him to taste and take what he desires.

The steam culminates further, and my eyes close as he sucks on my throat. Lost in imminent passion, I yelp when he ducks me under the spray.

"John!" I reprimand, almost choking while he laughs. "You don't need to practically drown me to perform mouth to mouth!"

"Beautiful, where I want your mouth is definitely not on my mouth. Now, shall we practice some cubicle copulation?" I nod enthusiastically. "And maybe we can end with your mouth not on my mouth," he suggests coyly.

I extract my legs from his middle, using his hard thigh to rub myself and kiss his throat. Stopping at his collarbone, I stare into his desire laden eyes. "Only if you promise to wash my back," I reply cheekily and throw the body puff at him.

"Angel," he placates exasperated since we're both aware he would walk through hell and back if I asked him to. "I'll wash whatever the fuck you want me to. But first, I need to get inventive, and you need to get dirty. Ready?" I grin because dirty with my man is always inventive, and I'm always ready.

I stand back under the flow, and run my eyes over his firm, beautiful length, admiring the heavy appendage now swelling under my gaze.

My attention is claimed when his hands wander my sides. Pausing at my breasts, his thumbs encircle my nipples until they are hard and extended. Pleasure turns to pain as he dips his head and takes one into his mouth. The suction of his extraordinarily talented lips is immense, and I grip the back of his head, pulling him closer, needing more. Obliging, as always, he tightens his palm around the swell of my breast and gently scrapes his teeth over my sensitive tip.

"John!" I gasp out when he sucks my areola into this mouth and licks my nipple. It's maddening, amazing and I feel my body starting to peak. He continues to tease my tip in his mouth, sucking and soothing. His other hand claims my neglected nipple, and it hardens between his fingers. Still stroking me, seeking, searching, I breathe out lasciviously, unable to control the urge to release the pent-up desire he's building within.

Ruined by sensation, his other hand glides down my side. Caressing my flesh to the point of insanity, he eventually pauses on my abdomen.

Desire infuses every cell, and I put my hand over his on my stomach and guide it lower. Lifting his head, his eyes darken, and he bestows my silent wish. Without warning, his flat palm roughly cups my sex. I slap one hand on the wall for ballast and the other behind his head, when his fingers rove my shape repeatedly.

"Darling, please," I whimper. He picks me up effortlessly and slams my back against the wall. The leg I used for my own personal gain brushes back and forth at my centre, stirring my aroused flesh, summoning divine expectation that will take me over the edge. My sex clenches as his hands grip my backside, breaching in between and lifting me higher around his hips.

"Show me heaven, angel," he commands hoarsely, exciting me further as he ghosts his finger around my opening.

I alter my position as his fingers work my folds, teasing my entrance again. Instinctively, I grip his shoulders and steady myself the second he encroaches my core. His fingers pump and stretch shamelessly, exploring deep inside, and I feel full and fulfilled with only a few touches. I dig my nails into his biceps, moving against him in a wave, seeking more contact, while his fingers persevere at my apex. My breathing becomes laboured, and my pants come out faster, harder, more determined than ever to reach fruition.

He extracts his mouth from my breast, and I cradle his head, engrossed by his hooded, heavily eyes.

"Come, baby. I want to watch." Spearing his fingers deep into my wet heat, I can't resist any longer, and I rasp out raucously. My spine curves back and forth, rippling sinuously against the man I love while he works me through the orgasm devouring me from the inside out. Opening my eyes, I stare into his. I want to watch him watch me because it feels incredible as the pleasure goes on and on.

He slides out with care and holds me close. My body is humming, but the urge to drop to my knees is all consuming. My hands act of their own volition, and I softly brush my fingers over his chest, before moving down to the cut ridges of his abdomen. Licking my lips, desire wins the battle, and I proceed to kneel. With one hand almost touching the floor, and my mouth aligned with his hot, teasing length, his hand unexpectedly sweeps under my chin.

"Angel," he murmurs huskily over the sound of water tapping the base.

"I want to," I whisper, pumping gently, relishing the heated throb he is producing. Daring to meet his eyes, my tongue darts out and I flick it over the head until he pulls me up.

"I don't want you on your knees, but you know what happens if you keep looking me at like that, don't you?" I nod quickly in confirmation. "Tell me what happens, angel," he cajoles, breaching my opening again, knowing how to make my body submit.

I slap my arm against the tiles and squeeze his fingers inside me. The wave of pleasure weakens me, and I mewl shamelessly. "I-I-" I pant out from the ecstasy compelling me, while his talented fingers bring me to intoxicating completion.

"Tell me." He takes a nipple into his mouth, sucks it hard, and release it with a pop.

"I get it hard," I breathe out anticipatory, thoroughly turned on.

"No, you get fucked because bad angels get punished." My core is tingling at the prospect of his punishment because it is punishment of the best kind. And to demonstrate, he lunges his fingers hard, showing me just how fucked and punished I'm going to be.

A slow, predatory grin stretches over his face, and he removes one hand from my centre and uses the V of his finger and thumb to tilt up my chin and stare into my eyes. My body trembles in response, and before I know it, I am being spun around to face the wall.

"Ready?" He kisses my neck, and pressurises his hand down my back, all the way to my tailbone. I lift my hips and bum in brazen invitation, and he rubs his hands over my wet thighs. "Good girl. Hands on the wall."

I reach forward and splay my fingers over the smooth surface, revelling in his gifted mouth at my neck. Trying to find purchase on the wet tiles, my head falls forward. Squeezing my eyes, still feeling the sensation seep into every crevice, he strokes between my cheeks.

"Beautiful, beautiful woman," he says reverently. He shifts my hair aside and kisses my nape as he positions himself behind me.

He kicks my legs apart, and one hand strokes low over my pubic bone, while the other grips my hip to hold me in position. His hard tip nudges my entrance and makes a smooth fluid insertion. I close my eyes as the first thrust pushes me against the tiles. Moaning loud on contact, I fist my hands tight and prepare to be fucked.

"What time will you be finished?" John shouts up as I pull the jumper over my head.

"I don't know," I respond quietly, descending the stairs. At my last appointment, I was there for hours, picking over my assault, or the *incident*, as we like to call it. I guess it's better than what it really was – GBH with intent. Possibly premeditated murder...

"Stop it," he mutters the moment I enter the kitchen.

"I'm not doing anything." I shrug, winding my arms around his broad shoulders.

He sighs unconvinced and rocks me. "You're thinking. Dwelling and drowning yourself in the past. I don't like it."

I chortle lightly. "And you think I do?" I mutter rhetorically and wiggle out of his hold. "What are you doing today?" I pivot and flick on the kettle.

He perches against the worktop and strokes his finger up my arm, causing me to shiver.

"Well, I'll probably be gone for most of the afternoon. I need to see a man about a dog."

"*A man about a dog?*" I hope that is a euphemism, although I know he'll never give up the truth.

"Hmm." He grins, studying me from head to toe. I glance down at my simple black jumper and faded skinny jeans until his eyes linger on my ring. I twist it tentatively and wonder if he is having second thoughts in the harsh light of day.

"What?" I ask, moving my head a little.

"Nothing, beautiful. After I've seen *a man about a dog*, I need to find out what time Jules' flight is landing."

The kettle begins to boil and steam billows under the cabinets.

"Crap, I forgot she was arriving today," I mutter, pouring the water into the mug.

"I'm sure you won't forget when you stunning ladies are splashing the cash in Knightsbridge." He snakes his arm around my waist and drags me back without hesitation.

"Definitely not! Now she really is a stunningly beautiful woman," I state playfully while removing the teaspoon from the mug and chucking it into the sink.

"Maybe," he says dismissively.

"There's no *maybe* about it. That woman walks into a room, and everything with a penis stands to attention. It's intimidating."

His expression turns serious, and he manipulates my chin to stare into my eyes. "Don't. She doesn't hold a candle to you in my eyes. Never has, never will. Never doubt that truth."

"I won't. I wasn't... Oh, never mind." I wave my hand submissively and step back, but he holds firm.

"Angel, I've wanted you since the first moment I saw you. There was never going to be anyone else for me, but you. You know, just like you, I also thought I knew what love was, but not even my ex-wife stirred this much emotion and longing inside me. What I feel for you will never be replicated or comparable."

A tiny sting taunts the back of my eyes because no one has ever said such beautiful things to me, not even my ex. But in this moment, enfolded in the arms of a man who has lived a life of service and dedication, witnessing things that one should never see and dare not speak of, I will never question his loyalty. I only hope when the time comes, when I confess my painful truth and the harsh reality that I had lived through all those years ago, I pray it doesn't destroy that loyalty beyond repair.

I stretch up and press a light kiss to his lips. My lids droop, and my head lulls back in despair when his mobile rings but he chooses to ignore it.

"What time's your appointment, again?"

"Quarter past nine."

"Do you want me to drop you off?"

"No, I'll drive."

Wrapping his arm around my shoulder, he walks us out of the room. Sliding into my jacket and fumbling through my bag for my appointment card, he steps behind me, the same moment his phone starts to ring again.

"Just one day," he says, glaring at the screen. "Just one day where it doesn't ring, that's all I ask."

"You ask for too much. Is that your *man about a dog?*"

"No, this is my man about the crown jewels."

I narrow my eyes. "What?"

He shakes his head, grins, then kisses the life out of me.

"Now you're distracting me on purpose," I grumble. I admit, I walk the line when it comes to his distraction method. I absolutely love to hate it.

"Hmm. Is it working?" he queries mischievously.

"No." My reply is curt, but I let it go. I pat his chest in a placating motion, grab his hand and lead him out of the door.

I climb into my Audi, start the engine, and press the button to open the window. Tiny droplets begin to splash the windscreen and darken spots on John's shoulders.

"You're getting wet," I tell him.

"Don't care," he replies and folds his arms over the window, ignoring the rain now coming down heavier. He lifts his hand to my forehead and gently brushes away my wayward strands. "Call if you need me."

I sigh, praying for the day to come when he stops saying that. "I'll be fine, darling."

"Alright, beautiful. Have a good session and try not to murder the shrink."

"I'll try," I reply sarcastically, but it comes out flat. But I'm not lying, I will try.

For him, I'll never stop.

Chapter 14

I CIRCLE THE busy car park for the third time and hit gold when someone vacates one of the front spaces. Usually, I pick a spot at the back, which is generally the quietest part. Not today, of course. Today, every man and his dog are out in force.

Reversing in, I apply the handbrake and remove the key. Pulling down the sun visor, I stare at my reflection. While I may not look my actual age, I feel it. And coming here every month drags me down a little further because there are only so many ways I can recant the *incident*.

I know one day, she will dig a little deeper, pry a little further, until I'm forced to divulge everything. And that is detrimental to my sanity because it means John may eventually find out from another source.

Stuart.

Except I must believe it will be from my mouth that the horrific truth will unfold. I know in my heart the good doc would never compromise his position or his integrity, unless absolutely vital. He's worked too hard to get where he is, but I doubt he will leave me to fester with my guilt if he ever decides to snoop.

I put up my brolly as I get out of the car and head towards the entrance. Walking through the labyrinth of corridors, the distinct, clinical surroundings assault my senses. All of them, from my smell to my sight, to my hearing.

Still, the most damning assault of them all is that of my conscience.

Reaching the crazy department, as I like to call it, the receptionist books me in. My eyes flit around the half-full waiting area, and I choose a seat at the back. I study the old pictures and NHS literature for the hundredth time when someone sits next to me. I politely move my bag then tip my head to the side. The dirty blonde hair, shapeless scrubs and white trainers speak volumes.

"Morning, Stuart."

"Morning. So, John told me he was planning to put a ring on it. And I see he finally has. Congratulations."

"Thank you." I stroke the stone in compulsion as he offers me a cup of coffee. "How did you know I was here?" I query, my earlier fears materialising again. Clearly, he has done some snooping. Or maybe he's spoken to John this morning...

"I didn't. I've just been to see the doc to have a patient referred for an emergency appointment."

"I see," I say, failing to hide my suspicion.

Stuart stands and downs the rest of his coffee. "I can keep secrets, Marie. It's part and parcel of my job, remember?" He eyes me carefully, before continuing. "Come and find me when you're done."

I hold back my sigh and nod. "Sure. What time do you finish?"

He chuckles sarcastically and rolls his eyes. "Oh, about four hours ago. Married to the job, unfortunately."

"Don't tell your fiancée that."

He runs his hand through his hair and cocks his head. "She knows. I think she just likes to play doctors and nurses with me."

I open my mouth but am saved a mortified response when Doctor Green enters the room. Stuart grabs my hand and looks between his colleague and me.

"One day, you'll learn to let go and trust."

"Maybe," I reply quietly and approach Doctor Green as Stuart toddles off down the corridor and gets caught up in conversation with someone else.

"Morning," I greet her.

"Yes, and you. He's a great guy, isn't he?" she says fondly, watching Stuart gesture animatedly with his hands, while he chats up a storm with a colleague.

"Yes, he is. He's a good friend, too."

I step into her office, remembering the first time I walked in here, after being coerced by my good friend of a doctor while I was still coming to terms with being the innocent bystander who got hurt for someone else's ill-gotten gain.

Of all the times I had dragged Kara to these places, kicking and screaming under duress, I never thought one day I would be the one sat here. If it hadn't been for the acts of one depraved man, I might never have been. But looking back, everything happens for a reason, and considering the recent turn of events, I've already had too much time to impart the injustice of the life I had run away from.

"Take a seat, Marie," Doctor Green says, opening the large file – *my file* – on her desk. She skims the notes of our last session, then flips to a fresh page. "So, tell me how you have been coping recently."

I shift in the seat and rub my clammy palms on my knees. "I've been okay, but there have been moments where I've wanted to escape and find solitude," I confess, starting with the most comfortable truth.

Leaning back, I continue to spew out the shit that mentally eats away at me. The shit I am too frightened to speak of. The shit that nobody knows about, and the shit that shall, inevitably, find the fan and hit it at full, unforgiving force.

"Sometimes I still don't know what to say to him. I say I'm fine, but I know he doesn't believe me."

Doctor Green presses the top of her pen against her pursed lips and flicks back a few pages. "During our last session, you talked about similar feelings you had when you left Peterborough."

"I remember." I sigh, but I really don't need her to jog my memory. I live with the nightmares every day. I remember them with vivid clarity, meaning I die a little more inside with each one passing.

"Okay. Do you want to continue?"

I nod in confirmation, because what's the point if I can't.

"For years, I've tried so hard to forget. I've tried to remember the good times and banish the reasons why I left. But it's no use because they're all an integral part of me. They've made me who I am, and the things I will now do to protect those I love. I failed once. I swore I wouldn't do it again, but I did. I'm the first person to say we learn from our mistakes, but sometimes, I don't think we do. Sometimes, I can't help but believe we are destined to fail repeatedly. To relive them, again and again, until, in another life, we get them right."

"And why do you think that is?" she asks curiously, taken aback since this is the furthest we've come in getting to the crux of my issues.

In a shameful tone, I admit a truth. "Because the fallen cannot be saved. Because we have sinned and need to atone for our guilt."

Her eyes widen, and she closes the file and drops down the pen. "What do you need to atone for, Marie?" I hesitate to answer as the clock chimes on the hour, confirming our time is up.

Ever the experienced shrink, she ignores the clock and prods further. "Is there something deeper you want to talk about?"

I avert my eyes, fixing them on the wall behind her. "I don't know if I can." I shrug and acknowledge frankly.

"Look, I know Doctor Andrews is a close family friend. While I'm not questioning his professional veracity, I do have to take into account what he may do when put under pressure. I know how it is; I've been there." She sighs. "Marie, I don't want you suffering in silence, but you really need to talk about whatever it is you're protecting. If not, all of this is for nothing."

My eyes drop down, and I swipe my hand over my forehead. "I know."

Ripping off a clean sheet, she jots something down. "I don't normally do this, but here's my home number. When you feel ready to talk, away from here and completely off the record, give me a call. I swear it will stay confidential."

She rests her elbow atop of her files and passes over the sheet of paper akin to an olive branch. It lingers ominously between us until I eventually reach out and fold it in four.

"I'll consider it," I say casually, but I know I can't not consider it. For years I refused to admit that I needed help. I refused to accept I was one of those people. Still, I'm the biggest hypocrite walking because while I forced this psychiatry on Kara, I never believed I needed the same professional help. I never wanted to let it in that I was also balancing on the precarious edge between sanity and insanity, and even the slightest slip could take me in either direction.

"Good." She stands and walks towards the door. "Same time next month?"

"Sure. Thanks, Doc." I dither and decide to give her something. "Marie?"

"Marianne Beresford. She's who I'm protecting. I'll see you in a month."

I stride down the corridor and push the lift call button. I tap my foot, waiting for one to arrive, and a few moments later the requisite ping resounds, and a set of doors open. As I gaze at my reflection in the mirrored control panel, I recognise the ever-present repression in my eyes. The things they've seen, the things they've done... In truth, I've been in a constant state of denial over the part I played in my past for years. I've always blamed myself, and I probably always will.

I step off the lift and march down the corridor, wanting to get this chit-chat over and done with. Reaching Stuart's office, I raise my hand to the wood, but it opens before I can knock.

"Hi. How did it go?" he asks as we walk back the way I came.

"How does any session with a shrink go?" The mild contempt drips from my tone and Stuart's brows lift, unimpressed. "It was stimulating, Doc! I feel thoroughly cleansed. I wonder how I ever survived without her," I say brightly and force a smile, although I'm annoyed that I'm being forced to justify myself to a boy that I'm biologically old enough to be the mother of – doctor or not.

Stuart presses the button for the lift, then rakes his hand through his hair. "Can't say I've ever heard it described like that before, but I'll take it."

The lift bell dings and we board in silence. As the doors close, confined in this box, I know I can't hide.

"Marie, I'm glad you made an effort to see her, but don't hold back, thinking I will find out. I'm many things, but I'd never betray your trust. The job I do puts a lot of responsibility on my shoulders. I see things I can't speak of. I hear things I must learn to forget. You understand what I'm saying?"

"I do; I just..." I stop because his concerned expression is an insult to us both, not to mention the words about to leave my mouth are as equally discourteous. "You're right, Stuart, I don't trust you enough. When put in a hard place - the same place Sloan put you in when he wanted the truth about Lorraine's health for the sake of his wife - you succumbed to the pressure and did something you had no right to do. I have to believe you won't betray me if John ever asks you to do the same."

"Marie, I won't-"

"No. The dedication you boys have for each other is admirable, but it knows no bounds. It's been proven on many occasion, and I'm not stupid enough to believe that when your hand is forced, you won't compromise your integrity. I'm sorry, so please don't take it personally, but I've got to protect myself. And John."

The lift stops, and Stuart steps out first. The tension grows and thickens as we walk silently outside to the car park.

"Are we good?" he asks as he unlocks his car and throws his bag inside.

"Of course." I fold my arm around his shoulder and impart my goodbye before he climbs inside and reverses out.

The dark clouds separate overhead, brightening what has become a dark morning as I drive out of the car park. Sandwiched between a bus and a refuse wagon in the tailback of traffic, my mind relapses. As I rehash the conversation with Doctor Green over and over, the desire to purge myself is overwhelming.

I know, irrespective of what happens going forward, the first card in the house is already preparing to fall. The structure has been on a slow, steady decline since my past choose to return to my present. But it dislodged completely the moment John's ring became a permanent fixture on my hand last night.

Chapter 15

I POTTER AROUND the house as the lunchtime news plays to itself in the background when the landline starts to ring.

I crane my neck at the display and sigh. Since I arrived home an hour ago, Kara has called repeatedly. It's wrong, but I've consciously ignored her because I don't want to divulge my whereabouts this morning.

"Hello?" I finally answer and cradle the phone between my cheek and shoulder, having perfected the art of multi-tasking many moons ago.

"Hi, it's me," Kara replies, sounding far too upbeat to the be the mother of a two-month-old.

"Hey, honey. Are you okay?" I ask, lifting the picture of Charlie and Jake. I wipe my finger over the dust and grimace.

"I'm fine, but Oliver and I are at the hotel, visiting Grandma Jules." The cheerful gurgle of her tot seeps down the line. "We wondered if you fancy coming over for a late lunch. We were going to go to the zoo, but it's too wet and miserable."

I take a fleeting peek at the window and the torrential downpour outside, but I know I can't blow her off. I haven't seen them in a week.

"I'd love to, and I've got something for you, too. I'll see you shortly, honey." Returning the phone to its base, I turn off the TV and run upstairs.

Fifteen minutes later, I tie up my damp hair and pull on a pair of jeggings and a long top.

As I lock the front door, I drag my hood over my head. Balancing the cake platter in one hand and the keys in the other, I rush to the car. Carefully putting the dessert on the passenger seat, I lob my bag on the floor and climb in.

I slow the Audi to a stop outside the hotel, and a porter ambles towards my door and opens it. Holding an umbrella – emblazoned with Emerson Hotel insignia – he smiles.

"Good afternoon, Marie."

"Afternoon, Paul. How are you?" I ask, juggling my bag and the dessert. He motions for the plate, and I pass it to him as I get out.

"I'm very well."

"Fabulous," I reply. Passing him my keys, he exchanges them for the plate and gets into my car. Entering the hotel foyer, Laura waves.

"Hi, Marie. Kara and Mrs Emerson are waiting for you in the suite. Do you want a hand?"

I purse my lips at the plate I'm carrying precariously. "No, but if you could press the lift button for me, I'd be grateful."

She falls into step with me as we approach the lift bank. Pressing the button, she smiles and turns back to the reception desk as a guest rings the ornate bell repeatedly.

"Sorry, Marie, but Sloan will slaughter me if I leave it unmanned." Her expression is guilty, and I offer her a smile.

"No, I understand. Go, on."

Laura scuttles away, her heels tapping over the marble floor, while the bell rings.

I board the lift and elbow the button for the penthouse, thankful the dessert is still in my hands and not smeared over the floor. As I exit in the private foyer, the penthouse door opens before I have even got out and Jules strolls towards me.

"Hey, lady!" she greets, using her pet name for me.

"Hi." I smile, as she lifts my hand.

"Happy birthday and congratulations. John told me this morning," she says, studying the ring. Pulling me into an embrace, she quickly pushes me back. "I see it's still raining."

"Why, of course. Welcome to England! Do us a favour and grab this, will you?"

"Sure," she says, taking the plate. "Oh, my bloody son!" She shakes her head in disbelief. "When did you find the time to make this?"

"This morning. I couldn't sleep. Seriously, don't worry about it. Baking is my thing, it calms the raging she-beast!"

Jules cocks a brow. "Isn't that what John's for?"

"Yes, but sometimes a man is no substitute for baked goods."

"True. Cakes take you on a high, always taste good and, sometimes, they last longer!" I laugh until she nudges my arm.

"Out of curiosity, shouldn't you have still been in the throes of passion, tangled sheets and multiple post-engagement orgasms this morning?" She peaks a brow in disgust that I have let all womankind down by not indulging in some serious sexual acrobatics with my intended. But little does she know I did. *Repeatedly.*

"That's not for you to worry about." I point at her.

"No, but since I'm still desperate, at least tell me you got some of the good stuff before you snuck out!"

"Wouldn't you like to know?" I quip tartly.

"Yes! Yes, I would!" she replies, unable to contain her own amusement.

"What's so funny?" Sophie asks from the doorway.

"Grown-up girl talk," Jules says flippantly. "One day you might be old enough to join in."

Soph inches towards us and slaps a hand on her hip. "And just how old is old enough?"

"Forty!" Jules counters, knowing Soph is a true force of nature. "Here, take this."

Sophie grabs the plate and walks back inside, muttering to herself about oldies and geriatric sex.

"She's such a handful," Jules says. "It's hard to believe that she and Kara even moved in the same circles at school. There is a definite difference in their personalities."

"Tell me something I don't know," I state and pad into the kitchen. "Hey, honey."

"Happy birthday!" Kara rotates around from the sink and beams at me. "Congratulations, too."

"Is nothing secret?"

"No, and thanks for the cheesecake, but I didn't ask for it."

"Congratulations for what?" Soph queries, but I ignore her.

"Thank you, and I know you didn't, so thank your husband," I tell Kara, the same moment my hand is snatched up. Urgent fingers tighten around mine, and I turn to see who has me at a disadvantage.

Sophie's eyes widen, exposing more white than should be humanly possible. For once, she is dumbstruck. I wait patiently for her to voice her thoughts before I can move on to the next romantically challenged woman vying to see if John has good taste.

The shuffle of anxious feet scrapes the hardwood floor, and Charlie has finally had enough of waiting when she nudges Soph's arm. "Say something or move!"

"Oh, it's gorgeous! Who knew GI Joe had such good taste!"

I chuckle and cover my mouth. *GI Joe...* She really has no idea.

"Although shouldn't you still be in bed celebrating? That's what Stuart and I did."

I roll my eyes, glad I've developed selective hearing over the years, and turn to Charlie, who is studying the ring meticulously, with Oliver on her hip.

"Marie, it's beautiful. I'm really happy for you and John," she says, sounding far from it.

"Thanks, honey," I reply sheepishly. "He suits you." I flick my brows as she sits Oliver in his high chair.

"Hmm, fat chance of that happening." She reaches for the bottle and sits in front of him with her hand poised. I avert my stare uncomfortably but don't dare broach the subject.

"What are all these for?" I ask, shifting the attention and pawing through one of the bridal magazines dog-eared on the island.

"Well, I thought it was about time I started looking at dresses and stuff," Sophie says and picks up a magazine showcasing a gown that costs nearly ten grand.

My mouth falls open. "Honey, I appreciate Stuart's a doctor, but that's obscene."

"I know, but it's stunning, isn't it? I was thinking of looking for something similar, but cheaper," she replies cheerily, proving her glass is always half full.

Charlie chortles and fights to get the bottle teat into the little mouth refusing to open.

"Even my dress didn't cost that much," Kara says, and Jules and I pivot simultaneously because she didn't get a choice in the matter. "Oh, Sloan told me, one night when we were..." She stops, her cheeks turning crimson before she mumbles an excuse and starts to clean the spotless worktop behind her.

I really don't want to know what they were doing, although I can guess.

"Oh my God!" Soph exclaims, fixing me with her excited, wide-eyed stare. "We could have a double wedding!"

My mouth drops open, because no. No frigging way.

"Soph, M will be married with a couple of kids running around her feet by the time you stop dragging yours!" Jules says, very matter of fact behind me. Thankfully, my eyes are down, focusing on my ring for her to notice my anxiety of such an audacious presumption. "Seriously, looking at dresses is one thing, but the day you finally set a date, I wouldn't be surprised if poor Stuart drops down dead from shock!"

I pitch my brow and glance at Soph, who shrugs. "So, I'll have to nurse him back to health! I'll have you know he loves my bedside manner!" The cheeky wink tells me far more than I need to know. And with all things that spew out of Sophie Morgan's mouth when the filter is detached from her brain, I'm at a total loss for words.

I inadvertently catch Charlie's eyes. They carry an identifiable glint of wistful longing, but sadness appears as she gets up and puts the bottle on the worktop. Leaning against it, both hands hardening on the edge, she sighs and then turns around.

"Honey, Jake will ask. Eventually," I add on the end because that man is backward in coming forward. Charlie and Jake have been in love with each other for over a decade. Why he hasn't got down on one knee already is a conversation I haven't dared to raise.

"But when, Marie? When will he ask?" Her tone is desperate, more so than I've ever heard before. "I'll be past my sell-by date by the time he gets around to it!"

"Sweetheart." Jules moves in front of her daughter and rubs her shoulders.

"No, mum. He'll never ask, because whenever he brings it up, Sloan gets creative in ways to make him suffer. It's not fair!" She wipes a fallen tear and storms out of the kitchen.

A cold ripple runs through me because I didn't want this. On the one hand, here I am. Forty-three, divorcee, with a rock on my finger that I was more than hesitant to accept. Then, on the other, there's Charlie. Twenty-six, in the prime of her life and desperate to be married. And the only thing standing in her way, an overbearing git who, unfortunately, is doing what all big brothers should – he's protecting his sister's best interests.

I glance between Sophie and Kara, who both wear guilty expressions, while Jules looks torn between wanting to swoon over my newest piece of jewellery and the need to comfort her daughter.

"I won't be long," Jules says, then leaves the room.

A gurgle interrupts the uncomfortable silence, and Oliver bangs his little fist on the highchair tray.

"Hey, now, Auntie Charlie will be back soon," Kara says softly, lifting him out of the seat. He screeches and kicks out his chubby legs as we move into the living room.

"What's wrong, my beautiful boy?" He sounds out again and simultaneously giggles when his mum passes him to me.

"Let's say, happy birthday, Grandma!" Kara nods ardently and punctuates the words, attempting to school them in his little brain.

Holding him tight, he beams at me. From his beautiful pink lips to his creamy, flawless skin and his full head of raven hair, he's his father's son through and through. He bounces up and down on my knee, until he shouts again, smacking his hand against my chest.

"Play nice, baby boy," his mum reprimands gently.

Enraptured by his innocent, inquisitive eyes, Kara lifts my hand to study the ring.

"It looks perfect. I knew it would," she murmurs. I cock my brow and she bits her lip guiltily. "John left it here for a while, so you wouldn't find it when you were cleaning."

Oliver squirms in my arms, and his little hand points. Kara, already knowing what her son is after, quickly leaves the room and returns with a plush teddy bear. My body falters, and a long-forgotten memory shunts back into my head.

"Do you fancy a late lunch?" Kara asks, bouncing the bear in front of an unimpressed little boy.

"No, I have dinner plans tonight, so I'm saving the calories," I say coyly. She is about to ask when Sophie bursts back to life.

"That's right, you don't want to be a fat bride! Right then, I think we need to have a girls' night out," she says, lounging on the opposite sofa, like a Roman Empress. She looks completely at ease as she picks up the well-used baby book that John gifted to Sloan. Evidently read, and seemingly not to be believed – if his early morning calls are still anything to go by.

"No. I do not party, club or rave!" I tick them off on each finger.

"But-"

"Or whatever is hip with the kids these days," I finish slowly.

Not to be deterred, she perches on the edge of the sofa. "But we need to celebrate your engagement, and yours and Kara's birthdays. So we need two nights out! Please, you know Kara always cries off. These days she uses Oliver as an excuse-"

Kara's shocked gasp blots out Sophie's unfinished sentence.

"Excuse me, but my son isn't an excuse! I'm a mother now, in case you haven't noticed. And while it was never really my *thing*, I can't just leave him to go party with you. And just to put it out there, you should be concentrating on actually getting down the aisle rather than getting towards a bar!" Kara growls at her and picks Oliver up.

"Sophie, I'm leaving this room now, and my *excuse* is that my son needs changing." She then hoists up her child and storms out.

Oh, for fuck sake, can this get any worse? Between Charlie crying a river somewhere within the suite, and Kara ready to go into battle with her best friend, I wish I hadn't bothered.

"I didn't mean it like that," Soph says with shame, practically tearful. "I just meant that we need to have a night out together. I miss her."

I stand and motion for Sophie to come to me. Dejected, she complies, and I pull her into my arms. "I know you do, but she's right. She has responsibilities now and one day, you will, too. I'll tell you what, if you promise me a *quiet* night out, I'll make sure she's there. Okay?"

She leans back, quirks her lips into a smile and nods. "Okay," she whispers as her eyes roam aimlessly. "Can you give me a minute while I grovel?"

"Sure. I'm going to go find out where Jules and Charlie are." Kissing my cheek, she edges towards the kitchen, where it is clear Kara is vexed, given the unnecessary banging of the drawers.

I wander to the foot of the staircase where Charlie is enfolded in her mother's embrace halfway up.

"Are you okay, darling?" I ask tentatively as I reach them.

"I'm fine," Charlie says, still upset. "I'm sorry. I didn't mean to make you feel bad; I just...just..."

"You just want to be a wife and mother," I state, very matter of fact. "So ask him. If he doesn't pull his finger out, then you need to. And if he drags his feet, you need to give him an ultimatum."

Horror consumes her pretty face, and she shakes her head. "No, I'll lose him."

"No, sweetheart," Jules says. "You just need to force his hand."

"But Sloan-"

"Never mind what he says. He doesn't control you. He can't tell you what to do. And let's not forget how he forced Kara's hand into marriage." I kneel on the step and tuck her face into my hands. "You're a grown woman, and you only get one chance in life. Follow your heart."

"I will," she whispers. "I feel so foolish."

I shake my head and appease her distress. "No, darling, you're just overwhelmed. But *I've* just done something very foolish."

Her expression is curious as her eyes shift between her mum and me. "What?"

I purse my lips and scrunch my nose. "I just promised Sophie a girls' night out." Charlie's eyebrows raise in surprise. "Two, actually. Although there's a chance it could turn into three on a technicality." I grimace and rise the same moment mother and daughter do.

"Oh, no," Charlie whispers in horror.

"Oh, yes. Come on, let's see if Kara and Sophie have made up." Charlie shakes her head. She's been in the middle of their rare stand-offs enough these last few years.

Entering the kitchen, Kara is sat at the island, nursing a mug of tea. Opposite, Sophie is sitting in front of Oliver in his high chair, feeding him. I pull out the stool next to Kara and take a sip of the waiting coffee. I almost chock when Sophie suddenly starts to make aeroplane sounds and waves the bottle around before baby boy opens his mouth greedily. Smacking his lips together, Sophie turns to see us all eyeballing her in surprise.

"What?"

"Nothing," we all chime simultaneously.

I raise the mug to my lips and continue to watch Oliver. He opens his mouth perfunctory when the bottle approaches and bangs his hand on the tray when it is too slow. A slight tension pinches my temple, and I fall back into an unspoken memory. My surroundings change from the present to the past, and I'm young again.

In a fleeting moment, I'm alive again.

"Marie? Marie?"

I whip my head around and blink rapidly at Jules. "Sorry?"

"What are you doing tonight? I was going to ask if you and John wanted to have dinner somewhere, but you said you had plans."

I grin. "I'm having dinner with the *clan*."

Jules throws her head back, laughs and claps. "Oh, good luck. You're going to need it!"

Kara scoffs and shakes her head. "Why are you laughing? They're nice, and Oliver loved the attention when we saw them last month, didn't you?" she coos at him, nodding her head, and he giggles infectiously.

"Actually, they're coming to us. Why don't you all come over? We can make it the first family dinner of the year."

Murmurs of agreement resound as a mobile starts to ring, and we all reach for our devices. "It's me. Hi, darling," I answer.

"Hey, angel. Louisa called to say she's coming over at half six."

"Okay, but we'll have a very full house because I've just invited the other *clan*. Make sure you tell the boys."

"Because we don't see them enough already?"

"I thought Lou might want to see them. Anyway, what time do you think you'll be finished?"

"Same as usual, but I have a few things I need to sort out. I'll pick up some extra food on the way." He pauses, the sound of shuffling paper resounds, followed by his growl. "Oh, for fuck sake! Parker!"

"Is everything okay?"

"Issues. Always fucking issues. Parker!" His growl is now a bellow. "Angel, I'll see you later, unless you get a call saying you need to bail me out. I swear heads are going to roll!"

"Okay. Anything specific you want on the menu tonight?"

"Before or after dinner?" he asks, full of insinuation. My eyes skim the room to find I have an intrigued audience watching far too intently.

"The road to ruin. Can we discuss this face to face?"

"Absolutely, but ruin when you're wearing it is a beautiful thing. How about I meet you in the bedroom later? How's that for face to face?"

"Ruin, Walker," I say playfully.

He laughs on the other end. "Just keeping you honest, beautiful."

"Bye!" I hang up quickly and toss the mobile down. "Ladies, it's been amazing, but I need to go!"

"Of course, you do. John probably wants to get in some fun time before the in-laws arrive!" Sophie says and is subsequently rewarded for her crass talk when Oliver spits a mouthful of milk in her face. I want to laugh, but since I'm not that cruel, I just speak the truth.

"That's a big mouth you've got, girly!"

"It's not my fault," she says, daubing a tea towel over her cheek. "My dad says I inherited my mother's dominant mouthy genes in the womb."

"Your dad is very fortunate," I say with a straight face and kiss baby boy's head. "I'll see you tonight, little prince."

Kara follows me out to the lifts and unexpectedly embraces me. Wrapping my arm around her back, it's nice she is finally able to touch and not suffer because of it. Holding her, my fingers dig lightly into her shoulder. As always, whenever she's allowed me close, she's unsuspectingly allowed me to pretend.

"I'm glad you said yes, by the way. Yesterday, John still wasn't sure what he was doing, and he said he wanted you really pissed off by the time you got home so it would make it that much sweeter," she confesses, embarrassed.

"I shouldn't admit it, but it was sweet. That was after I almost had a heart attack and nearly sprayed him with whatever is in those canisters he gave us all at Christmas. I guess that would've made for an interesting conversation with Doctor Green this morning." I step inside the lift and press the button to hold the doors open.

"I didn't realise you were still going." She fidgets on the spot, but I'm aware of her thoughts on counselling. It's a subject that makes her uncomfortable, and even more strange that she's studying it, albeit part-time these days. Still, I guess it's different being on the other side of the desk. All those years ago when I dragged her to the shrink's office, I never appreciated the effort she made in just getting through the door, irrespective if she talked or not. I now have first-hand experience of just how painful it is to lay out your heart and soul for someone to scrutinise and pick apart.

"Well, it makes John happy," I murmur.

"And that's great, but don't do it for him, do it for you."

"I'll try," I say as the doors close.

An hour later, I pull up in the driveway, apply the handbrake and climb out. As I open the front door, an old banger screeches to a halt. I drop my bag just inside the hallway and watch as the young lad removes a large box from the back and saunters leisurely up the path.

"Afternoon. I've got a flower delivery for you," he says, handing me the black device. Signing something that looks nothing like my signature, he drops the box inside the doorway. "Surname?"

"Dawson."

"Thanks. Have a nice day."

"You, too."

I shut the door and smile, loving John's romantic side. Ripping off the tape, the sides flop down, revealing a bouquet of flowers.

Dead flowers.

"What the hell?" I open the door, but the delivery lad has gone.

I bend down and root through the decomposing bunch until my fingers tangle in a ribbon.

Aged lilac ribbon.

Cautiously pulling the strands apart, the edges are frayed, the material stained. Closing my eyes, familiarity dawns, and I let it slide through my fingers. The ends finally come loose, and the flowers fall to the floor, revealing a small card hidden within the stems.

Snatching it up, the numbers and letters on the underside taunt me. Between the ghosts of New Years past, the old divorce papers, and now this, I can't bury my head in the sand much longer.

With a hardened resolve, I gather up the carnations, march into the kitchen and pull out a bin bag. Dumping the dead offerings in the bin, I smash down the lid. It's so easy to haul out the unwanted shit, but not so easy to dispose of it entirely.

My chest heaves and my lungs hyperventilate as I shiver and turn the card in my hand.

My tears can't be contained, and I slide down the bin, in broad daylight where any one of my neighbours might see. I'm utterly heartbroken, and now past caring because the lines have finally been drawn. It's been a long time coming, but I always knew it was a matter of *when* never *if*.

And as with all things in life, everything moves in cycles. After all these years, I realise I was imprudent to believe mine had finally ground to a halt. Imprudent to think vengeance wouldn't be coming. But the most remiss, imprudent thing I ever did was to give my love and trust to someone who didn't know how to return it.

He only knew how to destroy it.

Twisting the ring on my finger, inside, I know the bastard is planning to destroy me again.

When? I have no idea.

How? I don't even want to imagine.

But when he does, this time, I know I shall not survive.

I wasn't meant to the first time.

Chapter 16

I PICK UP the glass of wine and neck half of it in one. Twisting my mobile on the worktop, I press the standby button, and the screen illuminates, confirming what I already know – I have no missed calls or outstanding messages.

I sigh, down another mouthful and rub my forehead. It's safe to say I'm completely and utterly fucked off.

This afternoon, in the wake of the flowers from hell, I immersed myself in anything I could to take my mind off the reality. Namely, I decided to clean – something which rubbed off on Kara after a time. There's nothing quite like frenetically scrubbing a room to within an inch of its life to divert your attention. Because it's either that or close your eyes and become comatose to the world. And that's what I did after the cleaning failed to derail my thoughts which had fallen to the dark side of my mental spectrum.

Swiping my finger over the screen, I scroll through the call log. It has been months since my initial call to a man I never thought I'd need again, and two hours since the last. He obviously doesn't want to hear from me as much as I do him. Still, he's the only one who can help me. Whether he will or not, remains to be seen.

Downing the remaining wine, I'm honestly on the verge of crying. That's how anxious and isolated I feel. My heart is inexplicably heavy, and I can't decide if it's the events of the day - which are enough to give anyone a heart attack - or the fact I'm soon going to have a houseful of unwanted guests I intentionally invited over.

The door opens as I lean over the table, and a familiar presence sidles up behind me. His semi-hard groin pressurises the soft curves of my backside while he cages me against the worktop.

"What do you say, angel? Want to practice some kitchen copulation?" John asks in a husky tone.

"That's highly unhygienic. Not to mention our guests will be arriving shortly, and even your stamina isn't that good." I brush myself against him, cup his cheeks, and stare into his lust filled eyes.

"Very true, and I'm man enough to admit it. On the other hand, I do like a challenge, and I rarely lose, so one of these days I'm going to have you naked and writhing over this table. Mark my words, it's going to happen. I'm going to have you so hot for me, you won't be able to think straight." He smirks wickedly, but his apprehension from earlier is still there, marring his handsome features. Cupping my face soothingly, his lips ghost mine with gentle kisses.

"Are you ready to talk about what happened today?" he asks, finally addressing the state he found me in this afternoon.

My skin prickles against my clothing because he wasn't supposed to see me like that - a filthy, clammy cleaning mess, lying on the sofa, almost catatonic. He knows something is going on, and it won't be long before he starts to probe, but until then, I'll do what I do best – I'll lie.

"It was good," I reply half-hearted, spinning the wheel of deceit again.

"Good?" He sighs in annoyance. "Angel, you appeared to be on the wrong side of the living when I come home. That doesn't indicate a good session to me. I know you don't like to talk about it, but I know a few doctors who deal with PTSD. If you want I can-"

"Darling, I'm fine. I'm just so tired lately. After a good night's sleep, I'll be okay."

His jaw grinds in annoyance. "Are you sure it's nothing else?" he queries, his eyes piqued on my belly.

I inconspicuously roll my eyes. "I'm not pregnant. I have an IUD, remember?" I say, not missing the way his features subtly fall.

"I didn't say you were, but now that we're finally on the subject – thankfully, without contention - if you ever do decide to get it removed, I'd be elated." He leans forward and kisses my nose. "I want to be a father, and I'll do whatever it takes to achieve that with you."

My fingertips grip his arms, and I force a smile. "I'll consider it," I murmur, lying again, while a double knock echoes from the hallway.

I slip my arm around his waist as we follow the second persistent knock like a trail of audible breadcrumbs.

The sound of laughter and subsequent admonishment resounds from outside. As John opens the door, Louisa, his sister, waits on the other side with her third youngest daughter, Beatrice.

"At last!" John exclaims. "We were about to send out the search party." He winks and stands aside for them to enter.

"Sorry, Uncle J, it's my fault," Bea confesses, removing her coat and hanging it on the end of the banister. "Madam was being awkward." Her eyes cast down to the little pair of hands holding either side of her hips from behind.

"It's okay, sweetheart," I tell her, while John chuckles and bends down to play peekaboo with Katie, Bea's only child. "You're the first to arrive. Enjoy the quiet while you can."

John eventually straightens up, having failed to coax Katie out of hiding.

"Granny?" I smile at Lou and tilt my head as the little girl squirms and bends her knees, her hands fisted, nudging her grandma.

"I need to wee wee!" she proclaims in typical little girl quiet, which isn't quiet at all. "I need to go now!"

"Come on, madam," Bea says, swinging up her daughter and veering up the stairs. "We'll be a minute."

"How's she been lately?" John asks Louisa, who sighs.

"She's okay, but Katie's started to ask why she doesn't have a dad like her friends at school do. It breaks my heart for Bea. I wanted to have better than me."

John smiles sadly and shakes his head, but he can't fix this. From past conversations, I know towards the end, Lou's marriage wasn't good. So much so, not only did she change back to her maiden name, she changed those of her children, too. No mother does that unless something exceptionally terrible has happened to her.

And it seems that nasty cycle repeated with Beatrice. I'm covertly aware that Bea split up with Katie's dad when her daughter was too young to understand. By all accounts, it wasn't pretty. And by all accounts, she deserved better than what he was giving her – which was nothing but a broken heart.

"M, here you go. I didn't know what you liked," Louisa says, passing me a bottle of wine, killing the morose conversation.

"Oh, thank you. This is nice. I think I'll save it for later." I wink.

John guffaws behind me and moves us a little further down the hallway.

"What?"

"Nothing," he says, reeling me in. "But for the record, I'm not a fan of necrophilia, angel." He tips my chin for a kiss that's too indecent for an audience.

"No," I whisper. "But I do know you like drunken sex."

"Hmm, now that, I am a huge fan of!"

No sooner has one wayward hand squeezed my backside hard, a throat clears. We pull apart promptly, and John squares up to his sister, his arms crossed, his expression neutral.

"Keep it clean, little brother."

My hand instantly covers my face, because I think we've just been reprimanded. John, on the other hand, just shrugs.

"My woman, my house, my rules!" he replies flippantly. Lou's huff drifts over us, and my eyes volley between the siblings, like a spectator at a tennis match.

Louisa's smile stretches, and she shakes her head. "I love that you're in love, but not in front of little eyes." She glances up as small thuds beat over the landing and down the stairs.

"No running!" Beatrice calls out in a disapproving tone, following her child.

"Sorry, Mummy." Katie's little voice shouts apologetically on its descent.

"And say a proper hello to Uncle John and Auntie Marie, madam."

"Okay!" Katie sing-songs.

"Brace yourself," Louisa says, nudging my shoulder.

My head whips to the bottom of the stairs as the sprint of little feet slap the floor until a small pair of arms wraps around my calves for dear life. The action knocks me off balance slightly, and I grab John's waist hard under the impact.

Beatrice approaches and glances at her mum. Grinning at each other, Lou smirks.

Absolutely a Walker family trait.

"I think we'll leave you to it," Bea says. "Call it future practice." My mouth opens and closes silently while mother and daughter stroll into the kitchen, leaving John and me with a child we have no experience of.

Looking down, I grin at the small but mighty five-year-old. "Hi, Katie," I say sweetly and reach down to extract her from my limbs.

"Hi, Auntie Marie," she mumbles shyly. Finding her confidence, she moves around me and holds her arms up for Uncle J to pick her up, who happily obliges. My heart swells as she flops her small arms around his neck and rests her head on his shoulder.

"Are you tired, little one?" he asks, his expression playfully stern, not that she's old enough to know the difference yet.

"No," she whispers, looking at me. "Pretty." She then tucks her face into his neck. John grins at me, but a weird tension radiates from him.

"I want to see the baby," Katie requests in a muffled tone, and I run my fingers through her light brown locks.

"He's on his way, honey. But shall we call Uncle Sloan to find out where he is?"

Katie nods at that suggestion, and John wrangles with her, forcing her from the restrictive hold on his neck.

"Why don't you go and see what the rest of my clan are up to? It'll be the last time you get to speak before the crazy gang get here."

"Okay," I say, fascinated by man and child in front of me.

"I'll send in the rest of the women when they arrive."

The kitchen door is suddenly thrown open, and Bea stands there, her arms folded, her face a picture of annoyance. "My, my, Uncle J, anyone would think women never got the right to vote or the privilege of equal pay. Sexism is still alive and well in the Walker/Dawson house." She turns, then pivots her head back around. "Oh, and Mum told me to tell you that there are sharp knives in here, and we're not a bleeding *clan!*" The door slams, and I snigger, silently pleased he has just been put firmly in his place.

"Welcome to the modern world, darling." I peck his cheek and saunter away. "You chase up the rest. I'll be in the kitchen, donning an apron with the other little women."

He laughs and shakes his head. "Sure thing-" He stops and whispers something to Katie, who smiles and whispers back. "...Pretty," he says, blowing me a kiss and then strides into the living room. I shake my head because the man really doesn't need any encouragement, especially from a child who isn't even in double figures yet.

Louisa spins around, holding the lasagne as I open the kitchen door. "Wine, M?" she asks, placing down the hot dish.

"I really shouldn't, but why not," I reply as she moves around my kitchen. My eyes rake over the surfaces and the variety of dishes she has already laid out.

"Sorry," Bea apologises and bites her lip. "We've kind of just taken over."

"No, it's fine. It's nice to have help. God knows those boys can eat."

"Hmm, I remember when Dev still lived at home. I can't tell you how many loaves of bread I used to buy," Lou mutters sarcastically. "So, we haven't seen you since Christmas. I was expecting you when Sloan brought Kara and Oliver to see us last month. Right then, how's life, work?" She pours me a glass of wine, and I flick my finger to stop her when it touches halfway.

"Good," I answer, upbeat, snagging the glass she has slid in front of me. "Nicki and I have a potential new client, so we might be busier than ever soon."

"That's great. J didn't mention it when I called." She takes a sip of wine, her curiosity piqued.

"No, he's got *views* on it. Let's just leave it at that."

She rolls her eyes, and I grin, liking how the sibling's personalities are so very different.

I lift the glass to my mouth, mentally counting how much I've already had when she stares at my hand. I gulp, realising there is something else he has failed to mention.

"Bea?"

"Hmm?"

"Look at this."

My smile is uncontrollable as I glance at Bea and hold out my hand.

"Oh, my!" She gasps in delight. "When did this happen?"

"Yesterday," I confess sheepishly, devising ways to make John suffer for not calling them with the good-ish news first thing this morning.

"It's beautiful. Congratulations!" Bea says, hugging me, almost assisting in pouring wine down my front.

The doorbell chimes throughout the ground floor again, and I crane my neck to the door. "Incoming."

Louisa tuts. "They can deal with John. You're ours for the next few minutes." Her hand takes mine, and she lifts it closer, getting a better look at the ring. "I'm so happy for you both. I've always thought of you like family since we met. This ring doesn't make it any more official, but I adore you, M."

I smile; to have her approval is vital to me. When I first started seeing John, I knew he had a sister by the simple equation that Devlin is his nephew. When John said his sister was a mother of six and my age, I was terrified of what she may think of me. The words 'cradle robber' resonated in my ears, because at forty-eight, she is only five years older than me. And in some respects, she has accomplished so much more. I might be successful in business, but she has been successful in producing a beautiful family which, in my opinion, makes her richer.

"Thank you," I whisper. She encircles me in a loving embrace as commotion erupts from the front of the house and the kitchen door swings open.

"Now they can have you." Lou sighs in my ear as multiple feet enter.

I turn as Dev approaches with Nicki beside him. "Congrats, Auntie M," he says cheekily while Nicki grins. "Hey, Mum." He enfolds his mother in a hug while she tuts.

Nicki hesitates but lifts my hand. "Wow, it's beautiful. Did he do it right?" I nod, confirming he did indeed, even if *I* didn't. "Do you need a hand in here?"

"No, we've got it sorted, Nicki," Lou says, motioning her son's girlfriend over. It warms my heart that Nicki is very much a cog in their family wheel like I am. "I've not seen you in ages, sweetheart. You look lovely. Is everything good with you two?" she asks, nodding her head at Dev, who rolls his eyes at such presumption.

"Yeah, we're great." Nicki's eyes flit around the room. "Where are the others?"

"Heather's got a date, apparently. Amanda said she and Ed are too exhausted with the kids, and the twins are doing whatever crazy stuff the twins do!" Bea reels off the list of what her sisters are up to this evening while passing Nicki a glass of wine.

The sound of multiple greetings ruminates behind me, and someone takes my hand in theirs. Pivoting around to see who has me at a disadvantage – again - Remy smiles, accentuating his deep scars.

"Congratulations," he says, holding out his arm. I reach up and kiss his cheek, still mindful of touching his now healed lacerations.

"Thank you, darling. Did you bring Evie?" I whisper, not wanting anyone to hear just in case she refused.

"Yeah, she's listening to Park's infinite wisdom as we speak."

I pull back in horror. "You better go and make sure she hasn't left then."

Remy laughs, his finger and thumb rubbing his chin thoughtfully. "I'm sure *she'll* start educating *him* soon enough."

The door swings again, and Sophie flounces in, with Jules and Charlie just behind.

"Hello, ladies!" she says with dramatic flair, greeting Lou and Bea. "Didn't GI Joe do well!"

"That's Action Man, dear," Louisa counters as a familiar gait enters the already full kitchen.

"Did someone call for me?" John asks cockily and strides towards us with Katie still attached to him. He places her down, and she runs to her mum.

As John raids the fridge, the rest of the men stand in the doorway, seeing what the womenfolk are up to. "Here you go," he says, and hands out the bottles to the male occupants only.

Double standards.

Sloan waves off the offer of booze, grins and inches closer. Dressed casually in jeans and a polo shirt, with Oliver on his hip and Kara on his arm, he studies the ring intently, his dark head bobbing as he makes a show.

"Moment of temporary insanity or did you lose a bet?" He flashes his pearly whites, and I glare, ready to pitch a fit until his wife doles out my retribution.

"Sloan!" Kara slaps his stomach hard and claims their son. My eyes drift from hers to the doorway, where Tommy, Simon and Jake are all gawping.

Counting the number of bodies practically wall to wall, I'm reaching boiling point.

"I appreciate this house is bigger than most, but there are far too many cooks in my kitchen right now. Unless you are here to help, leave!"

"Christ, there's too much oestrogen in this room for me," Simon imparts. "Boys, grab the beer and get in the dining room where it's safe."

Simon disappears from the doorway, and Sloan and Tommy lead up the rear. Jake, on the other hand just stands there, and I flit my sight from him to Charlie, recognising her hopefulness and his hesitancy. With a look of panic on his face, Charlie huffs and brushes past him on her way out.

"Baby, we need to talk!" he says, scarpering behind her. I grimace, because 'we need to talk' are never good words - regardless of which sex dares to speak them.

"Is there a story there?" Lou asks on the sly, topping up my wine glass again.

"Hmm. She's ready to get married, but he's not ready to lose his testicles." My fingers curl around the stem, and I mentally calculate again. Is it three glasses now or four? Whatever, I don't feel tipsy. *Yet.*

"Sloan?" Lou asks innocently, wafting a tea towel over a bowl of steaming pasta.

"Sloan," I concur and leave her to it.

I loiter tentatively in front of the living room door and push it open to find it empty. I smile, happy that a lover's battle hasn't commenced just yet. Closing it ajar, Simon's voice drifts in from the dining room.

"Some of us are about to die of starvation!" he exclaims. "Do you want to get the little woman to hurry this along before I steal the milk from the baby's mouth? Some of us stood up a perfectly good ready meal to be here tonight."

"You're an ungrateful bastard." Remy laughs.

"You wouldn't dare say that to her face," Sloan pipes up.

"Damn right! Do you think I'm an idiot? That woman's fierce. She'll put me in a penguin suit and make me serve entrées again."

I purse my lips and pitch my brows; that's precisely what I'm going to do.

The collective laughter continues from the dining room as John steps out. He grins, and I motion for him to come hither. He advances slowly and grabs me. Walking us into the living room, he closes the door with my back and pins me against it. My body feels practically weightless in his arms, and I coil myself around him.

"Are you here to hurry the fierce, little woman along?" I ask sarcastically.

"No, I heard Jake and Charlie getting into it. Have they made up?"

I shrug and kiss him with more passion than I have all day. It's probably not the best time to do it, but I can't resist.

"Just one day. One day where there's no drama," I mutter as he sucks on my bottom lip. "That's all I ask."

"You ask for too much," he replies, repeating this morning's conversation verbatim. Squeezing me tight, his body hard pressed against mine, his partial erection digs into my pubic bone, and I selfishly rub myself against it.

"Fuck. How about we run out of here right now and find a quiet place where we can be alone?" he suggests.

I grin. "The road to ruin... Sounds perfect. Or you could practice patience." I catch his lips with mine, showing him that *I* have no patience.

"No such thing with you." His tongue dances with mine.

"My office is empty," I say, as his hands reach under my top and he strokes my spine, instigating a tingle to develop.

"Mine, too," he counters, his mouth dragging over my collarbone.

"My sofa is comfier than yours," I state, breathing hard. Swallowing my desirous gasp, he slams me harder into the door.

"My desk is bigger."

"Mine's tidier. Slightly." I reach down and find his groin. Footsteps move outside, but I can't stop my moan, and he puts his hand over my mouth to disguise it.

"I have a kitchen tab-" The word halts unspoken in my throat as the door handle catches on my side and pushes us back.

"Shit." John stumbles with me deeper into the room. My eyes meet Sophie's, and I gasp in horror, whereas she just stands there, her mouth curving up slyly.

"Oh, God!" I whisper and drop my head onto John's shoulder, still wrapped in a lover's embrace.

He quickly spins us around, shadowing me, and straightens my appearance, since my top is gathered under my breasts, exposing me. Lowering my legs from his hips, he gives me an apologetic look and turns.

"Keep it to yourself, Soph. I mean it!" he says harshly, pointing at her.

"I would never say a word!" she grins and promptly leaves.

"Why don't I believe her?" he asks flat and unimpressed. "So much for escaping. Come one, angel. The sooner we do this, the sooner we can get rid of them."

Chapter 17

AS I SLIP on the oven gloves and open the door, the heavenly smell wafts out, heating my forehead, creating a temporary sweat.

Removing the cannelloni, I set it down on the trivet, and grab a bottle of water from the fridge since I've already filled my wine quota. *For now.* Unscrewing the cap, I delight in the flow of the chilled liquid caressing my throat.

"Got another of those free?" My head snaps up as Stuart enters.

I study him carefully as he manoeuvres around the table to the fridge and roots inside for a beer. Downing more than half, his eyes eventually come back to me. The fine hair on my arms prickles and stands on end because I know he wants to talk about this afternoon, but I don't. Going over it again will just ensure it never rests.

Maybe it never has. Maybe it never will.

"Marie..."

Here we go.

"Stuart, please," I murmur.

"No, I want to say sorry. I did abuse my power, and you were right to call me out on it. You were also right when you said that if my hand was forced, there was a possibility I would do it again. And I would because just like you, there's nothing I wouldn't do to protect those I love. And that includes you."

I'm about to reply when giggling resounds, and Kara enters with Oliver, helping him to wave at me.

"He's getting grumpy being passed around in there."

Stuart smiles and shakes his head. "Come here, little man," he says, holding his arm out. Kara happily hands Oliver over, then she takes Stuart's bottle and sniffs it.

"God, I'm really not a beer drinker, but I'd love a sip of that," she says.

"Not while you're breastfeeding," Stuart replies, his attention on the baby.

"Spoilsport. Don't let Soph see you so comfortable with him," she warns, opening a carton of juice.

"Honey, it's all I've heard for months! I'm half inclined to administer the injection in her sleep to ensure she doesn't spring one of these on me." He chuckles, rocking Oliver to his chest, as Kara and I stare at each other in surprise.

"Stuart?" Kara whispers in horror.

He looks at her innocently, then realises what he has just said. "Sorry, that came out wrong. I love kids; I want a houseful, but we need to get married first. Call me old-fashioned, but I like order and balance. Maybe you can bend her ear and kick her backside into gear with the wedding plans?" he finishes on a question that isn't answered since the ruckus from next door heightens.

"Elope to Scotland." The words roll off my tongue playfully.

"Yeah, I can't imagine that will go down well." He laughs as steps approach.

"Hey." Sophie enters, wearing a loving expression, admiring her fiancé and child together. "Want a hand?"

"I've got him," Stuart says, while his future wife grabs a couple of dishes. Walking out side by side, Kara and I turn back to the worktops.

Pouring the chilli into a serving bowl, I throw her the tea towel, and she places the hot lasagne onto a plate. Doing this, preparing dinner, it feels like the last few years haven't happened and that we are still living together. Only the noise growing louder in the dining room ratifies that isn't the case.

"I need to talk to you about something," Kara says quietly.

"Sure, what's up?"

"Not now, but later, okay?" I nod while she carries the dishes out of the door, trying to fathom what she's nervous about.

I follow her into the dining room, and my eyes work over the table - the one we've had to replace twice since our numbers have doubled in the last two years. Seeing my anxious expression, Bea shifts the multitude of bottles and glasses so I can put down the hot dishes.

"God, that smells amazing!" Tommy compliments.

"Better than a ready meal, huh?" I smile and catch John's wink. His pride is clear, and I inadvertently see Jules looking between us, her expression one of joy. I know she is happy that John is finally in a stable relationship. It's no secret she is also anticipating there will be another marriage on the cards soon – and it isn't that of her daughter and the long-term boyfriend who really needs to get his arse in gear.

With a full heart, I glimpse around. Sloan and Kara are at the end, their heads together, as she feeds him garlic bread, much to his delight.

Next to them are Tommy and Simon, still very much a two for one deal. One is never present without the other and their brotherly bond - a bond that is stronger than any other at this table - is unfathomable. I've never asked how they met, but their absolute trust fortifies it is something that goes beyond just random acquaintances who eventually became friends.

Next to them are Remy and Evie. Watching them together, and the way she hangs on to every word reminds me of myself all those years ago. Depending on a man who I thought would complete my bleak world. But Remy isn't my ex.

Studying them inconspicuously, it makes me wonder if he has finally opened up. From the many conversations I've had with him over the last couple of years, I know he still finds their age gap an issue. Another issue is the girl's father, Andrew, who is on Sloan's board of directors. I know he doesn't think very highly of Jeremy, the man has even said as much to his face more than once.

"You okay?" John asks. I nod and fix my gaze on Stuart, who has now passed the baby to Soph.

"Right then, let's talk about the wedding since we didn't finish the discussion this afternoon," Charlie says, causing Jake to cower beside her.

"What wedding?" Sloan taunts. "It's been how long since you proposed?"

"Eight months," Stuart replies, shovelling food into his mouth.

"These things take time!" Soph wades in, defending herself.

"You've already had enough time!" Sloan retorts and turns to his wife, who drops her fork down.

"Like you have room to talk! At least Soph will have a hand in her wedding. I had fifty-nine minutes, remember?"

The table erupts into laughter. None of us will ever forget that day and the precision timing that almost had Sloan on the verge of a heart attack. More so, and not that Kara is aware, he thought there was a chance of her refusing.

Thankfully, that was never a possibility.

"That was fifty-nine minutes too long, my love. Or was it nine years too long?" he queries thoughtfully, lifting her hand and kissing her wedding ring.

"It was worth it, every minute," she says, her eyes flitting to their son.

I take my seat next to Charlie, and she dishes up two large bowls of chilli and covers them with cheese. As far as food goes, she's a girl from my own heart. I stretch across the table and grab four slices of garlic bread and more than enough dough balls for the two of us to share.

"What about me?" Jake asks from her other side.

"You're a big enough to feed yourself!" she quips, still upset.

"Yep, that's right!" His hand wraps around the side of her head, and he places a sloppy kiss on her cheek. She tuts but beams bright red at his insinuation, and furthermore when big brother eyeballs her unimpressed.

"Jacob, do we need to have another conversation?" Sloan asks, pointing his knife. Jake visibly shrinks in his seat and gives him the finger. "Didn't think so."

"Arsehole," Jake mutters.

"Language!" Kara and Lou say simultaneously.

A disconcerting silence grows until Tommy clears his throat and grins between John and me. "So, is it going to take you guys eight months to start planning?" he asks nonchalantly, and I baulk because *one day* didn't come with an expiration date.

"Shut it, sunshine," John mutters.

Tommy's hand raises in yield. "Hey, don't be so defensive. I'm just making conversation," he replies, with a mischievous glint in his eye. Ready to open my mouth with whatever words come out unrehearsed, John beats me to it.

"I'll tell you when; when you stop keeping Durex in profits, that's when!" He slams down his fork and picks up his bottle.

"Uncle John!" Bea hisses, her head jerking towards Katie, who is kneeling on the chair next to a smirking Sloan, trying to feed Oliver half of her dough ball.

"He can't eat that yet, honey." Sloan gently brushes his hand over her cheek.

"Okay." She pops it into her mouth with a grumble. "Mummy? Who's jurdex?" she asks, slapping her chips in tomato sauce.

Muffled sniggers ripple around the table, and I lift my eyes to Lou and Beatrice, daring to see their expressions.

"Marie, would you like two less at the table tonight?" Lou offers, her deadly gaze flipping between a contrite John and an ashamed Tommy.

I offer up a small smile in apology, but she just shakes her head. I guess having this much testosterone concentrated in one place is something she isn't used to.

"Sorry, ladies," Tommy says. "It just came out. We're not used to having impressionable ears at dinner."

"Speak for yourself," Bea responds, practically blushing. My brow lifts, and I give John a sideways glance to see his eyes narrow with a slight shake of his head.

"Seriously, though," Simon says. "Neither of you are getting any younger. I mean, you don't want to be pushing out John's offspring at fifty."

"Excuse me." I rise from my seat, my thoughts remiss that this wouldn't be brought up. Slamming the door behind me, I dash up the stairs and into the bathroom. Inhaling deeply, my hands clench the basin as the door opens tentatively to reveal Jules.

"Are you okay?"

"I'm fine." Except we both know that's a lie since sympathy is written all over her face.

"No, you're not. But I'll leave it – for now," she replies perceptively. "I'll see you back down there."

Her steps retreat as I turn back to the mirror, and for a split second, I see *her*. *Her* being the woman who has been incarcerated for an eternity.

I sigh, unsure how much longer I can keep up the pretence. Every day it gets harder and harder, and I dig myself in a little bit deeper, and one day, I know I will have to dig my way back out.

"One day," I murmur, and plunge the room back into darkness.

Approaching the dining room, Simon is waiting outside and my nape bristles.

"I'm sorry, M. I didn't mean to upset you," he says contritely, his beautiful mocha skin tinged crimson.

"No, it was just the realisation of the statement, darling. It wasn't you."

"Okay," he says, and flops his arm around my shoulder and holds the door open.

"Wait! Are you telling me you guys use my son as an instrument to pick up women?" Kara's appalled tone carries as we enter.

All eyes are on me as I shuffle back into my seat while Tommy, ever the laid-back optimist, shrugs and imparts his response.

"Absolutely. You've got to use whatever you can get. Besides, look at him! You handsome looking boy, you!" He wiggles his fingers at Oliver, who pouts sternly like Tommy is a raving lunatic. The kid has him pegged already. Plucking the baby from his mother's arms, Tommy blows raspberries on his belly, inducing a fit of giggles.

"Seriously, the fantasy of having babies that look this good is too great for some women to refuse."

"Really? Are they blind? He's not even ginger!" Sloan interjects.

"Irrelevant!" Kara's furious gaze cuts to her husband. "Tommy, my son isn't pulling power!"

"That's because you've never tried!" He wags his finger with each word.

Kara's mouth drops open sharply, but the admonishment waiting to be vented doesn't come as Sloan kisses away her reproach. I turn away, regardless of how much I love him, I don't want to see him manhandling my girl again. I don't care if he's her husband and they have a child, I don't want to see it.

"I'm so glad I have a daughter. Seriously, Kara, girls are easier than boys," Bea says, grinning at her daughter, who is now sitting on Tommy's knee, gabbing to Oliver and holding his hand.

"Oh, I don't know about that," Jules counters, levelling her gaze at Charlie.

"What? I was a perfect child."

"If you say so, honey. I have plenty of horror stories when you two were younger." Jules smiles thoughtfully, then gasps. "Do you remember when John taught you how to shave?" She addresses Sloan, who almost spits out the mouthful of wine he has just swallowed.

"Unfortunately. It was the day I realised toilet roll had a third use."

I laugh, but it's always like this; absurd conversation that rolls from one subject to the next. At some point, it comes back to work, but in between, I gain gems of information that I never knew before.

"Marie?" Nicki calls amongst the din.

"Yeah, honey?" I focus on her as she sits up straighter. Dev's arm relaxes over the back of her seat, while he strokes her hair.

"I put in a call to Richard Lowe's assistant to set up a meeting." I raise my brows. The way she is squirming tells me I'm not going to be pleased.

"And?"

"And within ten minutes of hanging up, he was on the phone, making a grand gesture of calling personally."

"When?"

"Next Thursday. Sorry, I should have told you sooner."

"Thursday's fine. Do you fancy leading?" I rim the edge of my glass with my finger, praying she agrees.

Her eyes widen in surprise. "Really?"

"Absolutely. I have complete faith in you."

"You just don't want to deal with him."

"That's right." I grin. "We'll talk about it on Monday. We've got plenty of time to prepare."

"Yeah, that's plenty of time to sharpen the knives, clean the guns, and give you both a crash course in self-defence," John says, reaching across the table to take the bottle Dev is offering.

"Damn right," Dev says, concurring with his uncle. "And when all that fails, I'm sure my connections might be able to source us a cannon to blow up the bastard's dirty den of iniquity."

"Devlin!"

Dev's head shoots round, and he gives his mother a sheepish look. "Ladies, I apologise for my language, but I'm not sorry I said it. That's what the man is. He's a dirty di-"

"Okay, who wants dessert?" I ask loudly, cutting him off. But nevertheless, dessert makes everything okay – even the prospect of dealing with Richard Lowe.

Time passes quickly, and Louisa and Beatrice call it a night when Katie starts to get grumpy and short.

"It's been lovely seeing you all. Next time see if you can get the others to come over." I release Louisa from my grasp.

"I'll try, but I make no promises. Katie, come and kiss Auntie Marie goodbye."

Katie, practically dead to the world, blinks sleepily and holds out her arms. Curling my fingers around her small head, I kiss her cheek.

"Sweet dreams, honey. And be a good girl."

"I will, Auntie Marie." She yawns and settles back into her mother's arms. I stand at the door while John walks them to the waiting taxi.

"Call me as soon as you both get home."

Louisa nods and kisses his cheek. She whispers something to him, and he turns back briefly. I smile suspiciously and wait as John stands on the kerb as the taxi moves off. He then jogs up to the house and palms my waist.

"Three down, ten to go. Want to give me a hand evicting them?"

I shrug. "What's the rush?"

"A kitchen table with your name on it!"

I guffaw and elbow him playfully in the gut. I sway my hips as I head back into the dining room, while he pretends to double over in pain.

"Is it too late to apply for the trainee summer scheme?" Evie asks Sloan as I take a seat.

My brows lift in surprise - this is the most personal declaration I've heard out of her all evening. Granted, she's engaged in the conversation. Not enough to become too ingrained, but enough to stay involved. Again, the fear she is too frightened to get too close rears its head inside my woeful heart.

"No, we have a few places left. Why?" Sloan replies.

Evie suddenly looks uncomfortable. "When I asked my dad, he said they were already taken." Her eyes drop to the table, and her long dark hair falls, shrouding her humiliation.

I look between Sloan to John, who are both wearing the same expression of disgust. Averting my gaze to Remy, he rubs his hand over Evie's, before tipping her chin up. An unambiguous, unspoken truth passes between them, and it's more than obvious something is going on with these two that Jeremy isn't divulging – not even to John.

"You don't have to apply, I'll give you a place. Call it a perk of having a father on the board."

"No," Evie replies, dejected. "I'd like to earn it properly. I want to stand on my own two feet without his interference."

Interesting, I think, overly interested as to why she doesn't want to ride daddy's rich, influential coattails. *Interesting* is also the word that John and Sloan use to describe Evie's dad. Although it's rare they discuss anything to do with Emerson and Foster openly, I know there are some misgivings on the board regarding the financial integrity of Andrew Blake. Namely, where most of his personal wealth comes from.

"I respect that," Sloan tells her. "My office, Monday at nine o'clock."

Evie's face lights up, then falls again. "Will you be doing the interview?"

"I shall be present, but HR will conduct the main. Be warned, there are certain aspects I will grill you on throughout."

"And I definitely won't be given special treatment?"

"No, you will be interviewed the same as every other applicant. If anything, you have more to prove."

She nods and smiles. "Good, that's what I want." She turns to Remy and beams, like the idea of being grilled by the CEO is something to get excited about.

"Park, are you taking notes of civility here?" John asks, ripping open a share size bag of crisps.

"No," he replies cockily.

"Pity, because I've got a job for you."

Simon groans. "No." His rebuttal is instant, but John ignores it.

"I need your charm services again."

"Again?" Simon shakes his head dramatically. "A man can't get a break at WS. I'm not the company debt collector. Jesus Christ!"

I smile, but I can relate - I despise chasing overdue payments, too.

"Hey, your God-fearing gran will shove that walking stick of hers where the sun doesn't shine if she hears you talking like that!" John says with a grin, uncapping a bottle and taking a swig.

"Yeah, yeah, what do you need me to do?"

"The arsehole who laid the dodgy tarmac needs chasing to finish it right. And since you're the one who recommended that wide boy, you can call him. And when you do, ask him if actually knows what he's doing. Did you even check?"

Simon shrugs. "He came highly recommended. He's a Jack of all trades."

John chortles. "Yeah, Jack of all trades and master of none, because I'm the owner of the newest off-road terrain this side of London!"

I shake my head in amusement and reach for the bottle of wine.

"Fine. Next time I won't suggest anything. God, at least I managed to get him on the cheap. My talents are so underappreciated!"

Remy cracks up laughing and slaps his hand on the table, while everyone sniggers and smirks.

"I'd rather have paid double to have it done right. And who lied and said you had discernible talents, sunshine?"

Simon grins, unoffended. He knows he can charm his way out of anything. "Like I said, underappreciated. Well, this chat has been inspiring, no wonder I lack confidence."

"No, no, sunshine, you won't be lacking *anything* with my size eleven rammed up your arse. Please, Park, I'm tired of arguing the toss with the bastard. Call him first thing, or you'll find yourself on civvy street, job hunting."

"Fine, but you owe me!"

John rolls his eyes as Simon stands. "Well, Marie, it's been fun. Thank you for saving me the loneliness of a ready meal, but the night is still young, and there are plenty of women out there who would love to cry on my shoulder. Anyone else up for a nightcap?"

Murmurs of approval resound and everyone, except Sloan and Kara, collects their things. Imparting my goodnights, I traipse towards the door.

"Remember, I want you on the blower first thing. No ifs, no buts. I want it done right, or he's not getting paid."

"I'll be on it, guv," Simon says with a salute. "Have a good night."

Closing the door, secure in John's embrace, I yawn.

"Tired?" he asks knowingly, setting the alarm.

"Hmm. Think we can give the table its inaugural testing another day?"

"Sure. Besides, the kids are going to stay tonight. Can't have Sloan getting any ideas. The last thing we need is more little Fosters plaguing the world and raising havoc."

"Impossible. You know that's a given, probably sooner rather than later."

"True," he says softly.

"Why wasn't I told they were staying tonight?" I ask, not out of annoyance, but again, because I'm being kept in the dark.

"Sloan's idea. He thought you might want to have your first experience of bedtime and morning with Oliver."

I smile at Sloan's thoughtfulness, while an anxious sensation overwhelms my chest. "I'd love to, but he's already asleep. The morning's good though. I feel I don't see them nearly enough these days."

John kisses me and pads down the hallway as I open the living room door. "Hey, darling," I say to Kara, who looks as tired as I feel. She pats the sofa, and I drop like a lead weight, as she snuggles into my side.

"I like that I can finally do this. Touch, and feel nothing but contentment. Having Oliver has made me realise how much I've denied you of that. I'm sorry."

I stroke my fingers through her hair and smile, but I will always forgive her faults. Unknown to her, she unwittingly breached a part of my heart that had been sealed for longer than should be naturally acceptable.

A long time ago, I steeled myself against the world. I was determined to walk through this life alone and into the next without tainting another with my poison. I swore that no-one would ever get back in. All that was annihilated the night I decided to get some fresh air from the drunk and wealthy and a homeless child crossed my path. It changed the course of my life forever. Seeing her, realising she was also alone in the universe, was the thing I didn't know I needed to pull me back from the downward spiral I'd been traversing for far too long.

She was just a child then, one who had suffered depravity that I could never imagine. Whilst we've both walked a path of pain, my own teenage experiences are nothing in comparison to hers. I had choices, and I made them. Except for one, they were all wrong. She didn't get that. She didn't get a choice whether she could scream or fight back, but she made a choice to accept a clean, warm bed for the night.

"It's okay," I tell her, then I remember. "Honey, what did you want to talk about earlier?"

She bites her lip nervously, and her eyes shift. "I've got a meeting with the vicar in a few weeks regarding christening Oliver."

"Oh," I murmur blandly because a christening means I will probably have to see someone I really don't want to.

"It feels a bit fraudulent since we don't go to church, but some of the mothers at the baby clinic say it's a good idea and Gloria keeps on asking, too."

"I bet she does. I thought she was retiring?"

"She did, but after two weeks with her hubby under her feet, she called Sloan and said she was going insane. Lucky for her, he too was being driven to insanity by Sophie, so it worked well for everyone."

"Good," I confirm, struggling to stay awake. Kara's fingers entwine in mine, and I fight against the inevitable until I finally give in.

And as I drowse off, I can honestly say there's no better feeling in the world than being loved by your child.

My eyes flicker open while the clock on the mantel ticks past midnight.

Creeping out of the living room, light floods from under the office door, and quiet voices discuss what sounds like business.

I tiptoe up the stairs and edge down the landing towards the spare bedroom. I carefully push back the door to find Kara asleep. In the portable cot beside her, Oliver is sprawled out, his tubby arms above his head.

I gaze sadly, fighting against a memory. "I did something right," I whisper. "I proved I could do it." With a content sigh, I close the door ajar and enter the bathroom.

As I dry my hands, I twist the ring on my finger, and the unbearable weight of my situation bears down on my shoulders. It's irresponsible, but the truth is hard to voice, and each time I've rehearsed my confession, the conviction to rid myself of it has been paper thin at best.

The truth is, I don't like the lying, deceitful woman I've become. She isn't me, but after existing inside a hollow shell for over twenty years, I don't know how to pull myself back from the abyss.

Turning off the light, I sluggishly descend the stairs. At the bottom, the men are still in the office, and the clink of glass is identifiable. Sneaking by the door, the talk stops me.

"I can't believe you finally did it," Sloan says. "I can't believe she said yes."

"Well, it wasn't without drama, that's for sure." John sounds exasperated, even a little annoyed.

I swallow hard. I know I shouldn't be listening, but compulsion won't allow my feet to move.

"Dom finally dug deep enough, then?"

John sighs. "No, he said he couldn't find anything else. And maybe there is nothing to find. He's got no reason to lie."

"Do you really believe that? What happened when you proposed?"

The crinkle of leather followed by intermittent steps proceeds the quiet calm until John fills the hollow.

"Let's just say what didn't happen. There's definitely something there; something deep-rooted. It's like she has a psychological fear of letting someone in. But I'll wait, forever if I have to."

"John-"

"No, don't you dare attempt to psychoanalyse and patronise me on my choices when yours are far from exemplary."

"I'm not. I just thought you were going to wait until she came clean."

"I was, but I've been hiding that ring for so long, I just couldn't wait any longer. I love her, kid. I've loved her for years, remember? And if you don't, let me re-jog your memory."

I perk my brows in query, although I shouldn't be surprised. If anything, that statement just gives more credence to my theory that he probably does have a file on me.

"I know. Look, don't take this the wrong way, but what happens when she finally lays down the truth. What if she tells you something you don't want to hear? Something that changes the way you feel?"

"It won't. Whatever it is, I'm telling you it won't."

"You say that now-"

"When Kara finally confessed the abuse to you, did it stop you from loving her? Stop you from wanting her?" John asks in a tone which would usually indicate a conversation is over.

"No, because I already knew. As did you. This is a completely different situation, and you know it. I don't want to fight about this, you know I love Marie, but I love you more. And if it came between you and her, you would always come first."

"I know, but it'll be fine, trust me. If I thought it was bad, I wouldn't have pulled out the rock."

And upon hearing that, I now wish he hadn't. I wish he'd left the thing in the fucking box to rot because it is bad. Far worse than he can ever imagine.

"Well, here's to a long, prosperous and hopefully, happy marriage. When it happens."

"Come here, kid," John replies, and the sound of backslapping fills my ears.

I tiptoe into the kitchen and gaze at the mess left in the wake of my impromptu family dinner. Emptying off the plates, I load the dishwasher and knot the overflowing rubbish bag.

Night cloaks me as I dump the evening's festivities in the bin, concealing the dead flower delivery from this afternoon.

As I slam the lid down, I concede I need a miracle. But more than that, I need a saviour; someone to protect me from what I know is inevitable. Years ago, I begged for the same thing, only he arrived too late.

Gazing up at the starless sky, tonight I'd do whatever it takes. I'd be willing to get down on my knees and beg a God I had forsaken for forgiveness.

Tonight, I'd sell my soul to the devil in exchange for my Faith.

Chapter 18

"WE'RE NOT IN Kansas anymore, Marie," Nicki says worryingly. "Or the Emerson."

"No," I reply amused. Standing in the middle of the ballroom, I'm completely mesmerised by the crystal chandeliers, vaulted ceiling and double the number of tables I am generally used to. I sigh and bite my lip as the enormity of what we're about to sign on for overwhelms me.

Taking a turn around the vast space, I envisage the patrons, the staff, and me – standing in a corner, terrified and wanting to hide.

I turn to Nicki to see if I can gauge her thoughts, but there is no gauging necessary since she is wearing the same expression of dread.

"Well, look on the bright side," she says with a shrug.

"And what's that?"

"At least they don't execute people at the Tower for crimes against the affluent and wealthy anymore." She breaks out into a smile, and I place my hand on her arm. Laughing together, lightening the impending load we have agreed upon, I lament.

"Just lie and tell me it will be great."

She rolls her shoulders and hesitates. "It won't be boring."

"Good enough."

In all the years I've been doing this, I've never had a room that could hold so many people. For the first time in my professional life, I feel like I'm twenty-six all over again, walking into the first hotel that gave me a chance and saw that I could shine.

"So, what do you think?"

Nicki and I rotate simultaneously as Richard Lowe's fake charm spoils the silence. He leans against the ornate door frame and surveys the room with pride. With his hands in his trouser pockets, he gives off all the airs and graces of a conquering king. I guess in these surroundings, he is.

"It's stunning, Mr Lowe," Nicki replies, and I breathe a sigh of relief, thankful that she hasn't called him flirty – yet. Give it time, it could still happen before this morning is through.

"That it is," he replies smugly.

He swaggers in, his confidence edging on arrogance, openly assessing us. His eyes linger intently on Nicki's slim fit jacket, pencil skirt and pinstripe top until he turns his attention to me. From my white blouse, buttoned to the neck to my navy slouch trousers, matching jacket and multicoloured brogues, this is the most androgynous and least sexiest work outfit I possess. I choose it with one purpose in mind – to repel the opposite sex. Namely, this member of it.

"Good morning, Nicole. You look lovely today." He takes her hand and kisses the back, and I note the subtle way she recoils. Letting go, much to her relief, he approaches me with a hasty step, and I brace myself when his lips curve. "As do you, Marie."

Holding out my hand, ready to get this necessary civility over with, his fingers squeeze mine, and his eyes slit when my ring glints under the lights. A flash of something plays on his face, and he steps closer, so close, his warm breath washes over my cheek.

"It's a pleasure to see you looking so ravishing this morning," he whispers, and my jaw grinds as he sniffs deeply. "You smell ravishing, too. I approve." I force a smile, although I'd rather pick up one of the chairs and smash it over his head.

"Good morning, Richard," I greet flatly, giving Nicki a sideways glance, feeling uncomfortable at her shocked expression. I brace myself because the bastard is being obnoxious on purpose. Why? I wish I knew. As I have previously said to John, I'm twenty years too old for his preferred tastes.

Consumed in my thoughts, light steps enter the room. "The conference suite is ready, sir," the woman speaks, then quickly turns on her heel.

Inside the boardroom, I gaze around in awe. Everything I've seen so far makes Sloan look practically destitute - and that's saying something.

The door closes, and I dally, purposely waiting to see where Richard will sit. He folds himself dramatically into the chair at the head of the table – exactly where I pegged he would – and leans leisurely, like a predator waiting to play with his food and devour.

Nicki sits a few feet away from him, and I place down my bag on one of the seats, spying the beverages in the centre. I fill two glasses with water and pass one to Nicki, before sitting.

"Right," Richard says firmly and opens his contract. "Let's begin."

"Mr Lowe, before we do, we would like to thank you for this amazing opportunity," Nicki says, leading the meeting as discussed. I admit, watching her involuntarily kiss his arse wasn't included in our pre-meeting preparations, and it's uncomfortable, to say the least.

Richard nods but doesn't comment. Instead, he flips the pages and clicks his pen incessantly. I groan inaudibly. The man isn't impressed. He's probably had his arse kissed so many times over the years he is now immune.

He looks up from the contract and levels his gaze on me. "Clause one, Marie?"

"Acceptable," Nicki replies, and my mouth curves, because he's determined to push her out, and she's determined to stay in. And I'm determined just to sit back and watch the power tug.

"Clause two, *Nicole?*"

"Acceptable, *Richard.*" She emphasises his name sweetly. "Although we would appreciate if, on the penultimate sentence, you replace 'all due care' with 'reasonable care'?"

His face scrunches up, before striking through his contract. "Acceptable. Clause three?"

"Acceptable."

"Four?"

Marking up the full complement of documents, I can't help but conceal a grin each time Nicki lays down her demands, and Richard is forced to change what is undoubtedly an unchallenged precedent. Time passes slowly, while Nicki and Richard debate the amendments and both sides of reasoning until we finally reach the end.

"I shall have my assistant make the changes, and the final versions will be emailed to you for approval and execution," Richard says, pulling out his phone.

I nudge Nicki and slide over my notes on the two clauses he has deliberately bypassed – for good reason. And probably for his own gain.

"Richard?" I call out politely.

"Marie, I'd forgotten you were here," he replies sarcastically, the sneer on his face dying a death as he puts down his phone.

"There are two clauses you have missed," I tell him with conviction, and flick to the first dogeared page.

"I haven't missed anything," he replies venomously, inducing Nicki to inhale sharply beside me.

"Yes, you have. Non-compete and non-disclosure are *unacceptable.*" I train my eyes on him, identifying his annoyance. "Unfortunately, we cannot agree to these in their current form."

"Why not?"

"Because it is unethical."

"Has Foster requested this?" he asks snidely.

"No, and with all respect, it is insulting you would suggest as such. Mr Foster, nor his associates, carry any bearing on our business or this meeting. I am requesting this as you cannot expect us to solely cater for your hotel and refuse all other propositions. Our livelihood and reputation are reliant upon our flexibility. If it is exclusivity you require, you will not find that outside of your own team, and I would urge you to reconsider today's meeting and annul the contract now."

Richard grunts and taps his pen hard against the table. A sour expression overtakes his face as he skims the clause. "Fine. I will have the clause amended."

"Good. I'll email you the wording, for your consideration, of course." My triumph is bubbling inside, but it may be short-lived. "Now, the non-disclosure clause."

"Thoughts?"

"My thoughts are that every event we successfully cater is a testament to our ability to provide a first-class service. We use that for publicity, the same way your establishment would. It is a marketing tool, and you cannot expect us not to disclose to potential clients the establishments we have already catered for satisfactorily." I glance over at Nicki whose eyes sparkle with glee, and she beams with pride. "We would ask that this clause is removed in its entirety."

Richard's eyes narrow, and long minutes tick by until he eventually strikes it out. "Acceptable," he confirms grudgingly.

An hour later, with the contract twice dissected and almost agreed, Richard leads us back into the ballroom. Nicki, wholly consumed in making notes, is in her own world as my hand is snatched up.

"Engaged?"

I'm stunned.

Lost for words.

"Marie?"

The spell is broken by his irritating tone, and I realise my mouth is still slightly open, failing to make any kind of response.

"Yes. Yes, I am, and I'm thrilled," I say defiantly, staring at him resolutely. His brow furrows, and he releases my hand instantly, almost like my touch is toxic.

"Second time lucky," he mutters under his breath, but I don't miss it.

"Excuse me?" I ask, my eyes narrow.

"I said, Mr Walker is very lucky." Turning abruptly, he makes his way into the centre of the room.

"What was that about?" Nicki jerks her head. I shrug in response, waiting for the sly bastard to turn.

"So, on the evening itself, I want everything pristine," he says, his tone harder than it has been all morning. "People pay an exorbitant amount of money to be seen at my events, and I won't have my reputation tarnished because you ladies experience cold feet. The event I want you to cover is in July. Four hundred guests. It is the wedding anniversary of a close, affluent friend, and I want it to go without a hitch. I will have my assistant call later in the month to determine menus and dressings. I trust the timing is acceptable?"

I nod, because what choice do I have? This man will either make or break me. *Slowly.* If this doesn't go smoothly, it won't be the stupid contract clauses I need to worry about. Putting food on the table and a roof over my head will take precedence.

"Of course, Mr Lowe." He glares at me as I revert back to formal address. "The successful conduct of the night is our utmost priority. You can be assured that your utmost satisfaction will be met."

Surprised, he strides back to us with predatory purpose. "Marie, I have no doubt in your ability, but my satisfaction, however, will be determined on the night." He opens his mouth again but is distracted by the ringing of his phone. Retrieving it from his pocket, his look of agitation is undisguisable. "Now, do you have any further questions?"

"Not at this time, Mr Lowe. I would be grateful if you could have all the details emailed across ASAP. We will be in touch if there is anything we need further clarification on. As soon as the amends have been agreed, the executed contract will be delivered to your office."

"Fine. Good day, ladies," he says, then turns on his heel and leaves the room.

"Well, that was charming," Nicki says, flipping open the contract as we stride out of the hotel side by side. "Good job, we only signed on for two."

"Indeed. I have a feeling he is going to make life hard for us."

"I think you're right. You, in particular," she says. "If we don't get the amends sent through by close of play, I'll chase up his assistant in the morning."

"Agreed. Let's start planning now. The less he has to complain about, the better," I say as we wait for the porter to arrive with my car.

"Done," Nicki says, jotting away in her planner.

Climbing into the car, I take a fleeting look back at the hotel in my rear view, mentally berating myself for thinking this would be a great opportunity on New Year's Eve. I entirely blame the wine and tequila, but Nicki is right about one thing: he is going to make my life hard.

Very hard.

I drop down the head of the food mixer and blast it on full power. Watching the ingredients churn together is bizarrely satisfying.

Honestly, it's the little things in life that make me happy. Such as a finding a dress that fits in a smaller size, or besting a dirty bastard in his own boardroom, or homemade cake. Now, cake really makes me smile.

This afternoon, feeling somewhat invincible after getting one up on Richard Lowe, I walked back through the door on cloud nine, determined to create heaven on a platter and feed it to John later. Hence the reason why my kitchen now resembles a bakery and every piece of cookware I own is out and primed.

I turn up the radio to drown out the ear-splitting noise, and my hips sway involuntarily to the pop music playing on the station.

Pottering around, washing the dirty crockery, and wiping down the worktops, a playful slap beats across my rear. My head darts around and John steps back, laughing with his hands up in surrender.

"Why, hello, Mr Walker!" I greet, fun and flirty, unable to mask my grin.

"Angel," he says, his eyes darkening as he glances around the unavailable space. He approaches mixer, turns it off and scoops up a bit of mixture on his thumb and licks it.

"Don't eat that! It's got raw egg in it."

"Hmm, Victoria Sponge?"

I nod and step forward. Kissing his neck, his attention is still diverted until his eyes flick up and he grabs the backs of my thighs and pulls them around his waist.

"Well, when I'm laid up with food poisoning, you can show me your bedside manner."

He perches me on the edge of the sink, and I throw caution to the wind, curve my legs around his hips and claim his mouth. Cradling his face, I glide my tongue against his in long, tantalising strokes.

"Very nice," he murmurs, lowering me back. Grasping his neck harder, I shall never tire of this. This feeling of being wanted and consumed. Lost in wicked, wayward thoughts, I shriek when he turns on the tap and purposely soaks my back.

"John!" I yelp. "I'm wet!"

"Words every man wants to hear from his woman."

He crushes my body to his and seals his mouth over mine, obstructing further complaint. He holds securely under my wet bum while I quickly unbutton my sodden blouse and throw it down. His eyes smoulder as he takes in my lacy bra.

"Hold on," he says hoarsely. Tethering my legs harder around his waist, my hands gripping his rock-hard shoulders, he fumbles with my trousers. "Fuck!" he hisses when the zip catches, and he tears them apart in frustration.

His eyes dart around and stop on the table, which is currently covered in flour and baking tins. Dragging his eager lips down my neck, he bends with me in his arms. The clatter of metal hitting the floor, and plumes of flour dust rise up, spelling out he has just wiped it clean – the Walker way.

Laying me on the table, he grabs the waistband of my trousers and drags them down my legs in a fluid motion. I stare into his eyes as he unfastens his shirt, and his predatory gaze causes me to inch back. The sensation of flour rubbing against my skin is forgotten when he rips off his belt and snaps it together. The sight alone is more than arousing, and I lick my lips hungrily. Seeing how much it has turned me on, he wraps one half around his hand and rids himself of his combats and boxers with the other.

The sun streams through the window, highlighting his broad physique. It outlines him perfectly, casting a halo of light around his frame. My eyes take a moment to appreciate what could possibly be the perfect specimen of man. Unashamedly tracking down his body, my insides develop that weak and giddy, excitable awareness as his chest expands and deflates under his desirous breathing.

He continues to wrap and unwrap the leather in his hands, and his muscles flex, from his arms to his chest, to his equally impressive abdomen. Wanting a better view of the rest of him, he groans when I purposely drop my knee aside and lift on my elbows. I lick my lip at his growing hardness, and a wanton shiver takes hold when he effortlessly ascends the table.

My eyes fix on the worn leather, still coiled around his hand as he looms over me. He palms my cheek and tilts my head back, then glides his tongue down my neck. I close my eyes and allow instinct to take over when he runs his nose down the hollow between my breasts, and he takes my nipple between his teeth.

"Oh," I breathe, but don't impart anything of importance since his action has me almost swallowing my tongue. I grip the sides of the wood as he sucks my tip into his mouth.

Hard.

"Oh, God!" The guttural plea escapes my throat and my spine bows, giving him more, shunting my peak further into his mouth.

Dragging his hands around my back, he unfastens my bra and rips it off. Throwing it out of the way, it lands on the hob. My first response is to pitch a fit that bras aren't cheap, but he has me beat.

"Perfect. The girls will appreciate that unforgiving bastard being burnt. Although, it does decorate nicely!" He smirks and kneads my breasts possessively. The ache between my legs intensifies, and I rub them together. "I'll take a view on the rest later."

I attempt to slap his chest, but he catches my hand and slides me closer. He lodges my centre to his and slips his hand between my lacy shorts and flesh. Drawing the skimpy fabric down my backside, I shuffle back and curl up one leg to get them off. When they land somewhere on the floor, he ensnares my arm and wraps the belt around my wrist.

"Bound together," he whispers provocatively against my cheek.

He carefully guides me back to the table and fixes one leg high around his waist, prompting a remarkable stretch. Pressing deeper, I begin to relax – insofar as possible on an unforgiving, rigid piece of wood.

"I missed you today," he says, staring at my mouth.

"Show me," I reply seductively.

No sooner have the words left my lips, he conquers and plunders my mouth. My thigh muscles constrict, and his hard length coasts up and down between my folds, sending me over the edge. My body spasms and the sensation ignites every cell and heats my blood.

Gyrating under him, he groans out as his tip pierces my opening then he pulls back. With a darkened gaze overcoming him, his fingers in our bound hands twist with mine.

"Ask for it, angel."

I rock my lower body up again, positioning him at my aching centre. My arms loll back until they hang off the end of the table and my breasts point to the ceiling.

"Fuck me, Mr Walker."

"With pleasure."

His fingers flutter around my core, dipping in and out frustratingly. Eventually, after far too long of leaving me hanging, he circles one inside and pulls it back out. Dragging the offending finger down his lip, he swipes his tongue across the tip, savouring the taste.

"Please…" I beg as he reaches under my back, raising my body higher and slides his hand under my shoulders. Giving up the pretence of being able to rein in his floundering self-control, he gives in and slams inside. "Oh, God!" I hiss out as he strikes me harder than he ever has before.

His hand under my back grips my nape for leverage, as he pumps back and forth inside me. It's punishing and unforgiving, and my body revels in it.

Inside, I want him to break me. I want him to tear at my dark places until I scream without shame.

Driving into me with conviction, the table creaks. Grasping my free hand on the edge, I attune my rhythm with his, until we are connecting and withdrawing in perfect harmony.

"Fuck, angel!" he grits out, claiming my mouth and sinking his tongue inside. My body starts to shake, the passion rapidly reaching combustion. "Let go, beautiful. Let go."

I stretch back, clamp my hand harder, and give him his request. Calling out his name, the radio still playing in the background is drowned out by my vocal overtones.

"Angel… Fuck!" he roars out, jutting hard, making me call out in the time as the second hit of ecstasy beckons. His heat radiates against my skin, and the surface chills my back while he continues to pierce me beautifully. Long minutes pass, until he finally slows, and lays over me. Loosening my legs but still clenching him firm inside me, he eventually begins to soften.

"Fuck, that feels good." He unravels the belt, and it drops to the floor with a clunk.

"I promised I'd have you over this table one day." Kissing my shoulder, his fingers tangle in my hair. "It's safe to say I'll never look at the same way again."

"No," I agree. I drag my hand over my damp forehead and steady my breathing as he slides down and pulls me up. He moves my perspired hair away from my cheeks and cradles my face. He starts to open his mouth but shuts it at the same moment.

"What?" I ask. He's been doing this a lot lately, seemingly wishing to express himself but never following through. His look is anxious, and I know whatever he does eventually say, I'm not going to like.

"Nothing." He holds me close and looks around the room. "It looks like a tornado just passed through here."

I smile and glance down at the charcoal tiles splattered with utensils and flour that I'll still probably be cleaning up in the days to come. "Hmm, you could say that."

He puts me on my feet and grabs his t-shirt. "Come here."

I lift my arms, and he drops it over my head, covering what little is left of my modesty. Pulling on his combats commando, he leaves the button undone and grabs my hand.

"Darling, no! I need to clean up and disinfect everything!"

"No point. I'll have you down and dirty in here at least once more tonight." He laughs and swipes his finger across my face and licks it. His head tilts to the side, and my worry dies when it finally registers what he has just said.

"Because the state of the kitchen doesn't already declare we've just done that?"

"True." He smirks and turns the food mixer back on. "How did the meeting go?"

"Nicki was amazing, she didn't give an inch! And Lowe wasn't playing fair at all. He thought he could get one over on the little women pretending to be businesswomen. He even brought Sloan into the conversation. Can you believe that?"

"Yes, because nothing that conniving bastard does surprises me." He hisses. "Look, angel, we need to talk." I hesitate because as I've said before, those are never good words to hear.

He leads me into the living room, sits on the sofa and pulls me onto his lap. Influencing me back, his fingers circle my abdomen slowly.

"Darling, what's wrong?" I ask, my body betraying me again, anticipating round two. Needing to regain some control, I tap him but fail to divert his hands. I suddenly feel sixteen again, remembering what it was like when love was new and exciting. Still, I don't need to remember, in his arms, that feeling never withers.

"I need to go away for a few days."

I jerk back. "Why?"

He shakes his head, probably thinking the worst of what is going on inside mine. "Just business. A mate needs a hand with something, so I'm taking Jake with me. I won't be gone long."

"How long?" I ask because right now, I'd prefer he didn't go. Considering the weird events and unwanted deliveries, I'd rather he stays here. Not to mention, the last time he left on business, I was assaulted in my own home.

"A week. I'll be back before you know it."

"I don't like it," I mutter but drop it. *For now.* "When are you going?" I twine my arms around him.

"In the morning."

"Well, I better get my fill of you while I can then."

I shift and straddle his thighs. Rolling my body down them, I unzip his combats and slide my hand inside. His hips jerk up, and he shrugs his trousers down his legs. The t-shirt covering me is yanked over my head, leaving me naked on my knees before him. I peer mischievously and lick my lips in readiness. Gliding my hands up his thighs, my mouth on a direct trajectory, he groans as I begin to get my fill.

"I want you on my tongue."

Chapter 19

THE RHYTHMIC TAP of the keyboard grounds me as I enter the names and numbers for the forthcoming Emerson event.

Flicking through Nicki's handwritten notes, my eyes drift lazily across the five by four picture beside the monitor. As I steady my tired gaze upon the frame, my fingers touch the glass, outlining the face of the man who has changed my entire world.

And the man who was supposed to come home yesterday.

Fighting the urge to call him, I input the same figures for the umpteenth time, before I give up and save the document. In truth, this morning is proving to be futile since my mind is currently elsewhere.

"Nicki?" I call out and gather up my things. Peering at the clock, the hand passes half-past twelve, and I grab my mobile as the landline rings. "Good afternoon, Dawson's Catering."

"Hello, Dawson's Catering. Fancy lunch?" Sophie's bubbly tone invades my eardrums. I smile because sometimes great minds do think alike. Albeit, sometimes she acts like she has cotton wool where her brain should be.

"You read my mind. The usual?" I ask, although pointless since it's their regular lunchtime stomping ground.

"Absolutely. Let me just convince the unreasonable sod he doesn't need me over lunch, and we'll meet you there."

"Okay. We'll see you in half an hour." I hang up, interested how she will convince Sloan. I admit I don't agree with her language towards him. He's been good to her, but yes, he is unreasonable. And often.

I stop in front of Nicki's desk, and my eyes skim over the neat, orderly piles – unlike my desk, which is just one huge pile. Guilt slaps me because, in this instant, I realise how incredibly unorganised I am in comparison. First Kara, now Nicki, no wonder she deals with most of the stuff before I even have a chance to see it. If I can't see it, I can't misplace it.

Okay, lose it.

"How are the table plans coming along?"

Nicki looks up and rubs her eyes. "After a while, I start seeing double, or I fail to see anything at all," she says miserably.

"Well, I'm tired of looking at that costs spreadsheet, so we're going out for lunch," I announce cheerily.

"Marie, I…"

Her eyes follow mine, and an anxious expression I can never place casts over her features. I've seen this look far too many times over the last few years. It's where she tries to cry off and says she's too busy.

"Nicole," I cajole, adjusting my bag on my shoulder. "All this stuff will still be waiting for us this afternoon, and tomorrow, and the next day. It's like the Forth Bridge – it never stops." I flippantly try to make light of it, but I'm not wrong. The thought of still doing this when I'm sixty or - God forbid - seventy, terrifies me. "Come on, we both could do with a fun afternoon."

"Okay, I'll drive."

I divert the office line to my mobile as Nicki quickly organises herself and follows me out. Pushing open the downstairs door, I almost collide with our postman.

"Afternoon ladies, there's one you need to sign for," he says, handing over a small wad of envelopes and the signature device.

"Thanks," I say and stuff them in my bag.

As I strap myself into the passenger seat of Nicki's Mini, my phone vibrates and rings simultaneously. I scowl at the screen and let him stew. He's the one who decided to traipse around the country for the last week.

Nicki grins in my peripheral vision as she slowly manoeuvres out of the car park and onto the main road. "I see where Dev gets it from."

"Honey, it's where they all get it from!"

Pulling up into a space at The Swan – Sophie and Kara's drinking establishment of choice, pre-Foster, Emerson's and every other ragtag integral member of Walker Security - I spot Charlie's Merc parked at the back.

I climb out, straighten my skirt and jacket, and sidestep the smokers congregated around the doorway - not in the designated smoking shelter.

I stretch up on my toes as I hold the door open for Nicki but am unable to find the meddling twosome.

"Honey, what do you want?"

"A diet coke, please," Nicki answers, craning her neck. "Hey, I see them."

I tilt my head and spot Sophie's highlighted mane glimmering under the lights. Worryingly, she looks half cut already. I narrow my eyes, but my fears that she has returned to her boozy lunchtime ways are unfounded because even from here, there is nothing remotely pissed about her. Sophie just naturally radiates life's good stuff. Her glass is always half full, and everything carries a shiny, silver lining. More so with the ring of a handsome, devoted doctor on her finger.

"Go on, I'll bring them over," I say, as Nicki digs into her bag for her purse. "Put that away. Do you want some lunch?"

"Sure. Chicken on wholemeal. Thank you." She strides towards the eatery section of the pub, and a few minutes pass until the barman approaches.

"Hi, what can I get you?"

"A diet coke and a glass of white," I reply and place our food order. Pointing to where I'll be sitting, he passes me a number.

"Anything else?"

"No, thank you." I stow my purse and proceed through the lunchtime regulars.

"So, what do you think?" Sophie asks the moment I sit down. I crease my brow seeing as her great mind is blatantly unaware that I have just joined the conversation.

"About what?"

"A winter wedding, of course!" she says in the tone she always uses when she thinks we should all be privy to the inner workings of her fantasies. "I can just picture it; long, flowing gown, snow in the background..." She rattles on with her daydreaming.

"I think it might chill your extremities." I pick up my wine and take a large mouthful. The way this conversation is going tells me I'll need it.

"I didn't think of that," she says, clearly mulling it over until her face lights up. "Good job, I'll have a sexy, skilled husband to thaw me out afterwards."

"Sophie!" Charlie and Nicki shout simultaneously, but she just shrugs it off.

"I still think we should do a double wedding," she squeals out.

No effing way!

I smile and shake my head. Sometimes, I still find it hard to believe that she and Kara bonded at fifteen. I vividly remember the day Kara said she had a friend from school coming over for dinner. After months of living with me, I finally made her go back. Honestly, I didn't think she would let anyone in, but the evening this little madam turned up on my doorstep was educational. And while she is and always will be a little too outspoken, opposites do attract. Truthfully, Sophie is owed a debt of gratitude. I don't think she realises just how much she helped Kara in those darker days.

"Let's not worry about my wedding for now," I say, taking another sip of wine. "Maybe we should just be grateful that you're finally thinking about yours."

"Jesus!" she exclaims. "Anyone would think I've been engaged for years!"

Charlie chortles. "By the time you actually make it down the aisle, we'll all be in our forties. I'll be an auntie to a football team if Kara allows my brother to have his way, and I'll still be unmarried and childless because said brother keeps threatening to castrate Jake!" Huffing out, she looks around the table, grabs my glass, and downs a large mouthful.

"Just get pregnant and take the risk. What's the worst he can do?" Sophie suggests like she is the voice of reason and logic.

"I've already tried that. Jake obviously considers his body parts more precious than me."

Meeting Nicki's eyes, she puts her hand over her mouth at the ridiculousness of this conversation. I, on the other hand, simply burst out laughing, remembering the last time Sloan threatened to separate Jake from his precious testicles. It's hypocrisy at its worst, especially since he has a hard time keeping it in his trousers when his wife is around. Yet, I shall never fault Sloan's ethics - he wants the best for his little sister.

"Chin up, honey," I tell Charlie, while Soph, on the other hand, just throws it out there. *Rudely.*

"Tell him to man up, or he won't get it up!"

Oh, for God sake! I murmur under my breath, performing better than a seasoned ventriloquist.

"So, your unforeseeable wedding?" I attempt to veer us away from the crudeness of this conversation, and where it will lead if it continues.

"Why don't you two just plan it?" Nicki says thoughtfully. "Kara's wedding was gorgeous."

"You should tell her that. I don't think she saw any of it after the church. Although I think she might be able to tell you how many cracks were in the ceiling," Soph says innocently, while I try not to choke on my own tongue.

"Sophie." I shake my head in warning.

"Or how firm the mattress was," she finishes in a whisper as I glare at her.

"Soph, that's inappropriate," Nicki says.

"Doesn't make it any less true."

"Look, enough of this depressing wedding talk," Charlie says. "Let's discuss the annual fundraiser."

I roll my eyes; that is as equally depressing. And as much as I love what I do, there's only so much I can take of hearing about canapés, overpriced fizz and petit flaming fours.

Our food finally arrives, and my eyes widen at the man-sized portions being placed on the table.

"Do you want to share?" I ask Charlie, who nods and picks up her vibrating phone.

"Why are you calling me?" she asks in a clipped tone. She scoffs, then hands me the phone. "It's for you."

I roll my eyes and take it. "Yes?" I snap.

"Well, that's a rude way to greet your future spouse," John replies sarcastically.

I laugh and pick at the bowl of chips. "I haven't answered for a reason. I never pegged you to rely on stalker tendencies to get my attention."

He tuts, disguising his chuckle. "I wouldn't have to if my missus answered her phone," he retorts.

"Is that so? Need I remind you that you're the one who decided to gallivant around the country for seven - no, silly me - *eight* days." I'm intentionally pressing his buttons, and as my eyes capture Charlie's – which are intrigued – there is no doubt my flippancy will be reprimanded. *Hopefully.*

"You're pissed off," he states correctly.

"What did you expect," I continue. "The welcome home committee when you returned?"

"No. I expected you naked and spread over the table, but I'm just wishful thinking, angel," he says playfully with a sigh. A sigh that I do, strangely, love to hear from him. It's a sigh of contentment. One he uses when he holds me, when he assures me of his love for me, and when he does beautiful, naughty things to me.

Shifting in my seat, I cross my thighs at my own naughty thoughts. I allow the silence to hang between us because I shall not be the one to give in this time. My submission is something I give up freely, but not today. I can't easily forgive him for leaving our bed cold and lonely for longer than agreed.

After a long pause, he finally speaks. "Come over. I've got a hand you can vibrate on and a desk you can disinfect in a few hours."

I burst out laughing, and glance around, seeing a few intrigue faces focussed on me.

"No, I'm not that easy," I lie.

"Oh, but you are, my angel. What if I said I've got an itch you can scratch?"

I pucker my lips in contemplation. "Tempting, but is that the best you can offer?"

"Hmm, what if I said the itch is below my stomach but above my knees? Is that tempting enough?" he asks, and a hint of breathless anticipation seeps down the line.

"Maybe," I whisper. I mentally run over what's still waiting on my desk, but to hell with it, because even my resolve can't refuse an incredibly sexy, ex-army officer when he commands my presence over his desk. "I'll think about it," I lie again.

"I'll be waiting patiently." He hangs up, leaving me smiling.

I pass Charlie her mobile back with a grin I can't disguise.

"Erm, your phone is ringing again," she says, nodding to my bag on the floor. I leave it to ring off. It doesn't take a genius to know it's him again.

"Honey, take the rest of the afternoon off. I'll see you in the morning," I tell Nicki, as I stand and smooth down my jacket.

"Why? Where are you going?" she queries.

"To see John," I reply, although it's pretty bloody obvious. Nicki nods, while Soph, yet again, calls it as she sees it.

"I guess your dessert is going to be some afternoon love. Remember to scrub his desk after you've finished!"

"Sophie," Charlie mutters in dismay at her brashness, while I eyeball Miss Big Gob hard.

"Big mouth, girly!" I say with a grin and a pointy finger.

She shrugs. "I've told you before, blame my mother. Have fun!"

Shaking my head, I give each a kiss on the head and call for a taxi. Standing outside, I smile, because this afternoon, John Walker is definitely serving me up some dessert.

Chapter 20

"KEEP THE CHANGE." I zip up my purse, thank the driver and slide out.

Approaching the security panel, I tap in the usual code, but it doesn't work. Jabbing my finger into the button, the faint hiss of electricity whirrs and the gates slowly open. As I pass through them, I note the lack of vehicles, which means Sophie's prediction, and my hope of so-called afternoon dessert on his desk, might be more accurate than we both realised.

I stride over the cracked tarmac with purpose and gaze up at the old façade. My smile refuses to be tamed when John appears at his office window. With a mug in one hand and an iPad in the other, his victorious expression grows. It's that bloody smug, I can recognise it from here.

And he is right to be because he knows I would never say no.

Still grinning, he points to the security camera, and I rotate as it moves up and down. I stick out my tongue at his abuse of using his toys to check me out. When it remains fixed on my face, I glance back up at the window to see him staring at the tablet intently and decide to really test him. Curling all but one finger into my palm, I politely stroke my jaw – giving him the finger with a smile. I laugh when the camera slowly moves from side to side, admonishing me.

I wave him off and concentrate on the click of my heels as I enter the decrepit building. Ascending the stairs leisurely, a dark silhouette shadows the nineteen-eighties glass door at the top. I push it open, and John props himself against the architrave, looking as dangerous and addictive as the day I first met him.

My eyes drop and roll down his body in anticipation. An involuntary moan leaves my throat and my mouth parts as my tongue caresses my bottom lip in desire.

"Are you lost, beautiful?" His thick, reverent tone causes heady expectation to spasm in my spine.

"I don't know. What's the reward for finding me?" My words are a whisper, adding to the tension and foreplay.

He holds his arms out confidently. "Six foot three of solid muscle and stamina, designed to make you come over and over."

Heat sizzles inside my belly. "Well, in that case, I think I've just been found."

Sauntering towards me, he tugs my bag off my shoulder, and the sound of paper and plastic slapping the floor fills the void. With a satisfied murmur, he curls an arm under my bum and elevates me effortlessly. Carrying me down the deserted corridor, he kicks the office door shut behind us.

"Now," he begins, kissing the digit I had shown him outside. "I can think of lots of delightful things you can do with this finger. All four and your thumb, actually." His hand dips low under my skirt, caressing the soft, supple flesh of my inner thigh.

With unhurried ease, I kiss his neck, ready to let my pent-up inhibitions off their leash. I take his jaw between my finger and thumb and turn his face towards mine.

"Maybe you can show me."

He smirks, deposits me on his desk, and pushes my knees apart. Standing in between them, his inquisitive palms snake up my waist, until they stop just under my arms. I bow my back instinctively, and brace my hands at my sides, while his deft thumbs circle my already distended nipples.

"Darling, the boys?" An air of poorly concealed desire consumes my murmured panic.

"They're all out, angel," he confirms, nuzzling my neck, sucking my soft flesh. "Shall we see how many different expressions these beautiful eyes can make?"

I breathe hard, expelling the air from my lungs, wondering how many indeed.

His thumbs press harder against my breasts and only relax when I release the moan that has built up in my throat. Thoroughly giving up the fight that has already diminished, he rakes his hands up my chest. He holds my neck, strong yet soft, and cradles my head.

I tilt back, trying to find purchase on the desk, as I wrap my legs around his hips. He peppers my jaw with hard kisses, grazing with his teeth and soothing with his lips.

Papers rustle under my body as he manipulates my prone position further until my back is flattened over the top.

Leaning over me, he smiles, accentuating his hairline scar – one of many war wounds carved into his skin for all time.

As he continues to stare deep into my eyes, his look of longing dominates, and it's enough to take my breath away.

"Please," I beg, desperate for him to satisfy the yearning inside caused by our temporary separation.

Stroking my forehead, his expression softens. "God, I'm so in love with you, it hurts. You'll never have to ask because I'll always give."

I close my eyes, drawing out the moment as he lifts under my back and slides my jacket down my shoulders. I wiggle it down my arms as he pulls it from under me and tosses it behind us. Touching his lips to mine, I open autonomously, and our tongues entwine passionately. The chill of the air conditioning tickles my chest as he unbuttons my blouse and parts the fabric, leaving me exposed. I squirm, the unparalleled desire of being irrefutably aroused and turned on is something that is far too easy to achieve with him - even if I am being stripped bare in his office, at risk of getting caught.

"Lift," he commands hoarsely, his large hands groping around my back. Obeying his request, my pelvis moves, like there is an invisible thread being pulled from above, as he unzips my skirt and slides it off. He drags his tongue down my abdomen, and I gently caress his face, ready for him to pleasure me in ways I'd never experienced properly.

Until him.

Kissing my thigh, he lingers on my knee and then pulls up a chair. Sitting down, he studies me in contemplation, stroking my leg lovingly. I squeeze my lids shut and wait for him to do something. *Anything.*

The tentative touch of his fingernail dragging up and down my skin is maddening, and I clench my fists as he trails it with no rhyme or reason. Slowly walking his fingers towards up my inner thigh, I am on the verge of sitting up and punching him until a thick digit teases my core and I mellow.

"Oh!" I cry, relieved, my body writhing in tandem with my laboured breathing. "That's good."

Spreading my legs wider, he finally presses his talented lips to my apex. My fingers tighten on the edge of the desk as he continues to mouth at my centre, over the thin coating of satin and lace covering me. Sliding his tongue in and out, my eyes roll, and I push forward to meet him continuously.

My body is ready to explode in a ball of heady fire when the first sensation canters through me like wild horses, unbridled and free. Moaning out blissfully, he slows down. I attempt to shift, but his large hand holds me firmly in place.

"Just close your eyes and feel, angel," he murmurs against my highly-sensitised swollen folds, eliciting a delicious vibration with each word.

I squeeze my eyes, ready to feel as an agile thumb slips beneath my knickers, and he strums my clit. I instantly jerk upon contact, and my body curves to the heavens willingly. The sound of fabric stretching fills my eardrums, and a thick finger presses into me a fraction. My hips lift again, chasing it, wanting it deeper.

"Good?" he asks, and I disobey his wish and stare back into his eyes.

"Amazing," I confirm under his darkened gaze. Manoeuvring me further down the desk, his skilful hands stroke leisurely.

"More?"

I nod and gulp, moistening my dry mouth and throat. "Oh God, yes."

Caging me under him, he slaps his hand beside my head and slams his mouth over mine. The fight to feel is on as he grips the side of my face. Locking me in position, he pilfers my mouth and swallows my enthusiasm. His hand slides into my hair, tightening in pleasurable pain.

"Harder," I request.

He retreats an inch or so and gazes with serious intent. "I'm ex-army, angel, everything I do is hard," he replies with innuendo.

"Prove it," I challenge.

"With pleasure." Finally, my knickers are being pulled down my legs, and he reaffirms just how hard his pleasure can be.

Heady, on the verge of another release, his thumb rubs over my swollen, slick folds, and he thrusts a finger back inside my centre.

"I love you," he whispers, choosing this moment to confirm his feelings. It's something he does a lot, but I can't fault him. It's no secret that sex is different for women. We need it for closeness and completeness. For a woman, there is no such thing as no strings attached.

"And I love you," I whisper breathless, stroking my hand over the back of his neck and tasting him. My tongue glides around inside his mouth, while my hips flex in harmony with his.

Circumnavigating his finger rhythmically, he builds me up to eventually bring me back down. I guide my hand down his chest and stomach and slowly unbuckle his belt and combats. As I skim my hand inside, massaging his hard, ready shaft, he replaces one finger with two inside me.

"I want this inside me."

I slowly stroke the head, before fisting him hard, and every cell under my skin explodes in pure fire. Breathing audibly, it is nothing against the sound of his trousers hitting the floor. Withdrawing his fingers, he presses his engorged tip to my opening and slams in.

"Oh, fuck, that's good!" he growls out, building his rhythm. The desk sways as he fucks me hard, and I clench my thighs tighter around him in response, but he stops me. "Too much, angel. Too much. Let me..." He groans out again. Plunging back and forth inside my tight walls with flawless, unrivalled abandon, my body jolts against the wood.

I rise up from the desk, which is now creaking in protest beneath us, and curve my arm around his shoulder blade. My other hand reaches between us, and I touch myself possessively as he removes my satin bra.

"Come on, baby. Come for me." Framing and squeezing my breast in his hand, he sinks his teeth into my peak, deepening the rampant sensation culminating in my core. I slap one hand behind me, and pivot my hips back and forth, riding him towards intoxicating oblivion.

"Darling... Oh, God!" I call out. "Harder!"

He grabs my waist tight and slams in and out, giving me what I want, fucking me hard, as per my request. His expression begins to turn feral, unleashed, and he exposes his teeth as the start of his release begins. His fingers cut into my heated flesh as he pumps furiously, efficiently using my body to fuck himself.

"Fuck!" he grunts out, swelling inside me, stretching me further. "Let go, angel."

With my skin on fire and my body pulsating, I smile in ecstasy. I constrict my thighs around his hips, ready to come undone, when a buzzer blares through the building, masquerading my moans and the sound of naked flesh upon flesh.

"No!" I cry out, disbelieving what the fuck has just happened while my impending orgasm disappears at the speed of light.

"Son of a bitch!" John hollers as the buzzer resonates again.

Pulling out painfully, probably more him than me, he drags up his shorts and combats, and rushes around, picking up my discarded clothes.

217

Still sitting on the desk, I slide down as he pulls my knickers up my legs. Holding my skirt at my feet, he gives me a forlorn smile.

"Hands on my shoulders, beautiful," he says, identifying my unfinished, unsatisfied and unbalanced stance. I hold him tightly as he covers my legs and bum and fastens me up - all the while the buzzer resounds unremittingly.

"I swear, whoever is at that gate is going fucking die!" He picks up the phone behind me. "Hold the fuck on!" He then smashes it down and presses the button to activate the gate. "Come here, darling," he says, gently this time.

Watching his frustrated expression, I laugh, finding hilarity in the situation, regardless of how unfulfilled I currently am.

"It's not funny. I don't leave my woman unsatisfied. Ever!"

And isn't that the amazing, beautiful truth that every woman wants to hear. In the years we have been together, he would rather forego a hundred orgasms just to give me one. He's said as much – and performed as such.

He strokes his hands down my chest, gently adjusts the cups of my bra, and positions my breasts inside. I try to slap him away since every touch just reminds me I'm already at boiling point with no way to release the pressure.

Buttoning up my blouse, I quickly slide into my jacket and look around for my bag. Remembering John had thrown it onto the floor before this failed endeavour, I run out of the office and down the corridor.

I snatch it up as the creak of the lift fills the emptiness, and I run back like a bat out of hell. Whoever is in there can't see me like this – caught in a compromising position, *almost* thoroughly fucked and *still* thoroughly dissatisfied.

I slam the door and turn to John. His obvious arousal is undisguisable and doesn't look like it is going away anytime soon. Not that he cares.

"How do I look?" I query, desperate to calm my perspired, slick appearance. I doubt even Elizabeth Arden herself could cover it.

John turns from the door, scowling at whoever has interrupted his playtime, and smiles. "Like a woman who has come twice on my desk, but a third would've been fucking beautiful!"

He approaches and grips my shoulders while I cake powder over my face until it is shine free.

"Who is it?"

"Jeremy. Tell me again why I hired him again?" He grunts, unimpressed, and stokes his jaw as an impatient knock shakes the door. "Yes?" He calls out but doesn't invite him in.

Unfortunately, as with all the men in this little motley crew, the door opens, and Remy sticks his head around it. He is ready to open his mouth but seems *aware* as he looks from me to John, to the desk and then back again.

My face flushes with embarrassment. I'm old enough to be the man's mother, and he's standing there assessing me like I'm a horny teenager.

"Hi, Marie," he greets in a weird tone. I smile, my face and neck burning out of control in shame. "Sorry, I'm interrupting."

John crosses his arms over his chest and gives him an unimpressed glare. The door closes, and John begins to kiss me his apology when it opens again.

"Oh, for fuck sake!" John shouts.

"Sorry, M, you dropped these." Remy flings my stray post onto the cabinet and slams the door.

"Boundaries, sunshine!" John shouts in frustration.

"That's rich!" I chortle. "You wouldn't know boundaries if they came up and bit you on the arse."

He spins around in surprise and grabs me. "Darling, I'm gonna go and see what he wants, and when we get you home, it isn't my arse you need to be worried about!"

He kisses me hard, and his tongue makes good on his promise as he uses it proficiently to demonstrate what he's prepared to finish. I swear I'm ready to release the built-up tension in my womb with this kiss alone.

Pulling back, he strokes my face. "You're a stunning hue of pink. I'll get you some water, cool you off."

"A Screaming Orgasm would be better," I retort innocently, then approach the cabinet and pick up the wad of letters. Hot breath tickles my nape, and I turn.

"When I've dealt with this arsehole, I'm taking you home, and you'll get your screaming orgasm. Repeatedly. As many as you can handle, until you beg me to stop." Claiming my mouth, he slaps my rear hard, then saunters out of the room.

I shuffle back to the desk and flick through the letters. The penultimate one causes my heart rate to accelerate. Any desire I felt is quickly vanquished as I rip it open. Skimming the page, the invitation to call the sender breaks my heart.

With my hand over my mouth, John's familiar stride thuds back down the corridor. I fight back the impending tears, unable to allow him to see this unprovoked change, and stuff the letter into my bag.

In my haste, I accidentally activate my phone, and the screen shows two unrecognised missed calls. The first was at lunch, which I presumed was John. The second was sometime between then and now. Between the calls and letter, this isn't a coincidence. It can't be, she knows I've received it because I signed for it.

I compose myself as John strides back in. "Let's go home, angel." I force a tight smile as he picks up his wallet and keys. "You sure you're okay?" His eyes narrow in question.

"Hmm. What did Remy want?" I ask although I'm not sure I will get an answer. And if I do, do I really want to hear it?

"Woman trouble," he says, but there is no amusement in his tone. And inside I'm glad because while he mulls over the issues with his boys, it is less time he has to fix his concentration on me. Especially since the tide has now definitely turned out of my favour.

I march with purpose out of the building, desperate to feel cool air on my skin, more for secrets unknown than being left sexually hanging anymore.

Settling into the Range Rover, I deliberately stare out of the window. John's hand squeezes my knee reassuringly, and I put mine over it, countering his false security.

"Angel?"

"I'm fine, really," I lie in my most convincing tone, and stare ahead at nothingness until our house comes into view.

A chill blankets my limbs as I step inside. I clutch my bag tight because it carries the catalyst that will eventually bring about the burn. Yet I know it can't be concealed indefinitely, since the past I hide is now compromised.

I look around the hallway and see it through different eyes. One day, this house and the man I love within it may no longer be my home.

A simple letter, one written from the heart with the best intentions, will be my unescapable downfall. It has shifted the axis that my carefully crafted world balances on, and now time is running out.

Maggie's letter is the beginning of the end.

Chapter 21

PICKING UP THE latest letter, which landed on my office desk yesterday, I slam it back down on the kitchen table.

It has been two weeks since the first letter arrived, and a week since the second. This is the third, and unlike the one last week, this one also came with another missed call yesterday.

I pull out a chair and slump into it like a lead weight, still wondering how she found me. Notwithstanding corrupt officials and those with connections, no one knows where I am. As far as most records are concerned, I no longer exist. The girl I was is gone.

Vanished without a trace.

I bury my face in my hands and stare at the paper. Calling her is the right thing to do, but I can't because she is an integral part of a past that broke me.

My finger taps against the dormant screen as I spin my mobile on the table. I glance up at the clock, wondering if I have enough time to make the call. And if I do manage to speak to her, what do I say?

Dialling the number, I wait for her to answer. I school the words inside my head, but *'sorry I haven't spoken to you in over two decades,'* or, *'how have you been? Want to meet up and chat about the good old times?'* probably isn't going to cut it.

"Hello?"

My eyes close in shame, hearing her voice after all these years. She still sounds the same, older, familiar, but the same.

"Hello?"

When I can't get my words out, my tears begin to flow. Covering my mouth, to mute my distress, she speaks again in panic.

"Marianne?"

"Maggie," I whisper and hang up.

Seconds later it starts to ring, and the sound is parallel to a warning siren in the silence. My body remains frozen in place until it rings off and a beep resounds. I inhale, harden my disposition, and with a shaky hand, I listen to the voicemail.

"Marianne, I'm delighted you called. I know you don't want to talk to me, but please call me back. I love you. I never stopped loving you, and right now, I need you. I need you so much. Please call me."

The timid, tearful message ends, and I toss the phone down. Splaying my hands over the table, I bend and press my cheek to the wood.

Two weeks ago, I was wrong. Her letter wasn't the beginning of the end. With her voice still ringing inside my head, hearing the three syllables again and again, as she spoke my real name for the first time in twenty-three years, it takes me back to the day the end really began.

It is a day I will forever regret because it was a choice I wasn't knowingly old enough to make.

At sixteen, I made the ultimate decision that will haunt me until the day I die. It was the day I decided teenage lust was worth more than my virtue. And when any girl loses her so-called virtue, there is only ever one reason behind it.

A boy.

Feeling out of body, having just taken the first real step back into my past, the kitchen begins to spin in front of me. Everything in the present fades to black, and the past returns with a vicious bite.

"Please, Dad, no!"

His hand slaps my face hard as my mother screams in the background. Cowering under the hatred of my father's glare, I know I deserve to be punished, but I don't deserve physical violence. Not like this.

"You've brought shame upon this family!" my father hisses, raising his hand again. I bring my own up to shield what could turn into a second blow, but instead, he turns and grips his hips, huffing and puffing. I stare until he spins back around and grabs me by my jaw.

"You're hurting me!" I cry out.

"You will not see him again, Marianne! I forbid it!"

"Please, you don't-"

The second, sharp slap to my face stings beyond belief, and I sway under the force as my knees buckle beneath me. I clutch my cheek and scramble back until my spine becomes one with the sideboard behind me.

My father's six-foot frame towers over me menacingly; his face furious, his fists rounded.

But this isn't the first time I have sat in this very spot, nursing injuries he has inflicted over the years. The first time was when I spilt nail polish on the carpet. The second was when I refused to go to church, and the third was when I got a C in science. And those are just the start. The last time he hit me, was when he found out.

Tearful, waiting for the monster to turn again, his heavy, nasal breathing eases, and he pads up and down in front of me.

"I mean it, Marianne. The last thing I ever expected was for you to become involved with someone like him!" he bellows.

"You don't even know him!" *I instantly regret it as his fury makes a slight return. Looking down at my lap, I curl my fingers into my palms.*

"He's from a good family, Daddy," *I say, hoping to appease him. Yet, I know that is impossible since the rumours making waves about the good judge's son are mostly founded. In truth, he is the quintessential bad boy his reputation claims him to be. And like any teenage girl with unrequited lust and hormonal tendencies, I'm immune from staying away like I have been told. God knows I've tried, but after sixteen years of growing up in this house, the allure to feel something akin to love is greater than pleasing my father and his judgemental flock.*

"That's debatable!" *Dad hisses.* "Tomorrow, you will tell him you are not allowed to see him again. And if I find out otherwise, there will be ramifications. Understand?"

I slowly look up at him. And with my heart breaking and my soul floundering, I nod.

"I. Can't. Hear. You!"

"Yes, Daddy," *I murmur, defeated.* "I'll tell him I can't see him anymore."

"Now go to your room!"

Picking myself up off the floor, my tears blind my way as I run out of the living room and up the stairs. I slam my bedroom door, and slap my hands against it, mournful for love I'm desperate to experience. And for love I've lost before it has even begun.

I throw myself onto the bed as my door opens and closes quietly, and then the mattress dips behind me. Rolling over, Maggie strokes her fingers over my tender cheek.

"I'm sorry, Marianne," *she says remorseful, and I tug her closer.*

"It's not your fault," *I whisper.* "He wants me to be like you."

As I stare into her eyes, we both know it's true. Over the years, especially when we hit puberty, he always wanted me to be more like Maggie; a good girl, one who walks the line and obeys as she is supposed to. Except, I'm not like her. I never have been, and I never will be – regardless that we are indistinguishable standing side by side.

When we were younger, no one could ever tell us apart. It's the downfall of being a twin, an identical one at that. With our blue eyes, blonde hair, identical features and even our mannerisms, there is nothing about us that you can separate. And while we share the same DNA and blood running through our veins, our daydreams and ideas are as far apart as can be.

She is the focussed to my flighty. The logical to my lustful. I think with my heart while she uses her head. And if I was more like her, I wouldn't be here now, feeling sorry for myself again.

"That's not true," Maggie says uncomfortably. "Don't say things like that. I love you. You'll always be amazing to me." Holding each other close, she strokes my sore cheek. "He really hurt you this time, didn't he?"

'Yeah,' I mouth, but don't dare say it out loud.

She sighs and pulls the duvet over us. Watching her nose and cheeks twitch, I narrow my eyes.

"What?" I ask quietly.

"What's it like?"

"What's what like?"

"To be held and looked at. To be wanted... by a boy." The silence grows between us, until she says, "What's it like to be kissed? I mean, really kissed."

With her wide-eyed anticipation, I recognise the symptoms of her loneliness. The symptoms of an undeniable urge to feel, to touch. And the symptoms of which I momentarily found a cure.

"It's nice. Warm, soft. Tantalising." A tingling tightens in my belly, just thinking about the way it feels. Maggie nods and touches her finger to my lips.

"I can't wait to be kissed," she says, her voice tipped with longing. "Or to be touched. To have a boy..." She drops her eyes, embarrassed. "Have you...done...anything?" She leaves the question hanging between us, and I squirm, uncertain how to answer.

"Just a little touching," I respond, entirely uncomfortable. Something in her eye glints and she sucks in her bottom lip.

"Have you done it?" she asks more firmly.

"No," I reply truthfully. As much as Joe and I have messed around, a little kissing here, a little fondling there, I'm still a virgin.

"Will you?"

I shrug in response, but the answer is yes. It is a natural progression once the boundary of my clothing has been breached. Not that I'm going to tell her that. She can make of my 'touching' confession what she will, but to divulge any further is a line I'm not willing to cross. She's still Daddy's favourite, not that she would tell on me, but I can't risk wedging her between a rock and a hard place any more than I already have.

"Are you going to do what Dad ordered?"

I sigh. I know what I should do, what I must do, but I know what I want to do.

"I don't know," I admit.

"I won't tell him anything, you know. You do whatever it takes to be happy. Whole. Loved."

I close my eyes, and realise deep down, she is as flighty and free-spirited as I am, but too afraid to act upon impulse and impetus.

And after tomorrow, I won't be acting on either when I tell Joe I can't see him anymore.

Fussing with my sundress, the bells toll loud overhead, drowning out the birdsong, practically deafening me. My hair blows in the breeze, my long strands lifting, while the refreshing draughts wrap around my bare legs.

I look over the churchyard as my father plays the good vicar of impeccable virtue, conversing with the other parishioners.

My eyes flit between the patrons until they latch onto Joe's gleaming red sports car, parked on the side of the road – a present from his godfather since he wrote off the one his parents gave him for his eighteenth a few months ago.

Excitement makes me giddy, but I tilt my head, allowing my hair to cloak my troublesome teenage eyes, and the way I cannot seem to control their drifting towards the forbidden.

I watch inconspicuously as the boy who is the current cause of my belly flutters climbs out of the car and props his long, lean body against the bonnet. He runs his hand through his dark, floppy hair, then folds his arms over his chest, accentuating his developing biceps and shoulders. I lick my lips involuntarily, unable to halt my reaction to him.

These days, he is more man than the boy I first talked to when I was fourteen, and he was sixteen. And boy, isn't that pleasing to my rampant, defiant hormones.

Joe crooks his finger, but I shake my head and mouth 'I can't'. Unperturbed, he shrugs and grins until his attention is caught by someone approaching.

Anger wells inside as Lucy, one of the parishioner's daughter's, strolls towards him. While I admit I'm beyond control as far as my emotions go, I'm nowhere near as obvious as she is.

I clench my fists the moment she strokes up and down his arm. He smirks, thoroughly enjoying her attention until her father calls her and she hurries away.

I bite my lip as I catch his gaze. His brow perks up, and he crooks his fingers to come over, but instead, I walk solemnly into church, feeling hurt and betrayed.

I slide into my usual seat at the end of the pew in the back row. My father glares when Maggie defies convention and joins me for the first time ever.

Her hand grips mine, and I squeeze it tight as my father takes his place at the pulpit, facing the congregation.

With his voice filling the room, I twitch in my seat. I can honestly say, sitting here in the house of God, I've never felt comfortable. This place has never held hope for me. It's a place that I've been forced to attend week after week, year after year. And while I do believe in God, I don't believe in the sanctimonious crap my father forces down my throat.

As I stare straight ahead, gauging how many more years of this I must endure until I'm free, the keystroke of the organ begins. My mind wanders, yet my mouth opens, knowing all the words of the hymn. Two verses in, I gasp when someone squeezes my elbow.

"Hi," Joe whispers cockily. His light brown hair is highlighted from the sun penetrating the stained-glass windows, and he runs his hand through it lazily.

"Go away. You'll get me in trouble!" I hiss out because I really don't need any more of that.

"Trouble is my middle name. It's yours, too. Last week in my car proved it!" My mouth falls open at his crassness, but he doesn't care. "Hi, Maggie!" he continues, causing her cheeks to blush beautifully.

"Hi." She smiles shyly, failing to concentrate the way we both should be right now, not being distracted by boys who I have sworn to stay away from.

I fix my focus front and centre until a hand drifts up from my ankle to my knee, causing a far too pleasant sensation to snake through me. I squeeze my legs together instinctively but ignoring him is impossible. And it's obvious my sister is also not immune as she giggles and taps my arm.

"Go. I'll tell Dad you felt sick."

I gawk at her, wondering why she is lying for me, assisting in my inevitable sinning.

"I can't!"

"Yes, you can. Go!" Leaning into me, she whispers, "Live, love, experience – for both of us." I kiss her cheek, then turn to Joe, but he has already gone.

I rise slowly and peek at my father, whose head is in the Bible, reciting his beloved scripture. Slapping my hand over my stomach for effect, I carefully walk out, methodical in my movements of my fake, instantaneous sickness.

I jog down the steps and look around, not seeing Joe's car where it was earlier. The rumble of an engine disrupts the quiet Sunday morning, and I dash out of the graveyard to see him gunning his car down the road. He slams to a stop directly in front of me and leans over to open the passenger door.

"Get in, gorgeous. It's time for a proper ride." His tone is suspicious, and I bite my lip. I know I shouldn't be doing this, but it feels good to be bad.

No sooner have I slid into the passenger seat and shut the door, the tyres squeal under his heavy right foot as he speeds off.

I gaze out of the window, my mind in turmoil as he strokes my knee. I shuffle, agitated, whilst that unspeakable tingling reawakens again.

"Okay?" he asks, but I can only nod. His hand continues to glide higher on my leg, and I grip the seat, trying to urge myself to stop reacting.

Ten minutes later, we pull up at his house, and I follow him inside the imposing property. Movement down the hallway piques my attention, and a door opens.

"Oh, you've got company," Patricia, Joe's mother, says with indifference and closes the door. I haven't seen her that much since we started seeing each other, but she hasn't changed since the first time in the park four years ago. She's still cold and heartless – at least towards Joe, anyway.

Joe scowls and turns with one foot on the stairs. "Ignore her. Come on."

He holds out his hand, and I stare at it, knowing if I go up there something in our relationship is going to change. And I understand exactly what that change is going to be seeing as I've never been in his room before.

"Are you scared?"

"No," I lie and follow him. I gulp in fear when he stops outside a door.

"We won't do anything you don't want to. But if you do, I'll make you feel terrific." His hand slides over my cheek, caressing the slight bruise I've tried to cover, and he presses his lips to mine. I moan into his mouth as he opens the door and tugs me inside.

Trepidation eats away at me as I glance around his possessions.

"Want one?" Joe asks as he fiddles with a roll up and I shake my head no.

I dawdle at the foot of the bed and trail my hand over the duvet. At two years older than me, I know he is experienced. I've heard the rumours of how many girls he's already been with. I've also heard stories of his so-called treatment towards them. But since he has always been gentle and sweet with me, I have trouble believing them.

Joe's arm slides around my front, and he rests his chin on my shoulder. "I want you, Marianne. From the first time I saw you, I've wanted you. Those other girls didn't mean anything to me. I was always waiting for you."

I turn around to see the lust and determination in his eyes. The second I nod, he slides his fingers beneath the straps of my dress. I automatically clutch the front because as much as I want him, I've never done this before.

"I'm scared," I whisper, practically tearful.

"Don't be," he replies gently. "I'd never hurt you." Palming my cheek, my fear is overtaken by the incessant need to feel. Intimately. My hands slacken on the fabric, and it falls away, leaving me uncovered, giving him the first view of my chest.

227

"Shit. You're stunning, baby," he says, his eyes dark, his breathing heavy as he holds out my arm to study me. He grins, his eyes still roaming before he pulls his t-shirt over his head revealing his slightly muscled torso.

"Tell me you want it. Tell me you want me to touch you."

I bite my lip, the reality finally hitting home, and I cover my chest with my hand.

"Joe, I-I-" I shake my head and quickly scoop up my dress, desperate to cover myself. I won't lie; I do want him, and all those things that are forbidden, but I don't know how to do this. I worry my lip, thinking he will laugh.

"Shush," he murmurs and rubs my shoulders. *"I understand. I know it is your first time."*

His head lowers, and he kisses me. His slow tenderness eventually becomes raw need, and he gathers my hair and wraps it around his hand, coercing my head back. *"God, I love this long fucking hair."*

Enraptured by the moment, my body experiencing what it feels like to be touched for the first time, I acquiesce. *"Just touching. For now."*

I slip my fingers into his and position his hand on my chest. He bends down and smashes his mouth to mine. Forcing his tongue inside, he possesses me brutally as he grips my flesh to the point of pain. I whimper the instant he rolls my nipple over my bra, and my body weakens, as a fantastic tremor seeps through me.

"Oh!" I cry out.

"Feel good?"

I moan in response, unable to articulate as an ache culminates between my legs.

"I can make you feel even better."

His words quickly transport me from the aftershock of my first real orgasm, and I stare wide-eyed. *"Joe, I-"*

"Just touching, I promise." He lulls his head and gives me a coy expression. It's one that should leave me frightened, but in my state of first time bliss, I'm ignorant to the little voice in the back of my head, screaming at me to end this. *"Trust me?"*

His fingers stroke my chest again, and I nod, too far gone to see my own stupidity.

"Yes," I whisper as I lie down on his bed. He grins at me as he opens the bedside drawer, tosses a condom on the pillow and then joins me.

I bite my lip in apprehension as the minute's tick by. Eventually, he reaches around my back and removes my bra. Pinning my arms out wide on the bed, he kisses the upper swell of my flesh, and I shudder in delight at the first touch of my bare nipple.

"Hmm, I wonder what else you'd like?" he queries, his smirk bordering on cruel. Sliding his flat palm down my belly, his other hand tilts my face to him as he tugs at my knicker band.

"Want me to make you feel good again?"

I nod, licking my lips. I shouldn't, but God, I want to feel that again.

"Say yes."

Wrapping my hand around his head, I pull him lower until his lips to mine. "Yes," I say in a heavy breath.

No sooner have the words been aired, he drags down my underwear. Touching me intimately for the first time, I dig my fingers into his shoulder.

"God, you feel amazing. I love you, Marianne. Do you trust me?"

"I trust you," I murmur.

And upon that foolish declaration, those three little words carried away any common sense I had remaining.

I jolt up and rub my forehead, my memories inundated.

Still, I wasn't wrong all those years ago, something did change that day. Something that shouldn't have, but I couldn't stop it. When you are so far over the edge, logic and reason flies out of the window. Along with something else I would never get back.

My virtue.

I inhale deeply as the words that have haunted me from the first moment I spoke them repeat over and over.

I trust you.

They were the words of a naïve fool who didn't know any different.

They were the words of a teenage girl who was desperate to feel.

Ultimately, they are the words I will regret until the day I die.

The front door opens and closes, and heavy boots clip down the hallway.

"Hey, beautiful," John says as he enters. "You've been crying." His eyes hold mine as he twists me around.

"I'm fine. I'm just remembering things," I murmur, drying my cheeks with the back of my hand.

He nods, although his expression is unconvinced. His lips press the top of my head as he picks me up and carries me up the stairs.

Standing in the bedroom, he strips us both slowly and holds out his hand. "Trust me?"

I edge towards him and press my face into his chest, calming myself in the rhythm of his heartbeat.

"I trust you," I whisper.
And in my life, no truer words have ever been said.

Chapter 22

I ROTATE ON my heels in the middle of the bathroom – one of three in this sumptuous, split level, five-bedroom, Belgravia apartment – and gaze in awe at the three shower heads over a bath big enough for two.

"Holy shit," I mutter, intimated by the grandeur. I reach out my hand but pull it back, thinking twice about touching anything in case I smudge the pristine finish.

The combined voices of the overenthusiastic estate agent and Miss Moneybags, talking prices and chattels, drifts in from the adjoining bedroom.

Taking a final look at the splendour, amazed at what the other half can afford, I leave the room.

As I enter the bedroom, Mr Collins, the agent, smiles at me with such zeal it makes me wonder if he thinks I'm his next sale commission.

Hardly likely.

Taking a peek at the glossy brochure in my hand, proudly displaying the seven-figure sum of this apartment, even the sale of my house - after redemption - wouldn't even cover one per cent of the deposit.

"So, what do you think?" Mr Collins asks, flailing his arms wide in true salesman style.

"I think it's incredible, but I'm not the one you need to be convincing."

I tip my head to Jules, who is dallying in the doorway, looking conflicted. She has worn this expression all morning, throughout various viewings of properties that cost millions of pounds each. I give her an encouraging lift of my brows, then leave her to her procrastination.

Walking the perimeter of the master bedroom, I open the wardrobe doors and cheekily check out some labels. Yep, whoever owns this place is wealthy beyond belief. As I close the doors, Jules jerks her head to the landing, and I follow her out.

"Thoughts?" I ask, as I smile back at Mr Collins, whose expression has gone from 'I've just hit the commission jackpot' to 'oh, shit, I need to try harder with this one'.

"I love it!"

I chortle. "At last! So why do you look so unimpressed?"

"Because..."

"It's too ostentatious? Too OTT? Surely it can't be too expensive!" I say flippantly, reining in my amusement.

Her head lolls to the side, and she gives me a look that could eviscerate me on the spot. Grabbing hold of my arm, she drags me through the hallway and down the stairs into the kitchen.

"Jules, what's wrong?" I ask as I lean against the units, waiting for her to speak.

She swivels around from the French doors that lead out into a small, high walled courtyard. "I'll tell you what's wrong. Since you abandoned me to mosey around..." Her head bobs comically. "That rude little man has been stuck to me like a fly on shit! If his hands wander near my arse again, my next home will be a prison cell!"

"He's just anxious for a sale... And maybe a wealthy woman. Besides, it wasn't so long ago you *were* desperate."

"I'm not that desperate!"

"Liar! We should ask him if he has a wife, that way you can kill two birds with one stone and stop trying to live vicariously through me." I grin, finally getting one up on her.

"Not funny, lady. He's a leech. Honestly, what do you think?"

"It's stunning. Truly. Are you going to make an offer?" I ask, repeating the same question I've asked at every other viewing today.

"Hmm, I think I am. I can see myself living here. I can see us right now, sitting out there with the sun shining while I ply you with alcohol." She smiles wickedly, and her lips pucker like a duck.

"You're wishful thinking," I retort.

"We'll see! Right, I think I'm going to go and make Mr Collins' day," she says ecstatically.

I give her a small smile, but I can't share her joy since I'm still waiting to hear about my own sale. It's been weeks, and neither I nor my solicitor, have heard a peep. I know I should call Veronica, but I'm not sure my sanity can take it if she tells me the buyers have pulled out again.

My eyes shift, and I catch Jules' frown. "Have you still not heard anything?"

I shake my head. "I dare not call her."

"To hell with that! I'll ring that useless cow for you. She can't just leave you hanging and then be all smiles and pleasantries when she wants that frigging invoice paying!"

"I know," I whisper, bracing myself to ring her at some point this week. Or maybe next...

"M?"

"Hmm?" I blink, casting aside the saga that is the sale of my once beloved money pit.

"I'm going to have another look around, and then have a chat with the agent."

I pat her arm and smile. "Okay," I say as the soft ring of my mobile leaks from my bag. Fishing it out, my eyes narrow as 'Private Number' flashes over the screen. "I really need to take this. Work," I tell her.

"You're always bloody working!" She strides out of the kitchen, and I lift my mobile to my ear as her steps fade.

"Hello?" I answer, my eyes trained on the doorway.

"Can I speak to Marie Dawson, please?" I gasp, recognising his voice as clear as the first time I heard it.

"Adrian? Oh, God." The words tumble over my thick tongue. I'm both shocked and relieved he has finally called. His timing is shit, of course. Not that any other time would be more convenient, but still. "I wasn't expecting you to call me back."

He sighs over the line. "No. Trust me, I wasn't going to. But I figured since this is only the second time you've ever rung me, it must be important," he drawls.

"It is," I stress, and rush to the door to see if Jules or Mr Collins are anywhere near. Hearing their faint voices echo, I dare to ask the only question that matters. "Where's-"

"No." He cuts me off sharply.

"No?" I reply, confused. "I haven't even asked anything yet."

"I know what you're going to ask. I've anticipated this call for a very long time."

"Please, Adrian, I wouldn't ask if it wasn't important." The desperation in my tone is apparent, but I'm not above begging if I have to.

"I know that, but why are you asking?"

"Because I've been receiving stuff."

"What do you mean by 'stuff'?"

"Divorce papers, ribbons, pictures. Where is he, Adrian?" I ask, firm, unwavering. My fingers clench my mobile, waiting for him to respond.

"Marie, I'm not legally allowed to discuss him with you. Nor am I at liberty to divulge his whereabouts."

My foot shakes, and my legs suddenly weaken. "So, that's it? I'm just supposed to sit tight and see what happens? Wait for him to one day show up at my door and finish what he started? Will you finally believe me when *I'm* dead at the bottom of the stairs?" I hiss quietly.

"Now you're just being dramatic. You don't even know if it's him."

Dramatic? Of all the words he could have used, that was the last thing I ever expected to leave his mouth, especially if he remembers how we first met. I wasn't being dramatic then.

I shake my head furiously. "No, I'm not, and it is. I'm unfinished business. He said as much in the cemetery that day."

"Marie, he isn't going to show up. For all he knows, you're still in Peterborough."

I let out an incredulous laugh. "No." I rub my forehead. "He knows I'm here. The bastard sent me a bunch of dead flowers, for fuck sake! He sent them to my *home*. He knows exactly where I am!" My voice is rising, and it's taking everything I have to keep my temper in check.

"That's impossible."

"It's not when you consider who his father is."

The line stays silent for an uncomfortable length of time until he eventually breathes in.

"Look, I'll see what I can find out, but my position still stands; I can't tell you anything. However, if you do keep receiving *stuff*, you need to report it down there and give them my name. That's the best offer I can give you, and the only one you're going to get."

"Well, that offer isn't good enough. I'm sorry I bothered you. I won't call again." Ready to hang up, his words stop me.

"That, I fail to believe. You only call when you want something. Years ago, you called me to sort out your runaway's fake ID, which I'll remind you I could have lost my job if anyone knew. I'm starting to think it's a Turner woman trait – call Adrian if you need something. Pile on the guilt, play on his conscience, he'll tell you whatever you need to know!"

"What do you mean?" I ask, furrowing my brow.

"I mean, I've had your mother calling me over the years, trying to track you down, and then last year Maggie called me out of the blue. How long has it been since you last spoke to them?"

I sway on the spot and cover my mouth as tears amass in my eyes. "Twenty-three years," I whisper, ashamed of the awful truth.

"You haven't spoken to them since you left?" he asks, shocked. "Why? What did they ever do to deserve that? They love you. They never stopped loving you!" His anger penetrates my sensitive eardrums, forcing me to remember.

"I couldn't," I say, breaking down. "My father-"

"Fuck your father! You know when Maggie called me, she didn't ask where you were, she asked if you were dead."

The acid in my stomach curdles at the unnecessary pain I have put her and my mother through all these years.

"I really think you should call her," he says obstinately. "Sooner rather than later."

"Why? What do you know, Adrian? I've had the Salvation Army chasing me, and then Maggie called me - *at home* - pretending to be a client, asking for a bloody reunion. Now she's writing me letters, begging for contact. I don't even know how she got my details!" But something inside tells me I do know because his silence is speaking volumes.

"Don't hate me, but I gave her your number. I gave her your address, too."

"When?" I ask through gritted teeth.

"When, what?"

"When did you give her my address?"

"Last year."

I pinch the bridge of my nose, my composure coming undone.

"I don't believe this. You can't tell me anything about Joseph, but you can give my information out to all and sundry when you're technically not at liberty to? You bastard! What gives you the fucking right?" I demand as a new awareness weighs heavy in my heart. "What do you know that you're not telling me, Adrian?"

He sighs. "I know enough to realise if you don't speak to her, you'll forever regret it. Do the right thing at long last - call her. Beg for forgiveness, but don't just ignore her. It will haunt you forever if you do."

I want to laugh. I have enough ghosts haunting me already; I don't have room for any more.

A rustling of papers seeps down the line. "Have you got a pen?" Grudgingly, I dig into my bag for my notebook. Jotting down the number, I'm fucking furious. I can't even begin to decipher what I'm feeling right now.

"Make it right with her, Marie, because you might not get another chance."

"Okay, I'll call her – on one condition."

"And what is that?" he asks knowingly.

"You tell me where that bastard is. This isn't a game. I need to know."

"No. Blackmail doesn't work on me. I won't be guilted into committing further acts that could affect my family. Remember, if anything happens, call nine nine nine. Goodbye, Marie."

"Adrian? Adrian!" The dead tone rings in my ears, and I slam the phone on the worktop.

Spying the knives in the block, it would be so easy to end it all now. And it wouldn't be the first time I've had suicidal thoughts. I drop my head into my hands as my unshed tears sting. Halting the first before it falls is worthless because it's just one more in the damn tsunami that is yet to spill.

"That's great, Mr Collins!" Jules' voice leaks into the room.

I quickly stuff my notebook and mobile into my bag and wipe my cheeks. I straighten and smile as she approaches me.

"Are you ready to go?"

"Sure." Linking her arm in mine, we walk down the stairs. Mr Collins leads the way, gushing relentlessly about the property – clearly forgetting he has a confirmed cash buyer just two feet behind him.

Standing on the pavement, Jules nudges me. "What are you doing for the rest of the day?"

"Nothing. Why?"

She winks and grins. "I think we need to celebrate. We need shopping, we need shoes, and we need wine. Lots and lots of wine! Come on, we'll stick it on the hotel tab and get George to take you home later."

I deliberate her proposition but ultimately agree. I know she'll ply and pry, but she can force feed me as much vino as she likes because nothing seems better right now than drinking away the harsh reality of a call that's left me in limbo.

Three hours and countless glasses of wine later, the hotel bar is beginning to look fuzzy around the edges.

Sitting at a table in the middle of the room, surrounded by a multitude of shopping bags, I lean forward. Unable to control my giggles, I place down my glass with a heavy hand, sloshing wine over the top.

"It's this big!" I grin, thoroughly pissed, focussing intently on my hands as I expand the gap in between them. Jules sits opposite, lounging, almost horizontal.

"And?" She nods, urging me on.

In some far-flung part of my grey matter, a little voice is goading me joyously that she's done it again. What? I have no idea, but shopping and wine – lots and lots of wine – was the best suggestion she's had in ages. I haven't felt this weightless or carefree in... Well, forever.

"And what?" I ask, pouting fondly at my glass.

"And how good is it?"

I smile, dreamily. "Very! It's very, very good!" I say proudly because it is!

She sighs. "I'm so jealous. I want very, very good. I'll be lucky if I get very, very bad again before I die!"

I shrug and down the remaining wine in my glass. "I might die from it!" I blurt out, not thinking since my brain cells stopped functioning correctly around two hours ago. I should've also stopped drinking about an hour ago – around about the time I stopped feeling movement in my face.

"Is it me or is it hot in here?" Jules queries as she tugs her blouse and fans herself.

"It's you." I scrunch up my nose and grab the bottle. Holding it up, something's not right. I upend it over my glass, thoroughly disappointed when only four drops dribble out.

"Who drunk all the wine?" I narrow my eyes in accusation at her. She waves her hand in the air like the Queen to attract the waiter's attention.

"Two bottles of merlot, please." Eyeballing me, I shake my head. "No? Make that three!" she says. "Charge it to the penthouse. Thank you ever so much!" she says appreciatively.

"Yes, of course, Mrs Emerson," the waiter replies with an uncomfortable expression.

I'd like to say what number bottle we are on, but I can't. I lost count somewhere between two and four.

Ten minutes later, the man returns, places the bottles down and scurries away. I grab one keenly but screw my face up when I see cork bits floating inside the neck.

"Shit," I mutter, but all is not lost as I spy the other two. I reach out for the second, eagerly fill my glass and stand, albeit a bit wobbly. Raising my arm high, I suddenly have the best idea in the world.

"A toast! Here's to expensive properties, handsy estate agents, arsehole detectives and bastard ex-husbands!"

"Hallelujah!" Jules cheers and downs half her glass. Shuffling in her seat, she tugs at her blouse again, and the buttons pop open. "God, it's not good being menopausal. I think it's getting hotter!"

"Drink more wine," I advise logically. With the glass to my lips, I smile and look around at the other patrons casting us curious stares. "Jules?"

"Yeah?" she shouts, causing the elderly lady at the next table to jerk in shock.

"Everyone's looking at us."

Jules' glazed eyes drift around the room, and she makes a show of pursing her lips at whoever dares to look our way. Tossing back her strawberry blonde mane, she waves her hand dismissively.

"Let them look. My family own this hotel, and I can do whatever the hell I like! And if *they* don't like it, they can drink elsewhere."

I nod slowly in agreement while a few guests heed her advice and leave. Reaching for the bottle again, I accidentally knock it over and watch in intoxicated horror as wine sloshes out in a red waterfall.

"For goodness sake!" the elderly woman hisses. She looks distraught, and I move closer, seeing spots of red on her cream skirt.

"Oh, I'm so sorry!" I drawl repentantly, as I rise from my seat, grab her skirt and rub it together. "It might wash out."

"Don't touch me!" the woman shouts, and I stand back and suck on my bottom lip, watching her rush out of the bar.

Okay then.

Sitting back down, I reach for the bottle again – slowly this time, because it's a sin to waste good wine – and pour another glass. As I lift it to my lips, Jules' eyes bulge.

"Oh! We've got company!" she announces gleefully.

"Who?" I ask, leaning back to look, but quickly right myself when the room starts to spin.

James, the hotel manager, strides towards us. He doesn't look happy, but I smile anyway because he's brought Sloan and John. Grinning like a Cheshire cat, I push out my chest, because John likes my breasts. I know this for a fact because he likes to use his tongue…

"What the hell are you both doing?" Sloan snaps quietly, standing in front of us with his hands on his hips.

I smile broadly at him because I do love my son-in-law. I love that he loves my Kara and my Oliver. I love that he loves my John, too, but he doesn't love him as much as I do.

"Sloan!" I hail, swaying where I sit. He glares at us, fuming, then looks around the room in anger. He can't be embarrassed – we're not that drunk.

"Sloan! Come and give your mother a kiss!" Jules offers, her chair falling back as she reaches for him.

I smile proudly, but James covers his face with his hand and rushes around to pick up the chair. Jules slaps her hand on his shoulder and digs her fingers in.

"Good afternoon, James! Have you been working out?"

"Hello, Mrs Emerson. I think it's time you ladies called it a day."

"Why?" she asks with her hand on her chest, tugging at her clothing again.

Sloan's eyes take on an evil glint, and he removes his jacket. "Cover yourself up, mother!" he demands, slinging the jacket around her.

I turn to John and stumble towards him as the room starts to spin again. I might be three – okay, six – sheets to the wind, but I'm still aware.

Sort of.

"Having a good time?" John queries, his voice hard, his expression sour.

"Amazing! We're celebrating!" I tell him. Catching my bottom lip with my teeth, I concentrate hard, until I remember what we are celebrating. "Expensive properties, arsehole police and bastard ex-husbands!" I count them off on my fingers. "Oh, and I'm going to yoga!"

His mouth compresses tight. "I see." Leaning into me, he yanks me closer. "When we get home, we're going to be celebrating something else," he adds darkly.

"Oh?"

Fantastic! Drunken sex the Walker way is out of this world.

239

"How many times I can spank your arse for doing this!"

Or maybe not.

"Let's go!"

He grabs my arm and jostles me out of the bar before I can even say goodbye. Marching us through the foyer and out of the hotel, a porter opens his Range Rover door, and John picks me up and lobs me onto the passenger seat. Blinking rapidly, slowly pulling over the belt, the other door opens. Patting down my legs, I remember.

"Darling, I left my shopping and my bag," I say, attempting to get out.

His jaw grinds, and he grabs my knee and then holds up my bag and throws it into the back. Daring to turn around, his anger is sobering a small spot in my brain. The car engine roars, and I close my droopy eyes and reminisce.

I jolt awake, tired and still inebriated, as the door opens. My stomach flips when John bundles me into his arms and carries me into the house. Tossing me onto the bed, I crawl into a ball.

"Marie?"

Lifting my heavy head, he stands there, furious, and I roll my eyes, feeling myself sobering up.

"Marie!"

I nuzzle my face into the pillow and groan. "Leave me alone, I just want to sleep."

"Well, tough shit, baby. That little fucking stunt you and Jules pulled isn't funny. I've never been so embarrassed in my life. People in that bar are regulars! It's humiliating that James had to call Sloan out of a meeting because his mother and mother-in-law were busy getting sloshed at three o'clock in his hotel. I never, ever thought you would stoop that low!"

I sit up quickly, hear something rip and open my mouth.

"Low? Oh, I'm sorry, but I think I'm entitled to get drunk once in a while and forget about all the shit I have to deal with!"

"You picked the best fucking place to do it! And what shit are you talking about? You deal in pastries and hors d'oeuvres. The only worry you have is curdled cream and stale bread!"

I see red, clamber off the bed, and get in his face. "Is that really what you think? You have no idea! At least Jules listens impartially. It's more than you ever would."

His jaw tightens, and he glowers. "Well, you'd know if you tried, but you don't tell me shit!"

"And this is why! You know what? I don't give a fuck because nothing matters anymore. *Nothing!*" My resolve snaps, and I burst into tears. "Get out! Just get the fuck out!" I scream and point at the door.

"Angel, stop," he says softly, shaking his head.

"I'm no goddamn angel. I'm a fucking sinner, the biggest one walking! Now get the fuck out!"

Inhaling with controlled precision, he rubs his nape, slowly walks backwards and out of the door. I throw myself back on to the bed, curl up in a protective ball and cry myself to sleep.

"Marie?" The little voice grows more persistent inside my head. "Marie?"

I groan groggily, still relatively numb and completely hungover. "I'm asleep," I mumble.

The mattress shifts, causing my body to roll and my empty stomach to do somersaults. Familiar arms tuck me into their hold, and as they rock me from side to side, lips caress my temple.

"I'm sorry, angel. If I promise to stay calm, will you tell me what happened today?"

I shift around, graze my hand over his five o'clock shadow and stroke his jaw. His thumb brushes under my eye, abrading the tear-stained skin.

"No, it's not that easy. And I didn't mean to embarrass you or Sloan, I just wanted to forget."

"Forget what?"

"My ex-husband. I hate him so much. I despise what he constantly reduces me to, and he's not even here." I close my eyes while my body floats back into the darkness.

"Where is he?" John's voice drifts further, and before I submit to sleep entirely, I finally give him a truth.

"In a place where he can't physically hurt me anymore."

Chapter 23

OLIVER'S JOYOUS LAUGH spills out in the silent graveyard, attracting smiles from other mourners, as I manoeuvre the pushchair over the manicured lawns.

The sun beats down overhead; the weather pleasantly warm. Spring is in the air, and the daffodils and bluebells are blooming around the borders.

"Shush," Kara says as he continues to squeal, and she unstraps him. Cradling him to her chest, he reaches for the flowers I have just passed to her.

"Hi, Sam. I thought it was time you met Oliver." Kara sits down on the grass with him in her lap. "We brought you something, didn't we?" she says, encouraging and engaging her curious four-month-old, and places the flowers on the ground.

"Oliver, no," she says firmly, foiling his newest attempt to grab the bunch. With a grumpy pout, he settles on his fist when he realises his mother won't let him have them. Sitting next to her, I stroke his hair and the thick raven strands blow gently in the breeze.

"I wonder who left those," Kara asks in suspicion, fixated on the wilted flowers I bought a few weeks ago.

"I did." I stare at her. "Every fortnight I come by, tidy up, and bring a fresh bunch."

"Oh, I didn't know."

"No, I guess I just wanted to make up for all the animosity between us over the years. It's my way of saying sorry," I confess. "If I'd have known this would be the outcome for her, at such a young age, I would've done things differently. I know it's easy to say that now, but I didn't want her to go like this."

"Hindsight," Kara mutters, as she extracts her hair from the chubby hand tugging it with all his might.

"Everything is wonderful in hindsight," I confirm. "But we don't learn from hindsight. We learn from the present."

In retrospect, I haven't learned from either. Way back when I should have opened my mouth and cried for help sooner. I should have screamed out the truth when John told me he loved me for the first time. And I should have done the same thing the night he proposed.

No, I haven't learned anything.

"I guess. I know she did a lot of bad things, but she gave me him." She nods to Oliver. "And she gave me his father, too. If it wasn't for her, I wouldn't have either of them."

"No." I shake my head, refuting her. "I think you still would have found Sloan. Or he would have made John find you... Again." I smile, wondering how the kid managed to stay away for so long. But I understand how - because she had to find herself before she could let someone else in.

I shift my eyes from the stone and look around. "She's finally at peace here," I state, recalling something else entirely.

"Yeah. It's a perfect spot."

Sensing the conversation is about to become a little too deep for comfort, I stand and brush down my jeans. Reaching for my grandson, he squeals in delight, his podgy arms flailing as I wiggle my fingers towards him.

"He's going to be handful soon." I blow a raspberry on his belly, much to his delight.

"Soon?" Kara replies incredulously. "He already is. You do remember who his father is, don't you? Trust me, he doesn't like being told no, either."

I laugh as we walk towards the church. Stepping inside, I shudder, remembering the last time I sat here at the start of the year. Kara smiles as the vicar waves at us from afar.

"I won't be long."

Left holding the baby, I walk between the pews. Oliver, wide-eyed, enraptured by what this place is, stops fussing and his little hand grips my finger. Kissing his cheek, his beautiful dark eyes find his mummy, now discussing the events of his upcoming christening with the vicar.

"Let's you and I take a seat, little prince." I sit him in my lap as Kara enters the private office.

Giving Oliver his feed, he sucks away with fierce determination, and his expression is Sloan all over. He's going to break hearts one day. I just hope I'm still around to see it.

With him settled in my arms, I pull out a hymn book. I absentmindedly flick through the pages and stop on one I remember well. Speaking the words inside my head, a soft hum emanates my throat. It's been a long time since I sang this, but it feels like only yesterday.

I close the book and peer down at the innocent eyes now struggling to stay awake. I hold him tighter, wishing, pretending, wondering why me. Closing my eyes, a masochistic memory taunts cruelly, and I allow myself to remember because for far too long I've tried to forget.

"Hey," Kara's voice tumbles into the past that has me ensnared. Jolting my head up, she is standing beside the vicar at the end of the pew. I rise carefully while she adjusts the pushchair and I lay Oliver down and strap him in.

"If you have any queries, Mrs Foster, please call the office." The vicar smiles at the little man.

"I will. Thank you."

My eyes lock onto her shaking his hand, and I'm impressed. It wasn't so long ago this would have been abhorrent to her. She would have run away faster than an Olympic sprinter going for gold.

I stretch the kink out of my neck and nudge her, but she doesn't move. Staring at the office, she looks ashen.

"We asked Sophie and Stuart to be his godparents, along with Jeremy. Is that okay?" Her voice sounds positively terrified.

"Of course, it is. Honey, it's your choice."

She fidgets, and I know there is more to come. Except this more, I can guarantee I won't be happy about. Long minutes pass, and I finally speak the words she cannot.

"You invited your mum." I wait for her guilty gaze to meet mine. "Good. She deserves to celebrate her grandson's christening," I say, before marching out. Every memory of the last twenty-seven years confounds in my heart. Each one starting beautiful, each one ending brutal. So much so, I can't turn around, because if I do, I shall break.

Lorraine Petersen, or whatever she is calling herself these days, has everything I ever wanted. She had a husband, who sort of loved her, irrespective that he was a despicable bastard. She has a daughter, who still found it in her heart to bestow love when she has no right to be deserving of it. But more than that, she has forgiveness. And I fucking despise the woman for it.

"Marie?"

My feet move faster, and I push open the door, and the breeze hits me.

"Marie, stop!" Kara calls again.

I compose myself and spin around. I don't say anything for fear of what hatred I might spew out.

"Look, I don't blame you for being upset, but this gives her hope. I'm not being malicious, and I don't want to hurt your feelings, but you promised me you'd try. I know it's hard for you, but please just try. For Oliver. *Please.*" Hearing that rare, begging tone come out, unnerves me.

"Okay," I yield. "I'll try. For you, more than anyone else."

The tension hangs between us as we reach the car. Kara fastens Oliver into his seat and stows the pushchair in the boot then climbs inside. Her hand hovers over the ignition, but she hesitates and turns.

"Kara, please don't."

"I'm sorry, but I finally have to. All these years, particularly the last few months, you've changed. It's subtle and unassuming, but something's different. When I left the vicar's office, you were murmuring softly, holding him like he was your own. Watching you with him, from the day he was born, you always knew what to do. In the past, whenever I asked, you'd blatantly change the subject, but now I'd like an honest answer. I have no right to it, but if you love me as much as you say you do, you won't deny me this."

"Kara…"

"When you were married, did you ever have a child?"

I press my palm to my throat, feeling like I'm being suffocated, and I dart out of the car, desperate to breathe.

"Marie!" Kara's urgent steps resound behind me for the second time in less than fifteen minutes.

"What?" I snap, throwing my hands out. She halts mid-step, recognising my fury. "What do you want me to say?"

"I'm-"

"Sorry? Don't be. I meant what I said years ago, you and Lorraine are lucky to have a second chance. But more than that, be grateful that someone up there saw you fit to have a beautiful child and an amazing husband who would walk over hot coals for you. When I was married, I had a lot of things. All of them were given and quickly taken away."

"I'm sorry, I didn't mean-"

I glare at her dauntless stance and drop my head. "Just get in the car and go!" I demand in a tone I rarely use - the last time being when we buried the woman a few hundred yards away.

"Please don't be angry with me." She reaches up and dabs the wetness teeming down my cheeks.

"I'm angry at a lot of things, honey, but never at you. You were my second chance," I confess, and place my finger over her mouth. "Not now."

"Okay," she whispers, her eyes drifting back to the car. "Can I have at least one truth?"

I sigh on a nod, fearful of what she will ask, but all I can do is brace myself for heartache.

"Is your ex really living in Peterborough?"

I open my mouth and confirm the single truth. "No."

"And does he have a fiancée?"

"That's two truths, but yes, he does. Of sorts." Refusing to drag her deeper into my fucked-up past, I take her hand and lead her back to the car.

"John." One word says it all, and she sighs in discomfort. "I won't say anything, but you need to do right by him. He deserves to know... Whatever it is." With that, she climbs inside.

Rounding the bonnet, her words rattle my core. Yes, he does deserve to know, whether he already does... Now that's a different game entirely.

I stare at nothing of significance as we leave the car park. The drive and the tension thickening between us is uncomfortable, to say the least. And in an attempt to avoid small talk, I pretend to be typing out emails on my phone, until Kara stops outside my house.

"I love you, honey." I embrace her tightly. "And when the time's right, I'll be honest."

"And I, you." She smiles sadly, but she also understands the importance of protecting secrets.

"Give him a kiss from me when he wakes." I get out of the car and watch as she drives away. Closing the garden gate, a familiar sensation prickles down my nape.

"Good afternoon, Marie," Mr Jenkins, one of the elderly neighbours calls out, tipping his flat cap in greeting. I smile and rub the back of my neck, as an awareness that I haven't detected in over two decades deepens.

"Hello, Mr Jenkins. How are you?" I ask and open the gate.

His dog, King – named after his Cavalier King Charles breed – sits obediently at his master's foot. I can't resist scratching his ears, liking the way he leans into my hand without fear.

"I'm very well. A little chilly in my old age, but nothing a few layers won't fix."

"True," I concur. "Well, enjoy the rest of your day, Mr Jenkins."

"Oh, Marie?"

I stop on my way back up the path.

"A lady was here earlier, maybe an hour or so. I noticed she had been sat in her car for a while. A red one, I forget the make," he says, trying to remember.

I wait with suspicious intrigue, mentally connecting the pieces that are now slotting perfectly in place.

It can't be.

Can it?

One of the good things about this street is the unofficial neighbourhood watch. There is nothing that goes on here without old Man J, or Mavis, next door, knowing about it.

John originally bought this house because all the neighbours were over a certain age. After witnessing the atrocities of war, he confessed he also wanted a quiet life. It's one of the reasons he chooses not to move since there is no better security than retired neighbours with twitchy curtains and not much else to occupy their time.

"It isn't like us to have strangers, so I thought I'd let her know I was watching and that you were out with your daughter."

"Oh, right," I mutter blandly. "Did she leave a name?"

"No, but she was surprised that you had a daughter. *I* was surprised that she looked *exactly* like you." His tone is inquiring, but I'm good at lying.

"Well, we all have a doppelganger somewhere in the world apparently. I guess mine is closer to home than I thought." I deflect quickly, but he isn't fooled. I can only pray the next time John goes out for his morning run, he doesn't come back with a new found knowledge from a second-hand source.

Mr Jenkins nods, but his wise eyes sadden. "Yes, I guess we do. Have a good day, Marie." He tips his cap and slowly walks with King towards his house.

I slam the front door behind me, drop everything and run upstairs into the bedroom. I loiter at the window, looking up and down the street from my vantage point. No red cars or blonde doppelgangers in sight, but that twinned sensation is still prevalent down my spine.

Leaving the room, my phone is ringing inside my bag where I dumped it in the hallway. My foot hits the bottom step the instant it rings off, and I pluck it out and redial.

"Hi."

"Hey, beautiful. How did today go?" John asks, and I wonder what part of today he is referring to.

Today, two people have become further embroiled in my past. While I'm positive John hasn't spoken to Mr J, I have to believe Kara when she promised she wouldn't divulge. I'm not worthy of her allegiance, but I want it all the same.

"Okay, I guess." I toddle myself into the kitchen and lounge over the worktop. My hand toys with the chef's knife in the block, removing and reinserting pointlessly. "And then it went downhill when Kara confirmed Lorraine is coming to the christening. Did you know?" The rancour in my tone is perceptible.

He stays quiet for a beat then breathes deeply. "Yeah, the kid mentioned it. Sorry, I should have warned you."

"No," I say, slotting the knife back in the block. "It's fine. I expected it really, but it still throws me whenever she speaks about that woman. Anyway, what time are you coming home? I was thinking of ordering a takeaway since I'm in no mood to cook. I don't think my sanity can cope with sharp knives right now."

He chuckles beautifully – that gruff, deep sound, soothing and intense. "I'm not, hence my call. Sloan's got something he wants my opinion on, so we're going clubbing."

"Clubbing?" I ask amused. "Darling, you're views on clubbing are identical to mine."

"We're just going to look at some plans, financials, boring shit."

"Is he buying another club?"

"Seems that way. Trust me, angel, I'd rather be trapped between your legs tonight, than trapped with the drunks in the seventh level of hell!"

"Oh, you sweet talker, you," I reply playfully, forgetting I am twenty years too late in the flirting stakes.

"I absolutely am! When I get home tonight, you'll see just how sweet I can be!"

"Promises, promises," I challenge.

He rattles on scandalously, and my body rejoices in both shock and seduction, until the bell chimes.

"Darling, there's someone at the door. I'll see you tonight. Oh, and don't be bringing any wanton, scantily clad women home, either! I need my beauty sleep to be at my best, and they'll just keep me awake!" I tease.

"Angel, the only wanton, scantily clad woman I want will be tucked away nicely in our bed, conserving her energy, waiting for me to deliver on my promises. And I will deliver, beautiful. Repeatedly."

I pad down the hallway as the knock becomes more persistent.

"One minute!" I call out. "And you, John Walker, better make good on everything you've just promised, mister."

"Better get your beauty sleep while you can, Dawson."

"Hmm. Have I told you that I love you today?"

"Can't remember," he answers cockily.

"I love you. Don't be gone all night."

"I love you too, angel. I'll see you around midnight, and wear something incredibly sexy and very, very sinful."

I grin and hang up, thinking of the sexiest, sinful thing I own that can be considered nightwear. A shimmery white thing he bought me on one of his many jaunts with Sloan and his pesky personal shoppers pops into my head as I open the door.

"Hello?" I greet, but my smile disintegrates rapidly.

Holy fuck, this isn't happening!

I stand in shock, studying the halo of pale blonde hair. My vision becomes unfocused, and I slap my hand on the architrave as I stare into eyes identical to my own.

"Hello, Marianne."

My mouth slowly falls open, and I lose all muscle function, coming face to face with a woman I haven't seen in twenty-three years. My limbs falter, and my knees weaken as shock takes control.

Unable to breathe, I grab my throat, while everything fades to grey. And my name is the last thing I hear before it finally turns black.

"Marianne!"

Chapter 24

"MARIANNE?"

COGNIZANCE RETURNS slowly, but the reality is mind-numbing, especially when I remember how I came to be unconscious in the first place.

All these years, I've successfully circumvented the truth. But the truth is unavoidable when it turns up on your doorstep and forces your made-up world to stop turning on its axis. When it makes you finally concede that you were wrong, to do all you did to ensure you could walk through this pitiful thing called life when everything had been ripped away in the blink of an eye.

Pandora's Box was always meant to stay sealed, but fate evidently deemed otherwise; biding its time before making me relive it in the worst way possible, and at a time when my life was finally beautiful and tranquil.

"Marianne?"

A coolness dabs over my forehead as the hallway drifts back into focus. Gazing up, bathing my forehead tenderly, caring for me when I have no right to receive her altruistic goodness, is the sister I never thought I'd see again.

"Marianne." She smiles beautifully, her features still identical to mine, right down to the hue of our shared eye colour.

I reach up and allow my fingers to drift over her delicately lined flesh. Gone is the fresh-faced nineteen-year-old I remember. Instead, cradling me is a woman who, unsurprisingly, has also aged identically to have I. Good genes are something our mother always prided herself on. We both used to laugh whenever she would say it, but staring at my mirror image, it's true.

"Maggie," I whisper and scramble up on my haunches. My hand covers my mouth; the shockwaves still crashing inside. "Oh my God!"

"Hi, Marianne," she murmurs, pain consuming her tone, as she tentatively edges closer and extends her hand.

I hesitate momentarily while everything else fails to exist. Embracing her as hard as I can, hoping beyond hope this isn't a dream - one where I am forced to relive the past in vain – I bury my face in her neck.

As I inhale her scent, I remember everything, including things I was far too young to. All the precious moments we shared, from our first days at nursery and primary school to the first day of high school.

Ultimately, I remember the last time I ever saw her. The last touch, the last smile. The last goodbye.

"I'm sorry," I whisper. "My God, I'm so sorry!"

"No, no, don't cry," she replies, stroking my hair. "Shush."

Digging my fingers into her shoulders, I'm fraught with both shame and happiness while she rocks me for what feels like an eternity.

"I'm sorry for passing out on you," I tell her, daring to touch her pale blonde locks.

She laughs softly. "No, it's my fault. I shouldn't have just turned up like this, but I *had* to see you."

I brazenly run my fingers through her hair, and her lips curve at my neck. In the last few minutes, I feel like a weight has been lifted. I feel lighter, more pliable; compliant even.

I pull back, and my hands frame her face while my thumbs stroke the apples of her cheeks. Suddenly the enormity of my situation hits, and I glance at the door, terrified. Twisting my head, her words soothe.

"Nobody saw you go down. Not even the little old man who challenged me a few hours ago. It's nice to see someone is looking out for you."

"Hmm, there's a lot of that on this street."

"I know the feeling," she replies. "Are you able to stand?"

"I think so."

I get up clumsily, my legs still unsteady as Maggie looks around with intrigue and removes her jacket. Unveiling her neck, I stare at her morbidly, or namely her attire, realising the control of the family patriarch is still dominant.

Maggie instinctively raises her hand to her throat, comprehending what I have noticed. She purses her lips together but remains mute as she follows me into the living room.

"I'll make us some coffee. Dash of milk and three sugars?" I ask, remembering she liked it akin to molasses.

She smiles, the same smile I remember, and it lessens the sickness inside me. I leave her examining the montage of pictures that have multiplied considerably from the living room, onto the hallway and up the stairs.

Hurrying into the kitchen, I close the door and press my head to the wood as the first of many tears start to fall.

"You can do this," I say rhetorically, debating if I will be shattered again when she leaves here today. Putting on the kettle, I dry my eyes and slap on my game face.

A few minutes later, slightly more composed, I clutch the mugs tightly, and shoulder open the living room door. Maggie is still perusing the pictures of my substitute family, but immediately drops the one of Kara and a newly born Oliver, when I close the door.

"She's a beautiful girl. You must be very proud."

"Yes, I am," I reply, but don't bother to correct her assumption as I sit down. She eyes the adjacent sofa but eventually chooses to sit beside me.

I stir my coffee repeatedly and wonder where to begin. Do I tell her again how sorry I am? Do I tell her the reason I never contacted her was that I was too terrified to? That I was ashamed to involve her further in the mess that was my life back then?

"I'm sorry." I snap back abruptly as her voice floats over the tense atmosphere.

"No, don't say that," I mumble, shame devouring me.

It's painful to hear her apologise for my actions because she has nothing to be sorry for. She is the other half of myself that makes me whole. All these years, the hollowness I felt inside was always the reckless abandonment of the sister I adored. Regardless, it wouldn't have changed anything; I still would have run.

Although my reasons were more than transparent to everyone involved, I owe it to her now to be truthful of where I was at mentally at the time. I had nothing. My life had left me with shattered dreams and excruciating nightmares that took years to overcome.

"Everything that happened before I left was of my own making. The choices I made were my ruin, and all I did was drag everyone down with me. The best thing I ever did for you was leave. You didn't deserve to be tainted with the same brush everyone painted me with."

My eyes drift down her neck, as she subconsciously strokes the contrasting white square. Aside from the obvious, her occupation could be ambiguous. With her fitted pencil skirt, tunic and jacket, she could just be another businesswoman. I guess in some respects she is – of the ecclesiastical order.

But as I stare at the clerical dog collar, she truly is my father's daughter, and I wonder when the sermon will start, and judgement will be passed down.

"I'm guessing you never read my letters then?" she asks.

I hold my mug mid-air, taken aback by her words. I did read her letters, and I replied to them all. But every response I received was written as though she had never read my rejoinder. And now I finally understand why – because she never did.

"I did write back. From the first letter telling you and Mum where I was, to the last when you stopped writing altogether. I replied to all of them."

She breathes in sharply. "No, I only received the first. It arrived when-"

"When *he* wasn't there to intercept it," I comment viciously.

"Why would he do that?" she whispers.

I place my mug down and sigh. I don't want to speak ill, but she needs to understand. Now more than ever.

"Because I was dead to him, which means he wanted me dead to you."

"No." She shakes her head.

"Maggie," I cajole gently. "In your heart, you know it's true. I've been dead to him since…" I exhale heavily and shrug my shoulders. "It doesn't matter."

Her eyes remain fixed, until they shift, absorbing the room and its contents. "I wish I'd have known. I would never-"

"No," I cut her off before she can finish executing her thoughts. "I know you wouldn't have contacted me, but I'm glad you did. But *how* did you find me?"

She glances down with a guilty expression. "Well, years ago I first tried the Salvation Army. I was inspired when they managed to track down someone from the village, and since you stopped writing to me…" She looks up and rolls her eyes. "I thought I would get them to do the legwork. It took a while, but they said they couldn't help; that the first place you lived in had been demolished and the landlord had passed, so there were no records."

My lips curve, remembering the squalid bedsit I wouldn't house rats in. The landlord, on the other hand, was lovely, and although he didn't know squat about running habitable accommodation, he was more than happy to take what little I had to put a roof over my head.

"So, last year I called…"

"Adrian," I finish for her. "I know. I've spoken to him. He wasn't particularly happy to hear from me."

Maggie smiles sadly. "No, me either, but he understood my reasons. He risked his position and integrity for me, Marianne. He gave me your address, but I didn't know what to do. When things took a turn for the worst last Christmas, I decided to give the Salvation Army another try, soften the blow as such, but they were slow, so I drove down to see if I could catch you."

I nod repeatedly. "I know about that, too. The vicar on my doorstep. The old lady next door asking if John and I were finally going to stop living in sin."

"Oh, I'm sorry," she says contritely.

"Don't be. They like to know everyone's business."

"When I was driving back up the A1, the woman from the Sally Army called me to say she had spoken to you, but she didn't want to pressurise."

I swallow a mouthful of coffee and put down my mug. "Oh, there was no pressurising. At first, she didn't want to say anything, and then *I* hung up on her in shock when she did."

"I am sorry, Marianne."

"It's Marie now," I murmur. "Anything else you'd like to confess?" I ask with a smile, uttering words she probably speaks on a daily basis.

She purses her lips sheepishly, and I wonder if she will own up to calling the house.

"Well, when all that failed, I came back down – only a few times. I never saw you, but I ended up following a man – your husband, I presumed – to that big, derelict looking warehouse. I didn't know what to do. I had your work number, but I didn't want to spook you, so I plucked up the courage to call here. I played dumb, acting as though it was your office."

"Hmm, I listened to your request for a *reunion*, and you've got it." She doesn't respond, and I'm glad because if she says sorry once more, I'm going to scream.

The silence slowly consumes, until she stands up and walks around the room, absorbing the life I've built without her.

"You look happy together. In love," she says, rubbing her thumb over a picture of John and me.

My mouth curves as I twist my engagement ring. "We are," I whisper. "Or maybe tomorrow I'll say we *were*." It's spiteful to implicate she has just destroyed my life, but I can't help it. Her head snaps back at my insinuation, and she looks horrified.

"He doesn't know, does he?" I shake my head no. "This was a mistake. I shouldn't have come!" Picking up her bag, she hurries out of the living room. I quickly moving after her, as her tears fill the hallway.

"Please stay," I request softly.

She turns and throws out her hand. "How can you ask that of me, now that I know the truth? I'm inadvertently destroying the good life you finally have by being here today. I should have just let it be. I should have just believed Father when he said you had forgotten about me."

I embrace her without a second thought and mentally drown in the flood of memories that have come rushing back.

"I'm glad you didn't believe him, and I'm glad that you're here. I am because now it means I can no longer hide. I've been trying for years to speak the truth. Seeing you here, inside my world, it makes me believe I can, and that I will survive the fallout."

Maggie wipes her eyes. "You know, I always prayed you would walk back through the door, and all would be forgiven. I used to sit in the graveyard for hours, hoping you would magically appear. I feel so ashamed that the reason I'm here, is the same reason why you felt you could never return."

She doesn't need to reiterate what was in her latest letter because I always knew the day would come.

"It's okay. Stay," I urge softly and turn on my heel, hoping she will follow.

I pace the kitchen floor, waiting for her to enter. Eventually, the door creaks open, and she takes a seat. Making a fresh pot of coffee, I place it down on the table and remove the cheesecake from the fridge that Sloan had requested yesterday. I meant to give it to Kara this morning, but I completely forgot the moment she arrived with a crabby tot.

I set the plate in the centre and pull out two dessert forks. "Here," I say. "I've found dessert makes everything better."

"It's good," she comments, cutting off a small piece. "But, of course, it is. It's what you do. You were always good at baking. It's the one thing I never really excelled at."

"It's not actually for me. My son-in-law asked me to make it."

Her eyes flash inquisitively, trying to piece together the puzzle. "Is the girl in the picture your daughter?"

I nod. "Kara. She is, but she's not exactly mine. I adopted her, so to speak. We crossed paths many moons ago. She was homeless, and I was surviving. We found peace and love in each other."

Peace and love? How many times have I heard that over the years and despised it? Now I'm bloody reciting it!

I devour more cheesecake – mentally promising to make the overbearing git another, should he ask – when Maggie's fork hits the plate.

"Tell me about your life. I want to know everything."

Collecting my thoughts, I know she's expecting a happy ever after I won't be able to deliver on. I open my mouth, prepared to unburden myself of the abysmal truth of the life I endured after the one that was heartlessly ripped away from me.

It feels like yesterday that I stepped off the train, carrying nothing more than a couple of changes of clothes and money that my mother had stuffed into my hand.

"After the funeral, I couldn't stay. Mum begged me not to leave. She even gave me money to ensure I wasn't walking the streets. When I arrived down here, I stayed in a hostel for a couple of nights, until I found the only place I could afford, and that was the cheap bedsit with a shared bathroom and kitchen." Looking up at her, tears glaze her eyes. "I signed on the dole and took every handout available. After a few months, I enrolled in college and worked any crappy job I could to dig my way back out of hell. I won't lie, I had it hard for a time, but I was always optimistic.

"Time flew by, and after I finished college and was finally making enough money to support myself, I worked for a small company who did wedding planning. Using the knowledge and contacts I had gained, and since I had no life-"

"Oh, Marianne," Maggie murmurs, knocking me off track.

"Marie," I correct her, then carry on. "And since I had no life or anyone within it-" my tone wobbles with pity "-I worked myself into the ground. Every spare penny I had, I squirrelled away.

"During that time, your letters became few and far between, until they stopped entirely. It hurt to think that you'd finally given up on me. But as with all things in my life, I buried it and set about finally owning my own home and business. I succeeded. While it still burned inside, I'd always believed I would never see you again. Until now."

"I really didn't think he would do that," she says, still disbelieving.

"No, but I did. After the first letter I sent you, I looked forward to receiving your reply. Like I said, I had nothing down here, and your letters became a lifeline for me. After a while, it became obvious something wasn't right, especially when you rehashed the previous letters. It's all so transparent now, but back then I failed to see the truth. Maybe I just didn't want to see it."

I place my fork down and swallow a mouthful of coffee. "What about you?" I ask, hoping she will divulge.

She shrugs her shoulders. "After you left, I went back to uni. For the first time in my life, I didn't know how to live. I didn't really fit in anywhere. So, I kept my head down and made it to graduation." Suddenly she chortles, recollecting something.

"What?" I ask.

She shakes her head. "It's embarrassing. You'll laugh."

"I promise I won't. Tell me."

"Remember when I said I couldn't wait to be kissed when we were sixteen?" I nod. "Well, I didn't get that first kiss until I was twenty-seven. You can guess the rest of the firsts I didn't get until then." She looks down, refusing to capture my gaze.

"I don't think that's embarrassing at all. I have my own confession. The first man I've been with since Joe is John. I abstained from letting anyone in for twenty-one years. Of course, John doesn't know that. I guess I'm also embarrassed to admit it. I think it's great that you waited for the right one – *the* one. God knows I wish I had." Her head raises at my flippancy, and she touches her neck instinctively. "Sorry," I apologise for taking the Lord's name in vain.

"It's okay."

"And family? How many children do you have?" I press her.

"I never had any children."

My mouth drops open at her confession.

"I got married at twenty-eight, and I found out I was pregnant a few months later. At six months, I miscarried. It took two more to find out I would never be able to carry to term."

"Oh, I'm sorry, Maggie. I know you always wanted a family."

She stares down at her plate and sighs. "The day I was told I don't remember anything, but somehow, I managed to find myself sitting on the grave, praying. For myself. For her. But mainly I was praying for you, having finally experienced the heartache of something so precious being snatched away. I appreciate it isn't the same, but I finally understood. Sitting there, I prayed you finally had a loving husband and a family who cherished you. That you finally had everything you deserved."

The clock chimes on the hour, resounding through the hallway. Maggie rests her chin on her hand, deep in thought. Sliding her other over the table, she links her fingers in mine.

"She's dying," she says sombrely, blighting the silence. But those two little words have just changed everything. "If she does, it will kill him."

"So I read," I concur flatly, squeezing her hand in consolation. "I know what you want me to say, but I don't know if I can see her again. *He* destroyed me. The two men that I loved killed off any part of me that was able to feel anything for such a long time. It made me faithless, Maggie, in more ways than one. There was no hope left for me."

"I understand, but I need you." Her eyes avert to the floor. "Mum needs you. She doesn't have long left, months maybe. They don't know, Marianne."

Anger rises in my chest at hearing her speak that name again. "Marie! My name is Marie now. I haven't been Marianne for over two decades. I left her in the cemetery, remember?"

"No, *Marie*. Marianne is the one who got up and walked away, but it's blatantly obvious your heart is still six feet under in that grave!"

"Don't!" I inhale sharply. "I live with that every single day. You don't know what you're asking of me. If I come back, it will bring up everything. *He* will bring up her, which means he will also bring up Joe because God knows he's another ghost who just can't stay dead and buried!" I hiss viciously.

"What do you mean?" she asks, her tone suspicious, her eyes narrow.

"I mean, the bastard has been sending me stuff. He is clearly bored of incarceration now, and evidently, he's feeling inventive and macabre. It used to be divorce papers every couple of years, but a few weeks ago, he sent ribbons. *Her* ribbons. He sent them *here!* I can surmise how he found me, but I'd like to know how he managed to get that stuff to me in the first place!"

"He's out. He has been since last Christmas."

"What?" I whisper, the room swaying slightly. "No, that can't be. You're wrong!" I shake my head, but I know she wouldn't lie. "I spoke to Adrian, and he said he'd find out."

"Adrian knows. I thought you knew. I thought the police would have told you. He's back in the village, living with his parents. He's out on licence, or at least that's what the gossips are saying."

My head is all over the place, finally comprehending the joyous expression on the face of the dancing queen on New Year's Eve. She was celebrating the release of her treasured bastard son. I should feel shocked, but I don't. She never showed an ounce of remorse for what he did to me. She even attempted to pervert justice when she took to the witness box in court. The things she said, the lies she spouted, lucky for me, for once in her life, dirty money couldn't bury the truth.

Maggie takes my hand, and her fingers skim over the diamonds in my ring. "John doesn't know any of this, does he?"

I shake my head in reprehension. "No, I haven't told him anything. He doesn't even know I'm a twin."

"What about-"

"No," I whisper, covering my eyes to hide the tears. "Nobody knows about her, Maggie. It's like she never existed," I reply, sniffing back my runny nose.

"Why did you never tell him? You're engaged. You've agreed to spend your life together. Why?"

Why, indeed? Fear, heartache? No, I didn't tell him because of the shame and guilt that I couldn't protect something that meant more to me than anything else in the world.

"Because he wouldn't understand," I admit tearfully. "He's ex-army. Everything he does is strategic and thorough. When he was in his twenties, he took on a job for a woman who had cancer. Eventually, he became like a father to her kids even though he was only nine years older than the son. Those kids are now in their twenties, and he's still their father figure. He prides himself on it. I've tried, many times, but I can't. To expose the truth is as good as packing my bags and leaving. He'll never forgive me for my failure."

"No, you didn't fail. You were an amazing mother. You know you were."

"I wasn't amazing enough to protect my baby. I failed." Pressing my lips together, my tears fall silently. Her stool scrapes over the floor as she stands and approaches. Sitting down next to me, I tentatively touch the collar.

"How long?"

She smiles knowingly. "You're deliberately changing the subject, but nearly fifteen years. When I left uni, I worked for social services, trying to help others find justice. After what happened, I wanted to make sure her fate wasn't suffered by others. Peter, my husband, saw I wasn't happy and encouraged me to follow my dreams. It might not be everyone's ideal vocation, but it's mine. I seem to be able to achieve more through religion than red tape. I'm proud to wear this." Her eyes flick down.

"You should be. And it's nice that she was your guiding light to try to make something right in the world." I give her a sad smile. "Tell me, are you happy now, Maggie?"

Her reciprocating smile is instant, brightening her face. "I am. I have a man who loves me, and our house is filled with love, notwithstanding it isn't filled with the children we would love to have. But right now, I'm happier than I've been in years because I finally have the other half of myself back. I've waited twenty-three years for this day. I won't wait twenty-three years for another one."

"You won't," I whisper.

"God has given us this day back. I want to stay in contact. Mum isn't the only reason I came. I came because a part of me has been lost all these years. There were times when I thought I could sense you and a little of what you might be feeling. Silly, I know, but I did."

Wrapping my arms around her, I don't want to let go. "I know exactly what you mean."

"Promise you will stay in touch," she reiterates.

I nod, feeling so much emotion just being with her again. Being close, being whole and complete. "I will. I swear."

A phone rings and Maggie lets me go and hurries out of the room. When she returns, she is tapping away at the screen.

"Peter." Holding her phone out to me, I grin. Her husband is nothing like what I expected. He's handsome, slightly greying, wise in his features. He's also large in the fact that he has muscle mass, not excess body fat. Definitely not what I expected for my sister. Then again, what would I know? A family reunion was never on the agenda for me. It is something I have purposely avoided for years.

"What does he do? Is in the church?"

"No, he's a solicitor. Look, I don't want to, but I need to go. Here," she says, removing a notebook and pen from her bag and scribbling down her address. "Call me. I know you won't come back, but I'd like for you to meet my husband." Her eyes flit to the hallway, then she looks back. "And I'd like to meet your family, too."

I wipe my eyes and agree. "I'd like that; all of it. Call me if Mum's condition gets worse, I'll reconsider my options then."

Walking to the door, she hugs me tight. "I love you, but now it's time to be honest with everyone else you love. Now that Joe is out, how long do you think you have before he turns up on your doorstep? He already knows where you are. I'll let you know if I see him, but please be careful."

"I will. And you're right, it is time."

"Your faith may not be the same as mine anymore, but it's time to find thyself again."

Kissing her cheek, I finally let her go. "I love you."

"I love you, too," she replies.

Watching her leave is the last thing I want. Wrapping my arms around myself, that familiar twined sensation is heightened, growing stronger with every passing second in her presence.

I walk her to her car and wait as she pulls away. Minutes later, when she has finally disappeared from my life once more, I rotate. My eyes lock with old Man J, standing at his front door. His expression confirms he knows my secret. Placing his hand on his heart, he smiles. I nod, a calm inside subduing the fear I should be feeling.

I stroll back into the house and catch my reflection in the mirror. Maggie's right - now *is* the time to be truthful. Whether it destroys the world I crafted in despair is a chance I'll have to take.

"Find thyself, Marianne," I reiterate her parting words.

Touching the glass, I didn't realise I was still lost.

Chapter 25

MY TIRED EYES flutter open as the early morning sun bleeds into the room from the gap in the haphazardly drawn curtains. I yawn and rub my eyes before stretching my neck to find John still slumbering.

Rolling over, I rest my head on my arm and stare at him. I didn't hear him come in last night; I was too far gone in my sugar-induced coma. After Maggie left, I spent the rest of the evening pacing and procrastinating. And making another cheesecake after I did the unthinkable and devoured the remaining dessert for dinner.

All of it.

In the aftershock of seeing her, I needed something. Something which will ensure I spend the next week eating salads to repent for being too indulgent in my quest for mental comfort.

Gently touching John's face, specifically his faded scar, I trace it softly. He moves in his sleep, and the mattress ripples. Drawing my hand back, his own comes up from resting on his front, and he quickly grabs my wrist.

"You're staring." Opening his eyes, he looks refreshed and wide awake. "Hello, beautiful."

"Hi," I reply as he kisses my fingertips, still preoccupied with the self-denial that I'm denying and drowning myself under. "What time did you get in last night?"

"About two." His palm trails up my side, paying attention to the curve of my hip and the dip of my waist. "I came home with a headful of wicked ideas, ready to fulfil my promise, but you were dead to the world. You didn't even move when I got in." He looks down my body at the satin shorts and camisole I'm wearing, not the tiny little white thing I originally planned to put on.

"I asked for sinfully sexy, and while these are a little restrictive for my tastes-" he tugs on the shorts, "-I'm sure I won't have any difficulty divesting you of them in due course."

"Really? You promised me that last night, and you didn't deliver." I test him.

"No, well, you know necrophilia isn't one of my preferred tastes." Something darkens in his irises, and his playful conduct morphs into seriousness. "Did yesterday get any better?" he asks, still worried about my state of mind since Lorraine bloody Petersen is darkening the horizon again.

"It was..." It was amazing and wonderful, and sadly, also terrifying. "It was eventful. Enlightening." My lips curl, remembering something from a lifetime ago.

"Beautiful." He caresses my cheek before swiping his thumb across my bottom lip. Teasing it against the seam of my mouth, I open without hesitation and release an anticipatory sigh. "I like that sound. It's the sound of things to *come*. Suck," he requests, his tone harder.

Stilling with his thumb in my mouth, I gently suck the pad, while he hooks his arm under my back and pulls me atop of him. His other hand curls around my shoulder and trails further down my nape. Ascending down the length of my back, he stops at my tailbone. Adjusting my position, he pressurises my pelvis into his. His hardness digs into my pubic bone, and I gasp, desire rising from within. His hot shaft pulsates, wholly attuned to every cell and nerve ending, prepping me for the inevitable.

"Darling," I breathe out, wanting more.

He grins at me, knowing precisely what *more* I want, and withdraws his thumb. He drags it further down my bottom lip and circles my stiff nipple. I throw my head back, revelling in his rough touch.

Capturing his talented mouth, his movements fight against mine, harder, stronger, while I feel down the contours and ridges of his torso. Feeling my way over the defined muscles of his lower abdomen, I stop inches from where I want to be. I shift back and stare into his dark, desire laden eyes.

"Want me on your tongue?" I nod because it's a start.

He throws the duvet off the bed, leaving one half dangling over the side. Sitting up, he relaxes against the headboard. With one leg bent at the knee, his foot planted the mattress, he palms my face. "I'll let you start this, but I'm finishing it. In you."

"In me and over me," I confirm, adjusting my position to fully explore him. I start at his forehead, and pepper his face with light kisses, teasing him, playing with him.

"Just like the first time," he says, as I reach his jaw. Nipping it a little, he smacks my arse, eliciting a sharp, instant tingle. *Everywhere.*

His palms find their way into the inside of my waistband, and he pushes my shorts down my legs. Finishing the job for him, I kick them off.

"Good girl," he murmurs. "And if you're really good, I might let you come on my tongue."

"Make love to me, and I might let you come on mine," I counter, nibbling his collarbone.

"Always, but first, we're doing it the Walker way. Cold and hard, then hot and slow." His fingers knead my backside, moulding over my shape and parting my cheeks. "This is definitely a hot and slow way," he says, stroking places that feel astounding when he pays them meticulous attention.

I grab his wayward hands and place them firmly on his stomach, but since he always has other ideas, he rubs one down his hard planes of muscle then fists it around his equally hard length.

"That isn't part of the plan," I murmur, rolling my tongue over his nipple, finishing with a nip and tug.

"I'm fulfilling my promise," he says gruffly. "And I always promise to give you the best."

I roll my eyes, annoyed that he likes to take control when he openly gives it to me.

Reaching my destination, I dart my tongue over his bulbous head and grip his thigh for support. My whole body is on fire as my lips caress the first inch, and a firm hand tightens in my hair. While the pressure is tangible, he does nothing other than massage my scalp. He doesn't control the action; he doesn't force more than I am willing to give. He's letting me play – my way. For now, at least.

"Fuck, angel!" he spits out when I take him all the way in and back again. Working my mouth over him, memorising the shape and feel of his most sensitive body part, I feel powerful.

Invincible.

Closing my eyes, doing what comes naturally, I continue to ease my mouth up and down, soft and slow, then hard and fast. Alternating my administration, my eyes flick up as his stomach muscles clench and retract. I smile, happy in my ability to make him react. His hand tightens further in my hair, almost to the point of pain, and I draw my teeth, ever so slightly, indicating him to lessen his grip. Thankfully, after all these years, our sexual tells are identifiable to the other.

I add my hand to the mix and roll and squeeze his testicles - his second most sensitive part.

"Shit! I can't… I need…" He doesn't finish, and neither do I, as he reaches forward and manoeuvres me up his front. With both hands high on my inner thighs, he circles my tender, highly responsive flesh. "I need to be inside you now."

He positions me quick and then slams me down on to him. I keen out in rippling moans, let it acclimatise, then move. I clasp my hands at the back of his neck and work my body over his, bringing myself from root to tip, over and over. Rocking my pelvis, building a rhythm, he pushes up from below, while I press down from above.

Never losing the connection, I shift closer to his tight arse. Unclasping my hands from the back of his nape, his dexterous fingers skim up my sides, taking the other half of my nightwear with them. He roughly curls his large hand around my breast, exposing only my areola and licks it. I sigh in delight and slide my arms behind me. My hips rotate in smooth, circular motions, revelling in the wonderful fullness filling me. He sucks my sensitive flesh into his willing, talented mouth, making me moan louder.

I dig my fingers into the mattress for stability behind me, while he groans and devours. Manipulating me backwards, my spine sinks into the softness of the duvet, and he hooks one leg around his hip. Curling his hand around my other knee, he uses one arm above my head to control the speed and intensity.

"Say the words, angel," he commands, and his hooded gaze compels me effortlessly.

"Fuck me," I reply, exhaling hard, my body desperate to ignite into flames around him.

Pushing my knee further into the bed, the pain is insignificant as he drills hard into my core for emphasis. Sliding back out, he performs to his remarkable ability again and again. My body is teetering on the edge; that fine line before passion and orgasm meet sinuously, removing one and replacing with the other.

"Come on, angel, I feel you fucking tighten around me. Let it go," he encourages. My back curves and my tailbone tilts, taking him deeper. "That's it, ride me hard."

"John!" I call out, my lungs straining for breath beneath my rib cage. "More…harder!"

He lets go of my knee and drags his palm down my leg. Sheathing my ankle in his hand, he sits back on his knees and brings my leg high, balancing my heel on his shoulder. He slowly descends, and the stretch in my hamstring is sublime. My leg continues to press back against my chest as he cages me in this unforgiving position.

"Give me those lips, beautiful," he orders, and I lean up and open my mouth. He coils his tongue around mine in a prelude of what's to come. He growls low and content, releases me and pushes back.

He repositions my leg, tilts his head and kisses the ball of my ankle. Rolling his hand back down the inside of my thigh, he strokes my swollen folds and flicks my clit. Lifting my backside, he guides his hard shaft to my ready and waiting core.

"Darling," I breathe out, clawing at the sheets, feeling his hot, engorged head at my opening. With his hands on my hips, he plunges inside. My body vaults in response, and my lungs release a strangled cry at the first thrust of the cold, hard fucking due to commence.

Working me into a frenzy, he controls the action with expertise, spearing me back and forth. My recurring moans grow louder, covering the sounds of our bodies connecting as he swells inside me and my internal walls tighten.

"Oh, God, that's good. Harder," I moan, staring into his eyes.

"That's it, angel. Eyes open, I want to watch."

My shoulders roll as desire claims every nerve and cell, bathing them in ecstasy. My eyes never leave his, because, I too, want to watch him, watch me.

"Fucking beautiful. Still going?"

"Yes! God! Come with me."

He smiles broadly and shakes his head. "Not yet. Want more?" I nod my entire body on fire. "You got it, baby."

Sliding my leg into the crook of his elbow, he moves inside me, stretching me further, adding to the tremors still pulsating in my abdomen. He reaches for my other leg and places my foot on headboard behind him. With a hand under my bum, he slides a pillow underneath me. Adjusting his body forward, one forearm beside my head, the other arm holding my leg up, opening me wider for his hips to sit comfortably, his slick front slides over mine.

"If this starts to get uncomfortable, darling, drop your leg. Ready?" I nod, and his hips retreat, and he finally begins.

I pressurise my foot against the headboard, as his fine body hair brushes against my front. I reach out behind me, finding nothing, until his hand curls into mine. Gripping it, feeling his unadulterated power throb inside me, we stare into each other's eyes.

This is more than sex. More than needing human touch, carnal or otherwise. This is love I didn't know existed. It's powerful and all-consuming. I might only have limited experience with men, and he might only be the second man I've let into my life, into my body and into my heart, but the best things come to those who wait.

And I've waited twenty-one years for this type of love.

Ultimately, I've waited twenty-one years *for him*.

I close my eyes, desire spreading from my belly in a wave of molten fire. A sharp thrust, one which causes me to whimper, hits deep and he tightens his hand.

"Okay?" he asks with a groan, easing down.

"Perfect. Keep going hard, don't stop. Don't stop."

Satisfied I am more than good with this, he ups the ante. He loosens my hand, drops my leg and slaps both hands aside my ears. "Spread wide, angel."

I part my legs further and place the other foot on the headboard. Feeling more than exposed, even with his body covering mine, he rears up on his forearms and looks down at where we are connected. His head dips, and he devours my lips. His tongue penetrates my mouth, matching the action of his length repeatedly impaling my core. The raptures consume and set me on fire. My body lifts from the pillow, seeking more and rises to meet his. Fucking me hard, with long, lingering, robust strokes of perfect, unwavering steel, it feels like time has stopped.

"Fuck!" he hisses out.

"Oh God, oh God!" I bracket my feet harder against the headboard, and the sound of cracking pierces the room. "Shit!"

John chuckles and rests his forehead on mine. "Come on. Squeeze me, angel. Show me heaven."

I cry out; the raptures electrifying me. The sensation is spine straightening, toe-curling and foot clenching. It's good. Too good. I intentionally crush his hips as I fold my legs around his back. Fighting against the coiling he must be experiencing inside me, he forces himself out and slams back in, roaring, letting go, riding the wave with me.

Dragging his head down to mine, I glide my tongue into his mouth, doing to him what he is doing to me. And I admit, enjoying every frigging second of it.

"Angel," he mumbles into my mouth. "Fuck, you feel good around me. Tighter, baby."

I squeeze internally, his hardness filling me beautifully. My skin is beyond perspired, causing a masochistic soreness each time my taut nipples rub against his chest. I drop my hold from his head and circle them between my fingers, fighting back the bite.

"God, these feel amazing!" Sensing his stare, I gaze up, seeing him enthralled. He taps a hand away, revealing my darkened tip that is turning a brilliant shade of red. Grinning, he swipes his tongue over it, lapping and soothing.

I gradually slow my grinding. My limbs finally admit defeat, and I flop my legs down. Holding my body up, I ease the pillow from under me.

"That was phenomenal. Amazing." He rakes his fingers through my damp hair. "Sinning with you is the best way to spend a morning." Pushing himself up on his hands, he withdraws with a little sting.

I roll over as he towers above me on his knees. My core contracts, wanting more, seeing his length is still firm and glistening from our combined arousal. I grin and slide off the bed, causing a trickle of heat to run down my leg.

"Hey, I'm not done with you yet!"

Swaying my hips, still very much turned on, I look back and jerk my head. "Why don't we kill two birds with one stone?"

I throw open the door and move across the landing into the bathroom. As I turn on the shower, the door creaks, and he enters. A smile curves over my cheeks and he reciprocates. Hoisting me up, I wrap myself around him, feeling safer than should be logical, considering today I'm going to attempt to start opening up. Whether or not anything of consequence leaves my mouth is another matter entirely, but the sentiment is there.

"These hurt?" he asks, gently stroking my breasts that are showing slight teeth marks.

"Marginally, but it was worth it."

Inside the large cubicle, the steam begins to billow as he grabs my body wash. Tending to my sensitive body parts with far too much precision, my lids close as a tiny flutter of orgasm resurfaces.

"What was the record last time?"

"Three, I think," I answer, unsure.

He quickly douses himself under the flow and cups my face. "I love you, Marie Dawson. And every day I spend with you, that love gets deeper." My mouth opens, but he shakes his head. "Don't say anything. I just want you to know that this is more than hard fucking and easy loving. It's the life I want with you. The future I want with you."

Shifting my eyes to the side, my aforementioned sentiment is prematurely calling.

"When I asked you to marry me, I didn't want to press it, but we need to talk, angel. A serious talk. One where we discuss where this is going. I know where I want to be, and I hope to God you want the same. Understand?"

The hot water pelts against the base, making my confirmation almost inaudible. "I do. And there are things I need to tell you. Things I've never told anyone. When I do, I need you to be impartial. Promise me that. Promise you will listen without prejudice."

He nods, his expression uncertain, then he kisses me deeply. So deep, in fact, my toes curl from the raw intensity of it.

"Now, two out of three isn't bad, but I'm thorough and disciplined, and I like a job done right. Trust me?"

"Always," I whisper. And in this moment, just like any other time when he has tested my loyalty, no truer words have ever been said.

I turn slowly, relax my forearms against the tiles and stick out my bum, silently requesting this amazing taboo. His hands rim around my thighs and then my hips. Pulling me back, his hard length moves between my cheeks, and I shudder in anticipation. I close my eyes as he glides in slowly and brings his hands to my front. With his fingers penetrating beautifully, I smile as my heated breasts press against the cold grout, eliciting a soothing, yet abrasive rub.

"Oh, that's good," I groan, tilting my neck, feeling his lips form a smile.

A short time later, my body shakes violently, my voice grows hoarse, and I call out incoherently.

As promised, he was thorough, disciplined and he definitely did the job right.

Chapter 26

ENTERING THE KITCHEN, John is leisurely perusing the morning paper, while devouring a pile of buttered toast in front of him. His eyes lift and roam from top to toe. I cock my head to one side in disbelief, because I think he's done enough ogling already this morning.

"Stop it!" I say friskily and pick up his mug of half-drunk coffee.

His brows peak, and he grins. "Would you like some coffee, angel?"

I remove the pint-size mug from my lips and give him my sweetest smile. "This is fine, darling." The sarcasm in my tone is evident, and I do nothing to disguise it. Secretly, he loves to be on the cutting edge of my tongue.

He picks up a slice of toast and prowls towards me. Evaluating his lustful stare, I think round three might be on the cards if I stay for much longer.

"Open," he says, with a hint of innuendo. I part my lips as he guides the toast into my mouth. Taking a bite, his eyes drift and darken. "Are those legal?" he teases, jerking his head to my tight yoga leggings.

"I don't know, you tell me. While you're doing it, what do you think of this?" I unzip my hoody and pull it down over my shoulders, flashing a little flesh and my equally tight fitted support vest. I smile when his mouth drops open. Yes, I'm very satisfied with this reaction.

When I bought these, on the proviso I would be the odd woman out in a room full of gym bunnies, it was a case of all the gear and no idea. Now, I know I made the right choice.

John's hands snake around my front, and he rests his chin on my shoulder. "Are you sure you don't want to blow off this shit, let me strip you bare and make good use of every available surface under this roof?" He wiggles his brows, his implication requiring no further explanation. "I can't guarantee they'll all be comfortable, but I can guarantee you won't complain. I might even let you keep the stretchy vest on since you're so proud of it."

"John!" I chide.

"What?"

"Sex is all you think about!"

He scoffs in disgust. "I'll have you know I don't only think about sex," he announces haughtily. "My interests are wide and varied."

"Such as?" I taunt.

He grins as he considers his next words carefully. "Such as I enjoy spreading you wide and fucking you in varied positions."

I chortle and shake my head. That response was ingenious. "Those are not hobbies; those are a necessity."

"Oh, God yeah, they're necessary."

"John..." I coax through gritted teeth.

"Fine! I have wide and varied interests in outdoor pursuits and leisure activities."

"Darling, hiking over a barren desert, under a scorching sun, toting an automatic weapon at Her Majesty's Armed Forces request is not a leisure activity!"

"No, but you have to look on the bright side." He smiles beautifully, accentuating his hairline scar.

"War *never* has a bright side."

"No," he says thoughtfully. "No, it doesn't. But regardless, I still have a strong interest in getting you horizontal, vertical and bent over backwards in every way possible." He shrugs his shoulders nonchalantly.

I reach up on my toes and press my lips to his nose. "Later."

"Seriously? You're going to be stretching out in all positions anyway, at least with me there's a prize at the end for your effort!"

"True." And yes, he does have a point. I'd much rather spend my first Saturday off in ages rolling around the already crumpled sheets, bathroom floor and kitchen table with him. When I agreed to this weeks ago – during my catastrophic afternoon piss-up - I wasn't in a sober state of mind to say no. After this morning's two rounds of sexual acrobatics, I already ache all over.

"John Walker, I would love to explore the possibilities with you, but I promised." I slip the fleece back over my shoulders and zip it up.

"I know, although I'm surprised you remember," he says, kissing my forehead. "What time does it finish? Maybe you came come back here and show me your new stretchy moves." His palms slide down my back and slip into my waistband.

"No idea, but I need to do a few things afterwards."

He pulls back slightly, and I tilt my head to the side. I don't want to tell him, but I know I need to.

"Angel?"

"I'm going to go to the house. I need to start packing up the last of the stuff."

He lets go and leans against the worktop, his hand over his mouth, his eyes weary.

"Darling, please. I need to do this. I need to go there and find closure. One day, it won't be my house anymore, and I'd rather do this on my own terms than being forced to do it at the eleventh hour."

"And that's fine. I want you to be able to leave it behind - insofar as you can. Look, if you get there and need someone, call me. That's all I ask."

"Okay." I smile, appeased. "I better go. No time like the present to voluntarily break a leg!"

He throws his head back and chuckles loudly. "Oh, I don't know. It means you could keep said leg elevated while I practice my bedside manner to perfection." Slapping my backside, he passes me my holdall. "Go, or I won't be responsible for what I do next. I'll see you later."

I pull up on the side of the road in the run-down industrial estate where Dev hires out his old gym. The adjacent barren land, also known as the car park, is full. Looking around, my eyes narrow when I see two identical Range Rovers at the back with personalised WS plates. I shake my head; this morning is going to be a disaster. Call it bad luck or call it intuition, but if those two ratbags are here, it can only end in catastrophe.

Gathering my things, I walk towards the entrance, but I'm immediately intimidated by a couple of toned, Lycra-clad women.

Inside, I look around and breathe a sigh of relief when I see Dev and Nicki chatting with a woman who looks like she belongs on the cover of Women's Health.

"Hi," I greet once I am in earshot.

"Hey, glad you could make it. This is Pearl, she's the instructor today," Dev says, removing his hoodie, exposing his ridiculously broad arms and shoulders. I'm not surprised, it isn't like I haven't seen him in a vest before, but it is still a revelation whenever I do.

As I exchange pleasantries with the incredibly fit, toned woman, I suddenly feel like a pygmy beached whale. Subtly glancing down at my attire, I should have worn one of John's old t-shirts to cover my forty-three-year-old skin.

"You look nervous. Is this your first time?" Pearl smiles astutely.

"Can you tell?" I laugh.

She·shakes her head. "Don't worry, this is the first time for a lot of women here today... And men," she states, turning to the other side of the old, desperately in need of a lick of paint, reception area.

I follow her gaze to the two reprobates grinning like Cheshire cats. Approaching them, Simon opens his arms dramatically.

"M, fancy meeting you here. Oh, and the beautiful Mrs E!" His eyes flick behind me, and Jules is at my rear, along with Charlie.

"Zip it, smart mouth! You're not too old to go over my knee," Jules says. With her hands on my shoulders, she twists me around and scrutinises me. I look from her to Charlie, feeling a little too centre of attention for my liking.

"Maybe you should skip this and take a nap instead?" she whispers. "You look like you've already had an extreme workout this morning."

I turn red through sexual mortification. It isn't often I get embarrassed like this. When the girls say anything untoward, I use wisdom as a weapon, but this woman sees everything. And she's my age, so I can't exactly scold either.

"Jules!" I snap and instantly look at a grinning Tommy and Simon, who heard all of it.

Great.

Brilliant.

"She's right, you do look tired," Simon says and nudges Tommy in the ribs, who bellows out laughing. "We should call the boss so he can take you back to bed." It's innocent enough, but there is no mistaking the underlying inference.

"Simon," I growl.

"What are you two even doing here?" Charlie asks, shoving her workout mat into Tommy's chest.

"The same thing you are."

"Really?"

"Absolutely!" Simon replies. "It's not every day we're openly welcome into a room full of scantily clad women, stretching in ways that can make us men cry. Hallelujah for tight, well fitted... Oh, man!" he exclaims as a stunning blonde crosses his path. He quickly moves after her, forgetting all about us.

Tommy, still amused by the whole situation, remains collected, watching his friend go for the prize, only to return a few moments later, plainly shot down.

"Not interested?" Charlie asks with fake charm.

"Charlotte, my beautiful little pixie, I'm too much man for that woman to handle!"

"You keep telling yourself that!" say quips, then follows the gaggle of women into the main room.

"Right, if everyone can find a space, we'll begin," Pearl announces.

I drop my bag on a bench and find a space at the back where I can proceed to break my legs in partial privacy. Laying out my mat, trepidation snakes around my body until Jules nudges me and lays her mat next to mine.

"Don't worry, Marie. You'll be fine," Charlie says, boxing me in on the other side.

"Easy for you to say. My old bones have got decades on yours, girl."

She is about to answer when her eyes narrow. "Oh, no. I do not think so."

"Oh, come on, Char!" Simon cajoles, as he and Tommy roll their mats out behind us. "You can't expect us to be at the front of the class. That would ruin the entire rear view!"

"Move it!" Charlie orders.

I quickly cover my mouth to hide the snigger that has just drifted past my lips.

"Char!"

"Don't 'Char' me! You're not looking at my rear view. In front. Now!"

"Problem, ladies?" Pearl speaks up, drawing every head in the room towards us.

"No," Charlie says sweetly. "They," she thumbs behind us, "were just moving."

"Fuck!" Tommy hisses under his breath, picks up his mat and lobs it down in front of Charlie. Simon follows suit, not making any kind of qualm about it, and tosses his mat alongside.

Finally, the class starts, and I get into the flow of it, using the beginners poses being demonstrated by her assistant until the tranquil is disrupted.

"Sorry, I'm late!" Sophie runs in, complete with the unique flair and drama she brings to every situation. Groans rise from the front of the class – from the ones who actually know what they are doing.

"Thank you, but please find a space and keep the noise to a minimum," Pearl requests in annoyance.

"What?" Soph asks. She rolls her mat out next to Jules' and gives us an innocent look. "So, what have I missed? Jesus, Marie! You look knackered already!"

"Why, thank you, Miss Loquacious."

In pose, I lift my head, and Simon whips around. "I think you'll find M's tiredness has J's name written all over it."

Sophie's eyes glint wickedly. "Oh, do tell!"

"Simon!" I whisper-shout, and he grins sheepishly and looks away.

I vanquish his implication from my head and proceed to re-join the class. After all, I've paid for this gentle torture, it would be a shame not to get my money's worth.

"Breath in, hold and exhale." Pearl's voice carries over the low sounds of breathing in the room. "Draw your breath deep into your lungs. Feel the tension leave the body and allow the calm to take over."

Tension and calm? These yoga types are a law unto themselves, but who am I to comment?

Twenty minutes later, with my tension banished and my calm flowing, I'm getting the swing of it.

"And reach up to the sky!" Pearl's voice echoes, along with the light slap of her bare feet over the floor. "Pretend there is an invisible piece of string, pulling you towards the heavens. Keep your core strong!"

My mouth falls open at her enthusiasm, but I follow relatively easy. Far easier than I thought I would.

"Now, the next pose is Adho Mukha Svanasana. Remember, if you're a beginner, please follow Rachel."

"What is that?" I ask anyone who cares to answer me. When it fails to get a response, I turn to Jules, who looks as baffled as I do.

"Downward facing dog," Charlie confirms, her body moving fluidly into the more advanced position.

"I think Marie's had enough of facing down already this morning!" Sophie sniggers.

"Oh, can you all just shut up!" I close my eyes to block them out and perform the beginner's pose, satisfied with my limited ability.

"Now, hands apart, stretch up and lean forward. All the way over, until your palms touch the floor in line with your toes. If you can't reach, just go as far as you can. We're going to combine the poses into the sequence of Surya Namaskara."

"Jesus, does she ever speak English?" I mutter, exasperated.

"Sun Salutation," Charlie translates again.

"We'll do the warm-up first and then a few rounds. Ready?"

Not really, but I'll co-operate.

With my palms together, poised for the sky, I send up a small prayer not to agree to anything while half-cut ever again.

"Got anywhere urgent you need to be, lady?" Jules asks as I throw my bag into the back of the Audi.

"Not really," I reply. My grand idea of going to the house isn't as appealing as it was this morning. Maybe it's because as time ebbs away, the fear inside - the fear I'm all about conquering - is winning the battle I have mentally already lost.

"Fancy a coffee and a chat?"

"Sure," I reply because I haven't seen her in weeks.

Inside the nearby greasy spoon, the smell of a full English is intense, while the fumes from the deep fat fryer sear my eyeballs instantly. It's safe to say I'm probably going to smell like a chip shop when I leave here.

"The usual?" Jules asks, and I nod and sit down.

A few minutes later she places down my skinny cappuccino and takes a seat.

"I'm sorry," she says compassionately.

"About what?" I dump two sweeteners into the mug and stir the foam out of it.

"The comments about you and John. If I had known it would become a running joke, I wouldn't have said anything. I'm sorry."

"It's okay. I'm sure I'll get over the mortification when I'm dead," I reply flippantly, hiding my displeasure behind the mug.

"M, stop it. John's an intelligent, gorgeous, sexy guy. Even I'm not immune to a good-looking man like him."

My eyes dart up, and I'm sure they are narrowing in suspicion. And jealousy. This woman has had him in her life for years. For all the talk that it was an innocent employment gig, her words have just insinuated it wasn't that clear-cut.

"Besides, the way Sloan's going on, I'll never have another good-looking man, so I'm already resigned to living vicariously through you! I'm desperate, remember?"

I grin and remember back to last year when she declared she had met someone in New York. Sloan, as you would expect, had a conniption. The lecture about safe sex, STD's and condoms he gave to his mother, is a conversation that should never be heard. And definitely not in the public arena, regardless if it was in front of family. After his little outburst, Jules stopped opening her mouth.

Nevertheless, she's beautiful, and she shouldn't have to face the rest of her days alone because her son can't handle that she needs some male attention every now and then.

A thought overwhelms, and I place my mug down. I shouldn't ask, but I can't stop the words tumbling off my wayward tongue. "Did you and John ever...?" The words stick in my throat.

"No. I can't even believe you'd think that let alone ask!" she laughs, but I'm failing to see anything funny.

"Sorry, I shouldn't have."

"Don't be. M, you're a beautiful woman, who's got an equally beautiful man. Believe me, the kids tried. Repeatedly. But he never looked at me the way he looks at you. I don't think he even looked at his ex-wife the way he looks at you!" The last word is spoken in amusement, and it warms me slightly.

I take a sip of my coffee, debating whether to ask her the newest question that is gaining momentum inside my head.

"What was she like?"

"John's ex?" Jules' eyebrows lift. "She was cruel. Not at first, although first didn't last long because it was pretty much over before it had even begun. But the things she did towards the end... She was a cruel fucking bitch, and that's not something I will say lightly about a fellow woman."

"What did she do?"

Jules fidgets, baring her discomfort of a conversation that was jointly orchestrated. "It's really not my place to-"

"No, I understand." I reach over and pat her knee. "Can I ask you something else? Something about John?"

Acute anxiety spreads over her face, suspicious as to what I will ask in the forthcoming minutes.

"When you hired him and told him about the beatings you and the kids were suffering, how did he react?" It is a question of personal desperation, but I need to know. I need to know what kind of reaction I might receive when I give him what I promised and expose the truth. About everything. My family; Joe; Faith.

Always my Faith.

"He was calm the day I told at our first meeting. Then the next day, he came to the house, and the kids let him in. The same evening when I finally got rid of the bastard," she says without a hint of emotion, referring to Charlie's father, Franklin Black. Who, as fate would have it, shares a colourful, entwined past with Kara's deceased father. "John finally let his emotions show. He was angry, and at one point, I'm sure he was ready to act that anger out. I think the kids being asleep kept him in check. Later, Sloan told me how he reacted when he saw their bruises. I felt like such a failure that I couldn't stop the bastard from hurting them, but I was weak; ill."

"Did he blame you?"

Shuffling her chair around, her expression widens from confusion to moderate understanding, clearly suspecting something. "No. Never. Marie, what are you...? Is there something you want to talk about?"

"No, no," I mutter. "I was just curious. I need to go." Scooping up my bag, she grips my wrist.

"John loves you, in every way a person can be loved. He would die for you. Don't ever forget that. When you..." She moves her head from side to side. "Don't be afraid to tell him whatever it is you need to. If he lashes out, remember the side of him speaking was the man who wasn't there to protect you, not the man you love, okay?"

"Okay," I confirm, press my lips together and say goodbye.

I jog back to my car, disengage the locks and get in. Retrieving my purse, I unfold the picture buried in the back.

"Faith," I whisper. Swiping my thumb over her face, I know it's time to set her soul free.

Then maybe mine can be, too.

Chapter 27

I REMOVE THE boxes from the boot and slam down the door. Balancing everything precariously, I cast my gaze over the street. Precious memories rush back in, and I'm mentally bombarded with all the good times I had had here.

Taking a breath, I open the door and drop my load on the floor. The aim that I was going to come over and clean every week regardless was a complete lie. This is the first time in years I have crossed the threshold.

Every few days, John gets one of the boys to come by and collect the post. I'm grateful, but today I need to close off the life I had made for myself. The life that I had salvaged from the tattered shreds of the broken woman who first stepped foot inside all those years ago, both excited and nervous to finally have a home of my own. One that I couldn't be kicked out of when I made a mistake. One that I wasn't occupying out of another's false pretences. No, this home was mine, and it's as empty now as it was then. And by the time I leave today, it will have gone full circle, and the life I worked so hard for will probably fit into a few boxes and bin bags.

Rolling the anxious knot from my shoulders, my absolution is weak at best as I remember the last time I was here alone.

An ominous chill consumes my body, and I jolt when a natural creak resonates in the silence. I sigh in fearful recollection as the almost authentic sensation of inhaling noxious fumes, followed by my knees hitting the floor, is too strong to forget. So strong, until I can't, and the memory returns with savage ferocity.

Striding up the path, my brain runs over the events of tomorrow. I halt with my hand on the door handle, noting the landing light on. Mentally retracing my steps, I significantly remember turning it off before I came out tonight.

"Marie?" Sloan shouts out from the limo.

"Nothing. I just thought I turned the light off earlier, that's all. I'll see you in the morning, honey."

Closing the door behind me, I drop down my bag and sigh.

"John?" I call out, hoping he has returned early and will be greeting me with nothing but a smile. It's something he likes to do as often as possible.

Honestly, I can't berate Kara for what I've seen or heard tonight. These days, I sometimes wonder what clothes were invented for since mine seem to decorate the floor more often than not.

A creak emanates from the living room, and I open the door and flick on the light. Edging inside, a sense of foreboding drifts over the atmosphere.

"John?" I call again.

"Guess again, bitch!" A menacing lilt speaks up behind me.

"SLOAN!" I scream out, as a hand smashes against the side of my face. Feeling my body collapse under me, I recognise the devil from the pictures John has shown me, as Deacon Black fills my vision.

My limbs are pulled painfully as he ties me up, and his cruel smile is the last thing I see before his hands wrap around my throat and his words echo inside my head.

"No one can fucking save you!"

And I believe him because I've heard those words before.

I gasp in horror and clutch my hand to my throat, attempting to stabilise my breathing. I edge towards the door where the penultimate act took place, but the calm I long to feel doesn't come.

As I stand here now, fighting back my fear, I wish I hadn't been so stubborn and allowed John to come with me today. Still, it's a blessing. The times he has asked me how I'm feeling - a question that still resonates from his lips to my ears from time to time - I lie, because he is unaware of the nightmares I still endure. And even though the bastard can't hurt me again, it is the depravity of what he did that ensures I will continue to suffer in silence.

Truthfully, I shall never forget the moment I came face to face with the devil.

The backhand across my jaw, my face smashing against the floor, and my limbs being incapacitated. The pain lingers deep, remembering his cruel laugh when I woke in terror. But not as deep as when he dragged me up the stairs by my arms, tied above my head, and the agony that reverberated over and over as my spine slammed hard against each rung. But above all that, the tortured sound of my own screams still echoes inside my head.

I suppress the tears and stare up at the ceiling, recalling the instant I thought I was going to be raped and murdered when he threw me onto the bed. The fear I felt was indescribable, and I finally understood why Kara ran when she confessed that he broke her, because that night, he broke me, too.

But no one knows how truly broken I am. And that's because I slap on the daily façade, urging myself to hold it together.

Inside, I need to be that strong woman who walks through life and doesn't look back. Except, I can't, because that strength has been replaced by a mental frailty I no longer recognise. That frailty was a side of myself I finished with a long time ago, and I left it six feet under along with my heart.

And the rat bastard dragged it back from the grave.

I run my hands over my face and pull myself together. Stretching up on my toes, I swipe my fingers over the door mouldings, and the dust darkens my tips. I chew my lip in contemplation, overwhelmed and not knowing where to start.

I pick up a box because the hallway is as good a place as any. I dump the phone and answer machine inside and collect up the remaining bits and bobs I have acquired over the years. Others may see them as tat, but to me, they are treasure; keepsakes that brought me comfort in hard times.

Nudging the kitchen door with my hip, I drop the box on the table and open the first cabinet. I cringe at the multitude of gimmicky gadgets I was seduced into buying but never used. Boxing them up without a second thought, I feel a sense of satisfaction that this stuff will be going to another good home when I take them to the charity shop.

I move from the kitchen to the dining room and pack away the last of the picture frames and the wall mirror.

Closing the door, another room bites the dust. Two down, five to go.

I step into the living room and lean against the door frame as a memory of John lounging with his feet up hits me. Months after we started seeing each other, he became a permanent fixture here. His boots were by the door, his clothes were in the wardrobe, and his toothbrush and razor were in the bathroom.

Now the roles are reversed, and I wish it wasn't so. I wish that night had never happened, and that it could all go back to the way it was. But that is something else that can never be.

Moving through the room, titbits of yesteryear come flooding back. Kara standing in front of the TV, giving the remote a workout to no avail. The way she stomped around the house when I made her go back to school in what she affectionately labelled the waiter's outfit.

Ultimately, I remember the way she curled up on the sofa, caving in on herself, day in, day out when it all turned to shit with Sloan the first time around. Then the second, and finally, the third and final time when she returned.

This room has seen it all, and its secrets shall live on with it.

The sound of the letterbox snapping shut rouses me from my reverie. Checking my watch, it has just gone two o'clock. I've been here hours, and regardless that I wanted closure, it's still taking longer than I would have liked.

I close the living room door and pick up the post. I flip over the missed delivery card and huff out. They didn't even knock, for crying out loud! I slip it into my bag and look up the stairs.

Gripping the banister, I inch up each rung and turn into what was my home office. Collecting up the junk, I do a sweep of the rooms then enter my old bedroom. These days, there isn't much left up here. Most of it John stripped out when I refused to return. I stop in front of the dressing table and look up because there is still one room to go. And no one has touched it in years.

Opening the loft hatch, I roll down the ladders and put my foot on the first rung. At the top, I flick on the light and squint as the musty space illuminates, exposing the years of junk I have stored up here.

I crawl under the eaves and pull over the first storage box. Unclipping the lid, I slam it back down instantly. These are things I never wanted anyone to see. Things that, inside, *I* never wanted to see. Pushing it aside until the very end, I drag the next one over.

Lifting the lid, this time I smile, seeing the photo albums inside. Setting them aside, I hold up the nineties striped knitwear, wondering what on earth I was thinking when I bought them. Deeming the box fit for charity, I continue to dig through the nineties and noughties clothing until I reach the box that houses Kara's old things.

Unknown to her, I never threw away the clothes she arrived in. I washed them and put them up here. Holding up the tatty jumper, I breathe in the stale scent; hers having disappeared years ago. Resting it in my lap, I know I can't keep them. I also know the charity shop won't want them either. Tears prick my eyes because I'm conflicted, but with a heavy heart I finally toss them aside - yet more items to rot in landfill.

Going through each remaining box, a lifetime of bills, property documents and mortgage statements, I finally close the lid on the last one.

I carry each box down the steps until the only one remaining is the one I don't know if I can face opening.

Dropping it on the bedroom floor, I sit on my shins and close my eyes. My heart and mind flood with emotion until I can no longer stand it, and I rip off the lid.

I stare at the contents and remove the framed picture my mother gave me all those years ago. My thumb glides over her shining blue eyes and blonde curls gently. God, it's been so long since I have seen it, I feel guilty that I have forgotten just how delicate and angelic she was. But how could I have forgotten? It's a stupid question of culpability, but I know how, because I kept her memory inside this box, waiting to be seen, to be remembered again.

I grip the frame tight and cradle it to my chest. Propping myself against the mattress, I stare blindly, realising I can't hide her any longer.

A faint ringing seeps in, but I ignore it and pick up the next picture. I smile at myself, only a child, in the arms of my sister, who, up until yesterday, I hadn't seen in over two decades.

"Maggie," I whisper, regressing back to the day it was taken, years before I turned my back on her, resolute in finding an existence that would not judge me.

I concentrate hard on the handful of memories, ending with the final one that put the nail in the coffin, as a loud banging rumbles throughout the house. I snap my head up, realising I have been crying, lost in time. I scramble up, wipe my eyes and run down the stairs.

Opening the front door, John is standing there. His smile evaporates instantly when he sees my teary demeanour.

"John," I whisper, my body shaking, threatening to take me down.

"Angel?" he asks with concern and quickly grabs me when my knees begin to buckle. His hands sit softly on my cheeks, cupping them while he assesses me.

"Just hold me." My body continues to shake against him, expelling every pent-up emotion that has chipped away at my soul for a lifetime.

I inadvertently stare over his shoulder as a car moves slowly down the street. My eyes track it, seeing the shadow of a ghost – probably a figment of my imagination since the past is lurking openly upstairs.

"Darling?" John murmurs as he gently shifts me aside and locks the door.

I shake my head, take his hand, and lead him upstairs.

"Is this going to be like the first time you seduced me into coming in here?"

I glare at him as he lingers in the bedroom doorway. Comprehending this isn't the time for jokes, he looks wide-eyed at the pictures I have left out. He bends down and reaches into the box and pulls out my old CD's - ones I had listened to over and over until they no longer played.

"Oasis, Blur, The Charlatans... The Verve. Great album."

"Hmm, that was my favourite."

"Why?" he asks, reading the playlist.

"I could relate to a lot on there at the time. Trust me, the drugs really don't work."

He smirks at my play on words. "Did you have the grunge combats and boots, too?"

My lips curve, because I did, and I wore them until they were threadbare.

He digs around in the box, and my heart shudders as he lifts out a picture.

"Wow, weren't you a little looker? All long blonde hair and blue eyes. I bet the boys were lined up outside your door," he says in jest, but I know he means every word.

I sigh in capitulation and choose my confession carefully. She may look like me, she isn't me, but he isn't aware.

"That's not me." I stare at him intently, waiting for the penny to drop. His face runs through a variety of emotions, unable to figure out what I am saying.

"I don't-"

"Understand? No, because I've never told you. That's my sister," I confirm and snake my arms around myself in cold comfort. His confusion is unmistakable, but it's clear he really doesn't know. Hope blossoms that he might be compassionate when I finally speak the truth.

"She looks exactly like you," he says confused.

"We're twins." I assess his expression. "Identical."

"What's her name?"

"Her maiden name is Turner. Magdalene Turner."

He breathes out in a whistle. "She's the woman who called the house," he murmurs. "I don't know what to say. Why did you never tell me?"

I shrug my shoulders and test the waters. "Are you angry that I didn't?"

"No! Fuck. Sorry, I didn't mean that. It's just a shock." His brow furrows, and his fingers splay over his jaw. "When did you last see her?" His eyes lift, encouraging my answer.

Do I lie and say it was when we were both younger? Or do I tell him the truth?

"Yesterday," I confess, knowing honesty is the best way forward from here. The truth is, I want him to know her, to eventually meet her. I want her to share this part of my life. Keeping her hidden was wrong. I've always known that.

"What do you mean, yesterday?" he asks tightly.

"She came to the house yesterday afternoon. She was at the door when you called me."

My blood turns cold when his expression reveals his shock and dismay.

"I'm sorry." I back away as the first unavoidable tear falls. "I can't..." I can't say what I need to because there is nothing that will make this deceit right, and the glare he is piercing me with confirms it. "Please, I'm sorry," I whimper. "Don't be angry with me. Please."

He rushes towards me, and his firm arms curl around my front, as he rocks me slow and steady.

"I'm not angry, angel. I just don't understand why you would never tell me about her."

"I was – *am* – ashamed. My life wasn't always like this. The amazing life I have with you? I never thought I would have that. I always thought I was destined to be alone. At first, I was alone by design, and before I found Kara, it was by choice."

He walks us to the bed and lays us down. I curl up on the mattress, and he pulls me into his chest. Removing a strand of stray hair from my face, he tucks it behind my ear.

"You promised," he says after a strained silence.

"I didn't know how to tell you," I confess, hoping empathy will prevail. "The last time I saw her we were both nineteen. A lot of things had happened in the years leading up to my leaving. Except one, none of them were good." I try to cover my face, but he tangles his fingers in mine and lowers them between us.

"What was the one good thing?"

My eyes smart instantly. Trust him to ask the question of which I'm terrified to give the honest answer to.

"I can't," I whisper. "I promise I'll tell you, but not now. Please understand." My tears echo in the room. The movement of the mattress beneath us, the natural sounds of the house, none of it hides my pain.

His hand slides over my hip and down my back. Hovering just above my backside, he tightens his protective hold.

"Tell me about Magdalene," he requests, a small smile playing on his lips.

"She's amazing. What she does with her life is so altruistic. She's beautiful, inside and out. Selfless, considerate, beyond generous. I feel inferior beside her."

"Why? What does she do?"

I sigh because I know his thoughts on religion. Just like me, he is faithless. Unlike me, his faithlessness comes from three tours of duty and horrors which once seen, can never be unseen. His idea of God left him when his comrades, his brothers in arms, were shot down in vain in a barren, sandy wasteland under an unforgiving, scorching sun. His faith vanished with the senseless bloodshed that made a desert run red.

"She helps others less fortunate in her community." I deviate from the truth, but not exactly omitting the reality of her profession. I must admit, it's still a shock to me that that is the path she has chosen. But she's happy, and that's all I ever wanted for her. For me, too. But it has been proven my happiness will never be found in black and white.

"Charity work?"

"Something like that. I've missed out on so much. She broke my heart yesterday, caring for me, forgiving me for everything I did before I left."

"What happened?"

"She came to tell me-"

"No, when you left. I presume you were nineteen?"

I nod, insofar as I can with my head nested to his chest. "The way I left wasn't pretty. The things that happened destroyed me, but I didn't have any other choice."

"Why did she finally make contact after all these years?"

"Because my mother is sick. Dying. She doesn't have long left, and my father isn't coping." I stare into his eyes, seeing the sorrow in them. Sorrow that he will feel acutely since his mother died when he was still a teenager and Louisa became both mum and sister. To add insult to injury, they both grew up fatherless after the man walked out when John was seven and Louisa was sixteen. It's a sad state of affairs, but my situation isn't theirs. I had my parents growing up, and yet, in many ways, I didn't.

"I'm sorry, angel," he says woefully.

"Don't be. I was close to my mum, but my dad... Well, we never had what you would call a good relationship. It was strained up until I was sixteen, then it was non-existent until I left." Sucking on my top lip, I wonder how far I can go before I can't turn back. "He kicked me out when I was sixteen. He told me I was dead to him."

John's eyes widen. "Say again?" he asks in anger.

"I made a mistake," I confess quietly.

"A mistake? Why, what did you do? It's not like you came home pregnant, is it?" There's a hint of mockery in his voice, but he has just unknowingly touched upon the truth.

When he first endeavoured to ask about my feelings towards a family, I shut him down. Over time, he's put two and two together and come up with five. It breaks my heart that he thinks I'm infertile. It breaks even further knowing that while I might still be able to have a family - more through medicine, than biology and natural endeavour - he still carries hope for us.

Truthfully, I've been a spiteful bitch, and I know I don't deserve anything he has given me.

Feeling his fingers brush my cheeks, sliding down my jaw to my throat, I close my eyes.

"I made a mistake," I whisper again, and I fall back into the day my evasive confession was my reality.

And my downfall.

Chapter 28

SLAPPING MY HAND over my mouth, the bile inside my oesophagus begins to ascend until I can taste the contents of my stomach in the back of my throat. I inhale deeply, aware this is just the start.

"Are you okay?" Joe asks from the driver's seat, rolling a cigarette.

Okay. It's a debatable word right now.

"We're still on for Saturday night, right? You told your parents you're staying over at Lynsey's again?"

"Yeah," I confirm, feeling wretched for the first time in my efforts to see a boy I am forbidden to - and involving my unsuspecting friend in the process. Every day it gets harder, and I don't know how long I can keep up the charade. Or how long it will be before someone sees us, informs my dad, and I have to face the consequences for the web of lies I'm spinning.

I know the house of cards will eventually fall and shall be floundering beneath them when it happens.

"Call me from the phone box when you want me to pick you up, yeah?" He lights the roll up, and the car fills with the putrid scent of cannabis. He's occasionally tried to get me to smoke it, but even I'm not that gullible.

"I can't. I don't have any money." I scrunch up my nose, feeling queasy.

"What happened to your allowance?"

"I spent it," I reply, unwilling to get into that conversation with him.

"Fine. Here." He digs into his pocket, producing a fistful of change. Opening my palm, he stuffs the coins into it. "Call me."

I nod and open the door, desperate for some fresh air. My action is refuted when he jerks my wrist hard. This is something that has been happening a lot recently. The changes have been subtle, but every day he gets a little more aggressive. I should be worried, because eventually, it may turn into more. But right now, I can't concern myself with something that is still a maybe.

"What was that?" he asks harshly.

"Yes, thank you," I confirm, a slight wobble in my tone, but my mind is on other things.

I stand on the kerb and watch as he guns the car down the street. As the rumble of the engine fades into the distance, I turn and look up at the house. My house. The house I grew up in. The one I can't wait to be emancipated from.

As I edge up the path, every sound is amplified. From the birds chirping in the dense tree canopy lining the street, to the throttle of nearby cars, right down to my feet, tapping on the stones beneath them.

Looking over the driveway, both of my parent's cars are absent. My father is probably still at the rectory, going through his work for the week. And my mother, who knows, since she has become the queen bee of the local groups for coffee mornings, knitting, helping the elderly, and whatever else she does to occupy her time now that she isn't running around after two energetic children anymore.

Still, I can't complain. Today, I'm entirely thankful they are not home already.

The church bells toll overhead, piercing the quiet afternoon with their melodic chimes as I unlock the door. Transfixed on the steeple in the distance, I wonder if I should start to pray again. My faith flew many years ago when I was far too young to become disillusioned and weary of life. Honestly, I feel like a fraud sitting in church every Sunday.

Inside the house, a hollowness emanates, giving rise to the sickness that has culminated in my stomach these last few days. I stare at my reflection as I drop my keys on the table. Assessing my appearance, this is the second time I have done this when no one is around. I study my face, trying to see if there is anything there that looks different. There isn't, of course, but I know there is. It isn't confirmed yet, but I feel it. And after today, I won't be able to bury my head in the proverbial sand or disguise it for much longer.

I pull out two pint glasses from the kitchen cabinet and fill each to the brim. I chew my lip, unsure how much is required. Surely two pints should be sufficient, but what do I know? I've never had to do this before.

Carrying them up the stairs, my mind drifts from calm to terrified incessantly. It is the fear of the unknown, and of a future that I don't think I will be alone in.

In the sanctum of my bedroom - which, fortunately, I don't have to share with Maggie - I put the water down on my dressing table. I toe off my shoes and shrug out of my jacket.

Picking up a glass, I down as much as I can, until my gag reflex begs me to stop. Allowing my stomach to settle from the influx of liquid, I upend my bag and reach for the box sat atop of my O-level books.

I turn it in my hand, before tearing it open and reading the instructions. Pacing up and down, I finish the first glass of water and start on the second.

Ten minutes later, with the glass drained, I perch myself on the edge of the bed. My leg shakes in a way it never has before. Lifting my head from the instrument of my impending doom, my stomach curdles repeatedly. Whether it is the acid churning or my fear coming out tenfold, I don't know.

Fed up with procrastinating, I pull out my homework - the stuff I should have been doing for the last week but haven't because more pressing matters have been on my mind as of late. Laying my language book over my lap, I'm unable to concentrate. I admit defeat and toss it aside after reading the same paragraph over and over without taking in a single word.

Twenty minutes later, my bladder starts to protest, and I leg it into the bathroom, white stick in one hand, instructions in the other. Placing the leaflet on the cistern, I send up a small prayer.

One I hope isn't in vain.

"Two," I whisper, as I sit on the floor and glare at the white stick, willing it to do something. "Come on," I urge, timing the minutes. "Three."

No sooner as the word left my lips, the window begins to change. Holding it between my finger and thumb, I inhale deeply and stand.

"Pregnant," I whisper.

The waters in my mouth are the first sign of what is to come, and I grasp the rim of the toilet bowl and throw up the remaining contents in my stomach.

Pregnant.

The result is final. It can't be changed or undone.

Rinsing my mouth, the girl staring back at me in the mirror is just as pale and sickly as I feel.

Lightheaded and in a daze, I can't remember walking the few feet from the bathroom to my bedroom. Nor can I remember how I came to be standing in front of my dressing table, now rubbing my belly, speculating how long it will be before nothing fits me. And how long it will be before I must confess my sins and face retribution for them.

The gravitas of my newly found situation overwhelms me, and my tears flow freely without a hope in hell of stopping them. Still holding the stick firmly, I stare at the little window, praying it might have changed or it could be a mistake. Or maybe it's defective, but I know that's not true.

My body is changing. It isn't just physical, it's mental and emotional, too. I feel different now than I did months ago. I didn't need to waste three weeks' worth of my pocket money on this to tell me what I already know.

When I finally plucked up the courage to enter the chemist, the pharmacist promised this was the best and quickest they had for sale. It was also the newest, and therefore the most expensive. I listened carefully, wanting to get the damn thing and get out of there, I then had to sit for twenty minutes and endure the safe sex talk. She also advised that if the test came back positive, I should make an appointment with my doctor as soon as possible. And as good advice as that is, I can't just go flouncing into my local surgery because they will tell my mother. Or worse, my father. I took far too many risks doing the same with the local chemist, but it is the only one we have.

But all those fears are now futile because I owe it to my unborn child to do the right thing - regardless of how brutal the fallout may be.

And since there is nothing further I can say or do to remedy my situation, I drop the stick into a carrier bag and shove it under my underwear in the drawer.

Shedding a solitary tear, I crawl onto the bed and ball myself up. As I wipe my cheek, I wonder what my future will be like now. Holding my growing stomach protectively, I wonder what our future will be like now.

Stretching out, a familiar presence lurks in the darkness of my room. Turning over, Maggie is curled up beside me, her fingers softly raking through my hair.

"Dinner's ready. Are you okay?" she asks in a tone that makes me suspicious.

"Hmm." I shuffle up the bed, until my back presses into the velour headboard and I flick on the lamp. "I'm fine. Why wouldn't I be?"

"I don't know. Maybe because I saw Joe in town and he said you were acting weird lately," she says, now sitting up with one hand behind her back. "Or maybe because I came home early from school and I found this in the bathroom." She holds up the test instructions. I instantly put my hand over my mouth to stifle my cry, having momentarily forgotten my new reality.

"Maggie..." I whimper.

"Don't worry, I got home before anyone else. Good job, really. So...?" She can't bring herself to ask the question, just like I can't bring myself to verbally admit it. Instead, I nod shamefully, then burst into tears.

The mattress moves, and she enfolds me in her arms and rocks me. Grappling my hands around her back, I cling to her, never wanting to let go. Pretending if we stay inside this little cocoon, the world will cease to exist.

"Shush," she soothes. "It'll be alright." But those are the words of a trusting fool, and I desperately want to believe her.

Except she's wrong, of course, because I have three options available to me. One, adoption; two, abortion; or three, the prospect of raising a child while still a child myself.

It isn't lost on me that the prospects of Joe buckling down and doing the right thing are minimal. I've heard rumours swirling again, but as with everything I don't want to face - including this unplanned pregnancy - I buried my head. Sadly, it also isn't lost on me that Joe, nor his parents, are going to take this news kindly.

And that is putting it kindly.

His behaviour of late is questionable. There have been plenty of times in the last few months when he has grabbed me with more force than necessary or said things that are hurtful. Not to mention his increased consumption of drugs and alcohol.

No, it isn't a matter of him doing the right thing, it's a matter of whether I will be able to raise a child single-handedly. I only hope it is the former that prevails and not the latter. Still, I won't get my hopes up for a happy ever after anytime soon.

Then there is also the other more fearful element of informing my father that his daughter is now with child. I can only imagine his reaction when the awful truth spreads that the good vicar's daughter is already on the road to ruin. Sixteen, unmarried and pregnant.

God, it sounds awful even inside my own head.

"How long have you known?" Maggie asks, pushing my hair from my tear-stained face, guiding me back from the precipice of my unwelcome thoughts.

"Officially, since about midday. Unofficially, maybe a month. I've just missed my second period, and I think I've started with morning sickness," I confess pathetically. "I didn't mean for this to happen. It was always safe, so I just don't understand!" I shriek, conveying my misery. Yet for all my excuses, I do understand. I understand very well when the moment of conception likely happened. It was the day I faked sickness in church, leaving home with my virtue intact, and returning without it. It was the day he led me to his bedroom and told me he loved me. It was the day I let my imprudence overrule, taking with it my common sense.

It was the day I had sex for the first time.

"What have you done with the test?"

"It's in my underwear drawer." I glance towards my dressing table.

"Keep it. The doctor might want to see it when you make an appointment," she says logically.

I shake my head, still believing I can keep it hidden. "No, Maggie. I can't, they'll tell-"

"You have to! Mum and Dad are going to find out anyway. How long do you think you've got before you're massive? Don't be so stupid!" she admonishes in a tone I have never heard from her before.

Growing up, it was always apparent which parent each of us took after. Maggie is a pacifist, just like our mum. She abstains from arguments and does as she is told. I, on the other hand, am my father through and through. Both of us like things our way, and we are both equally vocal in getting it. But two strong personalities don't usually bode well together, and this is also apparent whenever he raises his hand to me. He always denies it, if I ever get so rattled and speak of it, but it's true. There's also a chance he will do it again when he gains knowledge of my shameful indiscretion in the weeks to come.

Staring into Maggie's eyes, they are silently urging me to be more considerate of the child I am carrying.

"Fine," I say. "I'll book an appointment."

"Good. We'll bin this on the way to school in the morning." She shuffles off the bed and rights her jumper.

While I gather up my books, I make a mental note to start learning to my full potential again. Over the months, my interest has shifted from getting good marks, to spending every waking minute with Joe. Now that has changed. I know for the sake of having a future worth living – however that may pan out – I need to do better. For both of us, I think, caressing my belly.

"Magdalene! Marianne! Dinner!" Mum calls up.

"Crap, come on!" Maggie says.

"Maggie, I'm frightened," I whisper, ready to fall back into teary oblivion and hide.

She looks back and sighs. "I know, but it'll be okay. I promise." Holding out her hand, I take it and squeeze tight.

"Do I look okay?"

"Yeah. I'll deflect if need be."

We head into the dining room and take our respective seats - the same one we've been sitting in since we could walk and climb on our own. I shake out the napkin Mum insists we should use as a sign of good manners and lay it over my lap. As I reach for the potatoes, I grimace, praying masticated spuds won't be sprayed across the table if I can't keep them down.

"So, did anything good happen today, girls?" Mum starts the customary dinner conversation with ease, and Maggie and I instantly look at each other.

"It was eventful," Maggie says with a smile.

"Eventful? That sounds interesting," Dad replies.

"Hmm. I got a B on my mock exam paper. I consider that to be eventful." Maggie deflects easily, as promised.

"Good, but next time get an A," he mutters and turns his attention to me. "Marianne?"

"Erm… Enlightening." I supply my own take on Maggie's answer, while quickly thinking up something plausible - and enlightening.

"She got a B, too," Maggie replies, handing me the bowl of carrots and taking away the potatoes.

Dad smiles like he was suspecting I would get a D. Typical. I know I need to knuckle down, but I was never that bad, even if my head has been thirty thousand feet, floating alongside the clouds these last few months.

"That's fabulous!" Mum exclaims, full of the joys of spring that she has two well-educated daughters in her midst.

I inconspicuously bite my lip, fearing how she is going to react when she finds out one of her so-called educated daughters didn't realise her forbidden boyfriend hadn't worn the condom he conveniently produced until it was too late.

Settling into a quiet family dinner, the conversation eventually centres on our parents, discussing the usual boring aspects of their respective days.

Right now, I wish mine was boring, too. Because one day soon, the conversation in this house will be explosive.

Softy pressing my hand against my stomach, I know it's a given.

Chapter 29

AS I CARESS my little bump, now visible and growing more rotund by the day, I swallow down the waters lining my mouth.

"Please, stop," I whimper, unable to tolerate any more today. I feel dog rough, and since I have vomited up anything I've eaten, I'm also drained of energy. And because of this, I'm starving, more so than I've ever been before. I know it's the baby making me feel this way, but it's pointless to even try to eat when I can't seem to keep anything down.

I groan as another wave of nausea crashes inside my stomach. Rubbing my growing belly, whoever called it morning sickness lied. Or someone up there is cursing me because this is morning, noon and night sickness, and everything else in between. And lucky me, I've had it for nearly two weeks straight. How my parents haven't heard me retching at all hours, I have no idea.

I gaze up at the sky, part my lips, and take in as much oxygen as possible, hoping it will lessen my discomfort.

Sitting on the park bench, I pull out my packet of plain crisps from lunch and contemplate. I guess there is only one way to find out if these will make my stomach do the shimmies.

Tearing them open, the bland, salty smell drifts into my nostrils. My stomach churns instantly, and I put them down and wait for the queasiness to subside.

Holding my belly, I watch the multitude of mothers and their children make the most of the beautiful day. I study them, enraptured by the way they interact - easily and instinctively – and soon that will be me. A mother with a child, or a child with a child. It doesn't matter how you swing it, I will be looking after something that will depend on me for everything. I'd love to say I'm ecstatic, but right now, I'm terrified.

The church bells ring in the distance, and I peek at my watch; now is the time I would usually be finishing school for the day.

Needless to say, after my spectacular show of reverse consumption, my teacher sent me home early, fearing I would spread my 'tummy bug' to the other pupils. Fat chance of that happening. I doubt anyone would want what I have in my tummy - not at this early juncture in life anyway.

Yet regardless of that sentiment, I do want it. I have a miracle growing inside me, and it's a miracle I can't take for granted.

As I sat in class this afternoon, feeling my stomach roil until I ran out, I wanted to break down and cry. I never thought it would be this bad.

While I knelt on the toilet floor, my teacher behind me, holding my hair while I prayed to the U-bend and deposited the contents of my stomach, I was desperate to tell her my secret. I was dying to ask if this was normal. If I was meant to be sick this violently, this frequently.

Except I didn't voice any of that.

Instead, I heeded her advice and went home. Home, being the local park since I couldn't exactly rock up early. My parents, if they are in, will question.

I still haven't told them I'm pregnant. My mother, who should at least have an inkling since she has carried twins, is clueless.

Just last week she left a pack of sanitary towels on my bed like she has for the last four years since my periods started. And the last two months' supply I have passed to Maggie, who has turned into a mother hen.

It's been four weeks since I did the home test. Two weeks since Maggie urged me again to make a doctor's appointment, and one week since I did just that.

Next Friday, after I leave the surgery with confirmation I really don't need, there's a good possibility my parents are finally going to gain the knowledge that their child is with child. Next Friday, the awful truth, which doesn't sound so awful to me – that is if you forget I am sixteen, unmarried and have a boyfriend with a less than stellar reputation – they will know. And if our family GP doesn't inform them sooner, I shall.

My feet trudge slowly as I make my way home. Reaching the garden gate, I stall when I see both cars in the driveway. My mother's, I expected; my father's, not so much. As I open the front door, the quiet is unsettling.

"Mum? Dad?" I call out, and the faint shuffle of furniture seeps into the hallway.

I shrug off my coat and hang it on the rack next to Maggie's. Crap, I forgot about her. She's probably worried about me; she didn't know I left early today. We usually have most of our lessons together, but she chose Latin for languages, and I chose German. Therefore, when I started heaving mid-sentence in a language I'm probably never going to use, she wasn't there.

I untuck my blouse to disguise my tum and open the living room door. Maggie is sitting on the sofa, nice and obedient; her head down, her hands folded in her lap, and I look from her to my parents. Seeing their expressions, I know the shit is about to hit the fan.

"What's wrong?" I ask innocently.

Maggie's head lifts, and she gives me a sad smile, but her eyes linger on my middle. I bring my hands to my front, inconspicuously shielding my secret.

"I had a call earlier from the school receptionist," Mum says. "She told me you had been throwing up all day."

"Close the door and sit down, Marianne." My father cuts her off callously.

I timidly shut the door and bite my quivering lip as my eyes flood with unshed tears.

Turning around my father waves his hand towards the sofa, and I sit where he has indicated. I train my eyes on the floor and link my hands over my middle, acting compliant for the first time in a long time.

"I was putting away your laundry when I found this," Mum says hesitantly, revealing the white stick I paid a small fortune for. "Do you have something to tell us?"

My eyes close in resignation. I was wrong in my assumption of thinking they would find out next Friday. Today it seems, fate is working its trickery.

"I'm pregnant," I mumble.

"What. Did. You. Say?" My father's anger grows with each punctuated word.

I lift my head and look at Maggie. Her features crumple. Obviously, the noise I heard in the hallway was her trying to warn me. Her eyes meet mine and she mouths 'I'm sorry' before my face is abruptly twisted by my father's hand at my jaw.

"I'm waiting," he says viciously.

"I'm pregnant." Tears stream down my cheeks and I screw my face up. "I'm sorry. I didn't mean-"

My apology is cut short, and everything suddenly moves in slow motion. From the feminine gasp floating over the atmosphere to the sound of something slicing through the air, until a hard palm strikes my cheek. My head is forcibly whipped back, and I instantly grab my face and crawl to the other side of the sofa.

"You stupid little slut!" he shouts, raising his hand again.

"Norman!" Mum shrieks. "She's pregnant!"

But it's too late. Too little, too late. She never stopped him when he raised his hand to me before, why change the habit of a lifetime now. I love her, but some things are inexcusable.

My father's eyes grow dark, hateful, as I clutch my face and glare at him. His fists scrunch tight, and I know if I don't move that slap won't be the last today. Edging off the sofa, I put as much distance between us as possible.

"This is all your fault! You're too soft with them!" he says to my mother, and I watch in horror as his hand moves again and he strikes her jaw. I flinch as tears roll down my face. Judging Mum's expression, this definitely isn't the first time he has hit her, but it is the first time that Maggie and I have borne witness to it.

"Who's the father?" Dad demands, and my eyes instantly flit to Maggie for support. "Don't look at her when I ask you a question! Who. Is. The. Father?"

"Joe," I confess, knowing I will feel his wrath again for my betrayal.

"I thought I told you never to see him again!" His tone rises, and the last word is a spoken roar as he reaches for me again.

I move out of striking range, back myself into a corner and hold my arms over my belly. My father's eyes narrow, and I have to question how his adoring flock have never seen this side of him. The side that I've had to deal with for as long I can remember. I don't think there has ever been a time in my life when I haven't feared his reaction when I have done something by accident. Whether it be spilling something or having something I wasn't allowed to. Every time I have fucked up, no matter how big or small, I've been on the receiving end of his anger.

Wallowing in my thoughts, I'm not really paying attention until he says the word that makes my insides falter.

Termination.

"Book her an appointment," he orders Mum. "It needs to be taken care of before anyone finds out." But before he can say anything further, I make my wishes known.

"No, I'm keeping it!" I blurt out. "You," I say to my mother. "And you," this time with more venom to my father, "can't make me get rid of it. And I won't. You can't force me to have an abortion."

"Marianne, you're only sixteen!" Mum cries, nursing her jaw.

"Mum, if I'm old enough to make a baby, I'm old enough to raise it." I point out the logical at such a terrible time.

"Get out."

The two words cut through the fraught atmosphere, replacing the tension with silence.

"What?" I ask incredulously.

"I won't have that boy's bastard under this roof. Now get out!"

Horror washes over me. "But I have nowhere to go!"

"I don't care! I won't have it living in this house. Now, you either get rid of it before anyone finds out, or you get out!"

I slowly round the sofa, my hands out, pleading. "Please, Daddy. I'm not getting rid of it. It goes against our faith!"

"Faith? You have no faith!" He grabs hold of me and drags me into the hallway. Mum and Maggie run after us, crying, clutching each other.

"I always knew you were flighty and uncontrollable. Lead by hormones and dreams!" He hauls me towards the door, picks up my bag and coat, then shoves me outside. "Get out! You're not welcome here anymore."

"Please don't do this! I'm begging you, please!" I cry out, uncaring if our neighbours are watching.

"I can't hear you, Marianne, because you're dead to this family now. Leave, and don't ever come back!"

The door slams shut, and I pound my fists on the wood. My heart breaks over and over, and I'm sure there is nothing left inside to diminish. Turning around, my face tear-stained, my eyes beet red, I slam my skull against the wood and slide down.

"I'm sorry; I'm sorry. I'm fucking sorry!" I scream, until my throat is hoarse.

I curl up on the step while the afternoon slowly fades into evening. A clap of thunder brings the grey skies rolling in at speed, darkening the surrounding landscape. A flash of lightning cracks overhead, and the living room light turns on, illuminating the pristine front garden.

Standing up, I put on my coat and move to the window. Peering inside, Maggie is sat morosely on the sofa, her eyes trained on the floor. My father is sat in his usual seat, flicking through a newspaper, acting as though nothing has happened. In his eyes, it hasn't, because I no longer exist.

I lift my hand to the glass and, instinctively, Maggie looks up. Her eyes say it all and she mouths 'I love you'. Ready to do the same, a figure blocks her, and I gaze up into my mother's eyes. Tears wet her cheeks, and she presses her hand against the pane. I touch mine to hers, prolonging the last stolen moments until my father's hand clamps down on her shoulder and he shoves her aside. Scowling at me like something he has walked in, he draws the curtains sharply, and I flinch because it's finally clear he doesn't love me at all.

Maybe he never has.

Painfully aware that this door will never be open to me again, I turn down the path and slam the gate shut behind me. I run down the street as the rain pelts harder, soaking me to the bone. Seeking shelter inside the phone box on the main road, I dig inside my bag, source twenty pence from the bottom and call the only person I can.

"Yeah?" Joe answers after the third ring.

"Joe." I'm shaking like a leaf. The culmination of being slapped, dragged, and then kicked out, not to mention the abnormal morning sickness and the chill of imminent hypothermia, there isn't much more I can take.

"Marianne?" he asks without a nuance of concern, just irritation.

"I need you to come and get me," I say shakily, then tell him where I am. He hangs up, and I slouch down on the filthy, wet concrete.

It seems like I'm waiting hours until, finally, headlights brighten the year's old scratched glass. The door opens, and Joe stands there, hands on either side of the frame wearing a very ticked off expression.

"What's happened?" he asks, his annoyance morphing into concern.

"M-my d-dad kicked me out!" I reach for him, and he takes me in his arms.

"Why?" he asks flatly, uncaring considering the state he has just found me in.

"Not here." I shake my head. I know I need to do the decent thing and tell him like I should have done weeks ago when I first took that stupid test, but I can't risk not having somewhere to sleep tonight. It's selfish, but I'm not thinking of myself, I'm thinking of the baby. The baby is all that matters now.

"Here," he says. He puts his jacket over my shoulders and guides me to the car. Climbing in, he turns on the ignition and amps up the heaters.

We eventually pull up outside his house, and all the lights are off, suggesting nobody's home.

Typical Joe.

I follow him inside but grab his arm when he attempts to move us upstairs. "We really need to talk about what happened this evening."

"Sure," he replies nonchalantly, his arms moving around my chest. It is so indicative of the times he has held me, then talked me into doing something that was more beneficial to him than it was to me - ultimately putting me in this position.

Sixteen, unmarried and pregnant.

"Let's go upstairs and get you something dry to wear. I'm guessing that righteous bastard didn't put any clothes in there?" His chin jerks towards my bag.

"Don't call him that." Although why I still care is beyond me since that's what he thinks of my baby and me.

Joe flips on his bedroom light, and as always, the room is immaculate. Heading straight to the wardrobe, he pulls out a t-shirt and a pair of shorts and throws them on the bed.

He then lights up a roll up and stalks towards me, re-enacting the same moves he made on me the day we did it for the first time. Considering what I am about to tell him, it's fitting that we've come full circle.

He removes the cigarette from between his lips and takes my bag and jacket. Clearly not wanting to talk about what I am pressing for, he continues to try to get me out of my damp clothes.

"No."

"Don't be coy now. You never refused before." His hands continue to grope.

"I said no!"

"Just relax."

"I'm pregnant!" The words come out loud and firm - and far sooner than I intended.

"What?" The colour drains from his face.

"I'm pregnant," I whisper.

"No, you can't be. I always use a fucking condom!" He pinches the bridge of his nose.

"What's that supposed to mean?"

"Are you sure?" He deflects my question.

"Yes," I whisper again.

He throws his hands on his hips and gives me a look of pure disdain. Inhaling deeply, he stretches his neck. "Is it mine?"

And if there was ever a time I should've known that Joe didn't really give a shit about me, it should have been now, when those three little words of indignation left his mouth.

"Yes!" I bark out, disbelieving he thinks there could be anyone else. "How dare you!"

"You can't blame me for asking!" He fires back. "This isn't fucking happening. I'm too young to be a father!" He walks circles around the room. Linking his hands at the back of his neck, he stares up at the ceiling.

Scorching tears roll down my cheeks because I finally see. For all the hatred that my dad displayed this afternoon, it comes a close second to having the father of my unborn question my fidelity.

But at least I know where I stand now. And my wondering for the last month of whether he will be a part of the life we have created is finally confirmed.

"You'll have to get rid of it!" he says harshly.

I shake my head and step back. "No."

He grabs my shoulders hard and shakes me. "You have to!"

"No, I won't. I told my father I won't, and I'm telling you the same. No!"

"Marianne, see sense. How are you going to raise a kid?"

"We! We are going to raise a kid! And I said, no," I say firmly.

One hand drops, and he jerks his head. "You fucking listen to me and get rid of it! I'll give you the money."

"No, I wo-" My words dissipate as he slaps me across the face. I cover my mouth as he edges back, equally as shocked as I am by his painful feat.

Twice in one day - it can't get any worse.

I grab my coat and bag and run out of the room. Almost tripping down the stairs, I should have known. I should have fucking known. It isn't enough that my own father raised his hand to me, but now Joe finally has, too.

"Marianne!" Joe shouts at me, but I need to get out of here. "Marianne!"

My body is pulled back and a hand slams on the door in front of me. "Baby, I'm sorry. I'm sorry." He forcibly twists me around and tucks me into his chest. "I'm not thinking straight," he pleads. "I'm not thinking. Look at me." I look anywhere but at him, until he tilts my chin, and stares hard and unforgiving into my sodden eyes.

"I just need to wrap my head around it. It's the shock. I didn't mean to lash out. Am I forgiven?"

I nod gravely – my choices are limited. I appreciate the shock of hearing that he is going to be a father at eighteen. Still, it doesn't excuse it. Not at all.

I drop my guard and trudge back up to his room. The atmosphere thickens with every step we take, but what is done cannot be undone. That much is true.

"Look, get some rest. I'll be up in a while." Then he's gone before I can even voice my objection.

Standing behind the door, I force myself to walk away as soon as his steps fade into the bowels of the house.

I cocoon myself in the duvet and clock watch. One hour slips into two, two becomes three, and he still hasn't returned.

My brain trips from one terrible scenario to another, adding to my restlessness, debilitating my thoughts of a longed-for happy ever after.

Casting aside the anguish for the sake of my health and that of my child, I let the painful reality go.

Truthfully, in my heart, I'd settle for a beautiful lie, because it's got to be better than the nothing I currently have.

And unknown to me as I doze off, a beautiful lie is all I will ever have.

"Joe?" I jolt awake and throw my hand over the bed. Finding nothing but fabric, it's a sign of things to come; a half empty nest.

I tiptop onto the landing and down the stairs quietly but stop when movement emanates from the living room. Inching closer, the soft light flickers shadows over the walls.

"This is an absolute mess!" Patricia says, pouring herself a large glass of wine.

"It's finally nice of you to start caring about our son," Duncan retorts. "Maybe if you'd have shown an interest sooner, we wouldn't be in this situation."

"This isn't my fault! He's always been hard to control."

Duncan chortles. "Well if you'd have tried harder, earlier, he might not have been!"

Patricia huffs in vexation but ignores the comment. "Well, I wish he'd never laid eyes on her. She's ruined him!"

I bite my lip; they know. Joe's told them, and now he's gone.

"Now, now, Patty. You know it takes two. Our little precious isn't innocent in all of this. I doubt Marianne planned it."

"Oh, please, as if you aren't thinking the same! That's our boy you're talking about, and deep down he's a good boy."

Duncan strides across the room. "Yes, of course, he is. He's so good he's impregnated the vicar's daughter," he replies sarcastically. "Speaking of which, where is he?"

"He's gone to meet someone," Patricia says, waving her hand flippantly.

Duncan chortles, astonished. "Someone? It isn't enough that one of his girls is upstairs, homeless, and pregnant, that he feels the need to add another to the harem. He treats this house like a fucking brothel, and you let him!"

"That's uncalled for! He's young. Too young to be tied down."

A glass slams down and hurried movement forces everything I've just heard to be put back in my mental box as I move quickly towards the stairs. Jogging up them, I am at the top by the time Duncan reaches the hallway.

"I'm through bowing down to everything he wants and watching you turn a blind eye to it. He's going to ruin us. But this time, he's made his bed, and he will lie in it!"

"What are you saying?"

"I'm saying he's going to do the right thing. He's going to take responsibility. Do you want our name dragged through the dirt? People digging through our business? Our finances? No, I didn't think so. When he gets in, I want to see him. I don't give a shit how late, or early, it is. I'll be in the study, catching up on work." He strides down the hallway that runs the centre of the house and slams the door.

Training my eyes on the floor, I should be thankful that Mr Beresford is concerned with future events, but it doesn't help me in the present. Nor does it help me when I have just heard that I am one of many Joe is sleeping with. We never talked about exclusivity, but inside my heart - the one currently breaking from my own stupidity - I know I'm not the only one.

If I'm being honest, I think I've always known it. I now wish when I'd started seeing him I had gotten myself to the nearest family planning clinic and begged them to give me the pill. I wish I'd made sure he used a condom, rather than letting my lust overrule my common sense thinking he would.

Still, I can't blame Joe for my predicament entirely, I'm equally responsible, and I allowed it to happen. It's so easy to look back and right all the wrongs, but life doesn't work like that.

Closing the door softly, I stroke my belly and vow to do what's right. I know the only way I can give this child a home is to put my own hurt and humiliation aside. Even if it means ignoring the reality and putting up with being used and suffering further degradation.

As I promise to give my baby everything I can, I know that is another beautiful lie. As is foolishly believing you can have it all when there are some things in life you just can't give.

But the biggest lie of them all is the one you tell yourself when you believe the impossible to be possible. It is the unviable, elusive dream, and it's too fragile to pursue.

And eventually, I shall learn.

My eyes flutter open, bringing me back to the present.

Long gone are the arms of the man I adore, rocking me as I fell deeper into the nightmare I have lived inside of for almost three decades.

I rub my hand over my eyes, and the inside of the Range Rover gains focus. Softy touching my belly, the memory is far too real. But all those years ago I wasn't wrong. The dream I had of a beautiful life with my baby *was* too fragile to pursue. It was elusive and naïve, and less than three short years later, my beautiful lie was dead.

Unfastening my seat belt, the door opens, and John peaks his brow. "Nice timing, beautiful. Come here." He holds his arms open, and I thread mine securely around his neck. I let my head fall onto his shoulder as he carries me into the house.

"All done, boss." Simon salutes, striding down the hallway. "M, Jake will be bringing your car back soon. Have a good night." He shuts the door behind him, and John drops one arm from my back and punches in the code.

Carrying me into the living room, I curl up against him on the sofa, as he brushes the hair from my face and studies me intently.

"Thank you," he says, catching me off guard.

"For what?"

"For giving me a little piece of the puzzle that is you. I can't imagine how painful it was to leave someone you love, so thank you for sharing that." He gently twists my jaw and takes my lips in his. Falling into the exquisite touch of his mouth, my lids droop in rapture.

I sigh in contentment and slowly shift. Looking out of the window to the quiet street outside, hues of burnished bronze deepen on the horizon.

I shuffle off his lap, much to his disapproval - judging his discontented grunt - and pause when I see the picture of Maggie that I had shown him back at the house. I stroke the image and then the one next to it of both of us together.

"I had Park bring them over." He moves behind me and rubs my arms. "I should have asked if I could put them up, but she's no longer a secret, so her image shouldn't be either."

"No, I like seeing her here. She belongs here, in our home," I say with a smile. Staring into her eyes, the same vibrant blue as mine, she's not the only angelic, blue-eyed blonde who also deserves to be seen.

Horror fills me, and I rotate in panic. John grips my shoulders, his face plagued with confusion.

"Where are my boxes?" I ask urgently. "Where are they? Oh my God! Please don't say you've skipped them!"

"Calm down, angel. They're upstairs in the spare room."

Slight relief comforts me. "Did you look inside?"

"No, why?"

"Nothing, it doesn't matter." I lead him back to the sofa, suddenly feeling a hell of a lot older than I did this morning. John sits, tugs me over his knee and rearranges me on his lap again.

"Did I say anything?" I ask as I trace the vein at his temple, remembering the last words I spoke was that I made a mistake.

"No, you fell asleep. Do you want to talk about it?"

I press my cheek to his chest and listen to his steady heartbeat. "Not today," I whisper because there is no way I can withstand reliving that nightmare for a second time in a cognisant state tonight. That admission is for a time when I need to drag myself down to pull myself back up again.

It is an admission that will destroy, and ultimately, define.

As he cocoons me in his arms, I can't help but wish things had been different for Faith and me. If she had a man like John Walker for her father, it would have been amazing. Because he is amazing.

"I didn't always think it, but you're beautiful. Inside and out. Underneath this rough exterior, there is a beauty you rarely show. I'm grateful I get to see it. To share it, and to fall in love with it every single day."

John picks us up without warning and moves us up the stairs and into the bedroom. Tossing me on the bed in a playful throw, he climbs on, one knee at a time and envelops my body with his. Tangling us together, he cups my jaws, and peppers my face with soft strokes of his lips and tongue.

"No, Jake will be bringing my car back soon," I admonish. I will also not play the bloody martyr when I continually reprimand Sloan and Kara, and then do precisely the same thing myself.

He drags his mouth down my front, simultaneously undoing my zip and undoing me. Lifting his head, his mouth opens, but the familiar sound of my car engine ploughing down the street at speed stops him.

"John!" I push his shoulders, and he grins.

"Jacob is under strict orders to post the keys. He steps foot in this house when my woman is half naked, he's dead man walking."

I wait with bated breath as the car door slams, the letterbox snaps open and shut, and then another car pulls up. I drop my head back down; they really shouldn't have gone to so much trouble. I could have just gotten one of the girls to take me back for it tomorrow. As the second vehicle drives off, my hand is moved down my front, and John kisses my fingertips.

"Anything further objections?" he asks, and I shake my head in response.

With one hand behind his neck, he yanks his t-shirt off and throws it on the floor. Manipulating me up, he does the same with my yoga vest.

"Sure?" he asks as he swiftly removes the unattractive sports bra. He gives it a repulsed look before tossing it aside.

Circling one talented thumb over my nipple, a delightful pre-orgasmic bliss flares within. I relax down on my elbows, and slide one leg aside, inviting and invoking. Accepting my offer, he gets comfortable in the curve of my thighs, while my heel glides over his contoured backside and latches at his hip. Rotating my pelvis, his keen hardness digs in, tempting me.

"More," I whisper, while my hands move of their own volition.

"Always, now lie back. Eyes open, angel." I gaze at him as he unfastens his belt and pulls it from the loops on his combats. "I want you to watch. I want you to watch the way I fall in love with you over and over." He adjusts the pillows under my head, elevating my body up, smiling beautifully.

And then, until the darkness swallows the light completely, our shadows move and cast around the room while we fall in love.
Over and over.

Chapter 30

I CLUTCH THE missed delivery card and stride into the Royal Mail delivery office. As expected, there is a queue, and I am four deep within it.

Proceeding down the line, ten minutes and one irate man with a missing parcel later, I slide my card to the woman on the other side of the glass.

"I'll just grab that for you," she says and toddles off behind a makeshift screen. Tapping my nails on the top, she finally returns with a large box.

"ID?"

I flash my driver's license - the only thing that still bears my old address - and she lifts the glass to pass the item over.

"Thank you. Have a nice day."

As I walk to my car, I give the box a shake, and a soft thud emanates from inside. Sitting it on the bonnet, I unlock the doors and put it in the back. I pull off the side of the road, and stare at it in the rear view, debating what's inside. I haven't ordered anything, and if I had, it certainly wouldn't be getting delivered to the old house.

A touch of dread enters my psyche, but wondering is far too dangerous.

Half an hour later, I pull up in the driveway. Parking behind John's 4x4, I jump out and remove the box. I drop it down on the hallway floor and remove my jacket.

"Darling?" I shout up the stairs but receive no reply.

I pluck my mobile out of my bag and turn it in my hand. I already know it isn't going to give me some tremendous insight, but still, you never know.

"John?" I call out again, at a loss of where he is. I cast aside his whereabouts for a moment and carry the box into the kitchen and set it on the table.

Filling the coffee machine with water, I switch it on and let it run. Grabbing a pair of scissors from the drawer, I slice through the tape and pull out a handful of bubble wrap. I dig deep, insofar as I can, but it's all just packaging crap. To say I am beyond confused is an understatement.

The coffee machine beeps, and I drop the scissors and grab a mug. As I angle sideways to reach for the jug, my phone begins to vibrate.

"Hello, darling," I answer and stick him on speakerphone.

"Hey, beautiful."

"Where are you?"

"Out with a friend. The ignorant git didn't tell me he was coming down until he got here."

"Oh," I murmur, intrigued as to who this mysterious, ignorant friend is. If I thought he would play fair, I'd ask. But since I know I can't expect him to give up his secrets when I refuse to do the same, I leave it be.

"I'm just calling in to let you know I might be late for dinner."

"That's okay." I grasp hold of the coffee jug. "Anything you want to see on the table tonight?"

He remains silent for a beat then inhales – a very knowing inhale.

"What do I want on the table tonight?" he repeats in question. "That's easy, angel. You. Bare, wanton and writhing beneath me. Screaming my name until you're hoarse. Think you can accomplish that?"

"John." I chortle and shake my head. My cheeks flush, the colour spreading down my chest. I always deny it, but I do like his dirty talk. My body does, too, if the flurry of heat and sensation is anything to go by. It's burning anticipation that should be torture, but all it does is tempt and tantalise.

"You're scandalous sometimes," I tell him, but his innuendo has infused every cell under my skin.

"And you love it!" he chuckles. "But seriously, you, naked over that table is what I want to come home to every day."

"Well, then. I guess I better dig out the good lingerie and see what I can do," I reply, although I'm now also sizing up the table as an excellent place to writhe naked on tonight. And it wouldn't be the first time, would it?

"You do that. Remember, easy access is the key aspect here."

I slide the box back over and start to pull out the bubble wrap. There seems to be yards and yards of the stuff unravelling until the end finally appears. Balling it up in my hands, I lob it across the kitchen.

"Really? I thought you liked the chase of the game."

"I do but considering a certain part of me is hard enough to hammer nails right now, all I'm going to be able to think about until I get home is hammering you."

"That's extremely rude." I feign shock while he continues to assail my ears.

"That's the Walker way, beautiful."

I murmur my contentment, loving the way his deep, gruff laugh punctuates down the line.

"And there's nothing wrong with anything I've just said. I like my love physical as well as verbal and emotional. And I meant every word. When I get home tonight, you're never going to look at that table the same way again!" he says, his insinuation abundant.

"No, but you might want to tell that to the poor table. It might not survive another go," I retort and pour myself a coffee.

As I reach inside the box, my fingertips graze over synthetic, matted fur, like that of a stuffed toy. A morbid, long forgotten memory seeps into my brain.

"No," I murmur horrified, distracted; vaguely forgetting that John is still on the line. I swallow back the waters in my mouth as I glide my fingers around what I know is the neck and slowly lift it from the box.

A gasp leaves my throat as I first reveal the head, then the body, and finally, the stuffed legs dangling below it.

"Oh my God!" I breathe, while my limbs shake uncontrollably. My tears come next as my brain is bombarded and mentally assaulted.

"Marie?" John's muffled shout echoes down the line. And while I can hear him, the rest of me is frozen. Suspended in a time when this bear initially existed. That existence was brutal, coming back from the grave, plaguing the present, bringing with it the end of my current beautiful life.

"Darling, I've got to go!" I grab my mobile and hang up.

Hugging the bear to my chest, I turn abruptly and scream as my arm makes contact with the hot glass jug. Everything then moves in slow motion, and I watch, mesmerised, as the jug slides off the table and smashes over the floor, dousing scorching liquid over my bare feet.

My pain receptors register the full extent of the damage when the burning turns into a penetrating sensation.

I step back in agony and slouch down the unit. I drag down the tea towel and wrap up my feet, which are now burning and bleeding from the shattered remnants of what was John's fancy coffee jug.

Opening the freezer door, I pull out a bag of peas and lay them over my feet. The burning subsides as I clutch the toy in my arms, needing to find some comfort in the mess I have just made.

But I'm lying to myself because this mess has lingered just below the surface for far too long.

Crying into the head of the year's old toy, I take a better a look at him. Excepting the worn moth areas, he is still stained in the same places he had been, showing two years' worth of a little girl's love and playtime.

I grit my teeth as the pain radiates in my feet, and I slam my head back. The sharp pain is trivial, as is the pressure building in my sinuses.

As I drop my head down and stare into the black button eyes, blood trickles from my nose onto his musty fur. It's fitting because it wouldn't be the first time I have cried and equally bled into something that can't save me.

With light-headedness ensuing, the waters of my mouth churn, and the day we first met returns with clarity.

"Marianne?" Patricia calls out, or, as Maggie has taken to calling her, the wicked witch of the west. "You have a guest!"

The last word is an undisguised sneer, and the front door slams shut under the holler of my name again.

"Marianne!"

With one last look at my belly that is making me ridiculously front heavy, I yank down my vest. Pulling it over my stomach, it instantly rises. Pissed off that nothing fits me, my eyes wander, seeing Joe's shirt laying on the bed. I pick it up and breathe in the fabric. Breathing in his scent is the closest I can get to him these days. Sliding it over my arms, I leave it draped open and grab my maternity pack.

Trudging down the stairs, it has been over two months since my father showed me the door, then callously booted me out of it. During these last ten weeks, Maggie has been my rock. She has repeatedly risked her own neck to ensure I have someone I can depend on. She is the one who carefully packed my things and brought them to me. She is the one who held my hand a week later when the doctor confirmed what was already a fact. And she promised to be there, holding my hand as my first scan was conducted - which is today and quite overdue.

The glowing hue of my sister's hair shines through the glass door as I reach the bottom step. I shake my head, annoyed that the woman despises me so much that she has just left my flesh and blood standing outside.

Although I'm stupid to expect more, Patricia only pulls out the best hostess impression when it is someone who can raise her social status. And my newly found lousy reputation and bump of inconvenience are causing her to be the talk of the town in an entirely different light.

I shove the notion aside and open the door with a huge smile.

"Meet Mr Blue!" Maggie squeals, propelling the thing into my face while his arms and legs flail all over.

"He's charming, although the baby might be frightened of him," I state since it is probably bigger than a newborn. Possibly even a six-month-old... But what the hell do I know about the size of babies anyway? "You really shouldn't have spent your pocket money on him. You should have waited until after the scan. I mean, what if it's not a boy?" I brush my hand over my belly.

Maggie closes the door and grins at my tender stroking action. "I know, but he was the last one, and I couldn't resist. Besides," she says and jerks her head to my middle. "Look at how needy that bump is! I bet it's a boy."

I chortle. "Well, if you want to bet, it better be with chocolate buttons because I can't afford anything else!" I joke, but it's true.

Maggie grimaces at my pitiful hand to mouth existence and having to rely on a man and woman who consider me to be the destroyer of their son's life until she smiles. But since I'd rather not chit-chat about my impending life that will be 'less' of everything I can imagine, I ease the tension.

"It's a girl," I say with absolution, still rubbing my tum. "It feels like a girl."

"Pfft! What do you know what it feels like? For all we know, you could be having one of each! No offence but look at the size of you!" Her amused laugh dies a death in the grand hallway, and I gawp at her in horror. Staring at the other half of myself, how could that not have entered my foolish head? I've been remiss not to believe that history may repeat itself. Until now, it's a truth that hasn't occurred to me.

"Oh God, I feel sick!" I grab the bannister, but I no longer feel sick, I'm going to be sick.

"Crap, just breathe," Maggie says, concerned, fanning me with her hand.

I straighten up and grab her arms. "I can't do this. I can't!" Tears flood my eyes, the reality finally hitting home.

"What's all the commotion about? Have you two not gone yet?" We both turn simultaneously at the irate tone of Mrs bloody Beresford.

Maggie cowers instantly, and it doesn't give me hope. "We're just going, Mrs Beresford. Sorry," she mutters. "Is Joe ready to take us?"

I lift my head at hearing that because Maggie is definitely testing the waters. She might not be as flighty and wayward as I once was - once being the operative word - but she isn't stupid.

"No, he's gone out. He didn't say when he would be back. I guess you'll have to get the bus." On that note, she strides back down the hallway and slams the dining room door behind her.

"Marianne?" Maggie murmurs.

I shake my head and grab my coat. It's a pointless task because it's not like I can even fasten it anymore. Picking up my rucksack, I shove my documents inside, slide it over my arms and open the front door.

"So, how's the wicked witch of the west treating you?" Maggie asks, stretching her neck up to see what the next stop is.

I grip the bar tight and peer around the packed bus while being jostled left to right. The bell rings and the bus brakes sharply, almost throwing me into the man standing in front of me.

"Okay, I guess. She's still short with me, but I just try to avoid her." I huff out, feeling my back starting to hurt. An elderly lady smiles sympathetically, and I reciprocate, but I know what she's probably thinking - young, pregnant, stupid.

"Rather you than me." Maggie's voice breaks my procrastination, and I nod at her statement. I'd rather it be her than me, too. But honestly, it really is easy to avoid her. Their house is beyond huge, and she spends most of her time out socialising, doing whatever it is she does. I don't ask because I really don't care.

"We're the next one." Jabbing my finger into the button, we hustle our way towards the front. I breathe a sigh of relief when my feet finally touch the pavement. The bus moves away from the stop, and Maggie grabs my hand.

"Ready?"

"No," I answer without thinking. Am I ready to find out what I'm having? Yes, of course. Am I ready to be told it is two for the price of one? No, I'll never be ready for that.

We walk through the corridors to the maternity wing, and I book in. The waiting room is half full as I take a seat and wait to be called.

"Marianne Turner?" the sonographer calls.

I stand in typical pregnant woman fashion – front first, hand on back – and waddle towards her. Having to stand up on that flipping bus for an hour while it went around the houses has really taken its toll on me.

"Hi." I offer my hand. "I'm Marianne. This is Maggie, my sister." The woman does a double take, and I grin.

"Hi, sweetheart. If you'd both like to follow me." Leading us into an examination room, she goes through my documents and then helps me up onto the bed. I observe carefully as she sets up the equipment and turns on the monitor.

"Is this your first scan?" she asks on a turn.

"Hmm," I reply throatily as Maggie rolls up my shirt and vest. "Thanks."

"Right, if you just want to relax, I'm going to put some gel on your belly, and then we'll find your little one. It's up to you if you want me to tell you what you're having."

"Oh, I do want to know. We've got a bet on."

"I think it's a boy," Maggie says with a touch of excitement. "She feels it's a girl. As if you can feel it!"

The woman laughs. "Well, let's see who wins, shall we? What are you betting on?

"Chocolate buttons!" we reply in synch.

The woman laughs and reaches for a tube. "Good choice."

I shuffle, uncomfortable, when she slathers my middle with the gel. Holding a plastic thing like a wand, she glides it over my bump. "If you want to watch the screen, I'll point it out."

Turning to the monitor, the picture is ghostly, but there's something there. I study the screen, trying to see whatever it is she sees as she points out an arm, then a leg and then the head.

"What is it?" Maggie asks, more than excited. The woman looks at me, and I nod, dying to share this moment with my twin.

"What did you bet again, sweetheart?" she asks her.

"A boy!"

"You lost, darling. It's a girl."

Happy tears cloud my eyes, fogging my vision as they fall freely. Wiping them away, I press up on my elbows. "Is there just one?" I ask tentatively. The nurse glances between the identical double act in her room and moves the wand over my tum again.

"It appears to be, but it has been known that one baby can sometimes be hiding behind the other. I'll book another appointment for you in a few weeks, just to be sure," she says.

"When will that be?" Maggie queries, taking the initiative.

"Probably a fortnight."

Her hand grips mine, because we both know she won't be able to attend. Every year, my family rent out a small cottage at half term, and unfortunately, that will be in a fortnight. It's already planned, and I guess if I wasn't in this state, dragging the family name through the mud, I would've been going, too.

"It's okay. I'll be fine. I'll get Joe to bring me." I say to appease her, but we both know he won't – and that's the reality I need to get used to.

The woman looks uncomfortable at the scene playing out in front of her, and she hands me some paper towels. "You can wipe the gunk off now. I'll print you out some pictures."

Ten minutes later, with my stomach still sticky, I lower my vest and shirt. My eyes catch Maggie's, and I know what she is thinking.

"Are you okay?" she asks.

"Yeah, I'm good. We're good," I confirm, rubbing my bump.

"Do you think Joe will be happy when you tell him he's going to have a daughter?"

I roll my eyes. Honestly, I don't think he will give two hoots. If he did, he would be here now, rather than carousing – which I know he's still doing. It speaks volumes of what the future will – or will not - hold.

"Probably," I say, lying for him for no good reason.

Maggie nods uncomfortably and grabs my rucksack. "Mum gave me some money, so I'll get us some lunch. Don't go anywhere."

"I'll be in the waiting room." With that, she kisses me and leaves.

Putting on my coat, I leave the room and see the sonographer speaking with a colleague at the reception desk.

I take a seat in the waiting room as she approaches and passes me an appointment card.

"How do you feel?" she asks.

"I'm okay." She gives me a quizzical glance, knowing I'm lying my socks off.

"Will you be alone when you come again, or will the father be with you?"

"I don't know," I answer honestly. "The father isn't overly interested." I slouch in the seat and allow the pain to flow.

"Don't be ashamed, Marianne." She sits and takes my hand. "You're not the first teenage girl to get pregnant, and you won't be the last. I had my son when I was seventeen. My life stopped for a while but then I made it better for him. Don't think this is the end of your life. It isn't. It will be hard, but it will also be richer in ways you don't realise yet. Trust me." She smiles, and I wipe my eyes on my sleeve. "If you're okay to wait a little longer, reception might be able to arrange outpatients transport for your next appointment."

I nod. "Thank you. That's very kind."

"If you need to speak to us about anything, call the number on the bottom. It's been nice meeting you, Marianne. And if I don't see you again, good luck."

"Thanks."

She squeezes my arm and smiles before approaching another mother-to-be.

The television on the wall plays silently in the quiet room. Staring down at my feet, my leg shakes nervously. I wanted to know, and now I do. A girl. I smile, picturing a beautiful version of mine and Joe's combined attributes.

Running through the variety of names I have already picked out – alone – since Joe is also uninterested in that, I lay a protective arm over my stomach and decide upon what to finally call her. Repeating it inside my head, I hope she likes it. I hope she's proud of me when she is old enough to understand. I hope for so many things to be different, but the one thing I wouldn't change is the life I am growing. Of everything my father says I should be ashamed of, she will never be one of them.

"Hey!" Maggie skips into the room and halts when she notices she is disturbing the quiet. "Sorry," she mumbles, holding out an egg mayo and a bottle of water. "There's a cafeteria downstairs if you want to eat in there, or we could sit outside?"

I stand with my hand on my back for support and take my lunch from her. "Let's sit outside."

As we walk down the corridor, there is an unspoken air of energy wafting from my twin.

"What?" she asks, mouth full, exposing the half-masticated chunk of a cheese sandwich. Wiping the corner of her lip, her forehead creases slightly.

"Nothing," I murmur.

Outside, the sun shines bright, and we find a partially shaded bench under a tree. Sitting down, I realise it is becoming harder to get back up on my own. That's something else I might eventually need help with before this little one arrives.

"Have you and Joe decided what you're going to call her?" Maggie asks out of the blue, and I wonder why we have never discussed this. Everything else has been analysed in great detail over the last few months, but never names.

"No."

"No?"

"No. I mean, I've got a name I really like, but Joe..." I bite my lip, and my eyes instantly water, not enough to fall, but enough to sting.

"He's really not happy, is he?"

I shake my head, silencing the truth. "He doesn't care. And I know his parents only let me stay to save face and to make them look caring, but they don't want me there, either. I'm also pretty sure that Joe is seeing other girls behind my back."

Maggie looks pained as she lowers the sandwich and begins to open her mouth.

"No, it's fine. I know he is, but I'm just going to make the best of it. I'm determined to stay in school and do the best I can. It's the only way."

I sigh at my grand plan. It's going to be hard, harder than it has been for the last couple of months since everyone in school now knows I'm pregnant. I even heard a few girls calling me a slag the other day, but I don't care. No, actually, I do care, because I'm not, but I don't care enough to risk not having a future where I can eventually make my own way and make my baby proud. The sonographer was right, life doesn't stop, and I will make it better for us.

"What about Faith?"

"Faith?" I repeat, vaguely.

"Well, Dad's always saying you don't have any, but now you do. Besides, it's pretty." Staring at my twin, I smile.

"Faith." I let the name roll over my tongue, trying it out for effect. "I like it."

"Me, too. I can't wait to meet her."

I gaze into the distance and grin as Faith kicks against me, seemingly in approval.

"No, nor I."

"Faith," I murmur.

Grogginess clouds my vision, while my head bangs from the inside.

"Welcome back to the land of the living," Stuart says with concern as he slips a thermometer between my lips. "Leave that in a minute."

"Where am I?" I ask, disorientated, and shuffle to sit up, but he pushes me back down.

"You're still at home. Although if you hadn't have woken up, I'd have been admitting you. Lucky for you, now you won't get the privilege of spending the night in an NHS bed with the obligatory open back gown," he deadpans, trying to shed some humour on my situation. He removes the thermometer from my mouth, and nods, satisfied with the reading.

I sit up, hoping he won't push me down again, and baulk when I see my professionally bandaged feet.

"What happened?" I ask.

"You don't remember?"

"I... Erm... I dropped the coffee jug. Or maybe I knocked it off..." I rub my head, mentally retracing my steps.

"You did a pretty good number on your feet. I managed to remove the glass, but keep the dressings clean and stay off the heels for a few days, okay?"

"Okay," I whisper, looking around the living room. "Where's John? And why are you here?" I don't want to come across as unkind, but it really wasn't that bad. I don't think.

"He's finishing cleaning up the kitchen. My shift had just ended when he called to say you'd had an accident. He said when he got here, you were passed out holding a ragged old bear with your feet wrapped in a bag of peas and a tea towel."

"Where is it?" I ask in panic.

"Where's what?" he replies, his brows pinching together, his head moving from side to side in query.

"Mr B-" I catch myself quickly. "The bear. Where is it?"

Stuart stands with his hands on his hips and pivots towards the door. "I think John was going to put it in the washing machine."

Oh God, no! He won't survive the washing machine. It's pure luck he wasn't heartlessly binned years ago.

I vault upright and throw my legs off the sofa while Stuart attempts to stop me. Slamming open the living room door, I run with a pained hobble into the kitchen and stop abruptly when I see John leaning over the table with his head in his hands. He looks up, and for the second time since we have been together, his expression is forlorn.

My heart sinks, proverbially eviscerating in the acid lining my empty stomach, as he pushes off the top and walks towards me.

"You frightened the fuck out of me!"

"I'm sorry," I whisper; my apology laced with tears. He gently curves his hand around my head, cradles me to his chest and lifts me up. Depositing me on the worktop, I can't stand to look at him and lie, so I trail my eyes over the floor. Relief spreads through me, seeing a blood and coffee stained Mr Blue dumped in the corner.

I can't hide the relieved sigh that emits my mouth as my chin is tilted up. John looks down at the floor then back to me. I want to give vague answers, disguised truths and basically just plain lies, but I can't.

"Maggie gave that to me years ago. He was a gift."

He nods, a hardened expression taking over his face. Before he can impart any unwanted pearls of Walker wisdom, the kitchen door opens, and we both turn simultaneously to see Stuart shouldering his medical bag.

"I'll get gone. Make sure you keep those clean and take a few paracetamols if you need them. If they start to get infected, call me. I'll see you both later."

"Thanks, Doc," John says. "I'll walk you out. Don't you move," he says, kissing my forehead then follows Stuart.

As their muted tones seep into the kitchen, I stare at Mr Blue. The urge to jump down and snatch him up is profound, but since I know the pressure on my hurt feet will be immense, I stay put.

The front door slams and the intermittent beeps of the alarm system resound and then John walks back through the door. He bypasses me with a judgemental glare, bends down and picks up the tattered bear.

"This is more than just a gift. This caused what happened today. What's really going on here?"

I turn away, unable to speak, unable to move. I'm unable to do anything except sit here mute. "I can't." My voice is a terrified whisper, ringing loud in my ears.

"Can't or won't?"

"Both," I respond pathetically.

"Do you love me?" he asks annoyed. "Look at me. Do you?"

"Yes. You know I do!"

"Well, it's no longer enough. You say you love me and that you want a life with me, but you won't share your past with me. That isn't love, it's deceit. I've already had one woman throw me under the fucking bus, and I barely survived. But I'm such a fucking masochist because here I am, enduring it all over again!"

"Darling, I'd never-"

"Do that?" he finishes with a tinge of sarcasm. "You already are! You have been for years. The truth, Marie. You owe me that!"

I close my eyes, because I can't, and I won't. And he knows it when he huffs out his anger.

"Fine!" he bites out evenly. He drops the bear down on one of the stools and rounds his fists. I know he would never raise his hand to me, but how long can he tolerate living with me, loving me when I can't even give him a simple explanation is anyone's guess.

"I'm sorry." I start to sob.

"Don't be sorry, be honest!"

His roar cuts through me, signifying his tolerance has finally diminished.

And I know in my heart this is the beginning of the end.

"I'm going to stay with the kids tonight." He turns to the door, and I jump down, forgoing the pain and limp after him.

"John, please don't!" I beg, pleading with my hands. "Don't leave like this!"

"If I stay, I'll say things I regret, and I think what we have is worth more than that. It's worth fighting for. And if you feel the same, tomorrow you'll finally start being honest. I don't expect your entire life story in one sitting, but something - *anything* - is better than nothing!"

Turning his back to me, he disarms the house and leaves. The intentional slam of the door reverberates throughout the hallway, leaving me cold and alone.

I sit on the steps, hugging my knees to my chest long after his car has gone, hoping he will come back. Yet I know he won't.

Rearming the house, I hobble back into the kitchen and pick up Mr Blue. Cleaning off the blood and coffee the best as I can, I sit him on a stool, pick up my mobile and turn off the light.

Climbing into bed, I contemplate if I should call Maggie. It isn't that late, but it is unfair to involve her in yet another of my tumultuous episodes. That's all my life seems to be. Episodes. Some good, some bad, some I dare not speak of.

And this is yet another one.

Instead, I open a new message and tap away in the darkness. Re-reading the text, declaring my undying love to a man whom I dare not declare my undying secrets to, I delete it, because it's duplicitous and insulting, and he deserves more than that.

Curling up into a ball, I twist his ring on my finger and concede he's right. What we have is worth fighting for, but I already know he won't stay and fight when one half is unwilling to do the same.

Falling asleep, I recall a time I was more than willing to fight back.

And tomorrow, I must start again.

Chapter 31

"HAVE I EVER told you just how utterly brilliant you are, lady?" Jules says, looking around the ballroom in awe.

I roll my eyes at my glass of sparkling water. "Keep going," I tell her flatly, because who doesn't like to be congratulated. Usually, I'd be revelling in it. This morning, I just don't care. I know she's trying to lighten my miserable disposition, but there is only one person who can do that right now, and that prospect is slim to none.

Downing what's left in the glass, I turn my mobile on the table in front of me. The screen lights up and fades, and I wonder if I press the standby button repeatedly a miracle might transpire. It's the only thing keeping me going this morning. It's obvious my numerous voicemails, and single, simple text of 'sorry' aren't sorry enough because it's been fifteen hours since John walked out. And I haven't heard from him since.

When I called the kids this morning, Kara confirmed he was on the verge of exploding last night, and that he was gone before they woke up.

This doesn't give me hope since I know he won't yield. But there's no one I can bitch or shift the blame to because this is on me. And if he never comes back, that's on me, too.

"I knew you could work wonders, but I never expected anything like this!"

This coming weekend it is the Emerson annual fundraiser for abuse. Usually, it is held around March, but for various reasons, it has been delayed this year.

"Don't thank me. It's not my gig," I mutter and glance over at Nicki, directing the company she hired to decorate the room as they hang swathes of British racing green silk from the windows.

"God, she's wonderful. It's so... So opulent. It's going to look amazing!" Jules claps her hands together.

"Well, at least someone's happy." Giving up on the phone, I rest my head in my hands.

Honestly, I'd love to run out of here, but where would I go? My options are limited, seeing as the house I live in isn't mine. And when John does decide to return, there's a chance he might ask me to leave.

I'm jumping to conclusions, but considering he thinks I'm throwing him under the bus, I can't expect him not to do the same. And let's face it, his reasons are more than valid.

Ruminating on the various outcomes of last night, the chair beside me is ripped out from under the table. Jules plonks herself into it and yanks mine closer.

"Right, what the hell's going on? What's got into you this morning?"

I rub my eyes from my temples to the bridge of my nose. "John walked out last night."

"Say again?" she replies, dumbfounded.

I grit my teeth. "I said, John walked out last night."

"Yes, I heard that, but why? What's happened?" She looks concerned, and if I didn't know any better, and I crossed a line in the sand and asked her step over it, she would. But I do know better, and as with everyone in my life, I know she will stand beside John until the end. And that isn't lost on me.

"We had an argument," I tell her quietly.

Her face contorts in confusion. "An argument doesn't equate to walking out. What were you arguing about?"

I shake my head because she doesn't get to know that. She gets many things from me, but that will not be one of them. To divulge would genuinely be throwing John under his beloved fictional bus.

"It doesn't matter. All I know is he walked out, and I've not heard from him since."

Her nose screws up, and her mouth opens, but she is stopped by the determined stride approaching our vicinity.

Lifting my eyes behind her, Sloan is making a beeline for me, appearing less than impressed. I roll my eyes as the girls working on the decorations swoon and blush furiously.

Imbeciles, I think, but all I am doing is taking my bad mood out on everyone else, and that isn't fair.

But fuck it, life isn't fair.

"Marie, can I have a word?" Sloan asks impertinently, and for the first time in three years, I see the little bastard I first met before he became a family fixture.

I stand ungracefully and amble to the other side of the room. "Don't start, Sloan," I tell him before he reaches me.

His jaw grinds and his eyes narrow. "Fine, but you need to speak to John."

"I would if he'd answer my calls," I reply insolently but regardless if that statement is true or not, I won't be talked down to like one of his staff.

"I don't know what's going on, and I don't want to know. But what I do know is that I'm now a bottle of gin lighter because he was pouring it down his neck like his world was ending last night. Don't let whatever it is fester. I know from experience-"

"Sloan," I speak over him. "I appreciate your concern, but this is none of your business."

He glares. "Well, I think we'll agree to disagree there. Everything about him is my business. Whatever it is, you make it right, because if I'm forced to choose, he'll win. He'll always win."

Pain constricts in my heart upon hearing that, because if I ever wondered where I really stand with him, or any of them, I finally have it from the horse's mouth. I've always known it, but it's never been more transparent than it is right now.

Without thinking, I purse my lips in a sneer and use the only weapon I possess. "I admire your conviction, but who do you think Kara will choose? John, a man she has known for three years, or me, a woman who's loved her and risked everything for over a decade?"

On that, I turn on my heel. My stomach churns because I've just stooped low, so low, in fact, even I can't believe I have dared to put her in the middle. I would never, ever make her choose. But if she had to and she chose me, I'd do whatever it takes to swing that decision in the right direction – a direction that wouldn't be mine.

Halfway across the ballroom, my elbow is snatched hard, and I swing around to face a venomous Sloan.

"Listen up and listen good," he growls, sounding so much like John, it's scary. Leaning into me, his eyes turn black. "If you try to take her away from me, I'll dig up whatever fucking shit you're hiding and drown you in it. You can threaten to take my businesses, you can threaten to take my money, I don't give a damn. You threaten to take my wife and son, I'll rain fucking hellfire on you. Don't test me, Marie, because I'll burn you if I have to. Now, you need to speak to John, *today*, and make right whatever went wrong last night." He inhales deeply, and his angry glare morphs into a smile for the sake of appearances.

Leaving me where I stand, he approaches his worried looking mother and Nicki. "Wow, this looks great!" he compliments loudly and flicks back the sides of his jacket to put his hands on his hips.

"Thanks," Nicki replies uncertain, the same moment gurgling resounds, and Laura enters with Oliver on her hip. She makes funny faces and speaks baby to him while he giggles and smiles.

"Hey, little prince!" I greet, rolling my shoulders and moving towards them. I stroke the unruly mop of dark hair from his forehead, and Sloan pierces me with his glare. Apprehensive, wondering what he will do, he gives me a small smile of encouragement, rather than being the complete bastard he is capable of and denying me this.

Uncomfortable minutes tick by, until Sloan lifts his son from Laura's arms and smothers him with kisses.

"What are you doing here?" Jules asks him. "I thought you'd be at work already."

"We're going, but I've got a favour to ask." He grins gloriously at his mother.

Jules hesitates and caves. "When you smile at me like that I get suspicious."

"Good. It proves the Foster allure is still able to charm women into submission." He looks at his son and smiles. "It works on your mummy all the time."

I roll my wide eyes, because, yes, we know it works. He's holding the bloody proof.

"A little birdy told me you didn't have any plans tonight, and I thought it might be good for him to spend his first night away from home."

Jules slaps her hands on her hips and juts out her leg in a defiant stance. "He's already spent many nights away from home," she states, her tone devious, already clued up on what he wants.

"True, but not without us," he says, stroking his son's head, nestling him tighter into his chest. "And I would really, really like to spend an evening with my beloved. Just the two of us."

"Uh-huh," Jules mumbles. "Why?" She gives him her best vacant expression, wondering if he will bite.

I creep up to her side and slide baby boy's little hand into mine. Sloan sees the action and moves him closer, thankfully not holding that much of a grudge.

"Oh, come on, mother! Do you want me to spell it out?"

My mouth curves into a smile, and I press my lips together, suppressing my wicked laugh.

"Okay, fine! Because I'd like to make love to-"

"Darling, stop!" Jules spits out horrified.

And she's not the only one. I've seen them virtually naked together once in this lifetime already. I don't need further verbal illustrations to add to it.

"I really don't want to know, and yes, I'd love to have him tonight. But no drinking," she says when Sloan looks ready to speak. "I need you on standby in case he doesn't settle."

"Of course. We won't be doing much drinking anyway!" He winks and turns but calls out behind him. "Now, if you don't mind, we've got business to attend to. Say bye-bye to your grandmas." Sloan carefully waves Oliver's little hand in our direction as they walk away.

"Sloan?" I hobble after him.

"Yes?"

My body jerks to a stop at his harsh tone. "I shouldn't have said what I did. It was wrong, and we both know I would never make her choose."

He nods. "I know, but it wouldn't be your choice, would it?" He glances down at my hand and back up. "I feel your pain, I do. I know what it's like to wake up and wonder if the person you love will come back. I've been there, more than once. Just get over to the shed and make it right."

"What do I do if he won't listen?"

He sighs contrite – always an interesting look on him. "You make him listen. You do whatever it takes." With that, he carries his child out of the door.

Walking back into the ballroom, Jules meets me in the middle. "I bet you hundred quid she announces she's pregnant in a month or two. Anyway, let's get back to you and John. What happened?"

I ignore her comment and attend to Nicki as she rushes towards me, holding up my phone. "Veronica. She asked if you could call her back."

I purse my lips in annoyance. "How did she sound?" I ask cautiously.

Nicki shrugs. "Indifferent. She said it was urgent and requested you call her back in the next thirty minutes. Sorry."

Clenching my phone, I slam my fist down on the table and squeeze my eyes shut. I open them when I hear Jules calling my name.

"Oh, stuff this crap!" she says annoyed. "Come on!" She slides into her jacket and grabs my bag. "If it's so frigging urgent she can see you face to face. They can't leave you hanging like this!"

"What are you doing?" I ask, frantic.

"What *you* should have done weeks ago."

She drags me from the ballroom, into the foyer and out onto the street. George smiles as we approach the limo. Me, I'm terrified, whereas Jules is on a one-woman mission to end my money pit misery.

The car moves through the dense midday traffic as I sit and anxiously twist my fingers together. I haven't heard from the agency in months. They call whenever it suits them, but they've never returned the handful of calls I've made.

I gaze across at the shop front as George brakes on the other side of the street. Veronica, partially hidden by the property sales boards lining the window, gestures animatedly to her colleague.

"Right, lady, get in there and find out what's going on." Jules nudges my shoulder.

I clutch my bag and shake my head. "What if she says it's fallen through again? I might have a nervous breakdown. I'm not kidding; I can't take this today!"

Jules throws her hands in the air in frustration and climbs out. I stall inside, but not for long when she forces me out and across the street. My feet beat on the pavement, carrying me closer and closer while I train my eyes on the ground.

"*Marianne.*"

My name is a faint whisper on the breeze while the pungent scent of cigarette smoke wafts in my direction. Lifting my head, a man passes by me, but I freeze when his hand brushes mine, and awareness makes the fine hairs on my arms stand on end.

I pivot and stare at the stranger, who is now striding purposely in the opposite direction. My eyes narrow in recognition. His height, his build, the gait of his walk. The smoke... I release a shaky breath and wipe my hand over my forehead, my mind in instant turmoil.

"Marie, you coming, lady?"

I rotate back around to Jules, who is waiting impatiently in front of the office. I grudgingly shuffle towards her and push open the door.

"Marie! It's lovely to see you. I've been waiting for your call." Veronica quickly approaches.

"Yes, well, that's great, but what's going on?" Jules demands, reminding me of when Sloan commands authority. Veronica stops short, taken aback.

I pitch an awkward sideways glance at Jules – a silent request to back down – and she reluctantly takes a seat in the open plan office.

"It's nice to see you, too, Veronica, but what is going on? I haven't heard from you in weeks. You tell me I've got a buyer, and then nothing. I'm tired of this. I'm tired of your accounts department ringing me to settle an invoice of which payment is contingent upon a sale – a sale that still hasn't come to fruition. I'm sorry, but this is shambolic. If you can't sell my house, I'll find another company that can."

There, I've said my piece, and she can do with it what she will.

"I'm very sorry you feel that way, but we are doing everything possible to ensure a sale. The reason why I called is that I received some good news and some bad news earlier. Unfortunately, the prospective buyers had their mortgage application denied. They called late yesterday to confirm they wouldn't be able to proceed."

I close my eyes because it's the only way to contain my tears. I was right – I'll never be able to get rid of it. I guess it means I have no choice but to rent it out. I don't want to; being someone's landlord has never interested me. Regardless of what someone's application says on paper, the reality can be very different.

"And what's the good news?" Jules asks, breaking up my thoughts and forcing me to focus.

"Well." Veronica grins brightly. "A few months back, a potential buyer called to say he was interested in your house. Of course, it was already subject to contract, but I kept his details - just in case."

Why, of course, she did! She's thinking pound signs when I'm thinking sold signs.

"Anyway, I called him this morning to see if he was still interested, and he is! He's offering the full market price, *and* he's a cash buyer. He was willing to put a deposit down today."

"Okay," I mumble slowly, quietly. "That's great, but how soon does he want to complete?"

"ASAP, but he's waiting on the sale of the former marital home going through so it could take a little longer as he needs to sort out his affairs. He's moving down here to be closer to his ex. They split a few years ago, and she came back down here to live with her family. They've agreed for the sake of their kids he should be closer to them. I think he's hoping for a reconciliation. I'm a hopeless romantic, but I hope they make it work."

I give her an incredulous look. She doesn't give a shit about reconciling couples and bloody romance. She just wants her bonus!

A little finger tugs mine and I avert my eyes to Jules and watch her roll hers. She's thinking the same thing I am, since as we are both prime examples of what becomes of the broken-hearted.

"Well, at least something good has come out of it. Thank you for calling me, but from now on, I'd like to be kept updated. Regularly. Please send the new sales particulars to my solicitor *today*. I'd like this completed as soon as possible, then at least you can have your invoice paid."

Veronica's eyes narrow ever so slightly. "Understood. I'm taking the client for a viewing shortly. I presume that is acceptable?" she queries, submissive. Pissed off.

"Fine." I stand, ready to end this. "Right, is there anything else?"

Veronica rises from her seat, explaining she will contact me with weekly progress but telling me not to worry. From her mouth, those words are insulting. Wishing her goodbye, I all but run out.

I dawdle on the pavement a few feet away and bury my face in my hands.

"This is good, right?" Jules says. I nod reluctantly, but it isn't, not really.

"It will be when I have a signed contract and a definite date. Until then, it's not anything. I've been let down so much, I just can't find it within myself to get excited anymore." I eye my wrist, realising there isn't much time left. "We need to get back to Nicki."

Jules, understanding my unhappiness, comforts me in a loving hold. "Nicki is perfectly capable of organising this event solo. She learnt from the best. *You.* The last place you need to be is in that room, stressing when you don't need to. So, I think while I'm here, I might go shopping, but I think we both know what you need right now, and it isn't a new dress. Go on, go to him. Talk to him, make it right."

"Okay," I whisper.

I sit back in the car, while Jules marches off into the masses to abuse her bank account. My head lolls against the window as George starts the engine. I inadvertently fix my stare on the estate agents and watch as Veronica leaves the office, her mobile glued to her ear.

Palming my own, I scroll through the phonebook but contemplate for a second before pressing the screen.

"Hi," Maggie answers after a few rings. "I didn't expect to hear from you."

"I said I'd keep in touch. How are you?" I ask, watching the buildings pass by.

"Fine, busy. You?" she replies over the sound of children in the background.

"I'm okay. I just wanted to talk."

"Hmm, it's good to talk."

"You sound like an old BT ad."

She laughs beautifully. "Hmm, I remember those. Speaking of which, have you talked to John yet?"

"A little." So little, in fact, he walked out because of it. Not that I can tell her that. "I told him about you and that I left at nineteen," I confess, pleased at hearing her content yet surprised breath.

"How did he take it?" she asks with worry.

"Fine, kind of. I think he was more upset that I waited as long as I did." I pull the mobile from my ear when a high-pitched squeal almost deafens me. "Where are you?" I query as the screams grow louder.

"Oh, I'm volunteering at a playgroup. I'm currently surrounded by three dozen five and six-year-olds. Let me find somewhere quiet. Don't hang up."

I wait patiently, noting the background noise filtering through becoming more silent with each passing second.

"Are you still there?"

I smile, my eyes fixed on the window. "Yeah, I'm here."

"Did you tell him about Faith?"

"No, but I did tell him about Dad kicking me out. I didn't elaborate."

Maggie breathes in sharply. I know it hurts her to remember that day because I know she blames herself.

"How is everyone?" I ask, averting her anxiety with something more palatable, if not as equally painful.

Her drawn-out pause speaks volumes. "I've been meaning to call you. Mum's well, but she had a dreadful day last week. They upped her medication to keep her comfortable, but she's still coherent and aware of her surroundings. Have you given any more thought about coming to see her?"

I sigh. "Maggie, I-I..." I turn my eyes to the privacy glass and stare at my grey reflection. I'm being selfish by not going back, but I just can't.

"Just think about it, but don't take too long," she replies when words fail me. "I don't like to bring it up, but I said I'd let you know.

I saw Joe yesterday. He asked me if our Faith was still in the graveyard. The first thing I did was check he hadn't desecrated her grave."

I huff out. "It doesn't surprise me. He was always a bastard. His words cut more than his fists ever could."

And the last time they cut me beyond repair, I was laying on a cold floor, broken, beaten, and my Faith was dead.

"Marianne," Maggie whispers, but I don't want her sympathy. That heartache is hers to bear, too.

The car slows down, and the galvanised gates fill the window. "Maggie, I need to go, but promise me you'll call if she gets worse."

"I will but do something for me today."

I tip my head a little. "What?" I murmur, fearful.

"Confess."

I snort because that's the idea.

"I haven't been to private confession in decades."

"Confession can be whatever you want it to be. Today, I want you to confess to John. Nothing big, just something. Just one thing, give him that."

I gaze up at his office window, mulling over her request as I step out of the car. "Okay," I say. "But why?"

"Because you need to start rebuilding the world you abandoned. If you blurt out the truth when he is blindsided, he will jump from one conclusion to another. He needs to live it through your eyes to truly understand."

"Okay. I'll speak to you soon. I love you."

"I love you, too."

I put away my mobile, and tap in the security code and wait to pass.

Inside the building, I board the creaky old lift. The doors drone unnervingly, and I stare up at the ceiling, watching the light flicker. Seriously, if it broke down right now, it might be a blessing.

Minutes later, I reach the office door, thinking over what Maggie said. *Confess.* She makes it sound so easy, but I guess to her, it is. She deals with it every day in every way you can imagine.

With a surprisingly hardened tenacity, I punch in the code, and walk down the hallway but stop when I hear a familiar voice.

"Yes, because Robin Hood and his Merry Men have nothing on you guys."

"Just get us some tights and a skirt!" Simon laughs.

"Doc might be able to source us some dresses," Tommy retorts thoughtfully.

"I don't recommend it," Dev sticks his two penn'orth in. "Open back and scratchy."

I stick my head around the architrave to find Kara pointing at Jake, Remy and Dev, while Tommy and Simon are leaning over the desk. As always, rock music blares from the dock.

"God, I should've phoned in sick. I'm losing the will to live," Remy declares, blowing out his breath.

Jake turns and slaps his hand down. "My will to live vanished the moment I walked through the door. It's probably still sat in the car, waiting for me to return."

"Hi, everyone," I say with a grin.

"Thank Christ, you're here!" Dev says, almost relieved. "You need to speak to Uncle J. There's something seriously up his arse this morning. We've lost three clients because of him. I don't know what's going on, but he'll be happy to see you."

Hardly.

I think I'm the last person he's going to want to see. Instead, I give him a tight smile and glance at Kara, who gives me a concerned look.

Yep, she also concurs my thoughts.

"What are you doing here?" I ask her, diverting the conversation.

"Volunteering. They needed a skivvy."

Tommy clears his throat and runs his hand through his hair. "That's Girl Friday, little lady." He grins as she glares at him.

"Skivvy, Girl Friday, tea lady... What's the difference?"

"Plenty. And it's in your financial interest to be here."

Kara raises her brows. "True, but you boys forget this is the reason why I quit last time."

"Honey?" I say, garnering her attention again. "I saw Sloan at the hotel this morning. He said he and Oliver were going to tend to business. What's he doing with him today?" My brows raise in silent request.

"He's taking him to the office to meet everyone. He's been wanting to show him off for months." She smiles like it is the best thing in the world, but she is so proud of her boys, anything to do with them brightens her face.

"Taking him to the office?" Dev repeats in disgust.

"And what type of father takes his kid to work for a meet and greet with the minions?" Remy chips in.

"The devil!" Tommy says, hi-fiving Simon. I put my hand over my mouth unable to keep a straight face.

Simon picks up a can of coke, takes a swig and strolls over to Kara. "Just think, little lady, you could be getting replaced as we speak. They both have that dark, handsome, broodiness going on. And God knows the women in that office love Sloan. Many a woman has splashed out on expensive knickers in the hope he will remove them."

My mouth falls open, and I worry my lip, while Kara shoots him a look of pure derision. She always feared she wasn't good enough, and all that has done is validate those fears.

"Fine line, Si, and you're at risk of crossing it," Dev says, pissed off, fixing his concerned focus on Kara.

The door slams open behind me, and John walks in, his expression hard, and he jabs his finger at Simon. "That wasn't a fine fucking line, sunshine, that was a liberty, and she allowed you take it. The next time I hear that shit, I won't. You two-" he points at Dev and Remy, "-have got papers to serve. They're not going to serve themselves, are they?"

Oh shit, that was harsh.

"For fuck sake!" Remy chucks his pen on the desk, collects up some thick envelopes and jerks his head to Dev. "Let's go. John, do us a favour? Stop being a bastard! It's not becoming."

"Really? Is employment becoming, Jeremy?"

"Twat!" Remy responds, his scars pitching up.

"See you later, M," Dev says, but I don't dare reply. Remy follows him out and gives John the finger.

Fixing my eyes on Kara, she looks both concerned for me and upset for herself. I risk a look at John and instantly wish I hadn't when he gives me a hate-filled stare I've never received before and slams the door behind him.

I fight back my own upset because I need to ensure Kara's okay. Approaching her, I recognise the expression of uncertainty immediately.

"Don't believe any of that. Sloan would move the sun and the stars for you." I tuck a stray lock of hair behind her ear.

"I know," she replies. "Please, go speak to him. He's been like this since last night."

"Don't worry, darling. I'll make it right." Pulling the door ajar behind me, I pause when I hear Tommy.

"Sorry, little lady," he says, exposing his tender side. I smile because he's a good guy and the love he has for her is enormous. "Trust me, Sloan would never replace you."

"That would be like J tossing M to the wayside," Jake speaks up.

My eyes close in resignation because I feel like I already have been. First John, then Sloan.

"It's never going to happen," Jake continues. "They've been in love with you both for so long, it would be akin to missing a limb or having an organ removed."

I tiptoe away, trying to make myself forget that statement since it just confirms that John might already know.

I knock on his door, but it's obvious he is on the phone. I push it open slowly to see him standing in front of the window.

"It's a calculator, not a wand, sunshine!" he hisses. "Cash in hand? Are you having a laugh? I run a reputable business and what you've just suggested is fraud." He shakes his head and kicks the skirting board. "Cash, card, cheque, you've still got to pay VAT, mate." Pause. "Yes, it is that simple!" Another pause. "Well, go somewhere else then!" He slams down the phone and throws his hands on his hips.

While the company is reputable and competent, they're hardly choirboys. Sometimes, especially with some of Sloan's dodgy directors he's trying to boot out, they fly close to the wind. So close, I sometimes wonder when the strong arm of the law will stop their flight.

"Hi." My timid tone cuts through the atmosphere.

"What do you want?" John rotates on the spot.

I recoil in shock; he's never spoken to me so harshly before. I guess I shouldn't expect anything different. His anger is deserving and warranted.

"I wanted to see you." His brow creases, and he folds his arms over his chest. "Did you get my messages?" I query pathetically.

He snorts and looks down at his desk, laden with papers. "Marie, I'm busy. If that's all you wanted to know, then yes, I did. Now, I've got a million things to do and people to piss off, so unless you're here for something else, you need to leave."

Taken further aback, I train my sight on the floor. "Okay, I'll go. I'll talk to you when you come home tonight – *if* you come home tonight." The defeatist tone in my voice is there, and I know if I stay any longer, I'll break.

I hurry out and hobble down the corridor. Heavy feet pound behind me and John spins me around at the security door.

"Why can't I stay angry with you?" he asks rhetorically. "You make me goddamn crazy, but I'll never stop caring for you, loving you. I can't stand seeing you beaten... Broken."

I shake my head. "John, I'm sorry. You were right last night, it's high time I started to talk. It's more than long overdue. Look, we can talk later if you're under the cosh."

I look down without thinking, a tell he probably thinks is guilt. And maybe it is, but what I'm slowly learning is that I have nothing to feel guilty for. My life, the disaster it turned out to be, none of it was my fault. Aside from getting pregnant young, everything that came after was inflicted by someone else's hand. Maggie is right; I was an amazing mother, irrespective of the moments I doubted it. And even though I was biologically old enough to be a mother, the simple fact of the matter is I was a child raising a child, and I did it singlehandedly.

"No, we'll talk now. If given time, you'll regress. You made an effort to come here and here is where we talk."

"Is there somewhere private?" I avert my eyes down the corridor, then back to him. He nods, places his hand on the small of my back and manoeuvres me to the lift.

My anxiety grows as we descend into the basement. The lift eventually groans to a stop, and he guides me deeper into the musty bowels of the building. He taps in another code and pushes the door back, and I look around as he flicks on a light.

I blink rapidly, my eyes adjusting, as I spy an old sofa at the back, surrounded by boxes and crates. Sitting down, my brain sides with ignorance as to what I may catch from this tatty old piece of furniture.

"Is this private enough?" John drops down beside me and angles his body in expectation.

I nod and continue to study the room while I remove my jacket. We could be here a while, so I'd rather be comfortable.

"So, what do you want to talk about?"

"I've been thinking about last night. About you, us, my family," I say, voicing things I rarely find the strength to. His expression remains stoic, but I know those few words have piqued his attention. It isn't every day I openly admit my weaknesses, but whenever I have, he hasn't pushed for more than I am comfortable with.

I bend further forward and place my arms on my thighs. "My life story is long."

"I don't expect it all in one go, but the beginning is a good start."

I blow out my breath. "My father was – *is* – a hard man. Hard to live with, hard to please. Even harder to love." And I've never admitted that to anyone.

Ever.

"Tell me, angel."

"I was nine when he first hit me. I was punished because I spilt a bottle of my mum's nail polish on the carpet."

The sofa shifts and John's palm rests on the back of my neck. His fingers curl, and I shudder under his well-intentioned touch as he manipulates me back and tilts my face towards him.

"You relive this in my arms and nowhere else."

"John…" I whisper, my eyes flooding with tears. He kisses the top of my head, and I'm selfishly relieved that he can't stay angry at me.

"Angel," he says full of emotion, his cheek to my temple. "I'm not going to like this, am I?"

"No. You're going to despise it because it stands for everything you're against. But you need to hear it because you will eventually understand why I never told you. Just to reiterate, I never did because I'm ashamed of what I became. Of who I am."

He looks conflicted, and I wriggle my shoulders, breaking free. I can't do this if he is smothering me. Opening my mouth, I continue where I left off.

"He hit me again when I was ten because I didn't want to go to church. And again, when I was eleven because I got a C in science. When I was twelve, it was because I didn't tidy my room. Thirteen it was because I dropped a bottle of foundation I was forbidden to have on my bedroom floor." I hold his stare as his eyes darken, expressing his pain for my younger self who had to experience this.

"Maggie could do no wrong, even when she did. She was always the good girl in his eyes. It didn't matter how hard I tried to please him, it was never enough. And in the end, I just stopped trying altogether. I could have walked to the ends of the earth and beyond, and I would still be a failure to him."

John huffs and puffs in anger and hauls me onto his lap.

"No! I can't say all this with you suffocating me. You can't hate me one minute and then love me the next out of sympathy."

"This isn't sympathy, it's unequivocal love. And I've told you, you relive this, you do it knowing you are loved inside my arms. And I will never stop loving you."

"You say that now."

"No, I'll say it all the time. I will never, ever stop loving you."

My heart breaks, but it's irrelevant because he still loves me, and that's all that matters.

I gaze up at the rafters and hesitantly entwine my arms around him, amazed at how he can be so selfless in the face turmoil.

"What about your mother? Did she never stop him?"

I shake my head no, at pains to verbalise it. "I adore my mother, so I won't speak ill of her. But it wasn't so much that she didn't care, it was the fact she was too frightened to act upon it. That, I didn't realise until I was sixteen when everything culminated and exploded in my face. Literally."

His palms stroke my belly. "Is that the day he kicked you out?"

I nod. "I was a good girl, John. I worked hard at school. I did everything I was told to, but I was restless, desperate for something he never bestowed. I wanted attention, affection, but ultimately, I just wanted someone to love me. When I was sixteen, I finally found that, or something I thought was that."

I wriggle anxiously, and he adjusts his leg and plants it on the floor so I can get comfortable in front of him. Sitting up, his hands rub up and down my thighs in comforting strokes, making me shiver.

"When my father found out about the boy I was seeing, he slapped me and forbade it. I was heartbroken. I finally had a small taste of what I craved, and he was taking it away from me. The same way he took everything good away from me."

"So, what did you do?"

"I did what everyone does when you're told you can't do something – I carried on doing it. For months, I would sneak around, until the day he found out again," I tell him while thinking up something to cut out a big chunk of my tale.

For now.

"My dad told me I had to stop seeing him or leave. I begged him, but it didn't matter. That day he hit me again, but this time, he also hit my mother. It was in that instance I knew she was a secretly battered woman. I was forced-" I stop on a breath, silently crying a river.

I glance down, but he tips my chin up and swipes his thumbs under my eyes. "Go on, beautiful, I've got you." He wraps his arms around me and holds me tight to his front.

"I was forced to make a choice: my future or my family. And I choose. At the time, it was the only thing that mattered, yet I know now it didn't matter what choice I made. The outcome would always be the same. It was always going to be in vain because it was never destined to last.

"I ended up living with my boyfriend's parents. Life there wasn't much better, but I made the best of a bad situation. And I tried, John, I really fucking tried to make it work. I tried so hard, I even married the bastard! But as it turns out, I truly am my mother's daughter. Except, no one ever saw my bruises. He was clever, he beat me down, not just physically, but mentally and emotionally. He made me believe I was nothing, and I've suffered and sacrificed my entire life because of it."

"Fuck!" he hisses and stands, pacing in front of me.

"Skin heals, broken hearts mend, and eventually emotions become less fraught and torn, but memories never fade. And for a long time, I carried them like a shield. I used them as a weapon because I believed I wasn't good enough, that I didn't deserve to find happiness. But you proved all that wrong. And I want that, John, I want it all with you. I want to be married to you. I want to wake up every day and know I deserve to have you. But more than that, I want a family. I want a chance to prove I can do it right, that I'm not the person he made me believe I am. That I'm not too frightened to live, to take chances. I want it all."

He drops back down and twists my engagement ring repeatedly. And suddenly, I no longer care. I'm giving him the truth - albeit a diluted version.

He grips my shoulders and studies me keenly. "Angel, I'm overwhelmed that you're finally talking. Nevertheless, I'm fucking furious that every man in your life has taken advantage or abandoned you in some shape or form. And last night, I did exactly the same thing. I'm elated that you've finally admitted you want us to have a family. But what I don't want is you making a rash decision you'll regret. I think we both know it isn't going to be easy, or cheap."

I nod, but at my age I know I'll probably never get pregnant naturally.

"I don't give a shit about any of that, beautiful. What I do care about is you looking back in your late forties or fifties, saddled down with young kids you regret, and having you hate me for it."

"I understand that, but *I* don't want to look back in another ten years and regret that *I* never tried. Likewise, I don't want *you* to look back and resent me because *you* never had the chance. I know it won't be easy. That it could take months, years, maybe never, but I swear, I will never regret giving this to you. And regardless of what you believe, I *do* want to be a mother."

He kisses me hard, his thumbs circling my cheeks. Sliding my hands around his neck, I hold him tight. The kisses turn frantic and desperate, and when I tug on his shirt, he stops me.

"No, this needs to be the right way, and I'm not going to fuck you in my mouldy storage room with half my staff upstairs." He holds my face tenderly. "Look, I don't want you going back up in this state and raising questions. So, I'm going to go and apologise for being an absolute bastard, and then we're going to go home, have an early dinner and talk about this cordially. If we do this, you're all in. No *one days*, no half measures. It's all or nothing."

He lifts me off his knee and stands. "I once told Kara that you give the person you love everything. That anything less will never be enough. Now I'm saying it to you. You give me everything because anything less will never be enough. I'm all in, angel. And I have been since the first time I saw you."

I watch as he walks to the door and then walks through it. Sitting in the dank, dirty basement, on a sofa that is probably a health hazard, I stare into nothingness.

"I'm all in," I whisper.

Chapter 32

MY FINGERS TOY with the old pendant around my neck, while I flick through the pages of a well-read magazine, waiting to be called.

It's been just over a week since I poured my heart out in John's arms in his dingy basement. The same night, I told him more about my parents and the way my father ruled our house with an aggressive finality that was never to be challenged. I didn't impart anything further in respect of the unnecessary beatings, but I did answer honestly when he asked if my father was oppressive. I knew what he meant when the words left his lips, and he knew my thinly veiled answer when the words left mine.

Stoic, but visibly twisted from my painful truths, he said he would give me time. But time is fleeting, and now in short supply.

"Marie Dawson?" I put down the magazine and rise as the nurse looks over the waiting room with inquisitive eyes.

As per the receptionist's advice when I booked the appointment earlier this week, I prepped first. This consisted of ibuprofen with my morning coffee and porridge. And just in case the ibuprofen doesn't quite cut it, I've also bought a packet of fast-acting painkillers.

"Hello, Ms Dawson."

"Hi," I greet and follow her into the examination room.

Taking in the room, the last time I was here was seven years ago. In that time, the place has gone from being a murky light green to pristine white and cream. Granted, some things never change, and the metal, faux leather eighties chairs are the only things still the same.

"Take a seat." She waves over the two empty seats that have seen better days. "So, you're here to have your IUD removed?" She turns, crosses one leg over her knee and links her fingers.

"That's right," I confirm distracted, focusing on the walls displaying the usual NHS literature. From middle school basics of the human body to the image of a child in the womb, to the pictorials of the different forms of contraception available.

"Okay." She nods and twists back to the screen. "You've had it in for just over seven years. Are you experiencing problems with it?"

"No, I just want it removed. I've been on some form of contraceptive since I was seventeen. I think my body could use a break."

"That's understandable. Can I ask if you have had unprotected sex in the last seven days?"

"Yes, I have."

"I'm sure you're aware, but semen can live in the body for several days after intercourse. Are you sure you still want to go ahead? I can make a later appointment for you if you like?" She gives me an expectant look, but she really is preaching to the converted.

"I'm aware of the consequences, but I'd still like it removed today."

"Okay." Appeased by my declaration, she stands and draws back the curtain, revealing the dreaded examination bed. "If you'd just like to undress and hop up," she says as she tugs the roll of green paper at the end of the frame and covers the mattress.

I smile grudgingly and move past her. I admit I can't stand this. I appreciate she has probably seen hundreds of women naked from the waist down, but it's still embarrassing.

"Did the receptionist advise you to take anything before the appointment?" she asks from the other side of the curtain.

"I took some ibuprofen. I'm kind of hoping it won't hurt as much coming out as it did going in."

"There'll be a little discomfort, but otherwise it's relatively painless." She pulls back the curtain and puts on a pair of medical gloves. "Right, if you can lie back, knees up and relax, I'll have it out in minutes."

I roll my eyes, lie back and think of England. Hitching up my spread legs, I press my palms into the paper.

"So, what made you decide to get it removed?"

I consider my reply, while her hands touch places they shouldn't. The truth of the today is that this might be my last chance. Everything I've read on the internet tells me after forty the possibility of getting pregnant is roughly twenty per cent. I imagine mine could be longer since I've been on contraception for nearly two and half decades.

After much discussion this last week, I realise I've been selfish, not only to John but to myself. For too long I've played dumb, conveying the misguided idea that I couldn't give him something he desperately wants. At my age, maybe I can't. Maybe I have left it too late. I'm not expecting to suddenly fall pregnant in the space of a month or two, twenty per cent is very low, but if I don't try, I won't know. And I meant what I said, I don't want either of us to look back and resent our relationship.

However, if I do miraculously fall on, and if it happens before I have braced my heart in chains and found the courage to impart the final few pieces of my life to him, at least I won't have the choice to procrastinate over it any further.

"Marie? You still with me?"

"Yeah, sorry. My partner really wants children, and well, I know the chances at my age are probably slim to none, but you've got to try, right?"

"Hmm." She sounds suspect, but before I can say anything else, I flinch at a pinch inside.

"All done. How do you feel?"

"Fine, I guess," I tell the ceiling.

The nurse picks up my folded clothes and puts them on the end of the mattress. "I'll give you a minute to get dressed." The curtain draws shut, and her shoes squeak on the linoleum. I quickly pull on my knickers and jeans and re-join her.

"Before you go, you need to be aware that future periods may be longer, heavier and more painful. Obviously, you're no longer protected against pregnancy. When you do start actively trying, don't be disheartened if it doesn't happen. Unlike men, the older us women get the chances of conceiving lessen drastically."

"What are the chances? I've read twenty per cent on a range of websites. Is that accurate?"

"It's a broad guide, and there are exceptions, but a woman in her forties has roughly a fifteen to twenty-five per cent chance. Of course, IVF is an option, but really, it's a last resort." She thumbs through a few leaflets and hands them to me. Perusing the pages, I guess twenty per cent is still better than no per cent at all.

"They contain some good information with regards to preparing for pregnancy, extra vitamins, what to expect. The basics."

"Thank you." Sliding my bag into the crook of my arm, I'm ready to leave and head to the door.

"Marie?" She stops me. "Make sure you're doing it for the right reasons."

I smile. "I appreciate your concern, but I want a baby." There, again I've said it. I've repeated the words I had avoided forever when my choice was so blindsided by past events that, in a bid not to bestow the hurt I once felt on another, I sacrificed years of personal happiness. From the age of nineteen to forty, I led a celibate, solitary life. John doesn't know that he is only number two, but in my eyes, he'll never be anything but number one.

"I'm not patronising, but I've seen plenty of women cast their personal beliefs aside for love. It's easy to give in to someone else's wishes, but it's your body and your choice. Being a mother for the first time is hard at any age."

I rest my hand on the door handle and sigh. "I understand the risks, but I'm willing to take them. And I know how hard it is because it wouldn't be my first time. Thank you, have a nice day."

As I proceed through the busy waiting room, I send up a small prayer, praying that time is still on my side.

Pushing the empty stroller, I grin. Oliver - oblivious to anything other than being in his mother's arms - rests his sleepy head on her shoulder as she cradles his nappy-clad bum and walks around the department store, looking but not really. Doing the one thing she loathes beyond belief; she sits down with a huff on a vacant seat.

"I should have just got the pesky personal shoppers to do this for me," she groans, studying the cream dress hanging over the pushchair.

"And miss a day with me? I'm insulted!" I feign disbelief while doing the one thing I secretly love – shopping. How Kara never picked up the bug living with me, I don't know. I think I might have scared her when I took her to a store for the first time and bought her bras and knickers. She's never been the same since.

Kara rolls her eyes and rubs her son's back as he lets out a content sigh.

"He's got the right idea, hasn't he? Did he have early morning playtime with Daddy?"

"Hmm." She gazes down at her boy, completely in love, and slides back a thick lock of black wavy hair. "Sloan loves it, regardless of what he says. I offer to get up, but he refuses."

"Figures. I guess it's because he doesn't see him all day. Has he given any more thought to stepping down for a while?"

"Yes and no. He's just signed some huge deals, so he needs to be there. I don't mind, but I'd like to think I might see him a little more than I have lately. He's been in the office until midnight some days. There are times he sits and watches Oliver sleeping because he missed bedtime."

"Honey, it's not his fault."

"No, I don't mean it like that. We're lucky, I know that. I just think when we make this one a brother or sister, I'd like him to share some of the firsts with me." She smiles dreamily, thinking of something completely different, but I'm not brave enough to ask.

Taking a seat beside her, I twist her chin. "And he will be. What he does is for both of you." I tip my head between mother and son. "It's a hard sacrifice to miss out on moments he'll never get back. Knowing him, I can't imagine it's a decision he made lightly."

"No," she whispers.

"Are you?" I ask, levelling my steadfast gaze on her. "Trying to get pregnant?"

She shrugs. "Not purposely, but I need to talk to Sloan. He definitely won't mind, but it isn't just my decision."

I don't press for more because I'm not comfortable having this conversation with her. Namely, because I'm technically doing the same since John doesn't know I've had the IUD removed today. I can't imagine he will mind either, but still, I should have told him.

"How are you and John?" she asks delicately. It isn't often she enquires, but considering she was put in the middle of the standoff last week, I know it is out of concern – more for me than him.

"He's fine. *We're* fine, I think. I told him bits and pieces-"

"Bits and pieces that you've never told me," she states, very matter of fact.

I grind my teeth in annoyance, not because she has specified it, but because when I do tell her, I don't want her to look at me differently.

For a long time in her life, the only female role model she had was her mother, and she's no paradigm of a strong, independent woman. I wanted to be that for her, hence why I've always shut her down when she has raised topics I deem to be taboo.

"Honey, I will tell you, it's just-"

"Not the right time?"

I sigh in capitulation, not that I was going to say that, but still, I let it go.

"When it's right, I promise I will listen without prejudice. And I promise I will still love you after." Kara turns away when her mobile starts to ring, and she straps Oliver into the stroller. Fingering the screen, she shakes her head.

"What?"

"Sophie. She's complaining we're late."

Standing simultaneously, I link my arm in hers. "You know, the day you turned up with her for dinner, I thought the world had frozen over. You're both so chalk and cheese."

She laughs. "I remember. Feel sorry for me, she got me shouted at on the first day of school because she was busy telling me the teacher had a stick up his backside!"

I stop, shocked. "You never told me that."

"No, her bountiful pearls of wisdom leave a lot to be desired." Laughing between ourselves, we move around the fixtures to the cashier's desk.

"Have a nice day," I impart to the lady after she has handed over our purchases.

I stuff my purse into my bag as my phone beeps. Pulling it out, I activate the display and open the message. My heart rate quickens when I see Maggie's name and the message she has sent. Halting mid-step, her text of 'her condition has gotten worse', is pulling at my heartstrings. The statement of 'dad isn't coping', however, is not. Truthfully, that man deserves nothing from me. But knowing my mother's end is near, and now being able to appreciate we don't always get what we want in life, I contemplate if I can finally excuse all the wrongs he committed.

I've never told anyone my father wasn't the good man of the cloth they made him out to be. He was – maybe still is - exalted in our village, and I was nothing but the town tramp for a time. A nasty moniker that wasn't true, but he did nothing to protect me from that.

"What is it?" Kara's voice breaks the disturbing images that have rushed back into my head.

"Nothing. Just a marketing text." I grip my mobile tight as we leave the store. Heading towards the centre car park, I may be here in body, but my mind is currently one hundred miles north, remembering a life I left behind.

The sun shines bright overhead as we pass through the front door of The Swan.

I look around the busy bar, but Sophie is nowhere in sight. Ordering two pints of lemonade and a couple of bags of cheese and onion, I pass over a twenty and wait for the girl behind the bar to syphon the pop. Curling my hand around a glass a few moments later, Kara nudges my side.

"They're outside."

Pushing the stroller through the horde, who kindly allow mother and child to pass, I see Charlie and Sophie, lounging, decked out in sunglasses, laughing up a storm with Jeremy and Jake.

I follow behind, as the rare day of sun - in between the last few days of rain - beats down on my back. Placing the drinks down, I shrug off my jacket and lay it over my bag.

"Ladies, gentlemen," I greet and sit down on the bench.

Kara puts her jacket over mine, while Remy unbuckles his baby chum, who is now wide awake, and stands him on his knees.

"Hey, sunshine!" Remy says. Oliver, loving the attention, laughs and wiggles on his knees until Remy tucks him into his chest and reaches into the nappy bag for his bottle. Oliver bats it away unimpressed.

"No? How about this?" He pulls out a small jar of rice pudding and Oliver squeals in delight. "Oh, good choice, Mum!" Remy winks at Kara, who passes him a spoon.

I rest my chin on my hand, completely enthralled by this scary, scarred up man with a heart of gold, feed a child he looks upon like his own son. It's not surprising, Oliver is the shining light for everyone in his life. There is nothing they wouldn't do if Kara or Sloan asked.

Caught in the moment, I hiss as a twinge of pain stabs at my belly. I rub inconspicuously and avert my gaze to see if anyone has noticed.

"Come on, then. What did you both buy?" Sophie asks, tilting her sunglasses with her finger and thumb.

"A suit," I reply with a groan when the pain becomes stronger. I guess this is what the nurse meant when she said periods would be stronger and more painful. I'm not even due my bloody period for another week, and the side-effects have already started. I rummage through my bag for the painkillers, repeating my internal manta - it's worth it.

"A suit?" Sophie replies annoyed. "You always buy a flaming suit!"

Popping the pills into my mouth, I chase them down with a mouthful of pop and glare at her. "What do you expect me to buy? A thigh high, crotch-skimming, clubbing number?"

Charlie laughs and covers her mouth, while Jake has no airs or graces and guffaws, slapping his hand on the table.

"Don't be so defensive! I just thought you might go a little daring for once. You always wear a suit. It's boring!"

I swear she thinks I'm her age sometimes. Her ideas are ridiculous at the best of times, and downright ludicrous at others.

"Sophie, I'm forty-three, not twenty-three!"

"Forty-three *is* the new twenty-three!" Miss Garrulous replies with zeal.

"Hmm, and twenty-six is clearly the new six!" I retort although she doesn't catch on. She smiles, and I wave it off. I can't be mad at her. Even though her mother is not that much older than me, she has always said she sees me as friendly rather than motherly. I guess I should just be glad she doesn't think I'm over the hill.

"Soph, I'll have you know I'm wearing a suit, too," Charlie says and taps the iPad screen. "Urgh!"

"What is it?" Jake asks, tightening his hand on her shoulder, pulling her in to get a better view. "Oh, the boss is on the warpath, I see. Did you two little reprobates tell him you were taking an extended lunch?"

Sophie pulls a face. "He doesn't normally miss us."

I almost spit out the lemonade and wipe the corner of my mouth. "I can't imagine how that is possible," I deadpan.

"Understatement of the century!" Jake exclaims. "Soph, are you and Doc coming to the bash at the hotel at the end of the month?"

"No. We're having a romantic weekend in the Cotswolds."

Jake rubs his hand through his blond hair. "God, I'm in the wrong profession! He's making money hand over fist, while me and you," he motions to Jeremy, "are scraping the fucking barrel, installing systems, arguing the toss with tight bastards, issuing process demands and tracking down degenerates!"

"Language!" Kara interrupts.

"It's not his fault he's a doctor!" Soph exclaims.

"And you love to be his nurse!" Jake says knowingly.

"That's right, I do! How many emails, Char?"

"Ten. No, make that eleven." Charlie grimaces.

"What's he said?"

"'Get your arses back here now, or you're both fired! Right...'" Charlie stops, looking confused. "'Right' what? Oh, no, make that twelve. Now! 'Right now!'. We better go."

"He's such an unreasonable arse!"

"Hey, baby boy present, and that's his father, remember?" Remy says firmly, pointing the little plastic spoon.

"And that's my husband, remember?" Kara adds, thoroughly annoyed. It isn't often she makes any kind of comment because she is the first to admit how unreasonable Sloan can be, but she'll be damned if she lets Soph get away with far too much backchat.

"I didn't mean it like that, chick. You know I love him really." Sophie grins.

"Well, I'm glad to hear it. Because if it wasn't for him, you'd still be at a firm you despise, dating men who aren't worth your time." Kara gives her a pointed look as she and Charlie start to gather up their belongings and snuggle baby boy, who just looks annoyed at being disturbed from his pudding.

"I know; I owe him a lot. Marie, I'll call you, and we can go shopping for a dress for girls' night!"

"Crap," I say under my breath, forcing a Cheshire cat grin.

"No crying off now. I've got it all planned. I can't wait!" She claps her hands excitedly.

Moving around the table, Soph tells everyone goodbye, while Jake snakes his arm around his girlfriend's waist and plants a good one on her. Extracting herself from her man, Charlie waves as she high tails it through the beer garden, her phone now ringing persistently.

Jake plonks himself back down and necks the rest of his pint. "I think you might get that thigh high, crotch-skimming number, after all, Marie."

I shake my head. "Don't."

"Just making an authentic observation. John will love it," he says, reaching for Oliver, who Jeremy grudgingly passes over.

"Why did I agree to a girls' night out?" Kara asks.

I swing my head at her and smile. "Actually, you agreed to two. Deal with it, honey, because if she's making me wear a stripper dress, you are too!"

I open a bag of crisps, and pop them into my mouth, and watch Oliver smack his lips together and giggle at the big boys.

I smile and pull faces at him as he fusses in Jake's lap and stretches his podgy arms out to me. Reaching over, a knife-like sensation stabs at my abdomen, and I slap my hand on the table, sending the half-eaten crisps flying.

"Are you okay?" Kara asks, as Remy moves quickly and steadies me.

"I'm fine, honey, but I think I need to go home. I suddenly don't feel well."

Jeremy, the unlikely gentleman, takes my bag and grips my side. "I'll drop M home and see you back at work," he tells Jake. "Kara, I'll see you later. Take care of my sunshine."

I force a smile between the pain and the kindness of his speech.

"Call and let me know you're okay," Kara says with concern.

"I will, honey."

Walking through the beer garden, my steps falter as the pain comes and goes, leaving me nauseous and lightheaded. As I reach the car, I feel like my insides are about to drop out. After helping me inside, Remy folds himself into the driver's seat and starts up his Lexus.

"How's John been this last week?" I dare to ask the question that's been plaguing my conscience.

"Fine," Remy confirms, turning in my direction.

"I'm sorry he spoke to you the way he did." It comes out without thinking, but I feel the need to redeem myself. After all, it's my fault John spoke to him like shit.

"We all have bad days, Marie. John's are few and far between, but he has them."

"True. How are you and Evie?" I ask, equally curious and concerned.

"Good," he replies with zero elaboration. Single word answers are never good from these guys, but I know how uncomfortable he is talking about her. Still, I'll be damned if I let him stew on the hardship of loving a woman who is completely attainable, and in some respects, completely out of reach.

"Jeremy…"

"We're good, really."

"Really? I don't believe you."

He sighs and tightens his hand on the wheel as the traffic slows in front of us. "Marie, I know you care, but we're fine. I'm even learning to tolerate Andy Blake."

"Yes, but is he learning to tolerate you?"

He chuckles. "It's a work in progress."

I return his grin and turn back to the windscreen. Sometime later, in between tailbacks of traffic and polite conversation, I'm home. Unfastening my seat belt, I get out as Remy reaches into the back for my bag and hands it to me.

"Thanks, darling. I'll see you later."

As I stride towards the house, Mavis comes out of her front door, waving something with gusto.

"Crap, not now," I mutter.

"Marie, I've got something for you. It arrived this morning."

"Thank you, Mavis."

I take the letter and stuff it into my bag. Engaging in neighbourly small talk - small talk which always starts with the current street gossip and ends with the tenuous topic of when John and I are going to stop living in sin - her questions are always the same, as are my replies.

This time, however, just to pull on my already fragile heartstrings, she tells me she might not have long left and to get a move on down the aisle. Open mouthed, not having formulated the correct response to such an entrapment tactic, she does her usual – toddles off at snail's pace and shuts her door.

"Bye, Mavis," I whisper belatedly.

Crossing the lawn, I unlock the door. I lob my bag down, pick out the letter and slide my finger under the flap.

"What the fuck?" I mutter, lifting out the tiny plastic baby band. Horror suffuses me, while an instantaneous sickness mingles with the pain running rife in my stomach as I read the intended addressee.

Private and Confidential. Mr John Walker.

"Why?" I scream out. "*Why!*"

I slump down to the floor and kick my foot against the bottom of the bannister. Taking a breath, I lean forward and drag my bag off the step and pull out my phone.

"Hi," Maggie greets, sounding unexpectedly cheery considering her earlier message. "Sorry, I texted you earlier, but-"

"What's Adrian's number?"

She hesitates. "No, I can't."

"Maggie, please. I need to speak to him urgently."

"Why?"

I close my eyes, clutch the plastic in my hand and open my mouth. "The bastard sent Faith's hospital ID bracelet."

"What?"

"He sent it to *John*," I whimper, breaking down.

"Have you got a pen?" she asks firmly, without hesitation.

I reach into my bag and write the number on my hand. Promising to call her when I've calmed down, I hang up and dial the number.

"Taylor?" Adrian answers after two rings.

"Why didn't you tell me he was out?"

"Marie. How did you get this number?"

"How do you think? At least one person gives a shit if I'll still be breathing tomorrow," I spit out.

"Maggie," he says knowingly. "I'm hanging up, Marie. Don't ring me again. I told you, call nine nine nine."

"Adrian, he sent me-"

The phone goes dead, and I throw the handset the length of the hallway. Crawling into the corner, I clutch the plastic and cry into the floor, remembering the day my life changed forever.

Chapter 33

"OH-OH," I GROAN as a sharp, vice-like pain, develops in my belly. Pressing my hand to my bump, I wait for the sensation to ease down. "Play nice, Fay bear."

"I'm glad you agreed to come today," Mum says, sliding her arm around my back. I lean into her, appreciating the risk she is taking in still providing me with some sort of financial and emotional assistance since my father is still pretending that my bastard and I don't exist.

"I needed to get out. I've been cooped up in that house for weeks."

"Speaking of which, how are they treating you?" Mum picks up a two pack of Babygro's from the display, admires them, then deposits them into the basket.

I purse my lips, schooling my response. "Fine, I guess." Picking up a little stripy two-piece, I'm dumbstruck by the price. "It's not all sweetness and light, and Mrs Beresford has made it abundantly clear she doesn't want me there, but I can't be ungrateful. She feeds me and puts a roof over my head, so I guess I have to be thankful for that."

I trail my fingers over the little suit, then lay it on my bump and grab my purse. Digging my fingers through the coins - pennies and twos, not pounds and notes – I already know it won't be leaving with me. I tuck my purse away and catch Mum worrying her lip as the basket clatters to the floor. Guilt consumes me, realising what I've said, and the context in which she has interpreted it.

"Mum, I'm sorry. I didn't mean it like that."

She shakes her head. "No, I deserved that. I just wish..."

"Be careful what you wish for," I say, rather than listen to her voice all the wrongs she wishes she could right. She could chant them until she's blue in the face, but her wishes still wouldn't change anything.

"I know, but I wish it didn't have to be like this. This is a precious time, and I should be sharing it with you." She removes the two-piece from my very lively bump and puts it in the basket.

Coaxing me closer, insofar as my middle allows, I stretch my arms around her.

"She's active today."

"Yeah, a sign of things to come. I couldn't have a quiet, well-behaved baby, could I?" I smirk, and she shakes her head in amusement.

"No, I guess not."

"*Mum? Marianne?*" *Maggie calls, and I turn, but Mum stops me. Her eyes narrow, and she lifts her hand to my shirt collar and pushes it aside.*

"*What is that?*" *she asks firmly, pointing.*

I tremble, aware of what she has seen, and fix my shirt collar and move away in shame.

"*Darling, what is that?*"

"*It's nothing,*" *I mumble, but it's not nothing. It's the latest evidence of the bed of roses I'm not currently sleeping in. What started off small has escalated, and my earlier fears have finally come to fruition. It began when Joe slapped me when I refused an abortion. It was further cemented when his dad sat him down and told him he was going to do right by me. That night, three months ago, I knew what it felt like to cower in a corner, fearful for my life, while he rained down punch after punch. Since then, it has gotten worse. He's out drinking most nights. He comes home high, smelling of booze and perfume, and if I dare address his whereabouts, I feel the force of his fists again. Now, I've stopped asking altogether, because I'd rather live in ignorant bliss than wonder when my last breath will be.*

Frankly, Joe doesn't want this baby. He wordlessly confirmed it the last time he hurt me. I don't know if he remembers in his intoxicated state, but I'll never forget because a man only beats a pregnant woman if he wants a dire outcome.

And for all my mother's wishes, my biggest wish is that I had somewhere else to go, rather than living in silent fear every day.

"*Marianne?*" *Mum calls as I pick up the basket.* "*Marianne!*"

I stop dead and throw my arm out. "*What do you want me to say?*"

"*Why didn't you tell me?*"

I shrug, but I know what I say next is going to hurt. It's unintentional but unavoidable. "*Because it wouldn't change anything. I'd still be living at the Beresford's, and Dad would still be pretending I don't exist.*"

"*But if he knew, he would... He might...*"

"*No,*" *I whisper.* "*I'm already dead to him. And you can't beat what's dead. In the last four months, if I've learnt anything, it's this. I've learnt to speak no evil, hear no evil and see no evil.*"

With tears in my eyes, I know I can't leave it like this. I can't let her think this is all her fault. Inching towards her, I reach out.

"*One day, I know I'll have to choose between what's convenient and what's right. When that day comes, I will ensure mine and my baby's survival above all else. Until then, I will speak no evil, but I won't darken your door and put you at risk.*"

Mum nods, but she is far from pacified. She motions me closer until her breath blows on my cheek. "*Maggie doesn't know your father hits me. She thinks it was a one-off when he kicked you out. I want her to remain ignorant, but when the day of convenience ends, I want you to promise to come back, and I'll do what I have to." I nod, fearing that day may come sooner than either of us expects.*

"Okay." She rubs her thumb under my eyes and grips my hand. "Let's go find your sister."

"Oh, no," I whisper and drop the basket as I double over in agony.

"What do you think of these?" Maggie asks, full of excitement, holding a little pink dress over her chest, wiggling matching booties below it.

"They're great," I reply, short of breath, gritting my teeth to get through the pain, until the tremor in my abdomen finally wanes.

Maggie edges closer, and her smile fades, realising what's happening. "Marianne?"

I wave my hand. "I'm fine, really." No sooner have I said it, the pain comes back with a vengeance. "Oh, God!" I wail as another wave shoots through my belly, contracting my muscles. It feels like a vice is squeezing my middle.

I slam my hands down on a display of pink and blue crap, while my body falls forward, knocking every item to the floor. My huge belly presses against the cabinet, hindering a comfortable position.

"Oh, no! Mum? Mum!" Maggie cries out, tossing down the dress and shoes.

My eyes dart around the area with furious intent while I practically crawl across the floor. A member of staff rushes towards me, and I dig my fingers into her arm as she helps me onto a tub chair.

"It's too early. It's not time!" I pant. "Oh, God, that hurts!"

"Marianne?" Mum runs towards me frantically.

"I think the baby's coming," I idiotically state the obvious.

"Maggie? Call your father, tell him we're going to the hospital!"

"No, don't tell him!" I cry out, but Mum ignores me as she helps me out of the store.

The next hour is a blur as we manage to get from the shopping centre to the hospital. Pulling up outside, my father is already waiting with an auxiliary nurse.

"Please don't leave me!" I wail.

The nurse helps me into the wheelchair as Mum and Maggie are dragged away by my father. I reach out to them in vain and find nothing but air.

"Oh, God!" I grimace when another contraction rips through me like a tidal wave of knives. Crying hysterically, I grip the sides of the chair, causing my fingers to numb.

"Mum, please don't leave me! I can't do this alone!" I beg as I am wheeled into the maternity ward.

Mum clings to Maggie, whose face is distraught because she wanted to be there when I gave birth. We came into the world together, and this was another moment we agreed to share together. But our joint excitement is now laid to waste. Forcing my head up, I glare at my father, who has his hand on Maggie's wrist, holding her back.

"Please, Dad," Maggie whimpers. *"Please!"*

"Norman, please," Mum pleads in vain.

"I said, no!" he shouts with finality, giving me a pointed look.

"Marianne, honey?" The ward nurse rushes towards me, clearly fed up of the commotion, and glares with derision at my parents. *"There's only one person allowed in with her. So, who's it going to be?"*

"I am." Maggie instantly struggles to break free, disobeying him, much to his shock.

"No. We'll be in the waiting room," my father announces callously, and points for my mother and sister to move.

I stare at the nurse through watery eyes, mortified. Her look of revulsion at my father's actions is there for all to see. She smiles down at me as the porter pushes me into the room and the door closes behind us.

"Let's get you comfortable, sweetheart," she says, and I nod, heartbroken while preparing myself for another wave of pain.

"Please don't leave me," I beg as she helps me onto the bed.

"I won't, darling. I'll be right here with you the entire time. I'm not going anywhere."

I dig my feet into the mattress as I clutch the nurse's hand and bear down. Groaning out, I rest back as the contraction fades – but not for long.

"How many more?" I ask, sweating and shivering in pain I've never experienced before.

"You're nearly there, honey," the doctor says from the foot of the bed. *"Just a couple more pushes, and you get to meet your baby."*

Another contraction starts to build, and I scream out when it hits. Squeezing the nurse's hand, I grimace and moan incoherently through gritted teeth as my lower half feels like it is being ripped apart.

"I can see the baby's head, sweetheart. Give me another big push, Marianne. Just one more and it's all over!"

"I can't!" I sob, my eyes flicking to the clock. It's been four hours since I came in and they've been telling me 'just one more big push' for the last fifteen fucking minutes!

The next contraction hits and I push with all my might. Giving it everything I've got, the moment I've feared, and waited for, finally arrives. The sound of my wailing and panting is replaced by the unhappy cry of a baby being forced from it's nice, warm cocoon.

"You did it, Marianne!" the nurse says, who, true to her word, has not left my side.

"I did?" I ask tearful, relieved.

She smiles gloriously. "You did. She's beautiful!"

I lean up on my elbows, thoroughly knackered, but dying to see my daughter for the first time. I watch as they clean her up, weigh her, and bring her to me. Resting her on my chest, I cry tears of joy as she blinks at me.

"Hey, Faith. I'm your mummy," I coo, close my eyes and breathe in her scent.

"Marianne?" The nurse draws my attention. I smile proudly, stroking her forehead. "She's amazing, sweetheart. Have you picked a name?"

"Faith," I whisper.

"Faith is lovely. It's perfect for her," she says, writing 'Faith Turner' on the plastic band and attaching it to her tiny wrist. "Honey, we need to get you cleaned up. Do you want me to ask your mum or sister to come in?"

My happiness evaporates instantly, and I shrug. "Yes, but they won't. He won't let them."

"Your dad?"

I nod to hide the indignation and fuss over my newborn.

"What about the father? Does he know?"

Again, I shrug.

"Okay. I'm going to go outside and speak to your parents. I'll be a minute."

I cogitate, fearing what my dad will say when the nurse puts him on the spot for abandoning his teenage daughter in her hour – or four – of need.

Gazing down at my child, I smile, thinking of all the good things in life I'm going to teach her. My life might not be that good right now, but eventually, it will be better. It's got to be because it can't get much worse.

The door opens, and I turn to see Mum and Maggie. Maggie, as expected, looks excited at the bundle in my arms. She makes haste towards me, while the nurse returns with my father trailing pathetically behind her. I hold his gaze, as he loiters at the door, and for a second, I see something cross his face. It isn't his usual disappointment, but it isn't approval either. It's just something.

"Hi, Fay bear! I'm Auntie Maggie!" Maggie coos, and reaches for the baby, but then thinks better of it. The nurse, identifying my twin's hesitation, comes forward.

"Do you want to hold her?" I ask, and she nods, excited, before sitting in the chair the nurse has pulled over. Passing the baby to her, she holds her tight and whispers things only she can hear.

I smile at Mum, who kneels next to Maggie. She strokes Faith's forehead as she settles into Maggie's arms.

"She's gorgeous," Maggie says, verging on tears.

"She is," Mum affirms. "She looks like you both did when you were born." Her eyes shift across the room to my father, hoping this will soften him, but he remains stoic until he eventually leaves the room. I sigh, but I didn't expect more. "I'm sorry, honey."

"So am I," I reply, as Maggie passes Faith back to me.

"Smile!" The nurse holds up a Polaroid camera, and I grin, utterly drained, as the flash blinds me. "Has Faith got a middle name, sweetheart?" she asks, shaking the picture.

I nod. "Elizabeth, after my mum."

"Oh, honey," Mum says, wiping her eyes.

"That's nice. I'll leave you ladies alone, now." The nurse places the picture on the bed and shuts the door behind her.

"Mum, do you want to hold her?" I ask.

My mum laughs, showing her carefree side - the one she hides. "Absolutely. Come here, little one." She reaches for the baby and snuggles her. Sitting down beside me, she rubs my exposed knee. "My special girls," she says, beaming between the three of us, but her smile starts to wither.

"What's wrong?"

"I called the Beresford's. Patricia said Joe was out and she'd tell him you were in labour. I thought he would have been here by now."

"Wishful thinking," I mutter, but I really don't care where he is. As of now, he is no longer my priority.

Closing my eyes, exhaustion overpowers me, and I drift off to the soft sounds of my daughter in the background.

The day fades slowly into night outside, but there is only light in my heart right now.

I hold Faith to my chest, and she suckles away avidly. Getting her to latch on this afternoon was touch and go, but she's learning. We both are. I gaze down, absolutely in love with my daughter and the content noises she is making.

The door opens, and a nurse pops her head around the spine. "Hey. I see she's finally getting the hang of it. You're doing great."

"Thank you."

"I'm sorry to disturb, but you've got a visitor."

"Who?" I ask, having given up hope of Joe making an appearance. It's been over six hours since my mum called, and he's still not arrived.

"He says he's the father. Do you want me to let him in?"

"Sure," I reply.

"If you have any problems, just press the button. Someone will be straight in."

I furrow my brow at her departing words, curious why she is saying that. Seconds later, Joe walks in - swaying, slurring and smelling of booze. Now, I understand why she said it.

He moves into my line of sight and flops down on the chair. Leaning forward, he stares blankly at the child he has fathered. My heartbeat accelerates, frightened of what he will do in his current condition. Faith, sensing the change of ambience, starts to fuss at my breast, and I carefully extract her and cover myself up. I look at Joe and smile, hoping I can get something remotely pleased from him.

"Do you want to hold her?" I ask, hopeful. He stares at her a beat, completely impassive, then he levels his eyes on me.

"No."

"She's as much yours as she is mine." Appealing to his heart is the only emotional weapon I have left. And it might have worked – if he only had a heart to appeal to. "Joe, don't be like this. She needs her father."

"Yeah?" he drawls. "You should have screwed someone else then."

I sit back, shocked at how cruel he can be at a time when I – we - need him.

"That's not fair," I whisper. We've had this conversation over and over, but he still refuses to take responsibility. Let's be honest, I didn't get pregnant solo, did I?

Minutes pass, and he rakes his hand through his hair in annoyance. Faith fusses in my arms, and I slide off the bed and put her in the cot.

Joe observes my movements carefully, and fear claws at my heart as he stretches over and touches her forehead before picking her up. I don't know what he's thinking, but it's not like he can avoid her, is it?

"I guess she's cute. What did you call her?"

"Faith," I confirm, still shocked by his dejected demeanour, acting as though she is nothing to him.

"Fitting. You need as much as you can get with your family," he slurs while he cradles her.

My eyes flit over the bed sheets in disbelief, but I have no time to absorb it as he continues the verbal assault.

"I won't pretend, you know I didn't want a baby. All you've done is ruin three people's lives."

"You don't mean that. It's the drink talking," I say, as my heart sinks into my stomach acid.

He snorts angrily, puts her in the cot and staggers over. In a split second, his hand wraps around my throat, applying pressure as he gets up in my face.

"Do you need to learn another lesson about what happens when you think you own me?"

I quickly shake my head. "No," I whisper, and glance at the red button above the bed. His eyes follow mine, and he removes his hand.

"Good."

Walking back to the cot, he takes another good look at her before turning his intimidating stare back to me.

"My mother will be bringing you back to the house."

The house, not the home. He's never seen it as my home, it's just a house his mother and father allow me to live in.

He digs into his pocket and throws some notes and coins on the bed. "Ring her when you get released."

"Joe?" I call as he heads to the door. "We need to talk about where we go from here."

"Yeah, but I need to clear my head and get used to this."

Then he is gone.

I slide off the bed with a wince and touch Faith's tiny wrist. My thumb strokes over the plastic band, remembering the promise of giving my baby a beautiful life. And I'm determined I will, and I'll sacrifice everything to achieve it.

Even die for it.

Opening my eyes, curled up on the hallway floor, I stare at the plastic band in my hand. I stroke my thumb over the surface, reminiscing on the day I gave birth. I was terrified and alone.

And unknown to me back then, in the coming years, that would be all I knew.

Getting to my feet, I reach for the phone and dial. While I wait to be answered, the sound of tears floats through the atmosphere in a ghostly whisper. I stare at the foot of the stairs as an image I've shut out for years appears. Reaching my hand out, it vanishes just as quickly.

"Police operator?"

"Hi. I need to speak to someone about a restraining order," I say, my tongue thick in my mouth.

"May I ask who the restraining order is against?"

"My ex-husband. He's stalking me."

Chapter 34

I SHUT THE wardrobe doors and press my forehead against the wood. Daring to turn around, my eyes land on the bed where I've just laid down the cream culottes and matching jacket.

"It's only for a few hours," I murmur, trying in vain to conciliate myself. Still, it's not working. Not today, not yesterday. Not for the last week that I've been saying it.

I perch my backside on the stool, swipe translucent powder over my cheeks and grab my mascara. With a relatively steady hand, and my tongue poking out in concentration, I slick the wand across my lashes, functioning on autopilot. My mind is in turmoil, lost in the countless ways today will unintentionally beat me again.

"Shit!" I curse, as I smudge under my eyes. Picking out a cotton bud, I carefully remove the offending splodge from what was my meticulously made-up face.

Taking a moment to consider my appearance, in my life, I'm aware I've had far too many chances. And this is not the first time I've sat in front of a mirror, studied my reflection and suppressed my real thoughts. The last time, was the day of my sham marriage.

I glide my finger under my eye, and a glimmer of Marianne appears. At eighteen, she's still young and vibrant, and life hasn't beaten her entirely yet. But as I sit here, embattled with the twenty-five-year-old memory - having had the same amount of time to relive it over and over - less than a year later, she *was* beaten.

And in turn, I became battle hard, weary of trust, fearful of love.

Devoid of everything.

A shiver runs through me, and I rub my clammy palms on my thighs and stand.

Opening my underwear drawer, I pull out a matching set and slide the shorts on. As I pick up the bra, the door slowly opens. I rotate, half bent, half-naked, as John swaggers in, wearing two-thirds of his three-piece.

"Hey, beautiful," he says huskily, and motions for my bra. I hand it to him the same moment his arm slides around my waist. Tugging me forward, his mouth claims its prize. I submit further as his tongue tangles with mine, tasting me, teasing me, unfortunately choosing the wrong time to turn me on.

"Darling," I whisper and try to push him away, because his touch is maddening, setting me alight effortlessly. It's ineffective, of course, because my size is no match for his.

"Shush," he replies and slides the flimsy garment between us. I shiver in anticipation, unable to fight the attraction and constant need to feel him. For three years, this magnetism has never diminished, and for me, it never will.

His fingers manipulate easily, sliding the straps up my arms and fastening it. I moan instinctively, every cell under my skin igniting, rejoicing in blissful awareness as his hand slips inside the bra cup and he adjusts my tender breast. Positioning the other one, both hands then slide down my waist, until they reach the curve of my backside. He grasps my bum firmly, and picks me up and lays us on the bed. I wrap my arms around his shoulders and become lost in his eyes.

"Talk to me," he pleads, twirling a lock of my hair around his finger, studying me with intent.

I grow more uncomfortable as the silence builds between us, because what does he want me to say? What does he want to hear? Seeing I am unresponsive to his plea, he tries a different tactic.

"Angel, you haven't said two words about today all week, and that's not like you. I thought you'd be excited."

"I am," I whisper, and turn away, not wanting him to see the emotional conflict in my eyes. His hands tighten – an action that says he's going to say something and keep me restrained when he does – and I wriggle from beneath him.

"It's okay to be jea-"

"We're going to be late," I mutter, pushing him off me. I stand and grab my culottes. Zipping up the side, I'm reluctant to look at him as he waits patiently, watching my every move.

"Angel," he says tightly as I walk past him and pull a white silk blouse from the wardrobe. Brusquely removing it from the hanger, I'm spun around.

"Marie, stop this!"

I throw up my hands. "Can we please talk about this later?" My question is a demand, not a request.

Proceeding to put on my blouse, he squeezes his eyes shut momentarily before opening them again. Gripping his hips, his waistcoat clad chest heaves.

"Alright, but if I have to tie you down later to make you, I will. Of that, you can be sure." He turns to leave, but halts with his hand on the door frame and looks over his shoulder. His expression softens as he contemplates his next words. "I know your thoughts on Lorraine, so I can't imagine what you are feeling right now."

I pause, leaving half the buttons undone. I want him to stop because he's right, and he knows it.

"But I understand, angel. I really do." The soft click of the latch falls into place as he closes the door.

My body clenches in anger because he understands shit. He has no idea what it was like to sit awake night after night, watching Kara fight the demons inside her nightmares. Weeks after I took her in, they finally began to subside, but I will never forget when she cried out for that feckless, worthless mother of hers. I don't even think she remembers doing it, but she did. Honestly, I promised I'd try, and I have, but that's as much as my compassion will allow.

Fastening the last of the buttons, I put on my jacket and do a turn in the mirror. I flick my eyes to my wrist, already counting down for this day to be over.

As I walk down the stairs, John spins around at the bottom, suited and booted. If I wasn't on the verge of a mental breakdown right now, I would take a moment to admire his rare, shiny appearance. Dressed in a navy three-piece suit, it fits him to perfection, accentuating his tall, burly build.

He holds out his hand, and I grasp it tight. Exchanging a knowing look, no words are needed to confirm that he's got me; that he won't let me fall over the edge I'm currently teetering on.

With my lips pressed together, I stare straight ahead. I furrow my brow in agitation, and a frown pulls over my forehead.

I squeeze my hands into fists as the church comes into view. Releasing them, I rub them over my thighs. Unable to stop my fidgeting, I proceed to cross my arms, until it isn't comfortable and then I bring them to my head, brushing my hair with my fingers. Eventually clasping them together, I concern my mouth with them.

"Marie, quit bloody fretting!" I jump in shock at John's irritated demand.

He stops the car at the side of the road on double yellows - much to the audible displeasure of the drivers behind us - and I turn as tears spike my lashes.

"I'm sorry. I just can't seem to relax or concentrate," I say, refusing to admit the truth.

He slaps on the hazards, unclips my belt and pulls me over the gear stick onto his lap. "Angel?"

"I'm fine, darling. Really." His strong thumbs massage my temple, and he sighs.

"I know today is hard for you. There's no shame in admitting you're jealous." His eyes soften, and I try to look away, but he twists my chin.

"I'm not jealous!" I lie. His head lulls; his expression saying what his mouth isn't. When I fail to answer, his brows pitch together.

"Fine! You want the truth? You're right – I am jealous. I'm so fucking jealous, I can't think straight! I hate that I spent years raising that girl, caring for her when her own mother let her walk away at fifteen. I hate that I was the one who sat up with her, comforting her when she first started living with me. And I hate that that fucking mother of hers thinks she can waltz back in at will."

God, I could go on and on, but my chest is pounding against my rib cage, getting myself more worked up with every admission.

"I will never regret taking Kara in, but Lorraine… I hate that bitch, John. I fucking hate her! I'd do time for her!" I scream, finally giving up on my sanity.

He enfolds me in his arms and sways me as I cry. "Calm down, angel. Calm down," he soothes, breaking through my obliterated psyche, hoping I allow him back in.

"I am calm!" I cry in frustration, using my favourite line when I am anything but. And as much as I want to continue expelling my hatred, it won't do any of us any good.

"Don't think for one minute that Kara will replace you. She knows Lorraine was never a mother to her, but she's trying because she doesn't want it on her conscience that Lorraine will be alone in life."

I know all the reasons why she's doing it, but it doesn't make it any easier.

"I know; I just-" I pause, horrified, catching sight of myself in the sun visor mirror. "Can we wait here a minute? I need to sort out my face. I can't go in there looking like this." I wave my hand at the mess I've made of it.

He coaxes me forward and kisses each eyelid. "Sure, but you'll always be a raving beauty to me."

"You're biased," I tell him.

"No, I'm not." He gives me a coy smirk. "You illuminate a room, angel. You captivate in a way you don't realise. These last few years we've been together, I've noticed the way other men look at you. Desiring you, too afraid to approach."

"What?" I ask in bewilderment and incredulity since I've never noticed. Then again, I'm not looking.

"Hmm. I might be a masochist, but I like it. Aside from tricky dicky, I like that others find you attractive. I like knowing you'll never be going home with any of them. And I thank God every single day that I've got you, that Sloan never gave up on Kara because if he had, I would never have found you. I love you, Marie Dawson, from the first moment I saw you all those years ago." I open my mouth, but he stops me. "No, don't say anything. Just believe it."

I tease my fingertip over his jaw and tilt his chin. "I never believed in love at first sight. Instant attraction? Maybe. Lust? Absolutely. But never love, not until you. That first night across the ballroom, I remember thinking I'd lost my chance, but the next day when you came to the house... I acted like a bitch because you made me feel and want things I'd convinced myself I wasn't worthy of." I stare into his eyes and chastely press my lips to his. "Your crassness, your brazen display of control, you made me fall in love with you just like that." I snap my fingers.

He smirks with pride. "Really, like that?" He copies my action.

"Yeah, like that." I bestow him a kiss and shuffle over the seat. "Now, we really need to sort out my face. I don't believe panda eyes are currently in vogue." I pull out my small makeup bag, but before I can even unzip it, he has it in his hands. Rooting around inside, he pulls out my concealer.

"Lean over, beautiful," he says gently. Dabbing the wand under my eyes, he starts to blend, so softly, it almost hurts.

"Should I ask how you know how to do this?"

He grins. "Older sister, lots of nieces, and a very cheeky Charlie! What can I say? When she was a teenager, she had me and Sloan practising with her. Jules was too sick to do anything most days, so we indulged her. I don't think the kid has even told Kara how talented he is with the good old slap. I guess she'll find out when they have daughters."

"Well, your secrets are safe with me."

"So are yours, you know. Safe with me," he says in a coaxing tone. Yet no one will be safe when my secrets are told, or namely, discovered.

I remain mute, unable to articulate my conflict. Staring into his dark, mesmerising pools, he smiles intermittently, while a silent war wages on my shoulders between what's right and wrong.

"Do you need a few more minutes?" he asks, returning my makeup bag.

Yes, I'll always need those.

"No."

Sliding back on my seat belt, John starts the car, and drives the fifty yards or so into the church car park.

Everyone is congregated outside, including Sloan's part-time receptionist, Gloria, and her husband; George, his driver; and Kara and Sophie's friends from high school and college. Standing off to the side, a few feet away from the rest of the christening party, is Lorraine Petersen. With her dark hair up, her eyes no longer tired and her body evidently in a better state than it was the last time I saw her, my jealousy is heightened further.

John's hand squeezes my shaky knee in a comforting knead. Daring to make eye contact, his expression is still conflicted. As much as he wants to fight my battles, we both know that he can't.

"They're waiting for us, angel."

"I know," I say. "I'm terrified of the future, darling." My whispered confession cements my fears further.

Kissing the back of my hand, he holds it to his chest. "It'll be over before you know it."

I climb out of the car and unceremoniously slam the door. The brute force is indicative of where my head is still currently at. I'm drowning, falling apart under the belief that Kara will one day replace me. I know it isn't true, but it hurts. It hurts so much to hear her speak of her mother and to know that that woman will be sitting next to her... God, I can't even comprehend the evil things running through my head right now.

The last time I saw Lorraine, was when Kara insisted on travelling to Manchester a few years back when her father committed suicide. It was a road trip none of us wanted to make, and at Kara's insistence, for the few days we were there, I tried. I really did.

Still, I have no right to judge. Underneath the polished exterior I preen and present to the world, I am exactly like Lorraine Petersen. Just like her, I too once cowered in a corner, covering my face between beatings, until I couldn't take no more. And just like her, I couldn't protect my own flesh and blood, either.

A hand waves in front of my eyes. "Where were you?" John asks suspiciously.

"Nowhere," I reply distantly.

I clench his hand as I peer up at the façade, recollecting the times I had stood out here with a very nervous Sloan when he was secretly planning his wedding. The number of times he had me walking up and down that bloody aisle with him to ensure he knew what he was doing was torture. It was even more torturous when I stood with Kara at the fountain and endeavoured to soothe her nerves.

It's laughable considering marriage left a bitter taste in my mouth. It is something I neither wanted to relive nor experience again. The harsh reality is marriage scarred me for life. The beginning, the middle, and most definitely the end.

Approaching the small group, I force a smile. "Morning, darling," I greet Kara. As I reach out to embrace her, the flinch I thought was gone rears its ugly head. She steps back, and her eyes inconspicuously flit to Lorraine, and I realise it isn't the touch, it's the audience.

John was right, she is keeping up appearances. She doesn't want to hurt either of us, but that's impossible. I catch John's encouraging eyes and grind my teeth together.

"Morning, Lorraine." I wave her over. "It's great to see you again. You look very well."

Lorraine smiles indecisively and joins us. "You too, Marie. You look lovely."

"And you. That colour really suits you," I compliment sincerely, admiring her baby blue tea dress and matching jacket. A presence moves at my rear, and John fills my peripheral vision.

"Hi, Lorraine. How was the journey down?" he asks with genuine interest. I pat his arm and give Lorraine a small smile as I wander off, leaving them to discuss the delights of the UK rail network.

Loitering at the Wall of Remembrance, long strides disturb my solitude. From the corner of my eye, the shiny, black Italian leather brogues can only belong to one man. Sloan doesn't say anything, as he unfastens his suit jacket, flips it behind him and tugs on his trousers as he sits on the bench. Following his lead, I drop down next to him.

"I didn't want her here either," he confesses quietly, his faint American lilt coming through. "But I'll do anything for my wife. Even tolerate the intolerable."

I nod. "I told her I'd try, and I detest it."

Sloan's arm comes around my shoulders. "As far as I'm concerned, you're my only mother-in-law."

"Thank you, darling."

The stillness of the surroundings brings inner peace until a heavy gait approaches. "Hey, kid." John drags Sloan up and enfolds him in a man hug. "Everyone's waiting inside. What are you both doing out here?"

"Sharing common ground." The words come out without thinking.

He shakes his head in dismay. "That's a dangerous place for both of you. Don't risk losing her for the sake of spending one day with the woman."

A rush of feet resounds and Kara darts around the corner. "Are you all coming in? We're ready to start."

Sloan momentarily touches his hand to mine, then he stands tall and marches towards his wife. Kissing her lovingly, he guides her back to the front of the building.

"Do you think she heard anything?" I query, but John just shrugs and threads my arm through his.

Entering the church, the smell - the one of my childhood - hits me. And it's more potent now than ever.

I smile at everyone seated accordingly. Simon and Tommy are sitting alongside Stuart and Sophie, while Remy and Evie are in front. John points to a pew, and I slide over. Charlie and Jules on sitting on my right with Lorraine next to them.

I relax back as the ceremony begins. Staring up at the vaulted ceiling, I recant the vicar's recital word for word inside my head.

Oliver giggles and blows wet bubbles as he bounces up and down on my knee. Stuffing his podgy hand into his mouth, he drools.

"My Fay bear was also a very mucky pup," I whisper.

I frown at his christening gown, which is no longer in the pristine condition it was when his mother first dressed him this morning, and he gives me a stern glare, almost like he understands. He then makes a constricting sound and, moments later, the putrid smell invades my nostrils, causing my eyes to water.

"And she was stinky, too," I tell him as I get to my feet and catch Sloan's attention from the far side of the Emerson ballroom.

"Everything okay?" he asks when I am within earshot.

"Fine, but your charming son just deposited me a lovely present."

Sloan sniffs singularly, and his head jolts sharply. "That's a good one. I guess I shouldn't have started weaning him on sprouts last night." He rubs his jaw with his finger and thumb.

"Very funny," I deadpan.

"Here, I'll take him."

"No, I'll do it. I just need his stuff." Following my leader, Sloan places the nappy bag on my shoulder and passes over the penthouse key.

I adjust Oliver on my hip and spy John, pint in hand, in a raucous conversation with Stuart and Remy. He instinctively turns in my direction, and I point to the baby's bum and wave my hand in front of my nose. He grins, and in turn, points to the entrance of the room. I don't want to look, but my eyes drift to Lorraine, sitting on her own, looking uncomfortable and unwanted. I hesitate and turn back to him, but he is already by my side.

"Try. Please," he requests quietly, not to alert anyone else. "She knows she's not wanted here, but she came anyway."

I take a breath and give him a resigned sigh. "Fine," I reply as Oliver starts fussing. Apparently, he doesn't like having a soiled nappy as much as I don't like smelling it.

"Good. And be nice," he says, slapping my arse.

"I'll give you bleeding nice!" I retort.

Lorraine's her head lifts tentatively as I approach, and she forces a smile. "Hi," she says softly, her eyes lighting up, seeing her maternal grandson.

"Hi. I'm on a very delicate mission," I tell her. "Do you remember how to change a nappy?" I smile as she gets up. Her eyes cast behind me, and I glance over my shoulder.

"Maybe we should ask Kara if I can be with him first."

I twist my neck, almost painfully, and narrow my eyes. "Have you not asked to hold him yet?" Lorraine shakes her head no, and my heart breaks instantly, proving my compassion is not as unforgiving as I thought.

This last week, I realise I've been a selfish bitch. All I've thought about is *me*, and how her being here makes *me* feel. What I've failed to grasp is how *she* feels. Accepting couldn't have been an easy decision for her. She's not stupid; she knows she isn't popular among the masses. Of course, no one would dare say it to her, but how can she not?

"Come on." With a newly found resolve, I stride out of the room while Lorraine runs behind me to keep up.

"All done!" I affix the last sticky tab and hold Oliver up. He laughs, happy to have a clean bottom, and I pass him to his other grandma - his real grandma.

"Lorraine, take him," I say, while she backs away nervously.

"No, I haven't asked."

"Fine," I mutter.

Taking matters into my own hands – or out of them - I thrust him gently into her arms. As she gets comfortable with him, the angel and devil pitch a war of words on my shoulders. A side of me is still jealous to witness this, but the other side of me – the motherly side, the forgiving side - is happy. Happy to have done something that makes someone else smile.

I grin to myself, listening to Lorraine talk nonsense to Oliver while I bag up the mess and sanitise the surface.

"He's so beautiful," Lorraine says, full of pride as we enter the living room. She paces up and down, gazing at him in wonder. "He's got so much of Kara in him."

A small smile plays on my lips as I dispose of the incriminating evidence. After washing my heads, I brew some tea and join her. Dropping my backside onto the sofa, I feel a weird sense of responsibility.

As I bring the mug to my mouth, I dare to ask. "Why haven't you asked to hold him?"

She gazes down at Oliver and tenderly strokes the back of his head. "Because I didn't want to get my hopes up." The last word is finished in a whisper before she bursts into tears. I rise quickly, shocking myself when I wrap my arms around her.

"She wouldn't have said no."

She shakes her head and sniffs. "No, but her husband would have. Let's be honest, would you want me tainting your beautiful child? He's a good man, but he knows I was an unfit mother, that I couldn't save her."

I hide my flinch at her painful truth. But if that is the foundation upon which she is judging Sloan's character, then I'm fucked.

A chunk of Lorraine's hair falls over her face, and baby boy, seeing it as something new to play with, yanks it in his little fist.

"No, Oliver." He gives me an innocent look as I reprimand gently. Prising his inquisitive hand away, I face her. "Lorraine, Sloan doesn't think that," I circumvent the partial truth.

Again.

With a look of dejection, she wipes her eyes and sits, adjusting Oliver on her knee. "He does. You all do, really." I open and close my mouth. I don't know how to counter that statement. "When Kara invited me, I didn't want to come." She shakes her head in defeat. "I did because she made an effort even though I don't deserve it."

I pick up my tea and release a shaky breath. "When Kara told me she had invited you, I admit I was jealous – still am."

Lorraine chortles undignified. "You've got no reason to be jealous of me, Marie. You did what I couldn't; you protected my daughter. You gave her a real home, a life, a future. You gave her more than I ever could have."

My hand wobbles and I put the mug down, reality hitting hard from both sides. Because all the things I gave her daughter, I learnt in the cruellest way possible when I couldn't give them to my own.

"I envy you and the relationship you have with her. Biologically, she's mine, but it's not the same in truth. She's no longer my daughter, she's yours. And Oliver is your grandson, not mine."

My mouth falls open at her heartbreakingly sad assumption. Thinking up a delicate response, her tears float beside me as someone knocks on the door.

"Marie? Lorraine?" John's muted voice drifts in.

"Oh God," Lorraine mutters. "I don't want anyone seeing me. I don't want his pity."

"One minute," I call out. "Lorraine, don't leave just yet. Go back downstairs, and I'll be down there in a minute. Okay?"

She nods and flicks her longing gaze from Oliver before passing him over. She presses a tender kiss on his head, and that bleeding, breaking heart of mine cracks a little further.

Opening the door, Lorraine leaves the moment John enters.

"Lorraine?" he calls, causing her to pause in the foyer.

"I'm just going back downstairs." Her voice wobbles and she can barely look at him. Long, uncomfortable minutes tick by until the lift arrives, and she hurries inside. When the doors ding shut, I turn to him.

"Angel, I warned you-"

"I didn't say anything!" I cut him off, a little annoyed.

"Well, what was that?" He points back at the empty foyer.

"That was a mother who realised she no longer has a daughter."

The sting of tears builds behind my eyes, and I try to keep them contained, but I can't. Oliver, sensing the change, squirms in my arms.

"You were right – common ground is a dangerous place to be." John doesn't say anything as he embraces me with one arm and takes Oliver in his other. "She said some things that really hurt. They weren't meant to, but they did. I feel guilty, darling. I can already feel it devouring me."

"Angel, don't do this. Her lifestyle choices are not your burdens to bear."

"I know, but the hardest thing in the world is a mother confessing she's lost her child to another woman."

I'm shaking like a leaf. And I'm also conflicted, because I've spent over a decade despising her, hating her for the abuse that Kara suffered, but hearing her say that has broken me.

"Losing any child is hard – old, young, unborn," he whispers, his tone thick with emotion I don't understand. "God forbid, if you'd have ever lost a child, you would understand how she feels."

I stiffen because whereas Lorraine has just broken me, John has unknowingly annihilated whatever she left. The tears threatening finally fall. I grip him tight and press my cheek hard against his chest, muffling the sound of my anguish. Crying into his waistcoat while his hand strokes tenderly over my crown, my understanding is more profound than he knows.

"She made her choices, and now she has to live with the consequences. Don't cry for her, angel."

Except, I'm not.

I'm crying for me.

Chapter 35

I SCRUNCH MY nose and purse my lips together as I hold up the dress. The old adage of 'mutton dressed up as lamb' comes to mind.

Having second thoughts, I toss it on the bed and begin rifling through the abundance of black dresses I possess. When nothing stands out, I admit defeat and turn back to the dress that was purely designed with one purpose in mind – to attract the opposite sex.

Sliding it up my body, I reach around my back and begin to zip it up, when the bedroom door opens.

"Hey!" I clamp my arms over my chest and spin around. My annoyance dissipates as John closes the door.

"I thought you might need a hand," he says with a smirk and strides towards me.

I turn back around, and he drops a kiss to my nape. I blow out my breath silently when he taps my hands aside and slowly zips me up. His dexterous palms massage my shoulders, and he rotates me.

Looking down my front, I really wish I hadn't let Soph talk me into buying this last week. I really wish I hadn't done a lot of things lately, but this… This is my latest, most expensive mistake. And one I know John isn't too happy about, considering he has been looking at it hung on the door for six days and he is yet to make comment.

"How do I look?" I ask hesitantly.

His brows lift, and he moves his head from side to side. Taking my hand, he perches on the edge of the bed. Wrapping his muscular arms around the backs of my thighs, he squeezes my rear as I stand between his open legs. "Fucking amazing. I'm debating if I should let you out of the house wearing it. This thing should carry a government warning."

A small, incredulous laugh emits my throat. I put my hands over my face, desperate to conceal my embarrassment that I'm wearing something designed for someone twenty years younger than I am.

"It's too, too…"

"Young?" he finishes for me, already knowing what I'm thinking. He tugs me onto his knee and runs his hand over my cheek. "Angel, I don't know what goes on inside your head, but you need to get over this age complex."

"It's not a complex; it's a fact. I'm forty-three," I tell him - that being the real reason I'm insecure about wearing this tonight.

"Look at me," he says firmly. "You're beautiful, amazing, and very," his hands drag up my sides, "very," he stands, leaning his head, "sexy." His lips find mine, and he placates my anxieties with a long, hard kiss when the door opens again.

"Oh, sorry," Kara mumbles, mortified, before practically running back down the landing.

"Well, at least you're not wearing a sheet, angel." John laughs, and I put my finger over his mouth, silently requesting for him to shush. I don't need to remember that visual again.

As I pick up my heels, I catch sight of myself. Smoothing a hand down the dress, regardless of how old I currently feel, it does fit well.

"Yep, you're definitely sexy. Get here," he demands. Feeling rebellious, I shake my head and pout. "Get. *Here.*" This time his command leaves no room for frivolity.

Inching towards him, he bends down in front of me and lifts each leg to slip on my heels. He slides his hands up my ankles, higher and higher and he stands. Kneading my backside, instigating a little hum deep in my belly, he pulls me close, compressing my front to his and thrusts his hips indecently.

"When you come home tonight, I'm going to rip this fucking thing off and show you exactly how you make me feel wearing it."

I reach up on my toes and link my arms around his neck. "Promises, promises," I murmur, tangling my tongue with his before he picks me under my legs and carries me out of the room. At the bottom of the stairs, I reluctantly shuffle free and drop my feet down.

Entering the dining room, all the guys are sitting around the table playing cards with a wad of notes in the centre.

"You're cheating, you tight git!" Dev hollers at Remy, who grins, causing his scars to stand out prominently.

"Better luck next time, sunshine!" he retorts, picking up a can of coke, followed by his cards.

"Yeah, pipe down, Dev. Less complaining, more playing," Tommy says, wandering in with a pizza box in either hand. "You look nice," he says appreciatively.

"Thanks," I reply, still unsure.

"At least it isn't thigh high and crotch-skimming," Jake states, amused, and necks a bottle of water. I roll my eyes because *that* would have gone down like a lead balloon. And it wasn't for Soph's lack of trying, either.

"I see you gents have a hard-core night planned," I comment on the brink of laughter since the only liquid gracing the table is pop.

"Yep," Jake says with a boyish grin. "After we've cleaned out the soft stuff, we're going to start on the hard stuff – the baby's milk."

"I heard that!" Sloan's immediate rejoinder is loud and clear.

"Well, have fun." I shut the door as they all agree in tandem. Collecting my clutch from the hallway table, I stick my head around the living room door. Sloan is sitting on the sofa, his laptop on the coffee table, his son sprawled out asleep next to him.

"Hey, darling." I press a kiss to his head.

"Oh, wow. You look great. I can see why he's having a strop." He smirks and cranes his neck to the office wall. My eyes narrow, but if John's annoyed, he's not the only one. I didn't want to buy this as much as he doesn't want me to wear it.

"Fine, you tell her!" Kara sounds vexed as she steps into the living room. Huffing out, she shakes her head disbelievingly and tosses me her phone.

"Hello?" I bring it to my ear.

"Where are you?" Charlie asks from the other end.

"Still at home, but we'll be there soon," I confirm, feeling the exasperation starting already. I rest the phone between my shoulder and cheek as I kiss Oliver goodnight.

Listening intently, I'm suddenly one-third of a three-way conversation.

"Tell her to stop humping GI Joe and get over here! They're missing wine o'clock time!" Soph shouts in the background.

"Oh, for crying out loud!" Charlie grumbles in my ear while I slide into my jacket. "Did you hear that?" The poor girl sounds guilty. But seriously, the crap that comes out of Sophie's mouth sometimes leaves even me stunned.

"I did. I'm sorry, darling," I apologise on behalf of Miss Garrulous. "Is your Mum there yet?"

"Huh-uh," Charlie confirms. "She's waiting for you to arrive, so she can have some *grown-up conversation*." I shake my head because I'm far too conversant in precisely what 'grown up conversation' consists of. It's the conversation where she presses me about my sex life and pours alcohol down my neck to assist.

And it works - spectacularly.

"Okay. Try to keep Sophie away from the bar until we get there."

"Impossible," Charlie replies with zeal.

"See you soon, honey." I end the call and throw the phone back to Kara, who is currently being manhandled by her husband.

"The taxi will be here in five," she says, slipping into her jacket.

"Let me just say goodbye to John."

I knock on the office door and push it back.

"Yeah, just keep an eye out," he tells whoever he is speaking to as I enter. "I've got to go. I'll speak to you later." He hangs up and requests me to come hither with a flick of his fingers. Slowly walking around the desk, he curves an arm around my middle.

"I'm going now," I state the obvious, while he grunts petulantly. "Darling." I attempt to placate him and graze my finger over his hairline. "I'll call you when I'm on my way back."

"Are you kidding?" He laughs. "You're going out with the Sophie. You'll be so paralytic later, you won't know your left foot from your right, let alone how to use your phone!"

"Very true," I confirm, albeit some of us will be far worse for wear than others.

"Do something for me? Stay relatively sober."

"I will." I nod repeatedly. "I know you're not an aficionado of necrophilia." I slide off his lap when a car horn blares outside.

"Go on, go." He slaps my arse. "The sooner you leave, the sooner you can come back to me."

"Play nice tonight."

"Always do," he replies. Leading me out of the office, Kara is standing by the front door with Sloan lovingly wrapped around her. Commotion leaks out of the dining room, and she raises her brows, unimpressed.

"That said," John continues. "If they wake the baby, there might be at least one dead arsehole to contend with when you get home."

"That's fine, darling." I kiss him at length and rub my cheek to his bristly jaw. "But the less lifting, the better. And if you're really good, I'll even help you dig up the patio."

One extortionate admittance fee, three hours, and numerous songs later, I glance down at my watch as the hands sweep midnight.

The club is packed, and bodies are wall to wall. As the music ripples through me, I look around. The last time I graced one of these places, I was beaten black and blue, and almost watched my girl die.

Needless to say, the copious amounts of booze I've poured down my throat has been an aid in trying to forget that.

I down the last of my rum and coke and sway slightly, conceding I've reached my limit on what is merry and acceptable. Tapping Charlie's shoulder, she turns, and I give her my best charades impression of too warm and thirsty. She nods and motions to Kara and Sophie who are dancing in a corner together, and she moves towards them.

I stumble off the dance floor and dig my fingers into the back of a leather seat at the table we are occupying. I fan my hand over my face, ridiculously flushed, but also unexpectedly energised.

"Do you want a drink?" I ask Jules and Nicki, who both shake their heads no.

"Do you want me to come with you," Jules offers.

"No, I'm fine." I wave her off and make a beeline for the bar, desperate to rehydrate myself.

I tap my purse rhythmically on the top, the music inducing my hips to sway. I lean over, trying to catch the bartender's attention, and I inadvertently catch the attention of a man to my right instead.

"Evening," he greets in a thick Lancashire accent, his eyes roaming my attire.

"Hi," I reply awkwardly.

Truthfully, I don't like this. *This* being the meeting of people. Everyone is attempting to make small talk and appear to be an attractive, prospective partner. I guess my dislike is born from the fact I've never had to before.

Still aware of my unwanted company, in my peripheral vision the man's heavily - and crudely - tattooed hand moves closer. 'HATE' adorns his knuckles, and I roll my eyes, although I'm morbidly curious to see if 'LOVE' is on the others.

Risking a proper look at him, he is wearing smart dark jeans, a white shirt and a black blazer with the sleeves rolled up. His collar is open, exposing a crucifix inked over his chest. Continuing my observation, for no other reason than genuine curiosity, I spy the black and grey clock on this forearm.

"That's a compelling piece, but why is it handless?" I ask, surprised that something so intricate and stunning would be left incomplete. I don't have any tats, but I know I wouldn't want them on my body with two crucial elements missing.

ELLE CHARLES

His eyes meet mine and something flashes over them. Tilting his brow, he rests his arm on the bar and rolls his sleeve up further.

"It denotes the passage of time. Time spent; time remaining; time to reflect. It's handless because we never know how long *time* will last," he says mysteriously.

I purse my lips in contemplation. "Very true. You never know when your time is at an end. Anyway, it's very beautiful and captivating."

He stares at me for a beat, seemingly trying to figure me out. "Yes, it is *beautiful*." He emphasises emphatically. "I'm Kevin. Nice to meet you."

"And you. I'm Marie," I reply, but I could kick myself for giving him my real name. I guess I'm a little more inebriated than I thought.

Kevin smiles, and it's a look that is positively cruel on him. "Marie? A pretty name for a pretty lady. What are you having?" He tilts his head to the bottles lining the back of the bar, not cluing in that regardless of the polite conversation I've just struck up, I'm not looking for anything further.

"That's very kind, but you don't have to buy me a drink." I divert my gaze, wishing the bartender would get his backside over here, rather than chatting with his colleague when he has a full house to serve. If he was one of my staff, the door would be hitting his arse already.

"Look, I haven't been out much recently, and it's been a hell of a long time since I've bought a pretty woman a drink. Please." Kevin smiles sheepishly, and it makes me feel guilty for assuming the worst.

I sigh in defeat. "I don't want to sound presumptuous or lead you on, but I'm not available." I raise my ring hand, aware that the majority of the people here tonight are looking for a good time. "So, if you'd like to buy me a drink out of kindness, that would be very nice. Thank you."

"Fair enough," he replies. "It's rare to meet people who are honest these days. I respect that." Turning his back to me, he hollers at the bartender - loud enough that the little sod rolls his eyes and strolls over without urgency.

"Are you actually serving tonight, mate?" Kevin asks belligerently, and I avert my eyes, not knowing where to look.

"*Yes?*" The man answers his question with a question.

"A pint of whatever's on tap, and-" Kevin eyes me.

"A bottle of water, please."

"Water?" Kevin replies, incredulously.

I nod repeatedly. "Too much wine and rum. It's gone to my head." I twirl my finger at my temple for effect.

"And a bottle of water, mate."

"Sure, *mate*," the bartender replies sarcastically. Moments later, he returns, slams the drinks on the bar, and holds out his hand while Kevin slaps a twenty into it.

Pocketing his change, Kevin takes a swig of lager. "Cockney fucking twat!"

I grin. "He can't help being cockney."

"No, but he can help being a fucking twat!"

He downs another mouthful as I uncap the water and lift it to my lips, conceding he's right.

"Are you here with your husband tonight, Marie?"

"Oh, no, I'm not married. Yet," I add.

"Really, I thought you were."

I furrow my brow and shake my head. "No, I'm out with friends." I point to the table where I'm sitting.

His head bobs, counting. "Do you want to join us? We could all have a laugh tonight."

I follow his gaze to the other side of the club, where four burly, and very rugged, looking men are standing. Three of them are watching us with intrigue, while one has his back turned.

I inconspicuously chew my lip. On appearances alone, these men could be a little too rough-and-ready for us. And while Soph has the biggest mouth of us all, it's just that – all mouth. She wouldn't say boo if one of these guys accosted her.

"I'm sorry," I start my decline with diplomacy. "But none of us are single, and it wouldn't be fair to monopolise you or your friends' time tonight." I give him a sympathetic, yet honest reply. "Thank you for the water, Kevin. I hope you have a nice night." I smile and slowly edge away, but I only make it a few feet.

"Well, that's a damn shame, *Marianne*."

I spin around to see him wearing that cruel smile from earlier, while my own dies an instant death.

"What did you call me?"

He ignores me and reaches for my arm, but I angle my body away just in time. "I said it's a damn shame, Marie, because I've got a friend who loves demure blondes. In fact, I know he'd be *dying* to get his hands on you." He smirks and takes a long pull of his pint, still watching me.

The sinister glint in his pupils is unmistakable. Even under the strobe lights, illuminating every surface in sporadic sequence, an air of danger rolls off him. Flitting his sight between me, my friends and then his, it's clear he is mentally weighing something up.

"Goodnight, Kevin," I impart with determination, dying to escape when a hand touches my shoulder.

"Is there a problem here, Marie?" A man asks from behind me, and Kevin noticeably straightens, ready for the pissing contest.

"There's no problem, mate. Marie and I were just having a little chat," Kevin replies.

I turn to look at the man who has just saved me and my eyes narrow because there's something more than familiar about him. His features harden, but his venomous glare is still levied over my shoulder at Kevin.

"Well, your little chat is over, so walk away, *mate,*" he demands. "Now."

I don't dare glance back, but instead, continue to study the man who has thrown me a lifeline. The rumble of 'arsehole' and 'dickhead' seeps over the pulsating music, while my brain ticks over in its sobering state and plucks out the memory of where we have met

Attractive, dark-haired, articulate and exceptionally well-built. *New Year's Eve.*

"Thank you," I offer uncomfortably.

"You're welcome." He takes the bottle from my hand, and his all-seeing eyes absorb the room until they remain fixed on Kevin's gruff group. "Is this work or pleasure?" he asks distracted.

And just like before, I recoil at his query.

"Pleasure," I eventually confirm and stare back at the table where all the girls are now congregated, praying one of them to stand and see me.

"And your partner?"

"Oh, my husband is at home." The words roll off my tongue unambiguously.

"Your husband?" he replies, surprised, and draws his attention to my hand. I stroke my ring finger lovingly, but don't miss his subtle look of relief.

"Yes, women are allowed out without them these days. Anyway, thank you for saving me."

The man acknowledges my appreciation, but his attention is elsewhere as he strides away. With his phone to his ear and his hand gesturing wildly, he dumps my bottle of water before being swallowed up in the mass of bodies.

"Hey, are you okay?" Jules asks as I reach the table.

"Fine," I mutter, my eyes on the other side of the club where the delightful Kevin is now standing with his mates. "Why?"

"Nothing," she says. "I see you're making new friends. Who's tall, dark and *extremely* sexy?" Her flirty question is curious as she stretches up and cranes her head, searching for the mystery man.

I shrug. "I have no idea. I first met him on New Year's Eve at the hotel."

"Hmm, shame," she murmurs. "He was just my type. Although knowing my luck, he's probably gay. All the beautiful ones are." Sitting back down, her head jerks back. "What about him?" She turns her attention to Kevin's motley crew. "He's got a lot of friends with him. Maybe one of them is single…" Her voice drifts off in insinuation and horror fills me. "Come and introduce me. I'm desperate, remember?"

"You're not that desperate!" I spit out, trying to veer her away from whatever bit-of-rough fantasy is filling her head.

"Who's desperate?" Sophie shouts above the music, which I'm sure is getting louder as time ticks by.

"Nobody!" I respond with a wave.

Sophie downs the glass of wine in her hand and then grabs me. "Time to dance!"

On the dancefloor, strutting my uncoordinated stuff, I'm not the only woman who thinks she's auditioning for Flashdance. Going with the flow, my arms high, the thumping base of whatever is playing – some *new* chart hit that is actually a cover of a nineties classic – ripples through me.

I've convinced myself I'm having a movement of temporary insanity because I am absolutely not a dancer. I lack everything needed to be one – even on a nightclub dance floor with every other drunk. I have zero rhythm and zero spatial awareness, hence why my arm keeps hitting some kid who's definitely got moves like Jagger.

"Sorry!" I call out for the umpteenth time.

"It's okay." He laughs. "My mum can't dance either!"

I stop instantly, causing Jules to crash into my back. If I wasn't already sobering up before, I bloody am now.

And that comment is the reason why I didn't want girls' night to materialise. I'm too flipping old to be partying with the kids. Then again, I'm too young to be convalescing with the oldies, too.

"Hey, I didn't mean you were old!" The young lad hesitantly inches closer. "My mum's only forty-one!"

Jules roars out laughing. "Quit while you're ahead, sweetheart!" she tells him. The boy grins, his cheeks bright red, and he quickly grooves his way through the crowd.

Jules slings her arm around me, and we stumble off the dance floor. Laughing between ourselves, I pick up my glass of wine when we reach the table. Knocking it back, I grimace when warm liquid slides down my throat.

"Oh, that's vile."

"When's the infamous Roseby function happening?" Kara asks, and I nod and knock back another rum and coke. I swear this stuff is lethal. Tasty, but lethal.

"A month. God help us," I say with a wink at Nicki, who is very merry – more so than I have seen her in ages.

"It'll be fine. What can possibly go wrong?" she asks, and I give her a look that screams *everything*.

"Are we invited?" Charlie asks.

I shrug. "No idea. Although I'm sure Sloan could probably wrangle some tickets from flirty Lowe. The man seems hell-bent on showing all and sundry he has the best establishment in town. I'm sure he enjoys flaunting his wealth to his rivals."

"Right!" Soph stands with less poise than usual. Tossing back her highlighted blonde mane, she catches the eye of a passing fellow who visually approves. "I'm going to the ladies."

"I'll join you." I rise and squeeze my knees together, my bladder screaming at me.

"Me, too," Jules wades in.

"Again?" Sophie replies. "You both just went," she glances at her bare wrist, "two songs ago."

Jules rounds the table and throws her arms around Soph's shoulders. "Honey, this is part and parcel of growing old. First, you have lines to look forward to, then grey hairs, then a weak bladder. Except, you're lucky, you have someone to practice pelvic floor exercises and tightening of the abdomen with. I, on the other hand, will be having a very close, personal relationship with Tena!"

I snigger involuntarily and pick up my bag. "And on that note, I think I'm also going to call for a taxi and head home."

"No! One more dance!" Sophie says, linking her arm in mine as we head to the ladies.

"No!"

"Yes!"

"Sophie…" I say sternly.

"Marie, please." She flutters her lashes in desperation. "Just one more and I'll let you go."

I shake my head. "Fine!"

Standing in line for the toilets – unisex ones at that - the queue is obscene. Tapping my mobile, I dig my teeth into my lip in a bid to halt my dangerously full bladder from emptying itself involuntarily. As I shuffle down the line at snail's pace, Sophie and Jules talking crap behind me, I hold the handset to my ear.

"Good morning, beautiful," John answers, sounding far too awake at… I don't even know what time it is. Pulling the mobile back, the screen informs me it has gone one in the morning. It's definitely past my bedtime.

"Hello, darling," I reply, falling into comfortable bliss.

"Do you want me to come and get you?"

"No, I'll get a taxi. I was just calling to say I would be back soon. Hey!" I cry as Soph rips the phone from my ear.

"Evening, Sophie. Are you drunk, girl?" John asks, out loud, making me realise she has put him on speakerphone. I cover my face with my hands, mortified of what she is going to say. I can't imagine it is going to be polite – sozzled Sophie never is.

"Why, of course. Sorry, but Marie can't leave yet, we haven't had enough alcohol. Besides, we need to talk about you assisting with pelvic floor exercises and tightening of the abdomen with her. Apparently, it's part and parcel of getting old!"

John chuckles. "I think that can be arranged." He laughs, encouraging her. "Although Marie and I can discuss that privately when she comes home."

"No, you don't understand!" Soph exclaims, her face an absolute picture. Anyone would think her world had just fallen apart. "I need someone to talk to about this. It's very, very important!" She punches her fist in the air, exhibiting that drunken importance.

As she begins to open her mouth again, I see my chance and seize my mobile. She glares at me, but her attention is piqued.

"I know, you need to speak to Kara," she says seriously. "She knows plenty about it. Desks, offices... Boardrooms!"

I hold up my hand in horror and spin around. "Sorry about her, darling. She's been praying to the bottom of wine bottles all night."

"I'll call Doc and warn him. What state is Kara in?"

"She's fine. She's only had pop," I tell him. "Have Sloan and Oliver gone home?"

"Yep," he replies. "Give us a call when you're allowed to leave. Remember, sober and compliant. For us," he requests softly.

"I'll try."

"You better. I believe I have pelvic floor exercises I need to practice with you. And trust me, I'm more than compliant. I just need you in the same room. Preferably in around an hour." He then hangs up.

Ten minutes later, still ruminating on it, I unlock the cubicle door. Jules is waiting for me by the row of basins, but her attention is on the other side of the facilities.

"What?" I ask, washing my hands.

"There's a couple having sex in there!" she proclaims in a loud whisper, pointing to the other side of the facilities.

"Really?" I query, repulsed and yet riveted.

Suddenly, a loud, excitable moan emanates, followed by a male grunt and the door being jolted from the inside. Everyone present turns on cue, each unmoving as the grunting and sighing noises come and go with the intermittent banging. Sniggers rise above the sound of the hand dryers blowing and the water running, as the mystery woman reaches climax.

Loudly.

"Still desperate?" I tease Jules with a nudge and a grin. She purses her lips and nods sadly, and my good intentioned demeanour dissipates.

"What about online dating? Some of my girls are on a few sites. It's worth a try."

She runs her hand through her hair, the overhead lights illuminating her timeless beauty. "Tried it. There's only so many pictures I can take of ugly penises being sent to me. Seriously, do these perverts think they will actually get a date doing that?"

I shrug. "I don't know, the day John barged into my house, he offered to vibrate in my palm."

Her mouth falls open salaciously. "No!" She quickly moves closer.

"Hmm, hmm." I purse my lips. "Then he said we'd be dancing an intimate tango in the future."

"Oh, really?"

"What's got you two all hot and bothered?" Sophie asks, killing the conversation.

"Nothing." Jules winks. "We'll see you back down there," she says and links her arm in Sophie's.

I watch them depart in the mirror and run my finger under my eye. As expected, my makeup is shot. Touching up my face, I spritz on a little fragrance as a cubicle door opens behind me.

In the reflection of the mirror, I do a double take while every nightmare finally comes to fruition. My eyes expand, and everything happens in slow motion, as an arm hooks around my waist and hefts me back.

"No!" A hand covers my mouth and my spine slams against the wall. I emit a muffled scream, but his other hand wraps around my throat. Kicking out my leg, his knee lodges between my thighs, restraining me in the compact space.

"Hello, Marianne," Joe sneers, his face pressed up against mine. My first – and only – reaction is to fight back. And I do, but my attempts at emancipation are futile, and each try only gains me a moment of dizziness as he compresses my windpipe in retaliation.

"Imagine my surprise when Kevin told me there was a sexy blonde at the bar. It got me thinking back to my Marianne. Fate clearly moves in mysterious ways, because here you are. That said, this isn't the way I planned to see you again, and I've been planning this for a very long time." He smiles malevolently. "But Providence has predicted otherwise."

When my breathing labours, his hold eases, but not enough to escape. I rake my eyes over him. His build is more significant than what I remember, and his dark hair is now greying, and lines are clustered at the corners of his eyes.

The man standing before me is hard, far harder than the boy I was once in love with. No, this man has been battered by a difficult life of imprisonment and the hardship to survive. If he wasn't dead and emotionless inside before, he definitely is now.

"You've been a bad fucking bitch, Marianne," he says with venom, and my insides shrink because I remember my punishment for being bad. "I see you've been telling the police lies again. Sending them to question me, to harass me."

"I haven't lied about anything," I counter pitifully. "You sent me that stuff!"

He smirks and growls with vicious intent. "Prove it," he says innocently, then an expression of shocked surprise decorates his face. "Oh, that's right, you can't. No fingerprints. No DNA. My dad taught me well."

"Hurry up, for God sake!" Someone bangs on the door.

"What do you want, Joe?" I ask timidly, recognising the tone of young Marianne. He cranes his neck in thought, exposing a prison tat cut into his flesh.

"What do I want?" he repeats rhetorically. His expression hardens further, and he presses his nose to mine. "I want you to suffer."

"Because I haven't suffered enough by your hand already?"

"Not even fucking close! Do you know what it's like to be locked up for twenty-three hours a day for over twenty-three years?" I stare at him as he shakes me. "Do you?" he hisses.

"No," I whisper, terrified.

"No, you don't. You know my formative years inside were educational." He touches his lip in contemplation. "The number of times I was cornered and left for dead..." He stops and tugs his collar, revealing two large, jagged scars around two and four inches long respectively. "The names they called me, the things I had to do to survive... I ended up serving the full sentence without parole because of you. I've known murderers inside that served less."

"But that's what you are; a murderer!" I hiss in a truthful whisper.

He repeatedly tuts his disapproval, and inside my head, a little voice is telling me I might not make it out of here alive.

"Involuntary manslaughter," he says tightly. "It was never murder. After all, she was my precious daughter, too!" His tone is mocking because he never gave a shit about her – and he never let me forget it.

"You're a liar!" I scream as tears begin to sting my eyes. "You all lied! You, your barrister, your father. And let's not forget your mother tried to buy the fucking jury! But it didn't work, did it?" Joe pulls his arm back and rounds his fist, and I wait for it. "Go on, do it. Give me a reason to get you put back inside," I goad him foolishly.

"Hurry up!" The door rattles again, inadvertently saving me.

For now.

"Fuck off!" Joe yells as the woman rants about toilets and brothels.

He cracks his neck, and his expression softens. Fear pierces me because I don't recognise this side of him. Framing my face securely in his hands, he reaches back and wraps my hair around his fist.

"God, I've always loved this fucking hair." Yanking my head back, he swipes his thumb under my eye and then pops it in his mouth. "Your tears taste sweet, baby. I wonder if the rest of you still tastes the same as I remember."

The instant the last word tumbles over his lips, he slams his mouth against mine. Forcing his tongue inside, the undigested contents of my stomach threaten to ascend, and I bite down hard on his lip. As he staggers back in surprise, I rip the door open and run out as my name is screamed out behind me.

As I reach the top of the stairs that lead down to the main floor, my wrist is captured. A flow of hot breath causes the tiny hairs on my neck to stand on end, and I finally realise I will never escape him.

"And here we are again, baby," he says knowingly. Everything around us fades into oblivion, and we are nineteen and twenty-one again. Here at the top of the stairs, history may repeat itself.

"Push, pull, push, pull," he mutters indecisively, pushing me forward and dragging me back. He then spins me around and digs his fingers into my jaw painfully. "To fall or not to fall. Now that really is the question, isn't it?"

Turning away, the lights have dimmed throughout the club. The strobe lights cast random patterns over the room, and from an outsider's point of view, we could just be two lovers having a tiff.

"Retribution is coming, bitch; and it's coming sooner than you think. And when it does, you're finally going to understand what it feels like to have it all taken away." He walks back down the long corridor and becomes lost in the crowd.

I wipe my eyes and jostle my way through the dancers, drinkers and drunks. Nearing the table, Nicki is sitting alone, texting. She stands when she sees me, and I put on the performance of a lifetime and slap my clutch to my stomach.

"Marie, are you okay?" Her concerned eyes absorb my appearance.

"I've had too much to drink. I don't feel well. Can you tell the other girls I was sick and got a taxi?"

"Sure," She replies, sceptical. "Text me when you get home."

"I will. Goodnight, darling," I say, trying to sound like me, instead of Marianne – who is desperately clawing her way back from the void.

Collecting my jacket from the cloakroom, the air hits me as soon as I make it outside. Striding a few yards down the street, I can't hold it in any longer, and I double over behind a bin and throw up.

I slouch down on the dirty pavement as my tears flow freely. Pulling out my phone, there are a few texts from the girls asking if I'm okay. And one from John, telling me to wake him up if he's asleep when I get in. Ignoring them all, I inhale deeply as I dial and stroke my delicate jaw.

"Marie, it's three in the morning!" Adrian answers with disdain on the fifth ring. "This better be damn good."

"You wanted proof, and now you've got it."

"What are you talking about?"

"Joseph just assaulted me."

Chapter 36

"I'M OFF, BEAUTIFUL."

Soft kisses trail over my shoulder, and I roll over and yawn. "What time is it?" I ask, knackered, still recovering from my catastrophic night out.

"Almost nine."

"You're late!" I admonish teasingly.

"You're worth it!" He smirks.

I smile softly. "I'm glad," I tell him, hoping I'll still be worth it when the day inevitably falls into night. Figuring there's no point in ruminating over it any further, I open my arms and welcome him into them.

"I love you." I cradle his head into my neck, holding on for dear life because, in my heart of hearts, I know this time tomorrow, this might be a luxury I no longer have.

He releases a low exhale against my shoulder. "What's got into you this morning?" He withdraws to gauge my reaction.

"Aside from you?" I ask coyly. "Nothing. I just wanted to prolong this moment." Because little does he know, after I've purged myself later today, this moment might be all we have left.

He furrows his brow, kisses me hard and brings me up with him. Rolling my bare body over, he slaps my upended backside, then placates the non-descript sting with a brush of his lips.

"Tempting," he says, moving to the chest of drawers. "But unfortunately, I'll have to negate that offer. I've got a new client coming in this morning."

"Okay. What time can I expect you home?"

"The usual."

Lounging on the bed, arse up, I cross my ankles and reposition my hands in front of me. I watch John pocket his wallet, some change and his phone, performing the same monotonous routine he does every morning. His rakish gaze roves the length of me as he grabs his gilet from the wardrobe. With a charming smile, he crooks his finger to come hither, and I reluctantly clamber off the bed and meet him in the middle. Bending down he swings me into his arms and carries me out of the room.

"These are looking better." He gently strokes the line of bruising on my jaw. Thank you, Joseph effing Beresford.

"Hmm, I guess it will teach me to look where I'm going next time," I lie.

Again.

When I came home three nights ago, as per John's text, he was indeed asleep. Under any other circumstance, I would have woken him, but all things considered, I ended up sleeping in the spare room.

The following morning was interesting, to say the least. The part of the conversation where I said a fellow reveller opened the toilet door in my face was juvenile. Yet it was the only excuse I could muster. I'm still unsure whether he believes it, but he hasn't pressed further. I mean, stranger things have happened. I remember a few years ago, one of the girls on my staff had gone out to someone's thirtieth and the next day she woke up with a black eye and absolutely no idea how it had happened.

So, that is my defence; drunk and a door.

Depositing me in the bathroom, he cups my cheeks in both hands - evidently wary of putting pressure on my sore side – and bends to kiss me. His talented tongue swipes around my mouth, and he swallows my sigh while I stroke his back, memorising the feel of him.

"Are you sure you're okay?"

"I'm fine, but you better go before Simon calls."

"He already has. I'll see you this afternoon."

"I love you," I repeat sincerely. Again, because it might be the last time.

He smiles beautifully, then runs his hand down my face. His middle finger traces my profile delicately. From my forehead to my nose, over my philtrum, until he tips up my chin.

"I love you too, angel." His lips linger, and he retreats with a sigh. "I'll see you later."

I stare after him longingly and listen raptly as he thuds down the stairs. The alarm beeps, then the front door opens and closes.

Turning on the shower, I shift apprehensively in front of the mirror. I glide my finger over my jaw, fearful of every possible outcome that today will bring. Except it can't get any further down to rock bottom than it already is.

Truthfully, I deserve everything ounce of resentment that is going to come to pass. Karma has a lot on me, and I've always known that when she finally came to collect, she would be here a while.

A flash of sheet lightning illuminates the skyline as I stand between the French doors. An accompanying crack of thunder follows in a timely fashion, and I breathe in the faint aroma of sulphur from the oncoming storm.

The grandfather clock chimes in the hallway, and I sigh in surrender. In the forthcoming hour, a man I never thought I would see again will be sitting across from me, the same way he did over twenty years ago. Again, we will talk about things I'm pained to divulge. And again, I will sob through the heartache while he propitiates me with empty words.

Locking the doors, my eyes skim the table as I clutch the mug to my chest. Lined up alongside Mr Blue, are the long unforgotten documents I finally dared to touch again. Certificates of marriage, divorce, birth and death, together with police statements and a transcript of the trial are all neatly laid out.

Touching the wallets, curled and tattered at the edges, a sinking sensation stems from the pit of my stomach to my throat, bringing with it the unvarnished, caustic truth I was willing to take to the grave.

The faint, metallic taste envelops my tongue. It grows deeper, stronger, intensifying as the inside of my cheek burns from where the skin has been torn apart by my own teeth.

Joe breathes heavily behind me, and his figure casts a terrifying shadow from the Christmas lights strung around the door. I clutch my face, listening in terror as I drag myself across the floor.

Without warning, the beer bottle he has just battered me with smashes on the wall, and I sob, knowing what comes next. He hauls me up by my throat, and I cover his hands with mine, trying to prise his fingers apart, but it's no good. With a malevolent smile, he snaps his arm back, and he throws me onto the bed. Sitting across my stomach, I mentally catalogue every hit until the pain takes over and numbs my nerve endings. It's true, after a while, your pain receptors stop registering.

My head lurches from one side to the other, until he's fed up and administers the same unprovoked treatment to my chest and stomach. Balled up, floating in and out of consciousness, I stare at the ceiling through half-dead eyes, willing it to end. Each number I count silently brings it closer and closer. After an excruciating amount of time, the torment mercifully stops.

"Mummy!" Faith's distressed cry floats over my own tears from next door. With one last hit to my face, the bed lifts, feet move, and the door opens.

"And shut that fucking bitch up!"

Then the door slams.

Laying prone, my body now recovering from its second of the two regular beatings I receive per week, I know the only way to end this vicious cycle is death - whether his or mine. But I can't take risks, not ones of such magnitude when I have someone who depends on me, nor when I have nowhere to go.

Forcing myself up, barely able to move, I catch a glimpse of my reflection. I study the damage he has inflicted, uncertain how much more my body can endure. Touching my eye, further welts are already starting to form. It's not surprising; I bruise easily. Always have, always will.

I dig into the drawer and grab a pair of balled up socks. Unravelling them, I wipe my face and lift my fringe aside. My hair is crimson, matted with my own blood. Wincing, scrubbing at my hairline, I can't have her seeing me like this; broken, beaten.

Battered beyond recognition.

"Mummy!" Faith wails with determination again.

"I'm coming, baby!" I hobble onto the landing, using the bannister as ballast and push open the door. I smile, insofar as I can, and fight back the pain as my cheeks lock into position.

I limp towards the spare cot Joe always places her in before he kicks the shit out of me. I should be thankful that she doesn't have to witness what an evil bastard her father really is. Yet I'm more disappointed with myself that I'm not the strong, independent mother she deserves.

Blonde curly locks bounce up and down as she hauls her small body up using the side rails as leverage. I pick her up with a grimace and curl up on the bed - the bed I'm ordered to sleep in after Joe has finished using me in the one next door.

"I'm here, Fay Bear. I'm here," I whimper. "I'm sorry, baby. I'm so sorry."

"No cry, Mummy," she tells me, her little fingers prodding my tender eyelids.

As I stroke the hair from her face and wipe her tear stained cheeks, I know I need to do what's right at long last – something I should have done the day she was born. Something I promised my mother I always would.

I need to save us.

I need to save us before it's too late.

I rearrange the scarf around my neck and bite my lip as I study the exterior of the building. Pulling the baseball cap further down my forehead, I inhale deep and push open the door. My arm shakes under the weight; my muscles still weak and sore from the third successive beating I survived last night.

The truth I've always known has been a long time coming, but these past three days have finally validated that one day, my motherly instinct will be gone, and my daughter will be left to fend for herself with a monster because I know I shall be dead.

Looking around the stark reception area, every walk of life is present, including mine. But the young, once disillusioned girl was quickly stripped from me. I just wish I'd cried for help sooner. Still, I wouldn't have left. Not only because of the threats of social services that Patricia spewed at me but because I have responsibilities, ones that stay with you until the grave.

As I approach the enquiry desk, my resolve withers. If I do this, there is no going back. Pondering the pros and cons, I grab my stomach the same moment the waters in my mouth churn. I swallow the bile pooling in my throat while tears form in my eyes because I have more priorities than most girls my age do. And a test four days ago confirmed I have one more to add to the mess I need to find a way out of. Except, with connections in high places, even the police can be bought, and my being here could just be a worthless disaster.

With that thought weighing heavy on my mind, I quickly turn back to the door. Pushing it with the little strength I have left, my hat comes off, and a young constable blocks my path.

"Sorry, miss," he says casually. I timidly lift my quivering chin, and his expression morphs from pleasant to murderous.

My body sways beneath me, and I reach out, blindly searching for support. The constable steadies my fall and moves aside my overgrown fringe to reveal my bloodshot eyes, framed by blackened, bruised skin.

"Who did this to you?" he asks, his eyes working between the woman now approaching from the desk and me.

"Please help me!" My body starts to shake from the sobs rising up from the depths of my shattered world, and I fall into him. His arm comes around me, and he guides us through the waiting area, and into an interview room. Sitting opposite, along with his colleague, he pushes the box of tissues on the table towards me.

"What's your name, sweetheart?" he asks, his pen poised on the paper in front of him.

"Marianne Beresford," I whisper. Staring around the room, its clinical, utilitarian starkness provides weird, cold comfort. Pulling a tissue from the box, I blot it over my eyes and sniff.

"Nice to meet you, Marianne. I'm Adrian Taylor, and this is my colleague, Donna Bower." I nod, inconspicuously, biting my lip in fear. "Can you tell us who did that to you?"

A shiver creeps its way in, freezing my muscles, chilling my skin, causing me to regress. Yet I've come this far, and I need to see it to the end now.

"My husband," I confess shamefully, twisting the ring on my finger, speaking evil I never thought I would. I lift my head, showing the side of me that was always defiant. The side that started the downfall that finally brought me here.

"Your husband?" Adrian asks, perplexed, eyeing his colleague speculatively. "How old are you?"

"Nineteen."

The memory fades the instant the doorbell rings throughout the house. I squeeze my eyes momentarily and pad down the hallway. Opening the door, I brace myself. It's been twenty-three years, and apart from some greying and a little expansion around the middle, he hasn't changed a bit.

"Hi, Marie," Adrian says casually, his tone reminiscent of the day we first met. He was my saviour that day, he brought the light when the darkness was impenetrable and blinding.

"Hello, Adrian." I stand aside as he steps over the threshold. I take in his suit, noting he has risen in the ranks over the last twenty years. His colleague smiles and says thank you as I stick my head out of the door, checking for anything untoward. Locking it behind me, I motion my hand down the hallway.

"Please, come in," I say.

The men walk in front, and I watch as Adrian looks at the pictures on the walls. He stops at the one of Oliver and me, taken a few hours after baby boy was born, and turns in question.

"He's not mine," I confirm, and he nods and purses his lips tightly. I guess he thought I would have a perfect life these days. He thought wrong.

Unexpectedly touching my jaw, he assesses the dark patches. "Did the bastard do this?" I nod mutely as he grinds his teeth. "I'm sorry, Marie. I-"

"Don't," I stop him softly. "It's not your fault. We both know it's always been *when* never *if*." I turn on my heel and enter the kitchen.

"Would you both like a drink?" I flick on the kettle.

"Coffee, please," Adrian replies.

"Tea, thank you," his colleague requests. "Hi, I'm Detective Mark Chapman. It's nice to meet you." He holds out his hand, and I reach over the table and shake it.

"Marie Dawson, and you." I quickly turn back to the worktop and spoon out two coffees and chuck a teabag into the other mug. Pouring the water, I place them on the table and fetch the milk.

The silence is as terrifying as the words they are here to speak - and the ones I don't want to - wait to be aired.

"We all know why we're here, Miss Dawson," Mark says quietly.

"It's Marie, please."

Mark rotates the mug in his hands and surveys the kitchen. He stops when he spies the security camera in the corner. It's not hidden; it's not meant to be. It's a deterrent, not that it would stop anyone from taking whatever they wanted to if they broke in, but still.

"There's one in every room," I confirm, sipping my coffee. "My partner is very security conscious. He runs his own firm, so we play guinea pig with the tech sometimes."

"Those are expensive." His eyes meet mine. "Is it recording?"

"No, I turned them off for your privacy. And mine." He gives me a perceptive nod and then puts his mobile on the table.

"Thank you. Do you mind if I record this?"

"No," I reply as he activates the screen.

"There's no easy way to start this conversation, but a few weeks back I was passed some paperwork regarding a complaint you had filed for harassment. At the time, there was no real proof of who the perpetrator was, but you were adamant it was your ex-husband."

"That's right." I shift as his stare subtly changes.

"Upon review of the report and the *colourful* history of the suspect, the complaint was forwarded to the Peterborough force to follow up," he says.

"*I know,*" I emphasise, stroking my finger over the line of bruises. Mark leans closer, scrutinising the proof.

"Earlier this week, I received a call from my colleague regarding an alleged assault by your ex-husband in a nightclub three days ago," he says, flicking his eyes to Adrian. I breathe in sharply, trying to hide my crumbling façade as my eyes start to flood.

"I'm sorry," I whimper as I get up and grab a length of kitchen roll.

Mark nods sympathetically, his mouth compressing into a tight line. "Can you tell us what happened?"

Folding the sheet of tissue, I wipe my cheeks and sniffle. "I was out with some friends, and we'd been dancing and drinking, and I bumped into a guy at the bar. He had a handless clock tattoo on his arm," I tell them, touching my arm, seeing their intrigue.

"Prison tat," Mark confirms, but this I now know.

"I made small talk. I let him buy me a drink, and then he made a comment. He said he had a friend who would be dying to see me… And he called me *Marianne*. No one knows me as Marianne, so I left him. Later that night, I was in the toilets, and my ex-husband dragged me into a cubicle. He put his hand on my throat and pressed his knee into my crotch." I sigh in anguish and rub my fingertips over my forehead. "He told me I'd been lying to the police again, that he was being harassed and retribution would be coming."

"Go on," Adrian encourages when he sees me starting to flounder.

"He grabbed my face." My fingers stroke over my jaw instinctively. "And then he kissed me." I put my hand over my mouth, the memory is enough to vomit again.

"It's okay, Marie," Mark mollifies. "How did you get away?"

"I bit his tongue when he put it in my mouth, and I ran. I didn't get very far because he hauled me back at a flight of stairs. Then he threatened to push me again."

I stare at Mark, who blows out his breath. "And this is the only physical contact you've had with him?"

"Yes. His torment was always from afar," I murmur and point to the teddy and files sat on the table. "Over the years, he's sent me numerous copies of our divorce papers. It was always sporadic, and there was no pattern, until recently."

"Why did you never report it?" Adrian asks.

I shrug. "I don't know. Familiarity breeds complacency, I guess. Anyway, since January, I've had papers, flowers containing pictures of our dead daughter-"

"Your *dead* daughter?" Mark cuts me off, shocked.

"Yes." I nod. "Then that bear was delivered."

Adrian leans over and tentatively touches it, possibly remembering the last time he saw it. I stare at him, concurring his thoughts, recalling the way it dropped, moments before I did. Moments before the world shifted in the wrong direction and everything I had ever done, everyone I had ever hurt through my actions, was all in vain.

"Marie?"

"You know, I'm not stupid. It's always been in the back of my mind that one day he would come for me. He blames me for spending his life inside, so how could he not? I always thought I'd be informed of his release considering his conviction, but no, I didn't hear it from the police; I heard it from my sister." I take a shuddering breath. "Why wasn't I told?" I demand.

"I'm sorry, Marie, but I really don't know. That will be something you have to raise with the CPS and the parole board. But as far as they are concerned, in the eyes of the law, he's served his time-"

"I couldn't care less if he's served his time because he obviously hasn't learnt anything. And the prison board hasn't either! I fail to believe there isn't a procedure in place to mentally review if a prisoner is fit for release!" My tone is getting higher and higher the more agitated I become.

"Marie, every prisoner is assessed before release. Joseph was obviously evaluated, and subsequently deemed fit to re-integrate into society."

"'Re-integrate into society?'" I repeat scathingly. "I don't fucking believe this!" The words tumble off my tongue without restraint or grace. "I spent years been beaten black and blue by that bastard, and by his own admission when he held me against that toilet wall, his violence didn't stop while he was inside! I might remind you that the laws of this land saw fit to remove his freedom when he took away my Fai-" I stop myself because her name doesn't deserve to be said in the same sentence as his. She was pure, innocent. She's dead.

"I'm aware of his conviction and the way your daughter died. I appreciate how painful this must-"

"No, you don't!"

"Marie, calm down," Adrian cajoles, but I ignore him.

"Do you have children?" I ask Mark.

"Yes, two."

"Well, until someone takes them away from you in one of the most brutal ways imaginable, you can't possibly understand. And I pray that never, ever happens to you because you'll never know what it feels like to hold your child and watch her fucking die!"

I slump back into the chair. My elbows on the table, my hands nursing my jaw, and my fingers touch my quivering lip.

"You didn't watch her die," I whisper, while tears stream down my cheeks. "You didn't hear her last cry. You didn't see her lying there. Her neck broken, her head twisted the wrong way and the dead look in her eyes. And you definitely didn't see that fucking bear on the floor when her lifeless hand dropped it. So, don't tell me you appreciate how painful it is because you don't fucking know!"

Adrian grabs my hand and squeezes it, but his affectionate touch only causes me to shiver. Staring at Mark, his eyes are softer, more understanding.

"The day I first met Adrian, I was broken. Literally, broken. The night before I walked into the station, I had suffered a third successive night of abuse. Only this time it was different. All the other assaults, he did in private, never in front of Faith. But that night he beat me in front of her, in her room, while she lay in her cot. Watching, screaming, heartbroken. Her hands gripped the bars while I slumped to the floor, and all I could think about was her, wondering how long it would be before she became his victim, like I was.

"I remember reaching between the railings, and she touched my hand, reminding me I needed to survive. And I did. The next morning, I walked into the station, determined to do the right thing and save us, but my determination withered. I turned to run, but Adrian blocked my path and offered me a way out." I sniff singularly.

"Was this the day she died?" Mark asks.

I nod. "Joseph comes from a well-off family, and since my own had abandoned me, I lived with them. I guess you could say they covered up his transgressions, as they would call them. I was certainly told a time or two that's what I was. The only reason why they tolerated me, was because while their son was hurting me, he wasn't out muddying the family name further. They turned a blind eye to the beatings; they didn't give a shit about Faith or me. And neither did Joe.

"That afternoon, after giving my statement, his mother hit me the moment I walked through the door for having her son arrested. She told me if I was a better wife, he wouldn't need to punish me," I say with a laugh. "I always knew she was heartless. It also explains why Joe was cold and calculating. His mother loved money and status, and he was just something unfortunate that happened along the way that she couldn't use to her advantage.

"Anyway, I already knew I couldn't stay any longer, and I started to pack since Adrian had already arranged accommodation at a safe house for us the next day on the guarantee that Joe would be held overnight. But it never happened, because they released him."

"Come again?" Mark asks incredulously.

Adrian huffs out. "The Beresford's were – *are* - very well respected. A decorated judge and a wife on the board of everything. They have their hands in good, influential pockets. Without any substantial evidence, other than Marie's statement and my first-hand account of her appearance and demeanour, they deemed it wasn't enough to charge him since no formal complaints had been made prior. And add to that his father was making waves about personal prosecution if his son wasn't released. You know how complicated red tape can be."

Mark shakes his head in astonishment, and I roll my eyes.

"I didn't know he'd been let go and his parents had left earlier for a New Year's Eve party. It was almost midnight when I heard the front door go and he started shouting. I managed to call the police before he found us, but when he did, he looked feral. Monstrous. I still had Faith in my arms when he lunged at me. It all happened so quickly..."

My body is numb as I finally relive the moment my world fractured completely. The moment it was cruelly ripped away from me in the blink of an eye. The moment my Faith died.

I jolt back from the past as a hand touches mine.

"Marie? Are you okay?" Adrian asks.

I give him a sad smile while patting my cheeks dry. "Fine." I stand and stretch, feeling partially cleansed.

It is the first time in over two decades I have told this truth. I know I shall have to do it again in the future, more than once, but after speaking it and reliving it, I have nothing to be ashamed of. That bastard might have stood up in court and lied about my *terrible* mothering tactics to save his own skin, but he was wrong. I was a damn good mother. My only flaw was not giving Faith a better father.

"Do you guys want another drink?"

"I'd ask for something stronger if I wasn't on duty," Mark confesses, and I smile.

"I'm sorry I screamed at you. I didn't..."

"It's fine," he says, then turns to Adrian. "I just wish *you* had told me all this before we arrived. Reading it and hearing it are two completely different things."

"Exactly. I would have told you in an analytical, trained way, you had to hear it from a grieving mother."

Placing down some fresh beverages, I perch against the worktop and glance up at the camera.

"Look, my partner doesn't know any of this, so I'd rather you didn't just turn up at the door again. However, I would be grateful if you could take these, fingerprint them, test them for DNA, I don't know. But whatever you do, I'll co-operate, and if it means he goes back inside, then so be it."

Mark quickly downs his tea and picks out the papers and ribbon but leaves the bear. "I've got a friend in forensics who owes me a favour. I'll give you a call sometime next week with the results. In the meantime, if anything else happens, ring emergency and then me." He slides his card over the table. Picking up his mobile, he stops the recording and indicates for me to move. "I need to get a picture of those," he says, placing his pen under my jaw for scale.

"Thank you," I reply, relieved, my hands in prayer at my chest.

I walk them to the front door, but Adrian stops.

"If you ever come back up to Peterborough, maybe to see Maggie and your mum, give us a call. And one last thing? I'm aware your partner also has some very influential, wealthy connections. If that son of a bitch does show up here, don't let him do anything that will buy himself some time at Her Majesty's pleasure, understand?"

"Of course." I thank him for the last time and close the door.

I stand in the living room and watch as they drive off. Marching into the office, I open the laptop. Sliding the time cursor back, the recording plays at speed, from the moment they arrived to the moment I showed them out. I remove the memory card and twist it in my fingers. Dragging my hand through my hair, I know John is going to hate me, but it won't be any more than I hate myself.

I shut down the laptop as the landline starts to ring. WS flashes on the LCD panel, and I take a breath and answer.

"Hi, are you on your way back? We need to talk." I throw it out there before I can regress on my absolution.

"No," John replies bitterly. "And you're right, we *do* need to talk." My body stiffens instantly from his rancorous tone.

"Darling?" I look towards the door, expecting him to come barrelling through in all his unknown anger, but he doesn't. Instead, his next words slay me.

"I just had a visit from Joseph fucking Beresford, *Marianne!* Are you finally ready to confess your seedy fucking past yet?"

Chapter 37

MY FINGERS TIGHTEN on the steering wheel as I drive through the industrial estate. My stomach roils, and the acid culminating within threatens to rise and burn.

Slowing to a stop outside the gates, I retract my window, tap in the code, and wait for them to part.

I brake sharply as I roll into the yard. It would seem this little showdown is going to have an audience. All the boys' cars are present, along with Sloan's Aston and a convertible Maserati I don't recognise. This doesn't fill me with hope, because I'm about to enter the lion's den, and they will all undoubtedly side with John.

I remove the key from the ignition and clutch my bag to my chest like a shield. My eyes automatically flutter up to John's window and seeing him standing there, watching me with clear contempt, if my stomach wasn't already threatening to drop out, it certainly is now.

Entering the building, I take the stairs slowly because only a masochist would hurry to one's execution.

The rare silence blankets the atmosphere as I pause outside the office, listening to the heated voices inside. One I know better than my own, the other I've only ever heard twice before. Closing my eyes, I inhale deeply and push it back.

John rotates from the window, grasping the first opportunity to stick in the knife. "A gift from your husband!" he says through gritted teeth and throws a file on his desk.

"Ex!" I spit back because I'll be damned if I break in front of them. Lobbing my bag on the chair, the tension is thick.

We eyeball each other hard as a figure moves in the corner of my eye, and the man I met on New Year's Eve - and more recently, three nights ago - stands beside him.

I huff in disgust. "No names, no job descriptions," I mutter, my fingers curling into my palms. "Is that torch still fucking burning now?" I hiss at the man of no name. Yet I do know his name. I've known it for the last eighteen months.

"Dominic Archer," he greets, practically reading my mind, and I turn to John.

"You lied to me. And for months you've had your little dog follow me," I say reproachfully.

"*I* lied to you? *I* fucking lied to you?" he roars, and I flinch and retreat backwards.

"John, calm down," Dominic says in warning, his accent pronounced.

John brushes his hand over his face, visibly reigning in his composure as the door opens. I peek over my shoulder to see Sloan and Remy enter, while Tommy and Simon block the doorway.

"Are you okay?" Remy asks, taking a stance by my side.

It's apt, because the battle lines have finally been drawn, and John and I have gone from passionate lovers to warring factions in the space of just a few hours.

"You," John points at Remy. "Stay out of it! You," he points at me. "Start talking!"

I throw my hand out and approach him. "What do you want me to say? What do you want to hear that will make this right?" I cry in desperation.

"I want the truth! Three years, Marie. Three goddamn fucking years!" Picking up the mug from his desk, he throws it with force, and it smashes over the wall.

"For fuck sake, you're scaring her!" Sloan says, wrapping his arm around my shoulder in cold comfort.

"Good. Because maybe now she will realise her lies have just destroyed everything we've built! Do you have any idea what it was like to sit here and listen to that twat goad me? Telling me you were still married? Is that true? Or is your divorce just another figment of your imagination?" He opens the file and wafts a copy of my marriage certificate at me.

"We are divorced!" I seize the file and rummage through it. "It took me five years, but it was finalised!" I shout, not finding a copy of the decree. I huff out vexed and slap it down. "For years, I thought you knew. In my mind, it was a given. And considering you already knew everything about Kara, I suspected you had a dirty fucking file on me, too. God knows your resources are plentiful!"

I turn to Dominic to gauge his reaction. If I expected for a second he would feel guilty, I was mistaken. Instead, he just raises his brows sympathetically. My eyes close in resignation. *He knows*. He knows, and he hasn't told John.

"No, you don't get out of this that easily. You need to take some fucking responsibility for once!" John yells.

"Don't you dare throw this back on me! I never lied to you!" I round the desk and get in his face.

"You never fucking told me, either! In my book, *angel*, it's as good as lying."

I slap his cheek hard, and my short, sharp intake of breath carries over the tense atmosphere. Grabbing my wrist, he hauls me closer.

"But the worst part was hearing him tell me that you had a child together. A daughter. A daughter you've never disclosed."

My resolve deteriorates, and I swallow hard. I dare not look behind me as I don't want to see the derision I will be forced to face.

"Let me go, John," I whisper.

"Where is your daughter?"

"Let me go."

"John, stop it, you're hurting her," Sloan says firmly.

"Stay out of it!" John yells, staring wildly at me. My taciturn conduct is his undoing until he eventually crushes the silence.

"Where is your fucking daughter, Marie?" he roars again, finally letting me go with a push. Falling backwards, my world rewinds at high speed, and I close my eyes, waiting to hit the floor again.

Instead, my fall is saved by an unlikely ally.

"Don't touch me," I warn in fear as I quickly shuffle away from Dominic. Glaring between him and John, I retrieve the memory card from my bag and turn it between my fingers.

"My daughter isn't up for a family discussion. And after what I've been through today, there's nothing left to hide or to protect myself from," I tell anyone who gives a shit. "Believe it or not, I planned to tell you today, and that's why I called earlier. But my dear darling ex-husband beat me to it." I snort singularly. "The bastard even warned me." My fingers automatically drift over the row of bruises gracing my jaw.

John leans against the windowsill, and his expression turns from hurt and angry to empathetic. "What do you mean?" he asks curiously.

I shrug because it doesn't matter anymore. Joe has done what he promised. "He said I would suffer, and now I am. I should have taken him more seriously. I guess that's another failure. But personal failure is my friend, and it's also my foe," I whisper, ashamed.

Turning the card one last time, I toss it on the desk. "Watch it, John. Live it, like I've had to, every minute of every hour for the last two decades. If my heart wasn't already obliterated having to speak the truth today, you've just hammered in the final nail."

His eyes close in defeat because it hurts him to hurt me.

"You once asked why I never let you in," I say, evaluating his expression since it was a question he asked when he thought I was asleep. "But I always did let you in. The truth is I couldn't find a way out." Wiping away my fallen tears, I try to regain a handle on my composure. "When you calm down enough to watch that," I jerk my chin to the table, "just remember I live with the consequences every day. And every day since it happened, I've died a little more inside. One day, there'll be nothing left to consume, because my own guilt would've already won."

John pushes off the windowsill, his arms still folded over his chest, his muscles flexing angrily. I pierce him with a glare, while his features depict every emotion running rampant that he is controlling himself not to say. When he moves no further nor attempts to talk, my fury takes over.

"Fucking take it!" I scream, shattered. The floorboards creak, and I look over my shoulder, seeing everyone now watching the show with anguished expressions.

I pick up my bag and carefully place it over my shoulder. "I'm going home now. If you want to talk about this amicably and civilised, I'll be waiting. If not, and I wake up alone in the morning, I'll be gone. And I won't be coming back." I turn on my heel, but Sloan blocks my path.

"Marie, don't do this. Don't make the same mistakes I did. Please," he begs, and the sound of it kills me because it's the one thing in the world he despises above all else.

I gently place my hand gently on his chest. "Regardless of what happens, you and Kara will always be mine. Promise me you won't tell her. She deserves to hear it from me. Promise me." His growls low, verbalising the horrible position I'm putting him in.

"Marie, please, I'm begging you!"

"I swear you won't lose her over this. She will always choose you. And I'll do whatever it takes to ensure she does." Brushing aside him, I make it two steps to the door before his hand sequesters my wrist, and he vents his fury.

"Are you just going to fucking stand there and let the woman you love walk out of your life forever?" he yells at John.

I can't turn around. I can't witness the condescension John will levy, or the truths he will dare to speak when his hand is forced.

Sloan's grip slackens, and I dash into the corridor the same moment John finally gives him an answer.

"Yes."

"Bastard!" Sloan growls. Then his steps quicken and furniture is dragged over the floor.

I run down the stairs as the commotion of the men I have left behind echoes. I yank open the main door and crash straight into Nicki and Devlin. Dev instantly cradles my face in his hands, studying my weary, defeated appearance.

"Fuck!" he hisses, as he looks to the door and the shouting still raging from within.

"You knew?" I ask incredulously. My eyes catch Nicki's as she looks between us, bewildered as to what on earth is going on.

"Dom called me a few days ago conflicted, he never wanted to tell John. Please tell me he didn't."

"No, he didn't," I confirm. *My bastard of an ex-husband did.*

Dev lets me go and pulls Nicki in for a kiss. "Baby, take her back to ours."

I shake my hand. "No, honey. I'll be okay. Please, I just want to be left alone for now." He narrows his eyes and considers me carefully, not that I would expect anything less.

"Fine, but don't do anything reckless."

Reckless as in a moonlight flit? I bite my tongue, but the truth is you cannot flit when you've been evicted.

"I'll be home as soon as I can," Dev says to Nicki, then sprints into the building.

"Are you okay to drive?" Nicki asks.

"Sure," I reply, but who knows. I have no idea how I'm even still standing right now.

Climbing into the car, I start the ignition and peek at my watch. I can't believe it is only two o'clock. Truthfully, I want this day to be over, but I fear the end is going to be a long time coming.

"Are you sure you don't want me to come with you?"

I smile and touch her cheek. "No. I promise I'll be fine."

Nicki nods, compressing her lips. "It's not my place to ask, but what's happened?"

"Someone told John the truth," I whisper, hearing the shame in my voice. And it is shame because I should have been honest from the off.

The day I agreed to start something with him, I should have steeled myself to do the right thing. But as the months drifted by and I realised I finally had the love I'd always craved, I was selfish. I refused to risk anything destroying it. But it was in vain, because here I am, with everything blowing up spectacularly around me.

And it's all my fault.

"Is it bad?"

I stare at her unwavering. "Yeah, darling, it is. But I don't want anyone thinking ill of John. He was right to react the way he did. I would've done the same."

Nicki's eyes suddenly take on a worried, glassy effect, and she looks away. I sigh, and mentally question how long it will be before her truth comes to light. There's something there, I know there is, but just like me, she keeps her cards close to her chest.

"You know, I'm the last person who should be acting holier than thou, but secrets are a terrible thing. Kara and Sloan, John and me… Remy. We never know when the pain we want to keep hidden will be exposed. If there's something you need to tell Dev, do it sooner rather than later."

The silence thickens, and the only thing that can be heard is the hydraulic equipment in the scrappers around the corner.

"I'll call you when I get home, darling."

Reaching for my door handle, Nicki stops me. "My grandma told me many things before she died, but the one she always repeated was 'don't go to sleep on an argument'."

I mull over her statement, but tonight, I know that's precisely what I'll be doing.

"I'll see you on Monday, Marie," she says, and I give her a small smile because come Monday, there's a chance I won't be here.

As I slowly edge out of the gates, I brake and look up. John is standing at the window, holding something against his face. His other hand is flattened on the glass, and from here, it really does look like he is waving goodbye.

I rub my hand across the back of my neck and pull out a couple of tops. Removing the hangers, I drop them into the holdall and zip it up.

For the last few hours, I've roamed the house, remembering individual moments. The sofa, the shower, the kitchen table, and the countless days and nights of passion we shared in this room. On this bed.

Casting my heartbreak aside, I jog downstairs, drop the bag, and enter the office. Kneeling in front of the safe, I flick through the wad of files and pull out my passport and car documents. Sitting back on my calves, I don't know what I'm going to do. When I was nineteen, I didn't have a choice. I never expected to be trying to find my place in the world again at forty-three.

The landline starts to ring as I get to my feet, and I leave it for the machine to pick up since I'm in no fit state to chat right now.

"John, I know you don't want to talk to me, but I need to know you're okay. That you haven't done anything you'll regret. Call me, or I'll come looking for you. I'll see you later."

A single beep resounds, and I absentmindedly run my finger over my blemished temple, wondering where he is. Picking up the phone, I scroll through the call log and dial.

"John?" Dominic answers with relief.

"Where is he?" I ask instead of giving him the courtesy of a proper greeting.

"I was hoping he was with you. He stormed out of here hours ago, and he isn't answering his phone."

"Right," I whisper in dismay.

"Look, if he isn't home in a few hours, call me, and I'll put a search on him."

I slant the phone away from my ear. *Put a search on him? What on earth does Dominic do?*

"Fine, but if he isn't talking to any of you, do you really think he's going to rush home to see me?"

Dominic sighs on the other end. "Marie, today was a hard pill to swallow. For both of you. I've known about your past for a long time, and I choose not to divulge. I have my reasons. Just call me, okay?"

"Fine," I mutter and hang up.

Rotating the phone in my hand, I deliberate if I should try John again. But really what use will it be when I know he won't answer. Returning the handset to its base, the clock chimes six.

Six eventually turns into seven, seven turns into eight, and in my heart, I know he isn't coming back.

Chapter 38

SITTING AT THE kitchen table, shrouded in partial darkness, I lift the glass to my lips. The liquid chills my throat as I remember all the good times John and I have had here. We've eaten and laughed here. Debated and argued here. Kissed and made up here, and we've made mad passionate love here.

And tonight, we might finally end here.

Putting the glass down, the clock chimes. It's now nine o'clock, and John still hasn't come home. I've fielded calls left and right all evening to no avail. And I've sat here and rehearsed what I'm going to say. Regardless of how tonight ends, or how cleansed my conscience may be, I know I will have lost him.

The front door opens and closes, and I inhale deeply as his stride stops outside the door. I stare straight ahead, my determination resolute, yet my heart is already broken before the first word has left my lips.

In my peripheral vision, John walks past me and pulls out a chair opposite. Unsure of how to begin, after long minutes of silence, he slaps his hand down, causing me to jump. Picking up the glass, I down the remaining wine in one and pour another.

"Where have you been? Everyone's worried about you."

"Really? Are *you* worried about me?" he asks sardonically, and my mouth falls open.

"That's unfair," I whisper. "Of course, I'm worried. I love you, and that's never going to change, even if tonight is the end of us."

He slams his fist down and breathes harshly. I guess after everything that has come to light today, it's an injustice to tell him I love him when he is still coming to terms with my omissions. Still, it's true, and I've never lied about that.

"Start talking, Marie. The sooner we do this, the sooner we both know where we stand."

Studying his darkened silhouette, I already know precisely where I stand. I'm teetering on the edge of the precipice, preparing to fall.

"I was fifteen when I first started seeing Joe. He had just turned seventeen and was in sixth form. It started off harmless, flirting, sneaking kisses. It was fun and exciting, and at the time, he was patient and gentle. But more than that, he showed me affection, something I'd been starved of for so long." I sigh, and take another mouthful, feeling the effects of the two glasses I've had already.

"We were together for about six months before my father found out. One of his friends had seen us together in town. When I got home that day, he told me I wasn't allowed to see him again. But we all know when you're told to do something, you do the complete opposite. And even with my sheltered upbringing, I wasn't immune to wanting and desire. To feeling things that were deemed forbidden. And Joe gave me that. I thought I was in love, that I couldn't go a day without seeing him for fear that my heart would break. It didn't matter what my father would say, I knew better."

Looking back, it proves just how foolish teenagers really are. In reality, I knew shit. And if I knew then what I know now, I'd have done what I was told and toed the line.

"A few months later, when I was sixteen, I found out I was pregnant. I was terrified. For weeks I managed to keep it a secret until my mother found the test. My parents were upstanding citizens of the community so you can imagine the way my father reacted upon hearing his daughter was now with child. It was very much a personal disgrace to him. He hit me, called me a slut, and said I had to have an abortion. When I refused, I found myself disowned and homeless.

"Needless to say, Joe also wasn't happy when I told him. And to add further insult to injury, he also hit me and demanded I get rid of it. Later that night, his mother ranted on about how I had destroyed her son's life. His father, on the other hand, said he would make him do right by me."

Swallowing another mouthful of wine, the silence devours, until John taps on the wood, revealing his impatience.

"As the pregnancy progressed, it became clear Joe really didn't give a shit about the baby or me. I went to the first scan with Maggie. She was the one who came to the maternity classes with me when she could. But some weeks, I ended up sitting there alone. She chose the baby's name, and she bought most of the newborn stuff with her pocket money," I confess, feeling ashamed that she was the one to provide for my daughter when I couldn't.

"After a while, my impending baby bliss wasn't so blissful anymore. Joe was out frequently - seeing other girls - and I saw him less and less as the weeks passed by. Before the baby even arrived, he'd started to hit me. He was smart; he ensured he marked me in places that wouldn't be seen. A tap here, a dig there, until he got creative and used my stomach as a punchbag. I was seven months pregnant.

"At the time, my relationship with my father was still non-existent, but my mother was there for me, in a way, risking his wrath to ensure I still had one parent I could rely on. She was mortified the day she saw the bruises, but what else could I do? I had nothing, John. *Nothing!*"

He stands and flicks on the light. The brightness blinds me, and I squint as he sits back down and stares at me with such disdain that my tears finally fall.

"The day I gave birth, my romantic fantasy of Joe by my side, telling me how well I had done, was a dream I made myself believe. In my heart, I knew it would never happen. I spent four hours in labour alone. And subsequently, I gave birth alone since my father refused to allow my mother or sister to come in with me. I was a child giving birth to a child, and I had no one." I wipe my eyes as the harrowing and hideous memory of my father dragging my mother and sister away replays.

John puts his hand over his mouth, before slamming his fist on the table. I'd like to think it's anger for what I've just said, but it's probably annoyance that I'm not speaking fast enough to satisfy him.

"My mother called Joe's parents, but he didn't bother showing up until later that evening. He was drunk and swaying. He told me I'd ruined three people's lives, and then he threatened me as our newborn lay just a few feet away." I look up at him, surprised to see his expression soften.

"I then spent two days in the hospital alone, and I knew when I left, I would still be alone. Upon reflection, I was alone from the moment I met him. I was just a silly little girl to play with, but my getting pregnant put the brakes on that. Still, he never let me forget just how much I had destroyed his life."

I pick up the glass and swill the liquid inside, feeling just inebriated enough for comfort. Pouring it down my throat, it irritates my oesophagus, and I slam it down, breaking the stem from the body. It rolls across the table until it falls over the edge and smashes on the floor, giving me time to recollect the rest in my hazy state.

"A few months after I turned eighteen, Joe's father made good on his promise that his son would do right by me. I didn't want to get married, but the ultimatum I had been given left me no choice. So, on a dreary day, in the local registry office, I foolishly married him in a ceremony his mother arranged. I wore a cheap suit from the local market, and in return, he gave me a second-hand ring he found in a pawn shop for a tenner."

John's incredulous chortle reverberates around the kitchen. Seeing his reaction; his laugh, his subsequent head rub, it makes me feel so ashamed. Unable to look at him, through my own mortification that I truly fucked up my young life, I train my eyes on the window behind him.

"Continue," he snaps, nearing the edge of his control.

"That night, on what should have been the happiest day of my life, I laid in our bed alone, while he consummated the marriage with someone else. The next day, when he finally rolled up with black makeup smudged on his shirt, I dared to ask where he had been. In response, he beat me senseless, and it was a true taster of what was to come. It was the beginning of the end."

My sight drifts from the window to John, who scrubs his hands over his face and links his fingers together in front of him.

"What happened to the baby, Marie?" he asks evenly, yet his expression is one of disgust, of pity and shame.

I look over his shoulder because I don't know how to tell him. I sniff back my tears and shake my head, knowing he will never see it from my perspective. He will just see it that I couldn't protect her. He will tell me I should have done more, that I should have sought help. But I didn't do more because I was frightened of Joe's parents. And I was terrified social services would take Faith away from me, that they would call me an unfit mother. I couldn't take that chance, so I let him beat me instead.

The tears sting my eyes as I remember those dark days, and I put my hand over my mouth to conceal my sorrow.

John rounds the table and pulls out the chair next to me. He leans over and gently swipes his finger under my eye. "What happened to her?"

"She's not here," I whisper as my fingers touch the locket around my throat.

His forehead creases and he wipes his hand over his face. "Stop talking in fucking riddles. You're sat here, heartbroken, and still, you refuse to be honest!"

Unable to hold it in any longer, I break down in front of him. Crying for my daughter, for myself, and for the life I choose that has done nothing but bring me misery.

And it was all for nothing.

"Answer me, Marie!"

"I can't!"

"Why?"

"Because you wouldn't understand! You'll blame me. I was a child raising a child, but I was a good mother," I finish in tearful heartache. "I was a good mother."

He stands brusquely and kicks the chair. "Get out!"

"No, John, please!" I shake my head, experiencing déjà vu of the day my father kicked me out with the same request.

"Marie, I don't want you to hate me, but I won't be held responsible for my actions if you stay."

"I'm sorry. I'm sorry. I'm fucking sorry!" I scream; my throat hoarse.

"Sorry? Sorry is what you say when you've burned dinner. Sorry is what you say when you take off a wing mirror. Sorry doesn't fucking cut when I find out the woman I've loved for years has lied to me for just as long. And it definitely doesn't fucking cut it when she tells me she's had a kid with another man! *Years*, Marie. You've been lying to me for *years!*"

"I didn't want you to get hurt. I never thought I'd have to tell you!" I whimper in defeat.

"Well, you thought wrong, *angel!*" I shudder as he spits out the name that normally sounds so loving and revered. "What you've done has annihilated me. Now, leave. When I've calmed down, we're going to talk about this, and you're going to tell me *everything*. Understood?"

I sway on the spot as I stand, and he quickly reaches out to me. A flashback plays in my mind, and I see Joe's hand coming towards me. Horrified, my shoulders shake as my body withdraws.

John drops his arm instantly; his expression shocked. "I would never, ever, lay a hand on you!" he declares, but it doesn't matter because once imagined, it cannot be unimagined.

I rush to the door and rip it open. "I'm leaving, and I'm never coming back!" I stride down the hallway and fumble in my bag for my keys.

"You can't drive in that state." He takes another step and reaches for his phone.

"Why do you care?" I scream again and open the door.

The fresh air hits me, and it's a miracle I can even walk straight. The wind chill is sobering as I ungracefully clamber into the back seat and lock myself in. Rocking with my knees to my chest, my phone vibrates continuously, and I dig into my bag.

"Kara," I answer in tears.

"Oh, God. Please don't cry," she says. "I'm coming over to get you. Promise me you won't drive anywhere. Please!"

"Okay," I reply and hang up.

Resting my head on the pile of suit jackets I leave in the back, I cry irrepressibly.

And for the third time in my life, I know what it feels like to have your heart obliterated for something you love more than anything else in the world.

I stare up at the roof as headlights illuminate the inside of the car. I don't know how long I've laid here for, but John hasn't tried to talk to me again. It's probably for the best. If I was him, I wouldn't even want to be breathing the same air as me.

A light knock taps on the window, and I lift my head up to see Kara standing there.

"Hey," she says as I open the door and get out. Stroking my tear-stained face, she takes the car keys from me, and I stumble towards her Evoque. Climbing inside, I inadvertently glance at the rear and bite my lip in guilt when I see Oliver asleep in his seat.

Fuck!

Daring to look back at the house, Sloan is standing in the doorway, holding John's face while speaking to him. Watching them, it is so reminiscent of the day when Sloan kicked Kara out and the way John had to calm him down. But this is not then, this is now. And this is nothing in comparison to a few lies Sloan had been told – these are truths that I have intentionally omitted, thinking I would never have to confess them.

Kara gets in and starts the car, but her hand softly touches mine. "Sloan's going to stay tonight and make sure John's okay, but *we* need to talk."

The streetlights pass by as we drive out of the city. My hands shake nervously in my lap, and I glance over at Kara as she concentrates on the road ahead.

"I'm sorry," I say. "I know that isn't good enough, but I am. I'm sorry I was never truthful when you asked. I'm sorry I couldn't find the right words to tell you. No one will ever understand how truly sorry I am."

"You don't have to apologise to me. I know how painful the truth can be." Kara blindly reaches over and touches my hand, and I turn back to the window as the world passes by outside.

The soft melody fills the nursery as I stare down at baby boy. "Dream big dreams, little prince."

Picking up the baby monitor, I close the door ajar and trudge down the stairs. Stopping midway, I stare at the picture of John and me. The weight of the world sits heavy on my shoulders, but every justification I want to voice is duplicitous.

"Marie?" Kara's voice seeps up the stairs, drawing my attention.

"Coming," I reply and descend.

"Here you go." Kara places a mug of tea on the coffee table as I enter. Perching myself on the sofa next to her, I pick it up.

"I'm sorry you had to bring Oliver out tonight."

She smiles sadly. "It wasn't ideal, but he's none the worse for it. Besides, Sloan is under the impression you're going to leave and not come back," she comments curiously. "He refused to say anything further."

"Honey, don't be upset with him." I put down the mug and rub my hands on my thighs. "This isn't like before; he isn't purposely keeping you in the dark. I made him promise because you deserve to hear it from me. And if I can't make this right, he's terrified he's going to lose you. Before I do tell you, I need you to promise me that if John and I can't work this out and I leave, that you won't follow me."

"Marie, what the hell is going on? I can't make that promise!" she cries out.

"You must, or I'll leave right now. Whatever happens, I will always be there for you. You will always be my daughter, irrespective of which city I'll be living in." Her mouth opens in protest, but I raise my hand. "Promise me."

Her face falls. "I promise," she whispers.

"The other night when I disappeared from the club, my ex-husband cornered me in the toilets and threatened me."

"What?"

I shake my head - she can ask questions later.

"He told me I was going to pay for what I'd done to him. Today, he turned up at John's office pretending to be a client. He was spouting off that we were still married. He really turned John's head and filled it with lies." I feel wretched saying it, because they're my lies, too.

"Why would he say that?" she asks confused. "I mean, you are divorced, right?" Her hand covers her mouth. "Oh, my God, you're not divorced!"

"No, I am! Initially, he refused, but in the end, he had no choice. I'll never understand why he made it so hard – he never wanted to be tied to me in the first place." I take her hand and stroke her wedding band with my thumb. "You know what you and Sloan have is Elysium. You have the perfect marriage. Love, trust, commitment. What I had was hell, and Joe used the ring he put on my finger as free reign to abuse me."

Her eyes widen, having never heard me talk so bluntly before.

"But that isn't what put John over the edge. I had a daughter. Faith." Her mouth opens, but I raise my hand when she looks like she is going to say something. "This could take a while," I tell her.

Closing my eyes, I begin to rehash the past I had buried for the second time tonight.

Muffled tears float from beside me as I look at the clock on the mantel. The midnight hour is fast approaching, and tomorrow is on the horizon.

In the last hour, I've gone through every emotion possible, because to tell John is one thing, but to tell it to someone who knows what it feels like to have your choices removed, is quite another.

I shuffle on the sofa and face Kara. Tears stream down her cheeks, her eyes wet and inflamed. Reaching out to dry them, I feel cleansed in the worst way possible. But unlike earlier, I haven't held anything back, because she will not judge and find me guilty.

But there is still one part left to tell her.

Faith.

"That's unimaginable," she whispers. "I understand now why it's painful to talk about. I can't begin to fathom what you must feel every day, wondering if things had turned out differently."

I reach for her hand again. "If things had been different, we wouldn't be here right now. When you first started living with me, I'd long resigned myself to never meeting anyone. Every time you asked about my past or children, it put the fear of God in me. I couldn't bear the thought of telling you the strong woman you looked up to was weak and battered. I wanted to be a good role model for you, to prove

I was a good mother. I hated that you had been honest about your past when I couldn't do the same," I admit.

"I still remember the evening you called me to tell me you'd spent it with Sloan." Her cheeks flush a deep shade of pink, but she has nothing to be embarrassed about. "I was happy for you. Notwithstanding our call, I wasn't impressed that you had had sex with a man you'd only known for five minutes, but I was happy you were trying to live. And it made me realise that one day I would be on my own again.

"The day of the function you attended with Sloan – the one when you were supposed to be working? Well, John turned up at my house that afternoon to collect your things."

"I remember," she says. "I was going to kill you when I found out."

I force a smile; I expected as much.

"For the first time in twenty-one years, he made me feel desire I had convinced myself would never be mine. He made me feel alive again. I knew eventually I would have to tell him, but the longer I left it, the harder it became."

"I know how that feels," she murmurs. "Look, I'm not saying it's right, and I'm not taking sides, but John deserved to hear it from you, too. I guess it was always inevitable he would learn the truth one way or another, but I'm surprised he didn't already know. He knew all about me."

"I know. If I thought for one second this is how he was going to find out, I'd have done it years ago."

"Hindsight," she breathes out, rolling her eyes. How she loves her precious, bleeding hindsight.

"And she's still a bitch!" I reply sarcastically.

"Marie?" Kara suddenly takes on a sheepish expression. "It's getting really late, and Oliver will be up early in the morning, but there's one last thing I want to ask." I nod and chew my lip in anticipation. "What happened to Faith?"

I shake my head and squeeze my eyes. "Honey, I want to tell you, I do, but I need to speak to John first. I don't want him hearing it from a second-hand source. That's already done enough damage today."

She signs in resignation. Her lips form a tight line, and she acquiesces. "Okay," she whispers. "Can I at least have one final truth?"

I nod.

"Your ex-husband didn't leave you the business, did he?"

I shake my head no.

"And you didn't divorce due to his adultery, did you?"

"That's two truths," I tell her. "But no, I didn't." I stand and pace the room until I stop at the window. "I've lied about him my entire life. I've made up names, professions, even what he looked like. I said anything to evade the truth because I was ashamed."

Kara's head shakes behind me in reflection. "But why, of all people, did you feel you couldn't be honest with me? I mean, you even said he was engaged. You reaffirmed it months ago."

"He is!" I turn on my heel. "To her Majesty's Prison Service. It's the most enduring relationship he's ever had."

She frowns until her mouth drops open and it is clear she is piecing the puzzle together. "Oh, my God! Marie…"

"Honey, I'm knackered, and I've been through the wringer today. Let's go to bed. We'll talk in the morning."

"Okay." Kara agrees grudgingly.

Turning off the living room light, I wrap my arms around her as we walk upstairs.

"Are you going to tell John tomorrow?" she asks outside the guest bedroom.

"If he'll speak to me. Goodnight, honey." I kiss her cheek and close the door behind me. Stripping down to my underwear, I slide into bed and finally allow myself to cry.

A creak emanates from the landing as the door opens tentatively. "Marie, can I come in?" Kara asks.

"Sure." I pat the duvet as she enters in her pyjamas. She places the baby monitor on the chest of drawers, climbs in and strokes my temple.

"When you said I was lucky to have my mum back in my life, I finally understand what you mean. But don't misunderstand, because she can never replace you. You're my mum, and I'll always love you, regardless of what happens."

"I love you, too, honey. So, so much," I reply and snuggle into her.

As I drift off with one daughter in my arms, I dream about the one I didn't have for long enough.

It is twenty-three years overdue, but tomorrow, we will be reunited again.

Chapter 39

WAKING AT THE crack of dawn, the house is deathly quiet.

My bladder is screaming at me, and I dart into the en-suite and do what I need to. Flushing the toilet and washing my hands, I dig around in the vanity drawer until I find a new toothbrush. Brushing briskly, I turn on the shower.

Ten minutes later, on my knees, wrapped in a towel, I rummage through the chest of drawers. I'm relieved when I find some of my clothes and underwear neatly folded from the times I have babysat. But of everything I should be mulling over right now, clean knickers are a priority.

Sliding on my jacket, I stick my head out of the door and look towards the master bedroom. I tread lightly over the landing and into the nursery.

Sprawled out in his cot, Oliver shuffles in his sleep, and his arm flops back. As I bend down to kiss him, he moves, and I hold my breath, praying he doesn't open his mouth and wake the dead.

After a few tense moments, I tiptoe out of the room and down the stairs. Hurrying into the foyer, I swipe a set of keys and disarm the house. Locking the door behind me, I sprint towards the BMW and throw myself inside.

My phone starts to vibrate as I drive down the private lane. Pulling up in a layby, I retrieve my mobile to find a mass of missed calls and texts from John – the last being just a moment ago. Inside, a part of me is desperate to read them, but the other part of me wants to delete them since I can't imagine liquor-fuelled texts will have anything good to say. Leaving it on the seat, I move off.

Picking up speed on the quiet country lanes, I eventually join the M25. With my determination resolute, and my eyes fixed and unwavering on the expanse of road ahead, I change up a gear, put my foot down, and cruise up the motorway.

Two hours later, I stop in a supermarket car park as my phone rings on the passenger seat again. I shake my head – this is call number seventeen from John. Debating whether to answer, the ringing stops, and a text comes through. Again, I question whether to read it, but I know I can't avoid him forever.

With a cautious sigh, I open the message. It's the least I owe him after ripping his world apart yesterday.

Call me. I'm sorry.

A tear spikes my eye because I'm the one who should be begging forgiveness.

I hover my thumb over the screen, but I don't know what to say to him. How do I explain what I'm doing nearly one hundred miles north? God knows as soon as the words leave my mouth, he will think I'm running.

I'm in K's BMW. Turn on the tracking. I will explain.

Hitting send, I curse myself for forgetting the fundamental words that should have come first.

I love you and sorry.

I toss my phone into my bag, get out and enter the supermarket.

Perusing the flower displays, I choose a large bouquet of roses as my phone chimes again. Hunting down some bottles of water and a pack of dishcloths, I make my way to the checkouts.

Opening the car door, I carefully deposit my things on the passenger seat and open the latest message.

WHY ARE YOU IN FUCKING PETERBOROUGH?

I shake my head. Shouting and swearing at me isn't going to do any good, but I realise what he is thinking – my lovely, abusive ex-husband lives here. But what he doesn't know is that my daughter is also here.

I toss the phone on the seat, message unanswered, and turn the ignition as it starts to ring again. I glance over wearily because I won't tolerate being shouted at. Seeing Kara's name flash repeatedly, I connect the call.

"Hi, honey. I'm sorry I took your car."

"No, I don't care about that. Look, John's on his way to you with Jeremy. I don't know what state he's going to be in, but he downed half a bottle of gin last night. I'm not supposed to say anything."

"Okay. I'll talk to you later. Kiss Oliver for me."

"Wait! Where are you going?" she asks in a panic.

"To find my Faith. Don't worry, honey, I'm coming back. I love you."

She sighs, unconvinced. "And I, you. Call me and take care."

As I drive through the streets, my mind forces itself to remember the way. Entering the grounds, I park the car and step out.

Collecting up the flowers and cleaning items, my feet move. But this time, my mind isn't forced to remember, because I remember this place far too well. It is intrinsically ingrained within me in a way that nothing else is.

I remember the fortnight before the funeral vividly, when my mother showed me where Faith would be buried. I sat here alone for hours in the days that followed, contemplating if my father's words at the hospital the week prior would ring true. Of all the things he could have said, I didn't need scripture shoving down my throat, but I was fooling myself thinking he would give a damn. But maybe he was right after all. Maybe the fallen cannot be saved.

I take a breath as I stop and stare down in shame. "I'm sorry I've neglected you all these years, my Fay bear. I had my reasons, but I'm here now. Mummy's here now," I whisper, kneeling on the barren grave, standing out starkly in the midst of others with colourful flowers, wreaths and knick-knacks.

My heart breaks all over again as I stroke my hand over the marble, and I remember being that nineteen-year-old girl who was burying her two-year-old child. Wiping my tears, my phone starts to ring, and I lift it up and answer.

"Hi." My voice shakes. "How far away are you?" I ask before he can say anything.

"Rem, how long?"

"Forty minutes, give or take," Remy replies, his tone muffled. "Did you get that?"

"Yep," I murmur, trying to keep my tears at bay. "I'll still be here." Now I'm openly crying.

John sighs heavily into the phone. "Shit, angel. Why didn't you tell me?"

Running my finger over the engraved stone, the birds tweet overhead in the early morning sky.

"John, where did you think my daughter was?"

"I don't know. I-I-"

"Did you think I just dumped her off on anyone who wanted her, so I could gallivant across the country and finally live my life?" I grimace as the last word leaves my mouth, because, in essence, that's precisely what I did – I left her here and never came back.

And I'll never forgive myself for it.

"Look," he says softly. "I'll be there as soon as I can, darling. I'm sorry, please forgive me."

"I do, and I love you. I'll see you soon."

"Remy put your foot on it," John mutters, aggravated, as he hangs up.

Dropping my mobile on the grass, an old man approaches.

"Morning, Reverend-" the man stops when I turn.

"Morning," I greet. "Wrong sister. The Reverend is my twin."

"I can see that," he says with a knowing look, seeing double, no doubt. "Is she yours?" I nod, and he sits down beside me. "I've worked here for twenty years. After a while, you recognise regular faces. No disrespect, but I've only ever seen Reverend Booth and her husband here."

And isn't that the appalling truth? I feel wretched that someone has noticed.

"I haven't lived here since she died. I couldn't face coming back. That's awful, isn't it?" I query, not blaming him if he finds my actions repulsive. I put my hand over my mouth to quell my tears because if I don't, I'll be crying all day. I will never stop crying.

"Time passes so quickly, before you know it, ten years are gone, fifteen, twenty. Life moves fast." Offering his hand, I take it, and he squeezes tight. "My wife is buried not too far from... Your daughter?" he asks gently, and I nod again, grateful for his compassion. "I'm the only one who comes to her grave since we had no children. One day, I'll be next to her, and when that happens, my grave will also be austere, as will hers." Standing up, he wears a thoughtful expression. "God and nature will love what you leave behind. They will always be there for them. It was nice meeting you. Say hello to the Reverend for me."

"I will. Thank you," I say as he walks away.

Soaking a cloth, I wipe over the headstone, removing the grime. As I clean the front meticulously, in and around the engraving, my heart is heavy when I remember the bastard's name isn't on it. Shame fills me; he might as well have just left her birth certificate blank, too.

A small snap of a twig startles me, and I look up to see John and Jeremy standing three graves over, their bulky frames casting shadows over the stones. I lock eyes with Remy, who smiles sadly and approaches, leaving John standing alone, swaying unsteadily.

Remy squats on his knees, shifts a strand of my hair and kisses my forehead. "In this life, four women have inspired me to be a better man. My mother - obviously; Kara - a determined woman whose life was torn from her for so long; the woman I love – whose father would rather see me under a bus; and you. A strong woman with a heart that's big enough to put her own pain aside to do what's right." I raise my hand over my face. "To do this," he continues, looking at the grave. "To come back here and face this, proves you are all those things, Marie."

I nod, silently agreeing with him, because he's right; I am strong. From the age of sixteen, I've proved it countless times, but right now, I'm the one who needs someone to lean on.

"Does he hate me?" I ask, tearful.

Remy shakes his head and wraps his arms around me. I feel pathetic. I'm a forty-three-year-old woman being comforted by a man who is not that much older than what my Faith would've been today.

"No, of course not." Jeremey pulls back, still gripping my face firmly. "Marie, look at me. I'm not supposed to tell you this, but that man has loved you for almost as long as Sloan has loved Kara."

My forehead creases. "What do you mean?"

"I mean she wasn't the only one being followed. Just talk to him, explain, but don't grovel. This was your life long before he found a way in. And you did that – you let him in." He looks back at John, who looks very ashamed – and very hungover. "And he's aware you can just as easily let him back out. You lived without him once, he knows you could do it again."

"I didn't know how to tell him. How could I?"

"I know exactly what you mean. I still need to sit down with Evie and explain the truth. Like you, I'm putting it off as long as possible, because when she finally hears it, she will have to decide if she lets me stay in, or if she lets me back out. Trust me, *I know*."

I roughly wipe my already sore eyes. "Thank you, sweetheart. I mean that." He kisses my hand and stands, motioning John over.

"I need to get back. Evie will be wondering where I am. Marie?" I avert my eyes from John. "Can I take the beamer?"

"Sure," I confirm.

"Here," he says, exchanging keys. "He's probably still ten times over the limit, so don't let him drive."

I stand up and embrace him. "You're a good man, Jeremy James."

He quirks his brow in surprise. "I'm glad you think so. One day I might be calling on you when I need a character reference."

I fold my arms over my chest and watch as he turns and whispers something to John. Whatever is being said is causing John to look very pissed off.

"I'll see you later, M." Remy winks before striding away.

I rub my hands over my forearms as John inches closer. "I didn't know how to tell you."

He sits down on the grave and touches the headstone. "Only two?" he asks appalled, then soaks a cloth and wipes the sides. "Faith." The word carries over the peaceful atmosphere in a whisper. I reluctantly sit down beside him as my heart starts to beat rapidly, hearing him repeat her name with such gentle reverence.

"My Fay Bear," I murmur. I retrieve my purse from my bag and pull out the picture I always carry. Passing it to him, I stare at her face as he glides his thumb over it.

"Angel," he murmurs, stopping on her hair, which was the same pale shade of mine and Maggie's.

Biting my lip, memories come back, remembering her hair. The way it smelt, how it felt in my hands and all the times I had washed it and put ribbons in it.

"Faith." My whispered word drifts over her resting place. "Maggie thought it was pretty. And fitting, since our father wasn't convinced I had any," I say sarcastically.

The delicate stroke down my temple pacifies me, as John smiles. Turning back to the grave, I study him openly. The way he cleans each letter meticulously, showing such care and attention, that it makes my heartbreak. Her father should be the one doing this, not the man who should be back in London, throwing my things out of his house, calling me every name under the sun. But he's not. He's here, tending to the grave of a child that isn't his own. A dead child I've intentionally hidden for years.

"Some of the gilding is coming off here," he mutters, breaking my painful calm. "And here, too." He leans in closer, drops the cloth and dries his hands on his shirt. "I'll get someone to repair it."

"You don't have to," I reply, assessing the damage that has developed over time.

He adjusts at my side, and his hand covers my cheek. I sit back on my haunches, train my eyes on him, and open my mouth, but he puts his finger on it.

"No, angel, I want to. Not because I have to, but because she's yours and that makes her mine.

I press my lips together. "John…"

"God, I wish you'd told me."

"I know," I whisper. "I wish I had too. Maybe then we wouldn't be doing this, trying to figure out where to go from here, while you try to get your head around my lies." I pick up the flowers and begin to arrange them, but he stops me.

"No, angel, they're not lies. Secrets, yes; but definitely not lies."

"You've changed your tune." The words are out before I have time to take them back and I screw my face up. "I didn't mean it like that."

He rolls his eyes. "Yes, you did, and I deserve it. What happened to her?" I continue to fiddle with the petals, until he touches my hand. "Darling, please. I need to know." But I can't tell him the truth, not here, not where she might be watching overhead and listening.

I look around at the surroundings. The old man from earlier is tending the overgrown edges, and more people are entering, visiting their loved ones. Knowing this could turn into a scene of the worst kind, one that will guarantee my permanent expulsion from the place, I jump up.

"Angel, please."

I shake my head and pick up my bag as he stands. "Not here, John. I will not argue with you in front of the mourning."

He quickly looks around and nods. Holding out his arm, he hooks it around my waist and stares down at me. Skimming his finger over my jaw, he smiles, and I feel a fraction of inner peace for the first time in hours.

No, *years*.

Putting my bag on the bonnet, I shove my hands in my pockets and look around the services car park.

"When was the last time you were here?" John asks, striding towards me with two large coffees and two shots of espresso. He downs the shots first, one after another, then chases them down with a mouthful of cappuccino.

"The cemetery or Peterborough in general?" I query, knowing precisely what he means.

"Both."

"Well, both are the same answer. Twenty-three years."

I train my eyes on the ground, because if Lorraine thinks she is a mother of the worst kind, I know I'm not too far behind. She might have left her daughter to fend for herself because she was weak, but I left mine to slowly rot alone because I was too frightened of money and power.

431

"You buried her and never came back?" he asks, disbelieving. My earlier thoughts come back to haunt me because he's unintentionally calling me out.

"John…"

"How could you do that?"

"You don't understand-"

"You're damn right I don't! What you did for Kara, risking having your arse thrown in prison, harbouring a runaway. Everything you did, and still, you left your Faith alone for twenty-three years."

"You don't underst-"

"So, make me!" He cuts me off again. "Make me understand why the most amazing, selfless woman I've ever met, can suddenly turn into a heartless bitch in seconds!"

"That's not fucking fair!"

He slams the disposable cup down on the bonnet, grips his hips and walks an invisible line up and down.

"No, but it's the truth. And they're right, aren't they? The truth hurts!"

"You know, I always thought Joe's words cut to the bone-"

"Don't you fucking dare compare me to him!"

"But you can be a real bastard, too." I take a breath. "If it's easier, just drop me at the station, and I'll make my own way home. You were right; I don't want to hate you, but if you really want this bitch's honestly, the more I stand here, it's starting. Just get in the car and go, John."

He snaps his head around, marches towards me and pushes me up against the side of the 4x4. "No, you don't get rid of me that easily! I love you like I've never loved another, and yesterday your ex-bastard enjoyed beating me down. Now, I'm going to go into this shithole behind me and get us a room for the night, and you're finally going to tell me about Faith. And I want to know all about Joseph, his mother, his father. Everything. Understand?"

"Fine. You want it, you'll get it!" I march back into the café and yank out my phone. "Hi, I need you to do something for me. Can I come and see you tomorrow?"

Chapter 40

I TIGHTEN THE towel at my chest and finally exit the bathroom. John is pacing up and down in front of the window, remote in hand, deep in thought. Sensing he is being watched, he stops and throws down the controller.

"I ordered some dinner." He sits down at the small table and taps his fingers repetitively. I know he wants me to start purging myself, but I don't know where to begin. After a few tense minutes, I sit down opposite.

"We can sit here in silence for eternity if need be. We're not going anywhere until you talk to me."

"Joseph-"

"I already know more than I want to about the waste of space that is Joseph Beresford. Dom sent me an inbox full of shit about him. Yesterday, I sat in Richmond Park reading it."

"Oh," I murmur because I honestly thought he would've been in a pub getting tanked.

"Tell me about Faith," he asks, staring down at her picture again on the table.

The distant whisper of carefree giggles filters through my mind, forcing its way back from the void. The delicate memory of blonde curls billowing in the breeze and the scent of strawberries envelops my mental senses. A glorious smile instantly brightens my face, because, in my mind's eye, she's so real, I can almost reach out and touch her again.

"She was beautiful, John. So, so beautiful. Sweet and adorable, and every time I looked at her, I knew what love was," I tell him, touching the picture I no longer have to hide. "I didn't have her for long enough, and I'd give up everything for just one more day with her. Even just an hour or a minute. I took the time I had with her for granted, but like any parent, I never thought I would have to bury my child." I sigh sadly as he gives me a sorrow filled stare. "Before she died, I got to hear her call me mummy. And I'll always remember how she would smother me with sloppy kisses, and how she would pat my cheeks when we played."

He shakes his head, stroking the old picture again. "Strong genes," he says rhetorically, capturing my gaze.

"Yeah," I reply because Faith was my mirror image when I was little.

John's fist suddenly thumps down on the table, and he snorts angrily. "Did that bastard ever touch her?"

"No," I confirm. "He would beat me in private, until the day he completely broke me and battered me in front of her. She held on to the spindles of the cot and told me not to cry. It was that moment I knew I had to save her, and the following day I went to the police."

I stare at him with watery eyes, his sanity is hanging on by a thread. It is further confirmed when he shudders out a breath.

"I've read the death certificate, but I want you to tell me. How did she die, angel?"

And that is my undoing.

As I glance around the hotel room, with its scuffed walls, chipped woodwork and stained carpet, it's fitting that I'm going to air my most private confession in a dingy room, overlooking a grim motorway services.

Closing my eyes, I allow the memories of my Faith to rise from the dead. One after another comes and goes, until the penultimate one sticks.

"Play, Mummy, play!" Faith shouts from the cot as I finish packing the last few items into the bag. Taking a peek at the clock, it's almost midnight.

"Mummy!" she calls again, and I watch as she rolls on to her back and kicks her jammie-clad legs high. Using all her might to shift Mr Blue, she lets out a sound of discontent when he doesn't move her way.

Folding my arms over the top rail, I smile, realising these are definitely the terrible twos. But knowing my luck it will probably carry on through the threes, fours, and beyond.

"Come to Mummy, Fay bear," I encourage her, and she does what I call the commando crawl on her belly. Hoisting herself up, she bounces and reaches for me. I swing her into my arms, and the scent of strawberry shampoo from her bath earlier drifts into my nostrils.

"Bad Mr Boo," she says sternly, still unable to say blue. Although, bizarrely, she doesn't have any difficulty vocalising her other demands.

Bending down, I grab the arm of the bear and settle him between us. Adjusting her small body on my hip, she squirms, still wanting playtime.

"Baby, you're getting heavy," I tell her as she continues to grapple against me.

"Down, Mummy!" she demands in all her two-year-old enthusiasm.

"No, Fay bear. You need to get your beauty sleep, and we need to be ready when the policeman comes to take us to our new home in the morning," I say anxiously. But truthfully, my anxiety has grown over the course of the day. The only thing keeping me going is the fact that Joe has finally been arrested without bail.

In eight hours, we will finally be free.

I rock Faith back and forth and blow raspberries on her cheek, invoking fits of laughter, until playtime is forgotten.

"You're not going to go back to sleep, are you?" I ask her, and she laughs in response. "Didn't think so." I smile and kiss her cheek. "Let's watch the fireworks, baby."

Moving to the window, I draw back the curtains as colour paints the night sky. Faith's face lights up in delight since this is the first time she has seen fireworks.

"Pretty," she says, her little hand touching the pane, completely enraptured by the premature celebrations. I drag over her playpen and stand her in it with Mr Blue and go to grab the bag from the bed. As I heft it on to the landing, the front door opens.

"Marianne? Marianne!" The scream of my name echoes up from the hallway below as the door slams shut, and horror consumes me.

"Oh, no!" I whisper in terror. Dashing into the bedroom, I snatch up Faith, who clutches the bear's arm.

I lodge a chair against the door and fumble with the phone. Dialling nine nine nine, I wait for someone to answer as the sound of doors slam downstairs.

"Marianne!" Joe calls out, enraged. "Where are you? I'm going to fucking kill you!"

"Police emergency?"

"My name's Marianne Beresford, and my husband is threatening to kill me!" I tell her in panic. Quickly giving her the address, Joe's feet beat hard on the stairs, getting closer and closer. "Please hurry!" I throw down the phone and clutch Faith, who is still holding Mr Blue.

"I'm going to fucking kill you, bitch!" Joe screams out, and the adjacent bedroom door opens.

"It'll be okay," I say to Faith, who is crying hysterically. "It'll be okay." I stroke her hair repeatedly, trying to calm her down. "Don't cry, baby," I whimper in desperation as Joe stops outside the room.

"Open this fucking door!" he barks out, and the door handle rattles against the force of the chair.

Seconds later, the wood cracks and the chair flies back. Joe barrels inside and hurls himself towards us. I move quickly, skirting the perimeter of the room.

"You've been telling lies! Did you think they wouldn't release me?" His eyes widen in hate and fury.

I shake my head and my face screws up as tears flood my eyes.

It's too late.

"Joe, please, don't do this. Not in front of Faith!" My motherly instinct kicks in as he grabs me, and I hold her tight while he wraps his hand around my throat and squeezes. "I can't breathe!" I say, strained, suffocating.

"You've fucking ruined my life!" he says, walking us backwards out of the room and onto the landing. I tilt my head, causing my airway to constrict further when I see the top of the stairs nearing. "But not for much longer."

"Please, don't!" I scream. "Don't let us fall!"

At the top of the stairs, my heel rocks on the edge, registering the drop below. My arm tightens around Faith as tears stream down her cheeks, and she wails as the bear drops, bouncing off each step until he reaches the bottom and rolls across the floor.

Gasping for breath, I shake, terrified, as Joe pushes me back and forth with his hand at my neck.

"People fall down the stairs all the time. It was an accident," he says to himself thoughtfully.

"Somebody help me, please!"

"Shout all you want, bitch, but no one can fucking save you!"

"Joe, please! Don't let us fall!" I scream again. "Don't let us fall!"

His eyes flash black in cruel satisfaction while I continue to beg and plead for mine and Faith's lives. Pulling me back from the edge, he presses his nose to mine and huffs out in anger.

"Beg me!"

"Please! I swear, if you let us go, you'll never hear from me again. You can forget all about us. I'll never ask you for anything. Please!" I cry out. "Let us go!"

The instant the last word tumbles from my lips, his other fist shoots out, pummelling my face. My eye explodes in fire, my footing falters, and my body lurches back.

"NO!" I scream in vain, and the excited countdown from the neighbouring properties is the sound of my fate.

"Ten! Nine!"

My arms instinctively wrap around my distraught baby - now covered in my blood - determined to protect her at all costs, as we drop some thirty feet from top to bottom.

"Seven! Six!"

Halfway down, my arm smashes against a step, and the high-pitched wail of a terrified child turns to silence.

"Three! Two!"

My arms are empty the moment my body hits the floor, and my skull rebounds against it as I land in a crumpled heap.

"Happy New Year!"

The world weaves in and out of consciousness, and my body battles to stay alert, fighting hard against the darkness waiting to consume me.

"Oh, fuck!" Joe sprints down the stairs in a panic and stops at the bottom. He grabs hold of his head in his scrunched hands and screws up his face. "Fuck, fuck, fuck!" He screams repeatedly.

"Joe, help Faith!" I cry out as loudly as I can. "Help her. Please!"

He stands above me and shakes his head. "This is all your fucking fault! I'm not going down for this. You dropped her. You did this!" He then turns, cowardly running away from the scene of his crime. The door slams shut behind him, leaving me alone inside the cavernous hollow of the hallway.

"Faith?" I call but receive no response. The sound of her crying has long gone, yet it's still ringing inside my head.

It is a sound I shall never forget.

It is the sound of personal failure.

Auld Lang Syne seeps faintly into the house, and I press my cheek against the cold, hard floor. The silence is a revelation. A stark, cold awakening that will stay with me until the grave. For the last few years, the single most terrifying thing I've feared has finally materialised. And the stillness surrounding me tells me I have nothing left to fight for.

To live for.

"Faith?"

The pain throbbing at my insides is unimaginable. But it isn't the pain of the fall, cutting a resolute path through my limbs or coursing down my spine. It's the pain of a future I had once planned meticulously, but one I shall now face alone.

"FAITH!"

I hiss sharply as fire burns in my abdomen. Rolling over, it feels like my insides are about to drop out. As I lower my eyes to my jeans, heat leaks down my legs from between my thighs. A small patch of blood seeps through, but I have no time to be concerned about myself.

I turn onto my front and crawl over to Faith. "NO!" I scream out in vain. "Please, God, no!" Grasping hold of her lifeless body, I drag her over my lap. Forgetting about the pain cutting like knives at my stomach, I twist her head the right way and rock her, like I've done countless times in the past.

My tears fall in rivulets, mourning a life I couldn't protect. "I'm sorry," I whisper. "Please forgive me." The words continue to escape my mouth until I can't suppress the devastation and I scream them out in vain, praying for someone to save her.

Pressing my lips to her forehead, the front door slams open and multiple feet enter. A single set stop and a shocked gasp kills the empty, haunting sound of nothingness.

A crackle of electricity fills the air as someone finally speaks. "I've got two casualties..."

The voice fades away while the disorientation I was beginning to experience is instantly vanquished. Knowing we don't have much time left together, I forget the commotion flooding around me, and gently lean my head to the side and inhale her unique, irreplaceable scent.

The sound of sirens echoes in the distance and blue lights illuminate the darkness outside as I hold her tight. Minutes turn into seconds until a paramedic is in front of me. "I tried to save her." I cry as my heartbreak renders me inconsolable. But in reality, I was never enough to save her.

My arms slacken around her body in defeat, and the paramedic cautiously reaches forward.

"NO!" I scream, refusing to let him touch her and I tighten my grip again. Sinking my face into her neck, I keep my eyes trained on him. His frustration is identifiable; the hardness of his stance, the clenched hand on his hip.

Closing my eyes, every memory that has brought us here assaults me. I tried, God knows I did. I tried so fucking hard to escape this, but escape is futile when sanctuary doesn't exist.

"Marianne?"

I look up, acknowledging the soft call of my name to see a familiar face. He represents security. He represents a decision I made too late.

I stare at him and the handful of paramedics behind him, growing impatient to do their job. A job that is now decreed useless, because there is no longer a life here to be saved.

"They need to look at her, sweetheart," Adrian says sadly, already knowing, like I do, there is no hope remaining. I knew on the fall she wouldn't make it. I knew it when my own body hit the floor. And I knew it the instant the crying stopped to give way to the sound of deathly silence.

She never stood a chance.

And it's all my fault.

"Adrian," I whimper, shaking my head. "She didn't..." A wail leaves my throat, and I gasp for oxygen that I feel guilty for still being able to breathe.

"I know, honey. I know."

"No, you don't. I didn't protect her. I didn't save her!" I scream out. "She's...she's..." I can't vocalise the awful truth, and he knows it when he touches my shoulder in comfort.

"I know, sweetheart, but they still need to examine her. Will you let me hold her?" he asks with sorrow filled eyes.

I look back down at my baby, relax my hold and lift her up to him. The pain ravishes my body, and I release an agonising cry as he quickly takes her from me. He tenderly wipes the bloodied, tangled strands of hair from her forehead and carefully passes her to a paramedic.

With nothing left to apply my grief to, my own pain is unavoidable. I press my palms against my stomach as pain deepens in my belly. Another paramedic squats down in front of me and frowns in concern as I sit in a pool of my own blood.

"How long?" she asks.

"Nine or ten weeks, I think." It sounds pathetic, but I haven't been to see a doctor, although my suspicions have been there for a while now.

"What's your name, honey?"

"Marianne."

"How old are you, Marianne?"

My eyes meet hers when I answer. "Nineteen."

Her jaw tightens inexplicably, and she nods and snaps on some gloves. I gaze over her shoulder as she starts rummaging through her supplies.

Aside from the obvious miscarriage, my arm is also weak. I hadn't noticed it at the time, but just like my stomach, now that I have nothing else to fix my attention on, I feel it.

"Are you able to stand?"

I nod half-heartedly and grip her arm as a stretcher is wheeled towards us.

Just as I am about to lie down, I see Adrian in the corner of my eye, bending down to pick up the bear. But it isn't his action that piques my attention, nor the hard lines creasing his face, it's the way he clenches the bear tight, then closes his eyes and subtly crosses himself.

Curious, I press my hands on the stretcher and angle my weak body. My mouth slowly falls open in absolute fucking horror as a sheet of fabric is draped over my baby. But, again, it isn't the sight of the two men wearing bomber jackets with CORONER emblazoned across the back that is my undoing, it's the moment they adjust the sides of a black body bag and zip it up.

"Oh. My. God," I whisper, silently wishing He would take me away with her because there's nothing left in this world for me now.

"Marianne, no!" Adrian calls out.

"FAITH!" I run towards her, but the world disintegrates into black around me, and my body smashes against the cold floor for the second time tonight.

The faint pulse bleeds into my hearing, rousing me from the subliminal place where I have found a tiny fragment of peace. Shifting on the mattress, a doctor is milling around the room.

"I'm sorry, did I wake you?" She gives me a friendly smile.

"No," I reply hoarsely. Lifting my arm, I almost knock myself out with the plaster that has been moulded and set while I was out of it.

"Don't worry, it's a clean break. You should be out of that in the next six weeks or so," she says. "You have some extensive bruising, and aside from the gash to your temple and the broken arm, I would say you're a very lucky girl, Marianne."

I press my lips together in fury. That's not exactly a word I would use to describe my situation right now.

"Your family are here. I'll go get them for you. They're probably worried sick."

I suppress the urge to bark out a laugh. Two assumptions have been levied on me in the last few minutes; two that couldn't be further from the truth if she tried. Still, I must keep up appearances. After all, I can't have the good Father's name tarnished any further, can I?

Dropping my hands to my belly, I breathe deep. "Did I miscarry?" The words come out in a whisper, but I already know the answer.

"Yes, I'm very sorry. The trauma of the fall-"

"I know." I know precisely what type of trauma came in the wake of it, and I will live with it every day. And that's the hardest part because I don't know how I shall cope with it every day. To have something so precious suddenly taken away in the blink of an eye.

She bestows me a sympathetic smile, and the door opens, and Mum and Maggie enter. "I'll leave you alone." The doctor then leaves.

"Mum!" I cry, inconsolable. Mum drops her bag from her shoulder and embraces me.

"I'm sorry, darling. I'm so sorry," she says, heartbroken, her hand rubbing up and down my back. "I know you loved her more than life. This is all my fault. I wish I hadn't listened to your fath-"

"No," I stop her, while Maggie shuffles behind, wiping her eyes. She still has some respect for him, and until she experiences it for herself, I won't be the one to further strip away at his varnished façade.

"Maggie." I hold out my broken arm.

"Faith," is all she needs to say, because she was as much theirs as she was mine, regardless that my father refused to acknowledge her existence.

The door opens as I am comforted in the warm cocoon of my mother and sister, and my father steps inside. His judgemental, condescending eyes flit between the three of us. I feel myself cower under his disapproving glare until my mother turns and scowls at him. The show of disparagement he has for her is blatant. Once she was a meek woman, the type to stand behind him and agree wholeheartedly, whether he was right or wrong.

But I changed that.

Granted, before today, she was still the same in his presence. She would not open her mouth and dare to speak against him. But the path of destruction I had dared to venture down proved that she could still voice her opinion when the time called for it. And right now, it's calling.

Maggie, intuitively sensing something has just shifted in the family dynamic, slowly backs away from the bed.

"Norman, don't. This isn't the time," Mum says, but he ignores her.

The tick of the wall clock fills the uncomfortable atmosphere building between us. "Just spit it out!" I hiss maliciously.

"I forgive you, Marianne. Just like God will eventually forgive you."

I can feel my eyes bulge in fury that he is choosing now, while my daughter's body lays cold and alone on a mortuary slab, to do this. After what I have been through, I don't give a fuck if he, or God, forgives me or not.

"How dare you?" I grit out. "How dare you come here and say that to me? So easily you forget that you abandoned me when I needed you. I haven't done anything to be in need of forgiveness!"

"Still thinking of only yourself, I see. You have no idea the shame you have brought upon this family!" he raises his voice in agitation.

"What family?" I yell. "This stopped being a family when you kicked me out. I made a mistake, but it didn't warrant you throwing me onto the streets. I was sixteen! And regardless of any wrongdoing I may have committed in your eyes, I needed you!" After three years of my 'mistake' being shoved down my throat, I've finally had enough. "And in case you've forgotten, that mistake was your flesh and blood, too!"

"Enough!" he shouts.

"No! I don't care anymore. For years you forced your beliefs on me, but I've never felt like I belong in your world, and that's because I don't. I believe in heaven and hell. I believe there is a God, but I don't believe I will be banished from paradise for wanting to know what it feels like to love, to live. The last three years haven't always been great, but I've lived, I've loved, and I've lost - more than I ever thought I could. And your precious God can't change any of that."

Glaring at my father, he shows no emotion whatsoever. He has always been a hard man. A strong believer in his faith, never faltering in his robust character or will. And for the first time in my life, in this moment, I realise just how much I hate him for it. I hate that he can stand in church every Sunday and preach. I hate that he will console one of his congregation in their time of need, yet he will not practise the same with Maggie or me. And I hate, I absolutely fucking hate, that he thinks I deserve his forgiveness.

"You choose this life for yourself, and one day, God may forgive you for it."

"Get out!" I shout because there is nothing left here for him to dictate to. I've made my bed, I'll lie it in, but I refuse to die of his so-called shame in it. "I said, get out!"

I subtly glance at Mum and Maggie. I can't have them bearing the brunt of his rage again because of me.

"I love you." I reach out to Mum and embrace her.

"I love you, too. I'll be back tomorrow but call me if they discharge you in the meantime." She kisses my forehead and lets me go.

"Okay." I look over her shoulder, and Maggie steps forward.

"I love you, Marianne," she whispers and throws her arms around me. I reciprocate her hold and clench my hands on her shoulders. "None of this is your fault. You were an amazing mother and Faith loved you. Always remember that."

My eyes instantly water and I purse my lips against her neck. Regardless of her opinion, whether it is the truth or not, right now I all I feel is failure.

"I love you, too. Take care of Mum." Maggie's arms drop, and she gives me a look of sincere confusion. While she may not be aware of my reasons for saying it, the reality is valid. And there's a very real possibility she may see him raise his hand to Mum again tonight.

My eyes flit to my father, who stands ramrod straight.

"The fallen cannot be saved, but I shall pray for your redemption, Marianne."

A hard thump hits the bed, and I look down at the bible. I shake my head because its teachings – in his eyes – failed me long ago.

"Don't bother!" I chortle scornfully, pick it up and throw it across the room.

I turn around and count silently until they leave. I make it bang on four when the door slams shut.

With a sigh of relief, I force myself to climb out of bed. Edging towards the window, I press my forehead to the glass while the deluge of rain descends the heavens. All I can do now is think, and reminisce, and wonder what might have been.

I pick up the Bible and climb back into bed. Cocooning myself within the sheets, I flip through the pages, until I stop upon a verse I wish I hadn't. Closing it, I glance back to the window as the stark fluorescent lights overhead illuminate my hair, creating a golden glow. It's a paradox that is almost angelic.

Except, I know that's another lie since this angel has sinned. And one day I may find myself cast out of paradise, because the penultimate words of my father may eventually ring true.

Chapter 41

"THE FALLEN CANNOT be saved?" John's incredulous tone wheedles its way into my reverie.

I reluctantly open my eyes while a solitary tear rolls down my cheek. Stretching my neck from side to side, my eyes meet his. Wearing a shocked yet furious expression, his hand covers his mouth, seemingly in despair.

"That's one of the last things he ever said to me," I confirm in a defeated tone. "And he was right because I've spent years trying to repent and look where it's got me. It was all for nothing."

John inhales deeply and rubs his hand over his eyes, attempting to disguise his tears. This is only the third time I've seen him cry. The first when Kara was taken, the second when I was hospitalised after the assault, and today. And it breaks my heart that he is crying for a child that isn't his.

Still, it's probably a damn sight more than Joe ever did.

The sound of a lorry horn blares from outside in the rush of traffic. I open my mouth to continue, but I shut it again because it doesn't get any easier.

"Go on," he requests softly, unlike last night when he spat it at me.

"Two days later, Joe was arrested, and they charged him with murder and attempted murder. His father," I pause and laugh singularly in recollection. "Yet again, demanded they release his son. But this time they held him without bail until the trial. Four weeks later, on a cold winter's day, I buried my daughter, while he ranted at me from across the cemetery with a handful of witnesses who had already deemed me to be a terrible mother as well as the town slut."

"That son of a bitch!" He bangs his fist down on the flimsy table, inducing it to wobble. "Angel, I need a minute."

"No. I didn't get one, so you don't either. This is what you've always wanted, and now you've got it." I push the chair back and walk to the window. Gazing over the fields that frame the motorway, my faint reflection reflects back, and I raise my hand to my temple.

"That very same day, I boarded a train and reinvented myself as Marie Dawson. Five months later, I was forced to see him again at the trial where I was subsequently ripped to shreds in the witness box by his barrister. They described me to be an unfit mother. That I was more concerned about living my teenage years than taking care of my child. And his mother… My God! His mother concurred and gave a glowing repertoire of her son's kind, loving nature and genteel character." I impersonate the heartless bitch verbatim.

"A few white lies are easily seen through, darling," he says, causing me to glare at him undeservingly.

"A few white lies?" I repeat, my eyes wide. "John, the bitch went to town on me. It was a character assassination! She portrayed me to be a whore, spouting out that I was a heartless cheat and that Joe had done everything he could to save the marriage. She said I was a teenage temptress, determined to destroy the reputation of a wealthy family's only son because he had grown bored of me. She even made a comment that my own family were ashamed and that's why they refused to give evidence or even attend the trial. For two days, I had to defend myself against a barrage of lies. Truthfully, it would have been less painful if Joe had stood up and beaten me to death in front of them!" I huff out angrily.

"Obviously the jury didn't believe it."

I laugh in pity and amusement. "But they did. I could see it in their eyes with every cruel barb his barrister stuck me with."

"How did they manage to find him guilty then?" he asks curiously.

"Because he fell apart upon giving his evidence. The prosecution pushed him until he snapped. And as my barrister declared in court, you can't teach an old dog new tricks. Subsequently, Joe changed his plea to involuntary manslaughter when he realised his parents couldn't influence the outcome or buy the jury. He claimed diminished responsibility. He said he didn't remember much about that night, and that he had a *moment*. He was given a total of twenty-four years for involuntarily manslaughter and GBH."

"The bastard should have gotten life."

"Yes, he should. Still, I'm lucky. His behaviour inside ensured he served the full sentence, and Maggie confirmed he was released just before last Christmas." I rotate from the window and lean my backside on the ledge, my cathartic cleansing finally complete. "And that's all of it, John. All my sins laid bare for scrutiny."

"I wish you'd have told me," he says softly, and I shrug because I wish I had too. But wishing can't change the past.

"How do you do that?" I query, more to myself than him.

"Do what?"

"Explain to someone that you allowed your child to die? That you could have prevented it and didn't? How do you do that and not have someone judge you?"

His express mellows, and he furrows his brow. "I don't know," he replies after a long pause, possibly judging me.

"I tried, but I was too late. I contemplated going to the police sooner, but I was terrified they would take her away from me. He never left any evidence of his assaults so it would have been his word against mine. And the truth is I've never been good with words. What should I have said to make him stop? No? Please? Don't? Would they have worked?" I ask myself. "I could go on and on about what I should have said and done. Maybe if I had begged for mercy, she might still be alive today, and-"

"You would be dead instead." John halts my rumination. "And Faith would have been left with a monster."

"It's still my fault," I tell him.

He shakes his head, his face contorting in annoyance. "I don't understand why you keep blaming yourself."

My hands ball into fists, and I shake them in anger. "That's because you're not listening! Words get lost in translation."

"I don't-"

"I told him to let us go!" I shout out. "And he did!"

"Calm down, angel. Calm down!" He quickly moves in front of me.

"I told him to let us go," I repeat again, heartbroken. With his arms cradling me and his forehead against mine, he presses a kiss to my lips.

"Let it out, beautiful. I won't let you go."

Tears fog my vision and my nose runs unmercifully. I hiccup, pull back and wipe my nose with my hand.

"At least I don't have to pretend anymore. I can display her pictures in the house. I can talk about her openly. I can celebrate her birthday and mourn her death. I no longer have to lie my way through the darkest days in my diary."

"No," he whispers with a sad smile. Wiping away my tears with his thumbs, his thoughtful countenance turns solemn as he caresses my jaw. "Did he do this?"

I nod. "In the nightclub. I'm sorry I lied to you."

"No, I understand," he whispers again. "I was a bastard to you yesterday and the look on your face when you thought I was going to strike you... I swear I would never lay a hand on you."

"I know," I agree. "And I feel terrible for how I reacted, but I don't blame you. I can imagine how he taunted you for his own enjoyment. Like I said to Maggie weeks ago, his words cut more than his fists ever could."

He tugs me close, and peppers kisses over my face. It's soothing and loving, and I want to believe in long forgotten fairy tales. I want to believe we will get through this, but I'm not such an idiot to believe the recriminations won't run deep within him.

I curl my arms around his waist, press my cheek to his chest and close my eyes. "John, where do we go from here?"

"Angel, stop thinking. We'll survive this. I meant what I said, there is no end for us, only death. However, I do have one final question I want you to answer." I inch back cautiously. "Are you divorced?"

I release a sigh of relief. "Yes."

"So why is he bleating on that you're still married?"

"Because he never signed the papers, so as far as his warped mind is concerned, we are." He frowns in confusion, and I place my finger over his lips. "In the eyes of the law, it's been final for eighteen years. After Joe was locked up, I sent him fresh papers every month for three years, and each time they came back unsigned."

"Oh, he's a fucking piece of work!"

"You have no idea," I reply because I can't disagree with that. "Anyway, when I obtained the business loans, my solicitor told me I could dispense service through the court without his consent since we'd been separated for five years. So, I did. The day the decree came through my letterbox, it was the biggest relief I'd ever felt. I was free. I mean, I had been for years, but that day it was legal and binding, and I could start living again."

"But you didn't start living," John counters. "You've remained trapped in that place of desolation where he left you for two decades. You were still trapped in there an hour ago."

I inhale in resentment that he is spelling out what I already know. "I know, but for three years, it was just Faith and me, and then I was alone. But whatever happens when we leave here, whether we survive this or not, I have people who care. It's taken me years to see that, but I'm not alone anymore."

A strange sense of relief washes over me. I have given him what he asked for – I've let him in. As per Remy's words, it would be my choice if I let him back out, but I haven't. And by the time we leave here, I will know where I stand inside this man's heart.

Gauging him, I wonder if I will be house hunting alone next week. I wonder if the fallout will banish me into the cold. Regardless, I will never regret disclosing all of this, because the burden of truth has finally been lifted. Now, I no longer have to walk the fine line with my emotions or stress about if my secrets will be laid bare today.

"What about your parents?"

I blink a couple of times, bringing myself out of my procrastination. "What about them?" I ask quietly.

"I don't understand how any father could stand by and let his daughter be hurt and left to fend for herself," he says, repulsed. "Especially with a child."

"My father didn't want to know. My mother and sister were there for me when I needed them, but I acted like I had it all sorted because I knew my mum would suffer if my dad found out. Truthfully, there were days I struggled to cope."

A knock comes to the door, and John shouts for them to enter. Extracting myself from his arms, a member of staff pushes a trolley inside.

"I didn't know what to order, so I got a few things. I hope you're hungry," he says.

Striding to the bed, I open my purse and slip the gentleman a tenner for his gratitude.

"Thank you." He winks and closes the door.

"This isn't the kind of place you tip, angel," John says, sidling behind me. His hand drifts down my backside, and massages gently. I smile because his little gesture has inadvertently validated I haven't shattered everything. And for that, considering what he has had to come to terms with, I'm grateful.

"No, but hospitality staff get paid shit. He's earned it."

Perusing the plates, I don't know what I fancy. Choosing the dish of spag bol, I sit back at the table. My stomach churns upon the first mouthful entering it. This is the first meal I've eaten in... I can't remember, but there's only so long the body can survive on sympathy coffee.

"Do your family still live here?" he queries, and I almost choke.

"Why do you ask?" I swallow hard.

He shrugs. "I just thought you might want to see them after all this time."

"I do, but…" I sigh.

He stops cutting his chicken fillet and gives me a pointed look. "But what?"

"It's been twenty-three years, and it will be hard enough to see my mother again, but I don't want you getting on your high horse with Maggie."

"What on earth are you talking about?" he mutters. "I won't say how I really feel!"

I throw my arms up. "Well, that's a relief, isn't it?" I mutter sarcastically. "Just promise you won't air your views."

"What views?" He recommences slicing. "The only thing I never talk about is religion. You know that."

"Precisely. I didn't want you offending her."

Absorbing my words for a moment, he lowers his fork. "What? Is she part of a cult or something?" he asks flippantly.

I roll my eyes. "No, but I guess it depends on who you ask."

"You're not talking sense."

"My sister is a vicar."

"C of E?"

I nod. "My father is-"

"A bastard," he retorts, very matter of fact.

"I thought you weren't going to say what you really feel?" I ask, waving my knife, in exasperation.

He grimaces; he isn't used to holding his tongue. "Fine! I'll keep my mouth shut. So, your father?"

"Is also a vicar. Although I think he might be retired now - if there is such a thing. Knowing my luck, he's probably still preaching chapter and verse."

"Christ! Your family are all bible bash-"

"John!" I shout, silencing him immediately. His eyes flick to me, and I scowl, because whilst I turned my back on religion, I will never ridicule someone else for finding their strength in it.

"Tread carefully, Walker. I appreciate the things you've have seen in those lawless, godless countries you've toured in, and I wouldn't bestow that upon anyone, but the church, in all its different forms, means a lot to different people. People find their love there, their peace and strength there. I might be faithless and not garner the same views these days, but I wouldn't dare begrudge someone for believing. And I won't have my sister made to feel inferior because you have an opinion that is neither right nor wrong. So, when you meet her tomorrow, keep that talk to yourself," I admonish, as he slowly takes on a vacant, open-mouthed expression.

"Tomorrow?"

"I called her earlier. I wasn't planning on coming all this way not to see her. And not only her, but my mother, too. She doesn't have long left, and I need her to know that I never stopped loving her. And I want you there with me, so she knows I finally found the love I had always craved."

"Shit," he breathes out. "You know this isn't how I expected to finally meet the in-laws."

"No, but Maggie was determined to get her reunion," I mutter, reaching over to the food trolley for the chips.

I prop my foot on the seat, as John leans over and snatches up my ankles and puts my legs on his knees. Gliding his hands up and down my calves, he massages them leisurely.

"I always thought that I could get past anything that was thrown at me, but you... Just when I think I have you all figured out, you give me something else to chew on."

My breathing mellows, and I dip a chip in mayo and pop it in my mouth.

"You'll complain you're putting on weight next week," he comments, as I devour another.

I shrug. "Hopefully, next week I might still have a strong toyboy to work it off me."

"Toyboy?" he repeats in amusement. "I don't think four years qualifies me as toyboy material, angel. Seriously, is that really what you think?"

"I don't know. I guess it's what other people might think. What do I think? I think you are the most amazing man I've ever known. Do you want another truth?"

He raises his brow and looks uncertain. "I don't know if I can take hearing another one of those today."

I smile and pick up another chip. "I guarantee you'll like this one. You once asked me how many men I'd been with." I fall into a delightful reverie as he rubs my legs into hypnotic bliss.

"Go on, then. What number am I?"

Licking my fingers, I smile and press my toes into his hard thigh. "Two."

"Two?"

"You and Joseph. After losing Faith, I just didn't want to be with anyone. Love is painful, and sometimes you get nothing in return, so I choose a mundane, celibate lifestyle. That, and it was just easier to be alone."

After the last word has left my mouth, he lowers my legs and stands abruptly.

"John?" I murmur, wondering what I've said to upset him now.

He doesn't respond, and instead, he picks me up, and moves the four steps to the bed and throws me down. I quickly right the towel over my thighs for all the good it will do me. Still, if we are going into battle again, I'd rather not do it exposed.

At the edge of the bed, he carefully drops one knee down followed by the other. Crawling towards me with a slow, predatory pace, his body confines mine to the mattress.

"I like being number two," he confirms, huskily. "I like that I have the best of you. Something, by your own admission, you never gave him." He tucks his fingers into the knot at my chest. "Now, I'd like to make love to my angel."

"John, we still need to discuss where we go from here."

"We go forward. I promise I will never, ever speak to you the way I did yesterday. I will never bring up Faith, or any of this if we argue. Forgive me. Forgive me for all of it."

"Always," I manage to say before he steals my breath away. Claiming my mouth, his tongue rolls over mine, duelling together in the growing heat.

He sits up on his haunches and rips his shirt over his head. I shuffle up on my elbows and wrap my calves around his thighs. Stroking my hands down his chest, I trace the defined ridges with my fingertips, then fix my arms around his neck and force him back down. My breaths are already coming out laboured, while my head is hazy from his intoxicating pheromones.

Grappling with his belt, I tug it open along with the buttons of his jeans. Sliding my hand into his shorts, he's already hard, and I excite in the feel of him. My thumb brushes over his engorged head, capturing the accumulating moisture. Removing my hand, I lick my thumb innocently and smile.

"That's wicked, angel," he replies gruffly and divests himself of his jeans and shorts. Grabbing the front of my towel, he yanks it open. Positioning his knees at my inner thighs, he skilfully parts my legs.

A very naughty thought overcomes me, and I drag my finger from my lip down my chest. Circling my belly button, my body is on fire, and my core is already throbbing in anticipation of him entering me. I lower my finger teasingly, and I press it to my clit and brush slowly, methodically.

"If that was wicked, what do you call this?" I ask, elevating my chest up and using my other hand to stroke my nipple. His eyes darken desirously, and he reaches for my hand and places it on his hard length. Covering his hand over mine, he starts to pump.

"Sinning. But fuck, it's still worth it with you." He removes my hand from my apex and gently sucks on the offending finger. "It tastes good, too." And to prove it, he moves down the bed and places his mouth on my core.

I moan incoherently, my insides quivering as he pierces his tongue inside me and sucks my clit. I'm ready to fall off the edge into the sea of burning ecstasy with each lap and nip of his teeth.

Scratching my fingers over his hair, I rub my legs up and down his back, mesmerised by the feel of his taut muscles against my calves. Electricity spikes in my abdomen as he works me harder, and I squeeze my knees in response while I come apart hard and unremittingly.

"Oh, God!" I cry out and press my centre up to him. Holding my body down, he peers from between my legs and smirks.

He shifts onto his knees and thumbs my swollen folds in slow, firm strokes. Sliding two thick fingers into my centre, he sinks them in and out, preparing me for the inevitable, and I curl my hips in time. Wrapping his hand carefully around my throat, testing me, he captures my nipple in his mouth and sucks reverently until I can't take anymore. I let out another stifled cry as I press my head back and squeeze my eyes. My body continues to convulse in pleasure, and I twist the sheet in my hand, while my legs spread further in base response.

I rise up on my elbows, my body aching for him to fill it, and grip either side of his face and bring his mouth to mine. My tongue breaches his moist lips and fights for dominance.

Giving in to what I need, I reach down between us and palm his length. Moving in tandem with my hand, he throbs beautifully. Meeting his eyes, their dark and stormy blackness is captivating.

"Put me inside you, angel." Gently nestling him at my core, he nudges my tight opening, and I mewl at the feel of his tip breaching my already swollen, tender entrance.

"Hold on," he murmurs, and I grip him harder as he takes control and slams incredibly deep. So deep, in fact, my abdomen clenches and I moan in delight. In truth, as prim and proper as John sometimes likes to think I am, he also knows I do sometimes like it a little rough. Not enough to leave any lasting reminders, but to be controlled a little by someone you love is the most significant gift of trust you can ever give another.

My mouth parts and I dig my head back. Each exquisite plunge is a revelation because I've never felt this close or this potent, all-consuming connection before. It's a revelation because even my ex couldn't achieve the emotional bond I have now.

"Angel." John's strained tone pulls me back from the poignant precipice consuming my psyche. "Stop thinking."

I place my hands on either side of his cheeks and smile. "I'm right here with you. Always."

His expression changes with each ripple of his body inside mine, and he smiles and slows down. Inching in a fraction and receding back, he repeats this blissful torture until I'm a thoughtless, quivering wreck, ready to beg. Moaning out, I hitch my foot to his arse and hold him there while I mellow in the beauty of being fulfilled. But more than that, I mellow in the devotion he still has for me.

Time stands still as I rejoice in my internal revelation until he pulls me onto his thighs, forcing himself to penetrate me deeper.

His hand digs into my hair, and his dark stare burrows deep into my soul. All that was there before has finally dissipated, leaving nothing but love in its purest form.

"Do you want to know what I call this?" he whispers softly. "Paradise." I drop my head to his shoulder, and he grazes my chin. "Look at me, angel."

I look back up, and we stare into each other eyes. My breasts sweep over the fine hair coating his chest, while his hands make long sweeps up and down my back. Feeling my body spike yet again, I clamp my hand to his shoulder for leverage and twist him onto his back.

I sit astride him, and he grins mischievously and attempts to lift up, but I hold him down. Wagging his finger, I fall further forward, and he palms my breasts. My nipples, already painfully aroused, peak further, and he rubs and pinches them.

"Ride me, angel," he commands. Adjusting my legs around his strong, wide hips, I take him in a deep, satisfying thrust. I toss my head back and banish my inhibitions. Twisting my hips in a fluid motion, he grips my backside and slams me down harder.

"Don't hold back, beautiful," he says, playing my body so deep I can feel him hit my cervix. "Take what you need."

I straighten my spine, press my hands to his stomach and move fluidly atop of him. Moving in a figure eight motion, the fire ignites under my skin, and I spread my legs further as he slaps my backside before swiping a finger between my cheeks. Penetrating me gently, the awareness mounts and excites, and I move in a way to capture his touch in both areas.

Licking my dry lips, my throat ready to scream out, he swells inside me. Refusing to give in, not until I'm screaming the walls down, he tugs my nipple hard.

"Let go," he urges, pulsating, ready for release.

I shake my head and thrust my body up and down again and toy with his testicles, massaging and squeezing.

"Fuck!" he roars out and fills me with fire.

I continue to ride him until he abruptly withdraws and flips me over. He drags up my lower half and enters forcefully from behind in a swift motion. With his chest covering my back, I turn my head to the side, and his mouth finds mine. Digging my knees and forearms into the bed, fortifying my body, he influences me back until my bum is tight against his abdomen. With one hand on my chest and the other at my core, his strong body drives into me from below. I curl my hand around his as he mercilessly rubs my swollen clit while powering up repeatedly.

Dropping my head back onto his shoulder, I lose myself in the moment of being taken in every way possible, until the orgasm currently razing every cell, obliterates and I fall spectacularly over the edge.

"John! Oh, God!" I moan, convulsing. I press down further, needing him deeper, harder. *Forever.* An amazing shudder ripples through me as he licks up my spine to my nape.

"Let go, angel, that's it," he coaxes, nibbling the column of my throat.

Coming back down to earth, I jolt while he rubs the heel of his hand over my sensitive core.

"Too much, too much," I pant out, needing oxygen. Unable to hold myself where I am, I fumble for his arm and bring it around me. I crane my neck back, and he tilts my jaw to look at me.

"Beautiful, angelic and mine. Always mine," he says.

"Good, because I couldn't imagine my life without you in it."

He loosens his grip and slowly eases me forward. He withdraws, his length still firm, half-mast and throbbing, and I groan through a combination of desire and discomfort as he carefully lays me down. He settles on his side, and I fold my arms under my cheek and smile at him. Walking his fingers down the curve of my spine, he rims the small indentations at the base before drawing patterns on my bum.

"What are you thinking?"

"That I've made a lot of mistakes. With my family, with Kara… With you. Faith was never a mistake. Granted, the timing wasn't perfect, but she was. She was *my angel*. I guess the real reason why I threw caution to the wind and took Kara in, was because I needed someone to fill that gaping hole that had lived in my broken heart for years."

He rolls me onto my back, kisses my breast tenderly, before holding out my arm and pressing his lips up the inside. Eventually, he retreats back and smiles, highlighting his five o'clock shadow.

"We all make mistakes," he says and kisses me reverently. "And yesterday I nearly made the biggest one of them all. I'm man enough to admit when I'm wrong, and rather than forcing you to leave last night, I should have buried my own pain and let you air yours."

"No," I murmur sympathetically. I don't want him to continually rehash this, thinking it is an underlying issue. It will always be there, but I refuse to let it define us going forward.

I'm about to tell him so when he continues to air his own truths.

"I also have an intentional omission I need to confess. My ex-wife was my biggest mistake, and it cost me dearly. I've rarely spoken about her since she left, but the reason why I was so angry hearing you had a child yesterday was because she secretly aborted our baby at fifteen weeks."

My mouth slowly drops open. Now I understand why Jules said that John must be the one to tell me. From one mother to another, even when we both had babies fathered by monsters, abortion was never an option for either of us.

"Oh God, I'm so sorry, darling. No one should ever have to go through that."

"No, but in retrospect, I had a fortunate escape. It killed me to find out you had something I wanted. I didn't know where your child was, and Dom refused to tell me."

"Convenient," I mutter. "What an amazing friend he truly is; to allow you to wallow in your misery." I instantly regret saying it, because it just makes me a two-faced bitch when I conveniently did the same.

He shakes his head. "I know you hate him right now, but he did it to protect you. He said the less we all knew, the safer it was. He confirmed he had known about Faith and Joseph for years, ever since I first saw you and made a passing comment to him."

I sit upright and bite my lip since he has just partially reiterated words that Remy refused to elaborate on.

"Yesterday, Jeremy said Kara wasn't the only one being watched." I leave it hanging between us, wondering if he will give it to me straight. Tugging me onto his lap, he strokes my hair and studies me thoughtfully.

"When Sloan had me checking on Kara, there were days I would sit outside your house, hoping to catch a glimpse of you. It was wrong, but I was so drawn, I couldn't help myself. For far too long I watched you live your life from afar. And I was damn proud of you when you fisted that cocky shit who tried to assault Kara at her school disco."

"You saw that?" I ask in horror as he laughs.

"Yeah. I think I fell in love with you even more than I already was that night."

I shake my head. "I could have been arrested. It's nothing to be proud of."

"No, but you taught that little bastard a good life lesson on what happens to would-be rapists. No one would have faulted you for that."

"Maybe. And the day you forcibly barged your way into my house and offered to *manhandle my things?*" I smile, knowing I have the upper hand.

He breathes out content. "That offer was an excellent idea when I was sat in the car," he says, grinning sheepishly. "It took every ounce of control not to throw you down and do everything I'd fantasised about for years when I saw you were considering it."

"I wasn't considering it!" I lie.

He tips up my chin and brushes his thumb over my mouth. "Liar. Trust me, you would have called me more than an arse assaulting bastard if I had manhandled you. Up until that day, I wasted eight years waiting for Sloan to get his head out of his arse over Kara. Eight years that we could have been together. Looking back, I should have just planned to bump into you. It wouldn't have been hard, but I didn't out of respect for the kid. I once even had Jake hire you to cater an event so I could meet you, but you left early."

I stare into space and nod. "I remember," I murmur, recollecting the night Kara had a date from hell and called me in a state.

"I've waited eleven years to finally tell you all this," he says, staring into my eyes. Lifting my hand, he turns the ring on my finger. "I want you to proudly display this to everyone. I can't wait to see you walk down the aisle towards me. And I'll be holding your hand, telling you how amazing you are when you bring our children into the world."

I purse my lips together, crying tears of happiness. "I want all that, too."

He presses his hands to my stomach and studies my skin carefully. His inquisitive fingers follow the barely there, faint stretch marks – the only legacy of my pregnancy that he has never questioned before.

Kissing my hip bones, he massages my abdomen and taps. "You were never a fat child."

"No, I was as skinny as the days were long." I laugh.

Reaching down for the duvet, he covers us and wraps himself around me. Mouthing my neck, my eyes begin to close, and I hold his arm around me.

"How do you feel about tomorrow?" he asks quietly.

"I'm petrified," I confess.

"But you've already seen her recently."

"She's not why I'm petrified."

Chapter 42

"WHICH WAY?" JOHN asks, slowing down at the junction.

"Hmm," I bite the inside of my lip. "That way." I point right, having no idea where she lives.

"You don't sound too sure," he comments as he edges out.

"That's because I'm not." I turn to him, and he starts to open his mouth. "I haven't lived here for over twenty years. Things change." Opening the glovebox, it's empty. "Where's lying Lucy?" I ask, referring to the useless satnav.

"Locked in her cupboard at the office," he confirms. Closing the compartment, I scrunch my nose.

"This is like the blind leading the bloody blind. Did you or Remy not think to bring her on this little escapade?"

"No, darling. I'm sorry, my gin frazzled brain wasn't particularly functional when I kicked Sloan and Dev out yesterday morning and forced Rem into the car. Besides, she sends me in circles. Literally!"

Unzipping my bag, I pull out my phone and dial. "Hi," I greet when Maggie answers. "John's managed to get us lost." I smile broadly in response to his dirty look. Telling her the road of which we are currently driving blind on, she directs us, until some fifteen minutes later, we enter her street.

My heart is beating rapidly, and I clutch the belt at my chest and crane my neck as I see her standing outside a door six houses down. I can't contain my excitement, and I unbuckle prematurely, causing an alarm to ring out inside the car.

Before we have even stopped, I rip open the door and run at her full pelt. Halfway, I lose my footing on an unlevel paving stone and almost go arse over tit as I finally reach her.

"Maggie!" I cry in happiness and launch myself at her in a full body slam. Burying my face in her neck, I squeeze tight.

"Marianne," she whispers happily into my neck. I smile but don't reprimand her, because to her I'll never be anyone other Marianne, no matter how hard she tries with Marie.

The car door slams shut behind us and we both turn simultaneously to see John at the gate wearing an incredible smile. His eyes volley between us, seemingly trying to find a distinguishing feature. In truth, if not for the difference in attire, he wouldn't be able to tell us apart.

"He knows," Maggie says perceptively.

"He does." I give her a small smile. "He knows everything."

I curve my arm around her waist as we walk towards him. "John, this is Maggie. Maggie, John," I introduce them with blatant pride.

"It's great to finally meet you, Maggie," John says as he lifts his arm, uncertain if he should embrace her or shake her hand. Maggie, recognising his discomfort, touches his shoulder and plants a polite, welcoming kiss on his cheek. While she might be the mild-mannered vicar, she still carries the same fire inside that I do.

"It's nice to meet you, too," she says, stepping back.

"Well, I've heard a lot about you over the past few weeks." He grins, subtly absorbing her smart clerical attire of black tunic and trousers. His expression wanes inconspicuously, and I can tell he's cagey about being preached to.

Maggie brows lift, and she touches her collar, testing the waters of his distrust.

"And you," she says cunningly. "Hearing a lot about you, that is. Come on inside, I'll make us some tea." Giving my hand a final squeeze, she quirks her brow and turns. "Oh, John?" She looks back. "Don't worry, I won't indoctrinate you until the next visit."

I bite back a laugh, happy she still has the quirky sense of humour she did when we were younger.

She gives me a wink then heads back inside, leaving me standing with my subdued man.

"Well, there's not many things that can leave you speechless. Shall I invite her for Christmas dinner with the family?"

His brows tilt up in question, and he places his hand on the small of my back. Nearing the front door, I put my foot over the threshold, but he tugs my elbow.

"Angel, don't you ever jump out of a moving vehicle again. You could've been hurt."

I shrug with an innocent grin. "The car had almost stopped," I voice my case. "Besides, my sister is a vicar. She would've prayed and convened with God for my speedy recovery."

He laughs, impressed with my quick thinking, yet unimpressed with the end result.

"You pull that shit again, beautiful, you'll need more than a bleeding prayer and divine intervention when I've finished spanking your arse!" he says, rubbing my rear, before slapping it.

Hard.

Entering the house, I slip off my shoes. "Maggie?" I call out, my eyes flitting around, a nervousness creeping in.

"In the kitchen," she calls back.

I pad down the hallway, holding John's hand behind me when I stop.

"Are you okay?" he asks, faultlessly sensing my hesitation.

"Yeah, I am," I confess.

A glimmer of light catches my attention as I turn, and I stare at the picture of me, Maggie, and Faith. I pick up the picture as John body heat envelops my back and he lovingly rubs my shoulders.

"Faith." His fingers glide gently down the glass. "Mr Blue," he says knowingly, finally understanding the significance of the bear. "When we get home, I'll call around and see if we can get someone to repair him properly."

"John…" Salty tears instantly sting my eyes.

"Shush. Plenty of time to cry later, darling." I nod pathetically and wrap my arms around him. Caught up in the moment, the kitchen door moves back further.

"Are you two having second thoughts?" Maggie asks. Her happiness falters when she realises what we are looking at. Slowing approaching, she slugs the tea towel over her shoulder and smiles.

"Remember how we had to sit Mr Blue in front of her because she was covered in chocolate?"

I nod and purse my lips. "That was your fault. You spoiled her."

Maggie tuts and heads back into the kitchen. "That's what aunties are for!" she calls back.

I rub my hand over my face as John turns me in his arms. "Oliver is going to love her."

"Hmm, and the kids are going to need some divine intervention of their own not to kill her," I retort as he laughs and drags me into the kitchen.

Pulling out a chair, I smile when I see the Tupperware tub full of flapjacks and sponge cake on the worktop.

"I thought you no longer baked?" I ask, remembering our conversation over cheesecake months ago.

"I don't. One of the WI ladies made them for Mum," Maggie says, creating the perfect opportunity to broach *that* elephant in the room – amongst others. "Have some if you want. Mum will just pass them onto the staff."

I drop my eyes to my lap, not knowing what to say. I swallow, feeling like I have cut glass lining my throat as John rubs my knee.

"Don't mind if I do," he says as Maggie puts the container on the table and grabs a slice of cake.

"Babe, Victoria might have nothing on your sponge," he says between mouthfuls, snatching up a flapjack. "But you've got competition here. Tell me, Maggie, what does a man have to do to get one of those lovely WI women to hand over this recipe?"

"Mown the lawn, cut the privets and take her to Tesco," I quip, causing him to laugh.

"Just knocking on her front door might work, too." Maggie chortles as John winks at her.

"Don't encourage him," I plead. "I don't want to be responsible for giving some eighty-odd-year-old woman a heart attack."

"I don't know about that," John remarks. "She might die happy." He grins to himself.

Maggie laughs, puts down the teapot, then picks up a china cup. Sitting opposite, she watches intently as John interacts with me, shoving a piece of cake in front of me, of which I refuse.

"No? Liar, you love cake."

"I love being able to fit into my jeans, too."

Maggie clears her throat and lifts her cup. "When I saw you months ago, there were so many things we talked about. When I left, I still had a list of things I wanted to say, but now I can't remember any of them. I couldn't believe it when you called yesterday, but I'm glad you're here," she says, taking a sip of her tea.

"Me, too, but it wasn't exactly planned. Unforeseeable circumstances arose."

Her brows pitch together. "Joseph?" she queries.

"Unfortunately," I confirm, and turn to John, who scowls. "He finally decided to make his presence known."

"That's an understatement," John says, leaning back in the chair and looking around the kitchen. "The belligerent bastard turned up at my office."

"Oh, Marianne," she whispers compassionately.

"No, I didn't come here to talk about him, Maggie. I've spent the last forty-eight hours talking about him in painstaking detail. I can't do it anymore, and there's nothing left to say. Although there is something I need you to do." Her brow furrows, prominently lining her forehead. "I need you to tell him because I can't."

Maggie nods and unconsciously walks her fingers over the collar. I watch her intently under the growing tension until she eliminates the silence.

"So, what do you do for a living, John?"

"Commercial security, amongst other things."

"Other things?"

"Serving papers, locating people, that kind of thing," he says, pouring another cup of tea.

She lifts the cup to her lips and contemplates thoughtfully. "That sounds interesting and technical. Do you go to church?"

"No!" He laughs but reins it in. "I'm sorry, but no, I'm not religious. I'm ex-army. When you're discharged you either find faith that you're still alive or you damn God that your comrades are dead. I don't think there is an in between."

I cover my hand with my mouth, this was his expected reaction – and the reason I feared them meeting.

"Please, don't be offended. It wasn't meant as a slight. This," she says, touching her collar. "Makes some people uncomfortable. And considering we're now family, I just wanted to know your views on where I stand before I begin."

John gives her a half-cocked smile. "I appreciate your honesty, but neither the collar, nor the cross, nor the bible makes me uncomfortable. It's the holier than thou preaching I can't abide. Nevertheless, I have an abundance of respect for you, your religion, and your profession. And as long as this woman is by my side," he says, kissing my hand. "You will always have a place on the other. Always."

"Thank you." Maggie looks between us, and I nod my head in encouragement, causing her to sigh. "The reason I ask is that I don't know how much Marianne has told you about our family."

"A little, but maybe her opinion is a biased one."

"Or maybe it's not. Religion, regardless of which, is deep in some people. I may be a vicar, but I don't judge those who don't agree with my faith," Maggie says. "On the other hand, our father is very religious, and he takes the vows he made very seriously."

"Maggie." He puts down his tea and folds his arms on the table. "I'll be honest, I don't understand how he could abandon his young daughter and granddaughter, with a… I apologise for my language, but with an absolute fucking bastard! That's what I need to understand," he huffs out, and I reach over and stroke his hand. "I'm sorry."

Maggie smiles. "Don't be, I've heard far worst before. I've even used them a time or two myself. Our father was a very strict man, John, and our childhood reflected his views. If we misbehaved, we were punished."

I roll my eyes; *I* was punished, she never was.

I watch her as she continues to talk to him, describing our strict childhood, and our even stricter teenage years. Listening to her, it makes me finally see just how different we are, but how much alike we still are. Stupid not to be really since we both had big dreams and aspirations, and carried the same spirited fire inside growing up.

I pour myself another black coffee and sip it as she carries on.

"As we got older, we both grew more and more restless with the daily regime enforced upon us. Although I'd accepted the way it was, Marianne chose to fight against it. Eventually, she chose her path. Irrespectively if she chose wisely, she knew what it was like to love and to be in love. In some respects, I envied her that."

Love? Yeah, being battered, bruised, and ultimately pushed down the stairs with the one thing you would sacrifice yourself for, was definitely love.

Maggie turns to me with a sad smile. "The day Dad kicked you out was my fault. I tried to warn you," she says, almost in tears.

"I know you did," I whisper, remembering the sound of the chair scraping with vivid clarity. "I couldn't hide it forever though." I stand abruptly, because hearing Maggie purge her guilt is too much, and that memory still burns deep. And it always will.

"Do you mind if I sit in your living room?" I mumble, not waiting for a response as I dart out of the kitchen.

I push open the living room door, the first thing I see is a small cross on the wall. I slide my finger over the bevelled edge, feeling somewhat less faithless than I did yesterday.

Looking over the sideboard, my heart cracks further when I see the framed Polaroid of Faith and me, minutes after she was born. Regardless of the good times we shared, just the two of us, none of it matters now because the only real memory I have is the last.

And the most horrific.

I pick it up the picture and hold it close to my heart, wishing I had the living, breathing, flesh and blood version, not an image immortalised on paper, contained in metal and glass. I slide down the wall beside the open door and listen as Maggie and John continue to talk in quiet tones.

"I remember the day we buried her like it was yesterday. The mourners who turned up to get their last pound of flesh. The ones who pretended to care, when all they wanted was to see the town tramp finally get her comeuppance. Imagine a nineteen-year-old girl who had been forced to give up everything for nothing. The only good thing to come out of it was Faith – for the short time we had her."

"This is a lot to take in," John's voice drifts over the atmosphere.

"It is. The day we lost her, I realised my father's staunch views were jaded. And regardless of what he thought of Marianne, she is my blood, and that will always be stronger than my faith." She sighs deeply. "My biggest regret was walking away under my mother's orders after the funeral. If I had known then that I would not see my sister again for over twenty years, I wouldn't have done it. I'll carry that shame until the day I die." I drag myself up, hearing her voice vacillate.

"We all make mistakes, Maggie," John says soothingly. "So, how long have you been married?" he asks, consciously manoeuvring the conversation in a less painful direction.

"Fifteen years," she replies.

"Kids?"

I flinch the moment the question leaves his mouth. It's too personal to ask that of someone he barely knows.

"No." Her voice falters again, and I hear the fridge door open.

I traipse back into the kitchen, and Maggie smiles as soon as I enter and puts the kettle on. I give her an apologetic look, and she shakes her head.

"I'm sorry." John apologises as I sit next to him. "I didn't know."

"John, it's fine. It just didn't happen for us." She squeezes his hand in conciliation.

"What's that?" he asks, and I hand him the picture. "Always beautiful," he murmurs, gliding his thumb over the glass.

I look up at Maggie, who smiles and stands on his other side. "Do you mind if I take the picture out in the hallway and have a copy made?" She straightens instantly like I've said something wrong or she's remembered something. "Maggie?" I query.

"Come on. I've got some things I think you'll want." She nudges her head to the door and strides out. Curious, I drag John up with me and move after her.

On the middle of the stairs, I gaze in awe at the collage of pictures from my childhood.

"Another identical trait," John queries playfully, referring to our own landing walls covered in frames.

"That's my mum." I point to a picture higher on the wall. "She's beautiful, isn't she?"

He reaches up and pulls it down. "Yeah, she is, angel. How old is this?"

I frown. "I don't know. Thirty years, maybe. This is how I remember her."

A million thoughts fight for supremacy inside my heart, and I gaze at nothing of significance, pondering what she looks like now.

John hangs the picture back on the wall and tilts my chin. "Stop worrying. You've already done the hardest part." He kisses my nose, then turns me around. Caressing his hands over my hips, he pushes me up the rest of the stairs.

"Maggie?"

"In here!"

The sound of movement resonates from the bedroom at the end of the landing, and I cautiously move closer. Dallying inside the doorway, my face falls in amazement as I take in the contents. Maggie was right, I do want these. I want all of them.

I step inside and batten down my fraught emotions. Approaching a chest of drawers, I open the trinket box I had received one Christmas. The mechanical melody plays as I dig my finger around the dress jewellery inside and pick up a string of pink plastic pearls. A memory of playing dress up with Mum and Maggie assaults me, and I fist them tight.

"Marianne?" I put down the pearls and look over my shoulder. Maggie smiles and beckons me over. As she opens the wardrobe doors, my eyes flood with tears and I run my hand over Faith's old clothes.

"Where did you get all this?" I ask.

"Well, a couple of days after you left, Mum and I were in the supermarket, and the wicked witch waltzed right up to us, acting like nothing had happened, imparting her condolences at the loss of *our* Faith and your leaving. She prattled on about the pain of losing her granddaughter and Joe's innocence and said the real culprit would be caught. She made a big show and dance for anyone who was watching. Mum was incensed, and she dug into her purse and threw your wedding ring in her face and told her to burn in hell."

My eyes widen. "Really?"

Maggie nods with a smile. "She caused quite the scene. Anyway, a few weeks later, the wicked witch dumped all this on Mum's doorstep. She said it was rubbish, and we were lucky she hadn't burnt it," she says. "There's a load of other stuff in the loft, too. Feel free to take whatever you want. It's all yours anyway."

Inhaling deeply, unable to disguise my anguish, I stagger to the bed and drop down heavily. John quickly rushes towards me. Enfolding me into his arms, he holds me as I fall apart.

"Shush," he soothes, stroking my forehead. "It's okay, angel." His lips caress my temple as my body shakes uncontrollably.

"John?" Maggie blocks my line of sight and shares an unspoken look with him. Sliding out carefully from behind me, he walks to the door.

"Don't be too long, ladies," he says gently before leaving us alone.

The bed dips again, and Maggie lays down next to me. Face to face, she delicately brushes the hair away from the side of my cheek, the same way she did when we were younger.

Closing my eyes, tranquillity consumes me, and for the first time in a long time, I feel at peace.

"I'm glad Mum didn't bin them," I say quietly. "How is she?"

Maggie wraps her arm around me tight. "She's well. The prognosis is still bleak, but she's comfortable and happy, insofar as she can be."

"Does she know you found me?" I sit up and dry my eyes.

"No. I didn't want her getting her hopes up just in case you never came back. She talks about you all the time though. You and Faith. She'd love to see you."

I nod and bequeath her a smile. "I'd love to see her, too."

"Good." Maggie links my fingers in hers and strokes the back of my hand. "Are you not even going to ask about him?"

I close my eyes momentarily. "No, but you're going to tell me anyway."

She stares down at our hands and purses her lips. "He's okay. He's retired now, but he's still active in the church and the community, and he spends a lot of time with Mum."

I nod. "Does he ever-" I stop, because he would never ask about me. To even think it is preposterous.

"Actually, he does speak about you. He's never admitted what he did was wrong, but in the last few years, he's often talked about you with mum. And he's talked about Faith, too. I think he's finally feeling his guilt."

I sigh because I still want to hate him. And while a part of me always will, there's a small part of me that wants to forgive, because I don't eventually want to meet my maker with hate in my heart. But whether or not I can, is another matter entirely. I guess when the day comes that I finally have to face him again, will be the true reckoning.

A faint buzzing resounds, and I look down at my pocket. I smile when I see a text from Kara.

"Is everything okay?" Maggie asks.

"Yeah," I reply, as I open the gallery app and swipe through the collections. "This is my Kara." I shuffle closer and flick through the pictures. "That's her husband, Sloan. He can be a real overbearing git, and he likes everything his way, but he's an amazing husband and father. It took them a long time to get where they are."

"It sounds like an interesting story. They're a lovely looking couple," she says complementary.

"They are, and they make lovely babies, too." I pass her the phone to look through the snaps of Oliver. "He's a little cutie already. You're going to love him."

"Who's that?" she asks, and I tilt my head.

"Oh, that's Sophie Morgan. She's Kara's best friend. Absolute opposites, but they click. That's Doctor Stuart Andrews, Sophie's fiancé. They've been engaged for a while. And that couple is Charlie Emerson, Sloan's sister, and her boyfriend, Jake Evans."

"My goodness, there's so many of them." Maggie laughs at the next picture. "And these three handsome chaps?"

"Jeremy James, Simon Parker and Thomas Fox. They're John's ragtag boys." I smile and watch her swipe one picture after another.

"It's an interesting family," she says, handing the phone back.

"Hmm, and it's about to get even more interesting with a vicar and a solicitor to add to the mix." I grin.

The sound of a car leaks faintly into the room, followed by the distinct slam of a door, and a vague, muted voice.

"Oh, that's Peter. Come on!"

My feet slap hard on each step as Maggie drags me down the stairs. Reaching the bottom, John is studying the pictures lining the walls with more cake in his hand.

"What's wrong?" he asks.

The front door then opens, and we all turn simultaneously to see Maggie's husband enter. Dressed in his work suit, he looks between the strangers in his hallway.

"Sorry, I'll call you back," Peter says to whoever he is talking to and lowers his phone.

"Hello, darling," Maggie says, very prim and proper – using the same pet name as I do for John – and greets him with a polite kiss and takes his arm.

"Peter, meet Marianne, and her..." she stalls a little – who knows what he is to me right now.

"John. Her fiancé." He approaches with his hand out. "Nice to meet you, Peter."

"You, too, John. Congratulations."

Peter then turns to me and smiles. "Marianne. Gosh, I never thought this day would come. I've been hearing about you and seeing your face in this house for so long, I feel I already know you."

"Hi. I'm sorry we've just turned up like this. It must be a shock." I shake his hand, and he puts his over mine. I smile; Maggie seems to have found her equally gentle soulmate in Peter, and I have found my equally fiery soulmate in John. Clearly, the Lord's ways are not that mysterious after all.

"It is. One of the best kind. Please, don't worry yourself," he says, removing his jacket.

"You're early," Maggie says as she walks back into the kitchen.

"The office is a madhouse. I couldn't concentrate. Although it looks like I won't be getting anything done here, either."

I glance at Maggie, who looks from her husband and back again.

"Oh, sorry, Marianne. I didn't mean to imply you were a distraction."

I smile. "Yes, you did, but we'll get out of your hair for a few hours."

Maggie suddenly looks stricken. "You're leaving already?"

I nod. "Hmm, and you're coming with me." She squints at me, causing every fine line to run deep. "Would you take me to see mum?"

"I thought you'd never ask."

Chapter 43

MILES OF LUSH green farmers' fields pass by as I stare out of the window. Raising my hand to my temple, I can already feel the impending tension headache starting to take effect with vicious ferocity.

"Maggie, which exit?" John asks, slowly braking at the oncoming roundabout.

"Straight on, then it's your first left. You can't miss it," she replies. "You know you don't have to do this today, Marianne."

I feign ignorance because to say I'm ashamed is an understatement. The truth be told, if my life hadn't been turned on its head these past few months, I wouldn't have come back. I'd have lived and died in ignorant bliss, wondering what might have been. And the sad fact is, Maggie knows it too.

"Marianne?" Maggie's concerned tone burrows deep, cutting through my procrastination. Turning from the window, I note she is wearing the same expression I do when I'm contemplating. And procrastinating.

"Sorry?" I furrow my brow for effect as she grips my hand tight in comfort.

"I understand if you are having second thoughts."

"I'm fine," I mumble, while the irrefutable coiling in my stomach proves I'm lying.

"It's okay to be scared. I felt the same way when I first saw you again."

I scoff and rudely attempt to drag my hand away, but she is having none of it.

"I'm not scared," I reply curtly and fix her with a glare until she gives me a pointed look and I cave. "Fine! I admit it, I'm bloody terrified. Is that what you want to hear?"

I stare into the rear-view mirror, recognising John's concern that in this instant there's nothing he can do to ease my anguish. This, unfortunately, is a wave I'm going to have to ride out until the end. And I will either crash and be taken under, or I'll break the surface, and feel the sun caress my skin again.

"Marianne," she says softly.

"Magdalene," I reply, not so softly, and close my eyes in both tiredness and irritation.

When I refuse to acknowledge her any further, she sighs and jerks my chin. "To see you again has always been her dying wish. Give her that."

An icy sensation envelops, expanding down my throat and chest because she sees through me, and sadly, we both know that, too.

"I'm petrified to see her again, but today might be the last chance I get. I don't want to regress and then receive a call from you to say she's passed. I want to be able to look back and know, at long last, I've done something right for the first time. But more than that, I don't want her leaving this life and entering the next thinking I didn't love her enough to return."

My shoulders shake under my unintended confession, and Maggie shuffles closer over the leather and wraps her herself around me as I try not to fall apart. I tilt my head to the front and catch John's eyes in the mirror again. He mouths *okay,* and I subtly shake my head, because none of this is okay.

If I knew yesterday - when I was sitting in that abysmal hotel room thinking this was the right thing to do - that I would feel like I've been shattered again, I'd have got in the car and speeded south.

Still, for once I'm not lying. I may be terrified, and my insides may be threatening to drop out, but I am glad I'm going to see her again.

"We're here," Maggie announces, and I look up at the two-storey hospice as John glides the car smoothly into a vacant space. Maggie unclips her belt and reaches for the handle.

"Wait! She does know I'm coming, doesn't she?"

Maggie slowly moves her head and smiles gloriously. "No. Call it the element of surprise."

"Don't you look at me like that! The element of surprise? You said you would call ahead!" I'm seething, which is a good thing because it's momentarily diverting my apprehension. Although it's not stopping my gut from doing somersaults entirely.

"I was going to, but I thought better of it. And considering you've been contemplating whether or not to tell John to turn the car around, I was right to."

"No, I haven't!" I snap.

"Yes, you have!" she snaps back. "She's been reminiscing and talking about you for weeks. I didn't want to make any grand announcement and get her spirits up for you to back out." She huffs, grabs the cake box, and shoves the door open. "I'll give you a few minutes to compose yourself." She then shuts the door.

The acid in my belly churns unforgivingly as I watch her enter the building. I'm in desperate need of fresh air as the waters in my mouth culminate and a light-headedness ensues. Unable to take much more, I clamber out and sway when my feet touch the tarmac. John curses from the front as I heave and raise my hand to my mouth, and within seconds I am being curled into his arms.

"Breathe," he says as he picks me up and slams the door. Carrying me to a nearby bench, he sits us down and arranges me on his lap. He manipulates my prone position effortlessly, and I glide my arms around his neck.

"Irrespective of what she said, darling, we can leave if you want to," he says and rotates me around.

I frown in contemplation, but I can't leave, not when I've come this far. The finish is finally in sight; to forfeit now would be just one more cross I have to bear.

Long minutes pass in silence, and I keep my eyes trained on the hospice door, watching life come and go.

"Penny for your thoughts, beautiful?"

I shiver, unnerved by his soft touch tucking my hair behind my ear.

"Which one?" I mumble. "I doubt even Sloan has enough pennies in the bank to cover them all."

"Talk to me. Honestly," he urges softly. I curl myself tighter into his chest while he delicately strokes my bruised jaw.

"It's stupid, but I'm frightened. The last time I saw her, I made promises I didn't keep. I have years of broken dreams to atone for, and I feel guilty that I'm going to go in there and she's probably going to absolve me of all of them without begging or equivocation."

And that is the hardest, most detrimental part, because how can I accept her forgiveness when I can't forgive myself?

John tightens his arms further around my waist and sighs. "That's unconditional love, darling. That's what parents do. When Kara disappeared, was there any doubt in your mind that when she eventually returned, whether it be six months or six years, that you wouldn't forgive her?"

I turn brusquely. "No, because I understood the reasons why she ran," I tell him, answering my own question. He smiles in satisfaction that he has broken through, and grapples with me to get closer until my front is compressed to his, and I feel a restriction in my breathing.

"I love you, angel, flaws and all – the same way your mother does. She'll be over the moon to see you again." He tips my chin, and his lips consume mine in a very tender kiss. I close my eyes and grip his biceps hard, finally daring to dream of a painless future I may eventually call mine.

Footsteps pique my attention, and a throat clears. Reluctantly breaking apart, Maggie is standing a few feet away, blatantly embarrassed to have interrupted a very private moment. I give John a sheepish grin before advancing towards her.

"Are you ready to come inside?" she asks tentatively.

"Yes," I reply, psyching myself up to place one foot in front of the other.

Reaching the hospice reception, if I wasn't already aware my sister is a regular here, I am now. As we are stopped intermittently by other visitors, I confess, it's still bizarre to hear them address her as Reverend Booth, but I'm also damn proud of her, too.

John and I dawdle in the foyer as Maggie chats to someone. I take a moment to assess every aspect of the welcoming, homely setting while she is engaged.

"I'll come over sometime during the week. I'll call you beforehand," Maggie says to the man and waves goodbye. "Ready?" She points for us to follow her.

Moving through the corridors, a phone starts to ring, and Maggie reaches into her bag. Her stride doesn't falter, but her expression does. And if I wasn't so transfixed on her, I would have missed it, but I don't.

"Mum's in room thirty-two," she says, cancelling the call and plastering on a fake smile. I hang back as she marches off in front, and John takes my elbow.

"Angel?"

"Two guesses who that was," I mutter, then hurry after my twin, because it's easier to avoid reality when he isn't coddling me like I'm a piece of fragile, compromised glass; cracked and ready to break at any second.

Rounding the corner, my soul starts to feel weary as I glance at each door number we pass.

Twenty-five.

Twenty-six.

I mutter the numbers until I am standing in front of door thirty-two.

The long, forgotten voice of my ailing mother drifts onto the landing, revealing her excitement at Maggie's announcement that she has brought her a surprise.

I raise my shaky hand to the wood but drop it like it's a lead weight because I'm retreating, mentally regressing again.

I inch back, one step, then two, until I hit a solid wall of hard muscle. I pivot around and clutch John's jacket.

"I-I-" I feel the corridor closing in. I feel my lungs failing to function. I feel myself falling again. I feel a million things that are causing my heart to verge on shattering. "I can't!"

"Yes, you can," John urges. "Because my Marie is strong and beautiful, whereas my Marianne is fearless and willing to fight. And they are two sides of the same coin." I continue to grip his jacket tight until he prises me away. "I'm right here with you, angel."

I nod repeatedly and wipe my eyes. Finally regaining my mental strength, I push open the door. Maggie turns and motions me inside while the frail, shocked gasp of my mother echoes.

"Marianne?" Mum asks in disbelief and turns to Maggie who produces a beautiful, beaming smile.

"I told you I would bring her home," Maggie says proudly.

Mum shuffles off the bed, visibly in pain, and uses it as an aid to get to me. I drop my bag to the floor with a clatter and rush over to her when she winces in discomfort. Without hesitation, I hold her tight. Touching her for the first time after all these years, a barrage of emotions hit me tenfold. Her unique, memorable scent infuses my nostrils, and I close my eyes in recollection.

"I'm sorry, Mummy," I say, regressing, while my body shakes. Lost in the moment, everything I feared inside the car, outside on the bench and a few feet away in the hallway, no longer exists. I might be twenty-three years too late, but better late than never. "I love you. So, so much. I'm sorry I never came back."

"But you did," she says quietly, her voice frail, exhausted. "You're here now. I always knew you'd return." Her grip falters on my back, and as much as I want to prolong this moment, it's selfish to keep her standing in her condition. I pull back and gaze at her. Gone is the blonde curly hair I remember, now she is entirely grey. My hand cups her cheek, and I brush my thumb under her eye, tenderly tracing the age lines on her thin skin.

"I'm sorry I left it so long," I whisper.

Mum smiles, and motions for Maggie. "My special girls," she says sadly as Maggie joins our embrace because, in this circle of enduring love, one special girl is missing.

Faith.

Mum gives me a pained look and begins to open her mouth, but I stop her. "I know," I murmur, while Maggie rubs my shoulder.

"Ladies?" John's voice fills the quiet, and the three of us turn simultaneously to the doorway. Maggie nudges my side and nods at Mum, who, on the other hand, smiles with intrigue.

"You lied," she says to Maggie. "You brought me two surprises." Her blue eyes, still sharp and vibrant, shine in happiness.

Maggie chuckles as she assists her back into bed, and I grasp John's hand.

"Mum, this is John Walker. My fiancé." My pride is unambiguous as I guide him to the bed. Mum pats the mattress, and John gives me an unsure expression, but slowly edges towards her.

"It's nice to meet you, Mrs Turner," he greets her fondly, showing his sharpness that he hasn't forgotten the maiden name Maggie gave in her voice message months ago.

"Yes, and you, Mr Walker."

"John, please." He sits down on the precise spot she patted and winks at me. I smile back, my heart already overflowing as I absorb the room and its contents.

My eyes drift over the floral duvet cover, the matching curtains and the mismatched cushions scattered over one side of the bed.

I rotate without direction and double back on the chest of drawers. With a smile, I bend down and study the multitude of frames artfully arranged on the top. Numerous family pictures are proudly displayed; a portrait of Maggie and me aged five in identical dresses; one taken on our first day at primary school; and another from middle school. I rub my chest because it hurts to look at them. It hurts so much to remember that these are some of the good times before it all seriously turned to shit.

But the one I can't turn away from is the one of Faith. It was a picture that was taken when she had just started to walk. In clunky little trainers that Mum had bought for her, her arms are out wide as she balances in the photography studio. The cheeky smile I will always remember is etched on her cherubic face. And I remember seconds after this picture was snapped, she fell flat on her bum and wailed for an hour afterwards.

"Faith," I whisper, almost silent.

"Marianne?"

I reluctantly turn away from the drawers and drop myself into one of the spare chairs, alongside Maggie, who strokes back a flyaway hair.

"Thank you," she murmurs, slouching towards me. I wrap my hand around her head and run my fingers through her hair.

"No, thank you," I counter. "Thank you for never giving up on me." Leaning into her, the sides of our heads pressed together, we watch while Mum and John chat.

"Tell me about yourself, John. I want to know everything about the man that my daughter is overwhelmingly in love with. After all, I can tell a man like you will want parental approval," Mum says enthusiastically.

"Absolutely!" John chuckles nervously and begins to tell Mum snippets about himself.

Time passes slowly as we all indulge in a long overdue reunion. The conversation shifts repeatedly, and in between sighs of disappointment and laughs of joy as John regales Mum with both catastrophes and victories, I find my eyelids drooping until the need to sleep is greater than I can fight.

"Marianne?" I ruffle from my slumber, hearing my name, and I blink as I come to.

"What? Sorry?" I mutter and look up to find John and Maggie missing.

"I sent them for some beverages," Mum says and holds out her arm. I push myself up, climb onto the bed and place my arm across her middle. I carefully rest my head against her shoulder, and she strokes my hair softly.

"Sorry, I fell asleep. I'm just so tired, and-"

"No need to apologise. Your lovely man explained everything that's been happening. You know, the only thing I ever wanted before I left this life-"

"Mum, please don't," I cut her off, but she ignores me.

"Was to see you again. It was always my dying wish. Not a day has gone by when I haven't wished that I had never let you get on that train. I never thought I'd see you again. I've lived a lifetime of regret because of it, much like you have, I understand." She stares down into my eyes – those identical to hers – and they shimmer with impending tears. "John told me." I start to open my mouth, but she places her finger on it. "I'm glad I got to meet him, and yes, I approve. I'm proud and elated that you finally have someone who would sacrifice everything for you. And he would, sweetheart, he would die for you if you asked. And I can see you would do the same for him, too."

I sniffle. "I would," I tell her. "I have. I've emotionally died over and over telling him about my horrific past. I once thought he would judge me, but after all was said and done, he still loves me."

Mum smiles and presses closer. "Of course, he does, because it's ingrained in him. You do him a disservice thinking that he wouldn't. He's the type of man every woman wants. He's the type of man our Faith deserved for her father," she says without malice, mentioning her name for the first time. "And he's the man you've waited your whole life for. You deserve that unbridled, passionate love he wants to surround you with. Hold onto him, sweetheart, and never let go."

"I won't." I stare into her eyes, wondering if she ever felt that way about my father. I also wonder if she still bore the brunt his anger long after I had gone but dare not ask.

I snuggle her and run my fingers through her hair as the door opens and my father walks in with his head down, focused on his mobile. I swallow hard, still fearful of the man that once made me cower in a corner and would strike me for the slightest wrongdoing. Staring at his profile, he is still tall, but his frame has lost some mass. His dark brown hair is now peppered with thick strands of grey, having aged well the same as my mother.

A phone starts to ring, and he sighs, relieved. "Magdalene, why didn't you answer my call earlier?" His voice - still strong and resolute - carries the same air of authority I remember too well. His head lifts and his face falls, seeing I am not Magdalene.

"Hello, Dad." Contempt drips from my tone, and Mum stiffens beside me as I get up.

The atmosphere thickens as I approach him until he turns away abruptly. I chortle in disgust, in dismay, but regardless of how well he tries to disguise it, his action is indicative of his shame.

"Mum, is Marianne awake yet?" Maggie asks, entering the room with John behind her. "Dad." She stops instantly. "I didn't know you were coming today."

"Well, you didn't answer my calls," he replies tersely, showing his dominance, even in his seventies.

Maggie places the drinks on the drawers and addresses him. "No, I didn't," she states the obvious.

I edge back and catch John's guarded stance. He furrows his brow and shakes his head slowly. Incredulously. And while he would never strike an OAP, he'll be damned if he allows my father to cut me down again in front of him.

"As you can see, I'm busy. Dad, meet John, Marianne's fiancé."

"Hello," John greets him, cold and unimpressed, and holds out his hand. My dad simply stares at it, causing John to laugh singularly.

"Do you really despise your daughter that much that after two decades, a righteous man such as yourself can't even show an ounce of courtesy?" he asks with scorn, and my dad's eyes widen in shock, and he scoffs.

"Elizabeth, Magdalene, I shall return when you have finished with your guests." He then strides out of the room.

Maggie's hand touches my shoulder. "He'll be outside in the gardens. I know it's hard, but you should talk to him."

My mouth drops open. "And say what?" There is an array of not so pleasant pleasantries running through my head because now has presented the perfect opportunity for me to tell him to go fuck himself again. And, unfortunately, that might be as pleasant as it gets.

"Maggie," John starts. "With all due respect, his actions speak volumes."

"I know!" Maggie replies, throwing her arms out. "I just... Oh, never mind. Mum, I got you an Earl Grey." She picks up one of the cups and hands it to her, while John passes me a coffee.

"Thanks." I hold it against my chest and move to the window. Gazing over the landscaped grounds, my dad is wandering up and down, looking at something in his hand. I narrow my eyes in curiosity and put the cup on the windowsill.

"I'll be back soon," I tell them as I slide into my jacket.

"Angel?" John blocks my way and grips my shoulder. "He's made it perfectly clear."

I rub the back of my neck in acquiesce and anxiety. "I know, and now I need to do the same." I look back at Mum and Maggie, then peck John on the lips and open the door. "Don't worry, I won't start a war."

I stretch up on my toes at the French doors, casting my eyes over the orchid where I last saw him. Stepping out onto the patio, I pull my jacket tighter around my front and amble around the shrubbery. Just as I am about to give up hope, I see him sitting on a bench near a small coppice of trees.

"May I join you?" I ask.

My father looks up from staring at whatever has claimed his attention, and nods, bearing none of the condescension I received upstairs. I sit down beside him and catch a glimpse of the picture in his hand. It's the same one that Maggie has in her hallway. It's the picture of us both with Faith, holding Mr Blue, concealing her chocolate stained dress.

A frisson of hope blossoms in my chest. For all his talk that I was dead to him and he didn't want the bastard's child under his roof, he carries her picture.

I fidget, unable to relax in his presence, and stare off into the distance.

"I was wrong."

I turn, in shock, as he finally speaks the words I've longed to hear since I was a teenager.

"I was wrong when I kicked you out. I was wrong when I abandoned you. And I was wrong when I refused to stand up in court and tell everyone what an amazing mother my daughter was."

Pain suffuses my heart, and I cover my mouth because all the things I want to say are gone. I never expected him to purge his guilt, but now that he has, I don't know what to do with it.

"I realised a long time ago, if I had been a better, more loving father, your life would have been different."

In my teary, peripheral vision, his hand edges closer, until he eventually touches my knee and I flinch.

"I'm sorry, Marianne. I'll never be able to express the pain I've felt-"

"Don't!" I can't bear to listen to him when I know I can never forgive him. I thought I could, but I can't.

"Please?" he pleads, and I shake my head.

"No. We both know I could never please you. At sixteen, I tried to stay away from Joe, and I failed. At seventeen, I tried to do the best for Faith, and it wasn't enough. At eighteen, I tried to be a good wife, even though I knew my deceitful husband didn't love or even want me. And at nineteen, I tried to save her from the fall, I really did." I take a sharp breath. "I guess you could say I've failed at every turn, and it started with you. Now you finally find it in your heart to exonerate me, but it's not enough, because when someone kicks you down repeatedly, eventually you start to believe it."

Awareness swathes me, and I automatically glance up at Mum's window to see John overseeing from afar. I curve my lips slightly when he touches the glass, then I turn back to my dad. He looks ashen, undoubtedly feeling the guilt Maggie confirmed was consuming him.

"You are right about one thing though." Dad looks from the picture to me. "If you had been a better father to me, Faith would still be here. Every day since she took her last breath, I've lived in misery. Every night, when I close my eyes, the final image of her is the only one I see. And that's on you, too. You can beg for my clemency, but I'll never grant it. Likewise, I can't forget the cruelty and infliction we both endured because of your actions.

"I have a great life now. Someone who loves me, a thriving business, and an amazing family." Dad's head snaps up. "For the sake of Mum, and the little time she has left, I'm willing to show you respect and civility, but that's all you will get from me."

I walk away slowly and don't look back. As I make my way through the hospice, the hurt I'm feeling is a revelation. For a long time, I hated him, but now I just feel pity. And for all my fears that I didn't want to meet my maker with hate in my heart, I now know Dad will meet his God with guilt in his.

"Everything okay?" John queries as soon as I return, and I press my lips into a forced smile.

"Fine," I reply.

I approach Mum, who is openly flagging, and perch my bum on the bed. "We need to set off home soon, but I'll come back up weekly." Mum's face falls, and she tugs me forward.

"You promise?" she asks, sounding exhausted.

"I promise. And this time, I'll keep it." I cradle her cheeks and kiss her lips. "I'll call you every day. I want to know the most mundane things. What you've had for breakfast; what television programmes you've watched; which little old biddy is annoying you. Everything."

Mum nods and lets me go. As I step back, John steps forward, and they conduct a private, whispered conversation. Whatever he says has her grinning in delight, and she passes him a potted plant and kisses his cheek.

"We'll see you next week, Liz."

Liz?

I shake my head as Maggie passes me my bag. "I'll walk you both out," she says, and I blow Mum a kiss before I shut the door.

As I walk down the corridor, it hits me that this is the last place she'll ever see, and I slump against the wall and breakdown inconsolable.

"Oh, God!" I wail in absolute fucking agony that I may never see her again. Next week she might already be gone.

"Let it out, darling," John says, caging me to him. I cry in his arms for an indeterminable amount of time as people pass, and poor Maggie has to fend them off. Pulling myself together, I yank Maggie close and hold her tight as we leave.

"I want you to call me, daily, twice a day if need be, and let me know how she's doing. You, too. I'd stay longer, but I have-"

"I know. You can't just uproot without consequences." Maggie wipes my tear-stained cheeks and turns to John when he calls her name.

"Ring us if she takes a turn for the worst. Day or night, we'll be here in a couple of hours," he confirms.

Maggie nods and embraces him. "Of course. Have a safe journey back and take care of Marianne. She needs you."

"Always. How are you getting home?" he asks her.

"Dad will take me. One last hug before you go," she says, winding her arms around me, as John gets in the car and starts the engine. "I love you."

"I love you, too. Kiss Mum again for me when you go back up." Letting her go, I climb into the car. I stare as John reverses out of the space and reaches the main road until I can't see her any longer.

He rubs up and down my leg, and I stop his hand. "I'm good, darling. I won't lie; I'm feeling so much right now, but I'm good. Honestly."

He smiles beautifully, reminiscent of the first time I ever saw it. "Good, because we need to make a detour."

The sun beats down on my back as I sit on Faith's grave.

I watch John intently as he digs through the soil with his bare hands to plant the flower Mum gave him. Patting down the earth, he rubs his palms together before he stands and strokes the headstone. In the quiet surroundings, his murmured tones carry over the breeze.

"What are you saying?" I ask.

He whips around, drags me up and takes my chin between his finger and thumb and claims my lips.

"You're distracting me again," I grumble into his mouth.

"I am," he replies. "But what I said is for her alone. Are you ready to go?"

"Yes, but can we make another detour? There's another place I want you to see."

John whistles as he brakes on the opposite side of the street and cuts the engine.

I purse my lips and look upon the house. *The house*, not my former home.

"God, this makes the kids' place look like a Wendy house," John comments as he stares at the Beresford's opulent mansion.

"Yeah, it does." I gaze up at the window to the room that was my prison. "That was our room, mine and Faith's." I point to the second to last window on the right.

"Do they still live here?" he asks in a knowing tone.

"I think so. Why?" But I know why, and that I can't think about.

"No reason," he says and turns my head. "Today's been a good day. I don't want this to the be the thing you take away from it." He drops his hand to the gear stick and finds the biting point.

He's right to be worried, but it won't be because this house and its owners can burn for all I care. Still, there is one more thing I need to know.

"Darling, where do we go from here?"

He gently runs his thumb over my lips and lovingly gazes into my eyes.

"We go home."

Chapter 44

STANDING IN FRONT of the mirror in the toilets of the Roseby Hotel staff room, the exuberant, muted clamour of tonight's black-tie event resonates inside.

I sway to the obligatory big band offering, as I rake my eyes over my strapless black ballgown and smooth my palms down my sides. Critiquing my appearance after two hours of being on my feet, the light inadvertently bounces off the stones in my engagement ring, and I lift my hand in compulsion.

"One day," I murmur rhetorically, but one day has finally been and gone. And my declaration that I couldn't marry John without him knowing the whole truth has also been and gone.

It has been a month since my life was ripped apart and my soul was laid bare for scrutiny. A month since I finally made amends with my sister and my mother, and in some regard, my father. And a month since Joe polluted my world - and I've not heard from him since. I'd like to say I'm convinced he's done with seeking retribution, but I know him. And whenever I've raised it with John, he's told me not to worry, which in turn does make me worry, because how can I not?

Yet regardless of the issues still unresolved in my life, the last four weeks have been a beautiful awakening.

Granted, the first few days after we returned from Peterborough were painful, to say the least, and my sanity was hanging on by a thread when I imparted the awful truth to those I love over and over. But I survived. I made it through.

And I proved to myself that the fallen can be saved.

Twisting the ring on my finger, I was wrong all those years ago when I thought John might be the second reason why I would fall from grace.

In truth, he *is* my saving grace.

And he has saved me from myself.

Swiping powder over my shiny t-zone, I dab on some lip balm and chuck them back into my bag.

"Marie?" Nicki calls out with a tap on the door.

"In here," I reply as she enters, looking radiant in a calf-length green gown - which compliments her pale complexion beautifully -

and her blonde hair styled in a low, plaited bun. "Hey, darling. How's it looking out there?"

"Stressful. And flirty Lowe is on the hunt for you."

"Oh, joyful, joyful," I say sarcastically.

But really, we can't complain, we've lucked out so far tonight. He's been so busy entertaining his illustrious guests in his private suite – guests that we haven't seen hide nor hair of – he has, thankfully, left us alone.

"Tell me the truth, has he found a fingerprint on the silverware or an eyelash in his champagne flute?" I ask mockingly.

Nicki snorts undignified. "I think he'll always find a problem with perfection. Look on the bright side," she says, loving her bleeding bright side, just as much as Kara loves her bleeding hindsight. "After tonight we won't have to see him again. Seven more hours and he will be gone for good."

"That's still seven hours too long. Are you sure you don't mind?"

"No, of course not." She shakes her head, relieved. "If this is what it takes to run an event for him, I'd rather not, thank you very much. I don't appreciate being called at three in the morning to discuss red-carpet edge trimmings."

I roll my eyes and laugh. "Thanks, sweetheart. You look stunning, by the way."

Her eyes sweep down her front, inducing her cheeks to flush. "Thanks. You too."

Checking my overworked appearance for the final time, I flick off the light, lob my bag into the locker and make my way back into the congested ballroom.

"Oh, I almost forgot," she says. "Someone else is looking for you, too."

"Who?" I ask, but she just winks and flounces into the chaos. Standing tall, believing I can take on the world, I follow her out.

I stand on the outskirts of the room, cradle a flute of sparkling water and gaze over the sea of fake finery.

From one corner to the other, the smiles, the back slaps, the requisite pleasantries; all of it is fake ostentation to prove the wealth and power of London's elite. And all of it is proving blindingly clear that this is definitely going to be the first and last Roseby event we cover.

If the organisational aspect wasn't enough to leave a bitter taste in my mouth, the recent conduct of the owner has. I honestly didn't think he could stoop any lower than he did the day we signed the contract, but low and behold, his late-night calls and voicemails regarding the most inconsequential of details have proved he can. And after much discussion in the office this last week, Nicki and I have already agreed on the same.

I bring the glass to my lips and knock it back, wishing it was something a little stronger. Depositing it on the tray of a passing waiter, I take a leisurely stroll around the room.

Linking my fingers at my front, the usual habitual feeling of pride bubbles up from within. I might not like the man, but I aim for divine decadence. And tonight, that's precisely what Nicki and I have given him.

From the champagne coloured fabric adorning the Victorian sash windows to the silk tablecloths and matching chair covers. Even the lightening has been changed at our request, and a soft glow casts around the room from the crystal chandelier droplets, creating a romantic, intimate setting. Upon physical reflection, each piece is beautiful on its own, but as a collective, it is stunning.

I continue my evaluation as I hopelessly kill time. On the second pass through, my attempt to develop selective hearing to zone out the mundane political and financial banter is unsuccessful. The only successful thing I have managed to achieve is not getting accosted by flirty Lowe yet. But there's still time, and I can't avoid the man forever.

"Good evening." I turn and smile at the gent standing in front of me with a couple of glasses.

"Evening. I'm sorry, I'm working tonight, but thank you anyway." I politely decline as he offers me one.

"Actually, Ms Dawson, I know who you are. My name is Philip Barker. I was given your name by the receptionist when I enquired as to who catered tonight. I must say this room looks exquisite."

"Why thank you, but it isn't a solo effort. My assistant also has a very keen eye." I rock up on my heels, trying to locate Nicki.

"Oh, I'm sorry, I didn't mean to make you uncomfortable. I just wanted to approach you with a possible business venture. I suppose this isn't the best time to tout, is it?"

"No, I'm always interested, and I normally use these events to do the same. Please," I say in encouragement.

"Well then, I own a string of hotels, all of which are former country estates I've acquired over the years. Some date back to the last hundred years, others are from the eighteenth century. Each is unique in its own right, which means I need a very unique touch. To give you some idea, we accommodate everyone from ramblers to those seeking relaxation. We hold weddings, christenings, Christmas parties, conferences and anything else that is asked of us," he says with a laugh. "And I'm always looking for someone to cater for different receptions."

He puts the glasses down on a nearby table and dips into his pocket for his business card.

"Quite frankly, walking in here tonight, I'm already sold. I hope you will give my proposal some serious consideration."

Taking the card, my curiosity captivated, the idea of a grand seventeen hundred country pile, complete with upstairs, downstairs? Of course, I'm going to consider it.

"Do you live here in the city?" I query, hoping he will be up for a meeting sooner rather than later.

"No, my wife and I are only here for this evening. We will be leaving in the morning."

"Will you have time for a quick meeting before you go?"

"I'll make time."

"Fantastic, but I need to find my assistant to see if she is able to attend. So, if you don't mind, can I call you in the morning and we can come to you if that's acceptable?"

"Yes, of course." Philip smiles and clasps his hands together. "I look forward to hearing from you, Ms Dawson."

"Marie, please. I'll speak to you tomorrow, Mr Barker. Enjoy the rest of the evening."

"I will. Thank you." And on that, he turns and walks back towards his table.

I stretch up on my toes, trying to locate Nicki in the sea of glad rags, but hiss as pain spikes my leg. Flexing my foot, assuaging the tightness in my calf from my four-inch heels, I see something that makes me smile further, because I'd know that back anywhere.

There, looking completely uncomfortable is my knight in shining black tie armour. Biting my lip, I proceed through the attendees, cutting a determined path towards him.

I clear my throat, and John spins around. "Dare I ask how you managed to wrangle an invite?"

He grins beautifully, inducing my insides to spark to life with desirous intent.

"He's my plus one," Jules says from behind him, dressed in a stunning grey gown, with her hair intricately styled in a chignon.

"And we're just here for the free booze. You know, not that crap I serve," Sloan says, tugging Kara into his side. "That, and tricky dicky called me with complimentary tickets. I presume he just wants to flaunt his wealth as usual." He pivots and glances around the room. "Where is he, anyway?"

"Somewhere. Don't worry, darling, you'll get your pissing contest before the night is through, I'm sure," I say and turn to Kara, who is a vision in royal blue. I pull her into my arms, and she holds me tighter than she ever has before. No words are spoken, because we have talked enough in the last month, and there really is nothing left to say.

I press a kiss to her cheek, and my eyes latch on to her neck. I smile at the locket holding the picture of me, Maggie, and Faith. I gave this to her, for safekeeping, until the time is right to reclaim it. Or re-gift it, as she gracefully suggested.

"You don't mind?" she asks with worry. I shake my head; I can't think of any other place where Maggie or Faith would be safer.

"So, who has the pleasure of babysitting tonight?" I ask her, much to Sloan's muttered annoyance.

"Charlie," she says. "She needs future practice."

"There's going to be no practising! If Jake wants his balls to stay where they are, he can keep that to himself!"

I chortle, while Jules shakes her head at her son's dramatics. It's no secret that Sloan still treats his little sister like a child. But I guess it's hard to let go, especially when he found her the way he did years ago.

"God, you are such a hypocrite!" Jules says.

"Mum, I don't profess to be anything else!" Sloan waves her off nonchalantly. "But Jake is still going to be dickless if he decides to practise!"

"Darling, I love you, but this overbearing protectiveness has to stop. She's not fourteen anymore. She's a grown woman, and for your information, she and Jake have been *practising* for a long time." Jules smiles at her son, whose eyes narrow.

"Just wait until we have daughters. You can be overbearing and protective with them," Kara tells him with a sly smirk. His eyes fill with adoration, and he rubs her arm.

"Why do you want to kill me, my love?" he asks innocently.

"I don't want to kill you, just keep you on your toes," she says.

Sloan glides his finger down her cheek lovingly, he then tucks her into his side, and they walk towards their table. I smile, full of pride, as they move flawlessly, perfectly attuned with one another, invoking glances from the other guests who obviously know who he is.

Lost in thought, a faint, familiar touch plays upon my shoulder, but as I am about to turn, Jules tugs me aside.

"You better appreciate the visual, lady. You have no idea the heartache I went through this evening to get him looking this good. I practically had to dress him myself!"

I laugh, imagining the trouble just to get a tie around his neck.

"Is he always so petulant at these events? Are you even going to ask me to dance later, John?" She pouts, while he grunts.

I put my hand over my mouth but am saved the effort of a response as Devlin steps into my line of sight with his mother.

"Jules, us Walker men are too suave to dance – we blend, albeit very unsuccessfully this evening." And with that, he grabs his bow tie and yanks it with his finger. "It's a shame this shit doesn't come in camo," he says, earning himself a slap from his mother.

"Language!" Louisa says, then pulls herself together as if the last few seconds haven't occurred.

"Lou, you look gorgeous," I tell her, admiring the mauve dress accentuating her fuller figure, with the matching shawl and clutch.

"Well, when my wayward son calls to take me out for the night, how can I say no? He forgot to mention exactly what type of night it is. Good job I have at least one good dress. I feel I should be standing on the pavement with my palms out."

I bring my hand to my chest and laugh. "You really should come to some of the events at the Emerson. They're glitz but nothing like this. This is flaunting for flaunting's sake. Trust me, I feel out of place, too. But at least you're not dressed like the hired help," I say bemused, as fingertips drift tenderly over the back of my hand, summoning a delightful shiver.

"You look radiant, M." Louisa then turns back to Dev and nudges his side. "Now, will you at least promise me one dance with a suave Walker man tonight?"

"Oh, Mum," Dev whines, but graciously acquiesces. "One dance after dinner – a quick one. M, where's Nic?" he asks, and I look around the sea of people, still unable to spot her.

"I don't know; I'm actually looking for her myself." And with that, he kisses his mum's cheek and then proceeds to get himself lost.

"Well, I guess we're the odd women out. Again!" Jules says, casting her eyes head and shoulders above everyone else. "I think I'm going to mingle before the starters. Come on, Lou, let's see if we can find some single, attractive men to look at."

Flouncing through the throng, like mother like son, many a man bestows her with an appreciative nod or wink. And she's not the only one. Lou is also gaining some admiring glances.

Finally left in peace, teasing fingers tangle in mine, and I rotate around to John, who hooks his arm around my waist and presses me tight against him.

"You look absolutely astounding, angel," he says reverently, his eyes working over me. "The things I want to do to you... God, I wish you weren't working tonight." He cradles my cheeks, and presses his forehead to mine, staring deep into my eyes.

"Me, too. I should have called in sick," I whisper and place my hands on his forearms. I run my tongue over my bottom lip and tilt back. "I'll make it up to you. I promise."

"I'll hold you to that," he says coyly, gripping me harder. "One little kiss – for luck."

"Yours or mine?" I ask. "If Lowe sees me with your tongue down my throat, I'll be sacked on the spot!"

His face lights up in mischief. "Excellent idea. Why didn't I think of that? Pucker up, baby!"

"John, no," I say in amused horror, slapping his chest. "Seriously, he'll pop an artery if he sees the hired help in a clinch." I look around the guests to see if the leech is lurking in the shadows somewhere.

"I thought you decided to rescind on the second event."

"I have, but I can't fall down on the job, either. Irrespective of the final decision, I must maintain professionalism." I voice my case as the Master of Ceremonies catches my attention from the other side of the ballroom.

"Look, I need to go. Dinner will be served soon. I suggest you make the most of it because come tomorrow, you'll be back slumming it at the Emerson."

"I heard that!" Sloan says, flinging his arm around John. "You know *I hate* to break up a lover's tryst, but Lowe has just entered." He points to the doorway where the man is standing with a small group all dressed in their best with their backs to us.

John groans in annoyance. "I'll be right over there, and I'll be watching. If he tries anything, I'll chop his flaming hands off with the butter knife."

"A first!" Sloan exclaims with a coy grin.

I can feel the colour drain from my face, not sure how the masses will react if he gives them a first-hand lesson in Sharia law.

"Okay," I sing-song, and politely kiss John's cheek before Sloan drags him to their table.

Turning around, I finally spot Nicki waiting at the staff door with Ted, the compere.

"Sorry, Ted," I apologise on my approach and follow him down the corridor with Nicki by my side. "I think I've found your bright side, darling."

Nicki's eyes widen in question as I run through the short but sweet proposal of the lovely Mr Barker.

"Really?" she asks in excitement as we pass through the kitchen door. "Give me his card. I'll do a search on him, see what comes up. Did John find you? Have you told him?" she asks in between breaths.

"Yes, he did, and no, I didn't. He was too busy trying to get his tongue in my mouth!"

"Walker men," she snorts as we both stand in the busy kitchen.

Looking over the starters, the head chef jostles us out of the way and walks up and down the tables. He studies each plate carefully, before picking two up. Cocking his head, he drops them on the floor deliberately.

"These are shit! Do them again!"

"You have five minutes," Ted says to the chef, undeterred, tapping his watch.

"Shit," I say under my breath and meet Nicki's eyes. Her face takes on an undeserved guilty expression, and I bite the inside of my cheek as the chef rants about perfection to his embarrassed sous chef.

As the head chef barks out orders to his second in command, the staff fly around the kitchen to re-do the dishes that have failed to meet his impeccable standards.

Less than four minutes later in the fraught atmosphere, the head chef flicks his wrist, and the servers collect up the plates.

I bring my hand to my chest as my anxiety peaks. If these dishes aren't up to scratch, we're fucked. It doesn't matter that Lowe insisted on his staff doing the catering aspect. If he so much as sees something that displeases him, it will be Nicki and me in the firing line.

Shuffling out of the kitchen, I grasp Nicki's hand as we stand in the ballroom doorway. I count beats as the staff stand at the tables, a plate poised in either hand, waiting for the signal. In synchronised fashion, they turn in unison and place down the starters.

At the back of the room, I finally see Richard Lowe. He lifts his glass in greeting, and I nod in acknowledgement.

"I guess I can't avoid him any longer. Just six more hours."

"Let's go get a drink while we still can." Nicki gestures to the hotel restaurant.

Entering the empty bar, I take a seat at the far end of the room and look out over the street outside. A heavy shower pelts against the pane and the droplets fall under the lamppost, the light guiding each down to earth.

I crack my head from side to side and rub my nape. Catching sight of my reflection, I gasp as Joe's darkened silhouette appears behind me. I quickly grip the arms of the leather tub chair, push myself up and rotate. Glaring at the back of a man walking towards the bar, I put one foot in front of the other, but am stopped short when a woman approaches him and smiles.

"Hey, are you okay?" Nicki asks, ambling towards me with two glasses of wine.

I huff out and pinch the bridge of my nose. "I thought I just saw my ex."

Nicki looks over at the bar. "It's stress," she says, taking a sip. "Hardly surprising considering everything that's happened."

"Hmm," I murmur.

"What was he like?" she asks, and not for the first time either, which makes me wonder what she is holding close to her chest.

I raise my head and sigh. "At first, he was everything I ever wanted. In the end, he was everything I despised. I loved him once, and I played devil's advocate to stay with him. I lost."

She nods but doesn't push the conversation further. She, like everyone else, has heard all about my past misdemeanours for the last month, more so because I see her daily. Which means when she notices I'm mentally digressing, the tea, cakes and sympathy make an appearance. And as much as I love cake, it's playing havoc on my waistline.

Pouring some more wine down my throat, I lick the remnants from my lip and put it down. "God, that's dangerous."

"Hardly. Want another?" Nicki quirks her brows impishly. "We've got an hour until service is finished."

"I'd love one, but we really shouldn't."

"It's low alcohol, so it's allowed," she says and motions to the waiter for two more, plus some water.

I give her a small smile and touch my glass to hers. "To us."

"Yes. To ventures old," she says, her eyes roaming the room. "And to ventures new."

"To ventures new," I repeat and drain the last bit.

"Speaking of new ventures, when is your house sale going through?" she enquires as the waitress places our fresh drinks on the table.

"Three weeks. It can't come soon enough."

I slouch down in the seat, and we make small talk about anything and everything until the hour has passed, and the Master of Ceremonies finally finds us.

I slug my arm around Nicki's shoulder as we stroll back into the ballroom. Right on time, the dessert plates are being cleared from the tables and coffee is being offered.

"I guess I better go and find flirty Lowe. I think I've avoided him for long enough."

Nicki grimaces. "Good luck, and don't stand too close!" She laughs, but it's easier said than done.

I walk around the tables, deliberately breezing past John, who is sitting alone, fiddling on his phone while everyone else, including Dev and his mother, are on the dance floor. Trailing my fingers across his shoulders, a tap ripples over my backside and I drop my mouth open and feign surprise.

"Sinful," I whisper and blow him a kiss. He winks and turns back to his phone.

Passing through the line of bodies, my name rings through my eardrums like a warning signal.

"Marie!"

My expression morphs into delight instantly, and I slap on a beaming smile and clasp my hands behind my back.

"Good evening, Richard," I greet, praying I sound sincere as I edge closer to him and the woman by his side - who is just old enough to be his granddaughter.

"Go and get us some champagne." He shoots a glare at the young woman. "And don't rush back," he commands, and it takes all I have to keep my jaw from hitting the floor. The woman, on the other hand, hurries off perfunctory, not even batting an eyelid at being spoken to in such a derogatory manner.

I grind my jaw, staring with unease at the chair he has just pushed out. And, unfortunately, I'm left with no other option than to sit, considering there are still a few guests at a nearby table watching intermittently.

"Marie, I've been looking for you all evening," he says, almost charmingly, as he presses one hand between my shoulder blades and strokes his fingers back and forth. Cold shivers run down my spine, and I brace my body so that he can't feel the discomfort I'm currently experiencing.

Seriously, if my resolve to jump this shitty ship after tonight's event wasn't already absolute, it definitely is now.

Panic sets in the moment his other hand snakes over my thigh under the table. I automatically draw my attention to John, who is unaware of what's happening and is still engrossed by his phone.

"I must say you do look breath-taking," he compliments in a way that causes the fine hairs on every inch of my skin to stand on end.

My body stiffens further as he kisses the side of my neck. Jerking my head away, trying to keep my features neutral, his wayward hand ascends higher inside my thigh. I gasp in horror and jab my elbow hard into his side. Unperturbed, he straightens his shoulders and grins cruelly.

"Such beautiful, creamy skin. I wonder what it takes to give it some colour? Maybe I should ask Mr Walker? Or, maybe later this evening, you'll join me for a drink in my suite, and we can discuss our future relationship in finer detail, amongst other things," he ruminates salaciously, his forward flirting now on the dangerous ground of sexual harassment.

He strokes his finger and thumb over his chin and shuffles his chair closer until he has me cornered.

"I'm sorry, Mr Lowe, but after careful consideration, we have decided tonight will be the only event we will be catering for you. We, therefore, have no future relationship. Although I do have a query if you would be so kind to answer it?" Richard tilts his head. "Tell me, do you treat all your employees this way?"

"No, just the ones I want to fuck. And if you know what's good for you, you'll take me up on that offer. Spreading your legs and bending over my desk might just save you tonight. I'll give you some time to think about it," he says and picks up a bottle of wine.

Relied up and seeing red, I rise from the chair and lean down. Ready to open my mouth and hurl my uncensored opinion of him, a voice speaks up.

"Hello, Marianne." The snide words spear me because I knew it wasn't over, and he has chosen tonight to finally enact whatever retribution he thinks I deserve. Fixing my attention on Joe, the scar on his neck and the prison standard tats fill my vision.

"Ah, Marie," Richard says smugly. "I believe you already know my godson."

Godson?

I fall back, wobbly on my legs and clutch my stomach. I slam my fist down on the table, causing everything atop of it to reverberate.

"Why?" I glare from Joe to Richard. "You really are an evil, dirty bastard, aren't you?" I fist the table as Richard steps into my space. "Is this why you hired me? Is this how you get your fucking kicks?" I hiss, then pick up a random glass of wine and throw it over him.

"Marie, Marie, Marie," Richard says with a sigh, dabbing a napkin over his face and jacket. "I must say, I was absolutely intrigued by you on New Year's Eve. I could see why my godson fell hook, line and sinker. Although I could hardly reconcile the woman in front of me as the one who destroyed-"

"Save it!" I cry. "And you." I pierce my glare at Joe. "I hope you enjoyed prison because I'm going to ensure you get sent back there indefinitely!"

I turn on my heel and run between the tables as John catches me. "I'm done!" I turn back to see Joe and Richard sharing a drink as if nothing has happened.

"Angel?" John holds me securely while he peers over my head. "What the fuck?" he grits out, and my body is jerked to the side as he attempts to go after them. I glance over my shoulder as Richard and Joe, and now Joe's parents, all watch with triumphant smiles.

"No!" I twist John back around. "Lowe set me up. He's Joe's godfather. I never knew!" I hold him close, not wanting to cause another scene. "Look, I need to grab my things. I'll meet you at the staff corridor. Please, darling, I just want to get out of here," I plead, and he lets me go.

I run into the staff room, drag my bag from the locker and slam it shut. Plucking out my mirror, I rub my finger under my eye, already aware that nothing can save this look.

"Shit," I mutter and kick open the door. Reaching for the toilet roll, it's empty.

Left with no other choice, I bolster back through the staff door, catch John's attention, and point from my face to the ladies.

I shift anxiously in the queue, desperate to get the hell out of here. Five minutes and six women later, I finally close the cubicle door behind me. Dabbing my eyes with toilet paper, I sigh heavily and then flush.

Squeezing into the tiniest of spaces between two women perfecting their heavily made-up faces, I wash my hands. Staring at my reflection, I'm still incensed by tonight's revelations. Add to that the fact that Richard Lowe has not only set me up, but he also treated me like a slut. I always knew he was a despicable bastard. I just didn't realise the depths in which he would sink.

Turning off the tap, I shake my hands and shove them under the dryer. The noise is ear-splitting, and I run my hands back and forth, thankfully concealing the pointless, background ramblings.

"Excuse me, are you finished?" a woman asks, and I stare at her vacantly, until her question penetrates.

"Yes, sorry," I reply over the sound of toilets flushing, doors opening and closing and general chatter filling the space.

As I walk to the door, my imperfect world crashes at my feet for the second time tonight. It has been years in the making, but it had to come, and now it finally has.

"My, my, look what the cat dragged in!" Patricia exclaims, the practised venom rolling off her tongue smoothly.

Humiliation shrouds me as the surrounding din quietens, and all eyes are on us. Acute awareness prickles my neck, hearing the clusters of women whisper among themselves, exaggerating what might happen, and how they will miss it if they leave.

I shake my head, highly disturbed that some people will use another's misery for entertainment.

"What do you want?" I address Patricia, thoroughly fucked off.

"Well, after all the heartache you've caused, I finally want an apology!" Patricia shouts, commanding attention, instigating the excited chatter to grow louder. "After everything we did for you, don't you have anything to say to me?"

Oh, I have plenty of things I want to say to the bitch.

"Actually, I do." I step into her space. My eyes narrow, and I fight back the temptation to let rip and say all the things I've wanted to since the night she sat in the study with her husband and declared I had intentionally destroyed her son's life.

Instead, I'm going to cut where it hurts.

"I can forgive you for being a bitch to me. I can forgive you for all the shitty things you did to me when you knew how Joe was treating me. I can even forgive you for lying to the jury, and for setting me up for a fall tonight." Patricia's mouth curls up in victory. "Just know, that until your dying day, I will never, *ever,* forgive you for standing by your son and proclaiming his innocence when you knew damn well that he murdered our child in cold blood!"

While the words spew from my mouth, the area descends into a suspenseful hush, becoming so quiet, you could hear a pin drop.

"Goodbye, Patricia." I stride out as the noise grows again in wonder and accusation.

I rush back into the ballroom to John, who is walking towards me with Sloan, as the sound of heels clips behind me. I make it halfway when my hair is yanked back.

"How dare you, you little bitch?" Patricia screams at me. "How dare you think you can speak to me in such a manner after what you did?"

My entire body stiffens and my hands fist at my sides. I'm fucking furious that she has the audacity to forget the things that happened during the years I lived under her roof. The lies, the cheating. God forbid, the times she threatened to call social services to take Faith away if I dared to speak about the beatings. And by God, do I want to tell all and sundry the truth, but to lash out would make me no better than her right now.

Still, I will not stand here and take her sanctimonious shit after what her family have done tonight.

"After what I did?" I repeat, disbelieving she is going to play the innocent card. "I might say the same thing about you. You were never exactly the model mother, were you?" I scowl and move in front of her. "If you had been," I lower my voice. "Your son might not have ended up a convicted murderer!"

"You fucking bitch!" she barks out, and spittle showers my face. A swift whooshing slices through the tense atmosphere and her hand slaps hard across my cheek.

A stunned gasp resounds, and the big band slowly stop playing.

I press my hand to my inflamed flesh as heavy running approaches from different directions, and John spins me around and removes my hand. Looking up into his eyes, he glares at his palm and the streak of blood he has just wiped off.

"What the hell?" he hollers in revulsion, turning to the hundreds of guests all watching tonight's unrehearsed entertainment, of which, unfortunately, I am the centre of. "How dare you strike my wife?"

Patricia, unfazed and uncaring, struts towards us, but before she can open her toxic mouth again, Duncan grabs her.

"Darling, please, don't," I plead with John and place my hand on his chest.

"The bastard's parents?" he queries quietly, and I nod.

"Let's go. Let's not make this worse than it already is." My begging is futile, and I know it when he narrows his eyes at Duncan, who is still shielding his wife behind him.

John laughs, unamused, and shakes his head. "I don't beat defenceless women," he says firmly. "But for *that* thing," he points at Patricia, "I'd make a monumental exception!"

"Darling, please." I hold out my hand, willing him to take it, desperate to put as much distance between them and us as possible.

Upon hearing my plea, Joe swaggers towards us, putting on the guise of someone who belongs in this grand setting and not in a prison dinner hall.

"Now, your son, on the other hand, he knows all about beating defenceless women." John goads him, probably in the same tone that Joe did him a month back. "Maybe I should ask him for pointers? What do you say, Joe? How many senseless batterings does it take to get her to cower in submission?"

"Oh, no." I bring my hand to my mouth as Joe's misleading calm conduct begins to change. It's the same expression he would wear before he would beat me into capitulation.

Without warning, Joe suddenly launches himself at John, who pushes me aside in readiness. Shocked gasps ring out in the crowd as Joe lands the first hit to John's cheek.

"Is that all you've got?" John spits out, before swinging his arm back then forward. Smashing his fist against Joe's nose, he instantly slumps to the floor upon impact.

"You like to beat on women, don't you, you son of a bitch! Well, how about you try beating on someone your own goddamn size!"

John grits out as he bends down and grabs Joe by the collar and levies blow after blow to his face. "Come on, Joseph! You spent twenty-three in prison, sunshine. Did they not teach how to fucking fight inside, you hideous, evil bastard?"

"Oh my God! Somebody get security!" a bystander cries out.

I stand in horror as Dev and Sloan pull back a wild, worked up John.

"I'll have you arrested for assault!" Duncan yells as he removes a hanky from his pocket and tends to his son's bloodied appearance.

"Go ahead! I'll save you the trouble and call the police myself." John raises his arms in yield as two guards run towards him. "Do not touch me!"

"Get him out of my hotel!" Richard barks at the guards, who weigh John up for size, and clearly don't want to go there.

"You know," John says, shaking his finger, fixated on Duncan. "I'm surprised someone of your moral compass cares so much about the law."

Duncan, taken aback, puffs out his chest. "What's that supposed to mean?" he asks. "I'm a highly decorated judge and a purveyor of this country's laws and beliefs!"

John laughs acerbically, contemplating with his forefinger and thumb on his chin. "Values and beliefs?" he repeats thoughtfully. "Obviously our interpretations differ wildly because I believe that human life is priceless, and I value true justice when a crime has been committed. I believe in it so much, I'd vote to bring back the death penalty. Why should the rapists, paedophiles and murderers of this world be allowed to continue breathing in the free ride called prison?"

Duncan inhales sharply but doesn't respond. Instead, he reaches for his wife. "Let's go, Patty!"

"Remove *him*, now!" Richard demands yet again, forcing the guards to move.

"No, I don't think so," John says. He turns around, and the guards halt as he motions to me. He lifts my hand and kisses it before passing me off to Sloan. "I'm sorry for doing this, darling."

"Doing what?" I ask, fear rising from the depths of my heart, choking my tone.

John walks back onto the dancefloor and picks a flute of champagne off a waiter's tray. "Ladies and gentlemen?" he calls, garnering attention, taking this opportunity not to blend. "I'd like to apologise for my behaviour tonight, and to show there is no ill will, let us all raise our glasses in a toast. To the good judge and his wife!" he proclaims with false pride, tipping his glass towards a furious Duncan and a terrified Patricia.

"To the good judge and his wife!" everyone repeats, unaware of the cruel blow that is about to be delivered – if John's expression is anything to go by.

"Oh, shit," I whisper, as the multitude of arms raise under his command.

Sloan's grip tightens around my waist, and Kara appears at my other side along with Jules and Lou, and Dev and Nicki.

"I think any further invites from arsehole Dick are unlikely for us, my love," Sloan says with bemusement to his wife.

"I'm glad you think this is entertaining. This is my life. Not to mention my livelihood! I had a proposal tonight. That man is probably standing in the audience watching," I retort, but don't dare look around.

Sloan sighs. "I don't think it's entertaining at all. That bastard set you up, and that shit doesn't fly with me."

"I'm glad to hear it, but I'm still under obligation right now."

"Good thing I have an amazing legal team who have a proven record of rescinding even the tightest of contracts," he replies.

"Good," I tell him. "Because I'm going to need them. And a bottomless loan from you to pay for them!"

"Done," Sloan replies.

I stare wildly at John, who swallows a mouthful of champagne, puts it down on the floor, and then takes a relaxed stance with his hands in his trouser pockets.

"As a matter of fact, he is such a good judge and purveyor of the laws of our land, that when his son here," he jabs his finger towards Joe. "Was arrested for a crime he *did* commit – and if you aren't privy, it was GBH and battery of his young, fragile wife – the good judge coerced the police until his son was released without charge."

Ructions emanate around the room in a wave effect. I press my face into Sloan's chest when people start to turn, putting two and two together.

"Not your son, right Your Honour?" John mutters sardonically. "Tell me, Your Honour, what did your *innocent* son do after he was released?"

I pull away from Sloan's chest and glance at my former in-laws. Duncan squirms uncomfortably but stays mute, whereas Patricia looks forlorn and humiliated. And she should because she has lived her life under falsity and pretence. She has probably spent the last twenty odd years covering up her son's transgressions. And this evening, it was all for nothing.

"No? Cat got your tongue?" John taunts. "Well, let me rehash your memory. Your son attempted to murder his terrified, defenceless wife!"

The crowd ruffles further, some shake their heads in disgust, others, their mouths agape, disbelieving what is being played out in front of them.

"But the worst part?" John re-engages his audience. "Is that that lying, cheating, lowlife bastard over there, murdered his own child. *Your goddamn granddaughter!*" he yells at Duncan, causing every unsuspecting observer to flinch. "And what did you do, *Your Honour?* You, *yet again,* demanded his release when he was arrested."

The murmured exclamations and rumblings of discontent gain momentum, rippling loudly in the vast space. I turn slowly to see quite a few of the guests putting down their drinks, refusing to carry on toasting such a man, whereas others are preparing to leave.

"And that's not all. During the trial, you unsuccessfully abused your position to influence the jury. You flagrantly flouted the precious laws of our land and attempted to pervert the course of justice when you watched your wife lie under oath. She committed perjury, lied to your peers, and *you* backed it! Some might even say *you* instigated it."

"You son of a bitch!" Duncan shouts, humiliated. He propels himself towards John, who holds out his hand, while the guards stand between them.

"No, Your Honour, that bitch would be your wife, because if she had been a better mother, your son wouldn't have become a rabid dog that needs to be put down quickly." John strides closer. "And make no mistake, if he so much as coughs in the same vicinity as my wife, he'll suffer in a way that makes prison look easy. I promise you that."

Showing Duncan his back, John picks up his glass and holds it high. "So, ladies and gentlemen, one last toast to the good judge and his wife." Necking the last of the liquid, he opens his hand, and the glass shatters on the floor at his feet. The crowd, aghast and motionless, watch his every move as he strides towards us.

"Kid?" he calls out to Sloan, who nods and waves his hand.

"Excuse me, sir, you need to leave now," one of the guards says, far too politely considering what has just gone down.

"Don't worry, we're going," he replies and holds me close.

"Remove them *all*, now!" Richard continues to huff and puff, his face bright red, pointing at our little group.

I stare straight ahead as I walk calmly out of the ballroom. Reaching the foyer, Philip Barker is standing there with his wife.

"Oh, shit," I mutter.

"What?" John asks, his fingers squeezing mine instinctively.

"That chap offered me some events earlier this evening. I bet that offer is now off the table." I inhale then walk towards him. "Hello again, Mr Barker. I'd like to apologise for what you have-"

"Marie, my proposal still stands," he confirms.

"Really?" I ask in shock, looking at him and his wife, seeing no judgement whatsoever.

"Yes. Should you feel the need to discuss tonight, we can do it then, but I think someone wants you gone," he says, tipping his head to the tiresome guards.

"I'll call you tomorrow. Thank you," I say contritely and smile.

John removes his jacket, throws it over my shoulders and guides me to the door. "Trust me?" he asks.

"I trust you."

Chapter 45

I GRIP THE jacket over my shoulders as I stand, unwelcome, on the front steps of the Roseby. Gazing up at the sky, the heavens have opened considerably, and rain is falling in waves, bouncing off the pavements.

John's warm hand curls tightly around mine, causing an immediate frisson of excitement to ripple through me.

"Ready to get wet?" he asks coyly, his double-edged meaning more than implicit.

"Always." I grin, feeling young and carefree again. Holding the jacket over my head – although why is redundant since I no longer need to impress anyone – I skip down the steps and purposely land in a small puddle, drenching my calves. John rolls his eyes but smiles beautifully at my playful demeanour.

He tugs me into his side, preparing to leg it through the sodden streets when a car horn resounds. In the sea of identical black limousines waiting outside, George is standing beside his car under an umbrella.

"Come on." John grasps my hand, and we dash through the congested traffic.

"Evening, George." I dive inside as he opens the passenger door, grateful for a reprieve from the downpour.

"Where to, sir?" George enquires as John manoeuvres himself into the back. The car roars to life beneath us and pulls away from the kerb.

John winks at me as I divest myself of his jacket and drop it to the floor. "Home, George." He then activates the privacy glass with a cocked brow. No soon has the tinted panel fully concealed us from George's non-prying eyes, he drags me over his lap. "About tonight-"

"No talking."

Smashing my lips to his, he shoves up my dress, and a cold draught swathes my bum. Positioning a thigh on either side of his thighs, I crush my body against his. His hard shaft lengthens, vibrating at my core, and I rake my fingers over his closely cropped hair.

I gasp for breath the moment he exerts control, and his tongue invades my mouth, tangling and twisting with mine. I close my eyes as my body starts to enflame from the inside out.

My hands fumble with his shirt as I pull it out of his trousers. Undoing his belt, I flick open the metal catches and unzip him. Boldly shoving my hand inside his shorts, I sigh when I encircle his hot, silky shaft.

"Fuck," he curses, the same moment he moves his wayward hands higher on the backs of my thighs, and each palm grabs a handful of my bum. Kneading me hard, a dull ache spans my abdomen. I keen out, the instant he teases a finger between my flesh and flimsy knickers.

"Oh, god," I moan wantonly, desperate for him to consume me.

I thrust my chest closer to his face, and he yanks down my dress and bra simultaneously, splitting a seam in the process. Curling one large hand around my breast, he squeezes my areola and kisses my tight peak reverently. Two, maybe three, fingers breach my opening, plunging deep, stretching me flawlessly. It's so good, in fact, I can already feel my arousal drenching his hand, while the impending ache lingers dangerously low in my centre.

I feel empowered, and I stare into his eyes as my body begins to build magnificently. I pump my palm delicately over his throbbing length, while his talented fingers fuck me with impeccable skill. I slap one hand on his shoulder and the other on the roof for leverage. I roll my hips back and forth, taking him harder, faster. Deeper.

"Darling, I'm so close," I whimper, tightening my hand around him.

"Me, too. Lie back, beautiful," he orders, expertly guiding me over the seat.

I grudgingly let go of him and lay down. My bare back touches the supple leather, and I sink my shoulders and head into it, offering my bottom half up.

Unzipping my dress, he slips down my underwear. I automatically spread my thighs, insofar as I can, ready to accommodate him. I smile when he loses his balance as he tugs his trousers and shorts down mid-thigh. I shift my gaze in anticipation of him filling me. Or more precisely, fucking me hard in the back of the kids' limo, in the middle of a busy London street with multiple bodies passing by outside. Not to mention George driving.

Any further thought is obliterated when he throws one leg over his shoulder and positions the other on the back of the seat, exposing me to him completely.

"I'm improvising," he says wryly.

I rub my foot over his shoulder as he seizes my hips, hauls me forward, and aligns his engorged tip at my aroused opening.

"Please," I plead in wanton invitation. He slides himself in marginally, and the feeling of the first inch filling me is spectacular. I glance down at him sliding inside. My core contracts and my breathing becomes more perceptible. His expression is a heady combination of determined desire, and I know this look well - better than I know my own.

And I know all I need to do is squeeze.

Hard.

"Not yet," he says, reading me perfectly. As he penetrates little by little, my core soaked and ready, the car brakes sharply, forcing him deep in a swift thrust.

"Fuck, yes!" I shudder, revelling in every inch stretching me, while every ripple and beat excites me. I squeeze my eyes, desperate to keep my impending, orgasmic scream at bay. "Fuck me, that was good. Again, darling. I want more."

"You want it hard, beautiful?"

"God, yes," I confirm, as the fire between my legs dictates what it wants. And what I want, too.

Gripping the front of my thighs, he licks the inside of my knee, withdraws suddenly, and sharply glides back in. And it's utterly effing delicious.

My mouth opens in response, and I groan, unashamed. Meeting him hip to hip, I tweak my distended nipples, while the hunger in my centre deepens. "Oh, God!"

John smirks and puts his finger over my lips to stem my enthusiasm. I suck it into my mouth while I stroke down my stomach to touch my clit, needing to eviscerate in fiery passion.

"Fucking beautiful," he says, still ploughing into me with vigour.

Panting, minutes away from release, I brace my thighs and constrict him hard. His fingers pinch my waist tight as he throbs feverishly inside my aching walls.

"Sir?"

We both freeze instantly as George's static voice fills the cabin.

My face falls; the orgasm I earned in the next thirty seconds now obliterated. John's cheeks scrunch in annoyance, and he shakes his head.

"Fantastic fucking timing!" As he reaches over to the intercom, he impales me further under the action. And sadly, I'm unable to respond to the sublime feeling with George waiting.

"Yeah," John replies gruffly, placing his hand over my mouth to conceal my heavy breathing.

"We could be stuck in traffic a while," George states in an unusual tone, although I think he's more than aware of what we're doing back here. I don't think it is the first time, but that's something I really don't want to consider.

"Okay." John drops his head to my breast and chortles. "Are you okay to walk in your current condition?" he whispers.

I exhale grumpily. "Hmm. Are you?" I retort, looking down at where his unsatisfied erection is filling me. He nods reluctantly and gently pulls out, causing me to moan.

Quickly righting my appearance, I fasten my dress as he zips up his trousers, then search around the floor and seats.

"Where are my knickers?" I'm verging on panic, unable to find them. The last thing I need is for Sloan or Kara, or God forbid, Oliver, to unearth them unexpectedly in the future.

"I've got them," he replies slyly, tapping his pocket.

"Well, can I have them?"

"No, because it's one less piece to take off again in the next half an hour," he says, deactivating the privacy glass. "We'll walk from here. Thanks, George."

John takes my hand as he helps me out of the car and tucks me into his side. The rain is still coming down heavily, soaking us both to the bone, but it is insignificant. Turning to him, I reach up on my toes and find his mouth. Cradling his head lovingly, car horns honk at our display of unfettered passion, but I couldn't give a toss. I love this man with every inch of my being. I don't give a damn who knows it.

"It's a long walk home," I murmur.

"We're not going home," he replies, reciprocating the kiss before turning on his heel. Running behind him, my feet are aching along with my core – although that's aching for an entirely different reason.

As we turn at the end of the street, I grin in enlightenment, because I know exactly where we're going.

Five minutes later, hand in hand, we burst through the front door of the Emerson. I fuss with my drowned rat appearance - which is now truly beyond hope - as we stride towards James and Laura on the reception desk.

"Evening," Laura greets, her brow furrowing in curious question.

"Two free?" John asks, prompting James to toss him a key from under the desk.

"It is, indeed. Have a good night. I'll send up a hearty breakfast. Lots of carbs!" James says playfully, while Laura elbows him and smiles professionally. I cover my face in embarrassment, hoping neither of them is on duty in the morning when we do the walk of shame.

We board the first lift that arrives, and John ensnares me in his arms. Bending down to kiss me, his hands maul my back. The doors begin to close until they ping open again and an elderly couple enter.

I close my eyes in resignation because it would seem we can't catch a break tonight. I position myself against his front to conceal the raging erection prodding into my flesh. Taking a transitory glance between us, a naughty thought succumbs me, and I subtly rub my hand over him.

"Behave," he admonishes in a whisper, not yielding his own advice as he rubs my arms and gyrates his hips lewdly into my bum.

"Touché," I reply low.

Three floors later, the couple bid us goodnight. The moment the doors shut, I rotate without further hesitation and push him into the corner.

"Do you think Sloan will be calling us shortly?" John asks knowingly, recalling the day the kids were practically getting naked in a lift.

"Don't care." I shrug, untucking his shirt for the second time, breaching the space between material and man. I trace my fingers over his ripped stomach and snake my legs around his waist as he lifts me up.

Taking advantage of the position, he slams me back to the other side of the box and pillages my mouth brusquely. The brass bar encircling the perimeter digs into my lower back, assisting in holding me in place while he devours ardently.

Finally, the lift stops, and the door opens. Carrying me out, he unlocks the penthouse door and shoves it open. Kicking it behind him, I reach between us while he strides through the darkened space.

"The shagging suite," I murmur, nibbling his jaw. "How fitting."

"Quite," he replies with amusement.

Undoing his belt and zip for the second time tonight, I slide my hand back into his shorts. Hitching me higher up his body, he lodges my back against one side the dual aspect window, pulls up the skirt of my dress and brackets his body against mine.

He roughly shoves his fingers back inside my sopping core and lets out a possessive growl. "Still wet and ready. Fucking perfect," he says. "Slide me inside you, angel."

Twisting my neck, my cheek touches the cold glass, and the London skyline illuminates for miles.

I shift my hand between us and open myself for him. Removing my hand, he sucks my fingers into his mouth and flays me with a look of pure love. His dextrous hands manoeuvre my thighs wider apart to accommodate him until his hips are cradled tight. Aligning himself, he penetrates me in a quick, powerful thrust.

"Ah, Christ!" I exclaim, still very much turned on. But in truth, this man is my drug. One simple touch can take me over the edge. But this? This will annihilate me. And I summon the feeling of being burnt by the flames because his fire is the only place my soul has ever felt alive in two decades.

"John!" I cry out, my back hitting hard and repeatedly against the glass.

His fingertips cut into my backside as he influences my lower half further, and my shoulders to lodge uncomfortably against the pane.

I tighten my arms around him and scratch my nails lightly over his nape. His flesh slides against mine as a soft sheen grows under exertion, and I press my heels into his arse for traction.

The sounds of ecstasy fill the suite. The grunting, the panting, the slap of flesh against flesh. Combined with the flourishing need coiling in my abdomen, I know I can't hold out much longer.

My body shakes in bliss as he powers into me over and over. His body is an unrelenting force, and if I don't walk out of here full of bruises in the morning, I'll be lucky.

Actually, if I can walk at all, it will be a bloody miracle.

"Come," John growls, slamming up against me. His rock-hard length, hot and slick, ripples in and out.

"Harder," I find myself saying, although he's riding me to the point of pain already.

Pressing my nails into his shoulders, he gives me what I want, until I feel I'm going to split in two. Honestly, I can't continue to fight the inevitable, wanting to prolong it for no other reason than I want it to consume me. It's already consumed me; he's consumed me.

He takes the initiative, already aware exactly how to make me vocalise when he bites down hard on my nipple and laves it with his mouth. Unexpectedly, he drops down my legs, withdraws abruptly, and tears down my dress and bra. Turning me around, he pushes me front first, against the window, and I watch in reflection as he strips off his remaining garments.

A fleeting sense of horror stirs my sensibilities because anyone still working in the buildings opposite could see me; naked and flattened, nailed against the window and getting fucked hard from behind.

"John…" I murmur, now very alert.

"One-way glass, angel," he confirms, rearranging my hands above my head and pulling my bum back. Drawing a fitful line down my spine, he runs his finger between my cheeks, stilling me. It's not like we haven't done this before, and yes, I enjoy it, but it still makes me a little apprehensive.

"Not tonight," he says, placing one hand on my belly, before parting my flesh and re-entering me. I instinctively drive back against him, but he stops me. "I just want you to feel, angel. I don't want you to concentrate on anything other than how I feel inside you. How it feels when I take you over and over, and how it feels when you come on me. Now, close your eyes."

I reluctantly drop my lids, stretch out my fingers high above me and press my forehead to the pane. He holds my hips carefully as he reduces his tempo and makes a very gentle, but exposed kind of love to me.

I tip my bum up and part my legs further. I concentrate on the overwhelming collective of the coolness of the glass, the heat of his body inside mine, and the fire culminating deep in my core. I keen out as he hits deeper than before, and a cloud of condensation fogs the glass.

"That's it, darling. Come for me."

His fingers rub slow and soft down my stomach, over my pubic bone, until he draws unhurried, possessive circles over my clit. I draw my hand down and link my fingers in his, speeding up his ministration on my sensitive, slick flesh. I moan, in unashamed, beautiful torture, the moment his other hand copies the action over my tight, hard nipple, and I finally begin to let go.

"Oh, oh!" I rasp out, my core tight and heavy. I roll my body fluidly as fire razes every fibre of my being. My cries are guttural, and I come with ferocity while orgasmic overload consumes all my senses – just the way I intended it to.

My raw, unbridled cries continue to echo in the stillness of the suite, and I squeeze my core around him, and he roars out.

"Oh, fuck. That's good. Keep going." Pounding harder, my body slamming against the glass, I turn my head to find his mouth. Kissing him like my life depends on it, he eventually slows.

I flail lax at the window, his weight bearing down on my back. The coolness chills my hot flesh wonderfully. My body is depleted, drained of all energy; exhausted of all common sense.

"I love you, angel," he says quietly, and slides his arm around my waist and places his hand between my breasts. He withdraws carefully, and I feel empty without him inside me. Holding my back to his chest, he brushes away the damp hair plastered to my perspired face.

"I love you, too. And I shall until the day I die. There is no end for us, not even in death." I exhale, expressing how I really feel. I've wanted to say it for a long time, and now I can without guilt or regret. I lift my hand to the back of his head, curl my fingers and drag him forward.

"There's something I need to do," he says, as he picks up his trousers. Removing his mobile and wallet, he unveils a small velvet pouch.

My legs leave the ground, and he carries me up the stairs of the suite. Dropping me in the middle of the bed, he puts the pouch and his phone on the table and climbs in beside me.

Spooned together, he traces up and down my side, while I stare up at the ceiling. I yawn under his hypnotic touch until my breathing begins to level out, and my eyelids start to droop.

"Angel?" he murmurs, rimming my nipple, eliciting it to stiffen again.

"Yeah?"

He sighs heavily. "I need to apologise. I'm sorry I humiliated you tonight."

I arch up on my elbow, roll over and straddle his centre. "Darling, it's done, and I'll always forgive you, but why did you do it?" I query, flattening my palms on his taut stomach. He places his hands on my legs and shakes his head, apparently at a loss.

"Honestly, I don't know what came over me. Initially, I just wanted to get you out of there, but the moment I saw her drag you by the hair… No, no, no, that wasn't happening. And as much as I'd have loved to dole out the same treatment, and rag that vitriolic bitch across the floor like she deserved, that's not me. I couldn't lay a hand on a woman, regardless of how much she was asking for it. But at the same time, now that I know everything, I couldn't bear to see them stand there and gloat. Acting holier than thou with their heads held high. So instead, I decided to hit them where it hurts – their pride and social standing."

I give him a small smile. I'm not ashamed, and I don't expect him to grovel.

"You were amazing," I tell him, laying over his front, my ear to his heart. "I mean, I might not be saying that when Lowe is litigating me for breach of contract, but I was proud of you. I was proud that you kept your composure, and yes, it did get heated, but I can't blame you for that. You finally achieved what I had dreamed of for years. I would have just walked away, but you called them out for what they really are. And I will never, ever be angry with you for doing that for me."

He tugs me closer, and his thumb caresses my cheek, brushing away my hushed tears in the darkness.

"Angel, earlier when I said I had something to do…" he trails off and flicks on the bedside lamp. The room illuminates, and I squint and shuffle off him.

"I've carried this around for the last month, uncertain if I should ask." I kneel on the edge of the bed as he reaches for the pouch. Lifting my hand, he removes my engagement ring.

"This," he holds it up, "signifies what I want, but the woman I gave this to could only promise me one day. I don't want one day. I want forever, and I want it now." Pulling the drawstring of the pouch, he tips the contents into his hand. "This," he holds up another ring, "this is forever. This is now." Getting down on one knee in front of the bed, my hands come up in front of my face in a prayer position. "So, *Marianne Turner*, will you marry me?"

"Yes!" I cry out in exhilaration and haul myself into his arms. Spinning me around the room, tears of joy run down my cheeks. "Yes, yes, yes," I repeat, peppering his face with kisses.

"I want to spend the rest of my life with you. I've known it from the first time I saw you."

"Good." I rest my forehead against his. "Because I want to wake up every day and see your face. I want to watch when you teach our children to ride their bikes; when you teach our sons to shave; and when you lock up our screaming daughters when boys come calling. I want all of it."

Holding me effortlessly with one arm, he grins beautifully. "I think it's time we have that IUD removed, don't you?" He playfully pats my abdomen.

"Actually," I say on a breath. "It's already gone. I had it removed before the christening, but with everything that was happening, I just-"

"Shush," he murmurs. "So, there's a chance?" Putting me down, he tilts his head towards my tum.

I nod, feeling like the final weight has been lifted. "It's slim to none, but there's always a chance."

He grins gloriously and reaches for his phone. Intermittent beeps resound until the soft melodic cords of *The Drugs Don't Work* start to play.

"May I have this dance?" He holds out his hand, and I nod as he reels me in. Resting my head against his chest, we move from side to side to the song.

I smile when he begins to sing in my ear, remembering those painful days when I would do the same. Singing along about how if heaven called, I'd be coming too. But the lyrics that I could always assimilate to, the ones that genuinely hurt above all else, was that when Faith left my life, I *was* better off dead.

Now, inside the arms of a man who knows my tragedies and still loves me unconditionally, singing a song I love and hate in equal measure, one day, I know I will see her face again.

Breathing out, unable to disguise my tears, they roll down my cheek, soaking his chest.

"One day you'll hold her again, angel," he says, kissing my head and lifting me off the ground.

"I will," I murmur. "And you shall, too."

He swings me up into his arms as the song finishes and moves us to the oversized chaise longue near the window. Tangling my arms and legs with his, I feel at peace.

In the distance, a new day approaches with the midnight hour, and I welcome its arrival. Because once upon a time, when I was still in that place of desolation, waiting for the past and present to implode, my future was uncertain.

Now, as I stare at the horizon, I can finally look forward to tomorrow.

Chapter 46

I ROTATE IDLY on my heels as we join the end of the queue. Counting at least seven bodies before me, I scrutinise the menu board.

Debating between a cinnamon swirl or a pecan plait, I tap the side of John's thigh. His arms instantly circle my stomach, and his warm breath sweeps over my lobe as I twist.

"What do you want?" I ask, and he studies the board thoughtfully.

"A flat white and a toasted cheese panini. And throw a millionaire's shortcake in there, too," he replies nonchalantly. "Oh, and get me an oat cookie."

I blink in amazement, stunned at where he puts it all. Especially since it's only been a couple of hours since we had breakfast together.

"Anything else?" I query sarcastically as he drops his lips to mine.

"No, I've got to leave some room for lunch," he says in all seriousness, patting his infuriatingly flat stomach. "After all, my woman is now a fairly wealthy lady, and I do expect dinner at The Ritz."

"I'm not that rich," I mutter, trying to conceal my laugh. "How about a Marks and Sparks two for ten?"

Breathing out, he presses his nose to mine. "If you promise to serve me the dessert naked, I'll agree to anything," he says under his breath, triggering my insides to weaken. I touch my hand to his face, but his eyes avert behind me, and he straightens himself instantly.

"What's wrong?"

"Dom's here. I'll come back and grab the coffee, darling." On that, he cradles my face in both hands, rubs his thumbs over my cheeks and kisses me in the politest yet most indecent way possible. He touches my bottom lip before striding through the coffee shop, attracting a few wistful gazes here and there.

I gradually move down the queue and give my order to the barista. Waiting for the drinks to be prepared, the sound of the door opening and closing, chairs scraping the floor, general banter, and the hiss of the coffee machines, immerses the busy premises.

"Flat white and a cappuccino?"

"Thank you," I say to the man as he puts the drinks on the tray.

"Do you need a hand that?" he asks, proving chivalry is not dead.

"No, but thanks anyway."

517

I balance the tray precariously as I head towards the back of the shop. The closer I get, the conversation between my man and his closest confidante becomes more clear-cut.

"I see the crown jewels polish up nicely," Dominic says complementary, and I pause, pretending to hitch my bag higher on my shoulder.

"They do, indeed. Especially when the past isn't tarnishing the lustrous shine," John replies, kicking his chair back. He saunters over to me and takes the tray, brushing his fingers over mine.

"Are you okay?"

"Hmm," I reply as he winks and turns his back on me. I traipse behind him, finally realising *I'm* the elusive crown jewels he has discussed time and time again when he thought I couldn't hear.

I pull back one of the spare chairs and drop my bag on the floor. John places my cappuccino and pastry in front of me, and I catch Dominic watching intently, almost smiling as I remove my jacket and hang it over the back. Sliding onto the seat, I dump two sweeteners in my mug before stirring it for distraction.

"Good morning, Marie," Dominic greets with his Yorkshire brogue, forcing me to acknowledge him when I really don't want to.

"Hello, Mr Archer," I reply curtly and bring the oversized mug to my mouth as John gives me a resigned look.

I purse my lips in frustration; I'm putting him in the middle. It isn't intentional, but I just can't look past everything that has happened in the last eight months. This man had umpteen opportunities to reveal his identity, but he didn't. Likewise, he had the ability and knowledge to help when I needed it the most, but again, he left me to the ex-cons. Truthfully, I don't owe him anything.

"Angel," John cajoles firmly. It's a tone he's used for the last few days since he set this up and I've tried to argue my way out of it. His reasoning that he didn't want his bride and his best man scrapping over the wedding cake was enough to make me acquiesce. While I may not like being coerced into this little get together, for him I will always make an effort.

I clear my throat and put down my mug. "Good morning, Dominic. It's nice to see you again. How have you been?" I ask, lowing the shield of hostility.

Slightly.

"I'm very well, Marie. Thank you for asking, but let's not pretend. I'm not stupid, and I realise you're just being polite. I appreciate how incredibly uncomfortable this must be for you."

"That's an understatement," I tell the table, not daring to look at either man considering the chill that has just swept in.

"Angel, please," John murmurs, and I lift my head to evaluate his expression. It's not good. I raise my mug in front of my face to hide the indignation of being inadvertently told off.

"J, it's okay. I deserve that," Dominic says. "I'd rather clear the air now, and she's earned the right to say what she thinks."

"'*Earned the right?*'" I repeat in annoyance. "I've more than earned the right! Just tell me something – why didn't you tell me who you really were on New Year's Eve?"

"But I did - I gave you a clue when I said your full name, but you hadn't given it."

I chortle. "Oh, silly me for not picking up on that! I'll pay better attention next time."

Dominic sighs. "Honestly, what difference would it have made? Would you have gone home and purged your soul? Or would you have gone home, packed a bag and done a moonlight flit?" He gives me a levelled stare, daring me to confirm the former when we both know the latter would have prevailed.

"And the club?" I deliberately change the line of questioning. "You walked away and left me to fend off the wolves alone."

He sighs again in agitation. "Believe me, it was better that way. But even if I had stayed and dispensed my own form of retribution, John still didn't know. So, what would you have done?"

I shiver and avert my eyes, because regardless of how much shit I can spew at him, he's right, and there's nothing I can say that would change the outcome of either of those meetings. I would've run. I would've run so fucking fast I'd have put the world's best sprinter to shame.

"Look, I'm not your enemy, Marie. And I don't want every meeting to start and end like this. And trust that I will be in your life because J's in your life. There's nothing I won't do for him, and in turn, that also extends to you."

I nod and stare down at the pecan plait in front of me. It's no longer as palatable as it was when I ordered it.

"Now, let's start again. J tells me you have an amazing opportunity on the horizon."

I smile apologetically, and John reaches over and links my fingers in his. "Yes, a hotelier called Philip Barker. I presume you've already done a background check on him," I query with slight amusement. But after what Richard Lowe did to me, John and Sloan have already said that before I agree to anything, they will dig as deep as they can.

Or namely, this man will.

Dominic smiles. "Yes, of course." He puts a file on the table. "He's completely above board, in the black, and no skeletons in the closet with familial connections. In future, I suggest you call me directly." He flicks his brows to John; a look that confirms he is cutting out the middleman. "My number is on the front."

I pout slightly. I don't like this. *This,* being my life under a microscope. I see his logic, but still.

On the other hand, his time will indeed cost money – a lot of money, I would think - and I should be grateful that I get it for free.

I open the file and am surprised when it appears he has gone back generations. As I flick through a document dated seventeen hundred and something, it's obvious Dominic is thorough. Closing the flap, I drop the wallet into my bag.

"That's very generous, thank you, Dominic."

"Dom, please."

I smile and relax somewhat as I finally cut off a small piece of my pecan plait, admire it, then devour it.

With one ear on the pleasant, if not mildly weird conversation, which skirts the topic of coffee shop culture and how some American traditions have finally become a British way of life, to the current national obsession with politics, Dominic clears his throat.

"So, when's the wedding happening? Give me some notice so I can clean my suit," he says with a laugh.

I dart my head up because, with everything that has found the fan and hit it at full blast, marriage is something I have completely disregarded.

"M, are you sure you're ready for fifteen stone to be attached to you in holy matrimony?" He laughs again when John shoves his shoulder. "Hey, I wouldn't want your sorry arse attached to me until death. I've had to drag it out of the shit hundreds of times, sunshine!" he chides John, while I choke on the pastry as opposed to swallowing it.

"We've not started planning yet," I mumble between coughs, making a mental note to start looking at churches and registry offices this afternoon.

I down a mouthful of coffee to soothe the fire in my throat as my phone beeps. I delve down into my bag and open a message from Nicki, confirming a meeting with Phil Barker next week. Putting it on standby, I drop it on the table and finish the last of my drink.

"We don't need to actually plan the wedding. I've got a weapon in my arsenal that most don't," John says proudly.

"Ah yes, the sister. The vicar," Dominic replies. "And how are you finding that, you faithless sod?"

"Enlightening," John says honestly and smiles broadly. The truth be told, he has an excellent relationship with Maggie. They talk daily. Sometimes about his work, sometimes about hers, but mostly about my mum.

And my dad.

Deep in contemplation, my phone vibrates again. I furrow my brow in confusion as the screen displays the estate agents number. Although why they are calling me is superfluous since the sale completed yesterday.

"Hello?" I answer.

"Hi, Marie. It's Veronica Harris," she replies with her usual bluster. Or maybe she's just happy her inflated invoice has finally been paid.

"Hi, Veronica. I didn't expect to hear from you," I say as politely as possible. "While I've got you, have you received the invoice payment from my solicitor?"

"Yes, thank you. Marie, the reason why I'm calling is that I spoke to the new owner and he is missing the keys to the patio doors and the utility meters."

"Oh, okay." I dig into my bag and pull out my keys.

"Obviously," Veronica carries on. "He doesn't want to spend money on a locksmith if you have them."

"I'm sorry. Yes, I do have them."

"Would you be able to drop them off at the office today or tomorrow?"

I glance at my watch. "Actually, I've got an appointment this afternoon, and I'm closer to the house than I am to your office. I can post them through the letterbox on my way," I tell her, wedging my mobile between my cheek and shoulder as I twist the offending keys off the ring.

"Well, if you insist, but the buyer said he would collect them from here."

"I don't mind, it's my fault anyway. This saves us all time."

"Well, I'll let him know – thank you. I wish you all the best for the future, Marie."

"And you. Goodbye, Veronica." Hanging up, I stand and pluck my jacket from the back of the chair.

"Problem?" John enquires, taking a bite of his shortcake.

"No, an inconvenience. I forgot to hand over the patio and meter box keys last week."

John and Dominic look at each other speculatively.

"Are you sure it's safe to drop them off?" Dominic asks.

"I'm sure," I say. "Besides, Doctor Green is en-route, and I don't know complete closure, I guess."

"Angel," John says, holding me.

"I'm a glutton for punishment. You should know that by now. I'll see you around half past three. Okay?"

"Okay," he replies in an unhappy tone and kisses me.

Dominic stands and moves around the table. "I'll see you again soon, Marie. Take care."

"Yes, and you. I'll see you later." I turn on my heel and walk out of the shop.

Driving down my old street, the sold sign is still erect in the garden. I pull up in front of the empty driveway, noting there is no sign of life. And that's good because I really don't want to meet the new owner and hear how he is going to strip it back to its bare bones.

Climbing out of the car, the wind blows gently, and the birds chirp in the tree canopy overhead as I refamiliarise myself with the façade for the last time. Gone are my cream blinds, instead, yesterday's news covers the windows.

I fist the keys in my hand and stride up the garden path, but slow when I see the back gate open. Approaching it with caution, the lock and latch have been prised off. I back away, because something in my gut feels off here.

Opening the letterbox, a shadow moves on the inside of the glass. Soft steps then resound, and a woman appears from the side of the house.

"Hi. Can I help you?" she asks.

"Hi." I give her an awkward smile, but I'm instantly relieved and move towards her. "I'm the seller. The agent called to say you were missing some keys. I was just about to post them for you."

"Oh, that's great," she says, hand on chest, taking a step back, obliging me to step forward. "I thought I'd have to call out a locksmith."

"I'm sorry. I was under the impression the agent was going to call and let you know." I hold out my hand, my fingers desperate to hand the keys over.

"No, I've not heard from them, but they might have spoken to my husband." She edges back a little further and inconspicuously looks behind me.

The faint click of a door handle carries over the atmosphere, and I glance over my shoulder because something definitely isn't right here. I flit my eyes between her and the empty space behind me and place the keys on the window ledge.

"I'll just leave them there," I say, and slowly walk backwards.

I turn around, ready to run when a man blocks my path. I gasp in shock as the delightful Kevin digs his fingers into my shoulder and fists me in the stomach. The wind is completely knocked out of me, and I slump against him in pain.

"Hello, Marianne. Remember me?" he asks maliciously, exposing his teeth. I whimper, wishing I had listened to my gut and ran when I still could.

"Help me!" I cry out, hoping the nosy old bat next door can hear. "Somebody!" My arms flail out, and I scratch his face.

Kevin rams his fist into my cheek, and fire erupts in my jaw. I scream out continually until his hand muffles my pleas and he spins me around. I bite down on his fingers until I touch bone, and he growls behind me as blood seeps over my tongue.

"Bitch! Fucking bitch!" he hisses, shoving me forcibly through the gate. I hit the ground like a dead weight, unable to save my fall.

"Somebody help me!" I scream again, but it is weakened due to the numbness now taking effect on my face.

I crawl on my hands and knees, but a foot to my spine flattens me on the paving stones. With my chin smashed into the ground and my body braced, Kevin crouches on top of me. Fixing his hands around my throat, he drags up my head, partially obstructing my airway. I gasp out in shallow pants, while he breathes on me.

"Call Joe," he says to the woman standing in front of us, wearing a gleeful smile. She runs off into the house – through the patio doors – and I whimper. "And you? If you make any more fucking noise, I'll break your neck!"

And that's the last thing I hear before he smashes my face against the concrete. Pain explodes through my nose and forehead, consuming me as the world floats away and carries me into peaceful oblivion.

My lids open slowly, and I groan as the burning sensation deepens in my eye sockets and cheekbones. A familiar yet fuzzy ceiling rose gradually gains focus, and I concentrate hard, fighting the discomfort, as two becomes one. Swallowing tentatively, the metallic tang of blood registers in my foggy brain.

Daylight penetrates through the newspaper covering the windows, and I twist my head. Fire throbs in my neck, forbidding any further movement.

Working my eyes around the space, I'm in my old house. In my old bedroom. On my old bed.

I stare back up at the ceiling as my mind unravels place and time, until I remember how I came to be here.

Immediate panic fills me, and I keep my pained cry contained as I look at the closed door. Not hearing anything outside the room, I tug my arms above my head, but I cry out in desperation when they won't move.

Pressing my skull further back into the mattress, I catch sight of the thin rope circling my wrists, holding me captive.

Screaming out, defying the smarting in my face, I repeatedly yank my arms, trying to loosen the ties, until I am devoid of energy and determination. My elbows slump at either side of my head, and I sob because it's pointless.

I knew this day was coming. I made myself believe it was over at the Roseby, but inside, I know the true end is death.

And today, it may quite possibly be mine.

My bottom lip quivers as I continue to cry and fret. Kicking out my legs, which are not only unbound but free of pain, I vent my frustrated screams over and over, hoping the neighbours might hear.

"Help me! Somebody please!"

Each word is laced in agony, lancing the soreness in my sinuses further. I don't have to see myself to know that my eyes are swelling shut and my nose is most likely broken. This is physical pain like I've never felt before. For me, it's second to giving birth.

Opening my mouth, ready to brace and scream again, the door flies open. Joe leans against the architrave, wearing the malevolent grin I've come to remember him by. Pushing off the wood, he ambles inside and slams the door behind him.

"Oh, I'm glad you're awake. It means we can have some fun. You remember fun, don't you, Marianne?" His sneering tone grates on my senses, awakening each one further. Edging too close for comfort, I'm powerless to stop him. And even if I could, I'm not strong enough to fight him.

My tears sting my eyes, and I remember the last time I laid on this bed in tears was when I confessed my past sins to John. Now my ultimate sin is here, holding me captive, plotting what new, wicked hell he can bestow until I am no more.

Joe stops at the foot of the bed, and I instinctively press my body deeper into the mattress. Putting one foot on the end, he climbs up and walks until he stops aside my middle. Dropping to his knees, he covers my body with his and pollutes my nostrils with an exhale.

"I've waited a long time for this day to come. You have no idea how vengeance has eaten away at me. It consumes everything. Every minute, every hour. Every thought, every idea. And now that you're here, everything I planned to do has gone. But regardless of what I am going to do, the one thing you are going to feel, Marianne, is fear. And be sure that when you take your last breath, you will do it in fear."

"Fuck you!" I spit out because I don't want him to see that his words are having their desired effect. "John knows I'm here, and he'll come for me. And when he does, you'll pray for a quick death!"

He chuckles, until his smile downturns, and he lifts a knee and rams it into my side. I cry out, while my body strains to double over in my locked, laid out position. As my legs automatically kick out, he reaches behind me and grabs a knee.

"I always did love your fighting spirit, but the only one fucked here is you, because no one is coming to save you. You see, Marianne, this house was bought by Kevin. And I'm sorry to say, but he and his tart are now surplus to requirements. Besides, you can't trust an ex-con. And Kevin was garrulous at the best of times, so I couldn't just let them walk out of here. Twenty-three years in prison taught me well. I learned from the best that you *must* tie up loose ends. And you are the last." Leaning over me, I glare at him as he starts to untie the knots. "Don't think of trying anything. You do, I'll make you suffer in ways you can't imagine."

The rope burns as it cuts into my wrist, and he callously pulls it away. I rotate my arm and shoulder, wincing as the flow of blood rushes through my veins. Removing the bind from the other side, he cruelly yanks down my arm, and I screw up my eyes and howl in agony.

Catching my breath, I flick my lids up just in time to see his fist come down on my face. My body rolls over under the pressure while my throat emits a scream.

"Shut the fuck up!" He climbs off the bed and drags me up. Holding me by the throat, he shakes me and presses my back against the wall. My hands instantly find his as the pressure against my windpipe increases, asphyxiating me slowly.

The glint of my diamond engagement ring flashes in my eyes, and I lower my hand and twist it with my thumb. Mustering as much courage and strength as I can, I bring my hand up from the side. Blinded by my action, my hand strikes his cheek hard, and I deliberately press my palm into his skin and dig in my nails.

"You fucking bitch!" he hisses and throws me to the floor like a doll. Dragging my arm up, he rips off my ring and tosses it across the room. He digs into his pocket and pulls out the ring I last saw on a station platform when I requested my mother to get rid of it. Sliding it down my finger, abrading my skin further, he grabs me by the throat again.

"Til death us do fucking part!" He pushes me back, and I scramble away until his booted foot connects with my stomach. Kicking my arm and side repeatedly, the feeling of bone cracking steals my breath away, and I curl myself up as he launches into a full-blown assault.

I whimper in pain as time rewinds, and I'm no longer forty-three-year-old Marie, I'm eighteen-year-old Marianne, cowering in a ball, praying for the hate to stop.

With my hands shielding my face, I close my eyes, desperate for death to take me, so I don't have to live through this when his evil cuts through my hearing.

"You ruined my fucking life, you bitch. First, you gave me a fucking kid I never wanted, and then you put me in prison. If that wasn't enough, that bastard of yours humiliated my family."

I scream as he heaves me across the floor by my hair. I grab my skull automatically with one hand, while my other arm languishes at my side. I kick out my legs as he opens the bedroom door and he deliberately drags me in a way that ensures my side is jammed and scrapped against the door frame.

"My father is now facing investigation for misconduct. He could be disbarred. And yet again, you've ruined three people's lives. But today it ends." He grasps under my chin and stands me up. His fingernails pierce my flesh, and he secures his arm around my back.

"And you know how it ends, Marianne. People fall down the stairs all the time, and history has a nasty habit of repeating itself. And this time, if it doesn't fucking kill you, I'll break your neck myself."

Walking me backwards onto the landing, my arm – likely broken – hangs limply at my side. My fingers wrap around each of the wooden bannister spindles as I pass, pathetically trying to stall the inevitable, until they touch the end balustrade. I tilt my neck, insofar as I am able, and my body begins to shake, seeing the end in sight.

"Please, let me go!" I beg.

Once, begging worked on him. He liked to hear me plead in submission. He liked power, and he liked me under his thumb. Clearly, he still does, but today it is in vain.

"Beg all you want, bitch. But if you think you're leaving here in anything but a body bag, you're sorely mistaken." Pushing me back, my heels rock tentatively on the top step. "Now, say it again, Marianne!"

"Say what?" I ask in confusion, as every muscle tightens, preparing for my fate.

"Beg me. Beg me to let you go, and I will."

Foregoing the pain annihilating every cell and nerve ending, I fix my gaze on the stairs behind me.

Every second of the night he took Faith's life flashes before my eyes. It was cruel and calculated, and, without a shadow of a doubt, predetermined. But her destiny was doomed from the moment she was born, and that's on me because my fate to endure a lifetime of sorrow was also set from the moment Joe first showed an unexpected interest. I have spent a lifetime living in regret, wallowing in a past I can never change all because I said three, simple words which I thought would burrow into the cold, black void where his heart should be.

Let us go.

"Say it, Marianne. Say it!" he hisses viciously.

Let me go.

The words tumble around my head, but my mouth refuses to voice them because I know how it ends, and begging can't save me. It never could.

And the reality that has just hit me like a ball and chain is that Joe wants a long life. If he didn't, he would have ended it years ago behind bars. That or his body wouldn't have fought so hard to survive after he was shanked. But me, a part me died when Faith did. I accepted long ago I cheated death that night, but I cannot cheat it forever, and it's finally come full circle.

Still transfixed on the rungs, the faint rev of a powerful car engine moves down the street, bleeding into my eardrums.

I slowly drop my hand from the end of the bannister and bring it between us. My other arm hangs lifeless at my side, and if I survive this there's a chance there could be some permanent damage. Yet that is the last thing I need to be concerned about because the only real concern is death.

"Say the words, Marianne," he taunts again.

Turning back to him, his expression is taking on that of the predator who would stalk me before he struck, and I'm glad because it means he hasn't noticed.

"Fucking say them!" he yells, the white of his eyes widening with each squeeze and shake of my throat.

Rocking back on my heel, a car door slams outside and sirens approach in the distance. I smile at Joe, watching his eyes volley frantically between me and the bottom of the stairs. His body jerks as panic takes hold, and I curl my fingers into his belt.

"I told you he'd come for me. Now, let me go, Joe," I whisper.

No sooner has the last word left my mouth, *bitch*, penetrates my eardrums and his arm lurches back. His powerful fist tosses my head to the side as my molars explode with volcanic fire, and my mouth fills with blood.

I fall back into weightlessness, while the harsh realisation dawns on Joe. His hands grasp desperately at his belt, failing to remove mine.

"No!" he screams as we plummet.

Tucking myself into him, we twist halfway down. My body slams against the rungs and Joe's piercing wail fills the void as the front door is rammed open.

"MARIE!" The familiar, terrified cry fills the hallway, echoing throughout the barren bricks and mortar. Blood splashes over my face and a strange sense of relief consumes me as Joe's arms suddenly relax.

"Marie! Oh my God, NO!" John roars out again.

I hit the floor hard, and my head rebounds as my body crumples beneath me. Intense agony ignites, from top to toe, and the hallway falls silent.

The deafening hush overwhelms, and all I can hear is my own laboured breathing. I reach out in front of me, pressing my fingers into the carpet in an attempt to drag myself.

"I can't move," I say in pants. My tears fall uncontrollably as John grapples with the police.

"Don't move her! The ambulance will be here in less than a minute," one of them says, but his words are meaningless as John elbows him off and slides over the floor in front of me.

"He's army. He knows all about spinal injuries," Dominic's faint voice resounds in the void, and he appears in my peripheral vision and moves astride my back and firmly holds my hips. "Stay still, Marie."

"Shush," John says, his eyes red and wet. "Don't move, baby." His hands are firm on either side of my head, holding me in place.

"I can't feel my legs," I whisper, while my eyes shut of their own volition and the darkness calls for me.

"No! You stay awake. Look at me, angel. Don't you close your eyes. Don't you dare leave me!" he wails.

Opening my eyes, his cheeks are sodden, and I touch my outstretched fingers to his arm.

"I'm so tired."

"No, you keep your eyes on me. Don't you fucking close them!"

"I love you," I manage to say, unable to stay awake any longer.

"NO!" John's bangs his forehead to the floor and roars out in grief.

My body finally gives in to the oblivion summoning it, and I drift off into the nothingness as Faith finally calls my name again.

"Come to me, Mummy. Play with me!"

Chapter 47

A CONSTANT BEEP filters softly into my sub-conscience as my body emerges from the darkness.

My eyes flicker, unable to focus while incandescent light blinds me. And for a split second, I wonder if this might be the pearly gates of heaven.

"John?" I murmur groggily. Slowly raising a hand to my face, my nose feels massive. Not to mention I'm intubated. Lowering my fingers to my neck, hard, unforgiving plastic covers it.

I sigh, positive I'm not at the pearly bloody gates. I'm definitely in hospital because heaven would never be this brutal. Nor would it allow me to wake up with a dangerously full bladder.

No, this is the work of the devil.

Or the NHS.

Inhaling deeply, smarting snaps at my sinuses while the tell-tale clinical smell invades my nostrils. Although it's not as putrid and nasal assaulting as I remember since oxygen is also being pumped into me.

I squeeze my eyes, forcing myself to remember. Eventually, everything comes back with painful clarity.

The house, the bed, the fall.

Joseph.

"Hello?" I call out softly, finding my voice.

I lift my hands higher, feeling somewhat incapacitated, and crease my brow at the twin plaster casts. One from elbow to hand, the other covering all the way to my upper arm. This is obviously the encumbrance I feel.

Reaching down, searching for the hand control device I know these beds have, the urge to cross my legs is profound. Until, suddenly, the threatening of my bladder to empty itself is more than a passing thought and my abdomen cries a sigh of relief. And I know something is very wrong, considering I've just wet the bed and I can't feel it.

I groan in discomfort as I lean back further and look around. Unable to locate the flaming handset, I twist my head to the panel behind me. Yet another pointless exercise, because the emergency button is too high to reach.

"Help!" I stare at the door, willing someone to come in. Catching sight of the clock, the hands tick by, and ten minutes later, I'm still alone.

"Hello? Anyone?"

Touching my chest, my finger snags on a wire. Adjusting my gown, I outline it from my flesh to the machine monitoring my vitals. With pursed lips, I peel off the pad, and the machine starts to alarm out.

I exhale in relief as the door opens in a flurry of activity, and a nurse runs in with Stuart and John behind her.

"Oh, thank Christ!" John cradles my face lovingly, his thumbs rounding the apples of my cheeks. "Don't you ever do that to me again. God, I thought I lost you," he murmurs, touching his forehead to mine. "I thought I lost you."

"I'm sorry." I press my lips to the side of his face, and ripple my fingers over his hair, needing to ensure he is real. I've never been so happy to see him. I honestly thought I was dying when the light started to fade, and the darkness claimed me.

"Sorry to break up this happy reunion, but I need to check M's vitals," Stuart says, pointing John to the other side of the room. "Keeley, can you pull the blinds?"

"Sure, Doctor Andrews," she says and closes them. She then approaches the side of the bed, silences the machine, and places the bed controller I was searching for on the mattress.

Typical.

"It's good to see you alert and lucid. At least I'll now get some peace." He flicks his brows at John, lowers the bed guard and sits on the side. I give him a half-cocked smile and pick up the bed remote. Studying the symbols, the red emergency button stands out starkly, and I remember why I needed assistance.

"Stuart?"

"Hmm?" he replies, his concentration on my neck as he unfastens the brace.

"I remember everything," I confirm. "Tell me the truth. Was I paralysed in the fall?"

"Paralysed?" He shakes his head in confusion. "No. Why would you think that?"

I look at him and John, utterly ashamed. "I wet the bed," I whisper, almost silent.

"Sorry, M. What was that?"

I huff. "I said, I wet the bed!" I cover my hands over my face in shame and burst into tears. I can't help it; I'm old enough to know better. Grown women do not wet the flipping bed. "Well, if I'm not paralysed, why I can't feel it!" I demand, still croaky.

"Angel, calm down," John says, defying orders and sitting on the side of the bed. He takes my hand and rubs it soothingly, but I feel anything but.

Stuart sighs and pulls the stethoscope off his neck. "Marie, you've got catheters fitted. That's why you can't feel it."

I pull my neck back, neglecting to register the pain in my immediate disgust. "*Catheters?* As in plural? As in both ends?" I query, horrified.

"Hmm, hmm." Stuart smiles merrily. "So, how do you feel?" He nods encouragingly, expecting something charming to leave my mouth.

"Honestly? Like I've got tubes in every orifice!" I hiss out caustically, but it doesn't negate the fact it is true.

Stuart smirks while I glare at him. Oh, the little sod. He's enjoying this. If he thinks he's getting any further invites for a Sunday roast, he's got another thing coming. I swear I feel like my head is about to explode.

"I know that look, Marie. Don't worry, I'll have them whipped out shortly."

"Hmm!" I harrumph. "And these?" I lift my arms.

"Not as shortly." He smiles. Picking up my records, he goes the motions of checking the machines, taking my blood pressure, and other random bits I don't even want to think about.

Three hours later, having been given the all clear – and now minus tubes in every orifice – I have a full list of my injuries. It's pretty extensive reading, and yet it's not pretty at all.

I have been here for four days, and aside from the broken wrist and forearm, I have a concussion, overall body bruising - including ribs and lungs - and two missing molars. And according to Stuart's senior, I'm lucky. And yes, I am, because I'm here to fight another day. But there is still the elephant in the room that John is purposely avoiding.

I slap down the depressing read, shuffle myself up, and tentatively test out my reflexes. I give each limb a workout – namely a lift and a bend – and each ensuing groan of discomfort causes John to turn into a mother hen.

"Stop it," he says, holding up a beaker of water with a straw.

"I'm not five," I reply. "I can drink from a cup."

He furrows his brows in annoyance. "I know, but I take care of what's mine. So please, amuse me."

Taking the beaker, I give him his amusement. I set it on my lap, and stare at him pointedly, until he, predictably, turns away.

"We can't avoid it forever."

"I know."

"Tell me," I plead. "Please."

"Angel, it's too soon for me," he says exasperated and stands. "I thought you were dying. You were there..." He holds out his hands before he scrubs them over his face. "Then you said you couldn't feel your legs and you began to close your eyes. Then you stopped breathing, and I lost it. The police threatened to arrest me unless I calmed down, but I couldn't. I saw your light fading, your essence dying. I'd seen it so many times in battle, and I couldn't save them either." He roughly wipes his eyes, fists his hand at his mouth and blows out his breath. "The ride from the house to A&E was the longest twenty minutes of my life. I sat in the back of the police car, wondering if when I got there, you'd already be pronounced dead."

"Darling," I whisper, needing to soothe his heartbreak. And mine.

"So, you see, I'm not ready to talk about it. Not yet anyway. When I do, I want you to tell me everything. I already know he didn't rape you," he says, raising a brow, daring me to concur differently. I guess I should be happy because if Joe had, it wouldn't have been the first time. "But I know he didn't *not* touch you, either. Promise me, you won't omit anything."

"I won't, but something's you won't like," I say with a sigh, happy he doesn't want to hear it just yet. I don't think my strength or sanity can cope with an argument about the orchestration of my own fall, regardless that Joe was going to do it anyway. Maybe in a few days or weeks. Possibly months... Definitely not years.

As I ruminate on the foreseeable future, the door opens, and Stuart returns with Dominic and Sloan in tow.

"Nice to see you awake," Sloan says, and reaches down to me. I hug him tightly while emitting a content sigh. "I'm so glad you're okay. How are you feeling?"

"I'm fabulous, Sloan. I feel like I've gone ten rounds with boxing's elite. Evidently, you're okay, but how are Kara and Oliver?"

"Oliver's fine. Thankfully, he's too young to understand where his grandma is. My beloved, however, is climbing the walls. Needless to say, my mother's no help. She, too, is going off the rails demanding when they can see you. Be warned-" He wags his finger. "They're planning an invasion imminently."

I laugh and touch the tenderness in my jaw from my missing teeth. "Crap, that hurts."

"Hi, Marie." Dominic smiles as he steps forward from the window and drags over the chair. "I appreciate you may not want to talk about it, but we need to discuss Joseph. I don't know how much J has told you," he says, relaxing his position.

"I haven't told her anything," John confirms, short and uncomfortable.

"Right." Dominic nods. "About an hour after you left us in the coffee shop, Doc called to ask where you were. You hadn't turned up to your appointment with Doctor Green, and you weren't answering your phone."

I divert my gaze and stare down at my hands, consumed by my own discomfort that they are all aware I'm holed up every fortnight with the resident shrink. I'm not surprised; nothing is sacred where these men are concerned.

"Marie, look at me. PTSD comes in all forms, not just war. It's nothing to be ashamed of," Dominic says. "Anyway, Doc called J to find out where you were. And we all know the rest."

"Where's Joseph? Have they operated on him?" I query but don't know if I can take hearing he is being nursed back to health in the next ward over. I glance between the quartet as they all remain silent. "What? The last thing I remember was him screaming, then blood, then silence."

Dominic shuffles forward with his elbows on his knees and furrows his brow. "He didn't make it. On the fall, he smashed his head on the end of the bannister. It took out the majority of his front teeth, that's the blood you felt," he confirms. "However, the impact, the way in which he fell and the velocity... Well, it broke his neck. He died instantly. I'm sorry," he finishes with a forced smile.

"I'm not." I take in each expression, but I know they're not disgusted by my honesty.

"No, I mean I'm sorry that you won't get the justice you deserve. I'm not sorry the bastard's dead," Dominic clarifies.

"Poetic justice," I whisper. "A simple twist of fate."

"Very true," he replies.

I nod, deep in thought, until something occurs to me. "Before we fell, Joe said something about tying up loose ends. He said the man and woman posing as the buyers were beyond requirement. Are they dead?"

"Yes. The woman died of asphyxiation, strangulation probably. The man was found in the kitchen with his neck broken. Call it karma," Dominic says in a pleased, vindictive tone.

A shiver careens through me, and my eyes dart between them. "Is this going to come back on me? Am I going to be charged?" Panic surges up from within, because it's all above motive, and I have more motive for him to be gone than anyone.

"Angel, calm down. The lead detective has already spoken to all the officers' present, and he's confirmed you won't be charged. Of course, you are required to give a statement, but that's just procedure."

"What about his parents? Are they going to come after me?"

Dominic shakes his head. "No. Notwithstanding recent appearances, they washed their hands of him when he was inside. His father is currently under investigation for trial fixing and misconduct - courtesy of yours truly," he says, nodding at John. "And his wife is hitting the bottle hard, fearing they will lose everything."

"And my house?" I ask in confusion. "What's going to happen to that?"

He shrugs. "Legally, it isn't your house anymore. It belongs to a deceased ex-convict. The police are delving into his background, but they're positive it will be seized under the proceeds of crime act since he didn't have two pennies to rub together. They will probably investigate where he obtained the cash to buy it, although it's clear the Beresford's funded it – something else they will be investigated for. Eventually, it'll get auctioned off."

I shake my head. It's just hit me that the thousands I currently have sitting in my account from the sale is the Beresford's money.

"Dirty money," I whisper. "Even in death I can't get rid of him."

"It's up to you what you do with the cash." Dominic stands and straightens jacket. "Personally, I wouldn't think twice about where it's come from. But maybe that's because I'm a heartless, immoral bastard." His eyes flick to John who gives him an unimpressed smirk. "On that, I think it's time for me to leave." Advancing on me, he leans down. "Call me if you ever need anything, Marie. Day or night, you've always got my time."

"I will, thank you. But the next time I call, it will be for a suit fitting," I say with a smile.

"I look forward to it. Take care of him." He kisses my cheek politely, then embraces John with a slap on the back, before doing the same with Stuart and Sloan.

He then opens the door but pauses. "Sloan, I'll call you later in the week regarding our little problem." Then the door swings behind him as the room temperature drops a degree.

"Jeremy?" I query because it isn't a secret he is struggling with Evie's father. His work in progress isn't progressing at all.

Sloan's head swings to John in question, who nods.

"Partly," Sloan confirms. "Rem knows but keep it to yourself." And I will. I'll do whatever it takes to ensure Jeremy's tortured soul can sleep easy at night.

"Of course, but don't do anything that will send him over the edge." I glare pointedly at the trio until they nod in agreement.

"Right then, I think it's time we let M rest," Stuart says, and I wince as he pecks my cheek. "Sorry, I'll have a dental surgeon come and have a look and see if they can do anything. Sloan, let's go. Give them some privacy."

Sloan agrees reluctantly. Opening his arm to John, he shares a private moment with him, then kisses my forehead.

"Am I okay to tell my beloved and the family they can visit tomorrow?"

"Hmm, but I don't think it's right to bring Oliver, not when I look like this. Do you mind?"

"Yes, but I understand. I'll take him into the office. The secretaries will keep him entertained."

"Breaking hearts already?"

"Of course, he's my son." He smirks.

"He's lucky. Thanks, darling," I say as he and Doc reach the door with John behind them, literally shoving them out. "Oh, Sloan? Tell your mum to bring me a Walnut Whip and cake, lots of cake." He nods, and John locks the door behind him and dims the light.

"What are you doing?" I ask as he strolls back to the bed, slides his hands under my body and moves me over. "Am I so unpretty now you can't bear to look at me?" I pout playfully.

"You'll always be a raving beauty." Lying down on the bed, he carefully adjusts me until I am curled into his side. "Comfortable?"

"Very," I reply. I drift my fingers up and down his chest, and he snags my hand and tuts.

"Something's missing." Staring at him intently, he burrows into his pocket and proudly holds up my engagement ring. "One of the crime scene bobbies found it in the bedroom." He carefully slips it back over my finger and kisses it. "Jake had it cleaned and sanitised, but I understand if you want another. Three times the charm and all that."

"No," I whisper because this ring gave me the strength to fight back for the first and final time. Circling my finger around his Adam's apple, a thought snaps at my psyche.

"Did you call Maggie?"

"I did." He strokes my marred temple. "She's making arrangements to cover her ecclesiastical duties, but then she's going to come and stay for a few days. She told me if I said grace she'd ensure I was fed and watered in your absence. Maybe even get one of the WI ladies to bake for me."

I chortle. "God, cheap really is a Walker trait, isn't it?" I query rhetorically, peering up at him as he nods in agreement. "Well, it's going to be interesting." But I'm far from worried. In fact, I can't wait, because John and I have both intentionally omitted my sister's profession from all and sundry. Just the thought of what Sophie is going to make of her curls my lips in glee.

"These look better," he says, drifting his finger over my cheek. "The swelling's going down." Tipping my face up, he kisses me with such gentle passion I feel my heart is going to melt. "I'll love you until the day I die. No separation, no end."

"I'll hold you to that. I love you, too," I mumble against his lips, pilfering kisses before I curl back into him and close my eyes.

"Lunch!" a nurse calls out as the food trolley rolls into the room, bang on midday. "Ham or cheese?"

I crane my neck, feeling far less pain than I did yesterday.

"Cheese, please." Although both are subjective as far as hospital food goes. And I figure I've got less chance of food poisoning with dairy than I have with meat.

"Salad?" the man asks. Not waiting for my response, he lobs a bit of lettuce, two rounds of cucumber and a tomato on top of the bread.

Lovely.

With a smile, he passes me the plate with the sandwich that is so lacklustre it probably feels sorry for itself. I keep my expression neutral as I assess the two dry halves of bread and the processed cheese slice slapped in the middle.

"Madeira cake or a banana?"

I bite my lip. I should have fruit, but I really want cake. I volley between the two, and my decision is affirmed when he holds up a very green banana.

"Cake, please. Thank you." He places the plate on the table and leaves me alone. I'm halfway through the sandwich as the door opens.

"Hey! Come here!" I hold my arms out as Kara rushes in and holds me for dear life. Retreating, her face falls, and she begins to mentally catalogue my injuries. Lifting my arm, her expression saddens as she strokes the cast.

"Oh, God. When John called us, I thought-" She stops abruptly, unable to speak it and begins to touch her eyelids. "Now I know how you felt with me."

"Shush, honey. I'm fine, really." I pull her back into me and breath in her comforting scent. I stroke her hair softly, until the door goes again, and I divert my attention to see Jules, Charlie, and Nicki. Kara smiles, and I identify her reluctance, but she moves away.

"Hi, lady," Jules says, her arms wide, making a beeline for me. "Give us a squeeze." I wrap my arms around her as she buries her head in my neck. "I'm elated you're okay. When I got the call, I didn't know what was happening. John was borderline hysterical. I've never heard him so wild or heartbroken." She sits back and cups my cheeks. "You look well, all things considered."

"I'm better. Physically broken, but mentally healed. If there is such a thing."

"I know exactly what you mean. Here," she says and pulls a Walnut Whip from her bag. "It took me ages to find it. It's now Whip. Apparently, they removed the walnut."

"Really? But that's good because I never liked the walnut, just the whip."

"That says a lot about your personality, lady!" she winks mischievously.

"Mum?" Charlie speaks up, tired of waiting, and I put down the Whip and crook my finger.

"Give us a hug, darling. You, too," I say to Nicki, beckoning her over. Cosseted in their familial embrace, someone clears their throat. Breaking apart, a nurse stands in the doorway.

"You've got another visitor. You're only supposed to have two at a time, but I'll let it go."

As the nurse walks away, Maggie's head tilts around the frame. I gasp in delight and grin while she looks nervously at my other visitors.

"Room for one more?"

I catch sight of the girls, and each bears an interesting look, absorbing the new and shiny outsider in their midst.

I tentatively clamber up, testing my endurance. With one foot in front of the other, I slowly trudge towards Maggie, until she meets me halfway and catches me.

"Marianne," she whispers, and presses her lips to my cheek, squeezing me tightly. I dig my potted arms into her back, never wanting to let go again. Tears flood my eyes because this is the moment I've wanted for. Family, old and new, finally together.

"Marie?" Nicki calls softly, and I grudgingly turn from my twin's neck. "Are you going to introduce us?"

I let out a sigh of relief. "Sorry. Everyone this is Magdalene, my sister." I turn back to Maggie who holds me securely and guides us back to the bed. "Maggie, this is Kara, my daughter," I say with pride. "This is Jules, and her daughter, Charlie. And Nicki, my assistant." I point to them, but it's wasted breath. She already knows who they are.

Laying back down, I observe with a full, and finally whole heart, as my sister takes the initiative and makes her way around the women. I half listen to everyone introduce themselves, amongst other nonsensical anecdotes, and I smile.

Grabbing my phone, I tap out a message, informing John that Maggie has arrived. His reply is instant to say that he knows, and he will be over later.

As I put my phone down, an inhale of shock spikes my attention, and I drag my eyes up to see Maggie has removed her coat, exposing her attire. Jules eyes me quizzically, while Charlie and Nicki look ready to confess their sins. I fix my gaze on Kara, who sidles over to me.

"I think you and I need to talk again when you get discharged," she mutters humorously. "Does John know she's a vicar?"

I nod slowly. "Hmm, he met her when we were up in Peterborough."

"And neither of you thought to tell me? I feel our communicate is severely lacking lately."

I laugh. "Don't take it personally. We choose not to tell you all. We thought it would be a nice surprise."

"It is. She's lovely. She's you!"

Stroking her head and kissing her cheek, the door bangs open again, and Sophie flounces in, her hair big and bouncy, her personality ten times greater.

"You wouldn't believe the trouble of finding something good to read downstairs!" she exclaims, passing over a wilting bouquet and a tub of partially desiccated grapes. "Seriously, who wants to read death, destruction and geriatric detectives! Good job I brought you something." Her eyes are fixed on her bag as she whips out a book and throws it at me. I inadvertently catch Maggie's gaze as I pick it up and scoff at the cover.

"Soph, I don't need a smutty read," I say, recalling the time she gave Kara something similar.

Soph drags off her coat and tosses it over the chair along with her bag. "Yes, you do! Besides, that is an amazing book! It will make your bits tingle."

"I'll take your word for it," I reply flatly and chuck it aside, only for it to be picked up by an eager Jules, who quickly remembers we have a pious audience.

"Sorry, vicar," Jules apologies sheepishly.

"It's Maggie, please." My sister shakes her head. I know she's dying to laugh, but instead, she just lifts her hand in compliance.

"Vicar? Maggie? Am I missing something?" Sophie asks, joining the party late. With her hands on her hips, she pirouettes, and her eyes widen. "Oh!" Turning back to me, she opens her mouth and closes it.

"You're not seeing double, honey. This is Maggie, my twin," I say nonchalantly. Crossing one leg over the other on the bed, I watch with straight-faced glee as Sophie's eyes assess Maggie, until she sees her the collar.

"Oh, shit!" Rushing around the bed, she snatches the book from Jules' hand and stuffs it behind her back. "I swear I really don't read this stuff, vicar!"

"Soph, calm down. She is married and acquainted with sex. She can imagine what's in that book." I wave my hand at the read, and she hesitantly passes it to me. Skim reading the page, I close it. The crass words are burned into my retinas, never to be removed.

"Okay," I say slowly. "What have I missed? And where's my flipping cake?"

"I wasn't wrong – it's definitely an interesting family dynamic that you and John have."

Tilting my head, I grin at Maggie, lying next to me. It's been a couple of hours since everyone left, and John still hasn't materialised.

"What do you mean?"

"Earlier today when I called John to say I was here, he asked me to go over to his building. I finally met all of his boys. They're a rambunctious, fascinating bunch, aren't they?" she says humorously. "They were shocked to see me. I don't know if it was the face or the dress."

"Probably both, but they're good boys with hearts of gold. They would do anything for you. You'll like them."

"The gentleman with the scars has clearly got some stories to tell."

"Hmm, too many," I reply, but don't we all?

"The girls are lovely, too. I really like them, especially the cheeky, mouthy one. I think she might even be my favourite." Maggie laughs, squeezing my hand.

"I'm glad because they've got your number now and there's no escaping. Expect random calls and texts about the most arbitrary things."

She laughs. "Yes, I'm aware. Kara gave me a little insight earlier when we got coffee. Finally meeting her, I understand now why you took her in. I'm proud of you. You raised an amazing young woman."

"I did, but it's not all me."

"No, but Kara thinks so, and everyone else does, too. It takes more than biology to be a parent. Parents come in all shapes and sizes."

I'm about to reply when the door latch clicks, and John slips inside.

"Do you ladies want some privacy?" he asks, and Maggie and I both shrug and shake our heads simultaneously. "Okay, that really is disturbing."

Pressing his lips to my forehead, he sits on the chair, relaxes back and watches us contently while the light fades into a burnished red on the horizon outside.

"Did you tell Mum what happened?" I ask hesitantly. In her frail condition, I don't want to cause her any undue distress.

Maggie strokes her fingers up and down my arm. "I didn't go into any graphic detail, but yes, I did. Dad, too. It goes against our faith, but we're all glad that Joe's finally gone. Mum confessed she hoped he would die in prison."

I bite my lip as a shiver chills my body. It's hard to hear her speak like this, especially when, in her capacity, she is meant to be able to find mercy when there is none.

"Months ago, you told me to find thyself," I say with a yawn, my eyelids drooping.

"I know what I said, and you have, but go to sleep," she replies softly, kissing my cheek. "I'll be here tomorrow, and the next day, and the next. I'm never going to lose you again."

Holding her tight, my exhausted body begins to fall deeper. I close my eyes and beckon sleep to come quickly because I'm no longer afraid.

Long ago, I dared to dream.

I dared to have it all.

But my dreams are no longer fragile or unobtainable. They are no longer beautiful nightmares of a life that broke my spirit. They will now be beautiful reveries of a life that is yet to come.

Because finally, I can dare to dream again.

Epilogue

"HAVE YOU RECEIVED it?"

"Yeah, I'm looking at it now," I confirm distracted, opening the highly confidential file Adrian Taylor has emailed to me.

Flicking through the documents, the list of guilty charges is unbelievable. Yet, I can believe them, because the evidence levied against corrupt Judge Duncan Beresford - courtesy of Dominic and his equally corrupt connections - is damning. Protecting his dead son wasn't the only misdemeanour the immoral bastard conducted.

He had been receiving backhanders left and right for the best part of forty years in trial-fixing. Doing his utmost to disguise his dirty deeds, while sitting in court, purveying the laws of our land with vilification and bestowing judgment upon those who had committed far fewer atrocities. And all the while getting filthy rich off the back of it.

"Are you going to tell Marie?" Adrian queries, and the sloppy sound of chewing commences down the line.

I glance at the clock and avert my eyes to the ceiling – it's anyone's guess how much longer she is going to be. At this rate, the inevitable will happen before she even leaves the bedroom.

"Yes, but not today. I don't want to sully it for her."

Ever since Joe's death twelve months ago, not a day has gone by where she hasn't dwelled on what happened. In truth, I think she will always blame herself, carrying the burdens of a teenage girl who was too frightened to fight back. But she did fight back, in a packed courtroom, giving evidence against her ex-father-in-law, some twenty-five years too late. But justice prevailed. And just like his son, he too is also facing a lengthy stretch at her Majesty's Pleasure. And it couldn't have happened to a nicer bloke.

"No, of course not," Adrian replies. "She's been through so much this last year. How is she, anyway? I meant to ask Maggie when I saw her last week, but she got caught up with a parishioner."

"She's fantastic, mate. We find out today," I tell him, the excitement already swelling in my tone.

"Congratulations. Gosh, you two didn't waste any time, did you?" he chuckles.

I shake my head and chortle. "Absolutely not." But in reality, we wasted twelve years.

"I'm happy she's finally got the life she deserves. And you've given her that. It's just a shame you couldn't have given that to Faith, too," he says with heartfelt honesty.

I sigh, recalling the time he said the exact same thing when he turned up on our doorstep a week after Marie was discharged from the hospital. And again, six months later, when she met me at the altar.

"You're a good man, John Walker. One of the best I've ever met. Take care of her and call me with the news."

I smile and peak my brow. "I will. I'll catch you later, mate." I hang up, and turn the gold band on my finger, lost in memories.

Shutting down the laptop, I pick up the picture of our wedding day. Rubbing my finger over my angel in ivory, I smile. The same smile I'm wearing while dressed to the nines in my morning suit, tipping her back in a kiss. I've had hundreds of amazing days with my woman, but this was the icing on the cake. The day she finally became my Mrs Walker.

My eyes shift to the picture next to it, one of me standing in between the sisters, and snippets come back in high definition. Everything from the build-up, to the first dance, to the cake cutting. But the most prevalent memory is that of the weeks preceding, and the almighty argument of the century that ensued when Maggie refused to be the maid of honour. Not because she felt she was putting Kara's nose out of joint, but because she claimed she wanted the best seat in the house. That seat being front and centre, declaring us husband and wife.

Subsequently, it was an argument Marie lost.

And three months later, Maggie proudly tied us together in blissful matrimony. Inside a church that Marie hadn't set foot inside of in nearly three decades. In front of people who had tarnished her reputation. And in front of her father, who did a piss poor job of hiding himself in the back pews.

Notwithstanding the arrival of guests who weren't invited, our wedding was stunning. Every second of it, from the church to the reception at the local parish hall. Nicki did a fabulous job. The only part of the day that was blighted was the absence of her mother, who passed not long after the final assault.

"Darling, have you seen my pack?" Marie's shout draws me out of the memory.

"On the hallway table," I call back, hearing her feet finally thud down the stairs.

Strolling to the door, I dally and stare up at the wall. My pupils transfix on the large, framed picture of my wife aged eighteen and her two-year-old daughter that I'll never have the privilege of meeting. Not in this life anyway.

As always, I reach up and touch Faith. And as always, I hope her father's evil soul is rotting in purgatory for eternity, but even that's too good for him.

"Darling?" Marie calls out, closing the downstairs doors in her wake.

"One day, honey," I murmur, and shut the door behind me. Picking up the keys off the hallway table, Marie walks towards me with two bottles of water.

"Who was on the phone?"

"Adrian," I reply and lift my brows. She knows the trial verdict was returned yesterday, and it's something she has avoided. I feel conflicted whether to tell her until she nods, and a nervous expression afflicts her features.

"And?" she asks in a whisper.

"Guilty on twenty-two charges, including perjury and intimidation of the jury during Joe's manslaughter trial. He'll be sentenced next month, but regardless, he's going to do some hard time." Pulling her close, I run my fingers over her cheeks. "Don't." I don't need to elaborate any further, but thankfully, she shrugs and emits a small huff, unsure how to respond.

"Nervous?" I ask, blatantly changing the subject. She reaches up on her toes, and her lips claim mine in a soft kiss. A kiss to conciliate and comfort, but I can't tell if it's for her or me.

"No," she replies. Removing the keys from my hand, she places her bag on the table and picks up the pack. Attempting to stuff it inside, amongst all the random shit she always carts around, I take it from her and something catches my eye.

"Who are they for?" I ask in hope, reaching for them. She bats my hand away and gives me a crooked, secretive smile.

"You'll see." She gives me a once-over. "Darling, where's your jacket? We're going to be late."

Pot, kettle and bloody black, but what else is new in this house? Wishful flaming thinking is what it is.

She turns on her heel, and I roll my eyes as she flounces out of the front door. Grabbing my jacket and setting the alarm, I follow her out.

"I'll drive," she calls out, already seated with the engine running. Striding towards her, she gives me a huge grin, and I reciprocate and get in.

I furrow my brow while gazing out of the window intermittently. Keeping a conscious note of the time, I flick through the papers, one eye on the line of traffic as it begins to slow.

"Brake," I say out of habit, earning myself the dirtiest look known to man. "What?" I lift my hand in defence.

"I'm not even close! Tyres and tarmac," she says, pointing at the windscreen. "Besides, I've seen your so-called skills in that tranny van. And if you don't want to walk the last five miles, you'll do well to pipe down. I refuse to be stressed out today."

I tilt a brow and crease my forehead because she's doing a good enough job of that all by herself.

"What now?"

"Nothing." I clear my throat, knowing when I've been beaten, and drop my eyes back down to the papers. Doing the mental calculations, still hopeful I'm going to get the house in order in time, the indicators click repeatedly.

And prematurely.

I cast a sideways glance and narrow my eyes at her hopeful smile.

"Darling, do we have time for a detour?" she asks pointlessly, already making the goddamn detour.

"Sure," I confirm because I'd never deny her anything, not even this. For the best part of three years, she barely stepped foot inside the place. And for the best part of the last year, I've refused to acknowledge it still exists.

Driving through the streets, these roads come back to haunt me in reverse. The last time I was on them, I was sitting in the back of a police car, praying to a God I didn't believe exists to spare the woman I love and let me have the lifetime I deserve with her.

After months of legal wrangling and investigation, the house was finally auctioned off earlier this year. Again, through Dom's questionable contacts, I know far more about the people who bought it than the Land Registry would like me to. But I've never disclosed that to Marie. I felt it was best to let sleeping dogs lie since she never raised it.

Until now.

A cold sweat washes over me as she stops the car on the opposite side of the street, unknowingly idling in the same spot I did when I would watch her from afar for years.

Lost in bygone memories, the synthetic slide of material catches my attention as she whips off her seat belt and opens the door.

"Angel, what are you doing?" My panic is palpable.

"I want to see," she says, already halfway across the road.

"You can see from here!" I hiss out. "Get your arse back here now!" Running over the road, I stop when I see her staring at the 'for sale' hoarding in her former next-door neighbour's garden.

"That's really sad. She was a nosy old bat, but her heart was in the right place," she says, slowly walking towards her old house. I grab her hand and pull her back.

"Angel, you've seen it, now let it go." I hate myself for saying it, but this hasn't been her house for years, even when she still owned it. "It's over," I add, the same moment a people carrier slows down and manoeuvres into the driveway.

"Oh, no!" She spins around, hiding her face in my chest, while her belly crashes into mine.

"Careful," I say.

I conduct a grand show of pointing at the house for sale and roll my eyes at my own charade - all the while mentally cursing. One of the car doors opens, and two little voices shout at each other, inducing me to turn.

"No, don't do that!" Marie's muffled plea vibrates against my pecs.

"Hi. Are you looking to buy?" the woman asks, her eyes working between her rambunctious little boys, wrestling on the path, and us.

I smile and force Marie to turn around. I rub her arms up and down while she grips my forearm.

"Maybe. We're undecided if we want to move," I lie through the skin of my teeth.

"Well, to sway your decision, this is a lovely street. We've only been here for six months, but we love this house, and the neighbours are great." The woman smiles, and I return it while Marie's fingers cut into my flesh. "Alfie, Archie, stop it!" the woman shouts, causing her boys to apologise before chasing each other inside.

"Well, we'll take it into consideration. Thank you," I say, and walk Marie backwards with me.

"If I don't see you again, I hope you find what you're looking for." The woman then turns, calls out to her sons and closes her door.

"I already have," I mumble.

Opening the passenger door, I hoist Marie inside, before jogging around the bonnet and getting into the driver's seat. I hold the biting point and glance over at her, and she smiles, appeased.

"It's a home again," she whispers. Covering her hand with mine, she strokes absentmindedly, her eyes still fixed on the house. I turn her jaw gently and wipe away the solitary tear staining her cheek.

"Happy?"

"Very. Let's go, darling." Pulling off from the kerb, I drive slowly, giving her the last vestige of closure.

As I stop-start, rocking the clutch through the congested midday traffic, Marie taps away on her phone frantically. Huffing and puffing her annoyance, she inhales deeply and lets it out slowly.

"Have you heard from her?" I ask, finding a vacant space in the car park.

"She's on her way."

I get out of the car and grip her hand in mine as we head into the building. Anxiousness wells in the pit of my stomach with every step we take

"I need to sign in, darling." I let her go and look around the waiting room at the other couples. Sitting down, my knee shakes uncontrollably, until a small hand pats my thigh.

"Are you okay?" she asks.

"Fine," I answer far too quickly. Except I'm not fine; I'm nervous as hell. I wasn't even this bad on our wedding day. But today, I'm finally going to see what I've always wanted.

"I'll call Maggie again. Find out where she is." She fiddles with her phone as frantic steps rush into the room.

"Sorry, I'm late," Maggie exclaims, causing everyone to gape. "Care in the community, last rites, that kind of thing."

I snigger, still not used to the sense of humour that doesn't match the vocation.

Marie stands and embraces her twin, while the open-mouthed stares of shock continue.

"Maggie, you're scaring the civilians," I say in quiet enjoyment. Maggie casually shrugs and pulls me into a hug.

"Tough," is her low reply. "You look well. And very, very nervous," she says in a whisper. "Don't be. *We've* done this before." She waves to Marie.

"Mrs Walker?" a nurse calls from the mouth of the room, and the three of us turn simultaneously.

"Good morning," Marie greets him. "Is it okay for my sister to come in with us?"

The nurse smiles at the vicar giving him a pointed expression. "Yes of course," he replies, probably fearing divine retribution if he says no.

Again, something else that makes me snigger, because, by Maggie's own admission, she uses it to her advantage.

A lot.

"Bless you," Maggie says with sarcastic sincerity, as we follow him into an examination room.

Holding open the door for her, she turns to me and smiles. No words are imparted, and they don't need to be because I know the last time Marie did this, she did it with Maggie in tow because bastard Beresford couldn't be arsed.

And again, I hope his fucking soul is rotting – slowly, painfully.

The sonographer switches on the machine as Maggie pulls two chairs closer to the bed. I automatically grab Marie under the arms, lift her up and adjust the pillow. Unfastening her blouse, she attempts to bat my hands away, but I raise my brows, daring her. She rolls her eyes, wordlessly admitting defeat and allows me to get on with it. As I adjust her camisole and the biggest elastic band I've ever seen on her jeans, she turns to Maggie, who looks ready to burst.

"Remember the first time we did this?" she asks Marie, who beams at her. "Did you bring them?"

"Hmm, in my bag. Grab them and let's bet," Marie says as the man slathers gel on her stomach. "Oh, God, that's cold!" The man looks up and immediately glances at Maggie's back. "Don't worry," Marie placates. "I get a pass for taking the Lord's name in vain."

"Such presumption!" Maggie snorts, returning with the packet and clutches Marie's hand. "Right, I think it's a boy."

"Really? Again? No, it's definitely a girl. It feels like a girl," Marie counters.

"Pfft! Again, what do you know what it feels like? And again, you could be having one of each!"

My eye twitches and I lift a brow, watching the banter curiously. "Have you two already discussed this?" I query, because this scene is well rehearsed, and I'm secure enough in my masculinity to confess I feel left out.

"Hmm," Marie replies. "A lifetime ago."

Ah, Faith. Say no more.

"So, what are you betting on?" the sonographer asks, wheeling his chair over, equally as curious as I am.

Marie and Maggie wear identical smirks which I still find very unnerving. I don't think they realise just how identical they are. It's not just the face and stature, it's everything. It's the smile, the smirk, the eye rolling, the sarcasm. *Everything.*

"Chocolate buttons!" they reply in unison as Maggie lobs the packet on the bed.

The man chuckles. "Dad? Would you like to weigh in your opinion here? Do *you* want to know what you're having?"

"Oh, John, I'm sorry. I didn't think," Maggie says, looking abashed.

"It's okay." I shake my head in submission as Marie smiles apologetically and squeezes my fingers. While I know she is willing to go with whatever I want, I know that look. It's the one that confirms she doesn't like surprises - and it's the same one Maggie is also expressing. Yet another identical trait.

Ever since the test came back positive, after months and months of trying *and* failing, and then having to go through two rounds of IVF back to back, I've been saying I want a surprise. For the last three months, I've been agonising over this decision, but standing here now, I really do want to know.

"Let's find out," I confirm and wrap my arm around Marie's shoulders and take her hand.

The screen ghosts to life as the man glides the probe over her stomach. I'm mesmerised when shapes begin to appear, and it's no longer just a word in a window, it's now our child.

"Darling!" Marie gasps in happiness, clasping me tighter, almost cutting off the circulation to my fingers as our unborn makes his grand appearance.

"Look at that. That's our baby," I say in awe, not recognising my own voice. "Maggie, come here." I wrap my other arm around her as we all gaze in wonder at the screen.

"And here is baby Walker. Congratulations. Dad, are you sure you want to know the gender?" the man asks again for assurance.

I'm about to reply when the heartbeat echoes. I crane my neck in query, press my lips to Marie's forehead, and move around the bed. Edging closer to the monitor, needing to get a better look, I squint at the shadows. Studying the screen, the silent niggle in the back of my head gains momentum.

"Sure, but before you do, can you answer something for me?" The sonographer tilts his head back, awaiting my query. "How many are we having?"

His lips curve, almost wickedly, and he commences moving the probe. His eyes flit from the screen to Marie and Maggie, and then back again. Moving his hand over the monitor, he crooks his finger, and I bend down. Answering my query, I stand, ramrod straight.

"You're sure?" I ask, and he smiles and nods.

While I allow the imminent reality to sink in, Maggie's voice drifts distantly into my eardrums, asking the questions I've just had answered.

I grasp the back of the chair as the room starts to sway because there comes a time in your life when you realise you are truly fucked. And trust me, the words that have just left his mouth have confirmed that I truly am.

Fortunately for me, I didn't have to hear the identical gloating behind me, because I hit the deck in shock.

And I hit it hard.

And when I came to, I had the chocolate bloody buttons.

"Last orders!" the landlord calls out, ringing the bell with vigour on the side of the bar.

Picking up my pint, I knock back the last remaining mouthfuls, feeling more inebriated tonight than I have in the last two years. And I know I will still be recovering from this session until the end of the week since it's rare I play out these days.

I put the empty glass down with more force than I realise and yawn.

"Keeping you awake, Dad?" Park nudges my side and grins while I flip him off. "See, lads, this is what happens when your swimmers are inept. At least Sloan's boys aren't lacking in getting it right!"

"Park, we've had this conversation before – you won't be lacking anything with my foot up your arse! One of these days it's going to happen, sunshine."

"It's only a bit of fun, boss." Typical Park – can give it but can't take it.

I level my gaze on him. "It was funny the first time you said, but it hasn't been funny for the last fifty fucking times you've said it. Say it again, and I'll unleash the vicious little woman on you."

Park wilts, ever so slightly, because if there is anything in this life he's truly terrified off, it's Marie. Or, more precisely, her form of punishment.

"You really do hate me, don't you?" He grins innocently. "Do you want to see me serving canapés in a penguin suit again?"

I shake my head and slap him on the back. For all the threats he has endured from me over the years, I wouldn't be without him – any of them, the truth be told.

"Si, fancy a Jager bomb before his boot reaches your rectum?" Tommy asks, standing and stretching.

"Sure, get me two!"

"Anyone else want one for the road?"

The murmurs of acceptance and rejection ripple around our table, and I stretch my legs and get to my feet.

"Not for me. I'm going home to make love to my wife."

Remy laughs and slaps his hand on the table. "No, you're going home to change dirty nappies while your wife catches up on her beauty sleep!"

"Yeah, that too. But you've got no room to talk, sunshine."

"Touché. But just like you, I'm grateful for everything I've got now." He automatically touches the scar on his neck. Starting from just under his ear, it spans down his neck and ends mid-torso.

My lips compress instantly as my eyes fix upon it, and even in my moderately drunken state, the night he gained the newest addition to his collection will never leave me. Little does he know, many a night I've woken up in a cold sweat, remembering the dead look in his eyes. It's the same look my fallen comrades gave me for the last time in a bloody wasteland, and it's the same look Marie wore two years ago at the foot of those stairs.

Somethings in life you never forget, and the day he almost lost his is up there with the day I got married, and the day Marie brought our children into the world.

Deep in thought, I jolt when a rough hand slides around my nape. "Don't dwell on it, J." Rem presses his forehead to mine and sighs.

"It's hard not to." I slap his back and impart my goodbyes to the reprobates.

"Rem? Another?" Tommy queries as Sloan calls out for a lager.

"Yeah, half of whatever's on tap," Rem replies and lets me go. "Dom?"

"No, I'm off." Dom shakes his head and pulls out his keys. "I'll give you a lift home," he says, heading for the door.

Sliding into his gleaming Maserati, the engine roars, causing everyone in the smoking shelter to turn in awe. "You couldn't drive something a little less conspicuous, could you?" The irony rolls off my tongue, but I'm being serious. I might drive a Chelsea tractor, but this is ostentation at its worst.

"Says the man who has a 4x4 that rarely goes off-road. Besides, it's all about creating the right image."

"*'Rarely goes off-road'*. Have you seen my work yard?" I laugh.

Dom grins. "That's not off-road, that's shoddy workmanship. It'll teach you not to hire wideboys!"

"I didn't; Park did."

"And that lad's the biggest wideboy of them all!"

Touché.

I slouch down in the seat, insofar as is comfortable and gaze out of the window. My eyelids begin to droop as the sporadic flashes of the lampposts highlight the luxury interior.

"Have you spoken to Taylor lately?" Dom asks quietly, approaching a roundabout.

"No." I jolt up, sobering instantly. Even in my rare merry state, I'm not merry enough to talk about what I know is going to leave his mouth in the next ten seconds.

"Another attempt was made on Beresford's life last week."

"Did they get him?"

"Unfortunately, not. He's alive to see another day."

"Shame," I reply emotionless. "Maybe next time they'll try harder." It's an evil thing to say, but hate is a powerful weapon. There are few in this life I would wish harm on, but when the felons he convicted finally get him, I hope he suffers until the end. The day I hear he's no longer breathing, I'll hang the bunting in the back garden and throw a celebration party that will shame the Royals.

Dom taps his fingers on the steering wheel, effortlessly turning the car onto my street. "Of that, I think we can all be certain," he confirms with sincerity and looks up at the house. "Kiss your ladies hello for me. Tell M I'll be by for dinner on Sunday."

"Tell her yourself," I mutter. "Besides, maybe that's not the best idea. She's still annoyed about the dolly bird you brought around last month. Jules bashed my ear over it, too. Once again, some advice? You're too old to be picking up twenty-somethings in bars anymore. Find the right one, make her yours and live the life you deserve." I stare at him, the words sinking in.

"It's not that easy for me, and you know it." He turns to the window, indicating this conversation is done.

I grip the handle but hesitate in getting out. "Let me tell you something. When we dragged ourselves out of that desert, covered in our comrades' blood, carrying them home to ensure their loved ones had a body to bury, I didn't think it would be that easy for me either. You all laugh and joke about my inept swimmers, but I'd never change it. My entire world is inside that house, and I would kill for them. One day, I hope you find the same because you deserve it. You walk a fine line between worlds, and one day you may find yourself on the edge, praying for everything you should have done with your last breath."

He nods, reaches over and slaps an arm around me, patting my back. "I'll think about it. I'll see you on Sunday. No dolly birds, I promise."

Striding up the path, I turn and watch him gun the car down the street. Opening the front door, I remove my jacket and hook it on the rack. My fingers drift over the two little jackets hanging beside mine with the mittens threaded through the arms. Toeing off my boots, I kick them against the skirting board, next to the wife's collection of heels, and the matching sets of little booties and trainers.

Looking up at the ceiling, I pull out my phone and open the app for the monitor. I smile at the screen as I enter the kitchen and down a bottle of water.

Rearming the house, I jog up the stairs, and stop outside the nursery door, because I never trust that that app is in real time. Quietly pushing it open, the soft glow of the nightlight sweeps over the floor, and everything is indeed peaceful – for once. I close the door ajar and creep over the landing into the bedroom. Moonlight cascades through the haphazardly closed blinds, highlighting Marie's sleeping form.

I must confess, I do love the way she feels postpartum. Her breasts and hips have rounded slightly, not enough that it's noticeable, but enough that it's made her curves even better. For me, anyway. She's always been soft and supple, but if I have to live through one more fad diet that promises she'll be a size eight in two weeks, I'm going to slap her arse silly. Personally, I don't give a shit what size she is; she'll always be perfect to me.

Unbuttoning my shirt, I drop it on the floor the same moment she stirs. My grin stretches from ear to ear, watching her roll onto her back, giving me unfettered access to disturb her beauty sleep in the most delicious way possible.

Beautiful.

I hitch one knee on the bed and crawl slowly. Flattening my palms over her ankles, she murmurs, and I rub them up her legs, over her calves, and around her knees and thighs. A long, welcoming moan saturates my eardrums, and I part her legs gently, while her incoherent mumbling resounds louder, until she wakes and rises.

"Darling?" she queries sleepily.

"Shush." I blow the word out and press my lips to her soft inner thigh. Her fingers splay over my scalp, and she strokes gently. Working my mouth towards her centre, I delight in the fact that she is wearing a slinky little dress thing sans underwear. As much as I love the sexy lingerie she claims she doesn't have a penchant for, I love it even more when I find her bare and waiting.

"Sinful," I whisper. I run my tongue over her core, and her legs clench as I press the tip to her opening and suck on her wanton flesh.

"Oh, God. That's good," she mumbles breathless, automatically spreading her thighs for me.

Beautiful, indeed.

"Don't stop, darling."

I kneel back and grab her calves. Pulling her towards me, I press my face back into her apex. Savouring my tongue over her hot silky flesh, her laboured breathing fills the room. Elevating her hips with my hands, I pressurise my thumb on her clit. I continue to get my fill. Licking, penetrating and sucking, until eventually she shakes, and reaches the first climax of many to come. These days, we have to get it whenever we can, but one thing she can always be sure of – I'll never leave her unsatisfied.

All the promises I've made over the years, I've worked hard for every breath and every moan. For every touch and every shudder. For every precious moment she has seen fit to give me. I've earned every one.

"Oh God," she moans repeatedly.

Watching her delectable body writhe beneath me, my dick throbs uncomfortably, ready to explode. Taking a long lick of her, I direct my mouth over her pubic bone, across the C-section scar, higher and higher to her breasts.

I sit up on my haunches, needing to get a better position. I snag a pillow, situate it beneath her, and her chest lifts in invitation.

Palming both tits – because I am a self-confessed tit man, and hers are perfect - I squeeze them reverently before popping a taut nipple into my mouth. The texture and length forces my dick to harden further, and she mewls in delight. Everything from the waist down floods with pressure and I reach down and curve her leg around my hip.

"Put me inside you, beautiful," I request through a mouthful of luscious, pebbled flesh.

I groan when her small hand wraps around me, stroking and pumping from root to tip until her awaiting wetness sheathes me. Unable to submit control, the moment the first inch is filling her, I grab her leg and thrust inside.

Heavenly.

My angel keens out, her hips on the rise, grinding against me to prolong the sensation. I release her tit and reach under her back and pull her forward. Ripping the nightdress over her head, I adjust my legs to enable her to find a more comfortable seat and squeeze the globes of her arse. I pummel in and out, over and over, and she throws her head back in wild abandon. Her tits jiggle, advancing and retreating from my eager tongue, which is desperate to taste. Moving my hands up her waist, I watch her lose control, loving the way she drops all her hoity-toity inhibitions and surrenders in my arms.

Bouncing up and down on me, her flesh heated and perspiring against mine, her tits glide over my chest, eliciting a primal response. I dig my fingers into her flesh as my body hums and releases, until I roar out and empty myself into her, experiencing momentary relief.

"Turn over and crawl up the bed." I ease her off me, relishing the pressure of her tight grip, and flip her over. "Hand and knees," I tell her gruffly, putting her into position. I slide my hands from her shoulders, along the pale, creamy skin of her back and over her arse, and she releases a full body shudder in anticipation.

I lean down and lightly sink my teeth into one perfectly rounded cheek, before slapping it playfully. She moans in response, and I drag my lips from her delectable flesh to her tailbone. Licking and sucking, I wrap my fingers around her hipbones and pull her back. She widens the expanse between her thighs and lodges her bum in my groin. My dick jerks, ready to go again, but with this woman, I'd never expect anything less.

Stroking my dick over her clit, I align myself with her slick opening, piston my hips and plunge deep. I withdraw, teasing my head against her tender, swollen flesh, and roughly surge back in.

Manoeuvring over her, I clench the bedhead for ballast and power my hips harder, enjoying the sensation of her hot heat compressing tight and wet around me. I feel invincible as I slam as deep as I can go, then slide back out and repeat. Her body moves in sync with mine, chasing ecstasy, and I thrust vigorously, each time harder than the last until she cries out.

"Angel," I growl, slamming my body into hers, mindful of being too rough. But when she's as hot and wanton as this, I'm unable to stop. And I'll never stop.

As I pound into her, reading her tells instinctively, she shudders in time with me. My lungs are on fire as my body tightens in readiness.

"John!" she screams out, tightening around me beautifully.

I manipulate my hand under her stomach and lift her up. Holding her back to my chest, I pump my body up, while one hand reaches down to her centre, teasing her swollen clit possessively. Tilting her cheek, I claim her mouth greedily. My tongue breaches her lips, while the slap of flesh upon flesh resounds in my ears.

She rides up and down, her hot, wet core squeezing all around me. I can't hold back any longer, and I roar out my release. My loud groans are muffled by her mouth, and I rub my finger between her legs, before dragging up the dip between her breasts. I gently ease her head away and pop the finger into my mouth, causing her eyes light up.

"I want you on my tongue," she says provocatively.

She climbs off, forcing a guttural gasp to leave my throat, and pushes me down. Kissing me with fervour, she drags her lips over my front. Passion, stronger than a thousand burning suns, heats my blood and sizzles through my veins, observing the love of my life descend.

I prop myself up on one arm, and delicately massage her cheek. With the tip of her tongue grazing the head of my dick, my hips tilt spontaneously.

"Angel," I breath out, and close my eyes. I shudder as her lips move up and down my shaft, and her mouth takes me all the way in. "God, that's good, darling. Keep going, beautiful. Keep going." The moment she massages my balls, I'm ready to blow again. "Fuck, I'm going to co-"

"Dada!"

My eyes shoot open as my other name drifts from the baby monitor, killing all imminent sensation from the waist down.

"Fuck!" I curse, while the sucking on my dick stops. Marie grumbles, lifts her head and presses her hands to my chest.

"I'll go," she says softly, biting back a laugh. Kissing my lips, tasting our unique combination, I cup her head.

"No, I will." I reluctantly hop off the bed and drag a pair of pyjama bottoms from the drawer. Sliding them on, I turn back to where Marie is now laid on her stomach, her chin in her hand, her ankles crossed. My sight is instantly drawn to her arse, round and full, highlighted by the moonlight teeming through the blind gaps.

"That's mine when I come back." I point to the delectable backside I have every intention of biting and slapping until she's screaming my name and shattering the windows.

"What makes you think you'll be back?" she queries innocently. I purse my lips; she makes an excellent point. "After all, Daddy means fun."

I move back to the bed in a predatory stride and tug on her chin as the baby monitor broadcasts giggles.

"And Daddy has every intention of dirty fun with Mummy when he comes back. And I will be coming, angel. Make no mistake." Slapping her arse, I stride out of the room.

On the landing, I turn back with a smile. My woman drives me crazy, but after all these years, crazy in love is the best way to be.

Opening the nursery door, I flick on the bedside lamp. With my hands on my hips, I shake my head at the stern expressions concentrated on me.

As Lady Luck would have it, I have been blessed with identical girls. Wearing matching pink jammies, the only distinguishing feature to tell them apart is a small mole on Grace's cheek. A blessing now, although Grace may not think so when she eventually reaches puberty – God help me.

Now ten months, our special girls, as Marie calls them, are the apples of my eyes.

Georgia Alice, the most boisterous and vocal of the two, was delivered at ten past five on the eightieth of January, weighing five pounds, one ounce. Grace Amelia, who, just like her name is serene and elegant, weighed four pounds, ten ounces, and was delivered seven minutes later.

After months of Marie being put through the wringer carrying twins, especially being petite and forty-four, we opted for an elective caesarean. Or rather, it was pushed on us, much to Marie's dismay since she had some romantic idea she was going to push them out pain-free within ten minutes.

Personally, I was all for it the moment Doc started talking about worst case scenarios. And considering what we had to go through to have them, I wasn't about to lose them at the last minute.

"Dada!"

Strolling to the cot, Georgia is bouncing up and down, using the sidebars for leverage. Grace, on the other hand, is sitting quietly in the corner with a little pouty mouth. She may be the most laidback of the two, but she has that expression down pat, and I'm not an idiot to believe that it isn't a sign of things to come. Especially when I look at her mother and Auntie because those Turner genes are strong. And by Marie's own admission, she doesn't have well-behaved babies.

"Why aren't you asleep, little one?" I ask Georgia, who laughs at such absurdity she doesn't understand. I give her my best stern daddy glare - a glare which usually evaporates when the bottom lip wobbles, the nose scrunches up, and a teary 'Dada' comes out – and she starts to babble at me.

I sigh because the battle is already lost. Reaching out, wiggling my fingers, Georgia stretches towards me, and I lift her up and cradle her padded tush.

"Dada!" she shouts happily, knowing she's got her own way. *Again.* I'd like to say this is a rare occurrence, but it's not. Many a night, I've been walking a hole in the carpet because she wants to play at one o'clock in the morning when all I want to do is sleep.

"Baby, you need to go back to sleep because Daddy has had a bit to drink, and he's tired and slightly hungover already. Daddy isn't fit to play tonight," I say, trying not to breathe on her, which isn't hard since her tiny hand is persistently slapping my cheek.

"She's got you wrapped around her little finger." Marie enters the room, tying her robe. "Hello, my beautiful girl." Kissing Georgia's cheek and running her fingers through her wispy blonde hair, she reaches into the cot for Grace, who crawled over the moment she saw Mummy.

"Mama," Grace says as Marie plucks her up and blows kisses on her. She giggles infectiously, squirms and pats Mummy's chest.

"Hungry, sweet pea?" Marie asks, rocking her.

Not one to be missing out on anything, Georgia lurches for her mum, and I hold her securely and kiss her head.

"Come on, angel," I say, holding the door open. Carrying our jabbering girls back into the bedroom, I adjust the pillows on the bed and take Grace while Marie gets comfortable.

The moment she lowers her robe, Georgia automatically shows an interest. My girls can eat, but she's the greediest. I carefully pass her to Mum, and she latches her onto her nipple. I lie back with Grace over my front, her stunning blue eyes closing, while her sister sucks away with vigour.

I stare down at my littlest angel, snug against my chest, my hand securely cocooning her as she lets out a soft content sigh. Turning my gaze to my wife, lying on her side, with Georgia still sucking with ferocious fortitude, she places her hand over mine on Grace.

"I love you," she says, and I brush my thumb over her lip. "I love that you've given me a second chance at this. That you've finally completed me."

I close my eyes momentarily to stall the tears us men are not supposed to cry because it's a hard thing to hear. I never set out to be her knight in shining armour when I first saw her. I wanted to love her, and hold her, and feel her skin against mine when she screamed my name. She was strong-willed and beautiful, everything about her attracted me. She drew me in like a moth to a flame, powerless to escape having my wings burnt. Except, I didn't know just how broken she was inside when I would sit and watch her from afar.

"I love you, too, angel, but *I* didn't do this, *we* did." I stroke my hand over her cheek. Georgia fusses, lets out a burp and resumes eating.

Gazing in awe at the lives we have created, Marie's eyes drop down, and she smiles beautifully. It's an expression that now saddens me, and I need to remind myself daily that these are not her first. And I can only imagine the way she loved Faith. Jules has said it often, but Marie really is a natural mother. Born to care and nurture. To love and protect.

Running my hand over Grace's bum, I clear my throat. "Fancy another?"

"What?" Marie asks, taken aback. We've talked about it over the last few months, and I'd be lying if I said I didn't want to try for a boy. Granted, I'm aware she will probably be pension age when they are twenty, but I don't give a damn what anyone else thinks.

"Another baby. It's not too late for us. We might get lucky with just one." I internally grimace, because knowing my luck, I'll have another two girls to contend with. Not that I'm complaining. I honestly can't wait to chase hormonal teenage boys away from the front door when they eventually come calling. Or lock them in their rooms when they want to go out half-dressed, caked in makeup.

Marie sits up and rests Georgia against her shoulder, rubbing her back, burping her. "Hmm, or we might get lucky with three." And if that isn't an absolute passion killer, I don't know what is. "Darling, I'd love to do this again and give you a son, but I'm happy with what we've got. For now. Ask me again when they're one."

Two months. I'm agreeable to that.

Standing up, careful not to wake my sleeping beauties, I place Grace on the bed and take Georgia. I settle her next to her sister and stack the pillows around them like a fortress.

"Come here," I say, hooking my finger. Sliding my arm under her bum, I hold her against me and descend to the floor. On her back, I open her robe and kiss a line down her throat as she fumbles with my pyjama bottoms tie. Unthreading it, she shoves them down my thighs.

"This wasn't my intention, beautiful."

"No, but it's mine." She takes my lips in hers. "And I heard Daddy is tired, slightly drunk, and not fit to play tonight." She glides her hand down my semi-hard length. "I think Daddy lied." She smirks and rolls us over. "Now, you promised me dirty fun."

She straddles my abs and settles lower until I can feel my throbbing head pierce her hot centre. She presses down, taking an inch or so, before pulling back up.

This woman is not only the making of me, but she will also be the death of me, too. But by God, I'll go out with a smile on my face.

"This is the purest form of hell, angel," I tell her, settling my hands on her supple hips.

"Hmm." She licks up my chest, flattens her tongue over my nipple, and slides her luscious, wet heat back down on my dick. "But shortly, I'll take you to heaven."

Clutching the disposable cup, I knock back the last of the coffee, desperate to warm my chilly bones on this frigid night and toss it in the nearby bin.

I gaze up at the relatively clear sky, delicately peppered with twinkling stars, and seek out the brightest one. I sigh with a heart heavy because finally, these nights are mine. And tonight, we will mark the twenty-seventh anniversary of Faith's death.

With one last look above, I stride over the winding maze of gravel paths. Nearing our little late-night gathering, the sound of boisterous children playing guides my way.

"Daddy! Daddy!" Grace shouts when she sees me. My smile is instant, and I pick up my pace and jog towards her. "Kissy, Daddy!" she demands, toddling as fast as she can in her little pink, padded snowsuit.

As she makes a confident beeline towards me, I realise how much I miss the days when she and Georgia were both hesitant on their legs. The days when a topple would invoke tears and anyone would think the world was ending. The days when they would plod through the house, holding on to anything they could. And the days they would balance themselves, conducting what Marie affectionately called the mummy walk – straight legs, backs tilted, arms out in front.

God, I miss those days, because they remind me that one day, my little girls won't be so little anymore. One day, I'll wake up, and they will be young women who don't come running to daddy every five minutes. It's days like today when they do something that shows me just how quickly they are growing up, that I feel it the most.

But I'll always be daddy, and if someone so much as wrongs my girls, I will deliver the swiftest punishment known to man.

And I'll enjoy it immensely.

Meeting her halfway, I swing her up into my arms and smother her with kisses. She laughs maniacally, wraps her little arms around my neck and rests her head on my shoulder.

"Tired?" I ask her, gently tucking a strand of pale blonde hair back into her bunny beanie. She shakes her head no - causing the ears on the top to flop around - although I know she must be. Bedtime is strict in our house, and it isn't often we keep them up past seven, but tonight is special - in the most morbid way possible.

"Where's Mummy?"

"Don't know," she replies, jerking her head up as Oliver – who turned four last week, and is the absolute spit of his dad - runs towards us.

"Gracie!" he shouts, slowing down.

Not one to be left out – irrespective of how tired she may be - she wriggles in my arms and digs her leg into my rib.

"Down, Daddy!"

I reluctantly lower her, and she hurries towards Oliver, who takes her hand, and they run off together.

I grin as I watch them playing with a pile of fallen leaves. Jumping up and down and tossing them in the air, before deciding, in their infinite child wisdom, to roll in them. Yesterday, when Marie suggested this, I knew it was a bad idea. And watching my girl and her cousin covering themselves with dirt and God knows what else, I was right.

I avert my gaze from the little monsters because if I don't see it, I can claim diminished responsibility.

Striding back to our family gathering, Maggie is sitting on a blanket with another wrapped around her, rocking Sloan and Kara's newest addition, Benjamin.

Now six months old, it is clear the Foster genes are as equally as strong as the Turner genes. And Kara has long since resigned herself to the prospect of a houseful of boys while I've resigned myself to a houseful of girls.

Looking away from my sister-in-law, her husband, Peter, is sat next to her, deep in conversation with Sloan, probably talking shop, amongst other things.

I do a full one-eighty, searching for Georgia, who is nowhere in sight. As panic begins to set in, a familiar child's grumble piques my attention, and I spin around to see her stomping around the side of the church, her gloved hand in Kara's, who appears to be telling her off. My sigh of relief is mixed with my emotionally overloaded heart as I watch my other little girl with her big sister.

Georgia's clear sulking morphs into a grin when she spots Sloan and dashes towards him. With her hands on her hips, she kicks his leg until he lifts her onto his lap.

"Hey, darling." I approach Kara, but my attention is still on my daughter and son. I grin as the kid yanks her beanie cat ears. Georgia points her finger in admonishment, before playing with his hair and then settles on clinging to his neck.

"What did she do?"

"She ran off when I tried to put the harness on her. We had sisterly words. I hope you don't mind."

"No." I snigger. If my words don't make a blind bit of difference, Kara's aren't even going to register on the radar. "Don't suppose you fancy doing a swap for the night?" I ask playfully – if not secretly hopeful.

She moves her head from side to side with a terrified expression and laughs. "No. Your girls are hard work."

I'm reluctant to nod, but I do because I can't argue with that. "I blame your mother. And once upon a time, you weren't so easy yourself."

"True," she replies shyly. "Speaking of Mother, where is she? It's nearly time." She tugs on her scarf and looks around.

"I'll go find her, honey." I embrace her and kiss her cheek.

Putting one foot in front of the other, I look over my shoulder as Kara makes her way back to her husband. As she huddles down next him, smiling at his interaction with Georgia, I realise just how far we've all come in the last six years. The triumphs, tribulations and tears have all been worth it.

I pick up my pace, while a wave of cheers and revelry rings out from down the street. I slow my step when I see Marie kneeling down on a grave. Her soft words carry over the silent surroundings, and the moonlight bathes her beautifully.

"Angel?"

She turns around with a sombre expression. "Hi." She smiles and stands.

"Whose grave is this?" I ask, rubbing my hands up and down her arms before caging her inside them.

"It belongs to the gentleman who was the caretaker. The day you chased me up here," she says, making me relive the aftermath that followed her ex-husband's unwelcome visit to my office. It's a day I'd rather not talk about, and I've kept my word since – I've never held any of it against her. And I never will.

"He was nice to me when I needed it. When everything was stacked against me. He said God would love what we leave behind.

He had no family, so I thought I'd visit, say hi, and leave a gift." Her eyes trail to the large bunches spilling over in the two vases. She rests further into me, and I tighten my hold.

"I'm sure he's watching, darling."

"I hope so."

"It's a lovely gesture, and again, you are the most beautiful, amazing, selfless woman I've ever met."

"Really?" She places her arms over mine and grins. "You won't be saying that when our girls are giving you grey hairs."

"Too late, they already are," I confirm, having spotted a couple coming through these last few months since I turned forty-one. "And on the subject of our girls, your daughter is running amok."

She spins around and gives me an unimpressed smirk. "*My* daughter?" she replies sarcastically. "So, she's *our* daughter when she's good, but *my* daughter when she's naughty? Hmm?"

"Semantics." I grin broadly, tip her chin, and claim her lips. She moans into my mouth, and I fight the urge to find a secluded spot where we won't be disturbed.

The squeal of one - or both - of our girls floats over the atmosphere, and I reluctantly pull away and tuck her into my side.

"Just one day is all I ask," I say. "One day where there is peace amongst men – and children."

"I've told you before, you ask for too much. Come on, Mr Walker, *my* daughter is running amok." She pouts.

"Aren't you going to ask which one?" I raise my brow, and she shakes her head in response.

"I don't need to, but just tell me why we named her Grace?"

I laugh, and the sound resonates as we walk through the graveyard.

This last year has seen our girls grow into their own character traits, and with it, it would seem they have also had personality transplants.

A month short of their second birthdays, Georgia, once demanding and at the forefront of everything, is now laidback and mellow, and takes life as it comes at her. Grace, on the other hand, is a handful – and that's being polite. Hyper-aware, the centre of mischief and always on her feet. It doesn't take much for her to pitch a fit – and that's her mum all over.

Rounding the side of the church, Oliver and Grace are now running after each other, and both are covered in dirt.

"You can bath her when we get in since you've let her play in the mud," Marie says, very unimpressed, her brow raised.

I halt, tug her hand and shake my head. Grace will never go to sleep if I bath her. Bath time equals fun - duckies, bubbles and splashing.

"Hey, I didn't let her play in the mud – she followed Oliver's lead." I shamelessly place the blame on an innocent four-year-old.

She shrugs coolly. "Semantics, darling."

I close my eyes in defeat. My words always come back to bite me on the arse with this woman. Her cynicism is quick, and it never misses a beat.

"Where's Georgia? Have you allowed her to dig up the graves and swing from the trees?"

I shake my head incredulously and chortle. "Angel, it's going to turn me on immensely, but I'm going to tie you to a table and smack your arse red for the attitude."

"Chance would be a fine thing."

"Hmm, wouldn't it just. And if you must know, I left her with Sloan. She was clinging to his neck, charming him."

She sighs with dejection. "He wants a daughter like you want a son."

And isn't that the most talked about truth between the kid and me. While he and Kara still have time to expand their brood, time has slipped away for us. Over the last ten months, we've had two more rounds of IVF, but it doesn't look like it will be happening again. Each time we were told it was unsuccessful, it felt like a knife to the gut watching Marie blame herself for being forty-six and leaving it too late. In truth, as much as I would love a son, I'm more than satisfied with what I've got.

"Beautiful." I cup her cheeks in my hands. "You've given me everything I've ever wanted. It's taken years to finally get here, but I've now got a stunning, sexy wife; two amazing girls – despite they can sometimes be the naughtiest girls; a gorgeous home and a thriving business. I've got a perfect life." My verbal train of thought is cut short as Grace – head to toe in mud – and Georgia – still as pristine as the moment I dressed her – scream in delight and clap their hands simultaneously as a firework explodes overhead.

"Perfect?"

"Perfect." I wink, and plant one on her lips.

"Hurry up!" Sloan calls out, passing a sleeping Benjamin to his wife.

"Come on." I snatch up her hand and jog towards him. I let go of her and touch the top of Faith's headstone. Trailing my fingers over the marble, I smile.

"I kept my promise, sweetheart. I did everything I said I was going to do. I hope I've made you proud." I seek out the brightest star again.

Picking up a foil-wrapped jacket potato, I smile at Mr Blue, propped up against the headstone, while Maggie and Peter start to open the boxes. As I settle down on the blanket, gazing at my wife in contentment as she blows on a potato with Georgia - who giggles and puts her hands over her mouth when her little forceful blow splatters it in front of her - I know I have a perfect life.

"Sorry," Georgia mumbles as she blows again, and more spud sprays the blanket.

"It's okay, baby," Marie cajoles soothingly, stroking Georgia's head as she pouts, gives up on her food entirely, and runs to her sister and cousin. "You know, I was serious the other day. She's got your smirk down pat." Marie turns to me with an expectant look.

"Angel, she's a Walker – she's too suave to smirk. Although I think she's definitely inherited the Walker charm," I say coyly.

"Really?" she retorts and crawls over to me on her knees. "How about when they're asleep tonight you show me just how charming the Walker charm can be? My *things* haven't been *manhandled* properly for a while."

And if that doesn't pique my attention, I don't know what will.

I scrunch my nose and cheeks and feign improbability. "I don't know, it could be a late one. I'm on bath duty, remember?" I reply as Maggie stands.

"Come here, my little lovelies," my sister-in-law calls out, rounding up the three eldest, and starts putting extra gloves on them. With Peter and Sloan's assistance, they each light up a sparkler and hold them in the kids' hands. They laugh in wonder and excitement, drawing shapes and waving them in the darkness.

"Just so you know, if Oliver refuses to sleep tonight because of all this excitement, I'm passing him off to you," Kara says to Marie, who threads her arms around my neck.

"Actually, forget the charm and manhandling, and add babysitting to your duties. I need my beauty sleep."

I quickly snake my arm around her middle and drag her down onto my lap. "I will, and you can add one more smack to that quick-thinking arse, darling."

She sucks my neck seductively, while no one is looking, and volleys my words back at me. "I will, darling. By the way, what was that?" She nods at the headstone.

"I made a promise-" I am about to elaborate on that promise when our girls come bounding over.

"Mummy!" Grace cries out in exhilaration and plonks herself in her mum's lap. Georgia follows suit and throws herself into mine, while Oliver slumps into his dad's.

Sitting on the graves of Faith, and Elizabeth and Norman Turner – who just passed some six months back, and who, unknown to Marie, had bought the adjacent plots soon after Faith's burial - the first firework display of the night begins.

"Is Faith up there?" Georgia asks, pointing to the sky.

From the moment they started to cogitate, we've talked incessantly about Faith. Of course, they don't understand where their other big sister is, but it's our mission to ensure her memory lives on in our home, in our family and in the charity work Maggie conducts and the donations both Walker Security and Emerson and Foster now make. If we can stop just one child suffering the same fate, it is a success.

Marie smiles sadly, while Maggie and Kara both start sniffing. *Women.* I tilt back, noting the solemn expressions on both the kid and Peter. *Men,* too, but I'm also not immune as I wipe my eyes.

"She is, baby. She's the brightest star in the sky. Right up there, watching you," I tell her.

Marie inhales shakily but manages to control it as the kids wave up at the sky and shout hi to Faith.

"Darling? Your promise?" Her tone wobbles as she glances between the marble and her watch. Sadness overtakes her features, and I nestle her into my side and kiss her temple as it finally begins.

"Three years ago, I made a little girl many promises."

The explosions intensify, and colour dyes the dark sky while shouts ring out from the pub down the street.

I glance at everyone now looking at me in anticipation to reveal what I had sworn. I fix my gaze on my wife and twist her wedding band.

"I promised her I was going to marry her mummy."

Ten!

"That I was going to make you happy."

Eight!

"I promised to give you the life you deserved. One filled with enduring love."

Five!

"That you'd have everything you ever wanted or dreamed of."

Three!

"And I promised her that when I finally meet in her heaven, I'll be the father that she deserves. I meant what I said, angel - she's mine because she's yours."

One!

Happy New Year!

The opening chorus of Auld Lang Syne gains momentum from the boozer, and Marie's hand squeezes mine in confirmation that I've achieved every promise I made to a child who was taken far too soon.

The day I sat on this grave, planting the flower that Elizabeth Turner had asked me to, and those oaths tumbled from my mouth, I didn't know if I would be able to fulfil them.

The marrying part was easy – Marie was never going to say no - but everything else was interlinked and fundamental in giving her the second chance she had always secretly dreamed of. The second chance of being a mother and having a family.

In truth, she had already succeeded. She raised Kara to be a beautiful, intelligent, strong woman. And regardless of what the future held for us, in my eyes, she had never failed at being an exceptional mother – she'd already proven it time and time again.

But the day our girls were born, I fulfilled every promise as I held her hand and told her how amazing she was to have carried them, to have nurtured and kept them safe, and how well she was doing throughout the delivery. That day, every wish and dream we shared finally came true.

"I love you, angel. From the first moment I saw you."

"I love you, too," she replies and gazes up at the sky. "All my girls are finally together. It was always my dream."

"I know," I whisper, wrapping her tighter. "But you're not living in a dream anymore." As she settles into me to watch the display, I close my eyes and reminisce.

Over the last few years, she has often told me how she once dared to dream, how she dared to have it all. And she has often told me that

I wouldn't understand just how fragile and unobtainable some dreams can be.

But little does she know, when I would sit outside her house, spying on her for years, desperate to make her mine, I understand completely.

Because, I too, dared to dream.

And together, we finally have it all.

Follow Elle

If you wish to be notified of future releases, special offers, discounted books, ARC opportunities and more, please subscribe to Elle's mailing list.

Alternatively, you can connect with Elle on the following sites:

Website: www.ellecharles.com

Facebook: www.facebook.com/elle.charles

Twitter: www.twitter.com/@ellecharles

Bookbub: www.bookbub.com/authors/elle-charles

Instagram: www.instagram.com/elle.charlesauthor

Or by email:

elle.charlesauthor@gmail.com

elle@ellecharles.com

About the Author

Elle was born and raised in Yorkshire, England, where she still resides.

A self-confessed daydreamer, she loves to create strong, diverse characters, cocooned in opulent yet realistic settings that draw the reader in with every twist and turn until the very last page.

A voracious reader for as long as she can remember, she is never without her beloved Kindle. When she is not absorbed in the newest release or a trusted classic, she can often be found huddled over her laptop, tapping away new ideas and plots for forthcoming works.

Finally, if you enjoyed this novel, please consider sparing a few moments to leave a review.

Works by Elle Charles

All titles are available to purchase in print and ebook format.

The Fractured Series:

Kara and Sloan
Fractured (Book 1)
Tormented (Book 2)
Aftermath (Book 2.5)
Liberated (Book 3)

Marie and John
Faithless (Book 4)